Scorpio - a weapon of war o
precision. It was a type of small cata
crossbow, probably invented by the
developed by the Romans as an artil. ̲ ̲ ̲. ̲. was used
extensively by the legions, and could be operated by one man.
There were sixty such weapons to each legion; one to every
centuria. The scorpio was capable of deadly accurate fire over
100 metres. If used as an artillery battery from high ground it has
been calculated that a legion could fire 240 bolts every minute at
the enemy.

Author's notes and acknowledgements

This is a historical novel set two thousand years ago during the main political life of Gaius Julius Caesar, from 68 BC to 41 BC, based on his own words in his two books, his *Commentarii* on the *Gallic Wars* and the *Civil War*. I have tried to be as accurate as possible, but because of the distance of time not all dates are definite. There is a little background information in the Introduction concerning Romans and Gauls.

If I wrote this book in Latin not many people would be able to read it, and it would have taken me far too long to write. As the increasingly dominant force I have attempted to make the Romans speak as twenty-first century soldiers speak; with the Gauls being slightly more archaic. I have assumed that the psychological phenomenon known as the Stockholm Syndrome would have already existed two thousand years ago, whereby captives begin to empathise with the aims of their captors, and captors start to have positive feelings for their captives. In real life Caesar reported the dream described in the first chapter, and drew the same conclusion.

I have taken certain liberties. The Romans played many different board games, some involving military strategy, and using glass or wooden counters, but they didn't play chess or draughts. There were no early hours of the morning, the day being divided up into twelve hours, but the night divided into four separate watches.

I have had a great deal of assistance. I wish to thank Pamela Scruton who typed the original manuscript, and offered so much encouragement. Also thanks to my readers, Lauren Mulherron, Michael Boulton-Jones, Stephen Allison, and Anne Doig, for their help and advice; and to Rachel Allison, who solved so many problems. Especial thanks to my son Jody Mackenzie who designed the cover, and gave me so much help navigating my way round computers and iPads. He also turned my feeble tracings into proper annotated maps. Last but not least thanks to John, my husband, who has put up so patiently with an author wife who is frequently lost in her own thoughts of the past.

Cover Statue of Julius Caesar at the Roman Gate, Turin, Italy
       Italian/French border
       Photographer : Francesco Gibilisco

Introduction

The Romans

Gaius Julius Caesar was born on or around 100 BC into one of the oldest aristocratic patrician Roman families, the Julia. The family claimed to be descended from the Goddess Venus, and an ancestor of Romulus, the founding father of Rome. At the time Caesar was born the Roman Republic had already existed for centuries. The stability of the Roman political system and its gradually evolving and ruthlessly efficient army had enabled the Republic to expand with remarkable success. By the time Caesar became Quaestor (lieutenant governor) in Spain in 68 BC, Rome held sway over many conquered countries, huge 'provinces' extending from Spain in the west to Syria in the east.

The Romans were remarkable architects, builders, and engineers, connecting their well planned cities and conquered territories with roads and bridges. Roman cities were supplied with many civic amenities; plentiful water from long distances via aqueducts, efficient sewerage systems, temples, theatres, shopping malls, public baths, and amphitheatres for bloodthirsty displays. While they admired the Greeks for their arts, science, literature, and philosophy, they tended to regard most other peoples as inferior. The enslavement of war captives acquired during their conquests was regarded as essential, and the resultant forced labour increased the general prosperity of Roman citizens. More than half the population of the Republic were slaves with no legal status whatsoever.

The Roman Republic modelled itself on the Greek Athenian democratic system. Senators, Knights, and commoners made up a clearly defined class structure. The patriarchs of the wealthiest and oldest families became Senators and took their place in the Senate, the legislative assembly. The Senate chose two Consuls to rule for a given year. After their year of service they would be rewarded by full governorship of one of the many Roman provinces, a route to riches. In order to be considered for election as Consul, a candidate had to follow the 'cursus honorum,' the path to honour, during which time he would fulfil certain prescribed military and civilian roles. The two Consuls could only make laws if both agreed, (either could veto the other) and if the law was debated and passed by the Senate before sundown. There were also two tribunes of the people representing the common citizens, who also had the vital power of veto.

Caesar was born into a world where the invasion and conquest of other countries was considered a perfectly acceptable method of gaining power and wealth. As he grew up, however, the legal foundations of the Republic were already beginning to crumble. Military might had begun to supersede the rule of law. Legions of soldiers were showing loyalty to their general, rather than to the Senate, as the general was responsible for their pay, and the grants of land when the soldiers were discharged from service. Meanwhile, the common people were agitated and sought more representation. These disparate desires had resulted in a recent civil war, which saw the rise to power of Sulla the Dictator. He flouted many of the laws previously considered inviolate. Later Pompey the Great achieved astonishing political success by his military exploits. He became Consul, without following the cursus honorum. Filibustering techniques and other legal irregularities arose in the Senate. Although Caesar spent ten years of his life conquering Gaul to add to the wealth and status of Rome, his lust for power finally brought the Republic to a violent and bloody end.

The Gauls

The vast Celtic civilization stretched from Britain and Ireland to western and central Europe as far as the Danube. A large area was occupied by the Gauls (Gallic Celts) including most of present day France, part of Holland, Belgium, Germany west of the Rhine, and Switzerland. As the Roman Republic rose, this great civilization was in retreat, being pressured by invaders from the East, the Germanic tribes in particular. Gaul was divided into many Cantons or tribes, with boundaries often imposed by geographical constraints, such as rivers, and mountain ranges. The Gauls were agriculturalists, growing corn and tending cattle but were also famed for their detailed metalwork, and for their mining ability, producing gold, silver, and iron. The main exports were corn, cattle, precious metals, iron, hides, slaves, and hunting dogs. Trade and political treaties were conducted mainly with Britain and Spain, but increasingly also with Rome.

The Gauls had been in contact with the Greeks and Etruscans as early as six hundred years prior to Caesar's birth, as the Greeks gradually established colonies all along the western Mediterranean coast. Trade from Massilia (Marseilles) flowed up the Rhône, along the river valley routes, mountain passes, and across the plains, bringing Greek and Etruscan artefacts and copious amounts of wine. Vineyards were not established in Gaul at the time, so their love of wine might see a Gallic slave bartered for a jar of wine brought by the Italian merchants. Generally, urban civilization was highly developed and included both heavily fortified towns, and towns open to commerce, Bibracte, Lutetia, and Cenabum particularly. Towns were well connected by good roads and strong bridges. But the Gauls were more inward-looking when it came to spiritual matters, united as they were by their Druidic religion. Druidic priests were highly revered and were exempt from taxes and military service.

Individual Gallic tribes manufactured their own beautiful coinage, often following the Greek pattern of a horse or human head. Their highly developed decorative art appeared to arrive fully formed, derived from Greek and Etruscan artefacts. Elaborate patterns adorned Gallic pottery and jewellery. But their admiration for the Greeks did not stop at ceramics. The tribes in the southern part of Gaul increasingly adapted Greek and Roman political systems (although many of the northern tribes retained hereditary kingship). The Helvetii, Aedui, and Arverni had abandoned a monarchical system in favour of elected magistrates, answerable to a Council, and with public codes of law.

Pan Gallic councils involving all the tribes could be assembled, particularly in times of emergency. These councils were able to form general policies, and, if necessary, elect a military leader for the entire country, when threatened by an external source. In documenting his conquest of Gaul, Caesar paid tribute to the Gallic soldiers on their pride, passion and patriotism. His most dangerous opponent, Vercingetorix, he describes as fighting not for his own aggrandisement, but for his country's prestige and the liberty of all.

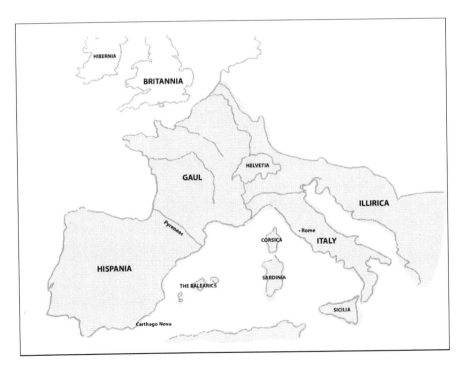

WESTERN ROMAN EMPIRE 44BC

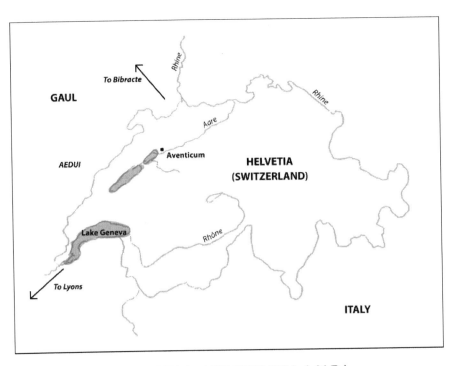

HELVETIA (SWITZERLAND)

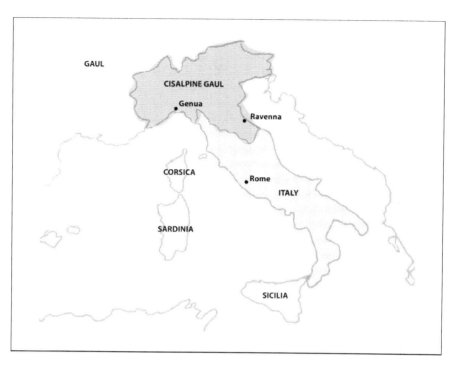

ITALY & CISALPINE GAUL

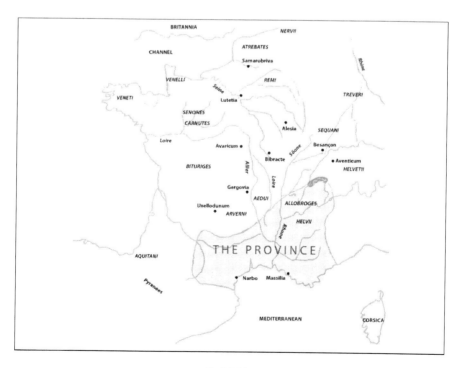

GAUL

Dramatis Personae

Italic script denotes actual persons.

The Romans

Gaius Julius Caesar
His Legates (Generals) in Gaul:-

> *Titus Attius Labienus*
> *Quintus Tullius Cicero*
> *Lucius Arunculaneius Cotta*
> *Quintus Titurius Sabinus*
> *Gaius Fabius*
> *Gaius Caninius Rebilus*
> *Marcus Antonius*

Avianus, a Roman spy
Gnaeus Pompeius Magnus
Gnaeus Pompeius, his elder son
Sextus Pompeius, his younger son
Licinius Crassus
Caecilius Scipio
Marcus Porcius Cato
Titus Pullo, centurion
Valerius, a legionary
Darius, a legionary

Titus Volusenus Quadratus, a Roman knight.
Claudia, his wife
Gaius Volusenus Quadratus, his eldest son,
Octavian Volusenus, his youngest son.
Borus, a household slave

Marcius Carvilius

Ursula, his mother,
Marcus Metius Celar, her brother
Senator Sperinus, her second husband
Andreas Carvilius, his younger brother,
Lucia Carvilius, his young sister

Hugo Domitius, friend of Octavian and Marcius
Flavius Domitius, his father, friend of Titus Volusenus

The Helvetians

Orgetorix, a Helvetian nobleman
Isolde, his second wife
Grandmother, (Dianthe) his mother
Coevorten, his eldest son from his first marriage
Metilaius, his second son from his first marriage

Allaine, his son from his second marriage
Eloise his eldest daughter from his second marriage
Chryseis, his middle daughter from his second marriage
Tzïnne, his youngest daughter from his second marriage
Nammeius, a Druid, his brother
General Divico, a leader of the Helvetii

The Aeduans

Guéreth, a noble
Diviciacus, an Aeduan prince
Dumnorix, his brother
Jayven, his only son

The Carnutes

Prince Acco
Prince Gutuater

11

Haetheric
His wife
Fáelán, his son

The Venetians

Drustan
Ninian
Cadell

Vercingetorix the Arvernian, commander in chief

Lucterius, leader of the Cadurcans

Drappes, leader of the Senones

Commius, King of the Atrebates

BOOK 1
MIGRATION

BOOK 1 : CHAPTER 1

Carthago Nova, (Cartagena), Hispania 68 BC

The city of Carthago Nova, founded on the South Mediterranean Coast of Spain by the brother of Hannibal a couple of centuries before, sat smugly on the isthmus, aware of its increasing strategic importance to Rome.

The port was surrounded on the southern flank by a natural deep water harbour, filled by so many merchant vessels of every conceivable size, it was difficult to discern the dark blue waters of the Mediterranean Sea between them. Swarthy sweaty men were busily engaged in unloading the varied cargoes amidst the screams of scavenging gulls. There were hauls of mackerel, netted from around the local coasts, to be used in the manufacture of the fish sauce for which the city was becoming renowned. There were exotic fruits, olive oil, grain, figs, grapes, and beans from North Africa, to feed the increasing populace. Huge blocks of varied coloured marbles were hoisted out and winched up the slopes, brought over from North Italy to help to beautify the newly constructed buildings, and pave the streets.

And from all parts of the Roman world, innumerable light-skinned and dark-skinned slaves were brought out from the stinking holds of ships, to be chivvied and kicked up the gang planks, desperate to see the light of day and feel hard land under their feet instead of pitching, yawing seas. The jetties resounded to the crack of the lash, and the cries and protests of the human cattle, as they were herded up the steep cobbles to the slave markets. Many of them were prisoners of war, others convicted felons. These fettered men were needed in their thousands to perform the dangerous works of mining, building, brick-baking, road-making, and all the other hazardous tasks required to increase the wealth of this ever-expanding city. Their lives would be short.

The streets followed the neat Roman grid pattern, incorporating houses, shops, taverns and theatres, built on the five little hills, rising to the imposing temple situated at the highest point. This building dominated the skyline, from whence Apollo, the Sun God, smiled beatifically on his many adherents below, and sent them scurrying to the shelter of shaded colonnades, or to seeking the cool waters of the public baths and fountains. It was very hot.

The city was in a state of great excitement. For the newly appointed Quaestor for Spain, Julius Caesar, had come for a visit. Everyone was talking about this up and coming young man from Rome, hopeful that he might consider granting the city Colonia status. The city fathers had proclaimed a public holiday in his honour. And having heard of young Caesar's reputation, who better to show him round the many civic attractions but Cassius Afranius, the handsome son of one of the Principal Citizens.

Julius Caesar stood on the temple steps looking far out over the busy harbour, and smiled in satisfaction. His role as Quaestor was proving much more interesting and lucrative than he had expected. Even from this distance he could see activity in the small fleet of sleek Roman warships. There were twenty triremes with banked oars, manned by marines and exhausted galley slaves, being readied to pursue and kill the pirates pillaging along the coast. But in the main the massive port was heaving with commerce. Public holidays were not allowed to interfere with trade. At Cassius's instigation Julius had already slipped on seaweed-encrusted steps, inhaled the foul smell of rotting fish, and nearly tripped over the interminable ropes straining to keep the big merchant ships and little fishing boats safely moored. Crowds of onlookers followed his every move, but were kept at a respectful distance by a wall of officious men wielding thick sticks.

Caesar had investigated the wharves and warehouses, and watched the emptied ships being reprovisioned, ready to take the precious cargoes of smelted silver, lead and iron back to Italy. He noted with approval the meticulous collection of harbour dues by zealous officials. Wealth was being created here. He would ensure some of it came his way. When this term of office was over, he would strive to be elected to the role of Pontifex Maximus, Chief High Priest of Rome. But it would take a considerable number of judicious bribes. Substantial bribes they would have to be, too.

He gave the slightest of signs to his lictor, the man who walked before him holding high the rods of the fasces, his badge of office. This caused a ripple of excitement in the crowd, who knew Caesar had the authority to order capital punishment. Not that there appeared to be any such requirement at the moment. The courts were closed for the holiday. But perhaps someone had displeased him, and would be dragged away, screaming his protests? No, the crowd turned away, disappointed. It looked as if Caesar was just going into the temple. No doubt he would be there for hours. They would have to wait for the games later in the day for further entertainment.

"Shall we go in?" Julius suggested to his companion. "I believe there is a statue here that I wish to see."

The two well-dressed young men bounded up the steep steps of the temple with the effortless confidence of the very rich, pausing momentarily between the huge pillars, glancing automatically upwards. The massive stones of the portico, carved in Corinthian style, seemed threatening, powerful with heavy menace. The chill air of the entrance struck through their fine thin wool tunics, making them suddenly shiver in unison. Cassius grinned in the shadows.

"Powerful Gods here," he whispered.

His companion made no acknowledgement, but walked purposefully forward towards the dimly lit interior. The sibilant murmuring of a service was in progress. The priest stared challengingly at the interloper, then hastily dropped his eyes in recognition.

Julius pushed through the congregation, which parted before him like the Red Sea, with Cassius trailing behind him. He made his way behind the altar to the far right of the temple, then stood silently looking up. He saw a black marble Colossus, clad in leather boots and a golden helmet. Stone folds of cloak draped over the statue's huge shoulders, fastened by a golden brooch. His eyes had been painted in, and stared far off through the temple walls to the countless countries of his conquest. He held no weapons, but his left hand casually clutched a thin gold crown.

"Is this what we came to see?" asked Cassius coming up, a little piqued that Julius knew something about his city which he didn't. "Who is he?"

"There's a plaque on the wall."

Cassius knelt down. "It's in Greek," he complained. "Isn't there a translation?"

Julius gave a tiny sigh of exasperation. "The statue is of Alexander the Great, conqueror of the world at the age of thirty three."

"He didn't do much at the age of thirty four though, did he?" said Cassius, getting to his feet.

"He became immortal, my dear Cassius." Julius turned his back on the statue, the voices, ritual and incense, returning to the fierce light of the temple entrance, the sounds and smells of the bustling city, and the residue of the gawping spectators.

"Now what?" asked Cassius, with some irritation. He was getting a little tired of trailing around after Caesar. He had hoped to be able to show his new friend over his city. Julius didn't take kindly to being led, apparently.

"Aren't those the new baths?"

Cassius nodded eagerly. "Yes, they're magnificent. Comparable to Rome, I assure you."

"Then shall we go for a swim?"

Julius sat on the steps, looking with open interest as the younger man slowly slipped off his tunic, smiled at him and walked to the pool-side, balancing delicately on lithe, muscular

17

feet. Cassius leapt swiftly into the air and executed a perfect, graceful dive, scarcely rippling the surface of the water, which closed above him. When his head broke the surface he wiped his face with his hand, grinned at his companion, then proceeded to plough slowly up and down the length of the pool, using lazy, seemingly effortless strokes. Arriving back, he heaved himself half out of the water, an elbow resting on the pool-side. Julius now sat with his feet trailing in the water.

"Aren't you coming in for a swim?"

"I'm quite happy watching you trying to impress me."

Cassius put a hand on his knee. "Am I succeeding?"

"No."

Cassius continued to smile, only the slightest constriction of his pupils registering the insult.

"Perhaps we should go then." He endeavoured to make his voice sound neutral.

"As you please," said Julius indifferently, and rolled onto his elbows, feigning interest in the swimmers on the other side of the pool.

Caesar glanced sidelong, as his companion pulled himself out of the pool and began to towel himself vigorously. He was pleased to see he had made Cassius angry. Good! He would make him furiously angry, and then spend the rest of the evening soothing him down. A more interesting challenge than Cassius had presented hither to.

Caesar lay back against the cushions while Cassius, satisfied, slept next to him. He put his hand out for the wine cup and drank deeply. The hunt, the chase, the final kill, his quarry never seemed worth the capture. The following night, after dinner, he kissed Cassius full on the mouth, bade him goodnight and walked off alone to his empty bedroom. His surprised servants hesitated, then followed. With their master in his present capricious mood, it was as well to be prepared for any eventuality. However, he dismissed them both as soon as he got into bed, and fell instantly into a heavy sleep.

He was dreaming, a dream of vast complexity. He knew it was important to understand the vital elements, but they slipped beyond his grasp. He floated in a boat down a long tunnel. People he knew were standing on the bank, waving to him, one holding an enormous sword. He needed someone to explain why. Ah, his mother stepped into the boat. She turned to him in great surprise. She was quite naked. He lay on top of her to squeeze the information out of her, pushing down her monstrous white breasts, her nipples under his fingers. He could feel her squirming under his thighs. He covered her mouth as she began to scream. He thrust himself into her.

He sat up in bed panting, drenched with sweat. He forced his mind to heave itself away from the nightmare. Vigorously he rubbed himself with the coverlet, then slipped out of the bed towards the window. The room was airless, stiflingly hot. He couldn't open the shutters, and was reluctant to summon a servant, as if they might read his thoughts. Without bothering to dress, he strode out of the room towards the garden. A lamp flickered in an alcove. Caesar paused on the threshold, surveying his new young secretary bent over the desk, scraping away at the parchment, still busy with the day's dictation. Silently he walked up behind the boy, and grasped his shoulder.

Philemon gasped in fright, jerking his arm, causing the ink to spill, ruining the work. Caesar smiled to himself. He would be able to have the boy beaten for that in the morning, if he so wished. He went over to the marble bench and sat leaning back, one foot on the cool floor, the other on the seat, the knee bent, thighs wide apart, a sexual threat.

"Here!"

Philemon came over promptly, and knelt on the floor before his master, keeping perfectly still, waiting for orders.

"I've just had a dream, Philemon, quite an extraordinary dream. I dreamt that I was raping my mother. What could that mean, do you suppose?"

A slight tremor shook the boy. "What would you like it to mean, Master?"

Caesar leant forward and briskly slapped him across the face. "I asked for your opinion."

Philemon hunted round in his mind. No answer seemed safe. "Could it be, Master, that your revered mother represents the earth, and that you are to conquer the whole world?"

Caesar lifted the boy's chin and looked into his eyes, pleased to see the fear, aware also of the hatred underneath.

"What a clever child it is, to be sure," he said softly, smiling. He stroked the boy's cheek with his thumb. "And such a beautiful boy, too," he added. "But look at this, there are shadows under your eyes, Philemon. You are working too hard."

"Yes, Master."

Dutifully the boy kissed his master's hand and rose to go. He walked over to the desk, unsure whether or not to put away the stylus and parchment.

"Leave it," commanded his master.

Relieved, Philemon withdrew, walking through the corridors to the slaves' quarters, his heart gradually ceasing to thud quite so loudly in his chest. There would be twice as much work to do tomorrow, and a spoiled parchment to contend with as well.

As he walked out of the room Caesar paused at the desk and picked up the parchment, handing it to the guard in the corridor with orders to burn it.

It was raining in the garden, a quiet, steady, warm drizzle. He strode over to the fountain and stood with his arms outstretched, head held back, mouth open. The soft raindrops gathered in his hair, and landed gently on his tongue. Raindrops fell on his oiled shoulders, coalescing, trickling slowly down his chest, speeding down the taut muscles of his abdomen. The moisture seeped into his groin.

He lay down on the soft earth, and started slowly to caress himself. He was seized by a sudden surge of sexual intensity. The power of all the world concentrated miraculously in his loins. He was the Divine Creator, descendant of Venus. His senses were overwhelmed; he cried out in ecstasy as he ejaculated into Mother Earth herself.

Gradually his breathing slowed, his pulses quietened. He lay still, absorbing the smell of wet leaves and grass, the heavy scent of drooping petals. His whole body felt wonderfully relaxed. Every separate muscle seemed to savour the past pleasure.

He was certain now he was destined for greatness. The message from the Gods was unmistakable. He rose up again, and leant with his back against the column of the peristyle, still warm with the day's sun. Tomorrow he would order the sculptor to start working on his bust. When it became his turn to take his place in the temple - here he smiled inwardly to himself - he wished to be represented a little more realistically than Alexander the Great.

BOOK 1: CHAPTER 2

Helvetia (Switzerland) 68 BC

Grandmother said that Father would be coming home soon, but she had been saying the same thing since the end of summer and now the snow was beginning to pile up against the shutters. Allaine was worried. There had been no messengers for a month. He could tell his mother was worried too. Although her stomach was getting fatter, her body was getting thinner, her expression perpetually anxious. The servants whispered and huddled in corners. He knew what they were saying, of course, that his mother was having another baby. If so she didn't seem particularly pleased about it.

"Brr, why is this room so cold? Allaine, come away. Close that shutter. Watching for your father will not make him come any quicker. You!" Grandmother poked the servant with her cane. "Light the lamps, you lazy slut. How can you see to spin in this light?"

She turned again to her grandson. "Allaine, come to me."

Her heart heaved at the sight of him coming towards her - he was such a perfect image of her husband; the same serious wide grey eyes, the same curls, though finer and blonder, the same deep intelligence.

"Tell me," she commanded. He leant against her knee.

"Mother is ill." He stated it as a fact.

"Mother is ill," she repeated. "Yes."

"And Mother is missing Eloise." His elder sister Eloise had been sent a long way away, to be brought up in the house of her betrothed. Mother and Eloise had both cried bitterly at the parting.

"Yes," Grandmother answered gravely. "She is missing Eloise."

"And Father is away, fighting the Germans. Dead, maybe, Grandmother?"

"It will take more than Germans to kill your father, my Grandson." She gave one of her rare smiles. He loved to see his grandmother smile. She still had all her strong white teeth. But she didn't smile often these days, spending most of her time, shouting, bullying, and cajoling the servants. With Father missing, they were apt to get slack.

"Grandmother, will Father be back for my birthnight?"

"Yes," said Grandmother decidedly. By the middle of winter he was certain to be back, alive or dead.

A horse seemed to give a large snort just behind them. Allaine ran to the shutters and threw them wide open again. There in the courtyard stood a jet-black horse, the sound of its hooves muffled by snow. The messenger had already hurled himself from the saddle and was rushing into the house. Two ostlers came running from the stables, agog for the news rather than for the horse. The maids wouldn't allow the messenger into the Great Hall until he'd taken his boots off. He approached Grandmother, and sinking down to one knee before her, he said,

"Madam, good news. The passes are held: the Germans are in retreat."

"And my boys?" said Grandmother, "my boys?"

"Madam, casualties have been very heavy." He dropped his head, his own brother had been killed. "But Prince Orgetorix is safe. And so are his sons."

Grandmother always knew what to do. "May the Gods grant peace and blessings to those who go before us."

"So be it, Lady," said the messenger. He kissed her hand.

A servant holding a lamp came through the doorway, followed by Mother and his two little sisters. Grandmother went immediately to her daughter-in-law, and put her arms around her waist, leading her over to the bench.

"Come my dear, come, sit down. It's good news, so the messenger has said."

Mother sat, one hand clutched to her side, pressing hard, the other holding Grandmother's hand tightly in her own.

His sister Chryseis pirouetted across the floor.

"Do you like my new dress, Allaine?"

"No," he told her.

She looked at him in annoyance. "Don't you wish you had dresses, Allaine?"

"No."

"I expect you do, really."

"What can you do in a dress?" asked her brother with scorn.

"It's not to do," she said, staring at him accusingly. "It's to look nice. It's to look nice for when Father comes home."

Allaine looked at her thoughtfully. He supposed there must be a use somewhere for small girls, but as yet he had failed to find one. He looked at Tzïnne, his younger sister, with slight concern. She was clutching some object close to her chest.

"Zinny, what is it? What's the matter?"

The little girl held out the object for his inspection, and the memory of her grievance caused the tears to flow again.

"Chrys broke me dolly," she said sniffing.

Chryseis put her hands on her hips, and stood staring defiantly at her brother.

"Well I didn't do it on purpose," she hissed.

Little idiots, thought Allaine to himself. Haven't they got more sense than to quarrel at a time like this? No, of course not. They were girls, wholly devoid of any sense at all. Grandmother was now firing off orders like a commander-in-chief. Servants, steward, and bailiff were hastily summoned. All must be got ready for the arrival of the conquering hero. This was a problem. Would Tzïnne, in fifty years time, be like her grandmother? If so, what would have wrought the change? He wished he could get some answers to all the questions that perpetually buzzed around inside his head. He broached the subject with Grandmother that night before going to bed.

"You need a tutor, Grandson."

"A tutor?" He looked enquiringly.

"Someone who teaches." She smiled. "When your father returns, we will make it a priority."

But Orgetorix had so much to worry him when he came home, that the question of the tutor did not arise for a long time. They'd held the passes, but the cost had been appalling, the carnage truly terrifying, the number of dead and wounded frightening to contemplate. The heavy snows had started already. There was no way he could repair fortifications and defences until the spring. Council had had to call up reinforcements, leaving pathetically few to till the land and harvest the crops. They were to institute rationing this winter, which would mean many petty quarrels to be resolved. Envy and malice would divide clan against clan, unless they were very rigorous, and he had no energy left to be rigorous. He was relieved that someone else was to be chief magistrate next year, but anxious lest they were not up to the task.

Still, how good it was to be home. He fervently hoped his brother, Nammeius, the priest, would soon seek out the pleasures of his own house. He was fed up with the man's constant carping in his ear.

Nammeius was quite unable to appreciate that the German king recognised no Druidic authority, and would be unlikely to give up the struggle just because a priest had so ordered it. However, he had ordained three days of thanksgiving for their deliverance.

Orgetorix and his depleted forces approached home to the sound of temple bells, and the deep Alpine horns echoing back from every mountaintop. As they passed through the mountain villages girls dashed out from the houses despite the cold, cheering and shouting, sometimes kissing and cuddling and more, crowning the soldiers with wreaths of leaves. His wagons held many of the wounded who were unable to walk, and these were distributed to each village, to be cared for throughout the winter.

Poor rations would make their wounds harder to heal. Orgetorix shook his head vigorously. He must stop thinking these miserable thoughts. There was a little time to rejoice, surely. But as soon as he saw his wife his heart sank. She had difficulty kneeling before him - he had to help her back to her feet again. He could see Nammeius looking sideways at her, a quick scowl deepening on his face. A weary foreboding moved in him.

After blessing the food Nammeius remained standing.

"I refuse to eat with this woman who calls herself your wife, my Lord Orgetorix. As can be easily seen, the woman is four months gone in pregnancy at least, yet by my reckoning we've been away for eight months or more. The woman is a whore and the child is a bastard."

Amidst the gasps of horror, Allaine's voice could be heard piping up clearly.

"What's a bastard, Grandmother?"

Orgetorix watched as his wife rose and went over to stand before the priest, bowing her head slightly.

"You wrong me, Sir, but I leave you to your supper."

As soon as she had gone Nammeius raised his hands in the air. "With the authority vested in me by the Gods, I order a family court. You will not speak to your wife without witnesses, Orgetorix."

Chrys looked in bewilderment from one grim face to another. "Allaine," she asked her brother plaintively, "what happened to the party?"

BOOK 1: CHAPTER 3

Helvetia (Switzerland) 68 BC

Allaine crouched on the bed with his arms round his little sisters. A black well of terror was bubbling up through the very centre of his house. Firstly, his grandmother had spoken in vengeance and fury to her son Nammeius, the priest, calling him many dreadful things, until he turned on her and threatened her death.

"How could such a wicked one spring from such a good man?" she wept, as she was dragged from the hall by the men.

And his father hadn't stopped it. Hadn't said a word. Just stared, empty and defeated. The maidservants were numb with fear, huddling against the walls, looking sick. When Uncle Nammeius ordered the children to bed, the maids fell over themselves in their eagerness to act as nurse, and then stopped, frozen with horror when he told them to stay in their places until summoned. Even though their rooms were far away, the children could still hear the screams and sobs as the maids were being questioned.

"Is it going to be us next?" asked Chrys, her teeth chattering with fear.

Allaine probed the answer with his mind. "No, they won't touch us. We're too small."

"What about when we grow big?" she sobbed.

"I won't let them."

Surprisingly, she believed him. He didn't make the mistake of believing himself. When the girls were finally asleep, Zinny sucking her thumb for comfort, he shuggled himself from under them, and went to fetch the furs. He peered at them closely, at their faces lit by the dim lamplight. He thought that maybe after all they did have some use. The girls lay huddled together, Chrys with her thick mass of red-gold curls tumbling round her head, Zinny with long black eyelashes delicately stroking her cheek, soft black hair spilling down, outlining the tiny ear.

A rush of love overwhelmed him, taking him by surprise. He bent over and kissed each cold cheek. Perhaps that's what they're for, he thought.

Lady Isolde awaited her fate with indifference. She felt too ill to care and too weak to fight her brother-in-law, who had always hated her with vicious intensity. Partly because he had wanted her for himself, and partly because of her influence over her husband. At times Orgetorix could make seriously rash decisions, often at the instigation of his brother. Sometimes, but not always, she managed to win him over. He had wished to send Allaine away to the college of priests, three hundred miles off in a distant land. She suspected that Nammeius had an ulterior motive, and wished her son dead. She kept her thoughts, she wasn't always right, of course. Sometimes her husband's ideas, so rash to her, became bold and successful in action and, she admitted to herself, made him one of the best respected and most popular men in the country. Is that the difference between men and women, she thought to herself. That men will risk everything - wives, children, servants, land - everything for the chance of success.

They sent for her in the morning, to be arraigned before the male members of her house, Nammeius sitting on his dais at the end of the hall, her husband and his two sons by his first wife, an assortment of cousins, and, she was horrified to see, Allaine, sitting gravely quiet at the end of the table.

She protested at once but Nammeius forestalled her. "It is right that he should witness his mother's disgrace."

She saw her stepsons lounging against the wall, glance up at her quickly and then look away. The trial was a travesty. She could see her husband become increasingly restless and agitated at Nammeius's questions.

No, she denied being pregnant, she denied ever sleeping with another man other then her husband, she looked straight at Nammeius as she spoke.

No, she hadn't seen her periods; no, she didn't know why. But she knew what a child felt like inside her belly - if this was a child it was so still, so silent, it must be made of stone.

The arguments went to and fro, getting nowhere. Wild theories were put forward. Isolde found she could not stand any longer, the pain was becoming intense. She begged to be allowed to sit, but was refused.

"You may kneel," said Nammeius. "A contaminated woman will not sit in the presence of her lord and master."

In the end it was decided that Nammeius should be appointed to determine the size of the foetus, and its composition.

"You will present yourself to me tomorrow, and submit yourself for examination."

"I will not submit."

"Isolde, you must."

"No, I won't, I won't." She started to cry.

Nammeius abruptly capitulated. "Of course your husband will be present, and your mother by marriage," he explained.

Allaine was bewildered by the questioning, and bewildered even more by his mother's defencelessness against his uncle. Why was his father not protecting her, speaking up for her? He thought his father loved his mother. Perhaps he couldn't love someone so ill and weak, and such a strange colour. But it makes me love her much more, thought Allaine to himself, I want to look after her, care for her, make her better, but I don't know how. Even Grandmother doesn't know how, and she knows everything.

The next morning Allaine crept out of bed very early. He went to his mother's room, where she was still deeply asleep. He bent over her, brushing her cheek delicately with his lips. He loved her so much. He crept under the bed, and lay there, stiff and cold as the morning progressed.

But when he saw her exposed on the bed even Nammeius felt some pity. Isolde lay gazing indifferently at the timbered ceiling with yellowed eyes, as his fingers delicately stroked her abdomen. The skin of her breasts was sallow, puckered and wrinkled where the flesh had fallen away, but her stomach was tense and bloated.

"I feel the woman may be right," Nammeius conceded reluctantly, "the child is made of either stone or wood."

"Well?" Orgetorix insisted.

"Desperate diseases call for desperate remedies, Brother," he spoke half-sorrowfully. He may be able to beat the child out of her. He flinched as Isolde turned her sardonic gaze on him.

"Why don't you just kill me and be done with it?"

"That is, of course, another possibility. A quick death is surely preferable to being devoured alive by a wooden child."

"No!" Orgetorix broke in desperately. "We must try anything, anything."

His mother turned on him. "Are you both mad? Are you both blind? Cannot you see the girl is dying? There is no child. Will you maltreat a dying woman?"

"Silence, Mother," said Orgetorix. "There are some matters of which you are ignorant. Affairs of this country do not always parallel those of Greece. My brother has knowledge of these things. We will leave it in his hands."

"Then I suggest, Brother, we first go to sacrifice, to appease the Gods."

As they rode towards the sacred grove, Nammeius found his mind churning over endless possibilities. Supposing the child stayed alive, even after Isolde was dead. That strange offspring may be capable of ruining the entire country. He would have liked some advice himself but couldn't think how to get in touch with any of his fellow priests quickly enough. Well, he would pray for guidance. The almighty powers of the heavens would show him what to do.

Allaine stayed still hidden between the bed and the walls.

"Help me, Mother, please help me," whispered Isolde.

"Don't I always help you, dearest child?" said Grandmother.

She picked up the handbell and rang it with vigour, ordering hot water and bowls to be brought, when the servants appeared in answer. Allaine watched with interest, as Grandmother removed some boxes from the chest in the corner. He continued watching while she carefully mixed the contents of the boxes into a bowl, and then steeped them in hot water. A pleasant and pungent aroma filled the room. Grandmother strained off the liquid and poured it into a little cup.

"Drink all of this now, Isolde," she said, gently supporting the girl with her arms, leaning her back against her own shoulder.

"Will it work quickly?"

"Yes, my dear, for you very quickly. You know Isolde, you are the best daughter a mother could ever have. When you are gone I will do my best to look after your little ones, and I will always tell them of their beautiful mother."

Grandmother carried on all morning, while Allaine got increasingly stiff, but he didn't care. She was telling all the old stories, how Grandfather had seen her in the market place at Massilia and demanded to marry her immediately; about her fear at coming to this new country; she told about the bath house, she told of her children, the happy times and the sad times, until at last she stopped.

"Come out now, Allaine. Your mother is dead. Kiss her goodbye."

So she had known he was there all along. Together they said the prayers for the dead.

"There. A blessed and peaceful end. She deserved no less," said Grandmother, finally drawing the sheet over her daughter-in-law's face. She squared her shoulders as she walked stiffly from the room. Now to break the news to her granddaughters.

The next day Nammeius had the corpse wrapped in a white sheet, interspersed with dried leaves of ash, oak and beech.

Allaine held onto his father's hand in the procession, his nailed boots slipping a little on the snow underfoot, which made everything silent. Nammeius had forbidden the sounding of any cymbals or trumpets. The body, grotesque under its coverings, was laid out on the altar stone and unwrapped. One arm flopped freely but otherwise the limbs were rigid, the knees bent, the yellowness of the skin much more obvious against the snow.

Allaine could see no resemblance whatsoever to his mother. The twisted shape seemed as perpetually dead as the stone upon which it lay. Nammeius ritually cleansed the sacrificial knife and lifted it high in the air, then brought it down in one swift movement, slitting the belly wide open. A glistening gush of liquid spouted from the wound, subsiding gradually to a thin trickle. Nammeius reverently laid the knife at the head of the altar, and raised his arms to heaven.

"Praise to the Gods," he declared. "The child has destroyed itself. The Lady Isolde may be burnt with due honour and ceremonies."

As if to make up for everything that had gone before, the funeral pyre was enormous. The speeches and ceremonies lasted for three whole days. When finally the guests had departed, and the ashes scattered, Allaine sought out his grandmother.

"What must I do now, Grandmother?" he asked.

She gazed back at him. It would have to be something to struggle with, to take his mind off these matters.

"You must learn my language, my Grandson," she announced.

BOOK 1: CHAPTER 4

Bibracte (Autun), capital town of Aeduan Territory, Central Gaul, 68 BC

Dumnorix was not sure how he had managed to get saddled with an eight-year-old brat. The boy seemed very determined. He couldn't imagine how he was ever to rid himself of him.

"I need to buy a tutor," Allaine had explained carefully. "One that speaks Greek."

He refused to accept Dumnorix's assurance that such a slave was unlikely to be found in the markets at Bibracte, even though it was the chief town of the Aeduans, and a centre of commerce.

"How do we know there's no such thing," Allaine said, with a trace of impatience, "if we don't go and find out?"

"Very well," Dumnorix became more cheerful, as an idea occurred to him. "While you're looking for tutors, I'll go and have a look at the girls. I need to choose a maid for my sister."

"You don't have a sister," Allaine pointed out.

"My mother, then," replied Dumnorix, with a grin.

"Doesn't your mother have a maid already?" asked Allaine, surprised.

"She needs another one," said Dumnorix, shepherding his charge towards the slave market.

Allaine tugged at his new friend's hand, and pointed out the man, with a small smile of triumph. The man was sitting on the ground, with his legs stretched out in the dust, a book unrolled on his lap. He was leaning back against the post to which he was chained. Closer inspection, however, revealed a decided disadvantage. The man's left hand looked to have been severely injured or crushed, lying cradled in his lap, grossly deformed, the fingers dark with bruised blood. He glanced up quickly as

Dumnorix squatted beside him, his right hand protectively holding the book, frightened it might be taken from him.

Dumnorix rolled the book up carefully, ascertaining firstly it was indeed written in Greek. He handed it to Allaine, and then addressed the man directly.

"Hello, what's your name?"

The man said nothing, just stared anxiously at his book.

"Well he can't speak Gallic; are you still interested?"

Allaine nodded eagerly. "It's alright, I've worked out a way. Watch." He held out the book, and pointed to it. "Book," he said. "You say it."

"Book," the young man repeated in his own language.

"See, is that right?"

"Correct," Dumnorix laughed. "I'll see if I can buy him for you. By the way, how much money do you have for this purchase?"

"Father will pay," Allaine said, confidently.

The dealer came forward to greet them, delighted to see two young nobles inspecting his merchandise.

Marcus Metius Celar, the slave dealer, was tall for a Roman. He held out his hand in greeting. He didn't believe in bowing and scraping like the Greek traders. He was proud of his business position and wealth. He was happy to help open up this wonderful country to commerce, and increasing contact with his own superior civilisation. Metius, though, had great admiration for his Gallic friends, finding them quick to learn and adapt. He thought highly of the state religion. Its mysticism and emphasis on personal revelation through spiritual contemplation, struck a resonating chord.

He recognised Dumnorix as the younger brother of Prince Diviciacus, one of the foremost nobles of the country. Here was a chance to impress.

"My dear Sirs, how can I help?" He turned to beckon imperiously to an interpreter, although his Gallic was becoming more and more fluent. There must be no mistakes, or question of misinterpretation.

Dumnorix explained. Metius looked at Allaine speculatively.

"The son of Orgetorix," he said pleasantly. "You wish to speak Greek?"

Allaine looked up and nodded.

"Perhaps you wish to learn how to buy slaves also?"

"Why not?" Dumnorix agreed, pleased. It was always useful to learn from an expert.

Metius turned to his secretary and spoke smoothly. "These boys are important. Get two chairs for them and a table. Give them some wine, use the glasses, and bring the prettiest girls." He might not be able to sell to them everything he had today, but at least he would be able to show them what was available.

Allaine sat on the beautifully crafted chair, feeling an inward pleasure as his fingertips traced the indentations of the carving. The Roman was treating them not with deference, but with respect. Dumnorix watched with delight as the pretty, confident maidservant came to them with a beaten copper tray, neatly stacked with wine jug, glasses and a little plate of cakes. He liked watching her graceful movements, as she fussed pouring out the wine. Allaine noticed her clothes, her black curls were pinned to the top of her head with a silver clasp, her dress was of wool as fine as that which his mother had worn.

While the man was being prepared, Metius talked to them about the glassware - how it was made, where it came from. The injured young man, now naked, was brought forward for their inspection. Metius rose, prepared to give the lecture.

"First," he smiled at them, "remember they are all fear, even the angry ones. Deep down, here." He held his hand out, palm towards the earth. "They are all fear. So, speak quiet, calm, move slow." His gestures emphasised his words, vividly expanding their meaning.

"Look." He pointed to the crushed arm, now somehow

much more apparent. "This man thinks only in his mind about this. Will he be hurt? So, first deal with wounds."

Carefully he showed how to assess wounds, deformities, and injuries, and then proceeded to explain the salient points of physical examination. He produced a man with a huge inguinal hernia to demonstrate that every part of the product must first be examined, and a boy who looked quite normal, but who became blue-lipped and breathless after the slightest exertion. Finally he took them inside and showed them the additional factors to check when buying a woman. But he didn't go into great detail.

"Come back another day," he suggested to Dumnorix with a glance at Allaine, "and I explain more. Now, most important. The price."

His secretary handed them two wooden tablets hinged by leather straps. "Tables for calculation. Assets. Can they do work? Light, heavy, skilled, unskilled. Can they read, weave, cook? Do they look good? Drawbacks. Age. Are they too young, too old? Infirmity, temperament, do they co-operate?" He pointed down the board. The man's reading ability seemed to be equally counteracted by the loss of an arm.

"Well, what is he worth?"

Dumnorix hesitated, conferred with the interpreter, checked a few points on the boards, and came up with the answer. "One hundred and fifty gold pieces."

"Correct, good. But remember also, sales tax. Which goes to your brother."

Dumnorix looked up with a laugh.

"And also my profit, most important. Two hundred gold pieces in total."

"Do we haggle?"

"No," Metius smiled. "It is a good price." Very good, he thought to himself, considering he had paid only twenty gold pieces to the pirates at Massilia. But then, he had all the problems of transportation. Astonishing how scarcity could force up a price so high.

"Very well. Will you keep the man safe for us please, and I will bring the boy's father back to complete the deal." Dumnorix walked over to where the man was writing out his name in the sand for Allaine. Noemon of Corinth.

"Did your father bring you all the way here to buy a tutor?" Dumnorix teased, as they strolled back to his brother's house.

"We're to fetch my big sister, Eloise," Allaine explained. "She was to be married, no betrothed," he amended. "But when the Germans attacked Besançon, her fiancé was killed, so Father wants her back again. I don't know why." He couldn't himself understand the implications of Eloise's engagement. How this was supposed to defeat the Germans when his father with his entire army had singularly failed to do so, was quite a puzzle.

Dumnorix ruffled his hair affectionately. "I see I shall have to teach you politics myself."

They seemed to spend all their time discussing the German problem, Dumnorix thought later that night at dinner when the subject occurred again. Their encroachments got worse year by year and their demands increasingly menacing. A pall of gloom hung over the company at the end of the discussion. In an effort to raise their spirits Dumnorix related the morning's events.

"I was impressed with Marcus Metius," he ended. "A better Roman than some of the others I've met."

Diviciacus smiled at him warmly. He had thought his younger brother to be getting a little too partisan, recently. For his own part, the thought of an alliance with Rome loomed pleasurably in his mind. He could see such enormous advantages, and perhaps a method of solving the German problem once and for all.

Helvetia (Switzerland)

The girls snuggled together under the furs. Eloise straightened out her legs, pushing her toes down to the cold part at the bottom of the bed. How lucky she was to be sleeping in this bed with her two sisters. If it hadn't been for the German king, if it hadn't been for the sudden raid, she might have been in bed with him, her betrothed. Her heart skipped a beat when she thought of it. It was terrible that he was dead, of course, he had been so alive, so big and powerful, his red mouth surrounded by the thick black beard. He had grinned at her from the other side of the table, taking bites of meat with his strong white teeth, licking the marrow out of the bones with his fat tongue, staring at her intently, then wiping his greasy fingers on his tunic. At the thought of him touching her, she shuddered. Oh, how pleased she had been to see her father. He had mistaken her tears for grief. He swore he'd find her another husband soon, but no, no, she had protested. She didn't want another husband. Her hysterical tears had led him to pet her and soothe her.

"Hush, hush, my precious," he said. "You're very young yet. We'll leave things for a year or two." It was after all only a betrothal, she was far too young for marriage.

Still, Eloise thought, there had been no mention since. Everyone had been too busy with the fighting. Perhaps she would escape for another year.

BOOK 1: CHAPTER 5

Rome 68 BC

The boys appeared to have exhausted all the possibilities of Marcius's bedroom. It was in a considerable mess. They had upended the bed to make a fort, and used the mattress as a siege terrace. The tripod had been turned into a battering ram, and now looked somewhat the worse for wear. A lot of water seemed to have got on the floor, and their clothes were soaked from the fight. Some of the feathers had escaped from the pillows and floated in the air. Marcius was presently engaged in puffing them up to the ceiling, before they had a chance to land on the floor. He rapidly tired of the exercise.

"What shall we do now?" he asked.

Octavian liked to be considered the leader, but wasn't sure he wanted to claim responsibility for the damage. His friend's new stepfather appeared to be rather stern. Just then a movement through the archway caught his attention.

"Shh!"

Octavian crept to the door, peering intently through the columns of the peristyle. He saw a small figure flitting furtively from column to column in the shadows. He turned and beckoned to Marcius, who crept up stealthily.

"Let's stalk him," Octavian whispered in his ear.

Marcius grinned in delight. "We'll be lions. We'll hunt him for our supper."

They slipped off their sandals, and crawled quickly from pillar to pillar on their hands and knees, making their tunics filthy in the process. They caught up with their prey in the atrium, disappointed but unsurprised to see that it turned out to be David. Unaware that he was observed, David carefully put down the wooden sticks he had collected at the side of the shallow marble pool and then, one by one, lowered them into the water, where they floated on the surface. All the time he did this, he kept up a running commentary.

The two spectators watched, fascinated.

"He's doing Jason and the shipwrecked sailors," whispered Octavian.

Marcius nodded. They'd been doing that part of the 'Argonautica' in school, with David sitting cross-legged behind them. To David's apparent consternation, one of the 'boats' had moved out into the middle of the pool. He would have to paddle if he wanted to rescue it, but somehow this seemed too awful a crime for a slave child to contemplate. He knelt hesitating at the pool-side. Octavian and Marcius hurled themselves on him, with loud roars. David screamed in terror, then burst into frightened sobs.

"Hey, David, stop it," Marcius protested. "We're not really going to eat you, we were only pretending. Don't be so stupid."

Octavian, who had by now confiscated the boats, was inclined to scold. "You shouldn't be doing this, you know," he said severely. "He'll get into frightful trouble if someone sees him."

Marcius couldn't be bothered to argue his slave's case. "Shall we have a shipwreck?" he suggested.

"Good idea." Octavian began arranging the boats in the pool.

"What about him," asked Marcius. "Shall he play?"

"Of course not," said Octavian. "You, boy, go and get us some cakes," he ordered.

Marcius's little brother Andreas appeared, sidling into the atrium from behind a pillar, hoping to be allowed to play as well. Octavian had already pushed him out of Marcius's bedroom. Unfortunately Octavian caught sight of him before his brother. Marcius was usually kind to his younger siblings, but always took the lead from Octavian, when his friend was around.

"Get lost, Andreas!" Octavian yelled at him. "Go and play with Lucy. You just get hurt, playing with us."

Andreas left before Octavian could shove him out of the

way. He made his disgruntled way to his little sister's room, and spent a miserable afternoon, thinking up horrible things to happen to David. He was outraged that Marcius should prefer a slave to play with him, and not his own brother. His childish pride was severely dented.

Octavian and Marcius had a wonderful afternoon. When David reappeared, with a plate piled high with cakes, they stuffed themselves full, Octavian even permitting David to participate. They used some of the remaining cakes as crew, balancing them carefully on the pieces of wood. But this often caused the boats to sink. They tried moving the resulting sludge at the bottom of the pool around with their hands, and had a sludge race.

Octavian's father, Titus Volusenus, was bitterly regretting the kind feelings that had prompted this particular social call. He had called round to see how his dead friend's widow and her children were faring, now they had married her off to Senator Sperinus, a man known for his bad temper. It was rumoured that Sperinus's own son had joined Pompey's forces, solely to escape from his father's rages. So far Titus had been thwarted in any attempt to see those with whom he was concerned, Sperinus insisting he accompany him first to the baths. He had been forced to spend the afternoon listening to a mishmash of conspiracy theories, and various tirades against people, some of whom were his good friends. Titus wasn't in the best of moods himself, when he accompanied his host into the atrium and saw the iniquities of his son.

Octavian was oblivious, he leapt to his feet, delighted to see his father.

"Hello, Sir," he beamed. "We've been having such fun."

"So I see," said his father, gazing round horrified.

Marcius, too, was pleased to see his father's friend, who had always acted more like a beloved uncle. Senator Sperinus surveyed the chaos.

"And just where are my servants?" he asked.

The edge in his voice at last brought realisation to both

41

boys. Marcius looked round at the atrium. It did seem a little disordered, and the cushions on the benches were decidedly wet, and smeared with cake crumbs, he realised. He gazed with dismay at his stepfather, not understanding the look of malevolence in his face. The steward appeared, all smiles and apologies, and quickly seized upon David as the obvious scapegoat.

"I'll have this wretch soundly beaten, my Lord," he said. "No doubt his carelessness has caused this."

"You can't do that," Marcius objected. "He belongs to Octavian." He would ask for him back tomorrow. He thought quickly. "I have to take full responsibility, Sir. We must have got carried away," an expression his mother often seemed to have used in the past, to excuse to his father, his occasional inexplicable behaviour.

Volusenus laughed aloud. "Carried away to Troy and back, I shouldn't wonder."

Later, at dinner, he had a chance to observe Lady Ursula. She seemed a little subdued, still possibly grieving for the death of her young husband. They had waited the bare minimum of six months before marrying her again. Perhaps not time enough to adjust to marriage with a much older man, he thought to himself. However, he was pleased to see she could want for no possible luxury. The house was beautifully appointed, the servants respectful and attentive. The good wine, though, seemed to have addled his brain, for when they set off for home, Octavian was attended by a little Jewish boy, but Titus couldn't for the life of him remember having brought such a child in the first place.

Lady Ursula lay in her enormous luxurious bed, awaiting her husband with dread. What would he be like tonight? Would he be pleased with her? Would he be angry again like before? If only she could find some way to placate him. His viciousness scared her, but when she had tried to be more conciliatory, more pleasing, he had struck her across the face and called her a harlot, yelling that she must have learnt such tricks in a brothel.

She hadn't dared look at Volusenus tonight, let alone speak to him. She didn't want another of those jealous rages, particularly not against her late husband's friend. That would have hurt her too much. What would she do if things got worse? She would have to be careful because of the children. She felt trapped like Persephone in an underground cavern. The last month he hadn't allowed her out of the house. Not even to shop. She turned nervously, thinking she heard footsteps. No, nothing. Perhaps, after all, he wouldn't come tonight. Perhaps she would have some peace. She drifted into an uneasy doze.

"Well, did you see her?" demanded his wife, as soon as Titus Volusenus got into bed.

"Yes, I saw her, of course I did."

"How is she? She's not been out of the house for a month you know. She hasn't answered any of my notes. I'm really worried."

"She's alright. A bit quiet perhaps. I didn't see the little ones, but young Marcius is a fine fellow. He was getting up to terrible mischief with Octavian, I'm afraid." Volusenus smiled to himself.

"And what's Sperinus like? Is he as black as he's painted?"

"He's certainly a bit grim." Titus Volusenus slipped his arm under his wife's head, snuggled up to her, and started kissing her cheek. "He seems to think the Senate is full of conspiracies."

"He's right about that, surely?" said his wife in surprise.

"Yes, I suppose he is." He leant over and kissed her lips. "Mm, do we have to talk about him?"

"Yes." She pushed him away. "What are we going to do?"

She could feel him grinning at her in the darkness. "You know perfectly well what we are going to do. We are going to ..."

"Octavian," hissed his wife.

"What?"

"Octavian!"

Volusenus rolled over and sat up. "Oh sorry," he said, with an apologetic grin, and gave his wife back the sheet, which she tucked neatly round her breasts.

"Octavian, would you mind giving us some advance notice of your presence in future?" started his father sternly.

"Yes, Father. I'm awfully sorry, but it's David. He won't stop crying."

"David?" his mother was puzzled. "We don't have a David, Octavian."

"He's just temporary," Volusenus assured her. He bent down and kissed the back of her neck. "Now don't move. I'll be back."

His wife chuckled.

He found David lying miserably still on the floor in the corner of his son's bedroom. He was curled up in a ball, naked, not even a sheet covering him. His head was resting on one hand, the other hand near his mouth, fingers limply curled, waiting to wipe away the tears which kept welling up under his lashes.

"We'd better organise some bedding for him," Volusenus started.

"No, we can't do that," Octavian said quickly. "He pees the bed."

His father looked at him in surprise.

"It's because he's a Jew. He hasn't got any skin around his dick to keep it in at night. He can't have anything!" Octavian finished, triumphantly.

Volusenus looked at his ruthless son with some misgiving. "Octavian, fetch the steward here."

Octavian looked at his father with surprise. Surely if anybody should be sent on messages, it should be David. But his father was frowning, and one must obey one's father after all. Volusenus wrapped David in a blanket, carried him over to his son's bed and sat down, settling the child into his lap.

"Firstly, David, peeing the bed has nothing to do with circumcision." The boy stirred slightly in his arms. "It's very common. You'll grow out of it. One of the bravest centurions I know, used to wet the bed when he was young."

David heaved a small sigh.

"Secondly, I will not hand you back to your master, until his steward assures me you will not be chastised for the misdeeds of my son."

Titus rejoined his wife to find her still wrapped in the sheet, propped on one elbow, staring into space.

"Where were we?"

"Ursula," she said. "She's only got that brother of hers, Marcus Metius. You know, the slave-dealer."

Volusenus pulled the sheet down, until it just covered her from knee to ankle.

"Venus reclining on a couch," he said, sighing with pleasure.

"I know he's a rich man," his wife continued, "but he's not much use to her in the wilds of Gaul, is he?" She looked down at herself in amusement. "Venus, indeed."

He smiled back at her. "To me you are more beautiful than Venus herself." He pushed her onto her back.

"Hush! You mustn't say such things about the Gods," she said, shocked.

He took no notice of her, but started kissing her neck, her breasts. When he got to her stomach, she spoke again.

"Promise you'll write to him."

"What?"

"Promise you'll write to Marcus Metius."

He sighed with contentment, cushioning his head on her abdomen as she bent her knees slightly, letting her thighs fall apart.

"I promise," he said. "In fact," he continued gently, "here's my hand on it." He smiled to himself as he heard her gasp in pleasure above him.

Senator Sperinus sat in his own room. He had been

drinking heavily for the last hour, trying to banish the ideas which haunted him. Again tonight he had caught himself looking at his wife, wondering if she was ogling Volusenus behind his back. He could feel the jealous rage starting up, flooding through his veins. He would have to stop these thoughts popping into his head, somehow expunge them from his brain. He mustn't quarrel with anyone again. He so regretted his words to his son. They had parted like sworn enemies, yet he was immensely proud of the boy. Surely he would do well under Pompey's command.

His physician had advised him to marry the young widow with her young family. But instead of improving matters, it had merely given him more fears to plague him. Could he be going mad? No. It was well known that the very contemplation of the idea proved sanity. He would leave his wife in peace tonight, and concentrate his thoughts on the speech he would make in the Senate tomorrow. He must endeavour to be kind to her, not be carried away by his feelings.

Impatiently he pushed the thoughts away. He was getting sidetracked already. Concentrate, concentrate. Julius Caesar. He was the present enemy, the present real threat, stirring up trouble among the Spanish colonists. His speech must resound round the Senate, supporting the Consuls. The legions must be sent to restore order. Wasn't the eldest Volusenus boy to go on Caesar's staff? What then could be the real reason for his father's visit this afternoon?

BOOK 1: CHAPTER 6

Bibracte (Autun) and Lutetia (Paris) 67 BC

Allaine could tell that Noemon's arm was paining him again. His slave's face was white, his mouth shut tight, and his body too rigid in the saddle. Allaine knew it always got worse in the cold weather, but he had bad need of the man's knowledge, and anyway he wanted him for companionship. Unfortunately, Noemon was a poor horseman at the best of times.

The road had been following the river for many miles, but now had swung westwards. He urged his horse forward to catch up with his brothers. The beast, though tired, responded gallantly enough, cantering up the hill, protesting, neighing violently when he reigned in, its snorting breath outlined in the frosty air.

"How much further," Allaine demanded, "before we stop?"

His half-brothers swung round in their saddles, both frowning with impatience.

"I warned you not to bring him, Allaine. He's been nothing but a bloody drag since we set out."

The road curved sharply down before them.

"Look!"

Allaine moved his horse cautiously to the edge of the escarpment. Coevorten pointed with his riding crop. "There, down there. Do you see?"

A thousand feet down the ground spread flat. Below in the damp valley he could see the pale gleam reflected from the walls of the fortified town, partially obscured by the smoke of a thousand fires, which filled the air below them in delicate horizontal bars of mist.

"That's Bibracte. Do you remember it?"

"Well, not much," Allaine responded.

"Another hour to get to the valley at least. But there's an inn. We'll stop there and rest if Father agrees."

Once at the inn Orgetorix ordered the slave to be wrapped in warm blankets, and set before the fire in an effort to ease him a little. It looked as if a wagon would have to be hired to fetch the man to Lutetia, otherwise they might find when they arrived, that the Gallic Assembly had finished its deliberations without the benefit of the opinions of the Swiss contingent. Fortunately such an eventuality was rendered unnecessary, for while the menservants were mixing the bowls of wine, and the maids were bustling around with plates and dishes filled with breads, meats, cheeses and eggs, a commotion was heard in the courtyard, the many sounds of horses and harness, the squeaking of iron-rimmed wheels over the icy cobbles. Marcus Metius strode confidently into the hall, attended by splendidly attired servants, and looking remarkably pleased with himself. He claimed immediate acquaintance with Allaine, gravely shaking his hand and asking if he had found his servant satisfactory, all the time using the Greek language.

Allaine was happy to respond in kind. He pointed out Noemon, lying on the floor in the corner, and briefly explained the present problem. Metius nodded, but made no comment. Ignoring the intimidating presence of the armed guards in the hall, he turned to Orgetorix, addressing him in fluent Gallic.

"I am honoured to meet you, Sir," he said, "but I am not used to local customs. Do we shake hands? Do I bow? Or," as he caught sight of the expression on the face of Nammeius, "perhaps I should go out of the door, and come in again on my knees."

Orgetorix laughed and shook Metius's outstretched hand. The man was dressed like a king after all - better than a king if truth be told, his tunic being heavily embroidered and interwoven with gold thread, his cloak lined and edged with fur. He looked what he was - a very wealthy man.

At dinner, when the boys returned from their inspection of the chariot and team, talk turned to the shocking state of the roads.

"Suppose your chariot had got stuck, Sir," Allaine asked, a little perturbed. "How would you have managed?"

"I've a convoy of wagons following me, Allaine, so I would have had my chariot dismantled, and finished my journey perched on a box in a cart. Very good for my soul, no doubt," he added with a smile.

Allaine was quite sure he would have done no such thing. He would at least have ridden one of the horses. Orgetorix wanted to know what goods he was importing.

"I have a quantity of good wine, Sir, and glassware. Worked leather, good olive oil and some perfumes and spices that can be a little hard to obtain here." He could see his audience was beginning to look interested. "And I've brought one or two antiquities that people might be interested in, perhaps."

"And do you stay in Bibracte," asked Coevorten with interest.

"I have a warehouse there certainly, but I intend to push on to Lutetia. I thought that while the General Assembly was in progress it would be a good opportunity to try and obtain permission to extend my trading posts a little further north."

"North and west, maybe," Orgetorix agreed. "You won't get far to the east - the Treveri like to keep themselves to themselves."

"But they must have much to export, surely," Metius said in surprise. He found it difficult to understand anyone not wishing to become better off. "Furs, perhaps?" he hazarded.

"Yes, but what will you give them in return?" Coevorten smiled. "They wouldn't thank you for perfume."

"Not even for their women?" Metius enquired. "Perhaps if you have time in Bibracte, you could visit my warehouse and give me your opinion as to what may be of interest, and what may cause me to be lynched in the market-place," he grinned.

Although Orgetorix protested this was highly unlikely, Metius was aware Nammeius didn't approve at all of his haul of exotica. "That's what would happen to me if I tried to sell your salt pork in Judea," he explained. "We traders have to be careful, we rely on goodwill alone."

This he ably demonstrated by presenting Allaine, at the end of the meal, with a soft leather bag. When the boy inspected the contents he found an exquisite silver hand-mirror, reflecting back his face with astonishing clarity.

"Thank you very much, Sir. I'll be pleased to give it to my sisters."

"Perhaps you'd better," Metius agreed. "Read the inscription."

"'To be used with spare......?' No," he hesitated. "'To be used with caution, remembering Narcissus.'"

"Excellent."

The rumbling of heavily-laden wheels presaged the arrival of the loaded wagons. Metius engaged to transport Noemon to Bibracte, and obligingly offered to take him with him to Lutetia.

"And perhaps, Allaine, you would like to ride in my chariot?"

"Sir, you are very kind," Allaine started.

"No," said Metius, "It's a trade-off. If I take you and your servant off your father's hands, I am hoping he will give me an armed escort to Paris." He turned to Orgetorix. "Once one leaves the protection of Rome, travelling with expensive goods sometimes becomes a little hazardous." Perhaps he shouldn't have said as much, but it was true after all. "Although, of course, I have a fair number of armed outriders, I have lost one wagon to bandits. So if you see any gypsy tents adorned with fine Persian carpets, you'll know where they got them from."

Allaine found Lutetia to be a very well fortified city on the banks of the River Seine, with a long strong bridge over the river, the upper part deliberately made of wood, so it could be easily fired in the event of war. The city was host to so many visitors, many had to be accommodated outside the city environs itself. The town was now surrounded by a large makeshift camp, with a multiplicity of little markets. All was well-ordered and policed, however. The city dignitaries had no desire for their town to become renowned for rioting.

When Allaine attended the assembly with his father and brothers, he was interested to see that there were several other children present - some the same age as himself, some older or younger. Perhaps like him they too were to be trained for the priesthood? He asked his father, but no. Their fate was much more uncertain, many of them were to be given as hostages.

His father tried to explain. The nation was in a perilous position at present. The Germans under their king, Ariovistus, had crossed the Rhine many times. Some Germans had stayed and settled. Every summer the raids penetrated further westwards, inflicting deep wounds on the soft flesh of Gaul, spilling her life blood, starving her of sustenance, while in the south the Roman Republic's expansionist policies loomed ever more threatening.

"There is only one answer to this, Allaine," his father explained. "The nation must unite. Every tribe, every canton. Old quarrels must be forgotten. Now that's easy for the Druids to say," he continued, "but not so easy for the states to implement. There'll be many agreements made here this year, and oaths sworn with hostages exchanged." He stopped, seeing Allaine's worried look. Why bother the boy after all. "They'll be alright, they'll be well looked after."

"But I'm not to be a hostage, am I, Father?"

"No, Allaine, it's difficult for us to make treaties. If the Germans overrun us, well, it doesn't much affect the rest of the nation. There's still another mountain range between them." Although he was beginning to have some ideas upon that score. "You're here to go to school, if they'll have you."

There was one other boy expecting to enter school, though, they found. A son of Ambiorix, one of the nobles of the Eburone tribe in the north. The boys looked each other up and down, liked what they saw, and decided to be friends.

Now his father had explained, Allaine could follow most

of the proceedings, although a lot of the northern language he found impossible to understand. If he got a chance he would learn to speak that as well. His new friend could teach him. Language was fascinating. Already he could dream in Greek and chat away happily to Grandmother - with a Corinthian accent, she teased him.

He'd also acquired a smattering of Latin, although Metius had told him all educated Romans spoke Greek for the most part. He thought, though, someone should tell the hostages they would be safe. Most of them looked apprehensive and miserable.

Noemon stood submissively two yards behind his young master, with head bowed, when Allaine was eventually presented. Orgetorix was proud of his son, showing, he thought, no trace of nervousness. The Arch-druid, however, knew better. He proceeded to interrogate Allaine thoroughly on his family, his upbringing, his education and his beliefs. The boy started a little hesitantly, but spoke well, in a clear voice, expressing his thoughts with mature reason, and a nice choice of words. Physically sound, too, this looked like promising material. They moved from Celtic to Greek philosophy. The boy had a good grasp of the basic principles.

"And I understand from Nammeius that you have a Greek tutor?"

"Yes," Allaine turned round to summon Noemon, who complicated matters a little by sinking to his knees on the floor. It had been one of his bad days, but the pain gripped him with such savage intensity, he could no longer think coherently.

Noemon recovered to find himself lying in a warm room, on a well-padded couch, wrapped in sweet-smelling blankets. He was being encouraged to sit up, and a cup with hot aromatic fluid was held to his lips. He was coaxed to drink; he swallowed the liquid obediently. He was pushed back gently against the pillows. The priest seemed to be giving his young master instruction. When he woke up again, he knew he had been answering questions, lots of questions, about his arm, about his capture, things he'd tried not to think about for years had come into his mind and been spoken out loud. His cheeks were wet; had he been crying?

He turned his head to the source of sound when he heard the priest's voice again.

"He's good. An unquestioning acceptance of authority is required to be successful."

"Does that mean most slaves are good subjects?" Allaine asked.

"Not at all. Many slaves are adept at hiding their minds deep down, as are most Druids, of course," the priest continued. "This is something we train for quite rigorously, with fasting as well as prayers and ritual. What do you think about fasting, Allaine? Most boys like to eat copiously, don't they?"

"Yes, Sir, that's so, but," Allaine hesitated, "I don't know the measure of my will, or the extent of my mind. It would be interesting to find out. I like to learn, Sir."

"Very well, Allaine, I will teach you." The priest turned his attention back to the slave. "Sit up now, Noemon, and look at me. Keep looking at me. That's right. Your eyes will stay open, even though your eyelids feel so heavy. Keep looking now. Good. So tired. Sleepy. You want to lie down."

When he was finally satisfied the slave had entered a deep state of trance, the priest instituted preparations for the amputation.

"And you think it unlikely he'll feel any pain," Orgetorix persisted.

Patiently the priest explained for a second time. "Only if I have convinced him this is the best course, only if he has appreciated that in its present state his arm is worse than useless, that the cyst will inevitably grow bigger. Well, Allaine, he's your slave, it has to be your decision."

But Allaine had felt the cyst himself. "This would have to happen, though, whether he can feel it or not, isn't that right, Sir?"

"Quite right."

All the same it was strange to see Noemon staring unconcernedly at his severed hand, lying limp and bloodless on the block. The stump scarcely seemed to bleed either.

"Noemon," said the priest, "in the next world your hand will be remade and reshaped so I will keep this for you."

The smell of tar filled the room as the servants brought in the bucket of scalding pitch. Noemon knelt on the floor in total submission, as his truncated arm was pushed down into the thick black hot liquid. Nevertheless the priest had taken the precaution of fixing chains to his ankles, and his right arm was tied close to his side by bandages. Still the pain failed to break the barrier. Allaine sighed with relief, and sank against his father's shoulder.

The priest thought it best to extricate his guests before the man had recovered his senses fully. After all, he couldn't keep him in a trance for ever. He arranged to keep him securely immobilised, however. He didn't want the man damaging himself by writhing around too much when in extremis.

Once he was admitted to the school Allaine and his new friend were put under the care of Vercingetorix, a charming Arvernian youth, who was kind to them, knowing how homesick they would inevitably be to start with. Allaine found it hard to say goodbye to his father and brothers. But Vercingetorix comforted him right from the first moment, brushing his tears away, and telling him of the excitements in store.

"I know it's hard to start with, Allaine. But it is only for half a year. Then we will go home for the summer, and we will travel together part of the way. You will love learning here. Our teachers know so much. And it's not all work. We play games, go hunting, train to use swords and spears. So don't be sad, my little one."

"Are you to be a priest, Sir?" Allaine asked him.

"No, Allaine. I don't think so. But I have learnt much while I have been here, and knowledge is never wasted, is it? This is my last year. I will be sorry to go in some ways. But life is an adventure."

Allaine agreed. At the beginning he often thought with longing of his home, his family, and his mountains. Gradually he got used to his new surroundings. Having Noemon with him was such a help. If he had any problems he discovered he just had to tell them to Vercingetorix, and miraculously they would be solved. He was going to miss him dreadfully next year.

BOOK 1: CHAPTER 7

Aventicum (Avenches)- Principal Town of Helvetia (Switzerland) 62-61 BC

The Swiss Council met in emergency session. The news was uniformly bad. Not only were they being pressed by the Germans to the east, evidence was pouring in from their agents that Rome had decided to take on the Allobroges in the spring, which, if they succeeded, would mean the annexation of the country as far as Geneva, right on their southern border.

"We're being crushed like a nut," one speaker complained. "Trapped in our mountains. One army we can contain, but two at once..." His voice trailed off. "Is there any possibility of placating Ariovistus the German king? Could we buy him off with gold perhaps? Or with corn?"

Nammeius rose to speak. "My dear Sir, a policy of disaster. Give him gold and he'll come back next year for more. Did you hear what he did to the hostages?"

No - few had heard. Nammeius changed his mind and sat down. After all they might be having to supply hostages themselves soon. General Divico rose to his feet.

"I feel we should be privy to any relevant information, Nammeius."

Nammeius got up again. "I've heard from reliable sources, having demanded hostages from the Sequani, Ariovistus met them with his army at a prearranged spot. Once the hostages were collected together and handed over, he selected the youngest - a boy of eight or ten - and had the palm of his right hand seared across with a red-hot brand." He had all their attention, he could see.

"The boy was the Chief's own son."

There were gasps of horror.

"Ariovistus said it was just a demonstration of what would

happen, should anyone presume to attack his forces or disobey his orders."

As he sat down the council erupted in a hubbub of noise. The chief magistrate called them to order. Orgetorix arose and stood quietly until every conversation had died down and all eyes were upon him.

"I move we give serious consideration to the total evacuation of the country."

He couldn't be heard above the shouting. He sat down. The chief magistrate spoke in his ear.

"I'll adjourn the meeting."

Orgetorix nodded. He wanted them to have an afternoon to think it over, for the idea to sink in, before he gave his reasons. For his own part he could see no alternative. When the meeting reconvened they were ready to sit quietly and listen to him. He went through the points one by one. Firstly the war of attrition with Germany was taking a heavy toll of their finite population. Year by year their young men had to go to fight, to be wounded or killed, leaving the fields to be tilled by the women and old men. Year by year less corn was harvested. It would take only one season of bad weather to leave them so short, the people would be semi-starved and their health suffer in consequence. They couldn't ask allies to come in and help protect their border - there wasn't enough land for foraging for an extra army.

"We can stay here, but we will either be massacred or have to accept rule from an external power, and make a treaty either with Germany or Rome. I don't feel there's much to choose between them, they are both noted for extreme savagery in their treatment of subject states."

He could see one or two heads beginning to nod in agreement. One of the young men rose.

"Sir, but where could we possibly go. It's hardly as if there were anywhere in Gaul uninhabited and liable to welcome us."

He sat to a ripple of murmured agreement.

"I have made tentative enquiries," Orgetorix started.

There were loud exclamations at this.

"I've seen this problem coming for many years. If we decide on this course, and I emphasize the point that I have no intention of acting without the consent of the people, we would be welcomed by the Sequani and the Aedui. Our combined forces would enable us to patrol the Rhine, and prevent the Germans from crossing the river."

He allowed time to let this information sink in.

"I say again, if this course of action is followed, gentlemen, we will be forced to destroy our towns and villages. Our homes and farms. To remove from the invading forces any source of shelter. But as we well know, the Germans aren't interested in husbandry. They wish only to steal our cattle, corn and women. To desecrate our sacred groves." His voice became higher and louder. "To besmirch our reputation, to destroy our way of life. Shall we permit this, gentlemen?" Of course they shouted, "No" enthusiastically enough. He would have to wait and see how the vote went. He sat listening to the speeches. Nearly all were in favour of his proposal. Both his elder sons got up and made short speeches, quite adequate, but he would be glad when Allaine was back with him. How he missed the boy when he was at school. He had ensured Nammeius was the penultimate speaker, with finally the highly respected General Divico succinctly weighing the arguments for and against. He went over to join them while the votes were being taken. It was already quite clear his proposal had almost total support. The idea of calling an emergency council meeting had been excellent, creating a feeling of panic and that action must be instantly taken. But of course the plan would take at least a couple of years to instigate. He hoped they had a couple of years to spare.

"Just how strong are these initial enquiries?" General Divico asked.

Orgetorix smiled to himself. The general was just as astute as ever.

"These states wish to become ever closer allies, Sir," he

replied. "In fact, Dumnorix, the chief magistrate of the Aedui, has agreed to marry my daughter, Eloise. If the vote goes for us, I will send for him straight away."

At dinner that night Orgetorix remembered to tell Eloise of the treats the fates had in store for her. A shame he'd forgotten to prime his mother with the information first. She was looking displeased. Eloise sat staring at the food in front of her, suddenly no longer hungry, while her sisters looked at her with interest.

"This Dumnorix," said Grandmother, prodding the air with her spoon, "what is he like?"

"A very popular leader, as I understand," Nammeius told her, "although, apparently, somewhat severe in his judgement."

"An excellent swordsman, evidently," added Orgetorix, mopping up the meat juices with his bread. "And a superb horseman. You should see his cavalry, a magnificent sight, well disciplined, well trained." He took a swig of wine. "And, of course, he's rich," he added as an afterthought. He glanced over at his daughter. What a beautiful girl. But still just a little timid. She should, of course, be deliriously happy at the thought of her good fortune. Well, well. Girls were a puzzle after all.

It was arranged that Allaine should join the bridegroom at Bibracte on his way back from Lutetia, and escort him to his bride, the other male members of the family meeting up on the Swiss border. Dumnorix stood up, took one look at him and burst out laughing when he entered the room.

"My word, but you've changed."

"No, Sir," said Allaine with a smile, "I'm just the same. A bit taller maybe."

Dumnorix held out both hands in greeting and kissed his future brother on the cheek.

"Ah," he said, spying Noemon. "The tutor."

Noemon dropped to one knee.

"I see you've changed as well," Dumnorix said, surveying

the man's arm.

"Indeed, Sir, for the better."

Allaine enjoyed being spoiled by the wealthy Aeduans, but even here, in the rich Loire valley, the talk was of war, of alliances to be forged, threats to be countered. There was still time for feasting, though, and pretty girls. Allaine was in great demand. He particularly liked Riona, a lively blonde who managed to manoeuvre herself a place by his side at dinner on more than one occasion. He enjoyed her conversation. She was the youngest sister of Guéreth, one of the foremost nobles, and had been taught to read and write. It was refreshing to talk books with a girl, Allaine found. She looked at things differently. He said goodbye to her reluctantly, but somehow didn't think he would be permitted to marry her. Apparently she was to be used to cement an alliance with a tribe in the North.

Dumnorix was delighted at the thought of having Allaine for company on the journey. He would make a charming companion, a little quiet and serious perhaps; he had to work hard to make the boy smile, but the reward was worth waiting for when his face lit up and the grave grey eyes sparkled with laughter. He found his young friend remarkably well informed, and the combination of Druidic instruction and Greek tutor had given him the knack of penetrating to the heart of an issue. Sometimes his arguments were a little too succinct for Dumnorix who liked to play with words.

"You have no poetry in your soul, Allaine," he complained. "You are purely prosaic. Now, describe to me your sister, but in glowing terms please. I don't want an anatomical description."

Allaine had been so enjoying the man's friendship, he had forgotten the purpose of his visit and wondered, just for an instant, which one of his sisters his friend meant him to describe. Of course it was Eloise.

"Is she like you?"

"How could she be like me?" countered Allaine, surprised.

Dumnorix looked at him in amusement. "Well I don't expect her to be six foot tall, but what's she like? Is she blonde? What colour are her eyes?"

Allaine thought hard. "She's blonde, certainly." He couldn't remember what colour her eyes were. "It doesn't much matter what she looks like, you're going to have to marry her anyway."

After riding for a mile in silence he relented. "I think she's very pretty actually."

Dumnorix burst out laughing and cantered off in high spirits.

He wasn't allowed to see the bride of course, until after the ceremony, but if the other two were anything to go by he was in luck, although it seemed unlikely for all four children to be beautiful. He was to have no mother-in-law evidently, Orgetorix contenting himself with a concubine for the past few years. His future grandmother-in-law, however, looked to be a woman of formidable character, but he had been well primed. So, coached by Allaine, he addressed her in her native Greek tongue and was instantly rewarded, Grandmother greeting him with enthusiastic affection. Inwardly she was much relieved. Last night Eloise had sat on her bed and burst into tears, and spoke foolish girl's thoughts of killing herself by jumping off a cliff or some such nonsense.

The young man looked perfect, clean-shaven with thick dark curls cut in the modern style, tumbling in layers down to the nape of his neck. Indeed when she watched him dining that night, with the members of her family, she found his table manners to be excellent. He ate delicately, using bread, knife and spoon, not only his hands, she was pleased to note. He was careful to have his hands washed and dried afterwards. He drank abstemiously, and his conversation was amusing, but never coarse. She was delighted with him. She thought it wouldn't take long before Eloise was delighted with him, too. If he hadn't been wearing dark trousers and the closed leather boots, he could have passed for a Greek from her home town of Massilia.

The wedding was hugely popular, the whole country celebrated. Allaine was permitted for the first time to assist his uncle in the sacrificial ceremony, invoking strength and fertility to the newly-married couple. Once Nammeius had selected the day most auspicious for the event, invitations were despatched to every noble in the country. Eloise found the feasting and noise of the first two days of the ceremony repetitious and irksome. She had very little part to play, merely to sit waiting dressed in her best, while outside in her father's hall and yard the serious matters went on, of arranging mutual assistance in the face of the external threats from Germans and Romans, interspersed with the eating and drinking more appropriate to a wedding.

By the third day Eloise was becoming increasingly nervous, frightened of what she might find when led to the altar by her father. She was dressed in a simple white robe of the finest wool, supplied in a bolt by Marcus Metius, and made up by her maids under the direction of Grandmother. It was pleated in the Greek fashion. Her father had presented her with a pretty necklace made from gold and river pearls. She had little pearl earrings in her ears, and a crown of flowers on her head. She clutched onto Orgetorix, and looked demurely down at the ground, afraid to look up. The rite seemed to go on forever. She felt so nervous. She now realised she should have either drunk less water at breakfast, or emptied her bladder more thoroughly.

At last her father took her hand, and placed it in her new husband's. His hand felt warm, and gave a comforting squeeze, which emboldened her to take a look at him at last. The young man was gazing down at her, smiling at her with a mouth of perfect white teeth. Now she was near him she was aware he smelt deliciously of perfume. Thank goodness Grandmother had bought some for her.

Allaine spoke the final words of the ceremony.

"You may now kiss the bride."

Dumnorix stopped smiling. He touched her face delicately with his fingers. "Allaine didn't do you justice," he whispered. "He said you were very pretty, but actually you are the most beautiful girl I have ever seen." With that he took her in his arms and gently kissed her on the lips, with none of the grossness she had seen at other weddings. The crowd erupted with cheers and laughter, and the musicians struck up for the dancing.

"I must just fix my hair before the dancing," she said in a panic, and rushed back into the house, leaving him wondering if he had committed some gross error of manners. But no, she was back by his side in no time. Her hair didn't look any different to him. It looked like spun gold, caught up silver clasps, making her look like a Goddess. She was smiling at him, looking very pleased with herself.

"Can you do our dances?" she asked anxiously.

"They appear to be much the same as ours," he laughed, and putting his arm round her slender waist, they took their place in the centre of the ring.

He took her that night with the greatest gentleness. Grandmother had made sure she knew just what to expect. Even though she found her husband so handsome, she was still disconcerted to be lying naked on the bed beside him, a man she had never seen before in her life. But he seemed so happy and cheerful, he made her feel comfortable, anyway. He told her to keep the flowers in her hair. He held her close, kissing cheek, neck, shoulder and breast. He gazed down at her, his blushing bride, and pulled the sheet up to cover her nakedness, to make her feel less embarrassed while they talked.

"Do you like me?"

"Oh yes," she smiled. Goodness, who could help liking him? He was gorgeous!

"That's good. Tell me all about yourself, Eloise," he commanded. "I want to know everything about you."

"There's not much to tell," she said shyly. She told him

about her brothers and sisters, and Grandmother. She told him with sadness, about the death of her beloved mother. She told him about her betrothal, and how frightened she had been of her betrothed.

"But you're not frightened of me, are you, my little love?"

No, strangely she wasn't. He was so friendly and gentle. She told him how apprehensive she felt about going to a new country, where she would know no one.

"But you will bring your maids, of course."

That was a comforting thought.

"All my relations are dying to meet you, Eloise. They will love you, just like I do. We have a lot of girls in our family, and I'm sure they will be friends with you. Not so many boys, though. We don't seem to be able to make boys. Perhaps you and I will be more successful. Shall we try, sweetheart?"

"Alright," she said, with a smile.

"Eloise, I swear I will make you the happiest girl in the world, tonight, and evermore."

She felt his strong arms round her. She sent up a prayer of gratitude to the Goddess Eostra, Goddess of rebirth and new beginnings. She felt so grateful to her father, for finding her this lovely man.

BOOK 1: CHAPTER 8

Rome 62 BC

The Senate was in uproar, everybody shouting, just Caesar leaning back against the steps, that aggravating smile on his face. But they weren't putting up with his tactics any longer. Cato rose to his feet, commanding silence and suggesting in his soft silky voice that the absence of Caesar, though he agreed it to be a negative concept, may well have the positive effect - he paused here waiting for the ripple of laughter to die down - of restoring order to Rome. Since with his presence, he emphasized the word, the use of filibustering techniques deprived the people of all laws of practical value.

Bibulus stood up and proposed bluntly that Caesar be suspended from the Senate. In contrast to the previous month's work, this decree was passed with celerity, its announcement being greeted with scattered cheers and applause. Caesar got up slowly, surveying the grinning faces on the benches opposite him, mentally marking each down for future reference. What fools they were to show their enmity so openly. He ostentatiously adjusted his magisterial robes, waited until the house had fallen silent to achieve the maximum dramatic effect, as always, and then made a stately exit. He walked out into the sunlit Forum. There were the usual crowd round the rostra, listening to the speakers. They looked at him curiously, wondering what had made him leave the Senate at such an early stage in the day's proceedings. He found the Lictors, his bodyguards, sprawled on the Senate steps playing at dice, their thick rods of office lying askew. He spoke to them quietly, noting with satisfaction how rapidly they sprang to attention. All the same he would have to maintain their discipline a bit better than this. He walked slowly through the throng of people, giving the Lictors plenty of time to make an adequate passage for him. He was distracted by a group to his left. There was Senator Sperinus being harangued by a youth who was obviously not even old enough to collect his toga yet. Caesar felt a slight stir of pleasure.

"Lictors, arrest that man at once."

Octavian gasped in shock as his arms were grasped and twisted behind him. He found himself being addressed by a stern man in the purple robes of a magistrate.

"What effrontery, how dare you accost one of our most noble senators in such a way. And in the heart of the Forum itself. Have you no respect? Have you no manners? Take him away."

"Where to, Sir?" asked the Lictors in surprise.

"I believe the prison for traitors to the state lies over in that direction." Caesar indicated with a broad sweep of his arm. He could see the boy was thoroughly alarmed. He walked over to the Senator and linked his arm through his, well aware that Sperinus loathed him.

"My dear Senator, what is the place coming to? I just can't apologise enough. It is, after all, my place to maintain civil order."

Sperinus tried ineffectually to disengage himself. "Really, Caesar, there was no need. No need at all, there was nothing about it." The disgusting fellow was trying to pat his hand now, as if he needed soothing. "Anyway, I know the boy, he is the son of Volusenus." Did Caesar really think he couldn't manage a boy of sixteen? "He was a bit over-excited, that's all."

Caesar had known perfectly well who the boy was, but he continued, "Ah, so you will not be pressing charges?"

"Charges? What charges?"

"Leave everything to me, my dear Senator. Permit me to escort you myself to the Senate and ensure your safety."

Sperinus allowed himself to be led away; it seemed the easiest solution. Why he then felt himself impelled to thank Caesar for his protection at the doors of the Senate he couldn't begin to imagine. He felt disgruntled for the rest of the day.

The next morning Titus Volusenus was summoned to appear at Caesar's house. Titus was having trouble maintaining his usual calm exterior; inwardly he was deeply worried. Octavian's servant had maintained that nothing particularly untoward had happened in the Forum, but there had been other garbled accounts giving much more graphic details. His wife had cried herself to sleep in his arms, convinced some terrible fate would overtake her youngest son. She seemed a little more resigned this morning. It was obvious, however, that she placed no trust in his abilities to sort the matter out. Fair enough - he wasn't a man of particularly high standing or wealth. He tried to marshall some thoughts in his head but gave up. Best first to ascertain the facts and then act accordingly.

Titus was feeling considerable trepidation when he was ushered into the magistrate's presence. Caesar had made sure he was clad in his full robes of office. He rose to greet his guest, a mark of great respect, and went forward, hand outstretched, smiling affably.

"My dear Volusenus, how delighted I am that you could come so promptly."

Volusenus was already taken aback; he thought he had been ordered to attend.

Caesar walked over to the side table, and poured out some wine into an exquisite silver cup, with a pattern of vine leaves chasing round the rim. He came back with it in his hand, and sat next to Volusenus.

"My dear Volusenus, this affair has been blown up out of all proportion. It is but a storm in a wine cup. Here, try this."

Volusenus accepted the wine, and drank. "It is excellent."

"I see you are a connoisseur. I like it myself. It comes from one of Pompey's estates. Near Naples."

There was a pause. Volusenus sat and sipped the wine. Caesar seemed to have forgotten why he was here, temporarily. Should he bring up the subject himself. Then he looked directly into the man's eyes and knew - Caesar had forgotten nothing. There was a moment of instant awareness, mutual recognition. Volusenus made the slightest movement with his hand, a tiny gesture of submission.

"About Octavian."

"Ah, yes, Octavian," said Caesar, still with the agreeable smile. "What a boy, eh? Well, my dear fellow, there's nothing to worry about. Having looked into the matter myself I find the affair has been greatly exaggerated. I've managed to persuade Sperinus not to press charges." He smiled. Volusenus had not been able to prevent that slight exhalation of relief. "So I am happy to deliver your son into your hands, as long as some suitable chastisement is provided."

"I'll deal with him myself, Caesar." Volusenus was anxious to go.

Now the matter had been settled Caesar did not bother to detain him. A pleasant man, he thought to himself, never likely to be an opponent. His boys, now, they seemed a little more interesting. The eldest, Gaius, a very junior military tribune, he found promising. Mentally he reviewed the events of the morning. His anger had subsided considerably. The message from the Senate that he was, in effect, forbidden to sit any longer as a magistrate, delivered in public, while he was in court, was presumably designed to cause him the maximal humiliation. And when he had refused to leave, he had actually been threatened with force.

Accepting the inevitable he'd dismissed the Lictors and then deliberately removed his magisterial robes before leaving the court, ensuring, however, that he was properly dressed again before he saw Volusenus.

He spent the rest of the morning with his secretary Philemon, reading the reports from Marcus Metius's agents. The one from Helvetia he found especially interesting. Affairs were, apparently, on the move in Gaul in more ways than one. He welcomed several of his friends in the afternoon, and told them that henceforth he intended to retire from public life. He gave orders that a section of the populace were to be heavily bribed to appear at his house the following morning, and to insist forcefully on his reinstatement. He would have to arrange for yet another loan. It was becoming apparent to him that when manipulation was not enough, the only method to achieve his ambitions would be by the resolute use of brute force. He knew the Gods would demand no less of him.

Volusenus could see that a night chained to the wall in the Mamertine prison had done nothing to cool his son's indignation. He adored this wilful, self-righteous, conceited boy of his, with his high-handed attitude to the rest of the world. His presumption, in thinking himself entitled to tackle a Senator, was breath-taking.

"Octavian, I don't often beat you, do I?"

"You don't ever beat me, Sir," corrected his son.

"I'm afraid I have to start now."

Octavian gritted his teeth and coped with it as best he could. When it was over he straightened up slowly and stood stiffly to attention before his sire. Volusenus touched his shoulders gently, gazing into his son's stormy face.

"Sometimes," he said quietly, "you have to do the right thing and suffer the consequences."

Octavian looked at him directly, his eyes nearly level with his own.

"He beats her, you know," he said huskily, the distress obvious in his face. "Lady Ursula, I mean. Not Marcius, or the children. But Dad," Octavian put his hands up to his father's shoulders now, "Dad, he said she's having an affair with David. He's had David put to death. David!" Octavian's composure broke at this point. He put his arms round his father's neck, and started to sob.

Volusenus held him as close as he could. Dammit, he couldn't even comfort the boy properly, his back would be too sore. He was almost as upset as his son. David. The boy had been an intermittent part of his household for years, Octavian and Marcius sharing his services quite amicably. David. If the boys wanted to know if bees stung when captured, David was told to hold one. David had jumped in the public fountain when ordered to find out how deep it was. David had been made to ride Octavian's horse first, to ensure the beast had a docile temperament. He had carried out the boys' orders with unhesitating obedience, even to the extent of raiding the kitchens for the honey jar, which got them all into hot water, but which laid the foundations for a radical overhaul of their various morals, duties and obligations. How anyone could believe the boy would be capable of .... They would have to be mad! He dreaded to think how his wife was going to take the news. She regarded David almost as a member of the family. Could there be any possibility of error?

"Are you quite sure of the facts, Octavian?"

"Yes, Sir, I'm quite sure."

Volusenus indicated to the servants that they were leave them alone. He guided his son to the couch. He didn't want to ask the next question.

"What was the manner of his death?"

"He was tortured."

Volusenus was silent while his son sat beside him, hunched forward over his knees, hands clenched tightly. Presently he sat up and rubbed his face.

"I'm sorry, Sir," he muttered.

"It doesn't matter," said his father absently.

What was he going to do? Where did his duty lie? The rumours surrounding Sperinus were increasing day by day. Everyone knew he was insanely jealous of his wife, but now, apparently, he had made a series of rash investments and stood to lose a considerable part of his fortune. Also, he was known to drink heavily when at the baths in the afternoon, and had once wagered a thousand gold pieces on the throw of the dice. Almost impossible to interfere between a man and his wife, of course, but oh, poor David. Still, even more impossible to interfere between a man and his slaves. What about Marcius, though? His son's friend. Was there anything he could do for him? And what about

Octavian's betrothal to Marcius's sister Lucy? They were both absurdly young, but his wife had arranged it to try and get the girl out of the nightmare, and under her own roof.

For a time Marcius had seemed practically to live in his house. He was growing up to be a remarkably likeable lad, but much less ebullient than he used to be. He spent more time at home recently too. Perhaps to support his mother.

"I think Senator Sperinus is perhaps going a bit mad."

"A bit mad?" exclaimed Octavian. "He's completely demented! I'd like to smash his fucking face in!"

"Quiet, boy. Don't let your mother hear you speaking like that." He hadn't realised Octavian could be so vehement. "I've already spoken to Senator Sperinus's brother."

"Have you, Sir?" asked Octavian, surprised.

"Yes, but I got nowhere. And I've written to Lady Ursula's brother, Marcus Metius."

Octavian was looking at him astonished.

"I'm not blind, you know, Octavian," he said, a little irritated. "I'm well aware of what's been going on in your friend's house. However, Metius hasn't deigned to answer."

Octavian hadn't believed his father would dare to interfere with the affairs of anyone of senatorial rank. He was quite impressed. There was obviously more to the old man than he'd thought.

"But at the moment," his father continued, frowning, "I cannot see a way forward."

Nor could Octavian.

"In the meantime we will ensure Marcius and his brother Andreas know they are always welcome in our house, while I consider what further steps can be taken."

That afternoon a letter from Senator Sperinus arrived, announcing all further communications between both families was to end. Octavian's betrothal to Lucia was to be terminated with immediate effect, as Sperinus thought him to be a malign influence on his stepson.

"Never mind," said Volusenus, "you'll be able to see each other again when you are both in the army." He didn't think Octavian would be all that bothered about Lucy, but his wife would be.

He waited until they were in bed that night before broaching the subject of David with his wife. He was feeling quite angry, an unusual emotion for him. He had discovered Caesar had ordered his son's arrest, after his powers as a magistrate had been removed. Titus believed Octavian's version of events in the Forum. He couldn't see what the boy could possibly be charged with, unless it was rudeness, not so far a crime against the state. To compound it all Caesar had sent round three enormous amphorae of that excellent wine, together with his amicable greetings to the Volusenus family. Titus was beginning to dislike Caesar.

Sperinus announced his embargo at dinner that night. But his public utterances were met with silence, Marcius, Andreas, and Lucy failing to give him the pleasure of seeing them upset. They had ceased to argue or shout their distress. It didn't make any difference after all. Sperinus paid attention only to himself. But later on, when the three siblings congregated in their mother's room, Lucy began to weep. Was everything to be snatched away from her? It had seemed to be the one thing she could cling to, that one day she would be married to Octavian, and escape this dreadful house for ever. Of course she would miss her mother and brothers. Her stepfather would be bound to put obstacles in the way of access. But she would have Lady Claudia Volusena as a mother-in-law. She adored Lady Volusena. She was sure Claudia would never put up with things like her mother did. There must be some way to get rid of Sperinus. What about poison, she thought, or a knife in him while he slept. But she knew she wasn't brave enough for these drastic measures. And when she discussed them with Marcius, he quickly dismissed such ideas. It was just too dangerous. They spoke in whispers, never sure which slaves might betray them.

"No, we can't poison him, or stab him, don't be stupid, Lucy. Do you think it will help Mother to see us arrested and executed?"

"We must do something. How can you bear not to see Octavian?" How could she bear not to see Octavian? Not that he came very often, and never to see her, always to see Marcius.

"His parents are taking him off to Greece, to see the sights, and to take his mind off David, so I wouldn't be seeing him anyway for quite a time." Marcius wished something would take his own mind off David. The poor boy's screams still haunted his dreams at night. And the feeling of helplessness would come surging back. If only there had been something he could have done. He wasn't allowed even to see him, even to hug him to his heart and tell him how much he loved him, and how he knew David was innocent of any crime, let alone the one for which he was charged. Maybe that would have made poor David feel worse.

Marcius knew also, that Sperinus's servants were bribed to spy on them, report any misdemeanours. If they tried to visit Octavian, it would be reported back. And it was always their mother who got the blame for everything, who had to endure the slappings, kickings, punchings, and beatings. It was always her fault for being too soft, or too strict, or any irrational cause at all. Trying to intervene made everything ten times worse. Well at least he could hug Lucy.

"I thought they were taking Octavian away, so he could get over losing Lucy," whispered Andreas. Marcius didn't want to enlighten him with Lucy present. He was well aware that Octavian only thought of his sister as a nuisance, rather than as a future wife.

"Anyway, they're taking him to Greece." He hadn't yet thought how he would be able to cope without Octavian as a friend. Ever since he could remember, Marcius had trailed happily in Octavian's wake. Octavian was always the one who thought of new adventures, new exciting games to play, new forbidden places to go and visit. He had other acquaintances, of course. Mentally he reviewed them. He couldn't see any of them taking Octavian's place, somehow. There was Hugo, of course, but he was older, sensible and steady. And, anyway he was about to serve his three years in the army.

"Sperinus is going to make me marry that disgusting ancient cousin of his," wept Lucy.

"You can't! He's sixty if he's a day! And he's fat and bald. I shall put a stop to it," Marcius declared.

"I don't think you can have any say in the matter, until you are eighteen," said Andreas. They seemed to be thwarted at every turn.

"Shall we try Uncle Marcus Metius again?" suggested Lucy.

"Why not? I'll have to think of some way to get a letter out of the house without Sperinus knowing about it." He thought he might trust the steward. He had come with them from their old house. Marcius thought he had an affection for his mother. But now none of the male servants dared to help Lady Ursula in any way.

"Listen, we've still got each other, and Mother. Somehow we'll pull through," said Marcius. Just saying it made them feel a little more cheerful. They kissed each other goodnight, and went off to bed. Andreas felt relieved. His brother was listening to him at last, paying close attention to his words. With no Octavian, and no David, Marcius would at last come to appreciate him. Andreas loved and admired Marcius with all his heart. But Marcius must never know his secret. He would carry it with him to the grave.

Caesar lay back on the couch, his mind busy as always, formulating plans. He wanted to be elected as one of the Consuls next year, to become unequivocally one of the two most powerful men in Rome, and afterwards receive a rich province to govern as a reward. He would need to find strong allies to trump his enemies in the Senate. Gnaeus Pompey, the brilliant military general, was returning to Rome for his Triumph, after his successful efforts at empire building in the East. Perhaps Pompey would agree to marry Julia, his beloved, but very young daughter. She would be better off in the care of an older man, who knew what he was doing, Pompey having been married four times previously. Also the fabulously rich Marcus Licinius Crassus had tentatively suggested a mutual pact between the three of them, to consolidate each others's interests.

The barber reached nervously for the tweezers. The order to render his master's body hairless seemed fraught with peril. Presumably Caesar had formed the erroneous impression that removal of his body hair would increase the sparse growth on his scalp. The barber knew better. He received a slash with the thin cane for any extraction that caused his master discomfort. Some shouts in the street outside the house caught Caesar's attention, but were not sufficient, evidently, for anaesthesia. The slave flinched from a stinging blow across his bare buttocks.

"That hurt," his master said softly.

Lady Pompeia walked into the bath house and surveyed her husband stretched out on the massage couch.

"There seems to be a riot going on in the street outside, Caesar," she informed him dryly. "Somehow I feel it may be connected with you."

"Thank you, my dear." He got up, crossed over to her, put his arm round her waist and kissed her cheek, oblivious of her inward revulsion. He was too conceited ever to discover her true feelings for him. She thought his increasingly naked private parts were beginning to resemble the dead ducklings hanging plucked in the cool rooms. She frankly couldn't understand his reputation in bed. He was just a selfish bastard. She had always preferred quality to quantity herself. Her friends wouldn't believe her, though, until they'd tried him for themselves, thinking she was merely attempting to preserve his virility for herself. He didn't appear to be virile enough to father any offspring on her though, despite his all-too-frequent attempts to do so.

Caesar had himself dressed carefully, the folds of his toga pressed neatly into place, his hair combed forward to hide the area of thinness. He had thought of obtaining his revenge on the Senate by using his position as high priest to declare a month of religious festivities. He laughed to himself. That would, perhaps, be a little childish, and severely disrupt the workings of the Republic. He ordered the attendants to open the shutters, and then sent a man through to the balcony to sound the horn announcing his imminent arrival. His agents must have spent a considerable amount of money - there was a swelling mass of people. A cheer greeted him as he walked out onto the balcony, although he was quick to note there were also one or two hisses. One had to be so careful with the plebs; they didn't like to feel they were being pushed around by their rulers. Better still to make them feel they were the ones doing the ruling.

Unlike the Senate, who were terrified of the mob, crowds never frightened him. He was an orator of consummate skill, aware of his power over them. He could change their mood and swing their opinion round almost instantly with skilled words. Sometimes he felt like a captain at sea, where the people's opinions coalesced to make a sort of ship, sometimes a sleek yacht that could be directed with only the slightest touch on the tiller, but often a heavily laden merchant vessel that had to be pulled and tugged round to face the ocean. He would launch such a ship against the waves of opposition of his enemies, into the gales of their ill-formed opinions.

He held up his hands until the crowd fell silent - they always wanted to hear what he had to say.

"Gentlemen, gentlemen, I fear you have been misinformed. I am holding no pubic banquets today."

"That's not why we're here, Caesar," yelled a voice from the crowd.

"Ah, we have a speaker, I see," said Caesar. "I give you

precedence."

The crowd laughed. They knew this was the way things were done in the Senate.

"Caesar, we're here to ensure you're reinstated as the people's magistrate."

Cheers greeted this, but Caesar held his hands up for silence again. "A good motion for debate," he said. "Now, who speaks in opposition?"

The crowd muttered to itself, but there were no volunteers.

"What, no one?" Caesar paused, surveying them all with a smile. "Then I shall have to oppose the motion myself."

The crowd was interested in this, especially those members of it who had been bribed to shout vociferously for his reinstatement. He spoke like an actor now, timing his phrases, pausing to let each one sink in.

"Gentlemen, it is my proposal that we abide by the decisions of the Senate. Our system of government has been perfected over hundreds of years." He paused. "Instituted by the father of our great city, Father Romulus himself."

At this point, some of the citizens cheered.

"We surely do not wish to return to the days of Sulla, the Dictator."

There was no mistaking the agreement on this count.

"I therefore propose the motion not even be put to a vote, but that everyone return to their houses. Or go for a picnic - it's a fine day," he ended cheerfully.

Amicably the crowd started to disperse. There didn't look to be much point in staying - nothing dramatic was going to happen if Caesar himself was to tamely accept the Senate's decree.

Later that afternoon a detachment of soldiers from the direction of the Forum came marching towards Caesar's house. Behind them came a deputation of Senators. News of the mob converging on Caesar's house had made them hurry to meet in session to put down this fresh threat to their authority. By the time they reached his house only a few idle spectators remained to see them.

Caesar feigned surprise when they paused at his door. "Are you coming to see me, Gentlemen? What an honour. Do come in."

Cato looked round, suspecting a trap, but Bibulus rushed in, accompanied by the others.

"My dear Caesar, we had word, something about a mob, commotion, even a riot perhaps. But, my dear fellow, we heard you spoke to them, and calmed them down and sent them all back home again. A most honourable course to be sure. We're delighted, Caesar, delighted, that you have such a high regard for the Senate, and that being the case, of course, with the agreement of everyone here," he hurried on in case Cato should disagree, "we wish to overlook any irregularities."

"What irregularities are those, exactly?" asked Caesar.

"The Senate, Caesar, wishes you to return at once to take your seat and be confirmed in your position as magistrate."

"Ah, how very kind of the Senate," Caesar said. He accepted a glass of wine proffered by a servant, and drained it to the dregs. He swung round to face his slave. The note of triumph in his voice was scarcely detectable.

"Boy," he said, "fetch my robes."

BOOK 1: CHAPTER 9

Lugdunum (Lyons) to Rome 61 BC

The eldest son of Titus Volusenus, Tribune Gaius Volusenus Quadratus, was enjoying the journey much more than he had anticipated. The orders from his commander had been clear. He was to meet a party of Aeduan nobles at Lugdunum and escort them to Rome. He must remember that they were friends and allies of the Roman people, and treat them with every respect and courtesy. The thought of nursemaiding a load of barbarian chieftains all the way to Rome and, presumably, providing for their every primitive whim, had been enough to make him shudder.

But he had been agreeably surprised. All his commands so far had been in the confines of the Republic, he had little knowledge of the northern peoples beyond the Alps. So it was something of a shock to discover just how civilised they were. In fact, he had to admit some of their possessions were most impressive, especially their exquisitely worked jewellery. But it was their minds that surprised him most of all. They were charming, witty and courteous, as they teased him unmercifully.

One of them Guéreth, a man of about his own age, could speak perfect Latin, but was nevertheless careful to use the official interpreters. Most of them had some working knowledge of Latin, but Greek was apparently their main second language, which several of them could both read and write. Gaius was very impressed with Prince Diviciacus, the Druid, obviously the most influential man amongst them. Apparently it was upon his instigation that the Aeduans had decided to seek the help of Rome in their battle with the Germans. Diviciacus had been invited to stay with Marcus Cicero himself, and was to be allowed to address the Senate. Not that it would get him anywhere, of course. Gaius couldn't imagine that Rome had any intention of going to war with the Germans, not at the present time, anyway. The legions were far too busy in the east with Pompey, who would be back home shortly for his Triumph.

Gaius had met them with a full cohort of six hundred legionaries at Lugdunum. They had then crossed the maritime Alps to Turin, and they were now following the Via Amelia, Via Flaminia and Via Cassia to Rome. Although he had been ordered to arrange for their return journey to be along the coastal route, Diviciacus explaining to him he wished to see as much as he could of the country, commensurate with a speedy discharge of his duties to his peoples. Of course, the necessity for quite so much obvious Roman military protection rapidly dwindled as they'd crossed the Alps, and they left behind the bulk of the cohort to be utilised again on their return.

The cities on their route had been given advance warning of the arrival of these important visitors. The hospitality had been of the highest order, but like him, few of the cities' dignitaries had appreciated that their guests would want to go to the theatre to see plays. The Aeduans found staged hunts in the arena deadly dull compared with the real thing. Even gladiatorial contests left them unmoved. Indeed, Diviciacus had to be tactfully woken at the end of one such performance, to give his speech of gratitude to the city fathers.

Gaius laughed to himself as he remembered the scene. These Gauls were adept at expressing their feelings, merely by adopting the right posture, without the need for words. They had draped themselves with weary elegance across the seats, their drooping shoulders indicating all too clearly their desire to be elsewhere. Tonight they were staying at the house of Verginius Rufus, who had provided an impressive banquet. It seemed the Gauls had taken a great deal of care in choosing presents to bring for their many hosts.

Rufus had been presented with pelts of an extraordinary thick, soft dark fur. Even the Gauls didn't know from which animal it came. They were assured the Romans had never seen anything like it.

"I thought not," said Diviciacus with satisfaction. "Only from the far north."

Gaius rose to make a speech. Tomorrow, he explained, they would be staying in the town of Bologna and the civic leaders had kindly agreed to host a mock hunt in the arena in honour of their arrival. Silence greeted this remark.

"How very nice," Guéreth remarked from his left.

"Perhaps you would convey our deep sense of honour to the city fathers," Diviciacus said, when this had been translated.

Gaius beamed at him. "But I've persuaded them to cancel it."

The laughter erupted without any need for a translation.

"We're going to the theatre instead."

They cheered.

"Bad Gaius, you tease us," said the youngest Gaul, and threw an apple hard at him. For which action, he was severely cuffed by the man sitting next to him.

Gaius caught the apple neatly, sat down and started to eat it.

"Have you any idea what we're going to see, Tribune?" Guéreth asked him.

"'The Birds' I think it is."

"And afterwards? The ladies, perhaps?"

"I'll see what I can do." These Gauls had an insatiable appetite for wine and ladies. They seemed to be able to handle large amounts of both, without ever getting drunk or showing other signs of over usage. Fortunately Verginius Rufus had provided both commodities on a lavish scale. The Gauls settled down to make a night of it.

Gaius was reading in the room assigned to him, when Guéreth sought him out later on.

"May I come in?"

"Oh yes, please." He was delighted to see the man. Finding Gaius's knowledge of farming non-existent, Rufus had taken himself off to bed. Gaius was missing the easy company of his fellow officers. Guéreth dropped onto the bed.

"I have been sent to apologise for that impudent youngster," he smiled, "and to ask whether you wish any penalty to be imposed."

"Jupiter, no. He was just being friendly. It doesn't bother me. Won't you stay, Sir?" he asked, as Guéreth rose to go.

"Don't you wish to speak to your Roman friends? You will be missing their company."

Typical of the man, Gaius thought, to show such sensitivity. "I'm no company for Rufus," he said, "as soon as he found I couldn't tell the difference between wheat and barley, he took himself off to his wife."

Guéreth settled himself down on the bed again. But now Gaius had got him, he didn't know what to do with him.

"How soon do you think we will reach Rome, Tribune?"

"Gaius, call me Gaius."

"Very well, Gaius, how soon?"

"We should be there in five days."

"I feel excited," said Guéreth. "You know? Like a boy with his first horse."

"Of course," Gaius agreed. "So do I, and I've lived there all my life until I went into the army. It is a wonderful city, so much to see, so much going on always. Shall I send out for the maps, Sir?"

"Guéreth, please call me Guéreth."

Gaius despatched his servant for the maps.

"Shall we be friends?" he asked. It sounded a bit childish but, after all, he was acting the part of ambassador. There mustn't be any cause for misinterpretation.

"Yes, indeed, Gaius, insofar as our countries will permit it."

Gaius nodded. It was an acknowledgement of his military status. He grinned happily at his new friend.

"Who knows, Guéreth?" he said, "after your chief has addressed the senate, perhaps our countries will be so friendly I will be joining you on the bed."

Guéreth burst out laughing. That seemed to knock down a few more barriers. They sat and chatted and questioned each other until the early hours of the morning, when both retired, equally pleased with themselves.

The next morning the youngest Gaul made a public, stiff and formal apology for the apple incident. This worried Gaius. This was getting out of all proportion. He patted the boy's cheek and told him it mattered not one whit. But from the youth's subdued manner for the rest of the day, he deduced that despite his denial of grievance the previous night, the boy had been punished anyway. So that evening, after supper was finished, Gaius appeared with a small plate which he carried carefully, and set down on a table in front of the boy.

"Sir, I return your apple, with compliments," he informed the astonished young man. "I've had it cooked into a pie. Aren't you glad I've refrained from throwing it at you?"

The Gauls chuckled appreciatively. Gaius sat down next to the boy, giving him a quick, sympathetic hug. He stayed with him throughout the evening. He remained quietly attentive to him for the rest of the journey, so that when they finally entered the gates of Rome the boy was almost back to his normal high-spirited self.

BOOK 1: CHAPTER 10

Rome 61 BC

Marcius awoke feeling appallingly sick. It took him a moment or two to appreciate he wasn't in his own bedroom. He became aware of the presence of several other sleepers around him, one or two of them making more animal noises than human. Very little light seeped through the shutters. The room was airless, and far too hot. His tunic was sticking to him, soaked through with sweat; the mattress he was lying on smelt of things too disgusting to contemplate. He sat up. That seemed to be a mistake. The ground rose up and swirled around, as did the contents of his stomach. His head felt terrible, something was thumping away madly inside his temples. He pressed with his fingers, and the throbbing eased slightly. He felt a strange sensation at the back of his neck, as if one of the sleepers was awake and watching him. Saliva gushed into his mouth - he was going to vomit and soon. There was no way he could stop it, he knew. He forced himself to stand, and blinked once or twice to try and get the floor to stay level. He made his way to a darker patch of wall, hoping it would be a doorway, stumbling once over a soft body.

He arrived at a landing with steps leading down, but no sign of any container. The message from his stomach was now overwhelming; he couldn't hang on any longer. He retched and retched. A vast quantity of fluids spewed out onto the floor.

"Oh for fuck's sake," said a voice. "Can't you puke outside?"

Someone appeared behind him. "Here, I'll give you a hand down the stairs."

"Oh thanks," said Marcius gratefully. "I don't feel very well."

"Yeh, we noticed."

His rescuer held his wrist, and tugged at him insistently.

84

They seemed to go down endless stairs.

"Jupiter, how many more?" said Marcius to the stranger in the darkness.

His companion laughed. "I think that was the fifth floor, but it's anyone's guess in places like this."

At last they reached the courtyard, but there was no cool breeze. The air remained thick, the stench became overpowering. They must be near an open sewer.

"Wait a bit," Marcius begged, as his companion made to move off. The waves of nausea overtook him again. A knot of pain collected under his ribs, increasing in intensity, causing him to double over.

"Is there a latrine around here?" he gasped. "Oh God, I need a latrine."

"There's something here," said his companion. "Oh, no, I wouldn't bother."

"Have you found it?

"No, don't bother." A leg was protruding from the alcove.

Marcius was sick again. And then again before they got through into the street. Once outside he collapsed, sliding down the wall, and ended up sitting on the pavement.

"Oh God, I wish I was dead."

His companion came up and squatted next to him. "Oh no, you mustn't die. At least, not till you've paid off your debts."

Marcius leant back exhausted. "I don't think I've got any debts."

"You'd be wrong there," said his companion. "You've got a lot."

Marcius experienced the same feeling he'd had in the room upstairs. There was something unpleasant in the man's tone, let alone his words. Abruptly he recovered his wits and looked around him. Where the hell was he? He had no idea at all. From the smell he must be in one of the poorest districts, somewhere near the Cloaca Maxima, the main sewer.

"Who are you?"

The man laughed. "You've got a short memory. I was your best buddy all last night, wasn't I? My name's Lucan. Remember now?"

Marcius shook his head. He didn't remember ever seeing the fellow before, and he didn't particularly want to see him again.

"Well, Lucan, it's been good to meet you. Thank you for getting me out of that place. I really want to get to my own house now. Do you think you could set me on the right road, perhaps? It's in the Palatine district."

"Don't you worry, I'll be with you every step of the way, Sir. Right to the front door."

Again that tone.

"Who are you, Lucan?"

"I'm a commissioner, a debt commissioner. I get ten per cent."

"What debts are you talking about?"

"You lost a lot of money last night. Don't you remember?"

No he didn't remember. He must think. He had gone out last evening with his brother Andreas. For once his stepfather had ascertained that Octavian's parents had taken him off to Greece, there was no longer any veto on his activities. They'd stopped at an inn to listen to an army recruiting officer. He'd had some wild idea of joining up immediately as a legionary but, as always, he'd oscillated between the desperate desire to get out of the house and away from his stepfather, and the realisation that he would be deserting his mother, and the others, not that he ever seemed to be able to do anything to help her. He would lie in bed at night and think of various ways of killing Sperinus, but the Gods knew what that would achieve. He would be executed and his mother would be left, and no doubt they would marry her to someone even worse, if that were possible.

At some stage of the evening he seemed to remember having a violent altercation with Andreas. Yes, he could see his brother's face begging him, pleading with him to do something.

86

To go home, yes, that was it. He wanted to go with the recruiting officer, yes it was something to do with that.

"How much money did I lose then?"

"One thousand, two hundred and thirty six gold pieces," said Lucan.

"What! You're joking."

Lucan shook his head. "No, no joke. I get ten per cent."

"You must be mad." Marcius could see the man's face, grinning. He didn't look mad, just very sure of himself. "I couldn't have lost that much money, I don't have anything like that much money."

"You'll find it," said Lucan.

Marcius began to feel panicky. His heart was racing, and his head swimming again.

"Who did I lose to?"

A syndicate, apparently, Lucan thought. With the recruiting officer, some men and other officers of the Sixth Legion. They'd had no compunction in dicing with the son of a Senator, presuming him to have unlimited funds. And Lucan intended to stick with him until the money was produced.

"Your Dad will cough up," said Lucan complacently.

If only he knew. Marcius stared into the distance. Disasters like this couldn't happen, surely. It was a bad dream. But Lucan had an awful reality. If only he could remember what had happened. Brief snatches were beginning to come back to him. He remembered grinning faces, now he could remember the dice as well. He must have been drunk out of his mind. Seriously out of his mind. There was no point in sitting here. He had to get home, get himself cleaned up and try and think. Try and work something out. He staggered to his feet.

"There's no use trying to run away. You won't get away from me."

"Run? I can scarcely walk, you fool. Give me your arm. If you're so worried about preserving me, you can bloody well be useful."

Dawn was breaking. The sky above the narrow tenements showed rosy. People were beginning to stir. He could hear distant voices. A boy pulled a laden mule on the road towards the river, the hooves sounding loud on the ground. A figure stirred in an alleyway, wrapped in a cloak, a bigger figure behind him.

"Andreas!" Marcius stopped abruptly. "What the hell are you doing here?" Marcius shook him roughly, getting rid of some of his pent-up aggression.

"We've been waiting for you," said his brother sullenly. "All night. I followed you from the baths, seeing as you wouldn't come home."

"Mother will be worried out of her mind."

"Aye," said a deep voice from the shadows.

"Shut up," snapped Marcius. "We'll manage without your comments."

"Aye, Master," agreed the servant.

Andreas giggled. "Come on, let's go home. Better still, let's find somewhere open and get something to eat. I'm starving."

The thought of food brought nausea back again. Andreas was alarmed to see his brother turn quite pale.

"Mark, what's the matter? Are you alright?" he asked.

"Oh God! I don't know what I drank last night, but it must have been very bad wine. No, stay there." He moved away a little distance and paused, hanging onto the wall. How could he have anything left in his stomach? Apparently the supply was endless. He could taste the bitter bile in his mouth. He felt quite weak. A strong arm encircled his waist.

"Master, there's a fountain down that end."

With his slave's support he struggled to the fountain. A patrol of soldiers marched down the street, stopping by the fountain. The decanus walked over.

"What's up, sonny?" he enquired jovially.

"Sons of Senator Sperinus," Lucan told him. "One of them's not feeling so hot, this morning."

The decanus was galvanised into action. Marcius sat and waited while plans were made and implemented, that involved his safe transportation back to his house. He was put into his own bed, and had only one more attack of retching throughout the day. Eventually the pain subsided and he slept.

He woke in the evening, the now familiar sensation of evil had become intense. He told his slave there was a man waiting outside the house. The man was to be brought in, as Marcius wished to speak to him.

"Feeling better, are we?" Lucan enquired, grinning.

He could produce witnesses and pledges. The amount was indisputable.

"And there's no good you thinking of killing yourself," Lucan told him. "These are gaming debts, debts of honour. They're to be paid. If not by you, then by your family."

Marcius sent him away again. He told his slave to arrange an interview with his stepfather on the following morning. He didn't see that there was any alternative.

BOOK 1: CHAPTER 11

Rome 61 BC

His stepfather listened to him, while he made his recital of events as far as he could remember, saying nothing, making no comment. Marcius finished and stood waiting. Sperinus looked up at him with his mad little eyes.

"You son of a bitch," he said. He got up. "You son of a harlot."

He hurled himself across the room and seized Marcius round the neck, squeezing his windpipe, trying to throttle him.

"Master, Master!" The slaves felt entitled to pull him off.

Marcius was shaken by the attack. He wasn't expecting it. Sperinus had never done anything to him before. His neck felt sore where those strong fingers had pressed in.

"I'm sorry, Sir." It seemed quite inadequate. "I'm very sorry, Sir."

Everyone was summoned to appear in the salon, the family, the servants, and the household slaves. Obviously something momentous was going to happen. Last time it had been David dragged away screaming. Judging by the faces of the missus and the children, nothing good was going to happen this time either.

Sperinus walked in, followed by his secretary. He was dressed as if he were about to attend a session in the Senate, his toga immaculately folded and pressed. He took his seat on the dais and then started to speak.

"With the power invested in me as the head of this august family, directly descended from the Goddess Minerva, I hereby order that my stepson, Marcius, be subject to emancipation. That his name be erased from every record in this house. That from henceforth he shall have no claim on me, nor I on him. Let there be no communication with him, from any member of my household."

He looked round at them all malevolently. There was complete silence. He got up and walked over to Marcius, and thrust his face up close. Marcius could smell his sour old man's breath.

"Now, get out!" Sperinus screamed.

"Very well, Sir."

Marcius turned and walked out of the salon, through the atrium, past the porter and into the street without looking back.

Gaius Volusenus decided that as his parents were away, he might as well hold the final party in their house, before his Gauls left Rome again. The steward had raised no objections. In fact it was quite obvious none of the staff would ever dare disobey the young master again. He didn't shout, he didn't threaten, he didn't need to. He'd gone away a boy, and come back very much more than a man, assured, powerful, commanding. Accordingly, the steward wrapped up the best vases, the delicate glasses, and the fine linen throws, and stored them safely in chests in the cellar. He made discreet enquiries, and discovered the barbarians had refrained from sacking Rome. Indeed, they seemed to have behaved with remarkable decorum, but, after all, they hadn't exactly got what they had come for, and this was their last night. As well to be on the safe side.

Perhaps it was a little more riotous, a little more noisy, perhaps there was a little more wine consumed, and the Chief, Diviciacus was evidently not expected.

Still, thought the steward gazing round benignly, if these were barbarians, then he'd welcome the invasion - they were a lot better behaved than most Romans he knew.

Marcius was gazing down into the depths of the river. He knew Lucan was somewhere behind him. Maybe he would surprise the man and jump. What would be the use, though, he thought, staring down into the Tiber. He could swim like a fish, and the river was so low at the moment even a child would have difficulty in drowning. He looked down at the turgid water of the side-channel. The river stank. There seemed nothing heroic about it at present. There was no answer in those decaying shallows.

He called on his creditors in the afternoon. A very unpleasant experience. They'd heard the news, of course, and saw their money disappearing. They weren't interested in the fact that he could sell his horse, and pay a little on account.

"We're not money-lenders," the recruiting officer told him. "We'll be off to the provinces shortly. You'll have to raise a loan from someone."

"Or sell yourself," the centurion suggested. They had all grinned, very aware that he would be hardly worth a hundred pieces, let alone a thousand. If only Octavian were in Rome! But they weren't interested in that idea either. They weren't going to wait for anyone to come back from Greece. He had been given the name of a money-lender. He didn't even get to see him. The porter wouldn't let him through. He knew his own father had other friends, but he hadn't seen them for years, not since he was small, and after this morning he had felt so disgraced. He still found his own behaviour inexplicable. It would have made more sense if he were a blood relation of Sperinus. Perhaps insanity could be caught off other people.

He heard a movement behind him. Lucan, he supposed. He turned round.

"Andreas!"

His brother ran to him, clung to him.

"You're not supposed to have anything to do with me."

"Don't be stupid."

Marcius half laughed and hugged his brother tightly. He might be young, but he was always so reliable, such a help.

"There's a party at Octavian's house," Andreas told him.

"Are they back?" Hope flared for an instant.

"No. They're still in Greece. It's his brother, you know, the one in the army. And some barbarians from the north. Come on, we'll go that way, shall we?"

It was good just to see Octavian's house again. The porter, recognising him, opened the door wide.

"Nice to see you, Masters," he said, obviously expecting them to go on in.

Marcius realised he'd had nothing to eat and he had no money. The porter's welcoming smile cheered him a little.

"Come on," he said to Andreas.

"Are we going in?"

"Why not? There's nothing to be afraid of here."

He was wrong though. Gaius Volusenus didn't look at all pleased to see them, even when the steward had explained who they were. After greeting them, he virtually ignored them. The steward thought he understood though.

"I'm sure, Sir, my Master would be happy for you to visit the house at any time while he was away. In fact he'd be delighted to think you were keeping an eye on things."

Marcius blushed a little. The steward was being very kind.

"I'm afraid the barbarians aren't quite as exceptional as we were led to expect," the steward continued apologetically. "They appear to behave quite normally to me."

However, he thought the young men would be entertained by the music and the dancers. He installed them at the side of the room, out of the way, gave orders that they were to be well looked after, and arranged for the girls to be a little discreet, until such time as the youngsters went home.

Marcius drank steadily; an idea was developing in his mind. They attracted one or two curious glances from the Gauls but were otherwise ignored. It was presumed they were performers of some kind. One of the Gauls did come up, and try to kiss Andreas, but was pulled away by one of his companions.

"No," they said laughing, "not them."

At midnight Marcius told Andreas to go home. "I'll be alright here. I think the steward will let me stay. He'll probably let me stay until Octavian comes back."

Andreas thought that was a good idea. "But what about the money?"

"Don't worry, I'll think of something."

Andreas, with his best company manners, said goodnight to Gaius Volusenus, and thanked him for a very nice party, which made Volusenus laugh at last.

"Isn't your brother going with you?"

"No, Sir. He's staying for a bit."

Gaius shrugged. Perhaps the boy was interested in one of the women. Well he could do as he pleased. He didn't bother him. Marcius was desperately wondering if anyone was ever going to bed, but gradually they began to drift away, taking the women with them. Unfortunately, the one he had been watching covertly all night, showed no inclination to move, being far too interested in trying to remove the last garment from his female companion. Marcius spoke to the steward. That particular gentlemen was supposed to be staying the night. There seemed no point in waiting any longer. It was time to act.

Guéreth watched the boy's approach with interest. He was aware he was being observed, aware also that the boy had been drinking steadily throughout the evening, although he showed no signs of it. The boy was walking purposefully towards him, with no trace of unsteadiness. Guéreth was a little surprised, when he dropped to his knees in front of him. So was Gaius Volusenus. He looked at Marcius with irritation. Guéreth reluctantly abandoned his lady friend. He leant forward, his hands lightly clasped between his knees.

"What can I do for you?" he asked.

"Sir, I wonder if you would buy me?"

"What a strange request."

"I need the money, you see, Sir."

"Why is that?"

"I'm in a lot of debt. I lost a lot of money gambling."

"Marcius," Gaius broke in angrily. "Is this some kind of a

dare between you and Octavian?"

"No, Sir. And this is a private conversation."

Guéreth laughed. "You wouldn't be able to say that, if you were my slave."

"No, Sir, of course not." Marcius flushed a little.

Gaius was really angry. What a bloody cheek the boy had, to come here and try to sponge off his Gauls. He had a good mind to have him thrown out of the house. He would do just that, as soon as Guéreth had finished with him.

Guéreth was finding the idea very entertaining. "And how much do you value yourself at?"

"I need one thousand two hundred and thirty six gold pieces."

"What," started Gaius wrathfully.

"Quiet, Gaius. We are having a private conversation." Guéreth turned back to the boy. "And what makes you think you are worth so much money?"

"I'm not," said Marcius. "Not here in Rome, anyway, although I can read and write, that sort of thing. I thought maybe there wouldn't be very many Roman slaves in Gaul."

"I don't think there are any," Guéreth smiled at him. "So it's your scarcity value, is it?"

"Yes, Sir. Something like that."

Guéreth stared at the boy. He could see it was no laughing matter for him. He could see Marcius was close to tears. He stroked the boy's cheek lightly with a finger.

"Very well, I agree."

Volusenus gave a howl of protest.

"Shut up, Gaius."

Guéreth ordered his servant to bring and count out the precise quantity of gold pieces. He leant forward again.

"Now listen, what's your name?"

"Marcius."

"Is that all?"

"Yes, Sir. Just Marcius."

Odd, usually Romans had more than one name, Guéreth knew that. "Listen, Marcius. Tomorrow morning we leave early. We are starting our return journey to Gaul. We will not be returning for a long time, maybe never. Do you understand?"

The boy nodded. The servant reappeared.

"The gold will be too heavy for the young master to carry."

"I'll send a servant with him," said Volusenus in exasperation. This was madness!

Guéreth was serious now. "So, Marcius, you may go and repay your debts. You must report to me very early tomorrow morning. I won't wait for you, you know."

"Yes, Master," said Marcius. He could hardly believe it could have happened. It had just been an idea, a straw to clutch at, and now he had made it real. He hoped they wouldn't set off too early in the morning, because he would have to wait for the courts to open.

"Guéreth, this is completely ridiculous. I'll raise the money for him myself somehow," Gaius interrupted.

Marcius felt the shiver of apprehension again. "Master, you won't sell me to anyone else, will you?" he pleaded.

"No. I give you my word." Guéreth turned away, and taking his lady friend by surprise, whisked off her last garment, to her squeals of protest and delight. And not having any expectation of ever seeing Marcius again, quickly forgot all about him. So he didn't see Marcius slowly get up and bow to him before leaving, or hear Volusenus's snort of disgust.

Marcius sat on the steps, waiting for the courts to open. As he had been waiting since the middle of the night, he was first in the queue. At least it was over quickly.

In the middle of the next day Gaius Volusenus walked into his friend's bedroom.

"It's time to get up," he shouted.

"Go fuck yourself," replied his friend, hugging the pillow.

"Your Latin gets better every day. More colloquial," Gaius said with approval.

Guéreth rolled onto his back and looked at him in consternation. "What's the time?"

"Mid-day."

"Merciful Gods!" Guéreth jerked up into a sitting position. "We should already be on the road."

"Fear not, my little one," said Gaius grinning. "Departure has been delayed until tomorrow. Apparently your inestimable chief and Marcus Cicero were discussing Platonic philosophy until the wee small hours. According to my steward's most reliable sources, they haven't yet got out of their beds."

"Good, a reprieve. Gaius, I think I will revert to Druidic custom tonight. Neither food nor wine will pass my lips."

"I didn't know you were a Druid."

"I'm not," Guéreth touched his head delicately. "But I feel I should be."

Gaius agreed. "I'll become a convert." He frowned at the steward, who had come through the door, and stood waiting for an opportunity to speak.

"What do you want?"

"Sir, I fear something a little untoward has happened."

"Well, go on, man."

"My lord Guéreth, your slave has arrived. I'm afraid he's not in a very good condition."

"My slave?" Guéreth said, surprised.

"Yes, Sir. The young man you bought last night."

"What!" Guéreth looked at the steward, stunned. He collected himself. "Bring him here at once."

"I wonder, Sir, if you would mind coming with me. It might be more convenient."

Guéreth leapt out of bed, thrust his arms into the sleeves of his dressing-gown, and followed the steward, with Gaius trailing in his wake.

There was a decanus in the courtyard, with a detachment of eight soldiers. They were guarding a naked prisoner, chained at wrist and ankle. The state brand had been pressed into the flesh of his buttocks, leaving an ugly blackened burn, reddened round the margins.

Marcius was in a half-fainting condition, in a state of shock; he hadn't expected any of this. Guéreth swung briskly into action, issuing orders.

"Get those chains off him at once. You, bring him to my room. Arrange for some wine and some broth to be brought. I'll need towels and dressings too. Jump to it."

Also, Guéreth wouldn't allow Gaius to enter the room. "He's my problem. I'll deal with him," he declared. "Now, lay him on the bed."

Marcius started to weep quietly into the pillow.

"Sir," whispered the steward, "the young master's brother is waiting on the other side of the road. I've seen him. Shall I fetch him in, Sir?"

"The boy that was here last night?"

"That's right."

"Very well. Bring him into the house, but not into this room."

"Sir," the steward had become increasingly deferential to Guéreth. "If the Decanus might have a word."

Apparently his orders had forestalled the decanus from handing over the official papers. "If you'll just sign here, Sir, to say you've received the goods undamaged."

Guéreth interrupted. "Who ordered him to be branded?"

"The court, Sir, it's always done in cases like this." He could see the barbarian didn't understand. "It's for your protection, Sir. For instance, say you was to be far away in one of the minor provinces, like. The lad might claim to the authorities that he'd been stolen, or kidnapped. Might even accuse you, Sir. That brand is your guarantee, like. Now, here's the rest of it, Sir."

The decanus handed over an engraved brass sheet. "You'll find all the details on there, Sir. Everything you need to know."

Gaius got more information out of Andreas than he knew what to do with. What a mess! How was he ever going to explain this to his father who, he knew, would be furious. He had been here on the spot, and let a disaster happen under his nose, without stirring himself to prevent it. It had never occurred to him that once the boy had got the money, he would proceed with the next part. He was quite sure it had never occurred to Guéreth either. The man had practically told the boy he was giving him the money as a gift and, of course, Gaius knew why Guéreth had been so generous. In some way it was to thank him for his friendship and hospitality; Guéreth thought he was doing something good. He could see from his friend's face, when he joined him in the garden, any ideas he had on that head had been dramatically changed by events.

"What does this mean?" Guéreth asked. "Emancipated by Senator Sperinus."

Gaius explained.

"You don't mean he's the son of the Senator?"

"That's exactly it."

"Jupiter!"

Gaius smiled. His friend was even beginning to blaspheme in Latin.

"This is worse than apples, Gaius." Guéreth glared resentfully at Andreas. Diviciacus was going to go stark raving mad at this news. "What have I done, Gaius? Started a war?"

"No, of course not. It's all my fault. God, what a fool I am."

Guéreth showed him the brass plate. "This can't be undone, can it?"

"No, Guéreth. There's no way it can be undone."

"Very well. Andreas, you may go and see your brother for half an hour."

"His ex-brother," put in Gaius.

"Afterwards I will accompany you to your house, and speak to Senator Sperinus."

"They've got an uncle, living in Bibracte, Marcus Metius Celar. Do you know him, Guéreth?"

"I know of him. A rich merchant and slave dealer, I believe."

"I think I'd better write to him, with your permission, of course, and let him know just what's happened." He thought if Metius were rich enough, he would be able to buy Marcius back. Maybe it wouldn't be so disastrous after all.

Sperinus was adamant. He received Guéreth quite courteously, and insisted he had no son or stepson by the name of Marcius. As far as he was concerned, the boy no longer existed. If Guéreth had a slave of that name, then let him watch out for treachery. He wished him a safe journey home, and bade him good day.

Guéreth walked slowly back through the house, busy with his thoughts. He still had time to be surprised, though. He had thought a Senator would live in some opulence. This was far and away the poorest furnished house he had been in. Instead of taking him to the road, the steward escorted him to a tiny courtyard. The lady sitting there looked up at him with red-rimmed eyes. The family resemblance was striking. This must be the boy's mother and the other one, the young girl looking at him with terror, must be his sister. Ursula found it difficult to speak to him, she was so overcome. Guéreth took her hand. He would look after the boy, he assured her. Marcius would come to no harm at his hands.

"I will write to you, Lady, and send you news of him."

To his intense embarrassment, she kissed his hands. He felt one of her tears wet his skin. The steward was pulling him away, so he quickly made his farewell. The steward paused with him at the door.

"My lord, I suggest that if you write, you do so via the house of Volusenus."

Guéreth looked at him. "Why is that?"

"I fear letters do not reach Lady Ursula. But messages can be arranged."

Then the steward handed him a tiny stoppered flask. "If you would give this to Master Marcius."

"Certainly. What is it?"

"His mother's tears," said the steward sorrowfully.

"I'll take the greatest care of it," said Guéreth, taken aback.

"Permit me, Sir." The steward laid the little amphora in a tiny decorated box, packed with wood shavings, and handed it solemnly to the attendant. He bowed deeply to Guéreth.

"It's been a great honour, Sir, to serve you," he said, before ushering him through the door.

Senator Sperinus looked through the spy-hole at his wife in the garden. So now she was having assignations with barbarian princes was she, now he had got rid of that handsome Jew-boy. He walked over to his desk and unlocked the drawer. He took out the many letters from Metius and arranged them in a heap. Then he took them one by one to the brazier in the corner, and watched with childish glee as the flames licked round their edges, flickered over the surface, flared up, and consigned the words to ashes.

Guéreth walked back through the streets so deep in thought, that at one stage he lost the attendants, and they had to come back for him. There was a good lesson to be learned here of course. He had been inveigled by the superficial similarities of their civilizations, to think he understood the Romans. Last night he thought he was making a light-hearted generous gesture, a token of appreciation, and he thought he had made it quite plain on his side, there were no conditions attached to the gift. But of his own volition, young Marcius had presented himself to the first court that opened this morning, and subjected himself voluntarily to that dreadful debasement. A man of his word. No, a boy of his word. He was only sixteen. How strange to think there was a legal system in this country, by which you obliterated your own son. Removed all trace of him from documents and inscriptions, as if he had never existed. Guéreth paused for a moment to watch, as some builders fixed a panel of white marble over the dark fissured brick of an archway. He would need to bear that in mind, in future. Admire the beautifully carved marble exterior the Romans presented to the world, but be aware of the hidden deep cracks, leading back to a much more primitive structure, built in past centuries.

As for the boy, he would find out tomorrow with what exactly he had landed himself.

BOOK 1: CHAPTER 12

Rome to Bibracte (Autun), Aeduan territory, Central Gaul 61 BC

The weather changed abruptly. Gusts of wind made the glancing rain sting his face. Marcius rode on, huddled in his hood, feeling cold, sore, stiff and miserable. His master was apparently in dreadful trouble, for having presumed to buy him, before consulting his chief. Volusenus had made it quite clear that Marcius was just one big problem. Marcius hadn't thought past selling himself. It had seemed such an unlikely thing to happen, the future hadn't occurred to him. He had just known that if he were to raise the money that way, he couldn't face staying in Rome. He had to go. And if it were to be tortured to death by barbarians in the north, or perhaps sacrificed at some primitive rite, so be it.

At nightfall they arrived at the country mansion where they were to stay. Guéreth dismounted, and walked over to the silent, sodden figure on the horse. He helped Marcius out of the saddle with his own hands.

He ordered the boy to be bathed and put to bed, then he reappeared later, with a servant carrying a tray of broth and bread.

"Sit up," Guéreth directed. He laid the tray across Marcius's knees. "Now eat," he commanded.

He sat on the bed and watched his new slave eat, with an approving smile. Marcius discovered he was very hungry. He'd had little to eat the day before.

"I didn't think it would be like this," he said, half apologetically, when he was half-way through.

Guéreth just laughed at him. "Finish your supper first. Then we'll talk."

His very presence made Marcius feel more cheerful. Guéreth seemed such a genial giant of a man. After he had been forbidden to see Octavian, Marcius had found no substitute for his friend's father. For the last year he'd felt helpless and powerless.

"Now, that's better," said Guéreth, when he had finished, handing him the napkin so he could wipe his fingers and face. "Firstly, why me?"

Marcius started to stammer his apologies.

"No, I want you to explain."

Marcius sat up, his arms round his knees. "Sir, the servants said you were leaving Rome. I don't want to be a slave in Rome."

"Yes, I understand. But why me?"

"The steward said you had won a great deal of money, and anyway you were a very rich man."

Guéreth reached over and patted his cheek. "Ah, good. What a sensible child you are. My chief does not think I acted sensibly, though. I'm in big trouble."

"Well, Sir, so am I," Marcius confided. "I can tell you, Gaius, I mean Tribune Volusenus, is pretty angry with me. He says it's all my fault."

"Well then, Marcius, we will prove to them that, on the contrary, this was a very wise decision on both our parts after all. Yes?" Guéreth reached out his hand.

"Yes, Sir." Marcius's hand was gripped in a strong clasp.

"That's good. When we reach my country, we will make this promise before the altar."

Marcius nodded his agreement. "Yes, Sir."

"Now," Guéreth continued, "Gaius tells me that you are great friends with his young brother Octavian, is that right?"

"Yes, Sir. We've been friends for as long as I can remember."

"Then before we leave here, perhaps you would like to write to your friend, and tell him what has happened?"

"Oh, yes. I would like that very much. Only..." Marcius hesitated. His voice dropped. This was his inmost fear. "Do you think maybe Octavian wouldn't want to associate with me, now

I'm a slave?"

"If that were so, Marcius, he wouldn't be a friend worth having. But Gaius thinks Octavian will be worried sick about you, so write to him with my blessing. I will make the arrangements in the morning."

"Thank you, Sir." Marcius was feeling more and more reassured by his master.

"These are my first orders. I wish you to learn my language. You will speak only Gallic during the day. After dinner you may speak as you like. I hope you're a quick learner," Guéreth added with a smile. "I don't want you dying of thirst."

To start with, it was really hard, especially when the youngest Gaul mixed him up by teaching him a lot of swear words. But having nothing better to do on the long rides, nearly all the Gauls came and gave him some instruction. Tribune Volusenus was surprised when he condescended to talk to him one day, and Marcius refused point blank to use a word of Latin, to the intense hilarity of his companions. At that point Volusenus washed his hands of him altogether.

Two incidents occurred on the journey. Once he awoke in the middle of the night and lay in the darkness. He could hear nothing but the sound of his master breathing. They had spent the day picking their way through the high pass of the Maritime Alps, and were sleeping in the primitive conditions of one of the new military forts. He felt quite isolated here on top of the world, hundreds of miles from his home and anyone he loved, cut off from all familiar things, and thrust into a new land, with nothing he could call his own to fall back on. Homesickness overwhelmed him.

Guéreth slipped out of bed and rekindled the lamp, walked across the room and knelt at the side of his softly sobbing slave.

"Come on, Marcius," he said. "Get into my bed."

Instantly Marcius rolled over on to his back, looking up at him with wide scared eyes, tense with unnamed fear. Guéreth sat on the floor and burst out laughing.

"What do you think I'm going to do? Rape you?" he said, ruffling the boy's hair affectionately. "You're cold. You need to be warmed up. Get up."

Guéreth was still chuckling as he wrapped Marcius up in the blanket, shoved him into his own bed, got in himself, turned over and went fast asleep.

Marcius found the next morning, to his intense embarrassment, that his master had shared the incident with everybody else. The youngest Gaul, grinning and with graphic gestures, tried to teach him the words for kiss and cuddle, and was progressing towards more technical detail, when carted off by his big cousin.

One morning he awoke just before dawn. He felt full of energy. He quickly dressed, taking care not to wake any of the sleepers. He trod softly to the door which the guard unbarred for him and went outside, wrapping his cloak round his shoulders. He sat on an enormous pile of logs, fuel cut ready for winter, and watched as the sky lightened in the east. Far away in the valley he could see the glints of the river. A large flock of sheep came round the corner along the road, jostling and shoving each other, bleating away. The shepherd paused, leaned on his stick, took off his cap. Marcius agreed it was a good morning and a fine view. The youngest Gaul came out of the door.

"Marcius! Pancakes for breakfast. Hurry up!"

Marcius sped inside, and went into the room where his master was still sleeping. He shook him vigorously. Guéreth sat up and yawned.

"Where's the fire?" he asked.

Marcius was gazing at him happily, a blissful smile on his face. "Good morning, what a lovely day. Isn't it a fine view? I understood it all, Master." He hugged himself with pleasure.

"You mean to say you woke me up, just to tell me?"

"No, Master. It's pancakes for breakfast, too."

Guéreth was pleased the boy's stiff patrician reserve was at last breaking down, in private at least. Guéreth made sure he didn't see much of Marcius for the rest of the journey. He allowed the youngest Gaul to take the boy under his wing, with a few basic instructions to keep them both out of trouble.

Marcius discovered that the youngest Gaul was a youth of some importance, Prince Jayven, Chief Diviciacus's one and only son. Under his new friend's guidance, Marcius went hunting, explored the countryside, tasted snails and frog's legs, got drunk and visited a brothel. All things one could do, it seemed, as a Gallic slave without his master appearing to mind in the slightest. Sometimes, he rightly surmised, his master was quite pleased to get rid of him for a bit.

Gaius Volusenus discovered he didn't want to say goodbye to his friends. He was glad, really, to see Marcius was going with them. Perhaps in the future he could use the boy as an excuse to make a visit, pretend he was enquiring into his welfare or some such thing. He knew such a journey could not be repeated. He had seen his country through different eyes, and was wiser for the experience. Diviciacus presented him with a gold ring, with a strange stone set in the middle, and made a little speech. He said the ring wouldn't open mountains when rubbed, or summon forth genies, but he hoped it would remind him of some good friends he'd made, and there was a list of their names. Gaius shook all their hands, and wished them good fortune. He'd said goodbye to Guéreth the night before.

He lined up his cohort, turned them to face the west, then marched them off on the road to Tarraco.

When the Aeduans arrived back in Bibracte, Guéreth found an invitation awaiting him. Would he kindly dine with Marcus Metius Celar, and could he see to bringing Marcius with him, Metius's nephew?

First Guéreth made sure Marcius had no objection to meeting his uncle in his new status. He thought the boy might be embarrassed.

"No, Sir. I would be very pleased to meet him. It's years since we last saw him. I can give him some news of my mother, and Andreas and Lucy, if it's allowed."

"Of course it's allowed. I'm not expecting you to remain dumb in his presence. That surely is the whole point of the invitation. He will probably want to see what I'm like, as well."

"Yes, Sir. But remember, you promised not to sell me to anyone else?"

Guéreth had been wondering that very point. He knew Metius was an extremely wealthy man. Quite able to afford a thousand or more gold pieces for a nephew, if he wanted him. Apparently Marcius didn't want to be the property of any Roman, not even an uncle. "Don't worry, Marcius. I keep my promises," Guéreth told him.

The next evening Guéreth took Marcius round to Metius's house. Marcius was struck by the luxurious interior, the beautiful wall paintings, rich hangings, silver lamps all lit, soft squashy couches, and a wonderful mosaic on the dining room floor, of a naval battle, presided over by Neptune himself. He began to feel slightly nervous. But after all, Guéreth was hardly going to make him kneel on the floor all night. He remembered sadly he had done that to David once, when he was cross with him for no good reason. He wished he could get a chance to put right the things he had done wrong in the past. He was so much more aware, now.

Metius came to greet them, his hand outstretched in welcome to Guéreth.

"My dear Sir, how delighted I am to make your acquaintance. I am deeply grateful to you for bringing Marcius with you. His mother must be very anxious about him." He stopped and turned to greet his nephew. "I see I shall be able to reassure her, that she need have no concerns about her boy's welfare. You seem to have acquired the Gallic habit of height, Marcius. The last time I saw you......well, it was many years ago after all. Now you tower over me."

Metius asked Guéreth if he had any objection to Marcius dining with them, knowing perfectly well the Gallic custom was to include everyone at table. Smilingly Guéreth shook his head. They were served a very good dinner. Marcius was cross-questioned closely by his uncle about his mother.

"I write frequently," said Metius, "but I have had no replies for two years now. I was wondering if the wife of a Senator wouldn't wish to acknowledge a connection with a slave dealer."

"No," Marcius was shaking his head vigorously. "It's not that at all, Sir. You should write via my friend Octavian's father, Titus Volusenus. My own father and he were great friends."

"Titus Volusenus. Is that Tribune Gaius Volusenus's father as well?" asked Metius.

"That's right, Sir. They have five sons, Gaius is the eldest, and my friend Octavian is the youngest." If he still is my friend, Marcius thought, with a sharp pang of misery. He continued to worry that Octavian wouldn't want to be friends with a Gallic slave, despite his master's reassurance.

"I know the name," said Metius. "Of course, I've met him. He was at the wedding, when my sister married your father, Marcius. I seem to remember he was the life and soul of the party."

"That sounds like him," Marcius smiled. "I think Senator Sperinus must destroy all your letters, Sir. My mother has been very sad to have had no communication with you for two years. I think she has been feeling a bit bereft."

"I remember now. Volusenus wrote to me some time ago," Metius exclaimed. "Something about my sister and your servant?"

"Senator Sperinus accused Mother of having an affair with my servant David. He was only fifteen years old. There's no way he could ever have done such a thing, let alone Mother, of course." Marcius was getting upset, talking about it.

"Go on, what happened?"

"Senator Sperinus had David tortured to death, and he beat

Mother with a dog whip. I think he's insane. He tried to throttle me when I told him about the gaming debts."

Metius was looking at him aghast. "But this is outrageous. She must seek a divorce. She must divorce him immediately. I will not have my sister abused."

"We have been urging her to do so, Sir. But she won't. She won't leave Andreas and Lucy in his hands. And of course if she divorces him, he will get to keep the children. She is worried he will start on them. So far he has left them alone. In fact I'm not sure he's aware any more that Lucy exists. He never mentioned her to me."

Metius was frowning. "I must think of how to help her." He remained lost in thought for a bit, then came to with a start, and remembered his guest. "Well now, Marcius, I wish to talk to your master, so run along to the library and read a book, or, if you prefer, take one of the women." Metius beckoned to the steward to assist.

"Now, Sir," Metius started when Marcius had gone. "Could you explain how this happened to Marcius?"

Guéreth told him as much as he knew. "I think myself, the boy must have been drugged. He says he rarely gets drunk, and never so much so that he no longer knows what he's doing, and he has never previously felt any urge to gamble. I have found him to be a nice truthful boy, and I believe him."

Metius then asked if he might buy him. Guéreth explained he had promised not to sell.

"He anticipated your request, and made his feelings quite clear, so I am not willing to overrule him on this. We have agreed he is to serve me for seven years. After that I will free him. If he then wishes to stay a part of my household, I shall be delighted to find him something useful to do. He tries hard to please me, and never makes the same mistake twice. He is beginning to be a pleasure to have around. And he is making great efforts to learn the language."

Metius smiled. "I don't think he could have chosen a better

master. With your permission I would like to keep in touch with him."

"Of course. Come and visit any time you like. You will always be welcome."

"I meant by writing," laughed Metius, "but I may hold you to that invitation. I will come and sell you some of my merchandise."

"I like your uncle," said Guéreth, as they rode back to their lodgings. "He may come and visit us."

"I wonder if he will do anything to help my mother."

"I'm quite sure he will, Marcius. He seems like a person who gets things done. Don't worry too much about your mother. You can't do anything at this distance. Leave it up to Metius."

BOOK 1: CHAPTER 13

Near Aventicum, Principal town of Helvetia (Switzerland) 59 BC

The girls stood in the doorway looking at their brother's room. Chrys always wanted everything to be perfect for Allaine's return. She looked round. Had she remembered everything? A large bronze bowl stood on the table with towels. The hot bricks in the bed had been wrapped in scented linen; the pleasant perfume permeated the room. She'd found some of the mountain flowers already opened, and put them in water in a little jug on the shelf alongside his books. Everything that could be swept had been swept, everything that could be polished had been polished with beeswax.

"Have I forgotten anything?" she asked Zinny.

Zinny didn't know why she bothered to ask, she never did forget anything. Nevertheless she walked over and rearranged the woven blankets. It was good to know this time Allaine would be staying permanently. Chrys was well aware her father needed support. He was becoming worried by the mood of his fellow-countrymen, as the preparations for evacuation became increasingly prominent in their lives. People grumbled, and looked for a focus for their complaints. Orgetorix seemed to have been manoeuvred by Nammeius and the other councillors into thinking he had to make all the difficult decisions. All blame to be shouldered by him.

Mutterings were becoming a little wild, people were beginning to forget the original motive for the evacuation, Chrys thought, and imputing to Orgetorix all kinds of ridiculous ambitions, as if her father wanted a kingdom, whether large or small. She knew he just wanted a chance of stability and peace. He wouldn't get it of course. But perhaps with the help of the Sequani and the Aeduans, they at least stood a chance. Orgetorix had been away much of the winter, carrying out negotiations, arranging for cattle and wagons to be brought into the country, encouraging the populace to be prepared to cultivate more land this coming season, to produce an abundance of corn to take with them.

Some Roman traders had joined the Greeks, and built a trading post in Aventicum. Marcus Metius had sent her father a masseur. Chrys didn't like him. She didn't think he was much good at massage, either. But he went out into the countryside, gathering herbs to make into poultices to relieve muscle aches and pains, and they had been very effective.

The ringing of harness in the courtyard caught their attention. The outriders heralding their brother's arrival were already dismounted.

"Come on," Chrys caught Tzïnne's hand, and they dashed off to welcome him, as happy and excited as children. There he was, tall, blond, grey-eyed, his smile slowly lighting up his face. The servants stood around them in a cheerful circle, as he hugged and kissed his sisters.

"Why do you two always grow so much over winter?"

"How can you say that?" his sister said indignantly, "when you've grown so much yourself."

He went off to make arrangements for his servants, and then made his way to the bath house, one of the many things he missed in the north. Zinny sighed in pleasure, they were to have him to themselves for a few days, they would be able to ask him everything.

Allaine had been almost beside himself with impatience waiting for the snows to melt in the high passes, so he could get home again. He found the self-control techniques he'd been taught didn't always work in practice. Perhaps they would be more effective when he was older. He looked at his sisters with considerable pleasure. They were quite different, Chrys with her grey eyes and thick curly red-gold hair, but Zinny dark, like

Grandmother.

"How was Eloise?" asked Chrys.

"Well she's a lot better than before. She's no longer so homesick." He smiled at the thought of his pretty elder sister and her young friend. Riona had decided to visit her, knowing Allaine would be there. He liked her more and more. The alliance with the North hadn't yet materialised.

"Is she? Is she having a baby?"

Allaine nodded. "Yes, and I'm to persuade Grandmother to go to her. Which will be quite a journey for an old lady, but no doubt she'll manage."

"Is she happy?"

"Oh yes, I think so. She's in love."

"Who with?"

"Her husband! Who do you think?"

Chrys looked at him under her long lashes. She didn't find that at all surprising, she was in love with Dumnorix herself. Who wouldn't be, after all? He looked simply gorgeous. Of course, he was well aware he looked simply gorgeous. He seemed to have flirted with everybody while he was here, even though he was getting married to her sister. She wondered when Allaine would get married, and who would be chosen for him. Whoever it was would be very fortunate, she thought.

"And are you now a proper priest?"

"Oh yes, I'm a very proper priest. I've made my first sacrifice."

"And what happened? Did it go alright?"

"Well I think it did," he said in amusement. "The lamb didn't get up and walk away afterwards, or anything like that."

"I don't like it," said Zinny.

"What don't you like, dear?"

"There's this huge part of your life that we don't have anything to do with. We only see you for half the year."

Allaine was touched. He hadn't realised the girls missed him so much.

"I thought you said last autumn, you were glad I was clearing off to the north again, because you were sick to death of me bossing everyone around," he said with a smile.

Zinny rested her chin on her fingers. "Well, there is that," she said.

"Did you go to Britain?" put in Chrys. "What did you see? Tell us."

He told them as much as he could. "There's this extraordinary stone temple. Enormous, like Carnac, only in a circle. No-one knows how it was built." He'd spent the whole of the winter travelling in Britain, and had been taken to the Holy Island itself. He couldn't tell them anything of the rites and mysteries, of course.

"But wasn't it dangerous travelling around so much? What are the roads like? Aren't there bandits, or gypsies?"

"No, it's perfectly safe if you're a priest. No-one will touch you. I could have travelled anywhere at all with no protection. Everyone would have taken me in and fed me. And made sure I came to no harm. They have enormous reverence for their priests. Even Druids from Gaul, though actually they think we're a bit inferior," he laughed.

The next night the girls decided to tackle the subjects worrying them most.

"Allaine, what do you think about this mass evacuation of the country? Do you think we're doing the right thing?"

"That's a very difficult question, Chrys. I've thought about it a lot." He smiled faintly. "My solution would be for the Romans to attack the Germans, but I haven't yet worked out a method to entice them to do so. Especially as the Senate have just declared Ariovistus, that's the German king, to be a friend and ally of Rome."

"Allaine, there's plotting going on. Maybe it always has been going on, and I've been too young to notice, but I have the feeling it's been getting much worse recently. They are saying things about Father I don't like."

"What sort of things, Chrys?"

"They say he's ambitious, too ambitious."

He looked up sharply at that.

"It's a bit frightening, Allaine."

No wonder the girls were glad to see him back. "Don't worry," he said, "I'll see what I can find out."

He kept his ears open that summer. He was too young to be considered of any importance, and also too young to be a threat. He attended the council meetings, and sat quietly listening. He discreetly sought the opinions of everyone he could. But he was already closely identified with his father, and thus many of his compatriots weren't very forthcoming.

There was a lot of news in from Rome. Caesar had caused the proceedings of the Senate to be published, so they knew what was going on in that city in minute detail. For some reason the Germans left them in relative peace, though probably Ariovistus had heard of their preparations for evacuating the country, and was minded to save himself the trouble of fighting for it, as he would be able to occupy it openly as soon as they had gone. As the summer months proceeded Allaine began to wonder if the record of the Senate proceedings were deliberately aimed at the Helvetii. Caesar was rumoured to have joined an informal alliance with Pompey, the popular and highly successful commander, and Crassus, the richest man in Rome, so that next year they could carve up the provinces between them. Caesar was becoming more and more high-handed in his actions, behaving more like a tyrant than a Consul. Every time they read of another of his bullying tactics, Allaine thought his father looked a little greyer and older.

It gave the people plenty to talk about, but also heightened their feeling of insecurity. The country was like a deer, being hunted by a lion from the south, and a pack of wolves from the east. Like the deer, their only chance of escape lay in running, but also like the deer there were barriers strewn in their path, political as well as physical. Evacuation was now taken very seriously indeed, possessions were being carefully wrapped up in the wagons. Allaine began to think they hadn't started running in time, when the news came that Caesar was to become governor of Trans-Alpine Gaul. Now his bullying tactics would be released not on the Senate, but on the world.

Allaine had spoken to Riona's father, wondering if he could possibly be considered a suitable husband, and obtained his enthusiastic agreement. But when he approached his own father, Orgetorix said no. He didn't think Riona good enough for his son. And at the moment there were far more important matters to attend to, rather than wasting time, organising weddings. Let alone Allaine soon wouldn't have a country to call his own. They would be under the suzerainty of the Aeduans. Anyway Allaine was far too young to consider marriage. He would have to wait until after the evacuation of the country. There would be much to do. Time to think of marriage later, when his people were settled in their new land. In reality, all these excuses meant Orgetorix needed his son by his side, concentrating on the affairs of the country, not of the heart.

The youngsters had been so busy, and the threats seemed to have disappeared, when the summons came that Orgetorix was to be arraigned for treason. He was to appear for trial at Aventicum in chains. He was accused of conspiring to become king. His children were taken by surprise. They discovered, though, that their father was very well prepared. He seemed to have expected such a turn of events, and had laid his plans well. Coevorten and Metilaius, his two sons by his first marriage, hastened to his side. He quickly dispatched messengers all over the country, mobilising his supporters. He appeared at Aventicum with a small army, but a well-disciplined and well-trained one. He made it quite clear he had no intention whatsoever of standing trial.

He summoned the council members to appear before him,

but none of them owned up to having believed the allegations in the first place. He strongly suspected Nammeius of being behind the plot, but could obtain no proof. So he called his supporters to remain on standby till further notice, and returned home to his worried younger children.

At dinner that night he attempted to explain. "The people are anxious, my dears. This is, after all, a huge undertaking, a leap into the unknown for many of them. Many of our people have never travelled out of their own villages. To be trekking across an unknown country fills them with dread. They are unsure of what they will find at the end of a difficult journey. Now they are faced with actually putting their schemes into practise. Of course there are problems to solve. But they need someone to shoulder their burdens of responsibility."

"But I don't see why they should accuse you, Father."

"Unfortunately, Allaine, all the problems have been ushered my way, so I appear to be taking all the decisions. The Chief Magistrate is not up to his job, this year. I suppose I may be becoming more autocratic. It is so much easier to issue orders, than to try to get everyone to agree. There really is no time for constant debate, but I will have to find a better appearance of our usual democratic procedures. I have assured the court that I will surrender all authority, once we have reached our destination."

Allaine wasn't sure this was a good idea either. He thought there would be innumerable arguments about land, once they had arrived. But as the conversation was disturbing the girls, he let the matter drop.

Although it was good Father was at home again, it meant in the future he would need to be surrounded by an armed escort at all times, making it appear even more that he was a dictator, if not a king.

BOOK 1: CHAPTER 14

Roman Military Garrison, Vicinity of Geneva, Spring 58 BC

Feeling very nervous, Octavian walked into headquarters, and approached his Commander-in-Chief, who was sitting behind his exquisitely carved Egyptian desk.

"Tribune Octavian Volusenus Quadratus, Sir. Reporting for duty. Hail Caesar!" he added as an afterthought. Drat, he had got that the wrong way round, he was sure.

Caesar sat looking at him from behind the desk, and said not a word. Octavian began to feel very uncomfortable. He still felt a little ridiculous in his stiff new uniform. He wondered if his stupid servant had put his uniform on correctly. Perhaps he was improperly dressed. Still his commander said nothing. Was Caesar perhaps remembering the incident in the Forum? He hoped not.

"Ah yes," said Caesar. "And who might you be?"

Octavian blushed and repeated his name and rank. Caesar leant back in his chair. "Let me see. Volusenus, Volusenus. I believe I'm acquainted with your maternal aunt."

"Really, Sir?" said Octavian. Was he supposed to remind Caesar that his elder brother was in fact serving in this very legion.

"What is her name now?" Caesar smiled gently.

Octavian panicked. Her name had gone right out of his head.

"I am right in thinking you have a maternal aunt?"

"Yes, Sir. I'm afraid I can't remember her name."

"I see. And am I right in thinking that one of your cousins is serving with Pompey?"

Octavian mentally reviewed his cousins. He supposed it would be Lucius. "Probably, Sir."

"My dear boy," said Caesar in mild rebuke, "you must learn to be more specific."

Octavian wanted to die of shame. What a fool he must look. A proper tribune came into the room, one that looked as if he knew what he was doing, walked with easy assurance up to his commander-in-chief, and saluted smartly with the customary greeting. A slight thrill went through Octavian, when he realised it was his elder brother.

"Ah, Gaius," said Caesar, with a charming smile. "You had better show your brother round the camp." He turned to smile at Octavian. "Come to dinner," he said.

"Oh, thank you very much, Sir," said Octavian.

"Not you, idiot," said his brother.

"By all means," continued Caesar, sweetly, "do bring him as well."

Now they were both looking at him; his brother with an expression of extreme loathing. He realised he was supposed to do something, but couldn't for the life of him think what. He didn't seem to be able to think at all. He looked desperately to his brother for help.

"Tribune," said his brother quietly.

"Yes, Sir."

"No, you just say 'Sir,'" snapped Gaius.

"Sir," repeated Octavian.

"Step one pace forward, raise your right arm in salute, repeat 'Hail Caesar', take one pace back, then turn round and march out of the room. Wait for me outside."

"He'll improve, Gaius," said Caesar.

"I should hope so, Sir." Gaius saluted impeccably, and marched to join his brother.

"What the hell are you doing here?" asked Gaius. "You're supposed to have joined Pompey's forces." It was the first chance he'd had to shout at his little brother, since he'd heard the news he was joining his own legion.

Octavian decided not to tell him.

"I suppose you think because I'm here, you're going to get a cushy number. Well you're not. So forget it."

He showed Octavian briefly round the camp as ordered, and after getting only monosyllabic replies to his questions, decided his brother was sulking. So he handed him over the Principal Centurion, who was told Octavian was in urgent need of basic training.

The Principal Centurion smiled in joyous anticipation. For him life held few greater pleasures than to be able to publicly ridicule a well brought-up patrician youth.

When Gaius got back to his quarters that night, he realised he'd forgotten to tell his young brother about Marcius. Oh well, he supposed the boys were in communication. When he walked into his room, he was delighted to see a bowl of shining red apples in a silver dish in the centre of the desk. He turned in surprise to his servant.

"Where did these come from?"

"They was delivered, Sir," said his servant woodenly.

Gaius selected an apple, rubbed it against his tunic and curled up on the bed. He took a bite. It was delicious and sweet. He lay back on his bed and laughed. He supposed he had better buy an orchard.

Octavian stepped smartly forward and saluted. "Hail Caesar! The ambassadors from Switzerland are waiting to see you, Sir."

"Thank you, Octavian." Caesar continued to write.

After a while he looked up at the tribune standing rigidly to attention in front of him. "You may dismiss."

"Very good, Sir. What shall I say to the ambassadors from Switzerland?"

"Ask them to wait."

He left them standing for two hours, until first one and then the other had to ask to be taken to the latrines. Eventually he received them on the parade ground. He was seated at a desk flanked by some officials. Once the ambassadors were standing in front of him, armed legionaries formed a complete square around them. Some of the ambassadors began to look distinctly nervous.

Caesar sat back in his chair, smilingly surveying them. His gaze came to rest on a blond, grey-eyed youth. Allaine stepped forward and bowed low, asking politely if he might act as interpreter. Caesar refused. He would use his own interpreters.

Nammeius began by congratulating Caesar on his appointment as Governor. Caesar's smile deepened. Looking at him, Allaine felt afraid. Give this man the slightest advantage, and he would do to you just what he had threatened to do to the Senate. Stamp right on your face.

"You will understand, Caesar," continued Nammeius, "that the whole of our Helvetian race wishes to move to the territory of the Sequani and Aedui."

They watched the smile disappear, as this was interpreted.

"Please don't misunderstand, Caesar. This is of course entirely with the consent of the Sequani and Aeduan people. Finding you have ordered the bridge at Geneva to be destroyed," The smile reappeared. "We wish to ask, to beg, your permission to cross the Province." Nammeius hastened on. "We will do no harm. Indeed we will be prepared to make reparations for any accidental damage."

"Your request has caught me by surprise," said Caesar.

Something made Allaine glance at the face of the young tribune standing behind his commander's desk. His expression was a puzzled frown. Octavian knew the news had come in a week ago. That, after all, was why they had destroyed the bridge. He was even more puzzled to see the young blond Gaul apparently smiling at him. He smiled back, before remembering to school his features to impassivity.

"If you would care to return in two weeks," he heard his commander say, "I will give you my decision."

Octavian could see from their faces, this had caused some consternation. Of course they would have to use up precious supplies of corn while they were hanging around waiting.

Allaine stared at Caesar. Caesar stared straight back with unwavering gaze. Allaine bowed formally and left with the other disconsolate ambassadors. Caesar turned to his secretary.

"Philemon, find out who the blond boy is. I like the look of him."

Gaius liked the look of him as well. What a strikingly beautiful youngster, with his tall slim figure, those huge grey eyes and blond curls. He seemed both graceful and intelligent. Someone to get to know.

In the afternoon Octavian was drinking in the officers' mess, when the Principal Centurion marched in, marched up to him, saluted and said "Sir, on the parade ground, in double-quick time."

"Piss off," said Octavian.

"Sir."

To his astonishment the centurion saluted, spun on his heel and walked out, leaving him staring open-mouthed at his retreating back. Octavian looked round at his brother officers. They were grinning from ear to ear, gazing into their wine mugs.

"Is that all you have to do?" he said incredulously. "Tell him to piss off?"

"That's right. Didn't take you very long to find that out, did it?"

One of them walked over to a board. "Your brother still has the record, seven days. You're second though. Well done. It took me three months."

"That says something about you, Hugo."

"Yes. It says when I take the soldiers out on parade, I know how to drill them properly."

Hugo grinned at Octavian over his wine mug. "Welcome to the Legion, Octavian," he said.

Helvetia (Switzerland) 58 BC

Orgetorix sat hunched over his wine, while his masseur rubbed the pungent oil into his skin. The confrontation had been ugly. He'd taken ten thousand men with him to Aventicum. That showed them pretty clearly they wouldn't get away with putting him in chains to stand trial. He felt the tension in his neck gradually ease as the individual muscles were gently smoothed and squeezed. The man was good at his job.

Orgetorix continued to stare unfocused. Which of his sons was stirring up trouble, or was it Nammeius? He wouldn't put it past him. The man had always been jealous of his power and authority.

"I could make you a nice drink, Sir, a pick-me-up, make you feel a bit more the thing, Sir."

Orgetorix turned to look at him. The man was smiling. "Very well," he agreed, "be quick."

"Right away, Sir."

The liquid had a strange bitter taste on his tongue, not quite like usual. Perhaps his slave was trying to poison him. He smiled to himself. He felt the soothing drug flow through his veins, enveloping him in inward warmth.

"Feeling better now, Sir?" asked the man.

"Yes. A lot better."

"Shall I send for your woman, Sir?"

He shook his head.

"How about a nice sleep, Sir? I'll call you if anyone comes, otherwise I shan't have to disturb you till dinner, Sir."

He allowed the man to tuck the furs around him and sank back gratefully. He relaxed, uncoupled his mind from control, and let his thoughts wander. So many problems floated to the surface, one after the other, but he couldn't be bothered to examine them tonight. He pushed them down again. He felt deliciously tired. His limbs were so light. He drifted into sleep. He sensed himself gently rising. He hovered over the bed. He could look down and see the form below lying straight out on the bed. But it meant nothing to him. Nothing at all.

His servant leant over him, peering closely. Nothing. No movement. Cautiously he raised one eyelid. The eye stared out, unseeing. Just to make sure he fetched the silver mirror from the oak chest, and held it close over the face. Nothing. No vapour. Nothing. Well, he'd done his job. He'd better skedaddle quick.

A group of youths stood on the hill watching the legion pass by. One of them picked up a stone.

"Go on, dare you."

He threw it. It landed with a dull thud against the leather-covered shield of a legionary. The soldiers carried on marching. The children turned away, bored before the last steel-tipped lance had faded from view. A detachment of cavalry moved from the main column and galloped up the hill, spreading like a fan. The children turned round curiously to watch. They saw the raised arms. Spears directed at them. For a moment they couldn't believe it was happening.

"Run, run!" one of them screamed.

They ran as fast as they could up the slippery grass-covered hill. They heard the first thud of the first spear, and the thick, short scream of the first victim, transfixed clean through the thin chest wall. The horses swept round in an arc and returned to the road.

The tiny bodies, pinned on the hillside, wriggled briefly and were still.

Noviodunum, Aeduan Territory, Central Gaul

Dumnorix lay on the bed looking at his beautiful wife. He thought she looked even more lovely, now she was pregnant. The maid was combing her thick blonde hair. Eloise studied herself in the bronze mirror, turning her face to catch the reflections. She smiled at herself. She thought she looked very nice.

"Come here," ordered her husband.

She looked at him quickly, then laughed and sent the maid away. She walked over to stand by the side of the bed, smiling down at him.

"What do you want?" she asked lazily.

"You know perfectly well what I want."

"I thought we were going out to dinner at your brother's house."

He caught her hand and pulled her down so she sat on the bed. He picked up her hand and played with the ring on her finger.

"Eloise, do you know you're the most beautiful thing that ever happened to me?" He pressed her hand to his cheek, then pressed the palm with his lips. He lay back again, still holding her hand, drinking in the picture she made. He loved the way he could still make her blush.

"Well I have had my suspicions." She answered his smile with her own. She adored him. He was so gentle with her, so tender. He moved his hand to where her stomach swelled under her dress and looked at her in surprise and delight, as the baby took the opportunity to kick vigorously.

"Another boy," he said, laughing. Gradually his smile faded and his eyes grew grave. He sat up abruptly, his arms around her, holding her tight, pressing her to him.

"Eloise, Eloise," he whispered. He was seized by bitter premonition. How could he keep her safe? How could he keep any of them safe?

Narbonne, Trans-Alpine Gaul

Gaius Volusenus had been told to tour the Province, and recruit as many men as he possibly could. Caesar had only one legion at Geneva. He sent for the three he had garrisoned in Italy, and hoped to raise two more. It was easy to see what was in his mind. He was looking for an excuse, any excuse, to march into Gaul, and thought with the Helvetian exodus, he had good cause. Or at least, could make it seem as if he had good cause.

General Titus Labienus, Caesar's second in command, had been left to fortify the banks of the Rhône. Gaius was quite glad to escape that work. He hadn't appreciated before joining the army, just how much engineering was involved. He carefully selected the centurions he was to take with him, one who was young, handsome and full of fun, and the other, a total bastard, but with a misleadingly fatherly air. Gaius told them to select a few personable looking legionaries, who were ready to lie through their teeth about monetary reward, the prospects of booty, and the conditions in the army. He was also provided with an army clerk, a fussy little man who kept meticulous records, and a medical orderly, who could carry out the basic medical examination, which each new recruit was required to pass. He wasted no time and marched them quickly down the path of the Rhône, and then along the coast to Narbonne. The city prefect was expecting him, and had been ordered by Caesar to give every assistance. So he was put up at one of the best houses.

The next morning they found a queue of willing applicants had already formed in the forum, massing on the steps of the Temple to Isis. Some of them had a parent with them. Swiftly Gaius opened proceedings. He found progress impeded by the clerk, who couldn't keep up with the paperwork. Gaius walked off to the city prefect's office and arranged to hire a couple more secretaries. There was nothing particularly for him to do, so he took himself off to the nearest inn and sat in the gardens, with a mug of spiced wine and a bowl of roasted chestnuts. An earnest discussion was going on behind him.

"Of course they don't let you keep dogs."

"But they have fighting dogs, don't they?"

"He isn't a fighting dog, Valerius. He's a hunting dog."

"But I'm sure he'd be useful," Valerius persisted. "Look how good he is at tracking things."

"Oh, don't be ridiculous, Val. You don't see a legion marching along with a load of animals. Supposing everyone wanted to take a dog?"

Valerius sounded desperate. "I'm not going if the dog doesn't go."

"You'll do as you're told, Valerius, and we'll have no nonsense."

Gaius turned round to survey the group, and caught the father's eye. "Is there a problem?" he said, coming over.

They all politely rose to their feet. Valerius had on a lead one of the most magnificent animals he'd ever seen, a beautiful long-haired golden hound. Most unusual, he'd not seen one like it before.

"Is this your dog?" Gaius asked, smiling. "He's a very handsome dog."

"Yes, Sir, Tribune."

"Perhaps you'd care to join us for a drink, Tribune?" said the father.

"I have a drink thank you, but I'd be happy to join you." Gaius pulled his seat up and they all sat down again. Valerius was anxiously gazing into space, stroking the dog's head, which was once again settled on his knee. The dog looked sadly at Gaius, with mournful golden eyes.

"Does your dog have a name?"

"He's called Hector, Sir."

"And you're hoping to join up this morning, are you?"

"Yes, Sir." Valerius looked as sad as the dog.

"I was just explaining, Tribune, that he can't take the dog with him."

"He'll pine," said Valerius. "He'll die."

"Jupiter, Val, he's only a bloody dog," said his elder brother.

Valerius merely looked mutinous. Gaius was feeling unusually tolerant. The work was proceeding well, without any effort on his part.

"A dog called Hector must be considered something out of the ordinary," he said. "A Hector should be a credit to any army. I'll take him, if you like. Would he stay with me?"

"Yes, Sir. He would if I tell him to." Valerius could hardly believe his luck.

"I suppose he takes a bit of feeding?" said Gaius, experimentally stroking the dog between its ears.

"No, Sir. He sits and looks sad and people give him things. You have to stop them, or he'd get too fat."

"Perfect," said Gaius. "Do you like horses, too?"

"Yes," said Valerius.

"He likes anything with four legs," said his elder brother, "even rats."

"Shut up," said Valerius.

"He does." The elder brother grinned knowingly at Gaius. "He had a pet rat once."

Gaius patted the dog. "I'll see you later," he said as he rose to go. "I'm afraid there's a long queue."

He wondered how Valerius would get on in the army. Not very well, he thought.

BOOK 1: CHAPTER 15

Helvetia (Switzerland) 58 BC

Everything was loaded ready in the wagons. They were waiting impatiently for Coevorten to arrive. Many of the towns and villages had already been put to the torch. A long column of beasts and people was winding its way through the length of Switzerland. Today it was their turn.

Fires, thought Allaine. Wedding fires, funeral fires, signal fires, and now this. The flames of total destruction. No sooner had Coevorten ignited the pyre that was to lift his father's soul to heaven, than he was to destroy everything Orgetorix had built up over the years.

Allaine was hating it, the whole awful process. The deliberate annihilation of his home, everything tangible that he loved, the sharply sloping roofs, the overhanging eaves with the house martins nesting beneath, the painted walls, the massive pine beams, the smooth polished floors, and his own haven, his much loved room. Not the bath house, though. At least one building would remain untouched. Grandmother was adamant about that.

Allaine felt a terrifying sense of loss at his father's sudden death. But also a certain relief. The Gods be thanked Orgetorix hadn't lived to see this, his country's devastation. Though maybe it wouldn't have affected him in the same way, as he had planned this exodus, right from the beginning. Allaine suspected his father sometimes had doubts as to whether this was the right course for his people. If so, he had never voiced them. Coevorten and Metilaius appeared to have no such misgivings.

Coevorten arrived, riding at the head of his cavalry. He dismounted in front of the little group standing before the servants. He greeted his grandmother first, then kissed the others in turn. He addressed Zinny.

"You're all looking very sad. You're looking at things the

wrong way. I'm surprised at you, Allaine. This is a wonderful new beginning for us, for our whole nation. The Gods have given us this opportunity. We must seize it with both hands. Cheer up, girls. The men of the Sequani, having heard of your beauty, are queuing up, begging me for your hands in marriage."

Chrys looked at him. He'd been making plans, then.

"Well, Allaine?" said his brother, as they walked off together to the sacred flames.

"We're running away," said Allaine.

His half brother paused and gripped his shoulder, staring into his eyes. "Allaine," he whispered, "repeat that remark in anyone else's hearing, and I'll have your throat slit."

Allaine stared back at him.

"You're a stubborn bastard," said Coevorten. "You'll swear an oath of loyalty to me tomorrow, Allaine." He should have seen to this before. "I'm the head of the family, now."

"Of course," said his brother.

Dumnorix listened to him in consternation. "Caesar wouldn't let you through, wouldn't let you across the Province?"

"No," said Allaine. "He kept us hanging around for two weeks, but it was just so he could fortify the river crossing. He destroyed the bridge at Geneva too. We couldn't get the wagons across."

"What now then, Allaine? You could go back, but hasn't everything been burnt?"

"I don't care, Dumnorix, I'd rather go back myself. I feel we're on a collision course. However, that's not what I've been sent to ask you. Will you explain to the Sequani, that we will be coming by the high pass route?"

"Of course, Allaine, that won't be a problem. What is the problem?"

"Food. We've no food, Dumnorix. We wasted two weeks doing nothing, waiting for Caesar's reply. It will take us far longer to get over the high pass route than we'd intended. We'll barely have enough rations."

"That's bad," Dumnorix was worried. "You know the harvest has been bad everywhere. And the rest?"

"My brother, Coevorten. I think if he doesn't get what he wants by negotiation, he might be prepared to use force. That'll alienate the Sequani, and your people as well, of course."

"Very well," Dumnorix said. "Allaine, I'll do my best and mobilise some corn supplies in the north of the country for you. I'll send you word."

Like the rest of them Chrys had had many misgivings before they had set out, before they had ever wrapped the first spoon. She felt every day was bringing a fresh disaster. There were so many problems to be surmounted. The two week's inactivity had been hard to bear, thousands of people sitting around with nothing to do but eat. And the increasing realisation that they were no longer in control of their own destiny. Their fate was at the whim of this man from the south, Julius Caesar.

Why hadn't they started out a year earlier, thought Chrys. She walked by the side of the wagon. Coevorten had insisted that she be near the head of the column.

"Your red hair will be a beacon to light us through the passes," he had declared.

She hadn't found this the slightest bit amusing. Only the small children, the very old, and the heavily pregnant were allowed to stay in the wagons. All the rest must walk, otherwise the paths were too steep for the mules and oxen. There were so many hold ups, so many cattle stumbled, wagons overturned, their progress got slower and slower, sometimes halting for an entire day, getting nowhere. Inactivity made them all cold at this high altitude. There were many deaths in the wagons. Old people with thin blood, little babies with no skin fat. They had started out with a conflagration behind them, and now their passage was being marked out by a long line of funeral pyres, receding into the distance.

Allaine didn't seem to mind any of it. He was remarkably hardy. He made sure Chrys was fed properly, that the servants were looking after her. Allaine rode back along the winding river of humans, animals and wagons. He was glad Chrys was at the front. Three hundred thousand people with all the accompanying animals, travelling through a high narrow pass, meant a lot of excrement underfoot for the walkers. He smiled when he saw his grandmother's wagon near the end of the column. She was sitting upright, sunk into her furs, her face inscrutable. She looked like a little wizened God, Serenos himself.

Zinny was delighted to see him, but she was being well entertained. Noemon was carrying on her lessons, she explained. She thought she'd learnt more in the last month than she'd learnt in the last year.

"This is certainly an Odyssey, isn't it?" she said cheerfully. "I wonder what city we'll found when we get to the end. It might prove to be greater than Rome itself."

A snow storm blew up, trapping the last quarter of the column and rendering them immobile for three days. The rest of the vast procession had reached the plains. The leaders ordered a council gathered.

"Aren't we going to wait for them?" asked Chrys in horror.

"No," Allaine told her. "I know, I know, but you mustn't worry. There are enough servants to look after them."

"There's too many," said Chrys, "and they're an undisciplined lot."

"Coevorten feels if we don't press on and get the corn, the leaders might not be be able to keep the people under control for much longer. The food is all guarded by soldiers at present. But as it runs out he's worried the soldiers may start to help themselves."

"What else?" demanded Chrys.

"They've decided to start pillaging the fields, rounding up

any spare cattle they can see."

"I thought we'd promised not to."

"Chrys, they have to make a choice. They feel it will be easier to deal with irate Sequani, than with irate Helvetians. We are to cross the Saöne, and pick up the corn Dumnorix has arranged. If we start pillaging there and alienate the Aeduans....." Allaine's voice trailed off. Really, it was all so hopeless.

"Well, we'd better wait for Grandmother and Zinny," said Chrys.

He took her hands. "They won't permit it, Chrys." Did she realise what a powerful bargaining counter she was? Probably not. He knew Coevorten was hoping to marry her off to the Chief of the Sequani's eldest son, though Allaine had heard he'd already got a wife.

By the twentieth day three-quarters of the populace were across the river Saöne.

It was pitch black beyond the circle of torchlight the servants carried through the woods. Zinny thought Grandmother was becoming strange. She seemed preoccupied by her bowels. It had been bad enough on the journey. She had insisted that the wagon be stopped when she performed inside, and no-one dared disobey her orders. But Zinny knew it had caused immense discontent to the vehicles behind, and so had allowed increasing numbers to pass them until they were the last. But now Grandmother insisted on performing in the woods. She seemed to have got it into her head that some of the urchins were peeking in at her, although Zinny knew it was impossible for them to get past the armed guard. Obeying her, as always, they had built a hut for her in the woods, while they were waiting for the river crossing to take place. Now they put down her carrying chair.

"I will not be taken unawares," she told Tzïnne, as she followed behind her maidservant, who was reverentially carrying the chamber pot.

Zinny smiled to herself. Quite an unlikely event, really.

She spun round sharply, she thought she heard noises in the distance, shouting. A high scream.

"What is it?" she asked the guard.

They all stood, straining their ears. The sounds became unmistakable. Screams and shouts, running feet, hooves stamping on the hard ground, the crash as a wagon was overturned. "Oh no!" said Zinny, dismayed, her worst fears realised. "They must have started fighting amongst themselves."

"No, Miss," said the captain of the guard grimly. "We're under attack."

His ears could pick out the sounds of metal on metal and marching feet. No riot could spread that quickly. The screams now appeared to be coming from all directions and they heard feet, running feet thudding through the woods. People were shouting and yelling in panic, cursing as they stumbled. The captain acted commendably quickly.

"You lot, form a wall. Extinguish that torch."

His soldiers formed a protective shield.

"Stay here, Miss. I'll find out what's happening."

Quickly he stripped off his armour and helmet, and took only a dagger in his hand. Ignoring the sounds of stampede, he made his way through the trees till he stood at the fringes of their camp. The Romans of course, but he'd never seen them in action before. He looked for a suitable tree and climbed up, lying along one of the thickest branches. The Romans had ringed the camp, and were systematically moving towards the centre, slaughtering everything in sight. The red of the camp fires reflected in their helmets. A ring of cavalry circled the site, making sudden acceleration as they speared an escapee. There were sporadic patches of hand-to-hand fighting, but basically it was just a bloodbath. Now he could hear another sound. A few cracks and rustles, then the thrumming of the fire growing louder. Sparks exploded in the air, a flame shot skywards. The Romans had fired the bridge. There was to be no rescue from the other bank.

They were making no effort to pursue anyone into the

woods. Very few must have made it, and he could see from the way the fighting was going, now clearly illuminated, that there was no likelihood of break out in any direction.

As soon as he could, he got back to his companions in the wood.

"We can do nothing, nothing, Miss," he said. "The camp's been overrun, not a hope. We are just going to lie low. Stay here, Miss, until daybreak. Then we'll see."

As soon as they could see he moved them deeper into the woods, staying roughly parallel to the river. The guards carrying the old lady's chair started to grumble, so he organised a roster. They made a little camp by a stream. He sent a couple of men out to get food.

"Don't waste much time on it, but see if you can find anything edible in the forest."

He went back to see what the Romans were up to. The sounds of carpentry resounded through the wood. As he approached it became difficult to remain concealed. He had the ridiculous idea at first, that the Romans were going to chop down the entire forest in their search for anyone who had escaped. He was filled with dismay when he saw what was happening. A fort had materialised as if by magic, complete with protective ramparts. He made his way quietly around the periphery of the wood. At the river bank much preparation was going ahead. With unbelievable rapidity a bridge was taking shape. He stood watching for some time. Every man was active, purposeful, disciplined. The sight was terrifying.

BOOK 1: CHAPTER 16

Aeduan Territory, Central Gaul

As soon as he had crossed the River Saöne in pursuit of the Helvetians, Caesar sent orders to his supposed allies, summoning the Aeduan nobles to present themselves with their cavalry at his camp.

"Yes, Sir," said the messenger, smiling as he replied to Diviciacus. "Caesar particularly wished me to emphasize that point. Friends and Allies of Rome. I'm to give you a list, Sir, of the people he's expecting to see."

"A list?" Dumnorix looked at him sharply.

"Correct, Sir. A list of all the nobles Caesar is expecting to see at his camp. I'm also to tell you that we shall need extra corn." He almost laughed when he saw their expressions.

"I thought you were bringing some upriver," Diviciacus objected.

"Yes, Sir, we've done so, but it's poor quality, and of course, we've got another five legions now, haven't we, Sir. That's a lot of bodies to feed." He smiled again. He had been told to bully them just a little.

"Thank you for your information, Tribune," Diviciacus said gravely. "I'll make arrangements for your stay."

"That's very kind of you, Sir, but I'll have to get back," said the Tribune. "I look forward to seeing you."

When he had gone Diviciacus sat down slowly, still in shock. "Over thirty thousand Helvetian dead," he said, "our allies, massacred in the night." He shook his head, bewildered. "How can we feed six legions? What have I done, brother, what have I done?" He rubbed his hands in despair. "Friends and Allies of Rome."

Dumnorix put an arm round him. "You did your best," he said pressing his shoulder. "What choice have we had, after all? Our infantry troops aren't even half trained. We are no match for

Roman legions. Not at the moment."

"We'll have to go then," said Diviciacus.

Dumnorix picked up the list. "Oh yes, we'll all have to go."

Octavian took a few deep breaths, straightened his tunic, and set out towards the Aeduan part of the camp, with an interpreter in tow. He shoved his way past the Aeduan guard with scant ceremony, and walked into the tent. Marcius looked at him in astonishment.

"Octavian," he said delightedly.

Octavian thought it best to ignore him. He took up a belligerent position, standing in front of Guéreth.

"Sir," he said, speaking too loudly. "The slave you have in your possession happens to be my close friend." He turned to the interpreter. "Translate," he ordered.

Marcius started to speak, but Guéreth held up his hand to stop him, and carried on placidly eating his supper.

"I therefore propose to buy him off you," Octavian continued. "Go on, translate that."

Guéreth gestured towards a stool, but Octavian shook his head impatiently.

"Perhaps you would care to name your price," Octavian finished. He had been waiting for an opportunity to say this for three years. Now it had come, he didn't think he had made a very good job of it.

"No," said Guéreth.

"No?" said Octavian, taken aback.

"No!" said Guéreth with finality.

Octavian turned to his friend. "Oh Marcius," he said, terribly upset. "Now I don't know what to do."

At that moment his brother walked into the tent, followed by Hector, and looked at him with disgust. "Jupiter! Not you again."

To Octavian's astonishment his brother sat down beside

Guéreth, put an affectionate arm around his neck, and kissed him on the cheek. "How are you, you old bastard?" said Gaius.

"I'm fine, Gaius," Guéreth replied smiling. "But we seem to have a problem." He gestured towards the two young men. "Octavian wishes to buy Marcius."

"Well, tell him he can't."

"I have, but he doesn't like it."

"Can't we send them away, or something?"

"No, Gaius. You know what happens when Marcius is allowed out," said Guéreth solemnly. "He'll sell himself to the nearest trader, and probably end up in Britain."

Marcius was grinning.

"And no doubt we will find we've offended every king in the country, as a consequence."

"I suppose you're right." Really, it was a pleasure to see how the boy had changed. He looked tall and fit, happy and confident. "We're stuck with them."

Jay, the youngest Gaul, walked into the tent. "Gaius," he declared in delight. "I knew it was you. Did you get the apples?"

"Yes, and I bought you an orchard."

"No, have you?" asked Jay, pleased.

"A very nice orchard, only unfortunately it's in Sicilia."

"Ah well," said Jay, "you can't have everything."

Octavian felt he was the only person who didn't know what was going on. Jay dropped to the floor, and put an arm round Hector, who proceeded to wash his face enthusiastically. Gaius pulled his hair.

"What's the news?"

"My uncle's not very happy."

"I don't blame him," said Gaius. "He's been put in a very difficult position."

"Your commander is very good at that." Guéreth spread out his hands. "We're to provide corn for six legions. That's like providing enough for three whole towns. And the harvest is bad this year. It's a problem."

"Jay, isn't your aunt Helvetian?"

"Yes, Aunt Eloise, she's a beautiful girl. She's the daughter of Orgetorix. He died very suddenly this Spring."

"Yes, I heard."

"And there's a wee baby, very blond, like his mother, and she's expecting another."

Jay looked thoughtfully at Gaius.

"Gaius, are you taking hostages from the Aeduans? Because if you are, I'll be one, won't I?"

"I've not heard anything about it, Jay."

"That's a pity," said Jay lightly. "I might have got to see my orchard."

"And if I had, I wouldn't be able to tell you."

There was complete silence. Jay looked at him steadily. His eyes were sad as the dog's.

"Octavian, Marcius, go away," Gaius ordered. "Jay, look after them, would you? Make sure they don't start any wars."

Jay and Marcius followed Octavian to his tent, Octavian giving a half hearted salute to the guard. As soon as they entered the tent, Octavian walked over to the bed, sat down on it, and covered his face with his hands, almost crying with vexation. He was so wrought up, and was now thoroughly deflated. Three years saving up for Marcius, and he'd got nothing. Three years! And now his big brother despised him, as well.

"Octavian, you can't do this," Marcius cried. "This is Prince Jayven, and he's fucking important."

Octavian peered up through his fingers at the young man standing in front of him with his arms folded across his chest, and looking highly amused. He rose up without enthusiasm. A barbarian! What was he supposed to do? Be nice to him?

"What should I do, then?" he asked Marcius, sullenly.

"You're supposed to salute him, for a start, and then offer hospitality."

Octavian just managed the salute, even worse than the one

to the guard. Then he twisted round to find his servant. He picked up a coin, and threw it at him.

"Oh, there you are, you dolt. Get some wine," he ordered.

"Won't you sit down, Sir?" Marcius suggested, as the servant returned, proffering the wine.

"It's not your tent, Marcius," Jay pointed out, enjoying himself hugely.

Octavian pulled himself together. "Please be seated, Sir." He dragged out his folding chair, and opened it up.

Once Jay was comfortably ensconced in the chair, wine cup in hand, Marcius sat down on the bed, and pulled Octavian down with him. Jay looked at the two friends with pleasurable anticipation. He could see Octavian wanted his friend to himself; he didn't want to share him with a barbarian prince. He knew all about Octavian from Marcius, how he was his best friend, how much he missed him. Marcius was quite loquacious when drunk. Though he made sure never to gamble.

"You two talk," Jay said, "I drink." He commandeered the wine jug, to make sure both the young mens' cups were constantly refilled. He listened to their conversation with interest.

Octavian poured out his woes. "Gaius is so stupid. He thinks I've come here, because I wanted him to make it easy for me. He doesn't think much of me."

Marcius grinned. "He never did." Privately he thought Gaius an idiot. "He hasn't a clue, has he?"

"Don't you want me to buy you, Marcius? I miss you so much. Maybe I could get Dad to do something." Though he couldn't imagine how his father could have any influence on Guéreth.

"No thank you. I don't want to be bought. I don't want to be called 'dolt', and have things thrown at me," Marcius said.

Octavian still didn't understand. "Of course not. Don't be daft."

"Anyway, you couldn't afford me. I cost one thousand two hundred and thirty six gold pieces."

"What!" Octavian was looking at him, aghast.

"How much did you save up for me, Octavian?"

"Four hundred." The funny side of it struck him. He laughed. "And you're not worth more than forty."

"Bastard," said Marcius, amiably, but he knew how hard it must have been for Octavian to save up such an amount in three years. "I'll tell you the truth. It is better to be Guéreth's slave, than to be living in the house of Sperinus. I worry about Mum and the kids, though."

"They're just about alright at the moment. Dad keeps an eye on things. He goes to visit, and won't take no for an answer."

Octavian had now had enough drink to get reckless. "Why are you so fucking important?" he asked Jay.

"I'm the only son of Diviciacus. Your foremost ally."

"So?"

"If you lose our support, the Senate rescind Caesar's command, maybe."

"Oh." Octavian thought a bit more. "Do you know why Caesar wanted to stop the Helvetians from crossing the Province, Sir?"

"He looks for an excuse for war, Octavian. Gaul is a huge fertile land, divided into many small countries, each with its own boundaries. He hopes to pick them off, one by one. Why do you think he now has another five legions?"

"Won't the countries join together?"

"Unlikely. We have a saying. For two Gauls to agree, is asking the wolf to be friends with the lion. Caesar has huge debts, from his political manoeuvrings. He hopes to pay them off by looting my country," Jay smiled.

"Perhaps he could sell himself to you," Octavian suggested with a grin. "And clear his debts, like Marcius."

At the thought the three young men all burst out laughing. They were still chuckling, when Jay and Marcius made their farewells, and left.

142

"Did you learn anything useful, Jay?"

"No, Father. Nothing we didn't know already. This Octavian's a bright spark, though. He will learn quickly, I think. But at the moment he has no information for us."

"Did you learn anything useful, Gaius?"

"No, Caesar. Nothing we didn't know already."

BOOK 1: CHAPTER 17

Near Bibracte, Aeduan Territory, Central Gaul

They were summoned to appear before Caesar. He was in a vicious mood. Diviciacus tried to remain dignified, but Dumnorix clasped his hands behind his back and stood with downcast eyes, looking like a naughty schoolboy.

"You Aeduans appear to be behaving with remarkable stupidity. I have ordered you to provide corn for my troops. So far none has arrived. Do you wish me to unleash thirty-six thousand Roman soldiers on your helpless towns and villages? I will do so if they're not fed. Your government has made an alliance with mine. I act as an instrument of that government." Caesar looked from one to the other. "I consider your inaction treasonable. Do you know how the Roman state punishes traitors?"

No-one replied.

"Their necks are pinned on the ground by a wooden fork, and then they are flogged to death. I see I shall have to arrange a demonstration."

Octavian listened to the interviews with shock. These were their allies after all. But this was the way Caesar treated the Senate, and now he had six legions. Octavian felt as if he had been dreaming all his life and had just woken up. In that instant he moved into manhood. Unwittingly he had become part of Caesar's will. Wielded by him like a club. An unstoppable force.

Only Diviciacus remained, the rest had been summarily dismissed. Caesar walked over to Diviciacus and stood, resting his hands on his hips.

"I want that corn within three days. If not I will start by executing your brother."

"It will be delivered in three days, Caesar," said Diviciacus, and bowing, quietly left.

Caesar watched him go. "Avianus!"

"Sir?"

"Have them both watched." He turned back to his desk. "Octavian! There you are, my boy. My God, you have to kick some people hard to make them work. Just like donkeys, aren't they, eh?"

"Yes, Sir," said Octavian.

"Tiring work belabouring donkeys." His slave secretary was sitting at a table. Caesar bent over him, putting a hand round his shoulder. "Philemon," he said, his face within inches of the slave's, "I'm going for a nap."

He stayed like that for a few moments, kneading the slave's shoulder with his hand.

Gaius Volusenus walked into his brother's tent in the afternoon. "We are ordered to dine with the Commander."

"Jupiter," said Octavian. "You don't think he's after me, do you?"

"What would you do if he was?" said his brother, dropping onto the bed.

"Kill myself," said Octavian. "He makes me feel sick."

"Read it back, Philemon."

The secretary obeyed. "Bursting into tears Diviciacus flung his arms around Caesar and begged him not to be too harsh in his treatment of his brother."

"No, further back," ordered Caesar.

"Diviciacus was an intimate personal friend of Caesar's, a man of exceptional loyalty."

"Yes, you can go from there."

Philemon read out the ensuing passage.

"It reads well, don't you feel?" Caesar asked Octavian.

"Yes, Sir. Very well."

Titus Labienus joined them.

"Are they back?"

"Yes, Caesar. The scouts say the hill can be climbed easily from the opposite side."

"Good. Then that's what you will do, Titus. You will take two legions with you. Set off in the small hours. You should reach the summit at daybreak. Take Dumnorix with you."

All had gone according to plan. They seized the hill with no opposition from the Helvetians. Octavian sat on the summit and watched the dawn come up. He could see the vast area of the enemy's camp at the bottom of the hill. A strange sort of enemy this. He could see dogs, women and small children. Men led the horses and cattle to drink before hitching them to the wagons.

"Hi," Dumnorix dropped to his knees beside him. He was holding a wineskin. "Drink?" he offered.

Octavian shook his head, he was still scanning the valley. Dumnorix pulled at the stopper of the wineskin with his left hand. Red wine flowed out of a narrow metal spout in a thin arc. Dumnorix re-stoppered the skin, and wiped his mouth with the back of his hand.

"Nice day," he said. He looked down at the small moving dots in the valley. Somewhere down there were members of his family. He could do nothing for them. Nothing to help them.

Labienus posted lookouts. He was to be informed directly they saw the first lines of Roman troops. He went off to roll himself in his cloak and sleep in the damp grass.

Dumnorix, too, lay back.

"You watch," he said to Octavian, "I sleep." And closed his eyes.

Octavian was fascinated by the activity below, and tried to concentrate on one particular group, but they were too far away. Gradually, all the animals were hitched, everything loaded. How many people were down there, he wondered. A hundred thousand? Two hundred thousand? They had slaughtered thirty thousand on the banks of the river Saöne. No, not slaughtered. Think of another word. Killed. Despatched. Defeated. His mind went on working of its own accord. Crushed. Annihilated. Slowly the Helvetians began to move forward. It was a strange sight. The huge mass was moving in one direction but there was no rhythm to it. Each part moved at a separate irregular pace. He couldn't compare it with anything, it was like nothing he'd ever seen.

"Do they know we're here?"

Dumnorix opened one eye. "Of course they do. They have scouts. And if they didn't have scouts, we would tell them."

One of the Aeduan cavalry commanders came up, conferring with Dumnorix. Octavian liked listening to the foreign sound of the language. He could understand nothing, yet Marcius could speak it fluently. That seemed so surprising. For three years he had been imagining the most dreadful things happening to Marcius, his letters containing the barest details just made him worry the more. He had been thinking all sorts of things - whips, torture, chains, starvation. Instead his friend appeared to have somehow grown in stature, managing to move with ease through a different civilization. Octavian felt absurdly cheated, as if he ought to have been given something to worry about.

Dumnorix finished giving his orders, and lay back to sleep again, the wine skin clutched to his chest. Octavian got up and walked to the far side of the hill. The Aeduan cavalry were arranged in neat rows down the hillside. The men were dismounted, mostly sitting on the ground. A small boy was going from one to another with the water jug. He offered some to Octavian, who drank gratefully, and managed to say "Thank you very much," in Gallic, as Marcius had taught him. The nearest horseman looked up in amusement. Gradually everyone stretched out to sleep, apart from the lookouts.

Octavian walked back to where Dumnorix was lying on the ground. He had taken off his helmet. Octavian did the same. He tucked his cloak up, to make a cushion for his head.

"Won't you burn, Sir?"

Dumnorix opened his eyes. "Probably. You're Octavian, aren't you? Friend of Marcius?"

"Yes, Sir."

"Nice boy, Marcius." Dumnorix rolled onto his side, and

went back to sleep.

At midday, Labienus was walking up and down just behind them, slashing the grass with his cane.

"Where is Caesar?" he demanded.

Three hours later, Labienus was in a towering rage.

"Where the fucking hell is Caesar?" he demanded of the world.

"Perhaps he stopped for a picnic," said Dumnorix.

It was very hot. There was no shelter. Perhaps that explained the murderous look in Labienus's eyes.

They found out in the evening that the Roman scouts had reported the Helvetians to be in possession of the hills.

"We should have used the Helvetian scouts," whispered Octavian to Marcius, later that evening.

BOOK 1: CHAPTER 18

Near Bibracte, Aeduan Territory, Central Gaul

Chrys now knew just how the sheep felt who were being driven to market, yapping dogs at their heels. As soon as they had discovered that Caesar had crossed the Saône, and in only one day, Allaine had gone with the Council leaders to seek peace. He had come back in helpless rage.

"It's hopeless, Chrys."

It was the first time she had heard him use those words.

"He means to make war on us. He wants hostages. Everyone you could possibly think of. You and me too." He saw the fear in her eyes. "We'll have to fight."

This time Caesar had insisted that he act as interpreter. He hadn't been very good at it.

Allaine lay on his back on his bed in the wagon that served as Chrys's bedroom. He could hear the gentle sound of Chrys's breathing next to him, and the occasional snores of her German maid, Greta, who slept on the floor of the wagon, beneath their feet. He stared up into the darkness. One or two holes had appeared in the seams of the cracked, tarred leather awning stretched over them for shelter. Pinpoints of starlight slipped through the slits. He could see a lighter darkness at the wagon's mouth. Outside the night was clear. The Gods could look straight down on them. No clouds obscured their view. He wondered what the Gods were thinking. Tomorrow night he would know. Tomorrow night he would be dead. Time then to review events, to get his thoughts in some sort of order as he had been trained.

It was now three weeks since the river crossing. Strange. He could still summon up the sense of elation he had felt as the first wagon rolled across the bridge, arriving in the Promised Land after that terrible journey. At last a chance to rest, recoup, regroup, replenish supplies, feed and feast. Time to plump up chickens and children. Some of the men were crying openly with emotion. Then, after twenty hard days of struggle with recalcitrant oxen, wayward horses, exhausted men heaving and straining, weakened by the steady diminution in rations, came the terrible night of the massacre. Their bridge of boats on fire. The maelstrom of the opposite bank. Their sense of rage and helplessness.

He had stood the next morning, looking across the river, to see the black smoke from pyres burning skywards. The funeral fires of his family. Grandmother, Zinny, his slaves and servants. He heard the dreadful organised sound of Roman legionaries, pitilessly spitting any remaining victims, their isolated screams sounding thin and far off in the smoke-scented air. He had to work hard to control himself, to stop the rage consuming him. Even this must be turned into a positive experience from which he must learn. He sank onto the bank of the river, and watched.

The Council ordered that the march proceed as quickly as possible. They needed to put as much distance as they could between themselves and Caesar's legions. Who knows, he might try to cross the river himself? The corn ration was now down to a third of its original amount, but the speed of their march meant little time could be spent foraging.

At Bibracte though, the Aeduan capital, Dumnorix had arranged corn for them. Three days later came the terrible news. It had taken Caesar only one day to build himself a bridge and cross the river in pursuit. His unencumbered legions were marching rapidly. The remains of the Helvetian foraging party arrived back at camp the following afternoon, shot to pieces by arrows from Caesar's cavalry. Now they had to negotiate.

Allaine rode towards the well-ordered enemy camp, accompanying Divico, the old Helvetian general who had defeated a Roman army forty years before. As they approached the camp Allaine tried to suppress the feeling of despair gnawing away at his stomach. The scouts confirmed that the Roman army had been in situ for one night only, yet there was no sign whatsoever of an encampment, just a huge wall of black earth. The spring green pasture ceased abruptly at the gash caused by the preceding twelve-foot deep ditch, spiked with sharp pointed sticks, slanted to skewer the enemy. The horses hooves sounded hollow, as they picked their way across the narrow wooden bridge that spanned the gap, towards the central entrance of the camp. The wooden doors swung open at their approach. They were expected. The long lines of black leather army tents perched on the ground, flapping gently like huge birds waiting to feast on some dead carcass.

The tribune was friendly, almost welcoming. "I'm afraid I'll have to relieve you of your weapons," Octavian said. "Just a temporary measure, of course."

Allaine told him that as ambassadors they carried no weapons.

But no, Octavian explained apologetically, this wasn't sufficient. They would have to submit to being searched. After he had been patted down, Allaine wandered over to stand beside the friendly tribune.

"It seems an odd way to welcome ambassadors," he remarked in perfect Latin. He sounded patrician, no trace of Gallic accent.

"I know," Octavian agreed, unguardedly. He frowned. "Of course, it's all designed to......." He hesitated.

"Humiliate," Allaine finished for him.

Perhaps even more startling than the fortifications, though, had been the appearance of Caesar's tent, which was furnished with the opulence of an oriental palace. The very ground itself covered with a beautiful rectangular mosaic. Geese, depicted in white marble, could be seen in the most realistic poses, strutting round the border, drinking water from a trough.

Caesar was seated on a chair that looked as if it had been carved from more solid marble, flanked by his generals who stood in full uniform. The implication was obvious - they should be kneeling there at Caesar's feet. Allaine had no intention of doing so.

He inclined his head slightly and stood, staring into those eyes, summoning up his own will. And it worked. His nervousness went. He felt surprisingly composed. The lines around the eyes crinkled, and Caesar smiled broadly.

"Ah, the interpreter." He was smiling directly at Allaine, inviting him alone to share in the spectacle, the play he was directing. Allaine lifted his arm in salute, taking care not to smile back, greeted him politely and then introduced his companions. Caesar leaned forward with interest.

"Divico," he repeated. "Have I the honour, then, of meeting Divico, the great Helvetian general, the man who defeated Cassius?"

"Yes, Sir, the same," replied Allaine.

"Well, what a strange choice for a negotiator," Caesar remarked pleasantly to Allaine.

With difficulty Allaine suppressed the desire to agree with him. He couldn't imagine why Coevorten had suggested the idea in the first place. The man was too old to think quickly, and the Romans might conclude such a choice showed aggression rather than conciliation. Caesar called for a chair to be brought for Divico - further emphasising the man's age.

On this occasion Caesar permitted Allaine to act as interpreter. But this turned out to be another piece of stage direction. Caesar looked only at Allaine, not bothering to turn to Divico to see what his answers might be. And his comments became increasingly provocative, the smile became mocking, contemptuous. Allaine was striving to keep his tone neutral.

"My general says, why do you continue to harass us. We have permission to cross this territory. We have a treaty with the Aeduans and with the Sequani."

"But you didn't have my permission," said Caesar.

"We don't need your permission. This isn't your country,"

152

snapped Allaine. He cursed himself inwardly. He'd succeeded in changing the atmosphere in the tent instantly. The soldiers all stiffened to attention.

Caesar stopped smiling. "Don't yell at me, boy. I prefer to hear your commander's reply."

By this time, too, Divico was becoming incensed.

"What gives you the right to attack us?" Allaine translated. "How do you justify the murder of thirty thousand people while they slept, old men, women and children? Did the Senate give you these orders?"

"On the contrary," Caesar replied, "my orders came from the Gods themselves. They have decided you must be made to pay for the crimes you committed forty years ago, with your unprovoked attack on the Roman soldiers."

"Unprovoked attack?" said Divico. "The man's mad."

"Also, as you chose to cross this country in direct defiance of my orders, I have to punish you, as a father must chastise a wilfully disobedient child."

At last Caesar looked directly at Divico.

"Perhaps the fellow thinks he should be congratulated on his great victory," Divico said.

"Now that's much better," said Caesar when this had been translated. "Now my terms are unconditional surrender, and here's a list of the hostages I will require."

The list seemed endless. Over six hundred named hostages. Every Council member and their families, anyone at all of any importance. The Helvetians would be left like a headless chicken. Allaine started to read out the list of names, but Divico put out a hand and stopped him.

"Tell Caesar," he said, "that the Helvetians demand hostages of others, but never give them."

They made their farewells and turned to go.

"Allaine."

Allaine turned round at the voice. Caesar had risen from his chair and was standing behind him.

"Allaine, 1 understand your brother has given very little for you to do at the moment. I like the look of you, my boy. I could make good use of you. Perhaps you would like to come and be one of my cavalry commanders."

Allaine was speechless.

"There's a lot of work to be done here in Gaul," Caesar continued, "and you'd be with friends. Your brother-in-law is already here."

"Sir, it's very good of you to ask me. Indeed I'm amazed that you should do so. But I don't think your actions have been exactly those of a friend."

Caesar broke in. "Your sister would be safe, however." He smiled at the look on the young man's face. "Think it over. Come and see me any time you like." And astonishingly he held out his hand.

Allaine was so surprised, he took it in his own, and nearly had his fingers crushed in the iron grip.

Just for a brief moment he let his mind play with the idea of being a cavalry commander in Caesar's army with Dumnorix. He'd found the news that Dumnorix was with Caesar hard to bear, until they started getting messages from the Aeduans, and then a few deserters and runaway slaves. The Aeduans hadn't been given much choice it seemed. Apparently Caesar knew a great deal about the Helvetians. He had known, for example, that Coevorten had refused to give Allaine any type of a command, despite his reputation as a swordsman, jealous, perhaps, of his increasing popularity with the people. To Allaine's intense frustration, he had been ordered to stay with Chrys, although he noted Chrys herself found this very comforting.

Chrys had a child in her arms. It lay still and thin in her lap, scarcely breathing.

"Is there nothing we can do?" she asked her brother.

Allaine felt the child gently, picking up a fold of wrinkled skin in his fingers. "It's more starvation, Chrys, than illness," he explained. "There are so many of them now. At least it makes up our minds for us."

"Why, what's the news?"

"We have to fight, today. The Romans are between us and Bibracte. Between us and our corn store. We no longer have any choice."

Allaine went from wagon to wagon, thinking to encourage the men and calm the women. But it was unnecessary. Now they had been told to prepare for battle the mood in the camp was euphoric. Soldiers were everywhere preparing their weapons, sharpening swords and spears, excited at the prospect of real action at last, a chance for revenge. The young men were grinning, thinking themselves immortal, chatting away about what they would do to the Roman prisoners they might take. The cavalry had been sent out early in the morning, and had already taken part in a few skirmishes. Caesar's army was drawn up on a hill only half an hour's march away. The council had met, the battle plan had been finalised.

Coevorten appeared. "The wagons are to be formed into an ellipse, to be used as a defensive barricade. You're in charge," he told Allaine.

To start with Chrys sat next to her brother and watched. She could see the Roman army on the hill opposite, stationed in three thick lines, one above the other, an impressive formation of disciplined men. Ten thousand of the front line gleaming in the sun. Ten thousand identical helmets burnished and shone. At regular intervals that were almost geometric Chrys could pick out the standards held high, identify each century, each cohort, each legion. Their uniformity was fearful.

"How many?" asked Chrys.

"Fifty thousand."

"How many of us?"

"Ninety thousand," Allaine sighed heavily. "But we're not a professional army."

"I can't see any horses."

"No." He couldn't either, which was puzzling.

"Are the commanders on foot, then?"

They heard the inhuman strangled sound of the trumpets, summoning the men to their deaths. The Helvetian lines inched forward up the hill, to where Caesar was waiting for them. The battle raged all day and half the night. Not a single man fled the enemy. To a certain extent the battle plan worked, but the enormous solid phalanx of Helvetians that ascended the hill was all too quickly broken by the hail of accurately thrown spears raining down on them from above. All the same, they continually regrouped and reformed, holding their ground as best they could until the sheer numbers of wounded forced them to begin to yield.

The Romans advanced slowly and methodically, leaving the second line to mop up the Helvetian casualties with a quick thrust of the short sword. Inexorably they advanced down the hill, pushing the Gauls before them. Still the retreat was orderly, the lines held. When the last Roman line reached the bottom of the hill, Coevorten struck. Fifteen thousand reserves smashed into the Roman right flank. They were now having to fight on two fronts simultaneously. Chrys could see the shock wave reverberating through the Roman troops. But she could see the line absorb the shock, regroup, mass, and slowly, so slowly, start to advance again. Chrys felt tears pricking at the back of her eye-lids. There were no more reserves. Nothing would stop them now.

Allaine became active, issuing orders. He had the wagons arranged with an inner and outer circle. Women, children and old men now at the very centre. He ordered water to be brought up. The wounded were being stretchered in, thick and fast. He wasn't going to let them die of thirst or loss of blood if he could help it. By evening the reservists had fallen back to the laager. Coevorten was unaccounted for. Allaine took command efficiently. They held the Romans off until midnight, hurling spears, stones, anything they could get hold of, from the top of the wagons to the enemy soldiers beneath. Poked at them too, with lances inserted between the wheels. Around midnight they heard the Roman trumpet sound, giving a signal they didn't understand. But the legionaries did. They all stopped fighting and retreated a little. There was the sound of shouting. Someone trying to communicate. A man pushed past to where Allaine was standing with one of his captives, sword in hand.

"Sir! It's the Roman general, Labienus, wants to talk."

Allaine looked at the man's exhausted eyes under his helmet. He smiled faintly.

"Splendid. He must wish to surrender."

The man smiled back at him. Allaine put a hand on his shoulder.

"You've all fought so well. I'm so proud of you. Tell everyone, will you?"

The man had tears in his eyes, as he saluted and stepped back.

Labienus looked with irritation at the young man standing in front of him.

"Order your troops to surrender," he said.

"On what terms?" said Allaine.

"On these terms. If you and your sister are prepared to throw yourselves at Caesar's feet and beg for mercy, out of the goodness of his heart he will refrain from having every man, woman and child slowly tortured to death."

"Thank you," said Allaine. "Perhaps you would convey to Caesar my sense of undying gratitude for his generosity. Now if you'll excuse me, I'll order my men to lay down their arms." His voice changed, cracked with fatigue. "If we have any men left, that is."

BOOK 2
INVASION

BOOK 2: CHAPTER 1

Roman Army Camp, Near Bibracte, Aeduan Territory

Allaine was becoming more familiar with Caesar's mosaic floor. He knelt with his sister's hand in his. He could see the geese now had their necks outstretched, hissing their warning to the young Roman soldiers. The highlights on the soldiers' helmets were picked out in gold, which gleamed in the myriad lit lamps.

"A most charming speech," declared Caesar.

They both looked up at him, the girl clearly terrified.

"And a charming sight," he continued. "I fear destiny has decreed that you two should be parted. It is my custom, however, always to be merciful if circumstances permit. I will allow you to spend the rest of this night together."

"Sir, what do the fates have in store for my sister?" asked Allaine.

Caesar's smile vanished. "I ask the questions," he said. "Take him away."

Chrys was sitting on a chair, with her hands tied in front of her when the protesting girl was brought in and led over to Caesar. He was lying full length on a couch. The girl quietened when she looked down at him. He had a thick gold chain suspended between his fingers and was swinging it backwards and forwards, making it sparkle and shimmer in the light. The girl looked at the chain, then looked at Caesar, then smiled.

He laughed back at her and patted the couch next to him. They released her arms. She sat quite still, while he leaned forward and fastened the chain round her neck. It was heavy and cold, reaching down to her breasts. He unpinned her dress at the shoulders and slowly, delicately, eased the material from under the chain. She gave a gasp of delight as the cold metal touched her skin. As Chrys sat watching, eyes wide with shock, he held the girl's left breast with one hand, while the other slid up to the back of her neck. Then he bent and kissed her lips, then her throat. He leant back a little to look at her again, continuing to caress her breast, his thumb circling the nipple, causing the pink flesh to pucker and pout. He dropped his hand to her waist and started to unfasten her belt.

"Here, hang on," said the girl. "What about something else then?"

She put her hand on his to restrain him and he understood. He rose and walked over to a chest, returning with a heavily jewelled belt stretched across his palms. The girl's eyes opened wide, her mouth an O of astonishment. She was going to be rich, very rich. She made no more protests when he pushed her back against the cushions. She helped him to unfasten her dress. He unwrapped her slowly, like a child with a present. She sat back naked, the curve of the necklace echoing the curve of her breast, her legs stretched out straight. Laughing he pushed her feet upwards so that her knees bent. With one hand he held the jewelled belt suspended in the air, oscillating like a pendulum. Gradually he lowered his hand until the end touched her stomach and slithered down her abdomen.

"Now it's time for you to open up, my pretty one," he said, pressing her knee down firmly.

Obediently, she opened her legs wide to his exploring hand, the gold belt glinting in her pubic hair. As he leant forward she could see Chrys over his shoulder.

"Hang on," said the girl, "she's crying. Look, her!"

A spasm of annoyance crossed his face. He got up and walked over to his prisoner. Her eyes were shut, tears were oozing from underneath the lids, trickling down her cheeks. A pity the girl was overwrought, because she was quite pretty. He very much disliked weepy females. He would give her as a gift to one of his young officers. He had, after all, promised to be merciful.

160

By the time he had finished, the girl was feeling decidedly sore, and her nipples ached from where he had pinched and squeezed. She rather hoped he wasn't going to be like this every night. Perhaps this was just because of winning the battle.

"Do you have any further use for this woman, Sire?" asked a servant.

Uneasily she caught his look of cold indifference.

"None whatsoever."

"Shall I take her to the men, Sire?"

"By all means."

She looked up in surprise as the soldiers came for her, and started to protest when the servant picked up the chain from between her breasts to lift it over her head. Savagely he jerked it tight round her neck, the links cutting deep into the skin of her throat. Her hands clutched ineffectually as she choked. Afterwards her neck ached dreadfully, and she couldn't scream, she could only make strange chirping noises like a hoarse bird. The men found it most amusing.

The scouts made their report. About a third of the Helvetians had survived the battle evidently. They had formed up and marched into the night, heading north-east.

"Are we to pursue them, Caesar?" asked Labienus. "Shall I give the order to break camp?"

There was a disturbance at the entrance.

"Get out of my way."

Dumnorix pushed past the guards with total recklessness, ignoring their drawn swords. He hesitated for an instant when he saw the circle of faces looking at him with glances unmistakably hostile, then walked over to Caesar's desk and stood, breathing heavily, making no attempt to salute.

"I believe my brother and sister-in-law were captured last night."

"Your information is correct."

" May I see them?"

"No." Caesar leaned forward, his elbows on the desk. "You may not."

"Why not?"

"Because those are my orders."

"Rescind your orders, then."

"No," said Caesar deliberately. "I will not."

Dumnorix leaned towards him. "You fucking shitface."

The gobbet of spit hung on Caesar's cheek, but he said nothing, just reached out his hand for a towel which an attendant rushed to supply. There was complete silence.

Dumnorix straightened up. "You fucking bastard," he said.

There was still no response. He turned on his heel and walked out.

Caesar continued speaking calmly, as if nothing had occurred to interrupt them.

"No my dear Titus, we will not pursue them. Our men fought with great courage yesterday. I must see they are properly rewarded. Our dead must be buried with full military honours, the wounded tended. Gentlemen, I wish our men to understand very clearly that their loyalty will always be well rewarded. And now there is a small matter I must attend to myself."

The centurion was addressing Allaine in an almost fatherly manner, while the legionaries were removing his clothes.

"Of course, you must realise there's nothing personal in this. Caesar bears you no ill will. In fact I happen to know he has a considerable respect for you. He was impressed with your defence of the camp. You must consider yourself merely as an instrument of punishment in Caesar's hands. You Gauls are proving to be a little slow on the uptake."

Behind the centurion was a young legionary, his face the picture of misery. He was to hold the irons. Despite all that was about to happen, Allaine registered the dejected face, and stored the information somewhere deep down in the recesses of his mind. The centurion was pleased. The prisoner had been surprisingly co-operative. He fastened a rough woollen cloak around the young man's naked shoulders.

"What's this for?" asked Allaine, with a ghost of a smile. "In case I catch cold?"

The centurion appeared to take him seriously.

"No. It's to mop up the blood."

It was difficult to make a dignified entrance, when the chains around his feet would only allow him to take small shuffling steps. Difficult to keep the dread out of his face, when he saw the arrangements made for his evening's entertainment.

"Ah, the interpreter," said Caesar, sounding pleased.

"Good evening, Caesar," said Allaine. Careful, his voice sounded tired. "Do you wish to offer me another job? As a general perhaps this time?"

Once again he caught the swift appraising look, the acknowledgement, the smile of secret shared. Caesar knew just how much effort he was having to make to stay brave.

The nightmare began. Each speck of time stretched out to infinity, like his limbs. The pain unendurable. How could it then get worse? And even worse, until he cried out against it, the unreasonableness of it. Now he was screaming, screaming, but it wouldn't stop, wouldn't stop. His mind suspended in agony. So much pain there was no thought. The world yelled in circles inside his brain.

Time compressed, pain lessened, just a little. A tiny little bit. A voice sounded loud in his ear, echoing round his head.

"The irons now, I think." "The irons now, I think." "The irons now, I think."

He could see again now. A face floated level with his own, grinning amiably. An ice-cold cloth mopped at his brow, causing him to gasp.

"That's it, son. We don't want you passing out on us, now do we?"

"No." Stupidly he found himself agreeing with the face. Reason returned with a rush. He started to cry quietly. "Bastards!

163

You bloody bastards!" he sobbed.

Caesar's voice cut in. "You haven't learned yet what it is to be conquered, have you Allaine? It means that I can turn you into anything I want. A creature with one eye perhaps. A cyclops. Or with half a brain, a simple animal."

The sweat was pouring off him again now, trickling down his forehead, through his eyebrows into his eyes, making him blink. His eyes were stinging with the salt.

"Touch him here. With the irons."

He heard his voice rising in hysteria, pathetic, pleading like a little child.

"Oh please don't. Please don't. Don't do it again. Not any more. I'lease, please."

And then.

"I'll do anything. I'll say anything."

The screams came again, the pain came again, biting deep, deep into his flesh. The screams got louder, the pain intensified, grew, obliterated, the world spun round, spun crazily, blackened and vanished.

He was listening to a conversation a long way off.

"I'm sorry."

"That's better."

"I'm sorry."

"That's better. Much better."

"I'm sorry, so sorry."

"That's better. More submissive. I like my boys to be properly submissive."

The apologetic voice started again. "I am sorry. I'm so sorry," he heard himself say.

Then Caesar's voice in answer. "There now, you're learning respect, Allaine. Respect for your superiors. You're doing very well."

The screams resounded round the camp. Octavian could

164

scarcely credit it.

"That's what he's doing?"

Gaius nodded. "I thought you'd better be aware of the fact, as our Aeduan friends undoubtedly are."

"You mean they'll harm Marcius?"

"Of course they won't harm Marcius," Gaius said in exasperation. "They're not like us. They're civilised."

Finally everyone was sent away, leaving him alone with Caesar. The worst part was yet to come.

He was still sobbing and crying with pain. Caesar sat close to him, and put an affectionate arm around his shoulders.

"A beautiful youth in chains always has the power to stir me deeply," he whispered. "Strong, yet so very vulnerable."

Allaine quietened immediately, sitting tense and fearful. Caesar held a bowl of wine to his victim's lips. Allaine drank obediently, gulping it down, desperate in his attempts to numb the future. His teeth juddered against the metal sides. The wine tasted bitter. A drug probably. Poison, he hoped.

"You're a good fellow, Allaine," Caesar spoke softly. Experimentally he began to touch his prey, caressing the back of his neck, running his fingers through the blond curls. He inserted the wine bowl into the chained hands. "There now. Have some more," he suggested.

Allaine tried to lift the cup to his lips, but his hands were shaking so much the wine slopped about in the bowl. Caesar had to steady him. Allaine drank again. The drug was beginning to work now. It was a delight to watch the lines of pain shade from the young man's face, to feel the tense muscles ease slowly, relax, become soft and pliant.

"Do you know what I'm going to do now?" Caesar enquired gently.

There was a long pause.

"The whole camp knows," said Allaine with weary resignation.

Caesar pulled the slumped body towards him, until he had Allaine resting against his shoulder, head close to his own. He was feeling sentimental, with a deep concern for this exceptionally brave young man. His arm tightened. How he longed for a son of his own. He loved his daughter Julia, of course, with a love too great for words. But a son........

However, it was never too late. Sons were born after all, even after a father's death.... Death, his own death ... Well no need to think of that just at present.

He had made them send his horse away before the battle. So his men could see he shared the risks equally. He could look at Death on the battlefield and spit in his face ... He would have to do something quick to appease the Aeduans, Dumnorix in particular ... but the gold ... there was enough gold to pay off his debts ten times over, and then plenty left to distribute as booty to the men. He'd better distribute some of the women too.

Allaine had quietened now, breathing more easily. Caesar frowned. He hoped the boy hadn't been overdosed with opium. There would be no pleasure in seducing a youth semi-comatose. He pressed at the edge of a patch of burnt flesh in the boy's groin. Allaine stirred, his eyes opened. A deep moan of distress broke from his throat.

Good. The youngster's silence was as insubstantial as a spider's web. One touch of the fingers could brush it away, revealing the tender hurt, the hidden pain beneath.

"Time for bed, I think, Allaine. I intend to teach you a great deal tonight about pleasure and pain. Reward and punishment. But fortunately, we have a long night ahead of us." He felt a deep excitement stirring in his loins. An intensity of pleasure he thought had passed with his youth.

Allaine was looking at him with wide grey eyes, drugged pupils dark pin-pricks. Caesar answered the unspoken question.

"Any mortal who is loved by a God, has to suffer, Allaine. And I'm afraid you will be no exception."

Caesar was in a thoroughly vindictive frame of mind the next morning. Gaius was ordered to arrange for the prisoner's disposal. He was to be transported to the military prison at Arles, like his sister.

The blond prisoner had been hurt so much, he could no longer stand. Gaius had to order him to be carried to the holding cell. He went over to see if the boy could be made any more comfortable. Allaine was lying naked on the ground, curled up in a ball of agony, face contorted with pain. The dreadful burn marks showed livid against his pale skin. The opium had worn off completely. He became defenceless, tense, and terrified as soon as Gaius appeared.

Gaius knelt at his side. "I'm so sorry about all this," he said. "Don't blame yourself. Don't despise yourself. You fought with great courage against it."

Pullo had told him how bravely the poor kid had tried to withstand the terrible onslaught on his body.

"But why?" Allaine asked huskily, utterly bewildered, his voice raw with distress. "Why? What had I done to him?"

Gaius explained as best he could, uncertain whether the explanation wouldn't make things worse for the poor boy. Now the youngster was slipping in and out of consciousness, the pain overwhelming again. He probably wouldn't remember any of this, Gaius thought to himself tiredly. Why was he trying to make things better? They couldn't be got better. He ordered a palliasse for the prisoner, anyway, and told the guards to find his clothes, get him dressed, and try and get some food and water into him, before the journey.

Gaius walked into the Aeduan headquarters. Dumnorix turned his back on him. Guéreth lay staring at the ceiling. Jay ignored him completely. Diviciacus looked at him with tired eyes. He had ordered his brother to be tied up the night before, and even his own men had agreed. They didn't want to hear another voice screaming out into the darkness. Gaius saluted.

"I thought you would like to know, Sir, the corn has arrived."

He saw it was quite hopeless. He felt like crying himself. He turned and walked wearily out of the tent.

Something hard struck the back of his head, and he spun round. An apple rolled away over the dirt floor. He knelt down and picked it up, then rubbed it slowly up and down his sleeve. He left with the apple still held in his hand. He walked back to his own tent, the elation of his brother officers and the men only served to underline his sense of profound depression. He sat down heavily on the bed. Hector ambled over to him, licked his fingers in sympathy, thumped his tail once or twice on the floor and then retreated, sitting back on his haunches next to Valerius. Gaius stared at the face of the dog, and the face of the soldier. They both stared back at him with the same sad eyes. Gaius leaned forward.

"Legionary," he snarled. "When an officer enters you are supposed to jump up, salute, and stand to attention until told otherwise. I mean now!" he shouted.

Valerius obeyed instantly. "I'm sorry, Sir, I wasn't..."

"Shut up!" said Gaius savagely. He let Valerius stand rigidly to attention for a bit, then relented, feeling better. "What's the matter, Valerius?"

"Nothing, Sir."

"Don't give me that shit. What's the matter?"

"Well Sir, it's nothing really. It's just the centurion says I need to be toughened up. So last night I had to....." He faltered for a moment, then started again. "I was ordered to assist the centurion."

"Soldiers have to perform a lot of unpleasant tasks, Valerius. It's their duty to do so as efficiently as possible. To obey their superiors. And not mope about afterwards. Do you understand?"

"Yes, Sir."

"Clear off, then."

"Yes, Sir."

Gaius knew there was a lot he should be doing. But he just sat still, gazing emptily ahead. He thought he'd better get drunk. A shadow blocked the tent entrance. Guéreth stood there, looking at him with an easy smile.

"May I come in?"

He was followed by Jay, and a servant carrying a large bone on a tray, which Jay ceremonially presented to Hector. Jay then curled up next to the dog on the floor. Guéreth served himself some wine, tasted it and said, "Good stuff this." He poured himself a much more generous quantity before sitting on the bed next to Gaius.

Guéreth opened the proceedings. "Gaius, remember we said we would be friends as far as our countries would allow us?"

Gaius braced himself. "I remember."

"Well to me," Guéreth continued, "I don't think this friendship is good enough. So I will be your friend, Gaius, even when you are putting that wooden collar round my neck." He paused, waiting for the import of his words to sink in. "I thought I should tell you in case you were worried."

"I was rather," said Gaius, a hand on his friend's shoulder.

Jay interrupted. "But when you do the same to me, Gaius, we will start to dislike you this tiny bit." Jay held up his fingers to demonstrate, then looked round the tent until he saw what he wanted. He got up and walked over to the dish. "This apple is bruised, Gaius."

"I'm sorry about that, Jay." Gaius could feel tears pricking the back of his eyelids.

Jay turned to him with a charming smile. "It's alright. I'll eat it anyway. Oh, here's your brother."

"Oh, for Gods' sake!"

"Don't you like your brother?" said Jay, surprised.

"No."

"I haven't got any brothers," said Jay with a sigh. "Only sisters." He thought for a moment, then grinned. "They're very pretty, though. Would you like to see them, Gaius?"

"Shut up, you horrible little brat!" snapped Gaius.

Octavian looked at his brother in shock. Surely their orders had been to be as polite to the Aeduans as possible, after the events of the last few days. But this particular Aeduan, the son of Diviciacus himself, didn't appear to be in the slightest bit bothered at being insulted.

"What will happen when we catch the rest of the Helvetians, Gaius?"

"I don't know. Massacre them too, I suppose. Anyway, that's the premise on which I'm working, and anything less than that will be a blessed relief." He looked at Guéreth. "It's the kids." And the blond prisoner, but he couldn't say that, he couldn't ever say that.

"Don't worry, Gaius, you'll get us to kill the children. Or maybe send Dumnorix all by himself."

They stayed for an hour, until Guéreth thought his Roman friend had cheered a little, and Jay could wring no more information from him.

BOOK 2 : CHAPTER 2

Lingones Territory, East Central Gaul

They were having trouble making him understand. He was a man lost. He could see the pity in their eyes.

"I'm sorry, Coevorten, deeply sorry," explained the chief, "but what can we do?"

Coevorden held the letter from Caesar between his fingers, the words jumbled and blurred. He gave up the attempt.

"Tell me what he says again."

"Caesar commands that no aid in any way be given to the Helvetians. He warns that anyone disobeying his orders will be regarded as an enemy, and will be treated accordingly."

"Look," the chief attempted to explain again. "We're not prepared for war. We have no troops mustered, no weapons sharpened. If Caesar marches here and starts to burn our barns, how can we stop him? Then we will starve too."

"We've marched three days and three nights," said Coevorten desperately, "stopping only for water."

"I know, I know, you've told us."

"Can you do nothing for us? Could you not even help the children? Please? The children are our future, and the future is dying before our very eyes."

The chief gave up. "Of course, of course we will help the children." How could anyone refuse such a request. "But go and inform your council they must make their peace with Caesar. There is no other way."

The chief was a little embarrassed when Coevorten knelt on the ground, and kissed his hand in gratitude.

"Sir, we will never forget this kind act of yours, I swear it. But I say this to you. If you're not prepared for war now, then be prepared in the future. You think Caesar will leave you in peace? Rubbish. The whole country spreads before him. He will have it all."

The remaining council members took little time in coming to a decision. The decision was made for them, they had no choice, no choice at all. Coevorten walked back down the long column of people, touching a child here, kissing a woman there, shaking a man's hand, explaining what was going to happen. They would beg for mercy. But explaining also, like a true prince, how wonderfully they had fought, what resilience they had shown, how brave had been their endurance. The council members would offer themselves up as sacrifices to Caesar's wrath, and beg that the people would be left in peace.

Caesar, mounted on his charger, surveyed the figures kneeling on the road in front of him.

"Perhaps a little more humility," he suggested.

Obediently they stretched out on the ground, their arms in front of them. Coevorten started to sob, choked with tears which ran from his cheeks into the earth. Caesar looked down at him with approval. "Now that," he observed, "shows proper contrition."

The ambassador walked up and bowed low. "Caesar," he said. "We have obeyed your instructions. Apart from giving a little food to the children, we have rendered no assistance to the Helvetians whatsoever, and beg that you leave us in peace."

He could see his words didn't meet with approval.

"When I give orders," Caesar said menacingly, "I expect them to be carried out to the letter. Not piecemeal. However, on this occasion I'm inclined to overlook the matter. Don't let it happen again."

The ambassador was profuse in his apologies.

"You others," said Caesar, "return to your people. Tell them to stay where they are until I arrive. I will deal with them then."

Once the Romans reached the remainder of the Helvetians, and had pitched their camp with their usual efficiency,

Caesar sent for the council members. They knelt at his feet, grimy and dishevelled, their clothes still marked from lying in the road. Inertia seemed to have seized them all.

"Here is the list of hostages I require," said Caesar. "As you will see, much the same as before. Here also a list of the slaves I believe have deserted to you. I wish them to be handed over. Tomorrow morning arrangements will be made for you to surrender your weapons."

"Yes, Sir. And then what?" asked Coevorten.

"After that, Coevorten, I will decide what is to be done with you all."

Well before dawn, Philemon was shaking Caesar awake.

"Well, what is it?" Caesar asked irritably.

"Master, one of the council members wishes to speak to you. He says it is urgent."

"Who is it?"

"His name is Coevorten, Sir."

"Very well. Send him in."

Coevorten came in, hating himself for doing this, but if Caesar got to hear some other way, the Gods knew what would happen to them all. He dropped to his knees by the bed.

"Well. And what is this urgent news?"

"Caesar, I've no wish to be doing this. I've no wish to be telling you, betraying my own men." Coevorten stared blindly into the distance.

Caesar sat up interested. This was Allaine's half-brother, of course. A fascinating family to be sure. "I'm quite certain you're doing the right thing to tell me, Coevorten. You have to give me the facts and rely on my judgement in these matters."

"Yes, Sir," Coevorten swallowed. "Six thousand, or thereabouts, have left the camp marching east. They are convinced we are all to be massacred tomorrow."

"Foolish," said Caesar gravely. "Very foolish. Well, well, Coevorten. I'm glad to find you so reliable. Now I'm sure you need your rest, after all these exertions. Off you go to sleep. I will have the matter attended to."

They dealt with the runaway slaves first. They were marched outside the camp, then each one was given a shovel and told to dig a deep pit, Centurion Pullo lashing out at them with his whip, if he didn't think they were exerting themselves fully enough in their own execution. A big wooden cross was laid out behind each pit. When Pullo thought the pits were deep enough, he ordered them to stop digging. The soldiers helped them to clamber out of the holes. They stood panting in the sun, dirty, sweaty and scared. The youngest one began to weep silently.

"Any chance of a drink, Sir?" asked one of them.

"None whatsoever," answered Pullo.

They were ordered to strip off completely, not that anyone would want their rags, but it was a tradition.

"Right, you lot," said Pullo to the little teams of legionaries. "Get this lot nailed on."

The centurion stood behind Valerius. "Now you're never going to get anywhere with his arms flailing around like that. Order these two to keep him still. Here you! Kneel on his wrist. Now, position the nail in the centre and remember, one good blow's a lot kinder in the long run."

Valerius obeyed. He was strong. The nail split the bones and embedded deeply into the wood. He was learning to suppress the sound of screams in his ears. He had thought the legs would be the most difficult, but as luck would have it, the boy had passed out. He got the nail right through the first leg, and into the kneecap of the one beneath with his first blow, and with the second, everything was fixed securely in place.

"Well done, lad." Pullo patted him on the shoulder. "You're coming on."

Valerius stood up, and looked at the boy's face. The eyelids were just beginning to flutter, as the brain registered the atrocity. Val wondered where he was going. Everyone swung to attention as Lucius Aemilius, the commander of Caesar's Gallic cavalry arrived. They were his slaves. He looked up at their faces twisted with pain, almost unrecognisable. He was a kind man. Ordinarily he would merely have had them branded on the forehead, meted out a certain amount of chastisement and then forgotten about the matter. But, as Caesar had reminded him, these boys had acted as spies, as well as runaways. An example had to be made. A pity. The ringleader was one of his own bastards, a man of whom he was particularly fond. He wondered what had induced him to run away. Dreams of freedom, no doubt.

After this Valerius was dismissed. He was lucky, they told him afterwards. A huge pile of wood had been gathered half a mile away from the camp. The six thousand recaptured men were marched or dragged to the spot. Each was then held still by two soldiers, while a third did the killing with one, two or three sword thrusts under the watchful eyes of the centurions. Good practice for the newly-recruited legionaries who took it in turns, quickly learning to hit hard and deep the first time. They made the prisoners themselves toss the bodies onto the burning wood, told that they either obeyed or would have a slow death rather than a swift one. The two Helvetian leaders were there, calming, coaxing, cajoling the men to co-operate, and accept their fate.

Finally, there were only the two leaders left. The legionaries watched as they embraced each other. Then, as one was led forward, the other raised his arm in salute and obviously made a short speech while his friend, or brother perhaps, was being executed. The men couldn't understand a word of it, but it impressed them nevertheless. Centurion Pullo got the interpreter to offer the man his liberty. He refused.

"He wishes to perish with his comrades, Sir," the interpreter explained.

Now no-one wanted to kill this man, standing ramrod straight in front of the rising black smoke of the pyre. Pullo drew his sword, walked up to the man and put a hand on his shoulder.

"You're brave, my friend," he said.

The man stared unflinchingly into his eyes. Pullo killed him with one quick blow, then pulled out his sword, and with it still dripping warm and red, saluted the man himself.

The rest of the Helvetians patiently awaited their fate. They had no choice in the matter. The severe punishments made it seem likely they would be sold into slavery. But Caesar had already spoken to Marcus Metius about this. Apparently the Helvetians were in such poor condition it would be unlikely many of them would survive a march further south to the Province, or Italy. And, Metius explained, he now had a large headquarters in Bibracte. A consortium, with warehouses. The Aeduans were his good friends and customers. He didn't wish to lose them. He certainly didn't wish to offend them by selling Helvetians. At last Caesar summoned the council members. They knelt on the floor in his tent. Each of them was to surrender his children to be held as hostages in Bibracte. The men were to line up and surrender their weapons. Then they were to return to their own country and rebuild their towns and villages.

"And make sure you rebuild them better than before," Caesar added. "I don't want the Germans to think they can invade Helvetia with impunity."

He ordered Coevorten to stay behind after the others had left. "You failed to tell me it was your own brother who led the men out of camp last night."

Coevorten knelt and said nothing.

"He was offered his liberty, but chose instead to die with his men. Yours is a courageous family."

Coevorten looked up. "And my other brother and sister?"

"Will remain in my hands," Caesar said. "But as you have shown such loyalty to me, you may keep your own children."

"Thank you," Coevorten whispered. To have to express gratitude to this swine! He would never get over the shame of it. And now he would have to beg.

"But Caesar, we have nothing to eat."

"Once you get to the Province, your neighbours will provide you with food."

"Caesar, there will be no point in rebuilding our towns and villages. Our children will not survive until we get to the Province."

"Very well, Coevorten. I'll see that the matter is dealt with."

"Thank you again, Sir." He found himself kissing Caesar's hand, just like a slave. He stood up to go. Well, he was a slave, in all but name, anyway.

Caesar sent for Dumnorix and Diviciacus. "I must apologise, Sirs," he said, "for not being able to return your close relatives, who must stay in my possession." He smiled to see their expressions. How he enjoyed exercising power over these barbarians. "However, to compensate, I intend to make you a present of all those who fought so bravely in defence of the baggage, and their dependents, of course. I believe there to be about thirty-two thousand of them altogether. I trust this meets with your approval?"

"You are too kind, Caesar," Dumnorix started, but hastily changed it to, "thank you very much, I certainly approve. We can find somewhere for them to stay, can't we, brother?" he said, turning to Diviciacus. "And then, perhaps find them some land?"

Diviciacus agreed. "Yes, indeed. Fulsome gesture on your part, Caesar. We are delighted."

Philemon had been given the Helvetian registers. They made astonishing reading. There were meticulous lists of the old men, women and children and also separate lists of men fit for military duties. Altogether three hundred and sixty-eight thousand set out on that mass migration and march of this year. One hundred and ten thousand returned. The secretary carefully opened files on the important prisoners and hostages.

"Allaine, son of Orgetorix," he wrote. "Interrogated by Caesar himself."

BOOK 2: CHAPTER 3

Bibracte, principal town of the Aeduii, Central Gaul: Besançon, principal town of the Sequani: Plain of Alsace

The news travelled fast, sounding the alarm all over Gaul. Caesar and his army sat squarely in the middle of their country, and showed no sign of budging. It was, Guéreth smiled at Gaius, a problem. With a view to solving it, Diviciacus politely asked Caesar if he had any objection to his summoning a general assembly.

"Not at all, my dear fellow. It would give me an opportunity to meet your distinguished countrymen."

To Caesar's intense annoyance, however, the assembly was held behind locked doors, a security so tight he quite failed to break it. He retaliated by inviting all the youngsters who were considered not old enough to be privy to their elders' deliberations, to be entertained in his headquarters. It was quite a party. His officers mingled with the guests, being charming and urbane, an interpreter always ready at the elbow should the need arise. To Caesar's pleasure, Jay acted for him as a sort of aide-de-camp, making introductions and acting like a staff officer. Jay came up to him laughing.

"This is a very good party, Caesar."

"Indeed it is, and I can thank you for helping to make it so."

"My father will be jealous to have missed it."

"The objective, however, Jayven, is not to make your father jealous, but to entertain these youngsters."

"Phooey," said Jay.

"Jay, you are incorrigible."

Jay looked at him enquiringly.

"No, don't tell your father I said that, and don't get it

178

translated."

Jay grinned wickedly and walked away. Caesar shook his head. Really, the boy was quite delightful, Gaius Volusenus was lucky to have found such a friend. He stood smiling to himself, looking around. He saw one young man admiring his chess set. He walked over to talk to him.

"It's made of jade," he said. "Do you like it?"

"It's beautiful," said the young man.

"Do you play?"

"Yes."

"Play now, then," said Caesar.

The young man looked surprised. "Why certainly, if you wish."

They played in silence for a while, both concentrating, the pieces falling slowly.

"I wonder what affairs the Assembly are debating," remarked Caesar, half to himself.

"Oh, I can tell you that," said the young man cheerfully. "They are arguing about who let the fox into the hen-house. Who made the hole in the fence." He looked at Caesar and smiled. "And now he's slaughtered five of the chickens, how are they going to get him out again."

"And how are they?" asked Caesar, interested.

"They hope if they tell him there's a goose in the field next door, he'll chase after that."

"And do you think he will?"

"Oh yes, he'll chase after it, kill it and eat it. Then come back, bigger and more blood-thirsty than ever."

The young man confiscated another of Caesar's pieces. There was silence.

"Not much chance for the chickens then?" Caesar concluded.

"The farmer will certainly have his work cut out," said the young man gravely. "And I fear there may be more casualties."

They played on.

"Who exactly am I losing to?" asked Caesar.

"My name is Vercingetorix. I'm from the Arverni. Is this a formal introduction?" asked the young man, "should I kneel or kiss your feet, perhaps?"

"I don't think either would be appropriate at this moment," said Caesar, smiling into his eyes. "Later perhaps."

Vercingetorix laughed, acknowledging the hit. They played on, oblivious of the sounds around them.

"Any news of Allaine?"

"What?" Caesar was taken aback.

"Allaine, Orgetorix's son. Any news of him?"

"You know him then?" Caesar countered.

"We were at school together for a bit. The Druidic College," Vercingetorix explained, "near Lutetia. Allaine is highly thought of. He's one of the healers."

"A healer. You mean a physician?"

"Yes, a physician. He has the power, even though he's so young."

"Well that's very interesting." Caesar looked down at the board. "I think I must resign myself to losing this game."

"Yes," Vercingetorix agreed, "I think you must."

"Allaine is fine, my young friend. And so is his sister. I have sent them to the Province for their own safety. And now as you have won this game, I must insist you keep the set as a reward."

The young man was quite disconcerted. "No, no. I couldn't possibly. It's far too valuable."

"My dear fellow, I insist," said Caesar. "And the next time you come, you must have dinner with me."

Vercingetorix proved quite correct in his assumptions. There was a lot of preamble, stuff about hostages and such, but the basic message delivered by Diviciacus was unequivocal. Caesar was to forget that as Consul one year ago he had declared Ariovistus, the German king, a friend and ally of Rome. If he wished to keep the Aeduan people on his side, and indeed the rest of Gaul, he was to declare war on Germany, and stop the repeated depredations across the Rhine. Caesar listened to it all with the appearance of the utmost gravity. The Gauls, no doubt, hoped the Romans and Germans would tear each other to pieces, leaving them the field. He became very gracious.

"My dear Diviciacus, I beg you not to distress yourself any further with worries about the Germans. I understand your concerns, and as your friend and ally I am determined to remedy the affair." He could laugh to see their faces. They hadn't expected him to be so gullible. Well, he would take great pleasure in proving young Vercingetorix right. He would come back more bloodthirsty than before. He wondered who that young man had selected for the role of farmer. One of his own heroes he supposed. He must try and find out which one. He thought that young man's judgement very sound.

The Roman legions were encamped outside Besançon, one of the richest towns near the Rhine. They had travelled by forced marches to cut off Ariovistus, and were now engaged in provisioning the army, ready for an all-out assault on the Germans. But the local inhabitants' descriptions of German military might seemed to have had the unfortunate effect of terrifying the wits out of the men. When the third officer appeared that morning, telling Caesar he was terribly sorry, but he had to attend to urgent business in Rome, Caesar summoned Gaius Volusenus, wishing to hear about the mood of the camp.

Jay had taken to following Gaius around, rather like Hector, so when the tribune came to headquarters to deliver his report, Jay stood hesitating on the threshold.

"May I come in too?" he asked.

"Of course, of course." Caesar beckoned to him delightedly.

Gaius turned round angrily. "No, Jay, you can get out." Gaius turned back to his commander. "Hail Caesar," he saluted impeccably. "I'm terribly sorry about this, Sir, he gets into everything. I'll throw him out."

"Leave the boy alone, Gaius. Just give your report in Greek."

"I can stay, Gaius?" asked Jay.

"You can stay, but shut up."

Jay grinned complacently.

"I'm afraid it seems to have started with the tribunes, Sir. They've got it into their heads there's no way we are going to be able to beat the Germans. The troops have heard that some of them are actually trying to quit camp."

Caesar nodded, "I'm afraid so."

Gaius grinned. "Maybe it would be better if they went. Evidently one of the junior tribunes is lying in his tent crying his eyes out. And the rest of them are making their wills."

"Just a moment," said Caesar. He walked over to where Jay was handling a Greek vase, one of his most prized possessions. Gently he took it out of his hands. "My dear boy, this is very valuable," he said, placing it back on the pedestal.

Jay drew himself up haughtily. "You think I'm a child. You think I break your precious vase. You think I drop it. I go!" said Jay.

"No, please stay," Caesar protested. "Of course I don't think you'd drop it, it's just, that, well, it's irreplaceable. I suppose if I see anyone touch it, I get nervous." He gestured with his hands. "Foolish of me, I know."

Jay was charmed. "It is very valuable?"

"Priceless," said Caesar.

Jay was puzzled. "How much is it worth?"

"It's worth a hundred Jays," said Caesar.

Jay grinned. "How many Caesars is it worth?"

Gaius cuffed him hard.

"Ow," said Jay.

"You're getting too bloody cheeky," said Gaius.

"Tribune," Caesar remonstrated, a little shaken. "This is

the son of our chief ally."

Jay hastened to reassure him, waving an arm. "Caesar, no matter. When I walk into the tent and Gaius say 'Oh God, no,' I know he loves me like a brother."

Caesar roared with laughter at that, "Well, well. So ill-treatment is a sign of affection, is it?"

"Only for Romans," said Jay mischievously.

Caesar watched Jay as Gaius continued to give him his report. The boy gave a little crow of delight when he discovered the gaming board was reversible, and smiled at the beautifully carved ebony and ivory counters he found underneath.

"My dear Gaius," Caesar said, when the tribune had finished his report, "if you are going to take that young man to your bed, make sure you don't hurt his feelings. I don't want an international incident."

They both looked at Jay, who was setting out the gaming counters. Aware of their gaze he stepped back quickly, arms outstretched.

"See? I'm not touching anything."

They continued to smile at him.

"Oh," said Jay, "you talk about me?"

"No, you conceited brat," said Gaius.

"One day you will," continued Jay. "One day I will be very important. You will give reports about me, Gaius." Jay stepped forward and gave the military salute. "Hail Caesar," he said. "See, I've practised." He beamed at them and went, nearly colliding with Octavian.

"What's this I hear, Octavian, that your mother has a bad cold?"

"No, Caesar. Not that I'm aware of." Octavian looked at his brother in surprise.

"Isn't this the news, that your mother has a bad cold and you must hasten back to Rome?"

"No, Caesar. I'm sure if my mother has a cold, my father will attend to matters." Octavian was getting used to his commander.

"Don't you want to run away from the Germans, Octavian?"

"No, Caesar. If you remember, Sir, I've really only just arrived."

The Aeduans howled with rage when Gaius told them the news. Ariovistus had agreed to meet Caesar, but on condition his bodyguard consisted only of cavalry. Caesar, therefore, ordered the Aeduans to give up their horses to the men of the Tenth Legion.

"I am most displeased," Diviciacus told Gaius. "Does Caesar not trust us to act as his bodyguards, after fighting a campaign with him?" He smiled at Gaius's discomfiture. "Of course, he doesn't, my dear Gaius, but I fear I shall have to reprimand him severely for this."

Gaius made sure he was a spectator at the subsequent interview.

Diviciacus bitterly reproached Caesar for his lack of trust in his closest allies. Caesar explained that he didn't wish to expose his dear friends to any treachery on the part of Ariovistus. Diviciacus took great exception to this. Was Caesar implying that the Aeduans were cowards who would run away from the Germans? No-one, Caesar assured him, could ever doubt the exceptional bravery and integrity of the Aeduans, but the Tenth Legion had always acted as his bodyguard and would be mortally offended if deprived of their role, thinking Caesar favoured his allies above his own men. He was sure that Diviciacus, as a great personal friend, a man whom he had always held in the highest esteem, would understand his predicament. If the Aeduans wished, he added maliciously, he would place them in the forefront of any ensuing battle to prove to them he knew he could rely on their courage under the most adverse circumstances. Diviciacus coldly told him that henceforth he would have great difficulty in persuading his men to fight alongside the Romans at all, and only with the most earnest representations would he prevent them from adopting an infantry role in future engagements. This action of Caesar's, he said, had belittled the Aeduans in the eyes of their fellow Gauls. It was a matter of national prestige.

Gaius felt quite sure Diviciacus could have carried on in the same vein for the entire morning. Eventually however, he allowed himself to be placated, with the promise of a greatly increased proportion of any subsequent victory spoils. Caesar knew when he had been out-manoeuvred. There was no way he could afford to lose these precarious allies, lest the Senate rescind his command. Rather pointedly Diviciacus invited Gaius and Octavian to dinner before he left the praesidium.

Jay stayed behind, perched on a stool, looking perturbed. "Caesar, you must understand, my father, he feels a little insulted."

Caesar relaxed, and stretched out, putting his feet up on a chair.

"My dear Jayven," he smiled. "We all go through a period when we think our fathers are fools, that other men know better. But listen to me, Jay. Your father is no fool. On the contrary. He is a very intelligent man. He knows I can't afford to lose you Aeduans as allies. I'm hamstrung by the Senate. So he has reinforced his position. Do you see?"

"No," said Jay, sounding puzzled. "Why can't you remove the Senate?"

They all laughed. "No doubt Octavian will be able to explain it to you tonight," said Caesar, highly amused.

Considering Prince Jayven had actually visited Rome with his father, Octavian was appalled by his apparent ignorance of the city's political institutions.

"What on earth did you do when you were there?" he asked indignantly.

"We partied," replied Jay with a grin.

"Don't let him fool you," Gaius said to his brother, pulling Jay's curls. "He knows more than he lets on."

"You have it correct, Gaius," said Jay approvingly. "I am a very intelligent man, like my father." He grinned at Octavian, eyes gleaming with mischief, making him choke on his wine. Marcius thumped Octavian's back hard, until he protested.

This being an informal dinner, Marcius was allowed to sit and eat with the guests, though he wouldn't speak unless addressed. He was finding his position increasingly invidious. He was well aware of Jay's sparkling intelligence, that he could speak Greek perfectly, and that he sat in Caesar's tent, patting Hector and looking sweet in order to keep his father informed of every move Caesar made.

Marcius disliked Gaius, and had no objection to watching him being taken for a long ride by Jay, but he found it disturbing to see Octavian suffer the same fate.

Guéreth, usually so easy-going, surprised the Roman guests by announcing that if anyone so much as touched his horse without his permission, he would personally wring their necks. Neither Diviciacus nor Dumnorix seemed at all inclined to put down this rank insubordination from a junior. Gaius made a mental note to make sure no Roman went anywhere near the precious beast. Of course, he remembered, Guéreth had bought the animal in Rome and paid a high price for it, along with Marcius.

But now the real reason for their guest appearance was apparent. Marcus Metius was ushered in, looking every bit the rich Roman merchant, exquisitely dressed in a toga of the finest wool, with the minimum of jewellery, but rings and bracelets selected for the high quality of stones and workmanship. The brooch he wore to fasten his cloak was the finest Celtic design, an intricate pattern of woven golden spirals.

Diviciacus effected the introductions, sure Metius knew, or had knowledge of, most of the other guests. Dumnorix greeted him with affection. Metius was a frequent guest at his house in Noviodunum.

"Did you hear what happened this afternoon, then, Metius?" Dumnorix enquired, "when Caesar met Ariovistus?"

"Insults were hurled on both sides," said Metius with a grin. "And a few stones as well, evidently."

"Two dogs fighting over a nice juicy bone," said Jay breaking in. "We are the bone, Octavian. I thought I'd better explain in case you didn't understand." And selecting a chop from the proffered dish, he offered it to Hector.

"No, Jay. We've got to stop feeding Hector at the table. Valerius says he's getting far too fat," said Gaius.

"Well you can try and get it off him, if you like," Jay grinned.

"Alright."

But a bone transformed Hector from a docile domestic to a savage snarling animal, who would fight to his last drop of blood. Gaius made one attempt, but was bitten for his pains. He retired hurt, shaking his hand vigorously.

"I hope this is not an omen," said Jay.

Gaius put his arm round his neck and whispered in his ear. "I can't scrag you here, but just you wait till I get you outside."

The prospect seemed to please Jay immensely. Diviciacus frowned them both into silence to allow his guest to continue.

"Ariovistus did make one rather telling point, though," Metius carried on. "Some of the most influential men in Rome have sent messages to him via their agents, to tell him Caesar's death would render them eternally grateful. If there are to be any further negotiations Caesar has asked me to participate, as I have had some dealings with Ariovistus. There is some suggestion that I go to German headquarters, with Gaius Caberus tomorrow."

Jay shook his head sorrowfully. "Putting your head in the lion's mouth." Jay dropped his voice to a loud whisper. "The Germans, Octavian, are the lion."

"Silence, Jayven," said his father.

187

Metius waited until the laughter had died down. "I think I agree with Prince Jayven," he smiled. "It seems rather a risky undertaking, so I'm glad to have this opportunity of discussing my affairs with you all present. If tomorrow anything untoward should happen, the lion should bite my head off, for example, I wish you all here to witness that I hereby adopt Marcius as my heir. My lord Guéreth, I understand from you, that you have arranged you will free the boy, after he has served you for seven years?"

"That's correct."

"I know from my nephew, and from my own experience, that you a very good man. One of the best. I don't think, or indeed expect, Marcius should be freed any sooner, whatever the circumstances, but in the event of my death, I wish you to act as guardian of my estates, and guardian to the boy, as well as being his master."

Guéreth nodded. "Very well. It's not a problem."

"Thank you. I'm grateful. As you know, I have other family obligations. The boy's mother, his brother and sister are in Rome. You are aware of the circumstances. You've met them. At the moment I can do nothing very useful."

"I will do everything I can."

"Thank you. We keep in touch via the Volusenus family. Here." Metius handed Guéreth a package. "This is a copy of my will, and letters to various acquaintances."

The evening ended on a very special note. Both Dumnorix and Jay ordered their harps to be brought, and they played and sang, singly and together for the guests. Gaius had no idea his friends were so talented. How little he knew of them really. Jay walked with Gaius back to his tent.

"Jay, why didn't you tell me you could sing and play like that? It was beautiful."

"Oh well, I thought maybe you would despise me."

"Why, Jay?"

"You know, the barbarians amusing themselves."

"Have I ever said that?"

"Oh yes."

They walked on in silence.

"You don't know me very well, do you?" Gaius said tentatively.

"I suppose not."

"Would you like to know me better?"

There was an infinitesimal pause.

"No, Gaius," said Jay. "Good night."

The next day Marcus Metius and Gaius Cabarus failed to return from German headquarters. They had either been killed or captured. It wasn't until the Germans had been broken in battle and beaten all the way back to the Rhine, suffering enormous casualties in the process, that they were found, being dragged along by their guards. A little shaken, a little shocked, but otherwise unhurt.

"Yes, indeed," Metius told them afterwards cheerfully, as they celebrated their victory in the officers' mess. "The lion spat out the porcupine."

Octavian groaned and covered his ears with his hands.

"And I, Octavian," said Metius, grinning at him amid gales of laughter, "am the porcupine."

Helvetia, (Switzerland)

Their neighbours, the Allobroges, had been remarkable, assisting in every way possible, welcoming the Helvetians into their own houses and treating them as favoured kinsmen. It made the difference between life and death. The chief magistrate's sons travelled with them, smoothing their path. Now the Helvetians crossed the frontier back into their own country. If only Allaine were there as well, to perform the rituals, conduct the sacrifice. Coevorten missed his family so much, not one of them left. Even Nammeius had succumbed on the journey. Not that he was ever close to his uncle, but he had occasionally offered good advice. Now he was alone, in charge of a nation with so many distraught grieving people. Oh well, he would just have to get on with it.

Here he was back in the vast bowl between the fantastic mountains. There were even a few cattle standing in the fields. The Gods knew where the beasts had come from. And scattered patches of bright corn - it would do for seed anyway.

There seemed to be increasing numbers of people - they must have run ahead of the main column. He rode through the streets of his city. Odd. There was one house nearly completed and several more well on. Through the market square, up to the blackened remnants of his own house. He steeled himself to look. His eyes widened in surprise. There they were, standing in front of the charred doorway, smiling through tears of happiness.

"Grandmother! Zinny!" Oh, thank the Gods, thank the Gods! He was overcome with emotion, even pleased to see Noemon! He could hardly contain himself.

BOOK 2: CHAPTER 4

Besançon to Rome, Winter 58 BC

The six legions were moved into winter quarters at Besançon. Now the Gauls knew why they had been forbidden to aid the Helvetians. Their corn was to be used to feed the Romans. There could be only one reason why Caesar was wintering the legions in East Gaul, and not in the Province. The fox was in the hen house now, and showed no sign at all of returning to his den. The chickens were squawking around in terror, wondering which one he was going to eat next. But no, Caesar returned to Italy. The fox would sleep till spring.

Caesar laughed aloud when he read the report from Metius. The northern tribes were rushing around making treaties, exchanging hostages, forming alliances. Well, let them. For a few months he would forget his barbarians. He arranged for the proper safe storage of his plunder, sent for his creditors and watched their faces with pleasure as his debts were paid in solid gold. He sent his friends lots of expensive souvenirs, and arranged for some extravagant presents to be sent to his son-in-law Pompey and Crassus, his dependable political allies. Then he wrote to Labienus.

The officers stood stiffly to attention. Their temporary Commander-in-Chief seemed in a particularly evil humour this morning. They were all aware Labienus hadn't relished the task of commanding thirty-six thousand idle men all winter in the wastes of North Gaul. Hungry men, too, probably. The corn supplies had slowed yet again.

Labienus prowled round them, head hunched forward, hands clasped behind his back, still holding the letter from Caesar. He stopped abruptly in front of Octavian.

"What is it you do exactly, Tribune, to merit a three month spell of leave in Rome, eh?"

"Nothing, Sir," said Octavian, taken aback.

"That's it. Nothing! Do bugger all, and you lead a charmed life. Gentlemen, learn the lesson!"

He walked towards his chair, then spun round. "Did you hear me?"

"Yes, Sir," they chorused.

He sprawled in Caesar's chair, then deliberately rested his boots on Caesar's elegant Egyptian desk. He stared at them, daring any of them to move a muscle. He kept them standing for half an hour, while he dictated the orders of the day to his secretary.

"Right, you lot," he said, when he had finished. "Caesar wishes two new legions to be raised in Italy. It looks as if we are going to be very busy next year. You are to set things in motion on the way to Rome, spend December, January, and February in the capital city, and return with the two new legions under the command of Quintus Petius. Is that clear?"

"Yes, Sir," they said.

"And a happy Saturnalia to one and all," Labienus ended bitterly.

"Thank you very much, Sir," said Octavian.

"Don't push your luck, sonny," said his commander. "I'm in a hanging mood today. Gaius, stay behind."

"Sir," said Gaius.

"The Aeduans are breaking camp. They're returning home for winter, lucky bastards. You're to travel with them."

"Sir."

"With any luck they'll slaughter you all, before you've travelled fifty miles."

Gaius laughed. "Is there anything you want brought back from Rome, Sir, apart from a couple of legions?"

Labienus lay back in his chair and closed his eyes.

"Warmth," he said. "Hot stone. Deep blue sky. Blazing sun. Smooth wine, really smooth, like a peach skin. Scented women, perfumed women wrapped in silk." He heaved a sigh.

"Warm blue perfumed women. I'll see what I can do, Sir."

Labienus smiled and then grew serious. "What do you think he's got in mind for the Spring, Gaius?"

"I don't know, what do you think?"

"Oh, I think we're going to annexe the entire country. You'd better find out what your Aeduans think of that."

Octavian thought it would be great fun travelling back with the Aeduans. He couldn't have been more wrong. Nobody said anything, of course, the Gauls were much too polite. But the parties travelled in separate groups, only Guéreth bothering to ride with them. Octavian began to think this was more for Marcius's benefit than anyone else's. Jay hardly spoke to them the entire journey, keeping with his own friends. When they reached Aeduan territory, the hostility became more marked. Diviciacus should have offered to put them up, but blatantly didn't do so. At least Dumnorix had the grace to apologise, offering the excuse that his wife, Eloise, being a Helvetian, might find their company a little trying.

They enjoyed their stay at Guéreth's house though, being entertained by his youngest sister, Riona, the only one still unmarried and at home. She was delightful, happy to welcome the charming young men, giggle at their feeble jokes and do her best to entertain them. They stayed for three days until Metius caught them up. He'd been transacting business elsewhere.

"So Caesar has allowed the Helvetians to return to Switzerland?" Riona demanded of her brother.

Guéreth didn't enlighten her as to the fate of Prince Allaine and his sister. He thought she would be upset. He'd heard she was fond of him.

"They've returned to their own country, yes, Riona."

"That's good," she smiled. She was so relieved. She would wait until Allaine visited his sister Eloise again. She hoped fervently it would be soon.

After dinner that night Marcius came to Octavian's room.

"Octavian? Damn," he said, catching sight of the slave girl. "Look, I need to talk to you. Tell me when you're free."

"It's alright, she can go. Shoo!" said Octavian, pulling back the blanket.

The girl shrieked, tumbled out of bed and made a dive for her dress, but she was too late. Grinning, Marcius held it aloft, screwed up in his hand.

"Marcius!" she said crossly, and spoke to him angrily in Gallic. When that didn't get her anywhere, she wound her arms around his neck, and pressed herself close to him. "Marcius," she said more pleadingly. She got her dress back after a long kiss. Once she'd got her dress on, he smacked her bottom, and pushed her out of the room, telling her he would see her later.

"She's sweet, isn't she?" he said.

"Mm. Your master's a very considerate host," said Octavian, leaning back, his head on his folded arms. "What do you want to talk about?"

"Octavian," Marcius laughed, he was so excited. "My master says I may travel to Rome with Metius."

"What?" Octavian sat straight up in bed.

"Yes. And stay for three months. Metius has business in Rome and has rented a house. I'm to stay with him. I'll be able to see my family. Isn't it great?"

"It certainly is," said Octavian, hugging him. "Weren't you clever, picking Guéreth for a master?"

"I was, wasn't I?" said Marcius thoughtfully. "He's very religious you know. The Aeduans all are. More so than us, perhaps."

"Are they?"

"He says he feels he was honoured, when I chose him. That there was something sacred about it." Marcius smiled. "Slaves don't usually get to choose their masters after all. He's giving me a fair bit of money too, but I'm not allowed to gamble."

"I should hope not."

"I never do, though, do I, Octavian? That's what's so strange. And I've never been drunk out of my mind, before or since. My master thinks I must have been drugged. I wonder which one of them did it, though."

In the morning they accompanied their host to the sacred grove, where the Ceremony of Departure took place, Guéreth treating Marcius as a son. Octavian found the ceremony deeply moving, as his friend knelt at his master's feet to receive his cloak, and then stood while Guéreth fastened it round his shoulders. The final embraces, good wishes, and they were heading south again.

Rome

Their quarters were luxurious. These city soldiers certainly knew how to look after themselves. The tribunes' dining room was furnished with couches, like a proper house. It was now nearing the end of December. Octavian was hoping that as time passed, memories would start to dim, and he would be able to sleep quietly at night. It was his birthday; the mess celebrated accordingly, and the party was in full swing. His brother stood up and made a horrible speech, recalling every time Octavian had said or done something embarrassing. Octavian wanted to stop him when he started making them up, but the others wouldn't let him. Gaius had a fertile imagination.

There were a variety of girls. Hugo got one dressed as an Egyptian. Freddy's was a black African with a flat nose and wide generous mouth. The agent brought the one allotted to him, and bowed deeply.

"A present from Caesar," he said.

Octavian laughed aloud. She was obviously meant to represent a Gallic prisoner. Her red hair was loose, with just a wreath of flowers. Her hands were chained in front of her with gilt chains. She was naked to the waist, the only dress she wore being a length of fine woollen material, pleated over her hips and fastened at the front with a huge Celtic brooch, just below her navel.

He pulled her down onto the couch beside him. She gave him one quick look with huge grey eyes, then turned away. She sat perfectly still with her head held up, her back as straight as a board. He could see the profile of her nice round breasts, little nipples pointing upwards, rising and falling with each breath.

"You're a lovely sight," he told her.

She gasped when he put one hand on the back of her neck, and touched her stomach with the other, caressing her gently. She seemed to be trembling. He wondered how she did it. Tricks of the trade, he supposed.

It looked as if she had been told to act terrified, but she was overdoing it. He had her on her back on the couch, but he couldn't prise her legs apart.

"Come on," he said. "Open your legs, sweetheart."

She didn't appear to understand him. He shook her shoulder. "I said, 'Open your legs.'"

She looked at him still with those big grey eyes. Apparently she didn't speak Latin. He looked down and swore at her. She was beginning to irritate him, dammit. He could see the others were progressing without any difficulty. Hugo had finished, and was grinning at him.

He turned back to her, exasperated, and slapped her hard across the face. "Open your legs, you stupid fucking bitch," he said, viciously.

"That's right, Octavian, you tell her."

At last she understood. She sighed and pretended to faint, her legs falling open. He tried to mount her, but didn't have any success to begin with.

"Not your night, Octavian," said Hugo.

"Either she's made wrong, or I am," said Octavian angrily. He explored with his fingers. Something gave. That was better, now he could manage. He finished quickly and lay still. It felt all wrong. The girl was motionless. He opened his eyes; there was blood on his fingers. Shocked, he lifted himself up and looked down at the girl.

"Gaius," he called out, "Gaius!" Others might think he was larking about, but Gaius recognised the cry immediately. His little brother was in trouble, and needed his big brother to help him out. Gaius stopped what he was doing, vaulted lightly over the next couch and its occupants, ambled up to his brother, and pushed him off the couch.

"Go and wash," he said curtly. He turned to the curious onlookers. "It's alright, just a practical joke."

Octavian moved to the nearest basin and scrubbed away at the blood, took a towel from the attendant, wiped his hands clean with religious zeal and walked back to his brother, still rubbing with the towel at his forearms, as if he were contaminated.

"Is she dead?" he whispered.

"No, she's fainted," Gaius replied. He was going to say something really coarse, glanced at his young brother's face, and changed his mind. "At least, I think she's fainted."

The girl was lying terribly still. She didn't appear to be breathing. He picked up a limp wrist. There was a pulse, though.

"Maybe she's pregnant, haemorrhaging inside." He could see a trickle of bright red blood.

"No, it's not that. Jupiter, I'm a fool. Why am I such a bloody fool?" asked Octavian despairingly.

"What then?"

"She's a virgin!"

"Well she won't die because she's been fucked, you ass."

"Shut up," snarled Octavian. Someone was coming up behind them. Octavian turned round in alarm. Their father stood looking at them, half smiling, half puzzled.

"What are you two up to?"

Gaius told him in one vivid sentence. The girl could be seen to be breathing now. Volusenus acted with commendable swiftness, pulling off his cloak and tucking it round the limp body. Her eyelids flickered, her eyes opened, closed again, then opened wide; colour flooded back into her cheeks. She moved her head a little, trying to focus. She saw three male faces staring at her. She took a deep breath and screamed - a piercing scream of primeval terror, pulling the war from the north back into the civilised south, invading the room. The sounds of terror echoed round the walls, bringing back dreadful memories, the thoughts they had suppressed, the carnage of the summer campaigns. The girl was making strange noises in her throat now. Little shuddering moans between clenched teeth. Volusenus wasn't sure which one of them needed more help - the girl or Octavian. They both seemed to be in an equal state of hysteria.

"You've got to help me, Dad," Octavian whispered in anguish. "Help me, I don't know what to do."

"It's alright, Octavian, it's alright," Volusenus reassured his son, then carried on talking in the same calm voice to the girl.

"We'll just wrap you up a bit better, shall we?" He sat talking to the girl all the time, stroking her hair and face. His actions seemed to soothe her a little, the sound changed to sobs.

The young men became useful, Hugo quickly coming to the rescue and dragging back the agent. Octavian flared up, beside himself with rage, when the agent couldn't find the key for the chains. He had to be prevented from choking him to death, his fingers gripped tightly round the man's thick neck, pressing the windpipe shut. Two of the others pulled him off. He stood trembling, still shaking with fury.

"Octavian," said his father angrily, "calm yourself. You are just frightening the girl more."

Gaius sent out for a file, but they managed to break the lock with a metal rod. They began to calm the girl, piece by piece. Volusenus had her on his lap now, cradled in the cloak. Gradually her sobs lessened, her head lay limply on his shoulder. To his astonishment, she went to sleep in his arms.

Octavian remained distraught till his mother arrived. She didn't seem at all surprised to be woken at midnight, and summoned to appear at the army barracks with a girl's dress. She acted as if she had spent her entire life in the officers' mess, giving her orders clearly and calmly. Finally she ordered Gaius to take Octavian and the other young men out of the room, telling him to bring Octavian to their house in the morning.

She stared at the sleeping girl. There were traces of tears still streaked down her cheeks; one side of her face reddened from the imprint of Octavian's hand. Volusenus looked at his wife and smiled. What a beautiful woman she was, and always so practical.

"Look," he said. "She's cried herself to sleep. It's the shock of course."

"I remember when Gaius fell off the wall, and broke his arm. What happened, darling?"

"Evidently the girl was a virgin. A present from Caesar for Octavian's birthday. The boy thought it was an act for his entertainment. You can't blame him too much. The other girls were all professionals, apparently."

"She's a lovely looking girl. Quite a present."

"I'd feel safer if Caesar stopped singling out my sons," said Volusenus.

His wife agreed. "Does she have a name?"

"She's called Chrys, according to the agent."

"Greek, then perhaps?" asked his wife.

"No idea."

"I've brought a litter."

"Shall I carry her?" asked Volusenus.

"No. I think we'd better wake her first, or she'll be frightened."

The girl woke quickly, looking at Claudia with great grey eyes which filled with tears.

"Hello, my dear, I'm Octavian's mother." Claudia spoke slowly, in Greek. "Now you are to come home with me. You'll be quite safe, I promise."

Chrys continued to stare. The lady looked like a Goddess, with a softly pleated dress falling from exquisite brooches at her shoulders, her hair piled in elaborate curls above a silver ribbon, necklace and bracelets heavy with jewels.

The lady said the same thing over again. "Do you understand, dear?" she asked anxiously.

Chrys sat up and looked around. There were two maidservants, otherwise the room was empty. The young men had vanished. She twisted round. She was sitting on a strange man's lap.

"And this is Octavian's father," the lady said hurriedly.

"I'm delighted to meet you, my dear." Titus put his arm out to steady her, but she panicked as she tried to stand up, and stumbled, then fell back weakly against the cushions of the couch. "Steady, steady." He gripped her hands tightly. "You're with friends. Can you understand me, Chrys? We're trying to help."

Chrys nodded weakly. "I understand. I understand the words, but I don't understand what's happening." She started to cry again.

"Nothing's happening at the moment, is it?" said Claudia, patting her hand. "Now I shall send my husband away, and then we will help you to get dressed. Then you will come home with me." Really, this seemed to be taking forever.

Chrys dredged up from her mind the start of the conversation.

"Who is Octavian?" she asked.

"He's our son."

Chrys stared at the lady, bewildered. Was this some strange Roman marriage ceremony she had gone through? Was that what Roman weddings were like? In memory of the Sabine women, she supposed. How she hated them. The force of the hatred inside her took her by surprise. She snatched her hand away. They were unspeakable barbarians! Worse than the Germans!

"I'd rather be dead," she said in faultless Greek, and started to sob again.

Lady Volusena realized this affair wasn't going to be at all easy to manage, but at least they had started to communicate.

Gaius dragged Octavian into his room, and kicked the servant out of the door. He thrust his brother roughly down onto the bed. Octavian dropped his head into his hands. Gaius knelt in front of him, and grabbed his wrists.

"Listen, Otto, listen. It happens all the time. Otto, stop this. Jupiter, it's what makes the world go round. So you were a bit rough to start with. Tomorrow you can be nice to her, buy her some presents, pretty dresses, that sort of thing. She'll come round in no time. Otto, don't do this." Gaius was beginning to get upset himself. He hadn't seen his brother like this for years. Then he remembered what to do. "Come on, Otto, it's me, Gaius, your big brother. Tell me what it is and I'll put it right."

Octavian lifted his head and looked into his brother's anxious brown eyes.

"I think I know who she is," he said.

"So, who is she? The Queen of Sheba?"

"In a way."

"Otto, do you want me to thump you?"

"I think she's related to Dumnorix. I think she's his sister-in-law. Orgetorix's daughter."

"Oh, bloody hell," said Gaius. He twisted round and lay back against the bed. "Oh, bloody hell."

"Gaius, I think something terrible's going to happen because of this."

Gaius did not contradict him.

Lady Volusena helped the girl to get dressed. They travelled together in the litter, the girl quite silent. When they arrived back at the house, they found a comfortable bed for her in the women's quarters. Claudia settled her for the night with her own hands. She sent her own maids to dress the girl the next morning, and then summoned her to her room. The girl still looked very pale, but even the dark circles under her eyes only served to emphasize her beauty, making her skin appear almost translucent.

Claudia talked to her, while she was having her own hair arranged.

"You do understand the position, dear, don't you? You are the property of my son, Octavian Volusenus. He's a tribune, you know, one of Caesar's staff officers."

The girl gave a gasp.

"Now you mustn't let that frighten you, dear. He's a very junior one." Claudia turned to look at herself in the mirror, "a little more to the left, I think, don't you? Now Chrys, I'm sorry my son was rough with you yesterday, dear. He had no idea you were still a virgin. He really should have been told. But he knows better now. He won't treat you badly again, I assure you."

The girl looked quite apathetic.

"We don't want to spoil his leave, now do we?" Claudia went on brightly. "I don't want to see you moping around looking miserable. The best thing for you to do, is to pretend to be cheerful even if you feel a bit low. I'm sure if you endeavour to please Octavian, he will treat you well. Splendid." The girl was beginning to look annoyed. "So I don't want to hear any more of this foolish nonsense about killing yourself." The girl was beginning to look angry. Claudia pressed on. "Just remember your manners, and don't forget always to be properly respectful, and mind your place."

The girl shot her a look of pure malevolence. Claudia hoped she hadn't overdone it. She didn't want her doing Octavian any harm. "Make sure there aren't any knives on the breakfast table," she hissed to her husband, "until I see how things go."

Volusenus came forward. Apparently they might be entertaining a real princess in their house. The girl certainly had a regal air.

"Good morning, Chrys," he said, holding out his hand.

"Good morning, Sir," she said. To her astonishment he kissed the tips of her fingers.

"Feeling better this morning?"

202

"No."

"You're honest anyway. Come on. I'm to take you to breakfast. We have it in the Solarium, these days. It's warmer."

"Will he be there?"

"Who, Octavian? Yes, he's always around where there's food."

"Then I don't wish to go."

"I'm afraid you have to, my dear." Titus guided her into the sunny room, and announced, "Chrys is joining us for breakfast."

"So I see," said Octavian. He was feeling different this morning, already slightly resentful that his parents had appropriated his property.

"Chrys, come and sit next to me, dear," said his mother.

"On the floor?" asked Chrys.

"No, dear. Of course not," said Lady Volusena, colouring faintly. "Come and sit next to me, on the seat."

Volusenus tried to coax her to eat some rolls.

"I'm sorry, I don't feel very hungry," said Chrys.

Octavian selected an apple from the bowl, and put it on her plate. "Eat it," he said.

She sat staring at it for a moment. "Is there a knife?" she asked, looking round.

"Allow me," said Volusenus. "You don't mind the skin, do you Chrys?"

She shook her head. He cut the apple into quarters, carefully removing the core, and then into tiny slices, as he had done for them all when they were children. Chrys stared down at the plate.

"It's alright, isn't it, dear?" asked Claudia.

"My father used to do that," Chrys said, her eyes swimming with sudden tears.

"All fathers do that," said Volusenus. "It's one of their main duties, as is supplying handkerchiefs to the female members of their family."

"Thank you." Chrys scrubbed at her face, and then started to eat the apple slices. She glanced surreptitiously at Octavian. He was engaged in spreading honey on a roll. He placed it in front of her.

"You can eat that too."

"Yes, Master," she said, with a touch of contempt.

"My name's Octavian."

"Do you want me to call you that?" she said in surprise.

"Yes, I do."

"Very well. Yes, Octavian." She made sure it didn't sound any better.

"Won't you tell us some more about yourself, please Chrys?" Volusenus spoke now. "Who is your father?"

"My father is dead, Sir. He was Orgetorix, one of the council members in Helvetia."

"Oh dear," said Lady Volusena.

"What do you mean, 'Oh dear,' Mother?"

"Well, wasn't he the man who made so much trouble for us?"

Chrys got up.

"Sit down," snapped Octavian. "No one gave you permission to leave."

"I wasn't leaving, Octavian. I was merely brushing the crumbs from my dress, from the roll," she added pointedly. "You certainly know how to humiliate your enemies, don't you?"

"Chrys, come and sit next to me," said Volusenus.

She walked round, and sat beside him on the bench. Volusenus put an arm round her waist. "So you're a princess, then?" he smiled. "We haven't had one of those in the house before." He looked across at Octavian, who seemed quite different from the night before. "We have five sons," continued Volusenus. "Octavian is our youngest. I'm afraid he's rather spoilt. I expect I should have thrashed him more when he was younger, but when you get to the fifth, you know, I think your arm wears out. I'm afraid you'll think the house is in a bit of a state, but it's always like that when they come home. Walk in the hall and you trip over a pile of spears, with bits of tack lying around the salon."

Octavian was beginning to look a little guilty, he noticed.

"I tell them to keep it at the barracks," Claudia broke in, "or at the stables. But it's like talking to a brick wall. And if the servants try to clear anything up they just get shouted at. Do you have any brothers, dear?" She could see Gaius shaking his head vigorously behind Chrys. "Well then, you'll know what they are like."

Volusenus kissed Chrys on the cheek. "It will be nice having you around, my dear. You're very pretty. I'm afraid I'm too old to do anything about Octavian now, but I can always get his big brother to sort him out."

"That's right, Chrys," said Gaius. "You just say the word, I'll sort him out for you."

She looked across at Octavian, but he didn't seem to be finding any of this amusing. He was inwardly cursing his commander, cursing Chrys too. Why did she have to look like that? She was a witch casting a spell on him. He wanted to touch her hair, touch her face, those big eyes, that luscious mouth, he wanted to kiss it. Why was she sitting there, looking at him like that, deliberately provoking him to behave badly. He wanted to ...

"What are you boys up to, today?" broke in his mother.

Gaius explained.

"But we'll be back tonight," put in Octavian, challengingly.

"Then I'll send out for some crabs. Octavian loves crabs," Claudia told Chrys. "All sorts of shellfish, really."

Good - thought Chrys to herself - perhaps he'll force me to eat mussels, then I can throw up all over his beautiful tessellated floor. She was smiling at him. Octavian felt his heart stop. The world swung into a different orbit. His life refocused. He felt dazed as if he were falling over the edge of a precipice. He clutched the edge of the table.

"Come on, get a move on! You're seeing her again

tonight." Gaius recognised the signs. Octavian was hooked. Oh well, thank the Gods the girl was his own property - things were bad, but they could always have been worse.

At this moment the steward walked in. "Pardon me, Sir, but there's an army clerk, wishing to speak to the young lady."

"How strange. Send him in," said Lady Volusena. "Somebody for you, dear," she said, still treating Chrys as if she were an invalid or an imbecile.

Gaius recognised the fussy little man. "Oh, it's you, Civilius. Surely we're seeing you at the barracks?"

"Yes, Tribune, of course. Just a little matter here that needs sorting out. The question of forms, you understand. I need a receipt for the prisoner's property and, of course, for the prisoner herself. I have all the papers here, Sir, if you care to look at them?"

Octavian looked through the lists. "You've got her down twice. Look, it says a slave on this property list."

"No, Sir, that refers to the prisoner's slave, of course."

Chrys wasn't following much of this exchange in Latin. She didn't know the language well enough.

"Do you have a slave, Chrys?" asked Claudia.

"I used to have quite a lot," said Chrys, "before they were all killed."

"No. It's just the one, apparently."

"Which one?" asked Chrys, urgently.

"Let's go and see, shall we? She's in the hall."

"Is that alright?" Chrys asked Octavian, anxiously. "Can I go?"

"I'll come with you," he said, springing up. He caught hold of her hand, and led her into the atrium.

"Jupiter," said Octavian, shocked.

"No," said Gaius behind him. "More like Juno, I should say."

"Oh Greta!" said Chrys.

"Oh well. Both wrong," said Gaius, grinning.

The woman was enormous, nearly six foot tall, with broad red cheeks, big shoulders and a massive chest. She was wearing a coarsely woven dress of undyed wool, with a man's leather belt instead of a girdle. She was clutching a sack with both hands. Despite her size she seemed quite intimidated, although she dwarfed the two soldiers on either side of her. When she saw Chrys her chest heaved with emotion, but she did nothing and said nothing until her mistress extended her arms, and spoke the ceremonial words of welcome. Then with surprising grace, she moved forwards to kneel at the feet of her mistress. Then they were laughing and embracing, the woman speaking a torrent of incomprehensible words, while Chrys attempted to soothe her.

Chrys turned a little shyly to the two grinning men. She didn't like to ask favours.

"Octavian, this is my maid," she started.

"I thought she might be," said Octavian, cordially.

"I haven't seen her for months, not since we were captured. May she stay with me, please?"

"We'll have to build an extension," said Gaius gravely.

"And raise all the ceilings," added Octavian.

"You'll have to buy an elephant for her, of course, Octavian. No horse would carry that weight."

The vision of Greta on an elephant caused Octavian to give a shout of laughter. Gaius was pleased with himself. He'd got one of them cheered up at least. Chrys wasn't smiling though. Octavian sobered up when he saw her grave look.

"I'm sure my mother will be delighted to welcome your maid into her house," he declared solemnly, but then couldn't help grinning again.

Lady Volusena took it all in her stride. "It will be very nice for Chrys to have her own maid with her again. Now Chrys and I will have a nice quiet day today. I'll take her to the baths this afternoon perhaps, and tomorrow you boys can take us into town, so we can go shopping."

"Mother, we've got work to do," protested Octavian.

"I'm sure you can spare your mother one day, at least," said Claudia. "And Chrys will be wanting to buy dresses and things, so you'd better come with us and make sure you approve her choice. Actually, dear, Octavian has no taste at all," she said when the men had gone, "but it will give you both a chance to get to know each other, won't it?"

Her husband had been adamant. The girl was to be treated as a honoured guest, with the utmost courtesy. Claudia wasn't at all sure what was to happen tonight, though, especially about sleeping arrangements. She had been worried about Octavian after Marcius had left. It had been bad enough with David. She shivered a little. It had been terrible with David, she amended. But when Marcius went too, Octavian had mooned around, not knowing what to do with himself. Then he had imagined himself in love with a most unsuitable creature and, forbidden by his father from having anything to do with her, had taken to writing execrable poetry, until he fell for someone else, even worse.

At least this girl was here, under her roof. If Octavian should fall in love with her, it would do no very great harm. Indeed, it might do him a great deal of good. He knew nothing whatsoever about girls. Nothing of their moodiness, or their bitchiness. He seemed to think only of their external appearance, as if one day he would be married to a dummy, without a mind of her own. Just a beautiful surface. The right woman would be able to manage Octavian easily. But the wrong one would do him incalculable harm, she thought.

Claudia looked around at her atrium and the bits of military equipment littering the floor. "All this," she said, with a gesture, "is to be put in a store-room. And if the boys object, you can tell them it's their father's orders."

The visit to the public baths had hardly been a great success, Claudia thought afterwards. She couldn't interest Chrys in the architectural merits of the building, or in the dresses and hairstyles of those matrons still clothed. And the crowds of voluble, chattering, naked women had stunned Chrys to silence. She could not be persuaded to discard her own clothes and take to the waters, or even suffer the mildest massage. Her colouring caused much talk. She was pointed out, stared at, and commented on, all of which shook her fragile confidence, and she became tearful again. Chrys was desperate to scrub herself clean from Octavian's contamination, but the oily waters of the public baths she found repulsive.

"Don't you have your own bath house?" Chrys asked in despair. "Do you always have to bathe with all these people around?"

"Of course not. If you would prefer to bathe at home, dear, we will go back," said Claudia with some reluctance, having caught sight of some friends of hers, and longing for a good gossip. Another day, perhaps, when the girl was more recovered.

Octavian spoke to his father before dinner, and made his position quite clear. As far as he was concerned the damage was done. Chrys was his property, and he intended to enjoy the possession of her. If his father wouldn't permit the arrangement, he'd take the girl off to the barracks and keep her there. Volusenus wasn't prepared to quarrel with his son at this juncture. After all, Octavian was right. Life couldn't be lived backwards.

"You must do as you think best, Octavian. Your mother and I would prefer that the girl stayed under our ..."

"Thanks, Dad," Octavian smiled at him.

Volusenus knew there was a lot wrong with Octavian, and suspected his son wanted to tell him, but didn't know how. So he started asking questions, delicate questions, probing around the edge, until at last it came tumbling out. It was Caesar, of course, as he had known it would be. They talked for a long time.

"They are a fine people, Father, these Gauls. They have a high culture. You should hear what Marcius has to say about them. Well you will hear. We could learn a lot from them, but instead we are smashing them to bits."

He told his father about the massacres. "Tiny kids, Dad, little blond things with blue eyes running for their lives and being unsuccessful. I can't stop thinking of them. Everyone'll hear about Chrys. It will get back to the Aeduans. Caesar has set me up as an instrument of punishment, to keep them in check, to prove he can damage them, even at a distance." Octavian took a deep breath. "I don't like being used by Caesar. I thought when I joined up I would be acting for the people and Senate of Rome, but instead I feel as if I'm acting against them."

"I can get your appointment cancelled, if you like," suggested his father.

"No." Octavian put his chin up. "That would be cowardly."

There was an emotional meeting with Marcius, when Metius brought him round to dinner that night. Volusenus hadn't seen the boy for four years. He looked so much like his father.

"Oh, this is so strange," Marcius laughed. "I never thought it would happen."

They were astonished to see how well he looked, how confident and happy.

"Yes, I gave Octavian quite a shock," he said. "I'm a better swordsman than he is now. He has to train with me."

He reacted differently when he learned Chrys's identity, dropping swiftly to his knees, kissing her hand, and greeting her in her own language. "And I have the honour to tell you, Madam, that I saw your sister and her two children only four months past, and they were all well."

"Well that is good news," said Lady Volusena, approvingly. "You'll be able to write to your sister, Chrys, and tell her you're safe. Perhaps she can come and visit us."

"Sir," Chrys said, ignoring this well-meaning idiocy, and speaking softly to Marcius in Gallic. "Have you any news about my brother, Prince Allaine? It was his birthnight yesterday." She had no idea why she had added this irrelevant information.

Somehow it seemed important just to say it, as if saying it would keep him alive.

"I believe he was sent to be imprisoned at Arles, Madam. But Gaius might know more. I'll ask him."

No, Gaius had no further information, Marcius discovered. None he was going to impart to the princess, anyway. Chrys was looking tearful again.

"What would you like to do tomorrow, Chrys?" said Octavian swiftly, slipping his arm round her waist.

"Go home," she said, looking stonily at the people in the dining room.

"I thought you would have had enough of being carted around by now," Octavian said irritably.

"Yes, dear," said Claudia, "now you've come all this way, you really must see something of the city. It's quite a sight you know. Now, Marcius, you must tell us everything. You would have come to us, darling, wouldn't you, if we hadn't been in Greece."

"But I did come here," said Marcius. "I gatecrashed Gaius's party. This is where it all happened." He looked round the dining room. "There," he gestured, "I knelt on that very spot, and my fate was sealed."

"What party was that, dear?" Claudia looked at her eldest.

"Just a few friends, Mother."

His mother nodded. No doubt that explained some of the otherwise inexplicable marks on the wall-paintings.

"It's weird coming back," continued Marcius. "I keep seeing things from two sides."

"How do you mean?" asked Volusenus.

"I keep seeing everything as if I were a Gaul myself." Marcius put down his wineglass. "They notice our faults more than our virtues. I suppose we do the same for them. They don't have a very high opinion of us. They tend to bracket us with the Germans."

"With the Germans?" Claudia was shocked.

"Yes, they don't think we are at all civilised, or civilised in the wrong sort of way. Materialistic, greedy, grasping. They think we are unnaturally cruel, and that we're cheats, with no sense of honour. They think as our soldiers are paid money, they are hired mercenaries, and they fight without principle."

"Give us some other examples," said Volusenus.

"The Gods, that's a good example. The Celts don't build temples with images of the Gods inside. They can't imagine why any God would want to come and live in a stone house built by a man. They think it's very rude of us to expect the Gods to come and visit us. They feel it's much more polite for us to go and visit them, so they look for holy places the Gods themselves have made. Mountain peaks, caves, groves in the middle of woods; they set their altars up there. Besides the big solemn religious occasions, they have little simple ceremonies for all sorts of things. The words are handed down. They're quite beautiful. I love the language," Marcius ended.

"And what is your master like? How does he treat you?" This was the anxiety that Volusenus had had, ever since Gaius told him about Marcius's enslavement.

"He's amazing, he treats me as if I were dedicated." He could see they didn't understand. He was forgetting how little they knew of Gallic culture. How little he'd known himself. "My master explained it. Gaul is a big country with many differing tribes. One tribe is usually at war with another. If a man is a warrior, and has been captured in war, he can choose to become a dedicated slave, a slave with special status. It is considered perfectly acceptable for him to swear loyalty to his master, even though previously they were enemies. I was taken to the altar, where Guéreth swore to protect me, and I swore to serve him. It's an oath that can't be broken by either of us."

"So are you treated specially?" Claudia asked.

"Guéreth is like a big brother to me. He treats me with nothing but kindness." Marcius looked over to Gaius and laughed. "Much kinder than a big brother, maybe. I got him into terrible trouble with his chief. Diviciacus was furious to think Guéreth had bought me without knowing who I was, or anything about me. But my master never blamed me at all. I think the world of him. He's one of the best men I have ever met."

Octavian found out more about Marcius's life that evening than he had found out all the time he had been with him in Gaul. He had been too shy to ask direct questions, but his mother had no such inhibitions.

Chrys sat upright on the couch on which Octavian reclined, gradually regaining her composure. It had been such a strange day. Her feelings were so confused. The house servants and the steward were treating her with marked deference, although she found it difficult to understand them, as they nearly all spoke only Latin. Her poor Greta was baffled most of the time. She was aware of the consideration and goodwill emanating from Titus and Claudia, but she didn't understand them either. Why were they behaving in this way? The contrast between her treatment in this house, and her dreadful treatment in the prison, was too great. And she knew she was going to have to face Octavian again tonight in bed, and she didn't know how she was going to cope. Her bath in the beautiful bath house hadn't helped at all. She still felt soiled.

However she was enjoying the food, surprised to find herself hungry, tasting flavours she'd almost forgotten about, and some she'd never met before, to Octavian's delight. He was trying hard to stay kind to her, despite her frigid demeanour. He was getting no encouragement. He suspected that pretty dresses and nice presents wouldn't make a great deal of difference, whatever his brother said.

Volusenus asked her what gave the Helvetians the idea they would be able to conquer the whole of Gaul. Chrys put him right, going into extensive detail, till she was sure he understood. He looked at her approvingly. She had considerable political acumen. Marcus Metius was happy to confirm her account, amplifying some points he thought needed further explanation.

After dinner Lady Volusena slipped her arm through Chrys's, and led her to Octavian's room. She stood there wrinkling up her nose in disgust. It smelt of leather, grease and sweat. There was a saddle on the bed.

"It's like a pig-sty, isn't it?" she said to Chrys. "I can't imagine how they pack it all into a tent."

"Oh, but the tents are huge, enormous," said Chrys. "They even have proper floors."

"No, dear. I think you must have dreamt that," said Claudia. "Well I've told Octavian you can hardly be expected to sleep here, and I've told him that if he brings a horse in I shall be most displeased," she added with a grimace at the saddle. "He used to keep a pet lizard once. It smelt terrible."

Chrys thought that was quite funny.

"So I've put you in here."

They entered a large elegant room, with a huge matrimonial bed in the centre on a platform. Greta stood in a corner, wreathed in smiles.

"I know it's not what your parents wanted for you, dear," Claudia continued. For a moment Chrys stood transfixed, remembering the man to whom she had been so briefly betrothed. "But you'll just have to make the best of it, and the sooner you get used to him the better, my dear. And although, of course, he has some really disgusting habits, well all men do, they are much the same, still he does have some good qualities. I'm not just saying that because he's my son, you know."

She stayed for a while and helped Greta get Chrys ready for bed. When Chrys was sitting up in bed, hugging her knees, her hair combed and arranged loose around her shoulders, the sheet tucked up under her arms, Lady Volusena surprised herself by giving her a kiss and saying, "Goodnight, my dear. May the Gods bless you and your children and your children's children, now and for ever." Something she would have said to a new daughter-in-law. Marcius must have put her in mind of it, she thought, as she left the room with Greta.

Octavian stalked in wrapped in a dressing gown, strode purposefully across the room, sat down on the bed, then couldn't think what to say all of a sudden.

"Hello again, Octavian," said Chrys, with outward composure and inward turmoil. Her mouth was dry with apprehension. She supposed if she didn't cooperate, he would hit her again.

He looked fully into her eyes and then away again quickly, as he noticed the slight swelling over her cheek. "Hi, Chrys," he said. He stared at the floor, took a deep breath and said he was sorry about last night and he was sorry he had hurt her.

"You see, I didn't know. I had no idea."

"I'm quite alright," Chrys interrupted, startled by the apology. "It doesn't matter." She wasn't going to tell him how much it mattered.

"Well of course it matters, you stupid girl," said Octavian.

Her eyes narrowed. A tiny flame of anger kindled inside her. That was good. It stopped her nervousness.

"Sorry, I didn't mean to say that. But of course it does matter. Everyone is going to hear about it. The Aeduans will be furious. I don't know what to do to put it right."

"You have to speak to my male relatives if you want to put it right. But I don't have many left," said Chrys, bitterly.

"Yes, I'm sorry about that."

She stared at him, outraged. "How can you be sorry about that, when you killed them?"

"I didn't kill them personally. I'm in the army. I was just doing my job." He looked at her with annoyance. This wasn't getting them anywhere. "Look, I know all this is hard for you."

"You don't know anything," said Chrys. She lay back against the pillows, staring wide-eyed at the ceiling as she tried to sort out her muddled thoughts. "I was betrothed."

"Really? Oh, well I'm sorry about that."

"Will you shut up saying you're sorry," she said in exasperation. "You're beginning to annoy me."

Octavian looked at her in amazement. Girls weren't supposed to talk like this, particularly not slave girls.

"I was betrothed to a man of the Sequani tribe. The son of the foremost prince. He had a face like a pudding and a big scar across his cheek." Chrys looked at Octavian's neat black curls and his smoothly-shaven cheeks. "He had lots of coarse brown hair that looked as if it had never been combed, and his beard had bits of food in it. He stank."

Octavian grinned at her, making him look more handsome than ever, she thought. He was like one of her father's deerhounds, with his big friendly brown eyes, that had come up for an affectionate pat, before returning and tearing the stag to pieces.

"I'm an improvement, am I?"

"At least you don't smell."

Octavian laughed, pulled off the dressing-gown and hurled it into the corner of the room. He turned to her, and was about to pull the sheet down from her breasts when he realized, just in time, that it wasn't an invitation she had issued, but a plain statement of fact. He stroked her bare shoulder. He wanted to worship her with his body. To touch her, kiss her, caress her and possess her. He thought she was the most beautiful creature he'd ever seen in the world, and she regarded him as a homicidal maniac that didn't smell. Chastened, he rolled over and rummaged around until he found the edge of the sheet. Then crawled under it and sidled up to her sideways until their flesh met. She was so smooth and warm.

"Lift your head up, Chrys," he said, "I want to put my arms round you." He rearranged the sheet, tucking it up under her arm again. He captured her hand with his own.

He nestled up close, his head on the pillow next to her. He started kissing her cheek.

"Tell me some more."

"Yesterday I was in prison, in the dark. With rats."

Octavian stopped himself just in time.

"And then they took me to those horrible, hard-faced women, beastly women. I didn't know what they were saying. And then," A tear collected under her lashes and rolled sideways down her face. He could taste it on his lips.

"Oh Chrys," groaned Octavian.

"And then this," she continued. "Light, space, a garden, people being kind. It isn't real. Tomorrow I'll be back in the pit. I don't know who I am, I don't know where this is. But it isn't real."

"Well I'm real," said Octavian. To demonstrate he held her chin in his hand and kissed her lips. But it didn't have the desired effect. He felt her body tense with apprehension. He was no longer a friendly dog, she thought, he was some rapacious animal, thinking only of that strange organ sticking up between his legs. He would manoeuvre himself into position, until he could thrust it up inside her.

He spoke quickly, reassuringly. "It's alright, Chrys, it's alright. I won't hurt you again. I promise." He had taken his father's advice and used one of the girls at the baths this afternoon. "We won't do anything tonight, I promise. Just get to know each other, shall we?"

He kissed her again. That was better, she began to relax as the threat was removed. He pulled her hips close to his own. Their bodies were touching from top to toe, all the way down. He let his hand rest on her stomach, doing nothing, just keeping still. Then he kissed her shoulder and snuggled up close.

"See?" he said. "I'm friendly. I'm not a wild animal." He sighed with pure bliss.

"Do I smell?"

"Mm."

"Do I?"

"You smell nice." He sniffed her neck and her hair. "Lovely, fresh," he said.

They lay still. "What's the matter, Chrys?"

217

"That prison smell, everywhere. On my clothes, on my hair, on my skin."

"No Chrys, you're fine. Everything's fine. Don't worry. Forget the prison, pet."

"How can I forget it? How can I forget any of it?" she asked in despair. "I've lived all my life not knowing that place existed, not knowing it was waiting for me. I'm so scared of it. I don't want to go back." She turned towards him. He knew what she was saying.

He held her tightly against his chest. "You're safe here. Perfectly safe. I'll look after you. You mustn't worry. You'll never go back there, Chrys, I swear it. There now. It's alright pet, it's alright sweetheart, don't worry. Don't worry."

He continued to stroke and soothe her, until she fell asleep in his arms.

Light filtered through the shutters. The girl lay still, sleeping quietly beside him. He crept out of bed, not wishing to disturb her. He pulled the shutters back, letting the pink dawn hues irradiate the room. He looked down at Chrys. A golden red tendril of hair drifted over her face, her long brown lashes rested delicately on her cheek, her lips were slightly parted. She looked so sweet, he thought. He was seized with the urge to possess her. He felt himself stiffen, become erect. He kissed her awake.

"It's alright, it's only me."

He saw recognition come into her eyes, but no fear. She was still soft and sleepy, making no resistance when he pushed her legs apart. Swiftly he moved on top of her and watched her face, while his fingers felt gently. As he entered, she moved her hips to help him. Concentrated pleasure surged through him. He lay still, in ecstasy as it ebbed away. He lifted his head to look at her.

"Are you alright, Chrys? I'm not hurting you, am I?"

She shook her head. She hated it. This invasion of her body, surrender of her privacy, feeling him deep inside her, his hard thighs against her own. She felt his lips brush against hers, the tip of his tongue enter her mouth. A tiny thrill flickered deep down inside her, gone again. As he started to move rhythmically, it came again. Fleetingly.

She looked at his face. His eyes were closed, his brows frowning, as if he were in pain. Presumably he wasn't. He gasped, clutched her tight and then lay still, his face pressed to hers. He withdrew and rolled onto his side looking at her, his hand cupping her face, touching her cheek.

"Why do I feel so much, and you feel so little?" he asked her.

"Was I doing something wrong?" she asked anxiously.

He thought about the professional women, their squeals of delight. Presumably it was all a pretence. He must remember to ask his father. He kissed her cheek.

'No, silly," he said, and bounded out of bed, walking over to retrieve his dressing gown.

At that moment Greta walked through the door, shrieked and walked out again. Chrys looked at him and started to giggle. He looked down at himself. A powerful but not a pretty sight. He put on his dressing-gown and came and sat on the bed, looking around.

"It's an enormous room, this, isn't it?" he said.

"You're not bringing any pet lizards in here," Chrys replied.

"I wasn't thinking of lizards," he said absently.

"Or anything else for that matter," said Chrys.

He turned to grin at her. His slave girl was getting very cheeky. He shocked himself by toying with the idea of spanking her beautiful bottom. Hurriedly he shoved the thought to the depths of his mind. Where do these urges come from - he wondered. He thought of his friend's stepfather. Wherever they came from they must be sent away again. She was looking at him, frightened she had said too much. He leant over and kissed her lips for the last time.

"Anything you say, dear," he said sweetly.

BOOK 2: CHAPTER 5

Rome, Winter 58 BC

Gaius refused point-blank to accompany them into town, knowing perfectly well that however selfishly he behaved, his mother would continue to love him. Lady Volusena had to content herself with Octavian and her husband. It was a bright sunny day, comparatively warm for December. They walked towards the Forum, the Temple of Jupiter dominating the sky-line. Chrys looked round astonished.

"It's like Corinth," she said, remembering Noemon's vivid descriptions of his home town.

"Do you think so?" said Claudia. "I suppose there are some similarities."

Chrys looked at her in surprise.

"We were in Corinth three years ago, weren't we, Octavian? Of course they've started rebuilding now, but it's really just a shell."

"Just a shell?" echoed Chrys.

"Yes dear. It's been virtually deserted for the last hundred years."

Chrys wondered if Noemon had actually been to Corinth. He had never said anything about destruction, or ruins. When they arrived near the city centre, Chrys was fascinated by the market stalls. The amount and variety of goods on display was astonishing to her. Octavian pointed out a canary in a cage, and offered to buy it for her. She told him tartly it was the last thing she wanted. He blushed at his stupidity and came back with some ear-rings.

"Octavian, they are quite hideous," said his mother.

"I don't know what we're here for," he muttered grimly to his father.

They turned the corner and came upon a fracas in the middle of the street. A heavily laden donkey had crashed into a market stall, causing the produce to roll into the gutter. The two men involved were squaring up to each other, yelling insults. Octavian waded in without a moment's hesitation.

"Shut up, the pair of you," he yelled. "You, stop making such a fuss about a few apples. And you," he turned to the man with the donkey. "It's obviously your fault. Stop arguing. Pay him thirty denarii in recompense."

The man started to protest.

"Do as you're told, or I'll have you arrested for causing a disturbance," snapped Octavian.

Grudgingly the man counted out and handed over the money to the satisfied stall-keeper. The man walked over to the small boy standing at the donkey's head, holding its bridle, and gave him a resounding box on the ear.

"It's all your fault, idiot," he said. "Now get a move on."

He looked up to see his path barred by Octavian.

"The boy is too small," said Octavian.

"He'll grow," said the man sullenly.

"You'll have to feed him then. Here." Octavian handed him a silver piece. The man looked up in surprise. "Kick the donkey," grinned Octavian.

The man laughed. Octavian walked off to find his father. Almost immediately he felt a small hand tugging at his sleeve. The boy gave him back the silver piece, and then bent swiftly and kissed his hand. Octavian looked up the road. The man with the donkey gave a salute with his whip.

"Where have you been, Octavian?" scolded his mother. "I want you to come with me."

"What for?"

"To carry something."

"What the hell did we bring them for?" he asked indignantly, pointing to their attendants.

A woman accosted his mother and he had to stop and wait. "Yes, she's Octavian's," said his mother's voice from behind him. "All the way from Switzerland. Yes, very pretty. A present from

Caesar. No, I've no idea what Octavian did to merit such a gift. I know, dreadful man, but what can one do?"

"That woman," said Lady Volusena when she joined her son again, "What impudence!"

Volusenus thought Chrys was looking a little tired. So he bore her off, with Greta trailing in their wake, to the island in the middle of the Tiber, looking like a huge stone ship, with the Temple of Healing in the centre. By the time Octavian and his mother joined them later in the morning Octavian was feeling thoroughly disgruntled. His affairs seemed to be being discussed all over Rome. His mother sat down on the bench, while he flopped onto the ground beside her.

"Don't do that, dear, it's not dignified."

"Mother, I'm sick to death of being dignified," Octavian said.

His mother thought of the time-honoured way to placate the angry male. She took a linen bag from the attendant standing behind them, took out a cake, and tucked it into Octavian's hand. This acted like a signal. A small knot of children came slowly towards them, arms outstretched.

"Octavian," said his mother apprehensively.

"Beggars," said Octavian, getting to his feet. "They're all over the place."

He picked up a stone and threw it. It landed where it was intended to, just in front of the group, but a flint flew off and struck one of the children on the cheek, causing a cut. It howled in pain and the group rapidly retreated down the hill. Chrys stared at the departing children. She said something to Greta who rummaged around in the bag, handing her mistress a purse. Chrys stood up and addressed Octavian.

"No wonder you let my people starve," she said, "when you won't even feed your own."

Now she turned to Volusenus. Claudia was sitting transfixed, a cake in her hand.

"Sir, if that were my wife, I'd be so ashamed, and if he were my son, I would disown him." Chrys stalked off down the hill.

Octavian made to get up to chase after her, but his father stopped him, grabbing his shoulder. "If you ever so much as touch that girl in anger while she's under my roof, Octavian, I'll throw you out of the house," he said grimly.

Chrys had the eldest boy by the hand. She emptied the contents of her purse into his hand, little silver coins. "Look, you can buy bread with this? Yes?"

Real silver! Yes, of course he could. He nodded, "Yes, Miss. Thanks, Miss."

She knelt in front of the bleeding child, holding out her arms. "Come. Let me see," she said. The little boy stopped crying at the sight of this funny foreign lady kneeling on the ground before him. He stood quite still and let the lady hold his face and examine his cheek. It was a nasty gash, down to the bone.

"Oh dear," said Claudia. Chrys twisted round. To her astonishment, her hosts were standing just behind her. Claudia was handing out the cakes to the amazed children.

"That needs a dressing," said Volusenus. "Don't worry Chrys, I'll get things organised."

Octavian was looking sulky. "I only meant to frighten them." He helped Chrys to her feet.

She started in Gallic. "It is my judgement,"

He looked at her in surprise, recognising the phrase. She continued in Greek, "that whatever your intention, your actions showed a wanton disregard for the consequences."

Octavian dropped on one knee, looking at her, half playing, half serious. "And the sentence?" he queried.

Chrys shrugged. "You must make reparation."

"Then the problem will be solved."

Marcus Metius called round to see Senator Sperinus. He was anxious to see his sister as soon as possible, after hearing

Volusenus was now forbidden the house. Metius was shocked by the impoverishment of furniture and fittings. When his sister had married the house had looked wonderful, opulent even. Now the place looked positively Spartan. The steward greeted him at the door with evident relief.

"Sir, how pleased we are that you have come at last."

Metius immediately felt guilty at this opening. But it wasn't easy to travel all the way back from Gaul. And unless he was buying and selling, he felt he was wasting time that could be put to better use.

"Is anything the matter?" he asked, knowing perfectly well that everything was the matter.

"Sir, my Lady is no longer ever allowed out of the house. She is not allowed to write to anyone, or have any visitors. The Senator seems to have the erroneous idea that she is conducting affairs behind his back. He has already ordered one slave to be tortured to death. My Lady is so reluctant to have any others put in the same position, she refuses to have any males in her presence at all, unless the Senator is there as well."

"What about my nephew and niece?"

"It is much the same with Miss Lucy. I believe the Senator wishes her to marry his male cousin, an objectionable old man, if you will excuse my saying so."

"Is the man mad, do you think?"

"Titus Volusenus certainly thinks so, Sir, but Sperinus still has powerful friends in the Senate. They rely on his vote, and so far he always votes correctly for them. So it has not yet been possible to have him declared mad. But he is mad, Sir. I can assure you of that."

Metius was not impressed with the way the Senator greeted him.

"Come to see your sister, have you? You sold me quite a bargain in her. I had no idea of her special abilities." Sperinus looked at him malevolently.

"Senator, I wish to see my sister, and also my nephew and

niece. I would like to assure myself of their well being."

"I'm afraid I can't allow it. They would be too unsettled. I've only just managed to get them in order again."

"What can you possibly mean?"

"You know perfectly well what I mean, Metius. I know they've been attempting to see that bastard Marcius. They think they have written to him. Well, they haven't. I've managed to intercept all their letters. And they make good reading, I can tell you. I won't have him near this house, do you hear me? If he approaches, I'll have him arrested."

"Sir, I must insist. I will see my relations. I will not leave this house until you produce them."

To his surprise, Sperinus capitulated, and summoned the steward.

"Bring my whore of a wife, and her bastard children here."

Metius was furious. "How dare you, Sir. How dare you speak of my sister and her children in those terms."

Sperinus shot him a venomous look. "You think your sister was virtuous when she married young Carvilius? She's a harlot, trained in a brothel. You knew that perfectly well when you had the temerity to marry her to me. My name, Sir, is besmirched by your sister. Sullied by any connection with your family."

"In that case I will take them all off your hands tonight."

"Oh no. You plot against me. You all plot against me. I know you. You want my money for yourself. Well, you're not getting it, not any of it, do you hear me?"

Metius looked at him in disgust. "You are completely mad. I will now exert myself to have you declared mad. I am a very rich man. I will not put up with abuse from you, and nor will my family. You have made yourself an enemy, a powerful enemy."

Sperinus looked considerably alarmed. None of his family had dared to raise their voice to him. This was a new departure. He started to whine excuses. "My dear Sir, my dear Sir, you misunderstand me. I fear my brain isn't what it was. I have strange fancies. I have bad dreams, very bad dreams. Sometimes I think I am sleeping and in a nightmare, and then find I am awake after all. You must forgive me if I have offended you. Or indeed your family."

Lady Ursula walked into the room, hand in hand with Andreas and Lucia. Metius could see that they looked well at least, although rather strained about the eyes. His sister looked far thinner than before. They stood quietly, like little mice. He went over to embrace them.

"My dears! How good it is to see you all. Ursula, my dear sister, I fear you have been enduring a difficult period in your life." He kissed Andreas and Lucy in turn. "I am sure you two have been a great support to your mother." He walked back to address Sperinus. "I am staying in Rome for three months, before returning to Gaul. I wish to make the most of my time by spending as much of it as possible with my family. So tomorrow I will send my attendants round to conduct them to the house I have rented. With your agreement," here he looked pointedly at Sperinus, "they will stay with me for the duration of my visit." He wasn't quite sure in his own mind whether his house would accommodate them all, with, he supposed, attendant servants. Well if not, he would just hire a bigger one.

"Yes, yes, you must excuse me. I don't feel so well at present. I think I must retire." Here Sperinus surprised his wife considerably, by going up to her and wishing her a peaceful night's sleep.

"Marcus, you seem to be able to perform miracles," said Ursula to her brother when Sperinus had left the room. She was half laughing, half crying with relief.

"If he changes his mind, my attendants will seize you all by force," said Metius grimly. "Apparently you are spied on here." Metius looked meaningfully at the servants. "So we will postpone discussion until tomorrow, when I have you under my own roof."

He didn't stay much longer, and went back to his house to ensure arrangements were made for his sister and her children's every comfort. Marcius was overjoyed to think he would soon see his family again.

Two nights later the Volusenus family were invited to dine with Metius. Lady Volusena was a little worried about Octavian. She had to remind him that he was once engaged to Lucia Carvilius. He appeared to have forgotten all about it. He was rather taken aback to find that his mother didn't think Chrys would be included in the invitation, and proposed to take her anyway. He couldn't stand to be away from her for very long. He found himself thinking about her constantly, which made Gaius shout at him quite a lot, when he was supposed to be working on raising new recruits, and instead stared dreamily into space.

Gaius didn't think Chrys was all that enamoured of Octavian. She appeared to tolerate him, but that was all. If he was to be away all day he thought she seemed relieved. He was certain she appreciated his mother's kind heart and practical help, but the one person he was sure she really liked, was his father. And the feeling was clearly mutual. They sought each other out, and chatted away about all manner of things.

Volusenus was fascinated by hearing at first hand from an intelligent observer, the political and economic workings of another country. He thought Chrys remarkably well educated. She knew much of Greek literature, philosophy, and astronomy. He wished his sons were as knowledgable, but none of them had shown any interest in politics, or any other academic studies, unfortunately.

Octavian walked round to ask Metius if he would be allowed to bring Chrys to the dinner. Marcius explained who she was.

"Dumnorix's sister-in-law?" said Metius. "Of course you must bring her. I hold Prince Dumnorix to be a friend of mine. We will show her every attention." He wondered whether he would be able to purchase her, and give her back to Dumnorix. But of course if Caesar got to hear he was interfering......perhaps, after all, better not.

When Claudia heard what her youngest son had taken upon himself to do, she was not best pleased. She went to find Chrys, and explained about the broken engagement.

"Is Octavian still wanting to marry this Lucy, then?" asked Chrys in surprise. Octavian had been telling her how much he loved her every moment they were alone together. She found him quite boring on the subject.

"No, dear, he has forgotten all about it. But I doubt if Lucy will have forgotten."

Chrys looked with interest at the quiet girl with the big brown eyes, that looked back at her in awe. This Lucy looked very young, not much more than sixteen. She didn't have a lot to say for herself. Octavian greeted her pleasantly enough, and then virtually ignored her, leaving his mother to do most of the talking. The men and Chrys spent the evening discussing events in Gaul, and speculating on what Caesar was going to do next.

"Nothing good," declared Chrys.

"I quite agree, dear," said Claudia. "Dreadful man. He does nothing but cause chaos wherever he goes. And when I think of what he did to Octavian........"

"Mother," shouted her two sons in unison.

"What did he do to Octavian?" asked Chrys.

"I'll tell you later, darling," said Lady Volusena.

The next morning after the men returned to army headquarters, Claudia related the story of David, and of how devastated they had all been at his foul death, especially Octavian and Marcius. Here Claudia had a little weep herself. And then how Octavian had ended up in prison.

"And of course after losing David, neither of the boys were ever quite the same. We took Octavian to Greece to try and take his mind off it, and then found when we came back that Marcius had sold himself to that barbarian gentleman. Octavian spent the next three years saving up enough money to buy him back." His mother had known all along what he was up to.

To Chrys this all shed new light on Octavian. There was obviously more to him than met the eye. Although to be honest, she thought to herself, what met the eye was very pleasant to look at.

Lucy cried herself to sleep, despite the lovely luxurious bed she was lying in. Octavian had barely looked at her; he was only interested in the barbarian princess. She couldn't blame him in a way. The princess was so beautiful, with her red gold hair, huge grey eyes, and creamy complexion. How could a drab of a girl like Lucy compete with a Goddess. And the Goddess had so much to say, which was clearly fascinating to all the men, none of whom could take their eyes off her to notice Lucy. And what could she talk about after all? She knew nothing of world affairs. She knew nothing about any affairs actually. And she could tell nobody about Sperinus. He had threatened to kill her, if she breathed a word.

But in the morning Lucy decided to take herself in hand. If she really wanted to escape from this hell, she would have to fight for Octavian. He was going back to Gaul quite soon, and Chrys wouldn't be going with him. Well Lucy would use the time he was away to make herself more interesting. She presumed he would soon tire of his princess. There had to be some particle of hope for her, in this world. If not, she told herself, she would simply have to try the next one.

BOOK 2: CHAPTER 6

Military Prison, Arles, Provence, Winter 58 BC

The centurion in charge of the prisoners had been given no explicit instructions. He presumed they were to be kept alive. It had been easy enough with the women. A few threats, a little minor violence and they became tame immediately. So safe, he fed one or two of the ones he favoured by hand, keeping their wrists chained together, making them take each piece from his fingers with their teeth. He kept them in their place, showed them who was boss, who was the master. He hadn't managed with the red-haired one, though. There hadn't been time to do a thing before she was packed off to Rome, together with a strapping great German woman.

One of the men was giving him trouble now, and would have to be dealt with accordingly. He was the son of Orgetorix, previously a prince - now a prisoner. The centurion rubbed his hands with the thought. The prisoner would need to be taught that there were no favourites here, the past no longer mattered. Well, he wasn't a tyrant like some he could mention, or a strict disciplinarian, but he did like a little bit of co-operation.

The guards sprang to attention as he walked along the corridor, the nails of his boots scraping and squeaking against the surface. A soldier pulled open the heavy oak door with the great iron ring. He went down the steps into the prison darkness. He could hear them rustling, he could hear the clink of chains, smell the stench of human sewage. Two gratings from the courtyard above let through some dimly filtered light, augmented by four pitch torches set in iron stanchions, their smoke smelling foully of resin. A further grating in the floor opened into a sewer. Once, years ago, after a lot of rain, the water had spilled up through the grating, so they said, and drowned all the prisoners. The air was so bad he ensured the guards down here were changed frequently, and their spell of duty lasted no more than ten days at a time.

The prisoners were kept in the large chamber to the left. The barrel-vaulted ceiling was so low, they couldn't stand upright. Each was chained by the neck to a ring embedded in the wall. They were given water every four hours, bread once a day and twice a week a broth made from the residue of the barracks kitchens and the leavings of the soldiers. If they all co-operated a shit-bucket could be passed from one to the other.

The guards tried to look as if they had been standing to attention all morning.

"Anything to report?" the centurion asked pleasantly.

"The blond one still hasn't eaten, Sir. Otherwise everything's quiet."

"Bring him out, will you?"

He had the prisoner stood under the grating, the light touching his hair and face, his chains sounding loud in the silence when he moved.

"What's his name?" asked the centurion.

The guards consulted the linen rolls. "Allaine, Sir."

"Allaine?"

"That's what it says here, Sir."

"Well now, Allaine. You've not been eating."

"No, Sir." Allaine didn't think he could cope with a confrontation.

"Why is that now?"

"I'm afraid I don't feel hungry, Sir."

"Are you sick?"

"No, Sir, I don't think so."

The centurion grabbed hold of his hair, and twisted his head roughly, one way and then another.

"Well you look sick," he told him. "The air down here. Terrible. And the food. Disgusting." He spoke to the guards. "Keep him isolated. I'll have to keep my eye on him."

Next they could smell it, as soon as the door was opened. The centurion could hear them straining at their chains. He came down the steps, followed by a servant carrying a platter on which sat a large leg of roasted pork. They'd had no meat for months. They could detect the smell of it over all the other odours. The aroma so powerful it made them drool, flooding their mouths with saliva. Guts started churning in anticipation. The guards weren't interested. The centurion had made sure they were well fed beforehand. The servant stepped forward and carved a tiny morsel. The guards and the servant followed the centurion to the deep alcove where Allaine was chained by himself, one carrying a plate with the meat, another carrying a stool which he set down beside the prisoner. The centurion sat down on the stool, and took the meat between his fingers, holding it an inch away from the prisoner's mouth.

"This stuff tastes a bit better, Allaine," he said. "Try it."

"No thank you, Sir," Allaine replied. "I'm not hungry."

"Go on," coaxed the centurion, "just a tiny bit."

"No thank you."

"Jewish, are you?"

He pressed the meat to extract the juices. He wiped the meat slowly across the prisoner's lips, so some grease ran down his chin. The prisoner swallowed but kept his teeth tightly shut.

"Allaine," said the centurion. "This is your last chance."

The prisoner just shook his head again.

"Oh well. Terrible waste of good food," said the centurion.

The guards removed the grating from the sewer, and tipped the meat into the blackness below where it must have stuck on a ledge, for they could smell it for hours afterwards. One or two of the prisoners were a bit restless that afternoon, and had to be quietened down with the whip.

Allaine leant back against the cold stone of the cell, reminiscent in a slight way, of the cool cave where he had practised delving into the recesses of his mind, probing down through the layers to find the self, the soul, the magic that made man above the animals. He knew he had set up another confrontation. But he had a little time now to prepare, to ready himself, protect himself even. Slowly, delicately, he laid out a shining white cloth. He placed his mind carefully in the centre, then started his descent.

The centurion stood in front of him the next day, one of the guards behind him holding a tray of roasted chicken legs, the other holding the evil-smelling bucket.

"No wonder you're not hungry, Allaine," said the centurion. "Apparently we've been doing everything wrong. You important people are different after all. We've been putting the food in the wrong end."

He peered through the gloom to see the effect of his words. The prisoner stared back at him blankly. He had no idea who the man was. He had no idea who he was either.

Arles, Provence, Spring 57 BC

Marcus Metius travelled back with the two new legions. It was too good an opportunity to miss with such a great level of protection. He was able to transport large amounts of valuable goods from Italy to the Province, to be re-routed over the Alps, and sold at a high price to the Gauls. They took the coastal route and stopped at Arles, the huge military complex, where Metius rented two large warehouses and had a trading post. They were to reprovision and pick up the new medical officer. Metius found that Caesar had ordered the prison to be cleared out in readiness for the new campaigns, and that his agent had bought the entire contents for ten gold pieces.

"Well you're either a fool or a genius," he told his agent. "Get them stripped down, cleaned up, and bring them in here one at a time. We'll see if there's anything worth salvaging."

There were one or two only, the vast majority of them had to be put down. When they led in the blond youth, something stirred at the back of Metius's mind. Recognition?

"And who's this?"

"No idea, Sir. Sorry."

"No name?"

"None that we know of, Sir."

The youngster stood erect, staring ahead with blank grey eyes. Metius walked over to him and stroked his cheek.

"He can't be very old, no beard yet." He frowned. The boy was prison-pale of course, and too thin. But there was no sign of any wasting disease, no sores, other than minor ones. If his hair was cut properly he would look quite presentable, almost Hellenic. Metius smiled at the thought. Homeric, even.

"The handsome Antilochus, tall as the house, with hair like golden corn, whom the splendid sun of the bright dawn killed," he quoted, pleased at finding a verse so apt. He turned round to fetch the ivory stick from the table, so he could examine the boy's teeth.

He heard the words of the next verse being spoken slowly behind him.

"Great Zeus!" The memories began to coalesce in his head. He said another verse at random.

Again the pause, then the boy spoke, slowly but without hesitation, picking up the verse exactly where he had left off. A Greek then, not a Gaul? Metius was puzzled. So many had been through his hands. It was so hard to remember.

"Look at me. Good. Now. What's your name?"

Again the pause.

"I don't know," said the boy in Greek.

"Where do you come from?"

"I don't know."

"How old are you?"

"I am nineteen years old."

"You do know some things, then."

"Yes, I know some things," the boy agreed.

He was also disturbingly docile. Not surprising perhaps, there were signs he had been appallingly treated at one stage. But the worst damage was in the body recesses, inner parts of arms, groin, and thighs. Metius paced round the room, impatient. Gauls,

Greeks, Greeks, Gauls. Gauls speaking Greek. He gasped and spun round. That was it. He was shocked now, when the memory came to him. He could still picture the bright child, the solemn intelligence. He looked sadly into the depths of the grey eyes. Now there was nothing there, just a wreck. Could anything be brought to the surface, he wondered.

He kept the youngster with him for a week. It was fascinating to see what he could do and what not. He could obey one command, but if given two instructions at the same time, he forgot the first one. He could write if told what to write. He wrote in Latin or Greek, but didn't seem able to tell the two apart. He appeared to have no memory at all for events. Names he should have known were meaningless to him. If he wasn't told what to do he did nothing, although fortunately he still remembered the rules of hygiene, and once shown where the latrine was, managed to take himself off there without mishap. Metius made discreet enquiries and found out all he could. Firstly he discovered that the centurion had been ordered to dispose of all the prisoners. He felt sure Caesar meant them to be killed. The youngster's loss of memory might prove helpful. He decided he couldn't do anything for the boy himself, he had no desire to mess around with politics either, and no wish to displease Caesar. He was hoping to get the army contract should there be any prisoners of war to be sold as slaves.

On the other hand, what a dreadful waste it would be if the boy were to be killed. Metius hated waste. Everything had a material value. It was merely a question of finding the right buyer. He invited the new medical officer to dinner, demonstrated the peculiarities of the former prisoner, declared that unfortunately the youngster would have to be sold, as he had no time to train him, and waited for the curiosity of the medical mind to emerge.

"Are you asking a lot for him?" asked the medical officer, with interest.

"My dear fellow, I couldn't. I don't even know if he's

safe."

"Oh, I should think he's safe enough," said the M.O. cheerfully. "He's quite a fascinating problem, isn't he?"

Metius smiled to himself. "You'll have to give him a name," he said, when the deal had been completed to the satisfaction of both parties. "I have to record the transaction, and give you a receipt."

"I'll call him Antinous," said the doctor. "It seems appropriate."

BOOK 2: CHAPTER 7

Aeduan Territory, Spring 57 BC

When they reached Bibracte, Octavian asked his commander for a few days leave. He told Gaius he was going off hunting, implying he would be with Marcius, and set off by himself without even an attendant, to Noviodunum, hoping he wouldn't get lost, and hoping that a solitary traveller would not be thought worth attacking. He had been making great efforts to learn the language, assisted by Marcius, but felt he wasn't making any headway; it was so different from his own.

"It will come," Marcius assured him. "It will fall into place."

He arrived in mid-afternoon, and asked how he could find Prince Dumnorix. He was directed to the courthouse, where the assizes were being held. Nobody stopped him when he went in, although he could see that he occasioned some comment. Several men were chained together at the back of the hall, condemned obviously from their expressions of fear. Dumnorix was sitting on a dais hearing a case. Octavian watched as an attendant went up to him and said something. Dumnorix looked up until his eyes rested on Octavian, then he gave a scowl of annoyance and spoke briefly to the attendant in reply. The man pushed through the crowds until he arrived at Octavian's side.

"Prince Dumnorix will speak to you now, if you wish."

"No," Octavian said, thankful that he understood. "Please, when it is finished," he said, gesturing to the hall. The man nodded in comprehension.

Dumnorix looked in surprise at Octavian when the message was delivered, but just nodded. A servant came now and led Octavian to a chair at the side of the hall. Another servant appeared with a side-table with bread, wine, and a little dish of hot spiced sausages that were quite delicious. Octavian sent up a prayer of thanks for the famous Aeduan hospitality. He had been very hungry, he found. It was late evening by the time all the cases had been heard, the condemned men led away, the litigants settled. Dumnorix got up and moved over to sit by the fireplace at the end of the hall, rubbing his face with fatigue. He beckoned to Octavian, who came and stood silently beside him.

"Greetings, Tribune," said Dumnorix, politely.

"I'm not a tribune at the moment. I mean, of course I am, but I'm not here in any official capacity," Octavian explained. "It's personal. At least I think it is."

"Go on," said Dumnorix, puzzled.

"I don't know what I'm doing, and I don't know why I'm doing it," said Octavian with an effort.

Dumnorix laughed. "In that case, do you mind if I have my supper while you work it out?"

"No, of course not."

Dumnorix ordered a chair to be brought for Octavian, then went to great pains to put the young man at ease, chatting to him about neutral matters, telling him what Jay had been up to, which made Octavian smile. Delighted to hear that Octavian was trying to learn the language. Here things slowed down considerably while Octavian tried to converse in Gallic. He was more successful, though, than he'd expected, and Dumnorix looked at him with approval.

Octavian stared into the fire, looking at the smouldering logs, while Dumnorix had his hands bathed and dried by an attendant. Then Dumnorix spoke.

"Now, Octavian, why are you here?"

Octavian looked round the hall, at the dais and the magistrate's cane laid out on the table, the chains hanging from hooks on the wall, the wooden whipping post at the far end of the hall. The answer shouted back at him. He got up, walked over to Dumnorix, knelt at his feet and spoke quietly.

"I've come to be judged," he said. "Nobody knows I'm here, no Roman that is. They think I've gone hunting."

Octavian frowned at the thought. Astonishingly lax really.

He paused, trying to frame the words. "I have offended against your family."

"Explain," said the quiet voice above him.

"Yes. Well we were in Rome, recruiting two new legions. You'll know that, of course?"

"Of course."

"It was my birthday. They arranged a party for me in the mess. They brought these women in, you see." Octavian broke off. "I can't believe how stupid I was. I just can't believe it."

"The women. Go on."

"They were all dressed differently. One like an Egyptian I remember, and one in those loose silk trousers, you know, that the Syrian girls wear." Octavian folded his arms across his chest, colour crept into his neck at the back.

"They brought this one to me. 'A present from Caesar.' I should have realised then, of course." His palms were sweating now. He started rubbing his arms slowly. "And, well, I......." He took a deep shuddering breath. "Well I suppose rape wouldn't be too strong a word," he said. The awful words dropped into the stillness of the hall.

"Who was it, Octavian?"

"It was Chrys." He had his hands tucked into his armpits now, his arms still folded across his chest. He felt as if he couldn't breathe.

"And where is she now?"

"She's at my parents' house. They haven't got any girls." He was unaware just how much information this sentence contained.

"And she was given to you, quite legally?"

"Yes."

"You've infringed no Roman laws, then?"

"No."

"And yet you seek judgement?"

"Yes, Sir."

Dumnorix sat back in his chair, folded his hands in his lap

and said nothing. Octavian felt his knees becoming quite painful. He wondered how slaves managed to keep it up all night. Because they had to, he supposed. Something he must remember for the future, if he had a future after tonight.

After a long while Dumnorix spoke. "Very well. Wait here while I make the arrangements."

Octavian hoped this meant he could sit down again and did so, massaging his knees. It was at least an hour before Dumnorix returned.

"Get up," he said abruptly. He took him by the shoulders and looked into his eyes. "Octavian, you will say nothing and you will do nothing. Merely obey. Do you agree to this?"

"Yes, Sir."

Dumnorix smiled. "Romans, the bane of my life. Come with me now."

They were riding for hours through a very dark thick wood. It was a cloudy night. He couldn't see the way at all, but his horse was tied on a leading rein. They must have travelled ten miles. He was beginning to feel really weary, when the trees opened out and they came to a glade. A huge grey stone altar was sited at the very centre. He could see a bunch of vegetation in the middle of the altar, mistletoe he supposed. Dumnorix dismounted quickly, came up and patted his thigh, indicating he was to do the same. He took his arm and led him to the altar.

"Now strip," Dumnorix commanded, quickly putting his finger to his lips when he thought Octavian was going to protest. "Hurry up, Octavian. I'm tired and I want to go to bed."

Quickly Octavian undressed. The attendant stepped forward and neatly folded his clothes up, placing them on the altar. He stood still, naked and shivering slightly. It was a chill night despite the cloud blanket.

"Now, hold out your hands, like this. Palms together, that's right."

The attendant held out the cords, and his wrists were tied

together very efficiently.

"Splendid," murmured Dumnorix. "Come on now." He pulled him over to a massive oak tree and reached up, dislodging the chain that was looped over one of the lower branches. Octavian was made fast to the chain. Dumnorix put a hand over Octavian's mouth, said, "Goodnight, Octavian." took his hand away, mounted his horse and rode off through the woods with his attendant.

Miserably Octavian listened to the sound of the departing hooves trotting down the path. He sat down on the ground. It was damp and cold. He looked longingly at his clothes on the altar. He wondered now what had got into him, what had impelled him like this, to submit himself like a lamb to the sacrifice. He wondered how many days it would take before he starved to death. Within an hour he realised he would be dying of thirst before he died of hunger.

The noises of the forest seemed to be getting louder. There was the constant rustle of leaves, the creaking of boughs as the wind caught the branches, occasionally the crack of dead wood. There was a very occasional burst of birdsong. Two little pin-pricks of light moved towards him. He was startled till he realised it was a vole or some such creature. There was a fair amount of pattering in the undergrowth, rabbits he supposed. He heard the high-pitched scream of some animal being killed by a predator, and the sound of a deer running. At last he heard the sound he had been listening for. The wolf howl, a long way off. He broke out in a cold sweat. He was very cold now. He jumped up and down a bit to try and warm up, the chains jangling above him. He heard the wolf again, a bit further away, he thought. Perhaps they'd give him a miss tonight. He hoped they'd wait until he was dead. He decided to sing a song to cheer himself up, enough to frighten a whole pack of wolves away, he thought. He had a pleasant rich baritone voice, and sang through all six verses. Then more softly he sang the lament in Gallic that Marcius had taught him. It seemed appropriate. It was the early hours of the morning, before he fell asleep completely exhausted, that he realised Dumnorix had said "Goodnight" and not "Goodbye."

A hand was over his mouth, he was being shaken awake. He sat up, looking round at a dozen grinning faces of cheerful young men. Dumnorix was smiling at him.

"Good morning, Octavian," he said pleasantly. He turned and said something to the other young men and they laughed. A warm welcoming sound. It didn't look as though he was going to be sacrificed after all. Dumnorix knelt in front of him and cut him free - with a very sharp knife, he noted, then helped him to his feet and took his arm. The group started walking through the forest. It seemed quite bizarre to be the only one naked, but no-one else was bothering. They were chatting to each other in a casual manner. In only a short time they came to a path under some huge overhanging rocks. Now he knew what one of the noises was last night. The sound of water falling. A lot of water. Dumnorix pointed him along the path, gave him a shove between the shoulder blades and said, "We'll see you in a bit."

The rest of the party disappeared down the hill. When he walked around the corner, he saw the path went behind the waterfall, which cascaded in a thick torrent into the pool below. He could see the others waiting on the opposite bank. He took a deep breath and jumped. The water was shockingly cold. So powerful, thrusting him down, down to the bottom, right to the very bottom of the pool. He fought and struggled, trying to get up to the surface. But the water hurled him back again. He had to breathe, he couldn't help it. He opened his mouth, his body jerked in shock.

Dumnorix never knew what made him look up at the exact moment, to see a body drop like a stone from the ledge, into the bubbling water beneath. He dashed to the side of the pool and dived in, fighting to get down as far as possible, as quickly as possible, using every ounce of strength. His hands groped, he clutched some hair, then a shoulder, then a wrist. He kicked up.

Someone else was there with him. Others, pulling and hauling, heaving them all out onto the bank, soaking wet. The breath knocked out of them.

Octavian heard a voice saying, "He's alive." Nice to hear that someone was alive. He started to cough and found he couldn't stop. When he did stop somebody thumped him on the back, and he started again. He found himself retching over the grass, expelling the chill pool water out of his system. He felt so cold though. He began to shiver. He was lifted up, dried vigorously, wrapped in warm blankets and laid out by a fire.

Nice - he thought drowsily - I'm being cooked now, which was good of course, but he didn't feel very hungry. He was lifted into a sitting position.

Dumnorix knelt in front of him. Octavian looked back at him with solemn brown eyes, saying nothing.

"Octavian, are you alright? You can speak now. Tell me. Are you alright?"

Octavian continued to stare at him, saying nothing. Then he pushed Dumnorix to one side and turned his head. More pool water. Perhaps now he could get warm. He sighed and sat up again.

"Here, give me that!" Dumnorix snatched the towel from the slave's hands.

Octavian sat passively while Dumnorix dried his hair, then patted his face gently with the towel.

"No-one has ever fallen from that path before. A child of three couldn't fall from that path," he said accusingly.

"I jumped," said Octavian. "Wasn't I supposed to?"

"By all the Gods," said Dumnorix. He sat in shocked silence, then put his arms round Octavian, and held him tight against his chest. "Octavian, Octavian," he whispered in his ear. "You're supposed to get a little wet, not drown."

Octavian sat very quiet, feeling foolish but happy, while Dumnorix patted his back.

"Don't say anything," he begged.

"But certainly I will," said Dumnorix, his face breaking into a smile. "Suppose we were to ride near a cliff edge, and people were unprepared for you to jump off. Before you do these things in future, my son, remember it causes a little alarm to your friends."

At the altar Octavian was dressed in his new clothes, which were lying on top. Expensive Roman clothes. He wondered who had provided them. The cloak, though, was of Gallic pattern, lined and edged with sable, and underneath the cloak was the sword. The sunlight gleamed on the blade as Dumnorix lifted it high in the air and said the benediction. This was the signal for everyone to yell blue murder, and wave their weapons and clash them together. Dumnorix handed the sword reverentially to Octavian.

"My son, here is your sword," he said. "Use it with honour and courage. Fight only with just cause, protect the weak."

"Yes, Sir," said Octavian obediently.

Dumnorix laughed at him and tousled his hair.

"You don't know what's going on, do you, Octavian?"

But he had a good idea. "I'm an Aeduan now?"

"That's right. You're an Aeduan. Come and have some breakfast."

BOOK 2: CHAPTER 8

Noviodunum, Aeduan Territory, Central Gaul

As they rode back to town Dumnorix explained. He, as the plaintiff, could bring the petition. Octavian, as the defendant would just plead guilty. A tribunal had been convened to hear the case. One had to spend a lot of time on one's knees in an Aeduan court, Octavian discovered. The deliberations took a long time. Eventually they were summoned to hear the result. Dumnorix translated for him. Octavian had caused an offence to the girl's family in that she was now spoiled and thus unmarriageable. He would either have to recompense the family, but as she was the daughter of a highly-respected nobleman, the fine would be considerable, or he could now marry her with the family's consent.

"Could you explain that I can't marry her," Octavian said, "because she's a foreigner, and Romans aren't allowed to marry anyone who isn't a citizen."

The answer came back quickly. That was no problem. He would marry her as an Aeduan; whether the marriage counted in Roman law was of no importance.

"Could you explain that she lives a long way away, in Rome?"

That was not a problem either. They could be married by proxy. He was told to go away, approach the girl's family and come back with his decision. Dumnorix took him to the tavern, opposite the courthouse. His entrance caused a stir of talk and laughter. They sat quietly drinking the warm beer. Dumnorix waited gleefully until Octavian plucked up the courage to ask for the hand of his sister-in-law. The fine was colossal.

"Certainly," he said briefly, when Octavian broached the subject. "Now, about the dowry."

At the end of the day Octavian found he was a married man, married to the girl of his dreams, that he was the owner of a

246

large estate, in some of the most fertile country in Gaul, complete with a house and several hundred retainers. Also a large sum of money.

"Which is just as well," Dumnorix told him, "because you have to pay for the banquet tomorrow night."

"I seem to be very well rewarded for having done wrong," Octavian said anxiously.

"No, Octavian. Certainly you did wrong. Your reward comes from putting things right. You're coming home with me tonight for a good night's sleep. Tomorrow you have to meet all your relations. And you'd better practise a few more songs," he added, grinning.

Some incidents Octavian found deeply upsetting at the wedding banquet. Prince Jayven looked at him in disgust, turned to Dumnorix and said savagely "For the Gods' sake! Don't say I'm related to him! A fucking Roman!" Unfortunately Octavian could understand the words. He wondered why Jay was so angry.

Dumnorix introduced his wife, Eloise, Chrys's sister. She wanted to know how Chrys was, and whether she could write to her.

"Of course, Madam," Octavian replied. "I would be so pleased. It would make her so happy."

"There is another matter, Octavian," Eloise said. "Guéreth's sister Riona would like to speak to you."

Riona came up and greeted him as a friend, then, holding tightly on to Eloise's hand, she said, "Octavian, do you have any news of Prince Allaine?"

"My brother," put in Eloise. "Chrys's and my brother."

"I'm so sorry," Octavian replied, feeling miserable to be the bearer of bad news. "I'm afraid he's dead. He died in the prison at Arles. I'm so sorry," he repeated.

Riona turned helplessly towards Eloise. They clung together. Octavian knew they were both crying.

"Leave them be," Dumnorix spoke quietly, and led him away.

Octavian said nothing to his colleagues when he returned with the corpse of a magnificent stag, courtesy of his new relations, but they would have to have been blind not to see the difference with which he was treated by the men of his new clan. He had some explaining to do when Diviciacus sent to his legate, to order him to appear before the Aeduan council. The legate seemed to think it a wonderful opportunity for Octavian to act as a Roman spy, so gave his approval. Octavian didn't bother to tell him till afterwards, that his grasp of the language was too poor to enable him to understand more than the rudiments. He was ordered, peremptorily, to take time off and learn the language.

He hadn't had to do anything, just stand up when his name was mentioned, as a graduate. It was nice to hear the scattered applause and friendly jeers from the others. At the next council meeting though, he was elected as a magistrate, not, he was told very firmly, as a priest. He could only hear cases, not conduct any part of religious ceremonies, for that he could only be a participant or spectator. The next day he found a huge bunch of mistletoe had been tied to the top of his tent pole, his badge of office. A sprig also always mysteriously appeared attached to his horse's harness, and he took to wearing some himself, pinned to his cloak brooch when he was called upon to decide disputes. The cause for his elevation to the judiciary rapidly became apparent. Any Aeduan could seek him out and petition him, but few bothered. It was too difficult to make him understand what they were talking about. But in the many disputes that arose between Aeduans and Romans, his authority proved invaluable. Instead of slouching around, yawning and looking insolent at disciplinary proceedings, the Aeduans now stood smartly to attention, and accepted his judgement without the usual furious gesticulations and protests, but with quiet respect.

None of the Romans bothered to enquire too closely about what he had done to achieve his Aeduan citizenship. When he said he had passed some sort of test out hunting, they accepted it without further questioning, even his brother Gaius, who should have known better. The sword which was stretched on a shelf in his tent was much admired. His close relationship with one of the leading Aeduan families was a fact only known to himself and the Aeduans. He knew that Diviciacus thought him an unnecessary complication.

Dumnorix made no overt show, just said, "Oh God, no," when Octavian walked into his tent. "That is the Roman form of fraternal greeting, is it not?" and made Octavian laugh. He insisted on teaching him a song in Gallic.

"That's my lament," he said. "You're to sing it at my funeral. None of my relatives can sing a note."

Octavian knew this wasn't true, but it was a good song, and when he knew the words he thought them quite beautiful.

Caesar joined his army in the spring. There he found a present waiting for him. A small blond page boy from Britain, and a message from Vercingetorix, the young man who had beaten him at chess, saying "Not so rare, certainly, but just as beautiful."

"Britain," said Caesar, turning to Labienus. "I've been thinking about that mysterious island, myself. A land made of iron and tin, apparently. Now where exactly is Britain?"

BOOK 2: CHAPTER 9

North East Gaul, Belgium, Summer 57 BC

The medical officer, Antistius Petronius, decided he would have to stop behaving like a child with a new toy. He was fascinated by his new slave, and could hardly let the man out of his sight, let alone stop playing with him, he thought ruefully. At first he had wondered if the youngster could feel pain at all, so expressionless was his face, and had then hurt him too much by mistake. The youngster had sat enduring silently. His first cry had been the sound of deep pain.

"Now, now, my dear fellow," said Petronius. "I'm ashamed of myself. I should have noticed sooner. Forgive me, forgive me."

The young man stared straight ahead, still in obvious pain.

"I'll tell you what, my dear fellow, I'll show you how to make it better. Is that alright, Antinous? Antinous, you say 'Yes, Master.'"

"Yes, Master," Antinous repeated obediently. He was looking at him now. Looking at him properly for the first time. That was good at least.

"First of all, a cold compress. That will reduce the swelling. Then salve. I'll show you how to make that later." He could see Antinous was watching his every move. "And finally, the bandage. There. Now, Antinous, does that feel better? Antinous?"

"Yes, Master," said the boy.

He found that his slave knew many Greek books. When he was given a verse of 'The Iliad' and told to continue writing, he continued until he ran out of parchment. Petronius thought he might have written the whole book. Similarly, with 'The Republic' and one or two plays. But when told to select a verse for himself, he sat staring blankly, appearing not to understand the request. He could answer questions, but didn't ask them. He could give facts, but not opinions. He was found to have the capacity to learn, though, Petronius was pleased to note. After he was shown how to do something, or where the wine was kept, he would fetch it without any difficulty. His face remained expressionless, he neither frowned nor smiled.

A few days later a man came in with a hand injury.

"Now, Antinous," said his master. "Do you remember what we did?"

"Yes, Master."

"Show me, then."

To his surprise, Antinous carried out exactly the same procedures that Petronius had performed on him. Indeed the bandaging - Petronius thought to himself - was, if anything, improved. This was excellent. If the boy could be taught and learn complex tasks, he would be an invaluable assistant.

And so it turned out. Petronius started by allowing him to weigh out and mix simple remedies, as well as roll the bandages. Then he had him assist at surgical procedures, by cutting surgical stitches, or holding retractors, or threading the needles. He taught him how to clean and dry the surgical instruments. The boy was so methodical and reliable, that he soon left the task entirely to him. Petronius found himself chatting away all the time to his slave, not only while he was examining the patients, making up remedies, or performing surgery, but also at night, while he was eating dinner, or in the baths, if no-one else was around. Every time he paused to say "Don't you agree?" Antinous would say, "Yes, Master." And every time he said, "Well I wouldn't, would you Antinous?" Antinous dutifully agreed, "No, Master," until one night when Antinous was engaged in braiding the sutures, and his master said, "And of course, Caesar's a perfect fool, taking on the entire Belgic coalition, don't you agree Antinous?"

"No, Master," said Antinous.

"No, my dear fellow. You should say 'Yes Master,'" Petronius corrected him.

"No, Master," said Antinous. "Caesar is not a fool."

Petronius laughed in delight. "Well, well, my dear fellow. So you commit yourself at last, do you?" He moved to sit opposite Antinous. "Perhaps you think I'm a fool for calling him one, do you Antinous?"

"Yes, Master."

"You think, perhaps, he's a dangerous man to have as an enemy?"

"Yes, Master."

"Antinous, you are quite right. I stand corrected." He looked at his slave. The eyes looking back at him were acutely intelligent. His rate of learning had been quite phenomenal. Petronius placed his hand on the boy's shoulder.

"Stop that a moment, Antinous. I wish to talk to you."

The slave was immediately attentive.

"That's better. You've done a lot, haven't you? Quite enough for tonight. Remember what I said? You must stop when you feel tired."

"Yes, Master," said Antinous.

He thought he detected a faint smile on the boy's face. In the first few days when Antinous had been given a task to do, he had carried on unceasingly, until told to stop. He had spent a whole day polishing the sword that Petronius had never used, and never intended to use.

"Antinous, I want you to try and remember now. How far back can you remember?"

Antinous paused, thinking. "The dealer?" he suggested.

"Yes. Good. The dealer. What was his name?"

"Metius."

"That's right. Can you remember before the dealer? Can you remember the prison?"

Antinous looked at the floor. A black pit opened before him; his mind teetered on the edge. He drew back quickly.

"Alright, alright my dear fellow. I don't wish to upset you. It's of no consequence."

Antinous looked at his master. He wanted to please this man, who had shown him nothing but kindness and compassion.

"I remember some things before. I think I remember them. It's hard to tell. I remember playing in the snow."

"In the snow, eh? You must have been living quite high up, I should think. You don't get a lot of snow in the lowlands of Greece. None, I would have thought. You must have been somewhere with very high mountains."

"Master, I don't think I was speaking Greek, I don't know why. I don't think I am Greek. Will it matter?"

"Not in the slightest bit, my dear fellow." He thought his slave was frowning a little. "You mustn't worry about this, my dear chap. You mustn't worry at all. I'm very pleased with you, delighted in fact. You're progressing splendidly."

Again the faint smile.

"Master, my mind is wrapped up in a cloth, like a pudding, tied with special knots."

"A part of your mind, Antinous, your memories, but not your capacity for learning."

"Some other part as well. I can't see what. The strange thing is, I know I tied the knots. I tied them in a special way. And the even stranger thing is, that I know how to untie them. I feel I know how to untie them, but I can't. The part of me that can untie the knots is paralysed. It won't work."

"Fascinating, quite fascinating. Well, my dear boy, should one of the knots work loose, I wish you would tell me about it. No matter if it doesn't, eh?" He patted his slave's hand. "You're going to tell me something else?"

"Yes, Master. I can understand what the Gauls say."

"The Aeduans, you mean?"

"No. All of them. Aeduans, Belgians, Aremoricans."

"Ah, but can you understand the language of the birds?" asked Petronius.

"No, Master."

"Thank the Gods for that," said Petronius. Ah, he had made the boy smile. That pleased him a lot. That pleased him very much indeed.

BOOK 2: CHAPTER 10

North East Gaul, Summer 57 BC; High Alps, Autumn 57 BC

Every fresh piece of information about the mobilisation of the Belgic coalition seemed to give Caesar increasing pleasure. He was in the best of spirits. He strolled round the camp chatting to the soldiers, exchanging witticisms and jokes, obscene ones mostly. Grinning, he told the Tenth they were now a cavalry regiment. Each legionary was presented with a gold badge depicting a horse's head, to be fastened to their breastplates. He was charming to the Aeduans, greeting them with effusive courtesy.

"I thought about you all when I was in Rome, and brought you one or two things I thought you might like. My dear Dumnorix, I have left your present in Noviodunum. You so much admired my mosaics, I have had one brought up for you. I thought, at first, the rape of the Sabine women." He paused here, to give a sadistic smile. "But then I remembered that possibly your wife would not approve, having the two little ones. So I have chosen the wooden horse instead. You'll know the story of course. You see? Here is the design for it."

"How very thoughtful," said Dumnorix.

"Not at all," said Caesar, "I always enjoy choosing the appropriate gift. So, Jay, come and see what I've got for you."

The horse was fantastic, pure white, from Syria, the saddle embossed with gold, resting on a deep purple cloth. The mane and tail were intricately braided with purple ribbon, the harness linked by silver medallions, depicting Victoria, Goddess of victory. Jay walked all round the beast very slowly, then came back to Caesar.

"Well, Jay, do you like him?"

"No wings," said Jay, dejectedly, shaking his head. "Ah well, you can't have everything."

"Jayven," said his father in warning.

Jay sank to one knee and kissed Caesar's hand. "With my father's permission, I will accept such a magnificent gift," he said. "And I thank Caesar for his graciousness."

"Not at all, my boy, not at all."

Jay rose gracefully to his feet and made a deep bow, before walking over to pat his horse's neck.

"A delightful lad. Exquisite manners," said Caesar to Diviciacus.

"Yes. Pity he keeps them so well hidden," said his father.

Jay trotted his horse up to them. "Caesar has mounted me. Am I now in the Tenth Legion?"

Diviciacus felt his stomach constrict. Surely the boy had gone too far now? One of these days he'd get them all hung.

Caesar looked up into Jay's grey brown eyes. What an innocent the boy was.

"Perhaps your father will give you a command this campaign," he suggested.

Jay smiled and saluted. He spent the rest of the day riding round the camp, jumping over all the obstacles he could find, and terrorising the servants, until an irate centurion reported him to Octavian, and he was summoned to appear before him.

Octavian had lost the day's reports. "Hurry up and find them, you dolt," he shouted to his servant as Jay walked through the entrance. "And then tidy this place up. It's a shambles." He turned round. "There you are, Jay. Look here, cut it out. You nearly hit the first centurion. Oh, you've found them, have you? About bloody time too."

"I'd rephrase that, if I were you," Jay said.

Octavian dropped the reports, stiffened and saluted. "Sir, there have been one or two complaints that some members of the cavalry have been practising manoeuvres inside the camp perimeter. Would it be possible, do you think, for them to continue this outwith the camp precincts, Sir?"

"I'll certainly look into it, Tribune," said Jay quietly, and left.

Octavian sat down on the bed. He felt a bit shaken, as if a spear had just whizzed past his ear.

The Aeduans discovered that their part in this year's campaign was to make war on their allies, destroy their towns, crops and villages and prevent them helping the tribes Caesar intended to smash with his legions. Most of north east Gaul. One tribe escaped the carnage. The leaders of the Remi were scared shitless and came and grovelled at Caesar's feet, handing over their terrified children as hostages.

Most of the tribes collapsed without much of a fight, but they nearly came to grief against the Nervii. Octavian was with Labienus when the Romans made their advance, down the hill, across the river, and up the other side towards the enemy's camp, which they captured with no great difficulty. Labienus was standing with a group of centurions firing off orders, when Octavian rode up to him and interrupted.

"Fuck off, Octavian. I'm busy," said his commander.

"No, Sir. This is important," said Octavian.

"It had better be, sonny."

"Look, Sir, at our camp." He brought up his horse and a mounting block. Labienus got up quickly and peered across the valley, cupping his eyes with his hands.

"Oh, by all the fucking Gods! What is he doing? Octavian, send the Tenth back, tell them to keep in formation, but to hurry!"

It was the turning point of the battle; they managed to wrest their own camp back from the enemy. But this enemy didn't run away. This enemy stayed and fought and fought, climbing on top of their dead comrades, to hurl spears down into the faces of their foes. This enemy didn't know when it was beaten and lashed out writhing in its death throes, still able to wound. It had been a sobering experience. They had been on the verge of defeat. Even so, the casualties were appalling.

They were camped outside Namur, in Belgium. The town had given up the fight before the first shot was fired, terrified by the intensity of the siege preparations. The piles of surrendered arms stretched from the city moat to the top of the city wall. In the morning the town opened its gates and submitted itself to the invading army. The legionaries rampaged through the streets, intimidating the inhabitants, violating the women or allowing themselves to be bribed not to. In the evening the bugles sounded the curfew, and the grumbling legionaries streamed out through the city gates, back to their tents.

Caesar was dining with his generals. "A remarkably successful finish to our campaign this year, don't you think so, gentlemen?"

There was a murmur of assent.

"This is an excellent wine you've brought us, Metius. I don't know when I've ever tasted better."

"I'm glad you like it, Caesar. I can bring you more, if you wish."

"The provisioning has certainly been much better since you've been around, Metius," Cotta declared. "Never campaigned on a full stomach before." He patted himself enthusiastically.

"Pity the troops don't agree," said Labienus.

"How do you mean, Titus?" asked Caesar.

"Well, they always grumble about the food, of course. Now they are grumbling that you're so damned merciful all the time, there's nothing to plunder."

"Yes. Well. The trouble is, Titus, our Aeduan friends do not have the stomach of Cotta here. I'm afraid the massacres of last year were a little too much for their sensibilities, shall we say? However, I take your point. Did I hear something?"

There were cries of alarm outside. The tent awnings were raised so they could see out to the town towering above them.

"That's the fire signals. Titus, go and have a look will you?"

"Caesar!" Labienus went off.

The sounds gradually died down. Labienus returned within half an hour and resumed his seat and his supper.

"A few of the inhabitants thought they might be massacred tomorrow, and tried to make a run for it. That's all. Nothing much."

"Were there many?" enquired Caesar.

"No, not many. A few hundred, Sir, perhaps."

"Oh, a bit more than that, judging from the cries and the noise, I would say, wouldn't you, gentlemen?"

They looked up, wondering what he was driving at.

"You make light of this, Titus, but to me it's a serious matter. The leaders of this town gave their word that the city had surrendered. It seems to me that the town has not surrendered. They have not kept their word. I fear the generous terms I had intended to offer them in the morning may well have to be rethought."

The face of the council leader was ashen. "Sold? Everyone sold? The whole town? Surely, Sir, you cannot mean this?"

"My dear man, what choice do I have?" said Caesar. "An example must be made after the treacherous events of last night."

The council leader looked bewildered. "I'm sorry, Sir, I don't follow you. What happened last night?"

"You are trying my patience a little," said Caesar, "I refer, of course, to the armed revolt."

"Sir, a few foolish young men. And they got nowhere."

"Because of the persistence and bravery of our troops. Don't argue with me, my good man, or you will suffer a much worse punishment. Go and inform your citizens of the fate that awaits them."

Marcus Metius outbid all the other dealers for the town's inhabitants. There were fifty-three thousand of them altogether, so the whole procedure took a considerable amount of organisation. He dealt with them in batches of five thousand a day. The old and chronic sick were put to one side to be freed immediately. They were given a small ration of corn, a little speech about their former master's generosity, and merciful nature and veneration for age, and left to crawl back into the town and die of starvation in the winter. Of the rest, he picked out a thousand of the best looking, best dressed, and best educated for himself, and disposed of the remainder in lots of a hundred to the rest of the dealers.

Those that were left became increasingly apprehensive while awaiting their disposal. The tales of the returning old men and old women did nothing to reassure them - stories of children parted from their parents, young girls being dragged away in terror, families torn apart. The populace became increasingly difficult to control.

The centurion looked at the queue of prisoners. They were jumpy and nervous, one or two of the women sobbing hysterically. It didn't look good. It made the men edgy, and unless the crowd co-operated, the more brutal the soldiers became. Pullo sent for Valerius. He remembered how well the young man had dealt with the terrified child hostages of the Remi.

"Well, young Valerius, what would your father do in this situation?"

Valerius looked at the people. Any animal sent to market tended to react in the same way.

"Move them over to the shade. Give them plenty of water. Give them something to eat. Dig a latrine trench."

"Alright," said the centurion. "Why not?"

"Don't bring the adults forward, bring the children. The cow will always follow the calf."

A little girl of about five was standing twenty yards away from them, sobbing noisily. She stood rooted to the spot when Valerius walked up to her. He unbuckled his helmet and popped it on her head, then swept her up into his arms. She was so surprised she stopped crying, and tilted back, trying to see what was on her head. She put both hands up to touch. She smiled when she realised what it was. Valerius smiled back at her.

"You look very nice in that hat," he told her. "Now where's

Mummy?"

"Mamma?" The girl's face crinkled and she started to cry again. It looked as though Mamma was lost.

Valerius carried her over to the table where Metius sat supervising his clerk, and explained. The sight of the girl seated on cushions, with the interpreters anxiously asking everyone of the whereabouts of her mother, did a lot to reassure the poor beasts about to be sold.

One of the Aeduans was brought into the hospital tent. An unusual occurrence, the Aeduans firmly of the belief - and with some justification - that Roman medicine was for the Romans and Aeduan medicine for Aeduans. The man had been injured and then fallen from his horse. His leg was swollen, discoloured, deformed and excruciatingly tender. The army surgeon made a cursory inspection, told Antinous to set up for an amputation, and went off for a drink while this was being done.

"My dear fellow, you did quite right to fetch me," Petronius said. "A leg is a leg, after all. Now if you would just enumerate the salient points to me."

He listened courteously while Antinous recounted the history and details of his examination. "Yes, yes, excellent. And you are of the opinion?"

"An abscess, Master. A deep abscess."

"And the site, Antinous?"

"Posterior to the gastrocnemius junction."

The Aeduan youth and his relatives were becoming exasperated by the procedure.

"Explain if you will, Antinous, that we are not yet all agreed on the correct procedure to be instituted."

Antinous explained, the young man becoming more voluble.

"Well, my boy?"

"He wishes you to know, Master, he did not seek our help in order to have his leg amputated. He's willing to submit to being

260

examined again. But he's not pleased."

"Of course not, poor fellow." Petronius smiled benignly at his victim. Then proceeded to inflict considerable pain, as he tested each muscle block.

The surgeon came back, a little bellicose. He looked at the table, and then at Antinous. "I told you to set up for an amputation, boy."

"Unfortunately, Ruteus, the patient doesn't consent to such a procedure."

"Oh, doesn't he?" said Ruteus. "And what does the patient know about such things?"

Ruteus walked over to stare down at the man's face, and shouted at him. "Your leg's black. It's rotting. If I take it off, you might live. If I don't, you'll be dead in a day or two."

"I'm not sure he understands you, Ruteus."

"No, probably not. Ignorant little bastards, aren't they?"

"I feel, myself, that the discolouration may be due to venous engorgement."

"What?"

"I feel it's a possibility. I wonder if, perhaps, we should try something more conservative."

"Something more conservative? By the great God Apollo!" Ruteus stared at him in disbelief. "Do you think I'm going to waste my time conserving a fucking Gaul! You can do it if you like. I'm off."

Petronius shook his head sorrowfully at the departing figure. "Surgeons, surgeons. A race apart I fear. If they see something bad they always wish to chop it off. Unlike us physicians, eh? Our role is to assist the healing process. At least he invoked the great God Apollo, Antinous, we must be grateful for that. Now, my boy, where would you make your incision? Yes, but if I were you, a little more laterally."

The following spring the Aeduan limped into the hospital block at Bibracte and presented Petronius with a little wooden box, filled with gold coinage.

"What is a leg worth?" he said through the interpreter. "More than this, I know. My thanks anyway."

Ruteus snorted in disgust.

The family were grouped round the harpist when Gaius came in, Octavian lying sprawled full length on the couch, Chrys sitting in a little wicker chair, feeding the baby.

"Darling!" Lady Volusena exclaimed. "How lovely to see you. Why didn't you let us know you were coming? Your room isn't prepared."

"It was a sudden impulse, Mother. I felt I just had to see you all. Is that my nephew?"

Chrys looked up with a smile of assent.

"Greedy bastard isn't he? Just like his dad. And what's this?" He took the instrument from the player's hands.

"A present from Dumnorix. He says he wishes the boy to grow up with some culture, which he feels he may not obtain from his paternal relatives. It's alright, Dad, I think he means Gaius."

"What an insult. I'm very cultured." Gaius handed the harp back with a bow. "Do I get to hold him?" The baby had finished feeding. "Who do you remind me of, now?" he said, gazing into the baby's face. "I know." He held the child alongside the bust of his grandfather. "Can you see the striking family resemblance?"

The baby was not impressed by this strange new man, who had plucked him from his mother's warm breast. He screwed his little face up, took a deep breath, let out a loud yell, and continued to sob with heart-rending choking sounds.

"Yes dear, everybody has already remarked on it," said Claudia above the noise. "Now give the baby back to Chrys."

"Here you are, Chrys," Gaius said, relieved. Chrys soon soothed the baby back to silence.

"He's very sweet," said Gaius. The baby did look very sweet now he was settled again. "So are you," Gaius added, kissing Chrys's cheek. "What's his name?"

"Octavian," said Octavian.

"Inspired," said Gaius.

Octavian had a whispered consultation with the harpist. Chrys looked up in astonishment as the familiar notes wafted in the air. Octavian started to sing. He sang to her alone, the beautiful Gallic love song that expressed his feelings immeasurably better than any of his feeble words. Chrys was entranced. She looked at her husband, and suddenly her eyes filled with tears.

"Oh, Octavian," she said.

Volusenus hadn't known how to react when Octavian told him he had married Chrys, and felt he no longer wished his father to continue with his attempts to betroth him to Marcius's sister Lucy.

"And what does your friend say?"

"He's not very pleased."

"You appreciate that this marriage has no validity."

"It has in Gaul, Sir."

"I'm afraid that hardly matters."

"Don't you think so, Sir? The estate she has brought as her dowry, brings me in four thousand gold pieces a year."

"Jupiter, Octavian, that's a lot of money."

"I'm well aware of it, Sir. A beautiful estate, too. In the lower Loire valley. Aeduan territory. There's a house and a lake. We could start a vineyard."

"What was this sudden impulse?" Octavian asked his brother, when he joined him in the bath house.

"A sudden impulse on the part of Chrys's friends and relatives to kick the Romans out of the high Alps. They succeeded too." He was silent for a moment. "Of course, we killed the hostages. The youngest couldn't have been more than eight. Valerius saw to him. Wouldn't let anyone else touch him."

Gaius turned to look steadily at his brother. "He got the boy onto his lap, and hid his sword in his cloak. Then he told the boy to look for the robin on the roof and, smooth as you please. Kid didn't make a sound."

Gaius disappeared under the water. He surfaced again and floated up to Octavian, water streaming out of his hair and down his face, which he dashed from his eyes with his fingers. "It was a close thing. They nearly had us that time."

"The Senate has awarded Caesar a public thanksgiving of fifteen days, to celebrate his conquest of Gaul," said Octavian.

"It makes you laugh, doesn't it?" replied Gaius.

BOOK 2: CHAPTER 11

Brittany, 56 BC

Caesar sent requisition officers to the Venetii and the other coastal tribes of North West Gaul, ostensibly to obtain corn supplies for the legions. Such a provocative move had the desired effect. The officers were seized and imprisoned by orders of the Venetian council. This was just the excuse Caesar was looking for, to make war. These tribes controlled the northern and western coasts, and thus all the trade routes with Britain. Caesar knew they would have to be completely subdued before he could make any preparations for his invasion of that watery island. He needed absolute mastery of the seas, which meant smashing the Venetii's huge fleet of ships, and preventing any aid reaching them from elsewhere along the coast, or from the lands on the other side of the Channel.

The ensuing naval battle under the command of Admiral Decimus Brutus against these rebellious Venetii and their allies, had been an enormous tactical success. Octavian sat with Caesar on the cliffs, watching while the more manoeuvrable Roman ships, manned by rowers, ripped through the enemy fleet like an Atlantic gale, tearing the enemy's sails to shreds with their grappling hooks. Then the Goddess Fortuna intervened. The wind dropped, the enemy's ships were becalmed, and the Romans were able to pick them off, one by one. Very few escaped.

The entire native population of these maritime tribes had then been sold, and all their councillors executed, to punish them for their temerity in seizing Caesar's requisition officers. How dare they object to feeding his legions!

After the naval battle Octavian had gone to the harbour with Caesar, to inspect the captured enemy ships. He had been ordered to find out all he could about Britain. A difficult task as he could understand nothing whatsoever that these men of Brittany said. Their language was quite different from that of

Southern Gaul, which he had so painstakingly learned to speak fluently.

Octavian returned to his tent, wishing he was back once more with his Aeduan friends. It was pleasant to be able to dip into a different world. A small group of legionaries was standing in front of his tent. He hurried up to find out what was going on. There were two prisoners kneeling chained on the ground, blond youths with sulky blue eyes and delicate bronze skin. They were identical.

"A present from Marcus Metius, Sir," the legionary informed him. "He didn't want to break the set," he grinned.

Jupiter, they must be worth a fortune, thought Octavian. "Why me?" he enquired.

"No, Sir, not just you. Each officer has been given a couple of good 'uns. I expect he thinks it's good for business."

"Well, you'd better rig up a post in front of the tent. They'll need to be fastened to something."

Octavian sat on the bed and ordered his slave to get him a drink. He had to shout. The man was so inattentive, perpetually lost in a dream world.

"Now get these boots off."

How was he going to find out about Britain? From these new slaves? It was the language problem again, he mused. He put his feet up on the bed, and leant back against the cushions. Marcius must have found it hard to start with, suddenly being plunged into an environment where everyone spoke the wrong language. Fortunate for him his master spoke such good Latin, fortunate for him that he had a good master. Octavian walked out of the tent and stood bare-footed in the sand.

"What do you think you're doing?" he said to the legionary struggling with the pole.

The man stood up, puzzled.

"Get the chains off these two, man, and hurry up. Then bring them in to me." Octavian walked back into the tent and yelled to his slave. "You'd better get a couple of mattresses brought in and put over at the back. Get sheets and blankets and make the beds up and bring me a tray, two mugs of wine, bread, meat, fruit, whatever. Hurry up."

The legionaries heard the shouting, and looked at each other uneasily.

"I thought he said we was to ..?"

"Yeh he did."

"And now we're to.. ?"

"Yeh we are."

"Fucking officers," said the other, spitting on the ground.

Octavian looked at their eyes again when they were led in. They weren't sulking. They were miserable, defeated, exhausted. They were much younger too, than he had thought initially.

He was awoken in the night by the sound of someone sobbing, which confused him to start with, until he remembered the prisoners. At first he couldn't see what was wrong. The youngster was curled defensively away from him. Then the brother pressed his hand against his chest, and gestured. A wound, drat. He wasn't making a very good job of these two. He wished his servant wasn't quite so dim. The man was awake now, so he sent him over to the hospital to see if he could get any assistance. Yes, there was a medical orderly.

Antinous put aside his book when they came in. "May I have his name, Sir, for the report?" he asked.

"I'm afraid I've been busy." Octavian felt a little guilty. "I haven't had time to find an interpreter." He listened, surprised, as Antinous started asking the boy about his name and questioned him about his condition.

"You speak their language," he said, pleased.

"Yes, Sir. It's similar to that of South Britain. This one is called Drustan."

Octavian was on the alert. How strange that a Greek physician would know the language of South Britain. He must

267

remember to question this man some other time.

"Do you wish to stay, Sir?" The man's tone was neutral, but Octavian realised how odd it must seem for a tribune to be bothering about his slaves in the middle of the night.

"I think I'd better," he said. "This will all be quite foreign to them, don't you think?"

"Yes, no doubt." The man spoke absently. He wasn't, after all, interested in Octavian, his attention was entirely for the prisoner.

There was an interruption. A little man appeared, rubbing the sleep out of his eyes.

"Do you need any assistance, Sir?" he asked the orderly. But the orderly just waved his hand in dismissal.

"Go back to bed, Pius. You have done far too much work today, already."

"What about the notes, Sir? You can dictate if you wish. You haven't had any sleep yourself."

"I can manage the notes perfectly well, so do as you're told, Pius. I don't need you just now."

"Very good, Sir." The little man bowed low to the orderly, and departed.

Octavian settled down - good to watch an expert at work, whether it was a metal-worker, horse-trainer, soldier or physician. He liked to see the exercise of skill. The orderly picked up the patient's wrist and questioned him quietly. The boy uncurled and straightened up like a snail emerging from its shell, the tension in the muscles relaxing. The orderly stripped the boy, and began his examination, which started at the head and ended at the feet, not forgetting the back.

"Even Venetians run away," said the orderly, with a faint smile. Then he wrapped his patient up in blankets again.

"He has three wounds," explained Antinous. "The worst one skating up the chest wall - a spear I should think. Quite a bad one in the groin, and a slight one along the front of the thigh. I can put a dressing on tonight and give him something for the pain, and treat him properly in the morning, when the light's good. He can stay here if you like."

"What does he think about that?" Octavian asked.

Antinous found out. "That's acceptable to him." He prepared the dressings, then he began to clean the wounds. It was painful.

Drustan turned his head to look at Octavian, and held his hand out to him in a wordless appeal. He looked so young, and so pathetic. Octavian grasped the hand in his own, prompted to speak, even though he didn't know the right words.

"It's alright," he said gently. "You will be alright with me, Drustan. Don't worry. There's nothing to worry about. I will take care of you both."

The boy gripped Octavian's hand tightly, and pressed it to his cheek. His eyes filled with tears. Octavian stroked the blond curls.

"Poor kid," Octavian remarked to the orderly. "Can you find out how old they are?"

They were thirteen years old, Antinous informed him. And did they fight? Octavian wanted to know. Yes, they were on one of the ships. They had fought in the sea battle, though they were so young. Their father was one of the executed Council members. This caused more tears to flow.

Octavian had the beginnings of an idea. Antinous finished with Drustan.

"I'll take a look at the other one now," he said.

"But there isn't anything wrong with him," protested Octavian. "Well I don't think so."

"I'll take a look at him," said Antinous.

The orderly was right. This one was hurt as well. Octavian found out that he was called Ninian.

"I wonder, if you can speak their language, would you ask them which type of slavery they choose?" Octavian said.

The orderly discovered they wished for dedication.

"Will you tell them, then, that I am greatly honoured by

their decision, and I will arrange it as soon as possible."

After Octavian had gone, Antinous sat looking at the fire, picking at his mind. How did he know about South Britain? What did he know about South Britain for that matter? He knew a lot about himself now. He knew his house, he knew his family, he thought he knew their names. He was sure he wasn't Greek. He thought he saw his father on a horse in great crowds of people, but still the key was missing. He could not find where he had hidden the key, yet it was a place so familiar.

One month later Octavian asked Petronius if he might hire Antinous to act as interpreter at the ceremony. The twins were solemn. They stood silently by the altar while the priest kindled the flames, poured the oil into the bowl, added the leaves of oak and mistletoe and then lit the oil. The flame flickered briefly. Antinous smelt the familiar scent. The priest lifted his arms and invoked the spirits of the earth. Two worlds fused, coalesced.

"Alright?" Octavian turned to the young man by his side, who looked as if he was swaying, a little off balance.

"An earth tremor."

Octavian hadn't noticed. He looked around. Powerful Gods here. I hope I get this right, he thought. There had been nobody's advice to ask on the subject. Marcius had no idea of the details. He had never witnessed this particular ceremony. And Octavian was too nervous to ask Guéreth, in case he was thought to be meddling in things which were of no proper concern for a Roman. He didn't relish the thought of being snubbed by the Gaul. The priest spoke again.

"Step forward, and give your name," Allaine directed.

Octavian obeyed. Allaine proceeded to guide him through the entire ceremony without mishap. It wasn't until much later, that Octavian found it at all strange.

BOOK 2: CHAPTER 12

Normandy Coast and Sea Channel, 54 BC

Octavian looked forward to the sea-crossing with increasing dread. The memory of last year's journey came back to him more vividly the more he thought about it, when he had spent both trips lying on the deck, retching. Gloomily he wondered what Caesar would do, after he had conquered and sold or massacred all the inhabitants of Britain. There was rumoured to be another large island off the west coast of the country, perhaps involving an even longer sea-voyage. And with weather apparently even worse, if that were possible.

He got no sympathy from his brother, who appeared these days to be perpetually hostile. Gaius had been ordered to survey the coasts last year before the first expedition, and had spent many days bobbing uncomfortably up and down in the Channel, while the surveyors investigated the possibilities of each harbour. Octavian knew also that his brother was sick to death of entertaining Commius, one of Caesar's protégés, who had been installed as a tribal leader. The man was always smiling, you couldn't tell what his thoughts were at all. Caesar seemed adept at finding the most nauseating, sycophantic council leader of each tribe, and installing them as king with his backing, at total variance with the Gauls' usual democratic procedures.

Jay was playing the harp in Caesar's tent when Gaius came in to make his report, but was asked to go on playing. When Gaius had left, Jay played and sang a sweet sad song.

"That was beautiful, Jay."

"It is the lament for your daughter, Julia. And this is for your grandson."

When he had finished, Jay knelt in front of Caesar and kissed his hand. "I've brought you a present."

"Have you, Jay?"

"It's small, not like a horse. Look."

"What is it?"

"It's called 'enamel.'" Jay put the ring in Caesar's hand, and closed his palm over it. "This ring comes from a grove, a very sacred holy grove, on a holy island. It has been blessed for you."

Caesar could see unshed tears in Jay's eyes. "You must wear this ring when you love your wife, and she will bear you sons."

Caesar pushed the hair back from Jay's high wide forehead, and held his face in his hands. "I would like a son like you."

"I'm a very bad son." Jay looked grave. "I do not obey my father's orders." He kissed Caesar's hands again, and got up to go.

Jay stormed into his father's tent with a face like thunder.

"Well, Jayven?" Diviciacus asked anxiously.

"Sire, there must have been an informer at our council meeting."

"That's bad, Jay, very bad."

"It has got back to Caesar that Dumnorix informed us all about Caesar's machinations, that Caesar had vowed to make him king, instead of you, to have an excuse to kill him. Caesar says he'll deal with him in Britain. Father, he has Eloise and the children. They are under house arrest." Jay stopped. His father looked so ill. He couldn't continue, just sat gripping his hands.

"He says he'll deal with you in Britain. He claims you are plotting to be king."

Dumnorix took his brother's hand. "My dear lord, he can deal with any of us anytime he wants to."

Diviciacus looked at him helplessly. "I know that. Of course I know that. What choice have we ever had, Dumnorix? I ask you, what choice? The country exhausted itself with the fight against the Germans. Look how many thousands of men we lost. Thousands upon thousands of dead young men. To what purpose? Can we be blamed for not wishing to destroy ourselves by taking on yet another powerful enemy?"

"He's worse than the Germans," said Dumnorix. "More systematic. Somehow that makes it worse."

Diviciacus pressed his shoulder. "You must go to him. Tell him you get seasick, tell him you have to stay here because of important religious rites."

"I can't see that being very effective somehow, but I will do as you say. I wonder if he intends to deal with all of us in Britain. How can anyone trust a man who seizes the German ambassadors? Even some in the Senate said he should be disowned."

"Brother, I may order you to flee the country."

"Sire, I don't wish to risk my children's lives. You know he watches every move I make."

"I'll find a way, Dumnorix, I must find a way."

Dumnorix sighed. "We failed our people, brother. We don't lack courage, we lack discipline, strategy. We need a leader, but it won't be me."

Six hundred ships had been built the preceding winter and were now assembled ready for the second invasion of Britain. But embarkation had to be delayed for a month because of the wind and the weather. The tribal chiefs became increasingly restless and edgy, as Dumnorix told them quite openly that they would all be slaughtered in Britain. They discovered they weren't allowed out of the camp perimeter. Not even to hunt. They were beginning to feel like trapped animals.

They were half way through embarkation, when the informer gave Caesar the message he had been waiting for. Dumnorix and some other Aeduan nobles had left the camp seeking to escape under the cover of general confusion. Caesar sent for Gaius Volusenus and instructed him to order the Aeduans to return immediately.

"If he resists," he said to Gaius, "kill him."

Dumnorix was waiting for them only five miles out of

camp. Jay was next to him. Gaius rode up to him and saluted.

"Sir, Caesar orders you to return to camp immediately."

"Tribune, I am a free citizen, living in a free country. I will obey no such order."

"Sir, I have orders to bring you back."

"I am a free citizen, living in a free country. I prefer to die on Gallic soil."

"Sir!" Gaius was desperate. "If you don't come with me, I have orders to kill you."

"Gaius, you are very stupid this morning." Dumnorix shook his head sadly and unsheathed his sword, holding it up. "I am a free citizen in a free country," he shouted and urged his horse forward.

Gaius threw himself sideways, knocked Jay off his horse, and they hit the ground together. It was the last thing Jay expected. Gaius succeeded in doubling his arms behind his back, and knelt on top of him, pressing his head into the ground until all the shouts had ceased.

"It's done, Sir," one of the men reported.

Gaius wouldn't let Jay up until his wrists had been tied behind his back, then he pulled him into a kneeling position, and brushed the dirt from his face.

"I can't take any chances with you," he said. But Jay was expressionless, looking beyond him through the horse's legs to his uncle's dead body, a spear shaft emerging obscenely from his chest.

Jay was hauled to his feet, but he pushed past the horses to stand by his uncle's side. Dumnorix lay on his back, his eyes wide open, his face unmarked. The torrent of blood gushing from his wounds had subsided, leaving only a trickle still dripping into the dark pool spread beneath his body.

Jay fainted.

BOOK 2 : CHAPTER 13

Normandy Coast, Sea Channel 54 BC

Labienus had taken the news that he was to stay behind with three legions, while the rest of them went swanning around Britain, rather badly. The first reports from Caesar were now coming back. Labienus stared at Octavian in pretended disbelief.

"What do you mean he wants me to build more boats? He's got six hundred already."

"Yes, Sir." Octavian was weary. He didn't feel like playing games. "Unfortunately, some of them were smashed in a gale."

"Why was that?"

"Well, Sir, you see it was because of the tide. And the wind," Octavian added as an afterthought.

Labienus decided his opponent wasn't worth playing. "Octavian?"

"Sir."

"You're ill. Go and see a doctor."

In the hospital block Petronius was conducting a post-mortem.

"You see, Antinous, as we suspected, the pleural cavity is filled with purulent fluid. Now, Antinous, does anything suggest itself to you that possibly could have been done to prevent our patient's death? Hypothetical, Antinous, I am merely being hypothetical."

Allaine smiled his usual faint smile. It was, after all, one of his master's pet theories.

"It does occur to me, Master, that if there were a method of effecting the drainage of this pus, it might have the same beneficial effects as draining an abscess elsewhere in the body."

"Antinous, do you know I believe you have something there," said Petronius. "I have found myself thinking along the same lines. Interesting that we should be in agreement. I think I will consult the engineers, and see if they can effect some kind of device that might render our theory a practicable one. Don't you agree, my dear fellow?"

"Yes, Master. I agree."

Petronius noticed Octavian. "Well Tribune, what can we do for you? You are looking a little green. You are ....?"

"Octavian Volusenus, Sir."

Octavian noticed Antinous looking at him. "You were good enough to help me with the twins."

Allaine nodded in remembrance.

Petronius was baffled. "The twins?"

"I left them in Britain. I have to go back, you see." He'd found the twins' amusement at his sea sickness a little hard to stomach. "My general has ordered me to report to you, Sir. He says I am ill."

Despite a thorough examination, Petronius could find nothing physically wrong. "I see you are in mourning," he said.

"Yes," Octavian agreed. He had sung the lament at the funeral.

"Well, well. Some lowness of spirits is perhaps to be expected. Physically you are a fine, healthy specimen."

"I don't suppose you have a cure for sea-sickness, do you?" asked Octavian in despair. It seemed so trivial.

"My dear fellow," Petronius said, "physicians have a cure for everything. Even melancholia. I will have Antinous bring it round to your tent. And hot bricks applied to the stomach under these circumstances can be most efficacious."

Octavian wasn't sure it would be easy to obtain hot bricks. Memories of the ship came flooding back. The cold sea breaking over the deck. Everything had been soaked.

"We would have the bricks heated before you go, and then stored in a chest lined with hay," Allaine put in. "I will have one made for you."

"Antinous, my dear boy, you know everything," said his master.

"I know how to keep warm, Master."

Petronius turned to Octavian with a smile. "He studies so hard I have to order him to stop. He overtakes his old master in knowledge, I fear."

Allaine shook his head at this. Petronius became confidential.

"His excellent results sadly annoy our surgical colleagues. Well, good fortune to you, Tribune. Let us know how you fare."

Allaine lay in bed at night. He imagined himself walking towards a tent. He paused at the threshold. He would have to force himself to go inside. The centurion was looming over him. "And that sister of yours, the red-head. Caesar has given her as a present to Tribune Octavian Volusenus. He should have some fun with her, eh?"

Allaine withdrew his mind from the tent rapidly. The emotion seized him so powerfully, he gripped the mattress in his hands and groaned. He would need to control it somehow, to pin it down. He had to wrap up the emotion in some bundle so he could carry on.

Revenge! The word acted like a balm, soothing him, letting his fingers relax. He would have to think of revenge. Formulate some plans. Imagine putting them into execution, even. That was better. He could breathe now. He would need to think of revenge, not just on the tribune, but on the whole lot of them. Every Roman. He thought about Petronius, and the love he had for the man. Now he would need to build a wall. Petronius on one side, the rest on the other. Mentally he started, brick by brick. He knew he wasn't quite sane, not quite rational. He knew he had to find some method to carry on living, impelled to follow his destiny. He thought of his work, the satisfaction of cutting into Roman flesh, the internal thrill of pleasure at watching the Romans suffer pain. Their agony helped to heal his. One day he would make one of them suffer so much, that he himself would become whole again.

Rome 54 BC

One of the servants came to tell Ursula that her husband had been found dead in his bed. She wasn't surprised. Nor were they. His condition had been getting so much worse. His ravings had become incoherent, his outbreaks of temper so violent that the magistrate, whom Volusenus had consulted on her behalf, had had no problem in appointing him curator furioso.

She told Andreas first, and then went in to wake Lucy, although they had discussed the matter many times. Lucy was awake when she entered her room. Hardly surprising, the servants were weeping and wailing, putting on quite a performance. She couldn't imagine any of them had much to regret at her husband's passing, and some of them would, no doubt, be freed in his will, if there were any money left after the debts had been repaid, which she doubted.

She looked at her pretty brown-haired, brown-eyed daughter and cursed Octavian and the red-haired barbarian who had ruined her plans. Would the boy ever come to his senses - she thought wearily. There were two babies now. Why could he not just keep the woman as his concubine, and be done with it. Lady Ursula had disliked Chrys intensely as soon as she had first caught sight of her, with her strange grey eyes and exotic coloured hair. What a wife for a Roman - the boy had gone native. She couldn't imagine how his father had allowed himself to be persuaded by Caesar that Octavian must stay on another three years in the army. The whole of Rome was agog to know the reason. It seemed unlikely to be Octavian's military prowess. Tongues wagged.

Lucy was quite sensible, she knew. She had taken the news of Octavian's defection with equanimity, superficially at least, though if her mother only knew, underneath she was heartbroken. She had loved Octavian with the love of a little girl towards an admired big brother. One who took no notice of her at all, barely acknowledging her existence. Which made it all the more important she try to win his affection - gain his favour, his attention. She succeeded occasionally, when he yelled at her to clear off, and she would skip away knowing she had been noticed at least.

Later on, when the betrothal had been announced, he had once or twice brought her presents, bought, no doubt, by his mother. But he had to give them to her. Even stay and talk to her for a little while, running rapidly out of conversation, as Lucy didn't know very much about the attributes of the gladiators in the arena, never having been permitted to see them. Or which chariot team she favoured, never having been to see them either. No, she wasn't allowed to read much poetry, her stepfather disapproved of most of it. And really, she thought, there was very little one could talk about with weaving and embroidery. So Octavian didn't stay very long. Now of course, she could converse on many different subjects. She had learnt a great deal in the past few years, under her mother's guidance. And Sperinus had left her alone at last, no longer capable of inflicting the secret torments on her body.

"I have sent for Titus Volusenus," Ursula told Lucy. "He will help us, as usual." However, everything may turn out for the best, thought Ursula. Life could hardly get worse than the last few years experience.

"Now, my dear, there's no need to feel sad. We will take the course we have all decided upon. We will join my brother in the province, where he will make us very comfortable, I know." Indeed she was longing to go to him, to be pampered. Only too thankful that he showed no desire, as far as she could ascertain, to marry her off to anyone else. She also felt the sooner she left Rome the better, in case her husband's relatives should make any objections. She was sure his disgusting male cousin had selected Lucy as a prospective bride for himself. She had terrifying thoughts about Lucy and Sperinus, but banished them from her mind. Impossible to believe. If she succeeded in disbelief, the problem would disappear.

Although Andreas had deferred his spell in the army, to be

with his mother, Caesar and his legions would be conveniently close when the time came for him to enlist. Should she tell Lucy about the marriage which Metius had arranged with the parents of one of the young officers in the Fourteenth Legion, Hugo Domitius, a friend of Octavian's unfortunately, but no doubt they could take steps to avoid him. No. She would leave it. Let her brother break the news. She didn't think Lucy would cause any fuss, but she couldn't face any more emotion at present.

Lucy wandered round the house, trying to work out what to take, and what to leave behind. She was glad to be going, she harboured a faint hope she might see Octavian in Gaul. And then perhaps he would notice her, see how much she'd changed. She didn't think she would stand any chance if Chrys was around, but with Chrys left behind in Rome, and Octavian lonely, maybe, wanting a nice intelligent sympathetic girl to talk things over with, who knows what might happen. She would miss Titus and Claudia a lot. Actually, to be totally honest, she would miss Chrys and the children. Chrys was clever, and was often able to explain things to Lucy. Especially politics. Chrys knew more about Roman politics than Ursula, or Andreas. Sometimes, Lucy thought, she knew more than Titus. And Lucy loved the children. She adored the children, they were so sweet. Octavian Junior was an affectionate clever little boy. She wondered whether she would ever have any children of her own. Not the way things were going. Sperinus had always been careful to withdraw, or abuse her in other ways. She felt hot with shame when she thought about it. At least she hadn't got pregnant. What would he have done with her? Killed her, presumably, as he had constantly threatened to do.

The two families had seen a lot of each other, once Sperinus had been confined due to his insanity. Indeed, Titus had offered to engage her to any of his other sons, none of whom showed any inclination to get married, to Claudia's disgust. But Lucy didn't know any of the others, and the idea of being

Octavian's sister-in-law was anything but enticing, so she had turned him down. She would have liked to travel north straight away, but Titus advised them to leave it till the spring, when the roads would be good, with less chance of bad weather holding them up.

One of the household servants arrived to ask her to join the others in the salon.

Titus rose from the table, walked over, and gave her a kiss. He thought she was looking remarkably pretty these days, once she no longer had to worry about her mother's treatment at her stepfather's hands. He turned to Andreas, and Lady Ursula.

"Now, Andreas," he started, "with Marcius away, you are acting head of the house, so you have to make the decisions."

"Yes, Sir. Of course." Andreas smiled his agreement, and sat up, trying to look properly decisive.

Titus then proceeded to make all the decisions for him.

"Although your stepfather hasn't managed to deplete his money any further for a while, there still remain considerable debts. I'm afraid even after your estates are sold, most of the household slaves will need to be sold as well, to leave you anything like enough to maintain this house. Half the proceeds will have to go to Sperinus's own son."

Ursula interrupted. They had all agreed.

"We will travel north, to Gaul, to my brother, Marcus Metius."

"Frankly, I'll be glad to see the back of most of the slaves," Andreas added. "They betrayed us often enough."

In the end they agreed to take the steward, and their own personal servants. The rest Titus arranged to be sold via a high class dealer. He thought a Senator's slaves, being thoroughly domesticated, would fetch a fair bit of money for the Carvilius family. He was sad to think he would lose their company. He thought Chrys liked it when Lucy and Ursula visited.

BOOK 2 : CHAPTER 14

Normandy Coast, Sea Channel 54 BC

Octavian fared very badly. He put to sea with the replacement fleet, but a gale sprang up almost immediately, and they could make no headway at all. He had a nightmare voyage. After twelve hours even his hot bricks were stone cold. Despite his plea, that he had no objection whatsoever to drowning, having tried it before, the captain wrapped him in a leather tarpaulin and attached him firmly to his bed, and his bed even more securely to the small cabin inside the bulkhead. The ship was being tossed about as if it were a plaything of the Gods. They had lost part of the rudder and all of the rigging. The horses in the hold were terrified, resulting in splintered bones and lacerated flesh, as they tried to free themselves from tack and stall. Their screams did nothing to soothe the fears of the men on board, even though they were experienced, having been picked from the Brittany coast.

This was a gale and a half. There was some suggestion amongst the crew, that the tribune might be sacrificed to appease the Gods. Then they remembered what had happened when they had harmed Roman officers before, merely imprisoning them. So they sacrificed the cabin boy instead, which had the desired effect, but which horrified Octavian when he found out later. He had assumed all Gauls were as civilised as his Aeduan friends. He would have to think about the twins a little more carefully in future.

They made landfall thirty miles down the coast. When Octavian returned to headquarters, he informed Labienus, that if ordered to put to sea again he would kill himself, which made his commander laugh. He sent for the twins to be brought back from Britain. Then went to off to report to his physician. The hot bricks had certainly helped when they were hot, but he couldn't imagine any medicine had been left in his body. He thought half the Channel was filled with his stomach contents.

He was upset to discover Petronius had caught a fever and died while he was away. Antinous, his slave, had been accused of using unorthodox treatment on his master's body, and had been flogged and sold accordingly. Octavian went off to see the slave-dealer, who was holding out for a fortune, despite the fact no-one was sure, at the present time, whether the man would survive the scourging. Apparently the surgeon Ruteus had performed it himself, having been so grief-stricken at Petronius's death.

Octavian returned to the hospital quarters, and walked over to the semi-conscious figure of Antinous, still delirious with fever. The slave was lying on his stomach on the clerk's bed, with his feet dangling over the end. His back was a dreadful mess of cuts, bruises, and torn flesh. Octavian picked up his hand. It was hot and dry.

"Are they saying he caused his master's death?" Octavian demanded.

The little medical clerk was heartbroken. He loved and admired Antinous so much. A man who was always unfailingly kind and courteous to him. And he thought Antinous's medical skills were astonishing. He was doing his best to nurse him, but he was only a lowly clerk. The slave dealer didn't appear to be that bothered.

"He carried out Antistius Petronius's orders exactly, Sir. I know, I was there. But the surgeons felt he should be made an example of. Ruteus said there was no way he would sanction such a dangerous medical experiment. The surgeons have always been jealous of him, Sir. His results are so much better than theirs."

There was no way Octavian could afford the price asked. Anyway, he had no use for a physician of his own.

"It doesn't seem fair that the man should be punished for obeying his master's orders," he said, thinking out loud. "But the dealer wants a small fortune for him. Where am I going to find someone with that sort of money?"

Allaine opened his eyes, and said, "Guéreth."

Octavian went off to see Guéreth.

"You could buy him yourself," Guéreth pointed out, "as you are joint trustee with Diviciacus of Dumnorix's children."

Octavian said he didn't think he should take any decisions by himself on such an expensive matter.

"Why don't you buy him for your own use?" Guéreth suggested.

Octavian told him. A report had come in. His twins had disappeared in Britain, together with a quantity of baggage. He would need to buy a couple of servants, and he wasn't going to have another dimwit like his present one. He had found the news about the twins deeply upsetting. He had been so sure they wouldn't run away.

"They will have been captured, Octavian. They would never break their oath, never. If they did, their own souls would be in danger. Alright, I'll buy your physician. I've arranged for my sister Riona to marry Tarleton of the Remi. I'm going back to fetch her just now, if you wish to accompany me. The physician will do as a gift to her husband. You'll be able to see your wards again."

Aeduan Territory

Riona came secretly at night to bid goodbye to her friend. They clung together, weeping. Both had lost the love of their lives. Riona had sunk in despair after discovering from Octavian that Allaine had died in prison. Eloise was shattered almost to pieces by the death of her husband, murdered on Caesar's orders. The girls' friendship with each other had helped to sustain them in their terrible grief, and united them in their love of Dumnorix's children. Now they were to be parted for ever. Riona was to be taken to be married to a man she had never seen in her life. And didn't wish to, either. She had no desire to see him at all, having heard he was old, fat, and lecherous, and had gone through two wives already.

Eloise was to try to get home to Switzerland, to safety, away from Caesar, with his assassins' swords and spears.

"You know, Riona, I have to make this last attempt for the boys' sake. But I'm so scared," whispered Eloise.

"May the Gods protect you, and keep you safe, my dearest friend. Good fortune, Eloise. You deserve it."

They kissed each other, and said their last farewells, knowing they would never see each other again. Riona prayed desperately to the Gods. No one else was bothering to help her darling Eloise. The priest she approached refused to say the prayers for protection. Too scared, the miserable coward.

Ridiculously Eloise found she was holding her breath, as if it would make any difference. She had told the boys they were playing a game, they were an invading army, marching at night to take the enemy's camp. The wagon and driver had been equipped and provided by Metius. She didn't trust him. But then, she didn't trust anybody. She knew as soon as Caesar returned from Britain, her children would be taken from her and killed. She would take this one chance for the sake of their father. And if things didn't turn out? Well, she would be happy to join him. She missed him desperately. The thought of never seeing his laughing face again, feeling his arms around her, pulling her close, loving her. She mustn't think like that. She must be strong for the sake of the boys.

The hooves of the mules were dulled with leather horseshoes, but even so, the creaks of the wagon seemed to shriek their presence to the world. She didn't find her terror begin to subside, until they were miles from the town. She had to travel solitarily. No chance of military protection. No chance of any protection from anyone.

They made good progress. To her surprise, Metius met them at the next village.

"I came to wish you good fortune," he said. "And I cannot allow my friend's children to travel on such a long journey without my protection. I believe we've given Caesar's agents the slip, my dear. I shall install a mother and two boys in your house to allay suspicions. You will travel with my wagons as far as Geneva, when my men will then escort you to Aventicum."

"You're very good, Sir." But she wished he didn't have such a loud voice. She was terrified a spy would overhear, and report back to Caesar.

As if he had read her thoughts, Metius dropped his voice to a whisper. "No, I'm not," said Metius. "That, I'm afraid, is my trouble. I fear that I'm usually very bad, so when I have the chance of doing some good for my friends I seize it. I was very fond of your husband, you know. There now," he said, as Eloise broke down. "There now." He blessed them all, and had a heavy chest installed under one of the wagon seats. Then he kissed her goodbye and the boys, and told them they'd best be on their way.

The wagon was half-way up the steep mountain road, stopped on the corner to rest the mules, when the horsemen caught up with it. The driver got down silently, and cut through the traces. The horsemen began to rock the wagon from side to side, ignoring the sounds from within, and finally heaved it over the edge where it bounced and crashed, smashing into the valley far below, a thousand feet down, stampeding the mountain sheep. The men didn't bother to look over the edge. There was no point. Nothing could have survived. They remounted their horses and rode back swiftly down the steep hill. Back to barracks.

BOOK 2 : CHAPTER 15

Atuatuca, East Belgium, Winter 54 BC

Allaine was seized with a furious jealousy when he was told where his new master had gone. Tarleton! That traitorous bastard! His girl to be married to that ape! With his anger came awareness that there was nothing he could do about it. Nothing whatsoever. Apparently he was to be given as a gift to this Tarleton. But he could plan. Various poisons came to mind. Poisons causing painful death. He enjoyed conjuring up images of Riona and her husband, dying in unspeakable agony, preferably on their wedding night. Of course, he would be suspected immediately, and would no doubt have to kill himself. But that thought no longer bothered him. It was inevitable.

The physician seemed to be unlikely to make a good companion while Guéreth and Octavian were away, Marcius thought. Antinous was in a perpetually foul mood, making no attempt to be friendly, quite the reverse. When Marcius attempted to be sympathetic, he was met with vicious sarcasm. The man ordered that his back be scrubbed with a cloth soaked in vinegar, then dressed with bandages treated with castoreum.

"Won't that be a bit painful?" asked Marcius, dubiously.

"As it won't be you that suffers, I can't imagine how it can be of concern," Allaine replied.

Thus Marcius was very relieved when they were eventually joined by Octavian. They were to pack up and go with Generals Sabinus and Cotta and the Fourteenth Legion, into winter quarters in Belgium, in Eburone territory. Guéreth would join them there with his sister, because Octavian was invited to the wedding. Marcius thought his friend seemed a bit subdued. Perhaps he was feeling miserable about Dumnorix again, having just visited his wife and children. He thought he'd better try and cheer him up.

"Are you looking forward to the wedding, Octavian? Lady Riona is such a lovely girl. I hope this Tarleton will make her a good husband."

Allaine stopped reading.

"She doesn't seem very happy to me," Octavian replied.

"Well, the gossip is that she lost her heart to some Helvetian prince, years ago, and has been stalling on the question of marriage ever since. I think my master decided to force the issue."

"Oh," said Octavian, showing no interest.

"Well, what do you think? Is your Chrys still more beautiful than her sister?" Marcius tried teasing his friend. "How were the boys?"

Octavian was silent.

"Octavian? What's the matter? Is anything wrong?"

"They're dead," Octavian replied flatly.

Antinous caused a diversion at this juncture, by dropping the book he was holding, which unrolled on the floor of the tent. Marcius and Octavian moved swiftly to roll it up. Marcius presented it to Antinous, but received no word of thanks. He turned back to Octavian.

"What do you mean, dead?" Marcius was shocked. He had often seen Eloise and her boys, frequent visitors to Guéreth's house, along with their father, Dumnorix.

"Caesar had them under house arrest. They escaped in the night, one night. So he sent the cavalry after them. No one would tell me exactly what happened, but there is a rumour their wagon was pushed over a cliff. Anyway I have been assured they are dead."

"What does my master think about that?" Marcius asked anxiously.

Octavian shrugged. "What's there to think? There's nothing he can do about it. Nothing I can do about it either. Just get on with things, I suppose." He noticed Antinous sitting staring at him. He thought the man looked a bit pale, still recovering from the scourging, he surmised.

"Perhaps you should go to bed, Antinous. You don't appear to be fully recovered yet."

"I think I might be a better judge of that than you," Allaine replied.

The legion was met at the border by the two chiefs of the Eburones, Ambiorix and Catuvolcus. They had brought as much corn as they could, the chief explained, but the harvest had been very poor, as the generals knew, because of the drought, and because, they forbore to mention, they had had so many men killed in the fighting, the amount of land ploughed and tilled was greatly diminished. The entire country was on the brink of starvation.

Ambiorix looked from the face of one general to the other.

"Jupiter," said Sabinus wearily to Cotta. "Am I sick of whining, fucking Gauls!"

Unfortunately the interpreter translated this before anyone thought to stop him. Octavian saw Ambiorix turn his head quickly away from the Roman generals, as if he'd been struck a blow.

"Tell him he'll supply us, or he'll have to answer for the consequences," Sabinus instructed the interpreter.

Ambiorix gravely apologised for the poor quality of his hospitality. He said he would do his best to make their stay a memorable one.

Within two weeks they had the camp properly fortified. What corn they had been given had been installed in wooden barns. The legionaries set about protecting the tents from the winter weather by building shelters of wood and thatch.

Octavian was a little worried about Antinous. He felt partly responsible for his present circumstances.

"He doesn't appear to relish the thought of being given to Tarleton," he complained to Marcius. "He has a very low opinion of him." Antinous's comments on his future master had been quite scathing.

"He has a low opinion of everyone. I was wondering why you had to palm him off on me," Marcius grumbled. "He speaks to me as if I'm a half-wit."

"He has a point," Octavian interrupted.

"Below the belt, Tribune," Marcius countered. "I'll get you for that when we start training again."

Octavian grinned, he was beginning to catch his friend up again.

"He's sarcastic, bad-tempered and vicious," said Marcius, though, of course, the man had done nothing. Well, anyway, not exactly been good company.

"I think he was very fond of his master," said Octavian. "He must be angry at the way things have turned out, being punished for obedience." Although, come to think of it, he didn't know if Antinous was fond of his master, merely that his master was very fond of Antinous. He didn't remember the slave showing any emotion at all.

Allaine told Octavian he was going out with the foraging party. Octavian had been doing his best to be civil to the man, and had so far refrained from losing his temper.

Octavian tried to be placatory. "There's no need at all for you to undertake such tasks, Antinous," he said. "Leave that sort of thing to the camp servants."

Allaine looked at him with contempt. "If I don't take the opportunity to collect the herbs growing locally, before the onset of winter," he explained, as if to a child, "I shall be reduced to treating my patients with grass."

"What about the camp apothecary?" asked Octavian.

"What about him?"

"Can't you obtain remedies from him?"

"I doubt if he'll hand them over free of charge," said Allaine, "and I have no money."

"And your instruments?" said Octavian.

"Nothing."

"Oh. Well I'm sorry about that," said Octavian. "I will see what I can do."

"How kind," said Allaine. "In the meantime I will go out with the foraging party."

The ambush came quite unexpectedly. Outriders appeared at the camp gates, announcing the imminent arrival of Guéreth and his sister. The gates were opened in readiness. As the cavalcade approached they came under attack. They were rapidly surrounded by enemy soldiers. Guéreth's horse received a spear wound, rearing up in terror, unseating Guéreth, who fell heavily to the ground. The Roman cavalry managed to mount a quick charge and scatter some of the enemy, before retrieving Guéreth and his retinue, retiring back into the camp, and shutting the gates.

Marcius came hurriedly over to Octavian.

"Where's Antinous?"

"He's gone. He went out with the foraging party. I should think they've been hacked to pieces by now," Octavian replied. Nothing was going right.

Marcius groaned. "Oh, no!"

"Why, what's the matter?"

"It's my master. He's broken his leg, badly. If ever we needed Antinous it is now."

"I'm sorry, Marcius. But surely one of the camp surgeons can help? They must know something about fractures."

"You wouldn't think so from the way they're mauling him about. His leg looks all wrong. They've put splints on, but he's still in so much pain. These surgeons don't care much about our allies, do they?" he ended bitterly.

Octavian shook his head in sympathy, but couldn't think of what else to do to help.

A little later in the afternoon, Octavian was looking down from the watch-tower. They were surrounded by a sea of enemy. Thousands of faces, drawn up at spear's length from the ramparts.

He could hear a shout, a message from near the front gate. Octavian sent a runner to headquarters.

Sabinus joined him on the watch-tower. "They want to talk, Sir," said Octavian. "They wish us to send out an envoy."

Sabinus looked at the enemy aghast. "No wonder they gave us so little corn," he said angrily. "There's no way we could withstand a siege for any length of time. We'd better talk."

The envoy came back looking grim. "Ambiorix says all the camps have been attacked simultaneously, all over Gaul."

"Go on."

"He says he owes us a favour."

Cotta snorted in disbelief.

"I know, Sir, but that's what he says. He says due to Caesar's influence, he had his son and his nephew returned to him. Evidently they were held as hostages by one of the neighbouring tribes. He is so grateful he's prepared to let us march through his territory, so we can join either Cicero's camp or Labienus's. He says he's prepared to grant us safe conduct, but can only do so through his territory. He feels then he will have repaid his debt to us, and also he won't have to feed the legion for the rest of the winter. He says again that his people are starving."

Octavian went to the council of war. Cotta was all for staying. Sabinus was all for going. Hugo, the Senior Tribune, sided with Sabinus, to Octavian's surprise. Hugo maintained there was no way they could withstand a siege for any length of time, and if all the other Roman camps were being attacked as well, there would be no chance of a relief force. The debate raged on and on until in the end the principal centurions got fed up and told their generals they didn't care what happened, but would they hurry up and commit themselves to one course or the other, unless they proposed splitting the legion in two, of course. At midnight Cotta gave in, deeply distressed. Octavian went back to his tent.

"Get ready," he said to Marcius. "We're marching at dawn."

"I don't believe it," said Marcius.

"I know. Mad, isn't it? Sabinus! What a fool the man is. I must say I thought Hugo would have more sense. Anyway. Get ready. I'm going to tell the men."

Octavian was riding beside Marcius, who was sitting next to the driver of Guéreth's wagon. Guéreth could hardly keep from crying out with the pain of the journey over the narrow deeply pitted roads. Riona and her maid could do little for him. Marcius had a sword across his knees. After a mile the column stopped. There was some sort of delay at the front. Octavian sat impatiently on his horse, wondering what the hell could be going on. His breastplate was rubbing uncomfortably against a deep cut on the side of his chest that he had neglected to do anything about. The sun was beating down on him. He felt hot and bothered, and took off his helmet for a moment, to wipe the sweat off his forehead.

A shower of stones came from nowhere. His horse reared up, his helmet dropped from his hands to the ground. There was no time to retrieve it. He heard the order 'Form a circle!' They must be under attack! Legionaries started to run back past him, attempting to get to the baggage train, striving to retrieve their most precious possessions, convinced the wagons and pack horses would be lost. Octavian yelled himself hoarse trying to turn them back into formation. Marcius gripped his sword tight, but so far they could see no enemy to engage. The fighting was much further forwards. Then another order, an unbelievable order came. "Throw down your arms! Orders of General Sabinus. We are surrendering!"

A small group of enemy horsemen trotted unmolested along the long line of troops led, apparently, by a standard-bearer. The sight of Antinous in the middle of them nearly caused Octavian to fall off his horse. Allaine was looking at him with some amusement.

"Good morning, Octavian," he said with a smile.

Octavian knew he had been struck on the head. He was

falling through space, hurtling into a void, he was drowning again. Once he rose to the surface, to the light, then he was pushed back under.

Back down to the black bottom of the pool.

BOOK 3
TRANSFORMATION

BOOK 3: CHAPTER 1

Quintus Cicero's camp, Belgium, Winter 54 BC

He couldn't move his head. When he tried, an agonizing pain seared through his neck. He lay perfectly still. He could hear voices whispering. He could make out occasional words - kept prisoner - once his own name, Octavian - to eat - nothing to eat - broken - something was broken. He couldn't see. He couldn't open his eyes. His eyelids wouldn't work. He tried to open them. He moved his head too much and groaned in pain.

"Octavian!"

He heard his name whispered again.

"Octavian!"

He tried to form words in his brain, but they wouldn't come.

Marcius was speaking now. "You bastard, you bloody bastard."

He wondered what he had done to upset his friend. He heard footsteps, the sound of a sharp blow, and the scream of a woman. Antinous's voice now. Sounding quite odd. As if something amused him.

"What do you say now, Marcius?"

Another slap, another scream from the woman, ending in sobs. Marcius sounded different, his voice choked.

"I'm sorry, Sir."

He must find out what was going on. He tried to move his arm. It seemed to be tied down. He groaned in frustration. Someone walked over to him. The noise resounded in his brain. His head ached with each step. Something dropped onto his mouth, some oil, and was rubbed across his lips. Strange, bitter taste. He attempted to speak.

"Who?"

He tried to move his arms again, unsuccessfully.

"I can't see," he complained.

He heard Antinous's voice. "No, Octavian, you can't see," he agreed pleasantly.

Octavian gasped and struggled against his bonds. He attempted to lift his head up, but the pain was excruciating again. He slipped back with a sob. He was being lifted up now. Made to sit up, despite the pain in his head.

"It hurts," he complained.

"Yes, it hurts." Antinous didn't sound as if this were cause for concern.

"Drink," came the command.

He drank. Wine, with something in it. Warm wine, with the bitter taste again.

"All of it."

He drank all of it.

"Why?"

"Be quiet, Octavian."

"No, why?" He cried out in sudden agony, as his face was pressed.

"I told you to be quiet, Octavian. You must learn to obey."

He was pushed back down again. Now he was floating on the water, a pleasant feeling. His limbs were floating, despite being tied down. He didn't mind being tied down. He didn't mind anything. He drifted into a dark tunnel.

He woke up, alert. The stuff was rubbed on his mouth again, and now on his cheek bones, eye-brows. He winced. A soft touch on the line of his eye-lids. The oil massaged gently from one side to the other.

"Open your eyes now, Octavian, and keep still."

He could feel the lids being pulled apart, and blinked painfully. A cool hand on the side of his face. Liquid dripped into his eyes, immediately soothing, the excess gently wiped away.

He turned his head a little towards the sound of the voice, and saw Antinous quite clearly, looking at him with a tiny frown of concentration.

"You're a mess, Octavian."

"What's going on?" croaked Octavian.

"There seems to be a bit of a revolt against Roman occupation at present," Antinous explained politely. "I regret to inform you that Ambiorix and his men attacked your legion. Successfully, as it turned out. You were taken prisoner. Ambiorix has very kindly given you to me, but he wishes you to provide some information about the exact disposition of the rest of the legions, and so forth. So while I am putting you back together, you may be thinking of your answers."

"Given to you?"

"Yes. You are my slave. I'm sure you'll be very useful when you're fully recovered. Unfortunately, that won't be for some time."

"Why? Why won't it be for some time?" He grasped at the last words, desperate to make sense of it all.

"Perhaps you'd better have a look at yourself."

He was lifted up again. Antinous held a small mirror in front of him. Octavian stared in disbelief at the grotesque bloody swollen mask that stared back at him. A great gash spread from his forehead, backwards into his matted hair. His eyes appeared red and distended, the puffy lids purple and blackened with bruising. He looked hideous.

"Not a pretty sight at the moment. Still, I'm sure we will be able to improve matters."

Octavian gasped, then groaned as the needle pierced his temple, biting and tugging at his flesh.

"Be careful to give me truthful answers only, Octavian. I don't want to have to hurt you more than is absolutely necessary."

"Don't you have to take some kind of oath?" Octavian cried out in despair. "First do no harm, something like that?"

"I'm not a Greek physician, Octavian."

"What are you, then?"

"I am your master. You will address me as 'Master' or 'Sir.' Look, Octavian."

298

Octavian stared in horror, as Antinous pulled up his sleeve, and exhibited the white scar lines twisting up his arm, like so many pale snakes.

"Look, my little one, see this? These were inflicted by your charming commander. I am sure you will enjoy being burnt as much as I did."

As Antinous approached him with the irons, Octavian could hear Marcius's cries for mercy blending with his own pleas. Antinous ignored them both.

"Oh, Jupiter, no! No! NO!"

They sat him up, sobbing uncontrollably.

"You've done very well, Octavian."

The terrifying sound of that quiet voice made him tremble again. He would do anything, anything at all to placate it. He'd said so, hadn't he? He'd screamed so.

"When you are a little fitter, I will take you to the altar, and you will take your oath of obedience. But in the meantime, I think you deserve a little more of this."

He drank the hot bitter wine eagerly, desperate for oblivion. He wanted to blot out everything, existence itself.

There was no warning. The enemy appeared out of the woods, thousands and thousands of them, surrounding Quintus Cicero's camp completely, but drawn up more than a spear's length from the palisade, Eburones, Nervii, Atuatuci, and all their satellite tribes. The Roman soldiers cutting timber in the woods for fuel and fortification, were the first casualties. Once negotiations had failed to budge Cicero, the Gauls built a rampart and deep trench in a matter of hours, and settled down for a long siege. All the roads leading from the camp were barricaded. None of Cicero's couriers were successful in crossing the enemy lines. No one got through to tell Caesar. The Gauls paraded their prisoners from the Fourteenth legion, and set them to work, building a siege terrace.

The centurion looked at Valerius coming into headquarters, and felt a knot of pride gather in his throat. The man was every inch a soldier. His military bearing proclaimed the professional. One with experience. One who took a pride in himself and his legion. Valerius had been his right hand man now throughout the summer campaign. He was as invaluable as Pullo had known he would be. Always there when needed. Quick to react. Carrying out orders with the minimum of fuss. Encouraging the others. Setting a wonderful example of courage. The centurion turned to General Quintus Cicero.

"This is the man, Sir."

Cicero looked the man up and down. He hoped to the Gods he would prove to be as good as Centurion Pullo thought he was. The situation they found themselves in was pretty desperate. Valerius gave an immaculate salute.

"Gentlemen, let us sit down. You too, Legionary."

When they were seated, the young man leaned forward. "May I speak, Sir?"

"Please do."

"If you wish me to get through the enemy lines, and get a message to Caesar, I'll do the best I can. But I don't speak their dialect, at least not well, Sir."

Cicero found himself impressed. The man hadn't even asked for a reward. The Gauls tortured the captured messengers with great glee, in earshot of the camp. Finding the next night's victim was proving to be a difficult task.

"Go and get kitted out, then, in something suitable. The letter to Caesar is in the hollowed-out shaft of this spear. Good luck. If you succeed," Cicero paused. What could you say to the boy? "I'll make you my standard-bearer."

"I'll do my best, Sir," Valerius replied.

He had nearly made it. Nearly got through the lines. He was on the edge of the wood when he was challenged. He tried to bluff his way through, but they were suspicious. He was knocked about a little, not too badly, but his mouth was bleeding. They led him to a barn, open on one side, two army tents pitched, one at right angles and one facing the open wall of the barn to make a courtyard. He could see armed men guarding a group of prisoners chained on the ground at one end. A man on a stretcher with his leg in splints. Another man, who looked as if his head had been kicked in, his face was blackened and swollen. A terrified girl, with her long blonde hair dishevelled, her dress torn. She was wrapped up in a cloak, weeping. And a man he thought he recognised - a man who thought he recognised him, so looked away quickly so as not to give away any information.

A man came out of the tent with a companion. A tall man, clean shaven, with blond hair curling to the nape of his neck, and cold grey eyes. Well dressed, in black leather boots, britches, and a cream sleeved under-tunic covered with an outer tunic of dark blue wool. He had a gold bracelet pushed above one elbow. He looked impressive, powerful, and cruel.

He pulled Valerius over to where a clerk sat at a desk, taking notes.

"Good morning."

"Good morning, Sir."

"You are from South Gaul, I believe."

"Yes, Sir."

"And what is your name?"

"Valerius, Sir."

"That is a Roman name, isn't it?"

"Yes, Sir. My father was a Roman, or so my mother says."

His questioner smiled at that. The man touched his face, examining the bruise on his cheek. His hand smelt fresh, astringent, of wintergreen.

"You've been hurt."

"I'm alright, Sir."

"That's good. Are you afraid, Valerius?"

"I'm afraid of you," said Valerius, honestly.

"Why is that?"

"It is you who controls events. Not me."

"On the contrary, Valerius, your future is entirely in your own hands."

"How so, Sir?"

"Did you come from Quintus Cicero's camp last night, Valerius?"

"No, Sir."

"See," the man smiled, "you could have said yes."

"Do you want me to write that down, Sir?" asked the clerk, puzzled.

"No, just the relevant answers," said the blond man.

Valerius stuck to his story. He was an auxiliary, attached to the Fourteenth legion. He had been out foraging with a party of others. When they tried to get back to the camp it was surrounded by enemy troops, so he had decided to make his way to Cicero's camp to tell him.

"And how many days ago did you set out?" asked the man.

"Five days ago."

"Are you quite sure about that, Valerius?" asked the man softy. "Perhaps you have lost track of time in the woods. Perhaps you have miscalculated the number of days. Take your time, don't rush. Think about it."

"I'm quite sure it was five days, Sir," said Valerius, looking at him steadily.

"Yes, well that's a pity."

If this was an interrogation technique - thought Valerius bitterly - it was very effective. It was difficult to stay confident under the gaze of those remorseless eyes. He could feel his heart beating faster. It thudded away so loudly in his chest, he was surprised no-one seemed to notice it.

While his clothes were being removed singly, and examined for hidden letters, two men brought forward a brazier, then set out a table on which they placed familiar and unfamiliar instruments. Valerius had seen them used - even used them himself once, until he was sick, and Pullo decided that part of his training could wait for a year or two. Finally, they removed his boots. He was left standing shivering, not just with cold. The blond man ordered him to be well wrapped up, and then immobilised on the table. He wondered what he meant at first, then saw the leather restraining straps attached to the table, as they wrapped him up in blankets.

"Is this his weapon?"

Valerius closed his eyes, willing it not to happen. He heard the exclamation, and the crackle as the scroll was smoothed out.

"I am writing this letter in Greek, so the Gauls will not be able to understand it."

Valerius could hear the tinge of amusement in the man's voice. Perhaps it will put him in a good mood, he thought, with an inward laugh at himself. He had volunteered for this. He must be stark raving mad.

Valerius could remember the occasion, years ago, when his father had thrashed him for telling lies. The man was standing like a stern God beside him.

"Remember I have already told you, Valerius, that what happens next is in your hands. Under your control. I don't approve of people who tell lies. But I understand your motives, and I won't punish you for it. But there must be no more lies between us, my lamb. It is very important. Now, did you come from Quintus Cicero's camp last night?"

"Yes, Sir." So he was a lamb, was he? One for the slaughter, no doubt.

"Then you will have heard your colleagues being tortured to death the night before?"

"Yes, Sir."

"It's alright, Valerius, that's not going to happen to you. No-one, that I know of, has ever been voluntarily tortured to death. You did volunteer to act as messenger, did you not?"

"Yes, Sir."

"Why was that?"

303

"I don't like being trapped." He gasped as he said it. It was ridiculous, yet it was the truth, as the man seemed to recognise. He nodded slowly.

"You're a brave man, Valerius, you have proved your courage. There is no necessity to do more. You don't have to impress me, or anyone else on this side."

Valerius was looking at him questioningly.

"The letter from your commander gives nearly all the information we need. There are just one or two points that must be cleared up. And after that, what do you suppose?"

"A quick death?" Valerius presumed.

"I think that is altogether too great a reward."

"Some kind of slow one then, you fucking bastard," said Valerius, his nerve breaking at last. "Why don't you describe it to me in detail, I'm sure you're dying to." He turned his head away, sharply. Angry now the man had succeeded in getting under his skin.

"You are no use to me dead, unless I have a need for glue, or dog meat that is."

"What do you mean?"

"Ambiorix has given you to me as a gift. You are my slave. However, I can hardly allow you to wander around camp at the moment. You will need to take an oath of loyalty to me, one which supersedes your oath to the army."

"I can't do that."

"I'm not giving you the choice. You can either volunteer to accept slavery, or I will force you to do so. Just as you can either volunteer the information I request, if not I will force you to reveal it. I am sure you must be aware that this," he gestured towards the instruments, "is always sufficient compulsion."

"Go to hell," said Valerius.

In the end, of course, he was begging, pleading, screaming desperately to be allowed to be a slave. Anything, anything at all to stop the dreadful pain.

"I'm afraid I'm not yet fully convinced of your sincerity," said the man.

As Allaine walked over to her, the girl started to sob.

"No, don't, Allaine, please, please don't," she begged.

Marcius joined his pleas to hers. "Look Antinous, don't hurt her, please don't hurt her. She's done nothing to you, has she? She's done you no harm."

"Since when has that had any relevance, Marcius?" Allaine asked.

He unchained the girl, and led her stumbling and weeping into the tent.

"Riona, shut up!" Allaine said sharply. She became quiet immediately. He could feel her trembling under his fingers. He sighed with relief. "That's better. What a noisy girl you are, to be sure." He pushed back the blonde tresses from her tear-streaked face, tucking them behind her ear. "Listen, Riona, I'm sorry about your maid. If she had obeyed me, and stayed in the wagon with you, I could have kept her safe. As it is, I'm afraid she didn't stand a chance, poor girl."

"Is she dead?" Riona asked fearfully. The terrified girl had hurled herself out of the wagon, straight into the arms of the rapacious troops.

Allaine thought of the human wreck he had found, the girl's torso almost torn in two.

"Yes, Riona, of course she's dead. She behaved stupidly, and suffered the consequence."

Riona gasped in dismay. "She was frightened. She panicked. I couldn't stop her."

"Well, there's no use blaming yourself, Riona. Unfortunately stupid people don't live long, at the moment."

Riona collapsed into tears again.

Allaine sighed. "Look, I'm sorry if you were fond of her, but it can't be helped now. So stop crying." He tried again. "Riona, Riona, stop crying." He waited until she had calmed down a little. "I may be able to get you another maid in a few days, a girl anyway. Now, over there, is a chest with some of your clothes. There is your bed, there are your toilet things. But in the meantime," he pushed her down onto a chair, "I suggest you look into this mirror, and try to do something about your hair yourself."

"Another maid?" she said tearfully, "for me?"

"Isn't that what you need? You girls never seem to be able to do anything for yourselves, do you? Always need a handmaiden, isn't that right? But this time, keep her close to you."

"Am I to be tied up?"

"No, but if you try and escape, I'll set the dogs on you."

She stared at him, terrified again. He brushed the hair away from her face once more. "I'm sure you wouldn't do anything so stupid, would you, Riona?"

She sat looking at him, breathing hard. "You're not being very nice, Allaine."

"We don't live in a very nice world, Riona. I'm sorry I was rough but believe me, you are safer with me than with any of those other men out there."

"But you've been hurting that poor man," said Riona, crying again. She'd had no idea Allaine could be like this, callous and cruel.

Allaine went over to the water bucket, moistened a cloth and came back. "You're a mess, my girl," he said. "Here, wash your face. He's not a poor man. He's a Roman soldier, one of the most dangerous and vicious animals in the land. Worse even than lions, they hunt in bigger packs, Riona, and devour everything they come across. Especially women and children. Remember that. Especially women and children. They're not like us." He picked up her hand then, and kissed the fingers. "But the only way I can see of defeating them, is for us to become like them." He released her hand and turned to go.

"Where are you going?" She panicked, not wanting to be left alone.

"I have things to attend to."

"Don't go away."

He stood looking down at her face. "Why? Do you want to be raped, Riona?"

She looked at him, speechless. He ran his finger down the side of her face, and chucked her under the chin. "Do your dress up. When I want you, I'll take you."

And bent down and kissed her lips. He walked out of the tent, leaving her numb with shock.

There were a few flurries of snow. The sky was leaden. Valerius had slept hardly at all, just drifted into the occasional doze, when the throbbing eased a little. He shifted in his sleep, and woke up again, as the lancinating pain seared through his shoulder. It had been dislocated yesterday. The pain rekindled the memory of the actual moment of unbearable agony when it was put back into place. Truly unbearable. The threat of its recurrence had brought the wall of his resistance crashing to the ground. He had become quite defenceless after that. He tried to ease his position but failed miserably, and let out a sob. His face felt cold where the tears were coursing down his cheeks. The man, whom he had agreed was to be his master, came and knelt beside him.

"Not doing so well this morning, Valerius?"

"No, Master." It seemed easier to say this morning, although he had been made to say it many times last night. He felt bone-weary, defeated, dejected. He swallowed suddenly, the misery catching in his throat.

"Here, this will help."

It did too. The sharp pains turned into duller aches. He could move a little now; he tried to stretch out his cold cramped legs. He slept. When he woke again the sky was much lighter in colour. He could hear the familiar camp noises, the sound of men being drilled. The language was all wrong, though, and that woke him with a jerk. Everything was all wrong.

A man knelt by his side, holding a bowl of something

smelling very good. Valerius allowed himself to be spoon-fed scrambled eggs. He couldn't manage to hold the spoon himself, but could hold the warm bread in his hand. He knew the man, he realised, Servilius, one of Cotta's personal servants. A gift, no doubt, to his master from Ambiorix. Perhaps his master was thinking of raising his own legion. Valerius smiled to himself.

"That's it. You're feeling better, aren't you? You are to be moved into the tent. Once the tribune's had his dressings changed."

"Tribune?"

"Tribune Octavian Volusenus. That's him over there. Looks a sight, doesn't he?"

Valerius agreed that he looked a sight. He looked appalling. His eyelids were swollen and black, his eyes red jelly, with little black dots of pupils floating in the middle. The top half of his face was a massive purple bruise.

"The one on the stretcher, that's Guéreth, one of the Aeduans. His leg's broken. And that's his servant over there, Marcius, and the girl in the tent's his sister, evidently."

"You're allowed to move around freely?"

"Yes."

"Then you'll have to try and get to Caesar."

The man got up abruptly, and moved away.

Octavian was lifted onto the table. His body didn't seem to be under his own control, any more. He was trembling, despite digging his nails into the palms of his hands to try and stop it. He broke down as soon as he was touched, pleading like a child not to be hurt. Allaine took no notice of him whatsoever, and proceeded to change the dressings. Then he started to unpin Octavian's tunic.

"Now let's get you stripped off," he said, without reckoning the effect his words might have on his prisoner.

Octavian panicked, thinking something else dreadful was about to happen to him. He tried to sit up, crying and protesting.

"No, no, don't! Oh, please, please don't!"

He found himself locked in the arms of his torturer, being soothed like a baby, as Allaine became unexpectedly kind.

"Octavian, listen to me."

"Please, please don't. Not again," Octavian sobbed.

"Octavian, listen to me." Allaine held onto the desperately frightened man. "Your clothes are covered in blood. Servilius will wash them for you. That's all. Nothing at all to worry about." Allaine caught Octavian's flailing arm, and gripped his hand. "Nothing to alarm you. Alright? Remember what we agreed? I won't hurt you, as long as you are good, and obey me."

"But you just have!" Octavian cried.

"Your dressings must be changed, and your wounds cleaned every day, to avoid infection. Believe me, you wouldn't like that to happen to you." Gently, Allaine began to massage the trembling shoulders of the terrified man. "Take some deep breaths, now, and calm yourself down. Nothing bad is going to happen, I promise you."

"I'm sorry," gasped Octavian.

"That's better. But you have nothing to apologise for." He glanced over to where Marcius was sitting, his hands covering his face, tears of rage and impotence squeezed between his fingers. Allaine placed his hand flat against Octavian's chest. He could feel his prisoner's heart jumping around like an erratic frog. He didn't want the man to die of shock; he would need to be more careful with him. His dreams of revenge had never envisaged this badly injured Octavian. "You will rest beside your friend for now," he said.

"Thank you, Sir," whispered Octavian, though afterwards he couldn't imagine why he should feel so grateful for not being tortured.

He was still shivering with cold and fear, when taken over to lie beside Marcius. Marcius was softly murmuring obscenities about Antinous under his breath, until pulled up short by Guéreth.

"Marcius, I have real need of you at the moment," said his

master. "You will behave towards Antinous with the utmost courtesy. But don't worry. If we ever get out of this alive, one day I swear to you I will kill him!"

Marcius became silent at once, as Allaine approached with a rough fur blanket over his arm, which he proceeded to tuck around Octavian's inert body.

"Are you warm enough, now?" Allaine asked. There was no response.

"Octavian," he spoke sharply. "Are you warm now?"

"Yes." There was a pause, then the gasping voice came again. "Yes, Sir."

"Good." Allaine felt inside the rug for Octavian's wrist, looking for the pulse. Satisfied, he tucked the hand in again, and gave the huddled body a gentle pat, to Marcius's surprise.

"Get some sleep, now," he said.

"Is he alright, Sir?" Marcius asked. The feeling of the pulse had worried him.

"He will be fine," said Allaine. "As long as he does as he's told, and obeys me, he will be fine." He looked at Marcius with his cold grey eyes. "And if he doesn't, he will be dead." He smiled to see the look of horror on Marcius's face. "Very unpleasantly dead."

Guéreth called out loudly, "Antinous! Just a moment!"

Allaine walked over to him, lips curled in contempt. "Well? What is it?"

"There is no need to keep Marcius chained. I swear he will remain with me. I give you my word he will not try to get through to Caesar."

"He would be an utter fool, if he did try."

Allaine stopped to think. Marcius unchained would make things a lot easier to manage. "Very well. Then you must order him to obey me. I have to be sure of him, if he is to be allowed freedom of movement."

Guéreth agreed. "Marcius, you understand? You must obey Antinous implicitly."

"Whatever you say, Master, of course," said Marcius.

"In that case, Marcius, come with me," Allaine said. "Let's see just how well trained you are."

After the chains were removed they walked together over to the barn. Allaine ordered Marcius to kneel at his feet. He was promptly obeyed.

"Listen, Marcius, Octavian and Valerius are now my slaves. The realisation of what that means hasn't yet hit them. But it will. After they have taken their oath of loyalty to me, I will train them, but I don't have much time in which to do so. They are bound to become very distressed for a while. They will find it difficult to adjust. They will probably feel suicidal at some stage."

Marcius looked up at him, horrified again. How he hated this man.

"Why are you doing this to them, Sir?"

"Revenge, Marcius. Revenge! And for that I need them to stay alive. You appreciate that if either of them succeed in harming themselves deliberately, or if you help them to do so, I will hold you, your master, and his sister to be responsible. And you will suffer accordingly. Is that quite clear?"

"Yes, Sir, quite clear."

Allaine spent an hour giving Marcius orders. "But it wasn't too bad, not too humiliating," Marcius told Octavian afterwards. "You know, just the usual things, bow, kneel, kiss hands." Marcius was relieved when it finished, though. At the end Allaine said Guéreth was fortunate to have him.

"He wants revenge," Marcius whispered to Octavian, when he woke.

"Why? Why? What have I done to him? I thought I'd helped him."

"Why did you want to help him, anyway?"

"Oh, because he helped me with the twins, he helped me with sea sickness. He said he wasn't a Greek physician. Who do you think he is?"

"I don't know for sure." Marcius was beginning to have the glimmerings of an idea, though.

Now Marcius was unchained Allaine showed him how to massage the muscles of Guéreth's broken leg, and what exercises were to be performed. At the beginning of their ordeal Marcius was made to assist, when Allaine reset Guéreth's fracture, and found the experience deeply upsetting. Guéreth screamed with the dreadful pain. Even worse was to come, when Allaine dealt with Octavian. Marcius hated Allaine with an intensity that made him feel almost sick. But he knew better than to allow it to show. Ostensibly he was a polite, well trained servant. Inwardly he writhed with anguish. He felt pleased though to be at last of great service to Guéreth.

"I am sorry you have to put up with this, Marcius," said his master, while perched awkwardly on the wooden bucket, which acted as a chamber pot. It needed both Marcius and Servilius to get him sorted.

"Well, Master, I've never been much use to you before. Just a nuisance, really. I'm so glad to be of real help now."

"You mustn't underestimate yourself, Marcius. I have always appreciated your devotion to me," Guéreth said. "But don't antagonise Antinous. I know you are hating all this. But keep your thoughts to yourself. I simply cannot do without you."

"Yes, I know, Sir. I'll be careful."

Between them they managed to get Guéreth cleaned up, and settled more comfortably. Riona came over to her brother with the water jug.

"Why do you call him Antinous, when his name is Allaine?" Riona queried.

Guéreth gulped down the water gratefully. He was finding his present situation intolerable, dependant on others for every little thing, his good nature sorely tried. Everything had gone wrong. His only method of staying sane was to imagine exactly what he would do to Antinous, that swine of a slave of his, when their situations were reversed. He pinned his hopes on Caesar, who would surely march to the rescue of his legions, as soon as he was informed of the present dire situation.

"His name is Antinous. He is a Greek physician. A very disobedient one, that one day I will punish."

"He is Prince Allaine, the Helvetian."

"My dear girl, Allaine died years ago, poor lad. He died in prison."

"Did you know Allaine, Guéreth?" Riona asked.

"No. I've never met him."

"Well I have. Lots of times. He always stayed with Dumnorix and Eloise on his way home from school. Antinous is Allaine."

"Rubbish! Wishful thinking, Riona. I heard you were fond of young Allaine, but I'm afraid wishing won't bring him back. He died long ago."

"Ask him, then. Ask him why Ambiorix is doing so much for him."

"He appreciates his surgical skills."

Riona smiled to herself, and walked back to the tent. She had known Allaine immediately. Her brother was in for a big shock.

A gale got up on the night, making the tent walls shudder and flap in the wind. There were a few splatters of cold rain. The sky was filled with dark turbulent clouds. Soon after first light another sound erupted, the far off crackle of fire. They could smell burning. A huge pall of smoke hovered over Cicero's camp. Allaine sent one of the guards to find out what was going on. He returned to say the Gauls had managed to set light to the thatched barns where the corn was stored, and the wind had carried sparks to the legionaries' tents. The camp was one large conflagration. Octavian thought about his friends, fighting somewhere amongst the flames.

Allaine invoked the Gods' blessings on the day's work. He then moved his equipment further into the barn, out of the wind, but he needed the light to operate satisfactorily. Octavian made no protest when he was moved onto the table. There was no point. It was going to happen anyway. He gritted his teeth, and hoped it would soon be over. He felt so ill and weak. Allaine called for Marcius to keep him still. Marcius held tightly onto his wrists, as Allaine removed the dressings, and scrubbed the scalp wounds vigorously with vinegar.

Riona approached, daintily treading through the dry leaves swirling round the barn, her skirts blown against her slender body, outlining her form, a few blonde curls able to escape from the ribbons that held them in place. She took a deep breath, and said, "Allaine, I would like to help you."

"How do you mean, help me?" Allaine gave her a swift appraising glance, but carried on cleaning the wounds. He thought she looked stunning, incongruously beautiful in the midst of her brutal military surroundings, with the wounded stacked against the walls, and watchful guards armed with vicious weaponry.

She raised her voice against the gale. "Well, I could cut stitches, or bathe wounds. Something like that."

"And what would your brother say to that?" He had to shout the words.

"You don't take any notice of my brother," Riona shouted back."So why should I?"

The wind dropped a little. They were interrupted at this juncture, as Octavian groaned aloud in pain, then let out a sob as Allaine smoothed salve over the burns.

"But you don't like me hurting these poor men," Allaine mocked her.

"But you're making him better, aren't you, Allaine?" Riona was anxious, and wanted reassurance that the Allaine she loved was still there, somewhere.

He changed tack. "Don't you girls faint at the sight of blood?"

"I think you'll find it's the men that faint." Riona was beginning to be angry with him now. "We girls get used to seeing blood; we see it every month." She was surprised at her own daring. Menstruation was not a subject much discussed in her brother's house. Never, in fact.

Allaine smiled ruefully at that. "I think you'll find it's not quite the same, my little innocent." Deftly, skilfully, he reapplied the dressings. "Alright, Riona, you can help. Go over to that man with his arm hanging off, and tell him he's next."

Obediently, she walked away. Now he had his girl back, Allaine found his jealousy of this Tarleton of the Remi was beginning to subside. He was increasingly impressed with his Riona. Not that she yet knew for sure she was to be his girl. He wasn't angry with her any more. She had acted throughout with a certain dignity, and here she was, not lacking in courage, either.

Allaine looked down at his victim, and smiled. He tied the bandages neatly round the remainder of Octavian's dark curls. Most of Octavian's hair had been cut off on one side, to facilitate the suturing of his appalling scalp wounds.

"You look very sweet. Now, Octavian. Let's see if you can walk back to your bed. Do you think you could manage, if we help you?"

Octavian looked down at the ground. It seemed a long way away.

"Yes. Maybe. I think so, Sir."

"Marcius, look. Support him like this."

Allaine hooked his arm under Octavian's, and held his wrist with his other hand. Together they walked him with difficulty into the tent. Octavian sank down thankfully onto the straw mattress.

"There you are, you have managed it," said Allaine. He walked over to his other victim. "And how are you this morning, Valerius?"

"I'm alright, Master."

"Then I'd better arrange to have you both chained," Allaine spoke unpleasantly, "in case either of you should wander away by mistake."

Tears were oozing from under Octavian's eyelids. He tried to wipe them away.

Allaine knelt down in front of him, and pulled his hands away from his face.

"Don't rub your eyes, Octavian. You will make them worse." Carefully Allaine mopped up the tears, and lifted his prisoner's chin. "Look at me, now."

Octavian obeyed him, but his eyes blurred with tears again.

"Alright," Allaine said. He got up and fetched a small flask from the table, returning to kneel at Octavian's side. "Now, tilt your head back, and keep still," he said. He administered more of the soothing fluid into both eyes, making Octavian blink rapidly. "Is that better?"

"Yes, Sir. Much better. Thank you." Octavian found himself feeling grateful again.

"Good." Allaine pressed his shoulder lightly. "And you'll feel better in a couple of days."

Again the affectionate gesture, Marcius noticed, and the reassurance. First the cruelty, then the kindness. Done on purpose? He wondered if he could do anything for his friend.

"Didn't Octavian help you, Sir, after Petronius died?" Marcius ventured.

The change was instantaneous. Allaine stared at him, eyes like flint. "Did he indeed? So where was he, Marcius when the rest of the Roman army were slaughtering my helpless relatives on the banks of the Saône? Having the night off? And where was Octavian when we had to stand and fight, or be annihilated?"

Marcius was silent.

Allaine said coldly, "Don't poke the fire, Marcius. You might get badly burnt."

"Very good, Sir," said Marcius woodenly. He hadn't helped, just made Allaine angry. He would need to be careful in future.

"Now, Marcius. Make sure they both eat."

"But you've had nothing yourself, Sir," Servilius said in concern.

Allaine frowned. "Haven't I? Oh, well, I'd better deal with this arm, first. I'll eat later, Servilius."

After he had served what little breakfast there was to his master and the two prisoners, Marcius left the tent in time to see Riona hurrying towards him, clutching a severed limb.

"I will not faint!" she told him, "I won't, I won't!"

"Let me take that, Madam."

"No, Marcius. He told me to put it on the fire. I must do it."

He accompanied her to the brazier. The wind was making the charcoal burn brightly, and the tips of the cautery irons glowed red hot. He watched as she threw the misshapen lump of flesh into the heart of the flames, and saw her give a convulsive shudder. The fire licked greedily around, charring the skin, the curled fingers straightening in an empty plea.

Riona was true to her word. She spent the rest of the day bathing and cleaning wounds.

"You have to be brutal," Allaine told her. "We are trying to prevent infection. The vinegar needs to penetrate the injured flesh. Here, watch me."

Riona learnt a lot about blood. She was astonished at the fortitude of the injured waiting to be treated. They knew only too well what was in store for them, from the screams and cries of the victim on the operating table. They tried so hard to be brave while she was dealing with them.

"Where have you been all day?" Guéreth demanded of his sister, as she entered the tent, with an exhausted Allaine by her side.

"I've been helping Allaine with the wounded," Riona said, with a slight air of defiance.

"Helping Allaine? Helping the enemy?" Guéreth was furious. "You slut! Flirting with him, I suppose. How could you do such a thing!"

Allaine had forgotten to eat. There were so many casualties to be dealt with. He felt a surge of rage. He picked up his riding whip, walked over to Guéreth, and slashed him across the face with it. Riona screamed. Marcius leapt to his feet. The guards drew their swords.

"Don't you ever call her that again," Allaine shouted into Guéreth's face. He turned quickly to grab Marcius by the wrist, and pulled him forwards. "And do you have something to say?"

Marcius looked at his master for guidance.

"No, he has nothing to say, you swine," responded Guéreth angrily, rubbing his sore face. "Leave him alone."

"Well, I have," Riona interrupted in anguish. "How dare you hit my brother. How can you do such a thing? He's helpless! Look at him!" Her eyes filled with tears.

"Be quiet, Riona," said Guéreth.

"You keep out of it," snarled Allaine, and turned back to confront Riona.

He stared at her. He had no idea why he'd reacted so violently. His anger subsided as he looked at the distressed girl. "Riona," he started.

"Eloise said you were cold and unfeeling," Riona continued, with a sob.

"Eloise said what?" Allaine was shocked. "Riona. Tell me. What did she say?"

Riona was scrubbing at her face with a handkerchief. Allaine walked over to stand in front of her. He held her by the shoulders and gave her a gentle shake.

"What did she say about me?" he asked again, with less vehemence.

Riona drew herself up. She would tell him the truth, and shame him. "She said 'Some people think he's cold and unfeeling, but actually he's the sweetest, kindest, most adorable brother in the world.'" Tears were spilling down her face again. "So where did he go, that kind man? I used to like him myself. Now you're not just cold, Allaine, you're cruel as well."

318

"I don't have any sisters left to be kind to, do I?" he said bitterly, "and for that your brother is partly to blame. He fights with Caesar against his own countrymen, the traitor."

"And am I a traitor as well? I'm an Aeduan," Riona demanded.

"No," Allaine said wearily. "You're a very nice girl, whose brother was idiotic enough to drag you into the middle of a war. Let's leave it at that." He told the guards to sheath their weapons, and went out to get washed.

Servilius poured wine into a wine cup, and proffered it to Guéreth, sinking onto one knee before him. "I'm sorry about that, Sir. I've found my master to become a little irritable after he's been working all day without eating. And, of course, he thinks the world of Lady Riona, doesn't he?"

"Does he indeed," snapped Guéreth, and sat brooding in silence for the rest of the evening. He was beginning to think Riona was right about Antinous.

The next morning at first light Allaine found his way barred by Riona, as he was walking to the barn to start the day's work.

"Have you broken your fast, Allaine?" Riona started.

"Not yet, my sweet."

"Allaine, promise me you will soon."

"Why?"

"So you won't hit my brother again." Riona's eyes filled with tears at the memory.

"I hit him because he called you a slut. I won't have it."

"Servilius said you hit him because you hadn't eaten. Guéreth is my brother. He can call me what he likes."

"Not in my presence," Allaine snapped.

Riona turned away from him, upset again.

Allaine gave in. "Oh, all right, Riona. Let's deal with a couple of the injured. Then we will have breakfast together. Will that please you?"

Smilingly she assented. He wanted to please her. So her Allaine was still there, somewhere. All she had to do was find him.

Octavian hated being chained. It made everything so awkward to do, eating, sleeping, shitting. The very noise of the chains disturbed him. He couldn't make a movement without everyone knowing about it. He loathed the feeling of utter helplessness, the humiliation of Marcius having to clean him.

"I suppose if it was the other way round, you'd just leave me to lie in my own shit, would you?" Marcius commented, with his usual unfailing cheerfulness. But Allaine hadn't touched him, as yet. Marcius collected some smooth stones from the ground outside, and scratched a rudimentary game board in the earth, but couldn't get either Octavian or his master interested in playing.

Allaine found Octavian battering his wrists vainly against the tent pole.

"Stop that now," he said quietly. "You are achieving nothing, except to hurt yourself."

Octavian looked at his tormentor. He felt so powerless and hopeless. He began to sob. Marcius watched him in anguish, hating to see his friend so distressed. But he could do nothing to help. Allaine picked up a rough towel, walked over to the table, and poured out a beaker of wine. He knelt on the ground in front of his sobbing prisoner.

"It has to be, Octavian. But it's just for a few more days. When you are fit enough to go to the altar you will be chained with words, instead of these. It will get easier for you."

There was no response. Octavian continued to sob.

"Here, stop crying. You are washing out the eye drops, and I don't know when I'll be able to get further supplies," Allaine added, tucking the towel into Octavian's chained hands. Octavian buried his face in it.

"If all else fails, the best thing to do is to get drunk," Allaine continued. "So drink this, now, and stop upsetting

Marcius." He took the towel away, fastened Octavian's hands round the cup, then helped lift it to his lips. Octavian stared at him with tired, still reddened eyes. He was finding his master's constant changing from cruelty to kindness deeply disturbing. He still felt a frisson of fear every time Allaine spoke to him. Though there had been no more torture, thank the Gods, the unspoken threat of it hovered in his mind.

"Good," Allaine said, as Octavian started to drink the wine. "That's better." He glanced across at Valerius.

"And how are you coping, my little one?" Allaine asked him.

Valerius couldn't understand why the tribune was so upset. Their master hadn't hurt them again, well, not much anyway, and only because he insisted on the dressings being changed every day. They were fed as well as rations allowed, given wine to drink at supper, and warm blankets at night. Alright, it was bloody boring, but that was army life. Complete boredom interspersed with moments of acute fear. At present he preferred the boring bits.

"I'm doing alright, Sir, I think." He smiled across at his master.

Allaine laughed, sat back next to Octavian, and put his arm round his slave's shoulder. "You need to try and copy Valerius. He's a true stoic."

Val wasn't sure what a stoic was, but as his master seemed to approve, he was glad to be one.

Octavian felt strangely comforted, as he leant back against his master's arm, aware he wasn't thinking straight, but unable to do anything about it. The wine, he supposed. He summoned up the courage to ask the question he hadn't dared to ask Marcius.

"They are all dead, Sir? Everyone in the Fourteenth legion?" He thought of Cotta, Sabinus, Hugo, all his friends, all his comrades-in-arms.

Allaine gave him back the towel. "There are some prisoners," he answered.

Octavian's hands tightened in the material. "Prisoners like us?"

"No, Octavian, not like you."

"How not like us?"

Allaine didn't enlighten him.

"Who are you, Sir?"

"I think you know, don't you?" Allaine said, still smiling, his eyes as cold as ice. "I am the enemy."

Octavian wondered why his enemy was gently rubbing his back.

Allaine's attention was drawn to the lines scratched in the earth floor, with the neat little rows of pebbles. He rose and went over to one of the chests, stacked at the closed end wall of the tent, and extracted two objects, a box, and a wooden board. He brought them over to Marcius,

"Here," Allaine said. "Try this. It might help to distract him, and it will be a lot easier to see." He went out, back to the barn and the injured, leaving Marcius staring open-mouthed at the chess set.

It was now fourteen days since he had been captured. Allaine held Octavian's face, scrutinising it carefully. Octavian's eyes were now practically back to normal, only the corneas still being a little discoloured. His bone structure had reappeared. The skin of his face was still yellowish in parts with the resolving bruising, but he was now recognisably Octavian Volusenus once again. Allaine removed the sutures. Painlessly, to Octavian's great relief.

"Good," Allaine said, satisfied.

"They look very red," Riona pointed out. She had told Allaine about Octavian, but it hadn't made any difference.

"It will fade, and his hair will grow."

Octavian still flinched a little, as his master smoothed the salve over his cheek bones, but now he could have his dressings changed without a murmur escaping his lips.

"I think he looks very nice," said Allaine. "Do you want him with a beard, or without?"

"I've no idea," said Riona in surprise.

"Well it's up to you. Keep still." He rubbed the salve over Octavian's lips as he had done for the past two weeks, Octavian making no protest.

"Why do you do that?" asked Riona.

"It's good, here." He smoothed some on her lips. "It makes your lips nice to kiss."

"You want to kiss Octavian?" Riona said, disconcerted.

Allaine laughed. "No, he doesn't look that nice. I want to kiss you." He took her in his arms and did so.

"Allaine!" Riona looked at him, amazed, when he released her. A rosy flush suffused her cheeks.

"I've waited five years for that." He smiled at her. "Worth the wait, though."

"You kissed me two weeks ago," Riona said indignantly. Surely that had meant something?

Allaine merely laughed at her. "Keeping score, are you?"

"Anyway, you were saying about Octavian," Riona said, still very pink cheeked.

"Oh, yes. Octavian," Allaine sighed. "Well, to explain, he's still quite ill, debilitated. His skin is fragile. He needs to be protected from the weather."

"From the weather?"

"From the cold. You valley people know nothing. It's going to be cold where we're going. You must learn to keep warm and safe," Allaine told her. He walked off and came back a short time later, with a man whose mouth was cracked and bleeding, his lips running sores. "This is caused by the cold. Cold makes wounds difficult to heal, as well," Allaine explained, "though the infection rate is less. Anyway, it's time to go, I think." He presented the man with the pot of salve.

The guards marched Octavian and Valerius a considerable

way into the forest, until they came to a vast open-air arena formed by the trees and a natural declivity. There was a huge ceremony or service in progress. There were various groups of men - some dressed in long robes, some in tunics, others with musical instruments. From Octavian's point of view the most arresting sight was that of his putative master officiating, being treated with the greatest reverence by the rest of the congregation. There was an ominous pile of wood at one side, with a huge wicker cage on top.

There was no running away from it now. Lady Riona was correct. The high priest behind the altar was clearly Allaine, son of Orgetorix. His own brother-in-law, if he did but know it. How he could also appear to be a Greek physician was something Octavian didn't care to consider further. His eyes were riveted to the wicker cage. With the wooden pyre that high, though, perhaps they wouldn't take too long to burn. He thought back to his recent suffering, the tiny area of body that had been seared, and the excruciating pain. He didn't want to be burned to death.

There was a pause. The mood in the crowd seemed to change, to lift and lighten. There was some laughter and cheery conversation, as they were pushed by their guards towards the altar. Allaine came towards them, and someone else took his place.

"Is that for us?" asked Valerius nervously, indicating the wicker cage.

"No, Valerius," Allaine spoke as if to a child. "If you remember you are here to swear an oath of loyalty to me. Have you forgotten? Do we have to start all over again?"

"No, Master," Valerius replied quickly. "I just hoped you hadn't changed your mind."

"No." Allaine gripped his shoulders, searching his face. "Have you changed yours?"

"No, Master."

Another pause. They all stood around waiting. With a shock Octavian realised they were waiting for Ambiorix, who appeared on horseback, and rode through the parting people. He dismounted, nodded to Allaine, walked up to the altar and proceedings began. Allaine said something to Ambiorix, who looked at the two Romans with an exasperated expression, and agreed to whatever it was.

"I'll translate for you," Allaine told them, as their chains were removed.

"Who gives these prisoners to be bound in loyalty to Allaine, son of Orgetorix?"

"I, Ambiorix, of the Eburones."

"Do you confirm that these prisoners were taken in war, that they fought with courage, and that their actions have not betrayed their country, nor their companions?"

"I so confirm."

Octavian knelt down, and repeating the translated words, swore to dedicate himself to the service of Allaine, son of Orgetorix, to lay down his life for him, if called upon to do so, to honour his name and obey his commands above all others. When he had finished, his master swore to protect him and his dependents, to nurture him, to care for him when he was sick, train him to be of use, punish him as occasion required and reward him likewise, and believe his word. When Valerius had gone through the same procedure, they were taken off to be dipped in a large icy clear pool. Octavian enjoyed it, he would quite like to have splashed around, but the guards told him cheerfully, to hurry up. Valerius didn't like the idea of being paraded, wearing only a towel.

"It's because you get new clothes," Octavian said, thinking back to the time he became an Aeduan citizen. But he was worried. They were dressed quickly, in good quality clothing, Octavian noticed, and warm boots lined with sheepskin. They had to bend their heads to receive the fine gold chain, the mark that they were the slaves of a prince. Finally, the hot, sweet, spiced wine. An ice-cold bath, vigorous rub down, warm clothes, hot wine. It was all done on purpose, of course, Octavian thought, to make him feel good. But his eyes were drawn inexorably towards the cage. His master noticed, and came to him.

"So, Octavian, no more chains. But remember, I will be looking for an excuse to flog you. To make sure you know I am the master, and you are the slave. Don't give me that excuse."

Octavian's solemn brown eyes were watering.

"You say 'No, Master, I won't.'"

"No, Master, I won't," Octavian repeated dully.

"How are you feeling? You look tired. You may ride back if you wish. Take my horse."

Allaine summoned the guards to escort them away. But the guards wanted to see the next part, so they hovered at the edge of the clearing.

They watched as each prisoner was brought up and scrutinised by their master, before being conducted to the wicker cage. One, who was sobbing hysterically, was rejected.

"A purist," said one of the guards to his companions, who nodded in agreement.

The prisoners were dazed, walking in a trance, each clutching a branch of willow in their hands. They weren't tied in any way. They were led quite unprotestingly to their death. Octavian caught his breath as ten men, holding torches, ignited the surrounding straw. With a whoosh, the flames shot skywards in an explosion of heat, the edifice collapsed in on itself, like a conjuring trick. There was nothing in the centre, just an incandescent glow. The guards remembered that these men weren't supposed to witness this spectacle. One of them pulled a face, another shrugged his shoulders. Too late now.

Allaine returned much later with the terrified prisoner, one of the newly recruited legionaries, apparently. He told Marcius the youngster was called Darius, rather inappropriately, and he could have him to help with Guéreth. And if Marcius could make him stop crying, he would be very pleased. Then Allaine noticed how drawn and weary Octavian was looking.

"Octavian, have you eaten?"

"Yes, Sir."

"Then go to bed."

"Yes, Sir."

Octavian looked uncertainly at Allaine for a moment, crossed over to him, and knelt at his feet, not sure what to do next. He remembered Marcius always made some gesture, to bid his master goodnight, but couldn't remember exactly what it was.

Allaine rose and placed his hands on his newly dedicated slave's head. He spoke the blessing.

"May the Gods bless you, and protect you and yours, now and forever more, Octavian."

Octavian found his eyes filling with tears again. Jupiter! Why did he have to keep crying all the time?

"You say 'So be it, Master,'" hissed Marcius.

"So be it, Master," Octavian repeated.

"Very good," Allaine said, a little surprised. "Now, can you say it in Gallic?"

Octavian repeated the phrase in Gallic.

"Excellent. Good night. Sleep well, Octavian," said Allaine.

Octavian bent his head, and kissed his master's hand.

"Good night, Master," he said quietly. He felt unreal, his world gone mad.

"Please, may I talk to him for a bit?" Marcius asked.

"Just for half an hour, then, if your master will allow. But remember, Octavian is still a sick man, he needs plenty of rest."

"Yes, Sir." Marcius bowed, and followed Octavian to the other tent, where they slept.

Under the watchful eyes of the guard, Marcius shook out the straw-filled sack that was Octavian's bed, to distribute the straw more evenly for him. He helped Octavian to strip. Octavian sat up on his makeshift mattress, hugging his knees.

"I'm a slave," he said.

"So am I," Marcius returned. He thought for a moment.

327

"So is Antinous."

They looked at each other, and both started to laugh. They soon sobered up, though.

"Mark, I don't think I can do this," Octavian whispered.

"If you kill yourself, or harm yourself, he will kill Guéreth, Riona, and me as well, in a not very pleasant manner, he said. We are the hostages for your life," Marcius explained. "And the guards are always present. There's no way we can all commit suicide simultaneously, is there?"

"I'll just have to get on with it, then, won't I?"

"You'll manage. Don't worry. It's not as hard as you think."

After Marcius left, Octavian lay in the half light, thinking over the events of the day, and the words of the oath he had taken. So Prince Allaine burnt Roman prisoners to death in a wicker cage. It was horrific. And he wanted revenge. Presumably being his slave was going to be pure hell, a slow painful path to extinction, probably. How was he going to cope? He had no idea.

The next day their master told his new slaves they would have to be trained quickly, as he didn't have much time, and he was afraid they wouldn't enjoy the process. They didn't.

Valerius's automatic reactions as a legionary had to be taken apart and reassembled. He found it more difficult than Octavian, and kept feeling stupid. Their master slapped, punched or hit them with a thin cane if they didn't obey his orders instantly. He took each of them for a day at a time. It was vicious treatment, but it certainly got quick results. Octavian found his mind wonderfully concentrated if the slightest mistake was met with instant retribution. After each session he had to stand, stripped and submissive, while Allaine checked him over carefully, told him he was fine, and usually gave him a gentle pat on the shoulder. In the evenings Octavian reported to a worried Marcius.

"What has he done to you? Are you hurt?" Marcius asked, consumed with anxiety for his friend.

Octavian made light of it. "No, just a few slaps. A bit humiliating, that's all."

He didn't want to burden Marcius with any more problems, but he found the forceful subjugation of his will to Allaine's a deeply unpleasant experience. Though it didn't seem as if he was to be destroyed, after all. Allaine made sure never to cause any permanent damage. All the same Octavian went to bed each night praying he would die in his sleep.

"You said it would get easier," he complained desperately to his master.

But Allaine just looked coldly at him. "I said it would get easier, I didn't say it would get easy. Would you prefer to be chained, instead?" Horrified, Octavian shook his head. "Well then, it's got easier, hasn't it?"

When his master gave him an apple one night as a reward for having survived the day without getting into any trouble, he felt like weeping with relief.

Allaine made Octavian put his hands down by his side.

"Now I'm going to hit you," he announced. "Don't move." He lifted his hand to slap him. Octavian instinctively raised his hands.

"No, Octavian. I said 'Don't move.'"

"I can't not move, Sir."

"Shall we return to the irons, then?" Allaine said. He paused, and waited as Octavian shook his head, appalled at the threat. "No? You say 'No, Master.'" He waited again while Octavian dutifully repeated the words, all too aware of his slave's increasing distress. "Then keep still, Octavian."

Octavian clenched his fists, and managed to remain almost motionless, as Allaine administered a stinging blow across his face. His eyes watered.

"Look at me, Cry Baby," mocked Allaine. "Hard, isn't it?" He ran his hands down Octavian's arms till he came to the clenched fists. "And stop doing that." He held onto his slave's wrists, and waited until the fists uncurled. "Slaves can't afford to look threatening in any way." He looked directly into the swimming brown eyes. "How do you like my training methods, Octavian?"

"I have never once punished one of my servants without cause," Octavian said resentfully.

"Well, it is good to know what a kind master you are. But of course on the other hand, you seem to have no compunction in thrusting your sword through women........? children......?"

Allaine stopped. There was no response. Octavian stared at him. The old feelings of shame and guilt lurched into his mind. His face reddened.

"Babies as well......... ?" Allaine continued. "Oh, of course. I forgot. They're barbarians, aren't they? Worthless creatures. Of no account. Whining fucking Gauls."

"You bastard," whispered Octavian, then looked at Allaine, aghast at what he'd just said. Now what hell had he let himself in for?

Allaine raised his hand as if to strike. Octavian flinched, but his master just lightly stroked his slapped cheek.

"You're in real trouble now, aren't you, Octavian. What are you going to do about it?"

Octavian looked at him in bewilderment. To his astonishment Allaine put his arms round him, held him close, and spoke quietly in his ear. "You've just called your master a bastard. Never a good move, Octavian. You're in deep shit. You've already been threatened with the irons." He felt Octavian stiffen with fear under his hands. "How are you going to get out of it?"

"I don't know, Sir." Octavian was lost.

"Well, think, my pet!" Allaine said urgently, as he released him. "What would Marcius do? What would anyone do with half a brain?"

"Apologise?" Octavian ventured, tentatively.

"Correct! Grovelling would be even more appropriate. So, now grovel, Octavian."

"What do you want me to do, Master?"

"Kneel down, touch the ground with your forehead, and say how profoundly sorry you are."

Octavian hesitated for an instant.

"No, you have to do it straight away. Believe me, it is a lot less bother than being whipped or burnt." Allaine could see Octavian was finding it hard. "Hurry up, my pet, or you will have lost the chance."

Octavian made up his mind, knelt on the ground, and did as his master suggested.

"I'm very sorry, Master."

"Well, you're not very convincing," Allaine said. "Now you have to plead with me, not to be punished. Go on."

"Please don't punish me," Octavian whispered, with bent head. He felt totally humiliated.

Allaine made him repeat the process until Octavian performed instantly on command.

"Good! You're getting there," Allaine said at the end, looking at the bowed head of the slave kneeling at his feet. "Get up, now."

Octavian stood before him, looking thoroughly dispirited.

"I've sworn to protect you, but by the Gods, you make it difficult!" Allaine frowned. "How long has your friend Marcius served Guéreth?"

Octavian was taken aback at the sudden change of subject. "Seven years, I think it is."

"Look Octavian, Marcius has been a slave now for so long he reacts well by instinct. We don't have the luxury of time. We are travelling to Switzerland. We will come across many people on the way. I have to keep you safe. Any jumped-up junior chieftain is going to try to upset you, get under your skin as soon as they find out what you are. You have to let it wash over you. You can think what you like, but don't let your thoughts show."

"Let my thoughts show?" Octavian repeated.

"I've been able to read your thoughts from the first time

we met," Allaine said. "Do you remember? You couldn't understand why Caesar said that our request to pass through the Province took him by surprise. You knew it was no surprise to him. You looked so puzzled."

Octavian stared at him. Suddenly it came back to him; the blond boy with the attractive smile, standing with the Helvetian ambassadors.

"The interpreter!"

"Yes, the interpreter. I wasn't much good at it," Allaine admitted. "So. We go back a long way, don't we?"

"Yes, Sir. I suppose we do," Octavian said, as memories came flooding back.

"A lifetime ago," said Allaine sombrely. He shook his head, as if to clear the past away. Octavian thought he sounded tired. He waited quietly for his master to perform the usual medical check, but Allaine merely touched his shoulder.

"You're fine, Octavian. Now, go and get washed before supper."

Octavian was about to obey, when he remembered. He bowed nicely, and said, "Yes, Master."

He heard Allaine sigh with relief, as he walked away.

"I think he's two people," Octavian said, when he was relating the day's events to Marcius later.

"How do you mean?"

"I think sometimes he's still Antinous. That part of him is, well, kind, if you like. But the other part is Allaine, the not very nice part. Actually, the downright cruel part."

Marcius thought about his friend's theory. "No, I think you're right, but you've got it the wrong way round. I thought Antinous was the vicious bastard."

"I hope you're right, Marcius. Because if we're going to Switzerland, we're going to see a lot more of Allaine, and a lot less of Antinous. He called me his pet today."

Marcius looked at Octavian, and burst out laughing.

"Some pet," he said.

Octavian looked back at him and smiled. Marcius always had the power to cheer him up. He felt a little happier. But Marcius knew his friend too well.

"What's really worrying you, Octavian? There's something you're not telling me."

"He's very tactile," said Octavian. "I wonder if his revenge will take some other form. You don't think he'll try and seduce me, or do something worse? You know, after what Caesar did to him? He said I looked very nice." But not nice enough to kiss, he thought with relief.

Marcius was reassuring. "You look infinitely better than you did, Octavian. But I think you're quite safe, unless he has a predilection for freaks." He looked at the huge scar on Octavian's head, and the stubble of hair beginning to grow back. "You still look pretty dreadful."

At supper that night Octavian sat staring into space, shredding his bread into coarse crumbs.

"If you are not hungry, Octavian, give your bread to someone else," Allaine said.

Octavian looked down. "Oh, sorry." He scooped the bread crumbs into his soup bowl.

"What is it?" Allaine asked him. "What's bothering you?"

"Sir, how far away is Atuatuca from here?"

"About fifty miles. It took us three days to get here."

"But I have no recollection of the journey." Octavian wondered anxiously why this thought had only just occurred to him. Allaine walked over to him and took his hand.

"Here. Can you feel this circular edge on top of your head? No, don't press," Allaine said quickly. "Feel gently now. The bone isn't yet fixed back to your skull."

Octavian looked at him in shock. He hadn't investigated the extent of his wound.

"The sling shot caused severe lacerations, but also a depressed fracture. You were unconscious most of the journey. I don't think you will ever remember much about it."

"Oh." Octavian tried hard to remember, searching his mind. "Wasn't I tied up?"

"Yes. The bleeding inside your head compressed your brain, causing cerebral irritation. When you started to regain consciousness you became very aggressive, trying to hit anyone who came near you, even Marcius."

Allaine realised Octavian was finding the information difficult to assimilate. "You're fine, Octavian. Don't worry about it. It is a common problem with head injuries. You are making an excellent recovery."

It got easier. The fear began to subside. Octavian started to watch Marcius, to see how he behaved towards his master. He noted the polite, respectful way Marcius always spoke to Guéreth. Marcius took no liberties, despite Guéreth treating him with great affection. They were clearly the best of friends, although still master and slave. But this slavery was never demeaning or humiliating. Octavian began to copy Marcius, and the other two Romans took their lead from him. He couldn't quite bring himself to act like Servilius, whose behaviour he found too fawning, too servile, like his name. Fortunately Allaine didn't demand such servility of him, just instant obedience.

Octavian found himself looking forward to the evening meal, which was taken in Gallic fashion with everyone, slaves included, present. After Guéreth had broken the bread and blessed it, anyone could speak and ask questions.

"Sir, why do you ask Guéreth to break the bread?"

"Because he's the most senior person present."

"But surely you are the most senior person present. Guéreth is your prisoner."

"But I am still his slave, Octavian, so how can I possibly be senior?" Allaine could see Octavian was disturbed. "I have sworn no oath of obedience to Guéreth. I am choosing to disobey his orders, therefore I will have to accept the consequences if he is ever in a position to resume power over me. You don't have that choice."

"And then what will he do to you, Sir?"

"Kill me, I should think, by one method or another," Allaine said, cheerfully.

"No!" cried Riona in horror.

Allaine looked at her in amusement.

"Do you remember my twins, Sir?"

"Yes, of course."

"They didn't return from Britain. Do you think they may have been freed by the Britons? They are allies of the Veneti, aren't they?"

"But they were dedicated, bound to you by a most sacred oath, Octavian. I'm afraid your twins will have been killed or captured. I may be able to find out. I have many friends in Britain."

But when he opened his mouth to ask the next question, Allaine said, "Enough now, Octavian," and shut him up.

BOOK 3: CHAPTER 2

Titus Labienus's camp, Quintus Cicero's camp, Winter 54 BC

Labienus had established his winter camp near the Rhine, fifty miles east of Cicero's, in the territory of the Treveri tribe. He lined up the all too few fugitives from Sabinus and Cotta's legion, congratulated them for their escape from Ambiorix's clutches, and questioned them closely about what they had experienced. Gaius looked from one to another.

"Did anyone see Tribune Octavian Volusenus, what happened to him?"

One man stepped forwards.

"I saw him go down, Sir. He was right at the back of the column, riding with that wounded Aeduan. It was a sling shot, I think, knocked him off his horse, and he was surrounded by the enemy, I'm afraid. There's no way he could have got out of it, Sir, even if he was still alive, which I doubt."

Gaius stared at the man. "And Guéreth, the Aeduan? He was wounded, you say? Did you see what happened to him?"

"No, Sir. But the wagon was completely surrounded. They didn't have a chance."

Gaius walked slowly back to his hut, trying to take it in. The Fourteenth legion destroyed. Unbelievable. But he must believe it. His little brother Otto gone for ever. Guéreth gone for ever, and Marcius as well, he guessed. He walked over to the chest, and took out the tiny wooden box. He smoothed out the parchment, the list of Aeduan friends given to him by Diviciacus, aeons ago now, it seemed. Several names were missing already. Then he picked up a reed pen and dipped the point in the ink. He noticed his hand was shaking; he had to steady it against the top of the chest. Carefully he scored a line through Guéreth and Jayven. Then, at last, he wept.

The courier stood before Labienus, and handed him the letter from Caesar. Labienus read it in disbelief.

"He wants us to march out of this camp to join him. Ye Gods, hasn't he heard what happened when Sabinus tried the same thing?"

"Yes, Sir. Of course. But Cicero's camp is under siege, still. Caesar has only two legions in the vicinity."

"Tell him to fuck off!" Labienus ordered. "Here, you, scribe!"

"Yes, Sir?"

"Write a letter to Caesar, telling him to get stuffed. I'm not risking my troops to save Cicero's neck."

"At once, Sir." The scribe sat and hastily composed the letter in more emollient terms. With trembling hands he showed it to his commander.

Labienus grinned. "Tell Caesar we're planning a surprise party of our own. Tell him we're going to give the fuckers something to think about. Isn't that right, Gaius?"

"Certainly, Sir." He could hardly wait. He wanted revenge, and soon.

Allaine was using the barn as hospital headquarters. Interspersed amongst the badly wounded waiting to see him, was a child of eight or nine. His father was with him, but Allaine sent the man away, and told him to return in a couple of hours. He then called Octavian over to help. The boy was crouched over his left arm, which was clutched to his chest. Allaine pushed the boy back onto the examination table, while speaking to him in a quiet voice. Octavian saw the whole body relax, the muscles flaccid. Allaine continued to speak softly, lightly stroking the boy's face and neck. The boy went to sleep. Octavian held the boy's arm still across a small table, while the wound was cleaned, sutured and dressed. A few more quiet words, and the boy was woken up to have his arm put in a sling, which was tied round his neck.

The boy was still in evident pain and looked unhappy, until it was pointed out to him that his arm had been mended. He then cheered up.

"Bring him back in two days to have the dressing changed," Allaine told the father.

"Will his arm be alright now?" asked the father.

"The future belongs to the Gods alone. One in four of these wounds breaks down," Allaine told him.

"Yes," persisted the father. "Will he be alright?"

Octavian could see his master was angry. "I've told you the odds, your child is no different from anyone else. If you wish to predict the future, I suggest you consult an augur."

The father didn't appreciate the significance of the slight change in tone, the narrowing of the eyes, but thanked Allaine effusively.

"That man's a fool," said Allaine to his retreating back. "What is he thinking of, to bring a child like that into a war zone. He'll probably bring the boy back in two days, with cow dung plastered over his arm."

"Sir?"

"They think if it's good for the land, it's good for everything else."

"And isn't it?"

"No, Octavian, it is not."

But Allaine was held in far too high esteem, Octavian noted, for anyone to disobey his orders, and the boy was dutifully brought back in two days. The edge of the wound was tender, the boy winced as it was dressed.

"Why didn't you make him sleep this time, Sir?" Octavian asked when the boy had been taken away.

"Why should I?"

"So that it wouldn't hurt."

"But that wasn't why I made him sleep in the first place. It was merely to facilitate treating his wounds. If he feels he can fall out of a tree with impunity, the next time he may climb so high he will break his neck. Pain is a necessity, Octavian. It teaches us not to behave stupidly. I thought you would be aware of that."

To Riona's intense annoyance, Allaine made not the slightest attempt to take her. He hadn't even kissed her again. Presumably he didn't want her. But she wanted him. Oh, to be married to Allaine, and not to the disgusting Tarleton. She scowled at herself in the mirror. Allaine had found her a maid, an untrained girl of ten or eleven from one of the nearby villages. But even having her hair dressed properly didn't seem to affect Allaine in any way. She continued her work with the injured. At least that way she saw a great deal of him, and sometimes gained his grudging approval.

Guéreth became increasingly irritable as the days went by, so frustrated by his disability, and angry that neither his slave physician, nor his sister took any notice of his edicts. So Allaine purchased three women, with some of the gold Ambiorix had given him, and kept one for himself, the other two being for the men. He told Guéreth he would be denied the privilege unless he co-operated. As one of the girls was a cheerful buxom wench, Guéreth became more amenable. But Riona was not pleased.

Allaine ordered a pair of crutches for Guéreth to try. His instructions were explicit.

"You will put no weight on that leg, otherwise you will cause it to refracture. But I will fix a weight round your ankle. We need some traction to make sure your leg doesn't shorten."

"How long for?" Guéreth asked impatiently.

"It will take six months altogether for your leg to be totally healed."

"Six months!"

"No weight bearing on the leg for three months. In the meantime we must make sure your muscles don't waste away. That's why it is so important to do the exercises. And whatever you do, don't fall over."

Allaine showed Marcius and Darius how to help Guéreth

up and to steady him, with their arms under his armpits. Now he could get around a bit on his crutches, he became more cheerful, but Allaine insisted armed guards always went with him, and only allowed him in the courtyard and latrine area. Aeduans were not popular, especially ones known to have fought with Caesar. Rations were not good. Allaine knew that a poor diet was not helping Guéreth's leg to heal. Ambiorix was correct when he said his people were on the edge of starvation. However most of Allaine's patients or their relatives brought food for them, and his women knew how to make the most of it.

One night at supper Allaine looked at Octavian curiously. His slave appeared to be rapt.

"Aren't you feeling well, Octavian?" Allaine enquired. "You haven't asked any questions tonight."

Everyone laughed. Octavian was gaining a reputation.

"I'm alright, thank you, Sir," Octavian replied. "But what are we eating? It's delicious." He looked sadly at the heap of shell left in his bowl. There was no meat left to extract, he'd eaten every scrap.

"Crayfish, aren't they?" Allaine didn't notice or care what he ate. A relative of one of the wounded had brought a pailful of them. "Don't Romans eat them usually?"

"Do you wish for more, Master?" said his woman, a fair haired girl from the Northern coasts.

"No, I thank you. Unlike Octavian, I do not like dissecting my dinner."

"I'm sorry, Master."

Allaine patted her hand. "It was excellent, my precious. Don't worry. Octavian can manage more."

"But the sauce. It's amazing. How do they do it?" Octavian asked.

The women laughed. One of them removed his bowl, then brought it back, filled again to the brim, while the other two told him how it was cooked, and fetched the herbs for him to see.

Their kindness made him cry again. He was getting fed up with it.

"Sir, why do I keep crying all the time? Do you know? I never used to. It's so annoying."

"There are two possible reasons I can think of," Allaine explained. "Firstly, you are in a very stressful situation. It's not like a battle, when the stress is over and done with, as soon as you win or lose. This situation has no end that you can see, which makes it much worse."

Octavian nodded. "Yes, I see." That all made sense.

"But I think your head injury is the main cause."

"Oh, why, Sir?"

"Head wounds are very variable in their effects. You could have been paralysed, or blinded. But they can also cause personality changes, memory loss, for example, disinhibition, or emotional lability, which is what you have. But you don't cry for no reason. That would be worrying."

"Oh." Octavian absorbed this new information. "You know everything, Master," he said.

"That is no more true now, than it was then," Allaine replied. "What do you think, Marcius? You know Octavian a great deal better than me. Has he changed at all?"

"I couldn't say, Sir," Marcius replied, without thinking.

Allaine spoke harshly. "Don't play stupid games with me, Marcius. I asked your opinion. Now give it."

Marcius swiftly pulled his thoughts together. "He's just the same Octavian, Sir, though a bit off balance, I think."

Octavian walked across to the bed, where his master was sleeping. He raised the dagger and struck repeatedly. Fountains of bright blood spurted into the air. Allaine was looking at him reproachfully.

"You can't trust a Roman," Octavian explained.

He was being vigorously shaken awake, a hand over his mouth.

"I think you were having a bad dream," Allaine said softly.

"You were making a lot of noise."

"Oh, Jupiter!" Octavian whispered. He sat up, clutching onto his master, like a man drowning. "Oh, Jupiter!"

He drew back a little. "Sorry," he said, still a bit shaken, the images vivid in his brain.

Allaine got up to reassure the guard, who was standing with sword in hand. "Go back to sleep, now," he said to some of the others, who had woken. He returned with a beaker of water. Octavian gulped it down, and then shuddered.

"Do you think dreams mean anything, Sir?"

"Yes, Octavian. It means you ate too many crayfish."

Octavian found himself increasingly enjoying starting the morning with an ice-cold dip. He wondered whether his own home's luxurious baths weren't a trifle enervating. It was strange to be experiencing good times, and be a slave simultaneously. Sometimes it worried him, but Allaine kept him occupied, so he didn't have too much time to speculate.

Valerius suggested he try again to get through the woods to Caesar's camp.

"But you've just sworn an oath, man!"

"They're not our Gods, though, are they?"

"What does it matter whose Gods they are? You've made a promise, now you must keep it."

"We're Romans, he's a barbarian," Valerius insisted. "A promise to him doesn't count. Don't you remember? When Caesar seized the German ambassadors, he said 'With these barbarians, the rules of civilised conduct don't apply.'"

Octavian grabbed him by the neck and shook him. "Listen to me, you bloody fool. If I give my word I keep it. If you disappear I'll tell the master myself, do you understand?"

"No." Valerius was bewildered. "You're an officer."

"I was an officer. For the moment I am a slave, and so are you."

Octavian thought there was no help for it but to try and

explain it to his master, but Allaine didn't seem at all surprised.

"Well I hope he doesn't do anything foolish. There's about twenty thousand pairs of eyes on you two, just dying for you to make one wrong move, so they can be confirmed in their suspicions that Romans are treacherous and have no concept of honour."

True enough, Guéreth had given Marcius that gold all those years ago, on the cheerful assumption he would never see him again, Octavian thought. Their reputation didn't stand very high amongst the Gauls.

The words "Allaine, son of Orgetorix" at the altar had meant nothing to Valerius. He had never heard of Orgetorix. It wasn't until Valerius was helping Allaine to dress after a dip in the pool, that he saw his master's naked body, and realised with an awful premonition of disaster, he knew exactly how each scar had occurred, had actually caused some of them himself. This was the prisoner in the scarlet cloak, not any old Allaine, but Prince Allaine the Helvetian. He felt sick, convinced Allaine might remember having met him before, at any moment. But as the days passed, and nothing happened, he began to hope his master wouldn't be able to differentiate him from any other legionary. After all, he thought to himself, we all look the same in uniform. He hugged this comforting idea to himself, and managed to continue to speak and act normally.

As the siege progressed, Octavian and Valerius found their relationship with the other camp servants becoming strained. They were jostled and jeered when they went to fetch water, the horses' feed mysteriously upset, some of the tack looking as if it hadn't been cleaned. Stupidly, Octavian omitted to report these matters to his master. One afternoon when Allaine returned to his tent, he found his Romans missing, and Marcius frantic with worry.

"They've been arrested and taken to headquarters," Guéreth informed him. "They attacked one of the camp servants

343

this morning. Unfortunately, one belonging to an officer. It's a problem."

Servilius, the servant who had previously belonged to Cotta, amplified matters. He was an anxious young man, eager to help. "If you please, Master, I believe they have been having a considerable problem with the other camp servants. In fact the tribune said he was deliberately jostled yesterday, when he went to feed the horses."

"What tribune was that, Servilius?"

"Tribune Volusenus, I mean your servant Octavian. That's the problem, you see, Sir. He's your servant Octavian, but he still thinks he's Tribune Volusenus everywhere else."

"And how does Valerius behave, Servilius, tell me that."

"Well, Sir, if anything he's worse."

"You don't think you could perhaps have given them some advice, Marcius?"

"Well I did try, Sir, but Octavian never listens to me. Never did."

When he got to headquarters Allaine found an irate owner with two youngsters, one of whom was sobbing, holding his jaw. Valerius and Octavian were under armed guard, kneeling on the ground. Valerius was still looking belligerent. Octavian experienced a sudden rush of emotion when Allaine walked in, which he recognised, with surprise, as relief. He knew they were in terrible danger, but Valerius still didn't seem to understand, telling Octavian the boy got what was coming to him. He deserved every bit of it, the lying little shit.

Allaine took one quick look at them both and then ignored them, walking over to the owner and apologising. "I believe my slave has caused your servant some damage. I will make reparation of course. May I have a look at him?"

The owner extended his arm in disbelief. "Look what the bastard's done to my boy. He's deformed, his face is all twisted. I don't know what the hell to do about it."

"I think I do. May I look?"

"Yes, of course, Sir. I was forgetting."

"What's his name?"

"Garo."

The youngster opened his eyes wide in panic as Allaine approached him, but was quickly soothed by the steady voice and the confident, competent way in which he was handled. His sobs lessened.

"Garo, I'm going to feel inside your mouth now. Your jaw is dislocated, it's not in the right place, it's been knocked out of place. That's easily dealt with, don't worry about it. But I want to make sure there's no fracture, that there's nothing broken, no bones, no teeth. Alright?"

Allaine felt the boy gag a little as his fingers probed into the angles of the jaw and along the gums, but he stayed still and co-operative.

"Good. Do you have a small cloth? Octavian, make that into a cold compress."

"Sir," Octavian proffered the soaking wet cloth.

His master sighed. "Squeeze it out, Octavian, and fold it into a neat small rectangular shape."

Octavian flushed with embarrassment, and obeyed.

"Now, Garo, I'm going to put your jaw back into place. It will make a grating sound, but I need your help." Allaine put the boy's fingers over the cloth, and applied it to the side of his face. "When I say 'Press' you are to press this cloth very hard with your fingers. Do you understand?"

Allaine gently slid his thumbs inside the boy's mouth, and then reduced the dislocation with one swift movement, before the boy had time to think. The clicking noise took everyone else by surprise. "Now you press," said Allaine, cradling the boy in his arms, as his sobs started again.

"What happened to the signal?" asked the interested owner.

"If he's waiting for a signal he's relaxed. He waits to brace

345

himself when I give the signal. It's difficult to reduce fractures or dislocations with rigid muscles."

"Really?"

"Yes. If he'd broken his wrist I'd say 'I will pull your wrist straight at the count of three.' While he's waiting for three, I reduce his wrist at the count of two."

The owner laughed. "I'll have to remember that."

"I'll think of something else for you," Allaine promised him. "Now let's see, is there any other damage? Some bruising. Quite a cut here on the gum and these teeth are a bit loose, but that should settle down." He took the boy's hands away from his face, probed along the jaw-line, made him open his mouth once or twice and then made him repeat the process. "Bloody but unbowed," he said, smiling as he ruffled the boy's hair and got an answering smile in return. "Now. What happened?"

"Look, Sir, I'm afraid I asked for a hearing," said the owner. "I was bloody annoyed, actually."

"I don't blame you. I'm very angry myself."

The owner was relieved. Now his servant was back in one piece again, he didn't particularly wish to offend the young chief by having asked for a court hearing.

"Octavian." He knelt, immediately obedient.

"Over there."

Octavian walked over to join Valerius, who was looking a little odd. At last - thought Octavian savagely. Perhaps he realises the mess we're in.

Allaine patted the uninjured youngster. "Now, will you tell me what happened this morning? Were you just attacked completely out of the blue, without any warning?"

"Well no, Sir." The young man blushed. "Well I suppose it was because of what we said."

"And what did you say?"

The young man looked at the yawning pit gaping at his feet. He remained speechless, blushing furiously. How could he possibly say it?

"Come on, spit it out," said the owner, getting cross. "It's only words. You're going to have to say it in court anyway."

The young man looked at his master, looked at Allaine, and went very pale. "I think I'm going to be sick," he said. He walked out of the tent and was.

"Powerful words, then," said Allaine to the owner. They noticed his patient was looking at him with terror-stricken eyes.

"We didn't mean it," the boy whispered.

Allaine understood. "It was about me, was it? An insult, was it?"

The boy gave a tiny nod.

"Bloody hell," said the owner.

"Something very bad." Allaine was gently stroking the boy's hair with the tips of his fingers, pushing back the fringe from his temple, lightly touching the curls behind his ear.

"We didn't mean it," the boy repeated, his eyes riveted to his questioner's face.

"And do you normally hurl insults at any passers-by?"

"No, Sir."

"Why these two, then?"

"Bloody hell," repeated the owner.

The other boy returned now, still looking pale.

"It's because they say things to us every morning, Sir."

"They?"

"That one, the one that grins all the time. He says something disgusting every morning. He thinks we can't speak Latin."

"Do you think that makes any difference?" asked Allaine.

"No, Sir, I suppose it doesn't."

"And what does the other one do?"

"He laughs usually, well sometimes he pulls him away," the boy conceded.

Octavian was kneeling before the presiding magistrate, his master at his side. He knew they were going to ask him, he knew the question was coming. He could feel his heart racing.

"And what did the boy say?" asked the magistrate.

"I think, Sir, some things are better left unsaid," said Octavian.

"I don't," said the presiding magistrate.

"He said 'Caesar shoved his prick up your master's bum.'"

"In Latin?"

"Yes, Sir."

"A well-educated lad," said the presiding magistrate.

"Yes, Sir," said Octavian shamefaced. No-one laughed.

"And he was immediately attacked."

"Yes, Sir."

"And did you take part in the attack?"

"No, Sir. I pulled him off."

"Very well. Stand down."

"I'm going to kill you," said Octavian, as he knelt again beside Valerius. His master cuffed him hard and he winced - the back of his head was still sore.

The magistrate found for the plaintiff and fined Allaine ten gold pieces - a reduced amount in consideration of the treatment he'd given the victim. Octavian was to have ten lashes, Valerius fifteen. Was this satisfactory to the plaintiff? The plaintiff agreed that it was and walked over to shake Allaine's hand.

"Little buggers," he said. "I'll thrash them."

"They were sorely provoked."

"It makes you wonder where they hear such things," said the owner.

"From their elders, I should imagine," said Allaine with a faint smile. The owner had the grace to blush.

"I hope you don't think the sentence too severe."

Octavian looked up.

"On the contrary," Allaine replied, "I think it unduly lenient."

He happened to glance at Valerius while Octavian was receiving his punishment. Something about the man's eyes made him walk over and push the hair away from the nape of his neck. There were a few red spots behind his ears.

"Valerius," said his master, "I too am going to kill you."

Octavian had difficulty straightening himself up, after bending down to pick up his clothes. Allaine crossed over to him, and had to help him to dress.

"Master," Octavian whispered, "Ambiorix." He could see the chief standing right behind Allaine.

"He's here to see if you two obey," Allaine said impassively. He looked at Octavian full in the face. "If either of you had hesitated for an instant, he would have had you tortured to death. I wouldn't have been able to stop him. It doesn't do to fool around when you are surrounded by enemies, Octavian. Life here is not one big joke. And in future, if Marcius gives you advice, make sure you take it."

Octavian was so ashamed. How could he have been so stupid as to go along with Valerius's idiocy? He was discovering that, far from being a joke, life felt most unpleasant when Allaine was displeased with him. Also that only ten lashes were required to make moving and breathing extremely painful.

Valerius was duly flogged, and then passed out when he was cut down. Allaine watched the proceedings without a flicker of emotion. If this was revenge it was poor thin stuff. He couldn't imagine why he'd bothered with any of them. He was wasting his time. Perhaps he should just kill himself, that would solve everyone's problems nicely. The youngsters came up to make tearful apologies. They knew they would be for it when they got back. Allaine patted their cheeks and told them not to worry.

He walked over to survey the unconscious figure of Valerius, and rolled him over to his side.

"He'll come round soon, unfortunately."

"Yes, Sir," agreed Octavian.

Riona came up to him as soon as they got back. "Allaine, I wonder if you would look at my maid."

"I suppose she's covered in red spots," Allaine told her.

"Yes, she is. Is it serious?"

"Sometimes. Keep her warm, give her plenty to drink. I'll look at her later on, but right now I'm a little tired."

"Of course, Allaine," said Riona.

He'd wasted such a lot of time today. Strange that such a little thing could be taken so seriously in the middle of a siege. It represented something he supposed, a desire to continue with the structure of society even as it was being ripped apart. As soon as news of his return reached the wounded, many came with petitions, asking him to see a son or a brother, or a friend. But he told them he could do nothing today, the light had gone. They were to stop the bleeding and he would see what he could do in the morning.

He thought about punching Octavian in the face and breaking his jaw, but even the thought didn't give him pleasure. He summoned him anyway, took him to a spot in front of the tent in full public view, and ordered him to lie on the ground on his face, until he was sent for.

He managed to get Valerius settled, and then went to join the others for the evening meal. Riona saw something, an expression in his eyes, that made her put her hand on his arm.

"What is it, Allaine? What's the matter? They're safe, aren't they?"

Allaine looked at her. "How could he be so stupid, so lacking in judgement?" he asked, his anger flaring up at last. "He acts like a child. He nearly got himself killed today. Val too."

"But it's all new to him, isn't it, Allaine," said Riona. "His world has turned upside down, and he's trying to find his place in it. He doesn't understand how much he is hated, here in the North. He's used to us Aeduans." She paused, wondering whether to say more. "Your sister Eloise thought a lot of Octavian."

Allaine was taken aback. "And why did Eloise think a lot of Octavian?" he demanded.

"Well, Dumnorix appointed him joint guardian of the

boys, didn't he? With Diviciacus." Her voice became husky, as she was seized with inward grief for her friend and her friend's sons. "The boys loved Octavian."

"What a great help that turned out to be," Allaine said in disgust.

A pall of depression hung over the group. No one dared to speak. Halfway through his supper Allaine put down his knife, stopped eating, and turned again to Riona.

"It's my fault. I must be partly to blame," he said, spreading his hands in an angry gesture.

"How come? How can you be to blame?" Riona asked.

"Octavian has made such a remarkable physical recovery, I wrongly assumed that he had recovered mentally as well. I will have to keep him closer to me in future, so he stays out of trouble."

He told Servilius that he and Octavian were to sleep in the barn, as Valerius was sick, and would probably disturb them in the night, otherwise. Servilius was appalled.

"Master, if you tell me what I should do, I can see to Val. Sir, you need your rest more than us."

"Tomorrow night, maybe, Servilius. We may have to take it in turns, it depends how bad he gets. And Servilius," Allaine continued. "You will stop calling Octavian 'Tribune.' Do it again and you will be in trouble yourself. Is that clearly understood?"

Servilius went pale, and stammered an apology.

"Marcius, you will assist Lady Riona, of course, as her maid is ill."

"Certainly, Sir." Marcius hesitated. "Will you allow Octavian to have his supper? May I save some for him?"

"I'm not that cruel, Marcius," Allaine answered tiredly. "He may have his supper, by all means."

Two hours later Octavian was kneeling at his feet again, very sore, cold and stiff. Allaine slipped his hand under the gold chain round his slave's neck, and pulled it forward.

"You are labouring under a misapprehension, Octavian, if

you think you'll escape being kicked to death out there, because of anything you've been in the past. This is the only shield that protects you."

Octavian was wondering, a little resentfully, why Valerius wasn't made to lie on his face. His master answered his unspoken words.

"Valerius is ill at the present, and is going to be much more so in the next few days," he said. "You'll have to manage yourself."

"Because he's been whipped, you mean, Sir?"

"No, because he's got measles. Now go and get something to eat."

BOOK 3: CHAPTER 3

Quintus Cicero's camp, Belgium, Winter 54 BC

"I've got a pain in my chest when I cough," said Valerius.

"Good."

"No, Sir. It's different."

Valerius, whose heroism against the enemy had become legendary, was terrified of illness, especially his own. He had been feeling alarmingly ill for the last few days, so weak he could hardly stand up. It frightened him. He had thought he was getting better, but today he felt worse.

"Perhaps you're dying of pneumonia."

Allaine continued writing his notes, which he kept meticulously, using neat Greek letters. Octavian's scrawl could be deciphered only by himself, and that with no great certainty, Marcius wasn't much better, and Servilius did far too much of the work anyway. When he had finished, Allaine examined his supposedly tough slave.

"You have pleurisy, Valerius."

"Is that bad?"

"No."

"Will it get better?"

"It may get better, it may get worse."

The hope, that being owned by a physician might render one immune to serious illness, was shattered. It got worse.

Allaine started working at first light, and continued long after nightfall. He made no charges for his treatment. The relatives of the rich men he treated were generous with their gifts, whether the patient lived or died. He accepted nothing from the common soldiers, the half-trained peasants who had taken up arms to defend their beloved country. They found it difficult at first to ask him for his assistance, feeling themselves unworthy to be treated by someone so exalted. No longer. His reputation and workload increased by the day. Now he invariably ordered Octavian to help him. He was dealing with a particularly difficult wound in the afternoon, caused by a spear through the neck. It was hard to keep the patient still, even with the restraining straps.

"Why don't you make him go to sleep, Sir?" Octavian asked. "Wouldn't that make it much easier?"

"I can't make everyone sleep," Allaine explained. "Perhaps I can put one in ten into a deep trance. It requires the unquestioning acceptance of authority, which isn't always forthcoming, even with foot soldiers. And it takes time, which is a precious commodity at present."

"Can you tell which ones to try, then?"

"Usually I have a good idea."

Without thinking, Allaine held out his hand for the next instrument he required. Octavian put a pair of forceps into his palm. Allaine paused, staring at his slave.

"I'm sorry, Sir. I thought that's what you needed." Octavian assumed he must have made a mistake.

"Yes, it is just what I need," Allaine said, slightly surprised. "Now, hold this retractor, here."

He put his hand over Octavian's, to show him how much tension to use. Octavian looked down at Allaine's warm bloody hand, covering his own, also sticky with blood. He saw the retractor protruding from the injured man's neck. He felt slightly sick.

When Allaine had finished, he told Octavian to explain to the man's relatives how to care for the wound and how to remove the stitches. He listened intently as Octavian started off using his master's by now familiar words. "There are four points to remember. Firstly, the future belongs to the Gods alone. One in four of these wounds breaks down....." Satisfied, Allaine moved away to wash before the next case.

It looked as if Octavian would become useful quite quickly. Allaine decided the more Octavian knew, the more helpful he would be. He called him over. He took a stick and drew the outline of a man in the earth. Riona wandered up to see what he was doing.

"Now, Octavian. Fill in the inside."

"What do you mean, Sir?"

"Draw in the organs, lungs, heart, stomach, liver, kidneys, spleen, intestines. How do they fit together?"

"Oh." Octavian hadn't the faintest idea. He drew a series of odd shapes inside the outline.

"The lungs and heart go in the top bit, I think. And the intestines go down here." He'd seen enough guts spilled out on the battlefield to be sure of that. What the hell was the spleen? And where did it go? Kidneys and liver, in the bottom section, he thought. "Er, something like that, Sir?"

"Let's find out if you are correct."

Octavian went pale. How exactly were they going to find out?

"Are you going to cut somebody open," Riona asked in terror.

"Yes. But they are quite dead, Riona. They won't feel any pain."

Riona steeled herself. "May I come and see, as well?"

"Why not?" said Allaine.

They all walked together to the barn, where a corpse was laid out on a trestle. Neatly Allaine opened up the chest cavity, and then the abdomen, talking and explaining all the time as he did so. Octavian was well used to the scent of freshly opened corpse. He was impressed with the neatness with which everything fitted together, and found his master's instruction fascinating. Riona found the sweetish smell sickening.

"It must have taken twenty years to form this perfect specimen of man, only for him to be destroyed in an instant," Allaine said. "It's such a waste."

"So what did he die of, Sir?" asked Octavian.

"Look at the back of his head. Apparently a stone from a

catapult. Always remember to examine the back of a patient as well as the front."

It was obvious, once they knew where to look. Riona thought she would prefer to cope with the still living, and said so.

"At least he died fighting for his country," Octavian observed.

"Hardly. He's a Roman, one of the prisoners, killed by his own side." Allaine picked up a fold of skin. "He's been starved. Look, there's nothing in the stomach, and the intestines are virtually empty as well. You can see the marks on his skin where he has been beaten."

"Then I should think his death was a merciful release," Riona said.

Octavian stayed silent.

The next day Allaine told Octavian to put a couple of stitches into a small gash on the patient's left leg, while he was suturing the more complicated wound on the right leg. This time he had managed to induce a trance state, so the patient was completely still. Octavian felt apprehensive, but did as he was told, and coped successfully, he thought, though Allaine said nothing.

As he was starting to wash the instruments afterwards, Marcius came hurrying up.

"Could you do that later, Octavian? My master's horse is being a bloody nuisance, and I need someone to hang on to him, while I apply the fomentation."

They sorted out the horse with great difficulty. Marcius didn't think the spear wound was showing any signs of healing, and now Val was too ill to give any further advice.

"Perhaps Allaine could help?" suggested Octavian.

"You'd be safer speaking of him as 'Prince Allaine', or 'my Master,'" said Marcius, "just in case."

Servilius appeared. "Tribune?" He flushed. "Sorry, I mean Octavian." He still found it difficult to say. "Could you give me a hand with Val? He's too heavy for me on my own. And he's too weak to help himself now."

The next morning Allaine summoned Octavian, and demanded to know why he hadn't washed the instruments as ordered. Octavian looked at them in dismay. He had completely forgotten. Marcius stood up for him immediately.

"It was my fault, Sir. I interrupted him."

This excuse quite failed to impress Allaine. "Octavian, I would be grateful if you could at least do one job properly."

"Didn't I do the stitching right, either, Sir?" Octavian had been worrying about this all the previous evening. It sounded as if he'd failed. He looked so downcast, Allaine was disarmed.

"Well, two jobs properly then. The stitching was fine, Octavian."

Octavian squared his shoulders and prepared for the worst. "I'm truly very sorry, Sir. I'm afraid it went out of my head. I'll do them now, unless you wish me to be punished first?"

"Why?" Allaine asked sharply. "Are you thinking of making the same mistake again?"

"No, Sir, of course not." But how on earth could he have forgotten a task so vital? What was the matter with him?

Allaine took hold of Octavian, and pushed back the hair over his forehead with the tips of his fingers, revealing the angry scar beneath. He gave a small sigh.

"Look, I appreciate you have been plunged into the middle of things, when you are not yet fully fit yourself. But when you do something, think of what exactly you are trying to achieve, and don't stop until you have succeeded. I would rather you do one job well, than two jobs badly. If you find it all too much, with Valerius being ill, I will co-opt one of the prisoners to help you. Think about it, and let me know."

"Yes, Sir. I'll do my best."

"That will make a pleasant change," said Allaine, as he walked off, aware that he was being a little unfair. Clearly Octavian was still some way from total recovery.

Octavian looked at his departing figure and let out his breath slowly. He felt thankful there were to be no physical consequences. His back was still sore.

"He makes me feel so small, like a six year old," he complained to Marcius, who was finding it all quite funny, now the immediate danger to his friend was over.

"You sounded like one, too," jeered Marcius, grinning with relief.

"Well I happen to know he is exactly the same age as me. We even have the same birthday."

"How do you know that?"

"Chrys told me." Into his mind came the vision of Chrys, as she had been on his birthday, sobbing her heart out for her dead brother. Which is why they had called the new baby Allaine.

"He's brilliant, isn't he? I wish I'd been owned by someone like him all my life," added Servilius.

Marcius sobered up immediately, and exchanged a meaningful glance with Octavian. It seemed such a paucity of ambition, just to wish for a good owner.

"Don't you ever dream of being free, Servilius?" Octavian asked.

Servilius gave a half laugh. "What use is freedom, if you've no work, no money, and nothing to eat?" He looked from one to the other of his companions. "I was free once. My father sold me when I was nine years old. We were starving. Three failed harvests in a row, and the tax farmers took what little we had. I was the eldest, but Dad didn't get much for me, not enough to keep the rest of the children alive through the winter. I was too thin. I didn't look good." He turned away abruptly, as the bitter memories surfaced, still feeling it was somehow his fault that he had failed to provide sufficient money for his little brothers and sisters.

Octavian laid a hand on his arm. "I'm sorry, Servilius. That was a facile remark I made. I wasn't thinking."

Servilius sniffed back the tears. "Look at us," he said. "We have warm clothes, thick cloaks, good boots, food, and women, too. That's never happened for me before. Never. I want to stay with Prince Allaine always, if that's possible." He could see the others weren't convinced. "He provides for you as well, Marcius, and he doesn't even own you. Anyway, he's right, as usual. We could do with some help at present. Val is really sick, and it's taking all my time looking after him."

Octavian took the cleaned instruments over to his master, and said it would indeed be helpful to have some assistance. Allaine summoned the guard, and told two of them to escort Octavian to where the prisoners were being held.

Octavian looked about him with interest. Allaine had kept his Romans well away from the fighting, so he had seen little of his surroundings. The Gallic camp was extraordinary, a complete shambles, with no attempt made at fortification. There were hastily improvised tents in disorderly rows, horses tethered here, there and everywhere, scavenging dogs roaming about, camp fires tended and untended all over the place. Unlike the well-ordered hospital barn with its neatly dug outlying latrine pit, there appeared to be haphazard piles of human excrement lying on the ground, as well as horse manure, and dog shit, all of which Octavian took pains to avoid. But the smell of human faeces was heavily overlaid with that of woodsmoke. A continuing enormous bonfire, in front of an altar on the edge of the camp, disposed of the dead. There were numbers of men milling about aimlessly, resting from the fighting, getting drunk, although others were busy, sharpening weapons. Despite his master's strictures about children and war zones, there were many youngsters of varying ages, mostly thin, and ill clad, and some very young indeed.

Just as with the Roman camps, no sooner had the siege begun than all sorts of ancillary bodies started to appear. The merchants hoping to supply Cicero's legion, regrouped and returned to supply Ambiorix instead. There were heavily guarded stalls selling overpriced food, stalls selling booze, stalls selling clothes and boots removed from the dead, tents selling sex with shackled women, as well as all the usual camp servants, ostlers, armorers, farriers, blacksmiths, leather workers, carpenters. Even an optimistic slave dealer or two turned up.

The prisoners and the troops were engaged in enlarging the earthworks, the deep ditch and rampart all round Cicero's camp. Some prisoners were also being made to assist in completing a siege terrace, under a hail of bolts shot from the catapults inside the camp. Octavian was unprepared for the sight that met his eyes. A group of men were herding the prisoners, forcing them to work, hitting them with the flat of their swords, or beating them with sticks if they noticed any slackness. Octavian spoke to the guards, and was told he could pick any prisoner, whichever one he fancied. Octavian looked along the rows of starved, dirty, soiled, defeated men. Most of them were looking shamefaced, down at the ground, but one was staring straight at him. He was almost unrecognisable. Octavian walked over to him. What to do? What to do? He must think quickly.

"Hello, Hugo. Have you had measles?"

Hugo looked at him as if he was mad. Despite the odd missing hair and livid scar, he knew this warmly dressed, booted, bearded man was Octavian, but couldn't understand how he had suddenly materialised.

"Hugo, have you had measles? Answer me!"

Hugo spoke slowly, with difficulty, his speech slightly slurred. "What are you talking about, Octavian?"

"Measles! Lots of red spots, and a fever, sore eyes, a chest infection, that sort of thing. Have you had it?"

Hugo couldn't begin to think why this should matter, but he gave the question his consideration. "Yes, I think so."

Octavian heaved a sigh of relief. "Right, you're coming with me." He ordered the men to remove the chains around Hugo's ankles. The other prisoners began to get an inkling of what was afoot. One of them called out to him, "Tribune, Tribune, what about us?" They pressed forwards desperately, only to be beaten back. Octavian raised his hands in despair. There was nothing he could do.

"Merciful Gods! Is that the best you could come up with?" Allaine remarked, when he brought Hugo back to their quarters.

"They all look pretty dreadful, Sir," Octavian said, "but this one says he's had measles." Which was true, at least.

"Has he, indeed. Well, at the moment he's covered in lice. Riona is not going to be very pleased about that." Allaine made a cursory inspection of the infested prisoner, frowning a little, while Octavian stood by, consumed with anxiety, and unsure how to proceed if his master rejected Hugo.

"Still, it shouldn't be too difficult to sort out," Allaine concluded. "Servilius, take him outside. You'd better strip him and burn his clothes, and then you must shave his head, beard, armpits and pubic hair. Try not to stand too close to him. Report back to me when you've done it."

A little while later Allaine walked out to inspect the naked hairless man. Hugo's thin body was covered in contusions, welts from whip marks, and bruises of varying size and colour. His boots had been taken, so his feet were in a terrible state, ulcerated and oozing blood from multiple cuts.

"I'm afraid you are going to look a bit strange, and smell a bit strange," Allaine told Hugo, who appeared to be quite stunned. "But this will get rid of the lice. Here, Servilius, put this lotion on all the shaved areas. It's best to apply it with a brush."

"I can do that, Master," Octavian offered, thinking Hugo might need a familiar face.

"No." Allaine was impatient. "It needs to be done thoroughly." He could tell from Octavian's stony look that he had offended him with the implied rebuke. "You're not yet totally reliable, are you, my pet?" he said gently. "You need a bit more time."

Octavian felt a flash of fury. So his punishment was to be

treated like an imbecile! He had thought to tell Allaine about Hugo, but decided it might be better to leave well alone.

The bewildered Hugo certainly looked very odd, but he smelt quite pleasantly of lavender. When Servilius reported back to Allaine, that Hugo was by now thoroughly disinfected, Allaine ordered that he was to be provided with some warm clothes and serviceable boots. "And you'd better get the girls to feed him, something simple to start with, soup, bread, eggs, that sort of thing. He looks half starved." He didn't think the prisoner was going to be much help.

Allaine had hoped to have set out on his journey home by now. He found he had no desire to see another six thousand Roman legionaries slaughtered. There had been no more captured messengers for several days, which meant someone had got through. He was pretty sure Caesar would be on the march soon, and didn't want to delay. But Valerius became too ill to move. He was feverish, then toxic, with sweat pouring off him, floating in and out of delirium. When his previous rapid breathing became true breathlessness, he heaved and struggled for air, his lips blue, the muscles of his neck stretched in a membraneous web. Allaine sat him up in bed, leaned him against Octavian, punched a hole in his chest wall, and to Octavian's utter amazement, drew off a bowlful of straw-coloured liquid.

Valerius breathed more easily that night. His colour improved and he seemed to be getting a little better over the next few days. Then he got worse again. The cough became thicker in his throat. The breathlessness increased. He seemed confused, found it difficult to swallow, said his throat hurt. The coughing became weaker. Octavian and Marcius looked at each other in consternation. They had no idea what to do to help the invalid. Octavian hoped his master knew.

Allaine detected the change in note of the breath battling in and out of the sick man. He feared it was going to be a another long night. He made his arrangements accordingly.

"Servilius and Hugo, take your beds, and go and get some sleep in the barn. Take the women as well. Marcius, go and ask Guéreth if you can stay here, for tonight. Octavian, you will stay with me."

Allaine walked over and knelt on the floor beside the mattress. Valerius was propped up as much as possible on cushions, but it no longer seemed to make any difference. Valerius opened his eyes.

"Am I dying?" he gasped.

"You may be." Allaine moistened a cloth, and carefully bathed his slave's face.

"Tell me what happens when I am dead."

"You will stay asleep until I fetch you, then we will go on a long journey."

"Master?" Valerius clutched feebly at his master's sleeve.

"What is it, Val?"

"Will there be dogs there?"

"Yes." Allaine spoke decisively. "There will be dogs there, Valerius."

"Don't go away, Master," Valerius begged. He could hardly gasp the words out.

"I'm not going anywhere, Val," said Allaine. He reached for his slave's hand, and held it in his own. "I'm staying right here."

"I can't breathe," whispered Valerius. He started to cough.

"Lean against me. Here." Allaine pulled him forwards, and propped him up against his own chest, with Val's head resting on his shoulder; the thick phlegm rattling in the sick man's throat.

"Cough!" Allaine ordered, and punched his back. Valerius put an arm round his neck, and clung to him, coughing feebly. After a while his arm slipped down again, flopping onto the bed. His breathing became imperceptible. Allaine lowered him gently onto the mattress. There was no sign of life.

"Damn you, Valerius!"

He brought his fist crashing down onto the man's chest. The body remained motionless, and then gave a convulsive heave. The lungs tried to fill with air. Allaine pushed his fingers along the moist tongue to the back of the pharynx, and then hooked around the obstruction. Valerius made a strange musical sound like a horn, as the air rushed into his lungs. Allaine pulled out some of the dirty greyish membrane, then wiped his hand on the cloth. He was more successful the second time. Valerius coughed. Allaine pulled him over to lie face down, with his chest across his master's lap, and his head tilted towards the floor. Allaine thumped his back hard. Valerius gave two or three juddering breaths. His colour turned from dusky to pink. He coughed again. Allaine bent over him, clearing his mouth with the cloth.

He stayed like that all night, sometimes clearing the pharynx, sometimes forcing Val to cough. When Octavian was convinced they were both fast asleep, he woke his master up. Allaine stared at him, with gradual recognition. He looked down.

"He's still warm," he said softly, fingering Val's thick black curls.

"Yes, Master," Octavian said. "He looks alright, doesn't he? He's breathing more easily. He hasn't coughed for a bit, and he's a good colour, isn't he?"

Allaine jerked upright, and gazed in stupefaction at Valerius. He could see his slave breathing sweetly, his colour nice and pink. He exhaled slowly.

"I didn't think he'd make it through the night."

"No, Sir. Nor did we. You perform miracles, don't you?" Octavian said. "May we get him to bed?"

Allaine nodded. He wanted to say that no, he didn't perform miracles, he merely helped the healing process. He was too exhausted to be bothered to speak, however. A little while later Octavian came to him again.

"Master, your bed's ready."

Allaine looked at Valerius, looked at Octavian.

"Thank you for your help, Octavian," said Allaine. He lay

down on his bed, overcome with fatigue, as Octavian began to undress him.

BOOK 3: CHAPTER 4

Quintus Cicero's camp, Winter 54 BC

"Jay!"

Octavian got no answering smile.

"Where's your master? Go and tell him I'm here."

Jay had managed to quarrel with Guéreth, and captivate Riona, before Allaine returned, carrying a strange-looking puppy. Jay got to his feet and bowed.

"Sir, I believe I'm a relative of yours."

"News travels fast. I will be with you in one moment." Allaine found Valerius sitting woebegone. His chest still hurt very much when he coughed. Being told his sternum had been fractured by his master in his own best interests, didn't make the pain any better.

"Here, Valerius, you'll have to train this. If it chews anything of mine, I'll thrash you."

"What is it, Master?"

"Some kind of hunting dog from the north. I told the boy I didn't wish to deprive him of it, but unfortunately he already has another four."

"The one with the injured arm?" asked Val.

"That's right."

They watched the puppy, with its unsteady legs, sniff around the floor.

"It's going to be big, Sir." Valerius held out his fingers for the puppy to lick. "He's a lovely fellow, aren't you? What's his name?"

"You'll have to think of one."

"Ajax?"

"What do you think, Riona?" asked Allaine.

Riona thought that was acceptable. She liked Allaine asking her opinion about these small domestic details.

"Ajax it is, then," said Allaine. Politely he apologised for

366

the delay to his visitor.

Jay explained who he was. He told him he had come to join his forces, and would put himself under Allaine's command.

"That's good of you, Jayven. I'm afraid I have no forces."

Jay shrugged his shoulders. "There will be plenty of men willing to fight under you."

"I don't fight. Octavian, bring some wine."

Octavian poured the wine, and remembered to bring it on a tray, for a change.

"What's he doing here?" Jay asked.

Allaine waited until the wine was safely in Jay's hand.

"He's a relative as well."

Octavian stood rooted to the spot. So his master had known. He wondered which of them had told him. He looked to see if there was any emotion in the cold grey eyes, but met only indifference. Octavian was beginning to realise, that although his master might spend days nursing a sick slave, he had little feeling for the man, but only cared about winning the battle being raged in his body. Although that didn't explain the puppy.

"Octavian," Allaine snapped his fingers. "Here."

Obediently Octavian walked over to kneel by his master's chair, schooling his features to impassivity. He was determined not to give Jay any sense of gratification at his new status. Allaine's hand rested lightly on the back of his neck.

"He seems well trained. All done by kindness?" Jay asked, his eyes alight with laughter.

"No, of course not," Allaine answered, perfectly serious. "I wasn't quick enough to prevent him being wounded. He was badly hurt. That made it easier for me."

"Why don't you fight, Sir?"

"I'm a Healer. I can't do both."

"What are your plans then?"

"To return home. To ensure my master has a functioning leg." Allaine paused, sipping the wine. "Marry Riona. Nothing beyond that."

Guéreth and Riona sat stunned. Jay didn't notice. "May I come with you?"

"I would like that very much," Allaine smiled.

"Then I think you should make a move soon."

"I would have moved before, but one of my servants became sick."

"What do you mean, marry Riona?" Guéreth recovered his powers of speech, and interrupted in fury. He was incensed.

"Exactly what I said. Unless, of course, she would prefer to marry this Tarleton of the Remi. Then, no doubt, I would have to find a way to hand her over."

"I wouldn't," said Riona quickly.

"I forbid it. Do you hear, Riona? I absolutely forbid it. He is my slave." Guéreth glared at Allaine. "You think my sister will marry a slave? She will not!"

"But I have her father's permission. I don't need yours," Allaine said. "I believe my sister is married to my slave. So what's the problem?"

He could feel Octavian go rigid with tension under his hand, and he could see Marcius becoming increasingly worried.

Guéreth looked at Allaine in consternation, knowing he wouldn't lie. "But my father's been dead for three years."

"I asked him five years ago."

"Then why didn't you marry her?" Guéreth challenged.

"Because my father wouldn't consent. He said I would have to wait until after the evacuation of the country. He was right, as it turned out." Allaine looked across at Riona, "Anyway, she was very young, and I was only eighteen."

"Well, I wish you'd told me," said Riona, smiling at Allaine.

"The only reason you're still alive, Guéreth, is because you are also going to be my brother-in-law."

Jay was surprised by the depth of animosity between the two men. The atmosphere was becoming strained. He thought a diversion would be in order.

368

"So do Romans make good slaves?" he asked mischievously, drinking his wine and grinning at Octavian.

Allaine laughed, and relaxed a little. "You should ask Guéreth. He has had Marcius much longer than I've had these." He surveyed his slaves. Valerius was asleep, with the puppy in his arms. "They're not much use at present," Allaine admitted ruefully. "I'm hoping they will improve. But it will be some time before Valerius is fit again. He was very ill."

"They wear the chain."

"They have no real understanding of its significance."

Octavian stared at the ground, feeling humiliated.

"They are intelligent, though. They learn quickly, and they try to do their best. They have been hurled from the top of the mountain to the bottom. But already they are starting to climb up again. Isn't that right, Octavian?"

"Yes, Sir," Octavian agreed. He began to feel a bit better.

Allaine got up, walked over to the side table, and poured out more wine. He gave a cup to Guéreth, another to Riona, and a third to Octavian. "So let us drink to the family," Allaine suggested, "as we are all related, or will become related. Don't look so worried, Marcius."

"To the family," Jay agreed, "quite a diverse group, aren't we?"

"Mostly Aeduans," Allaine replied, smiling.

Guéreth drank as well, despite his antagonism. There was no way he was going to waste good wine, looted from Sabinus's own stores.

"Do you have your father's permission to be here, Jay?" Allaine asked.

Jay spread his hands out. "My father and I no longer agree." Jay gave a quick smile. "Well, we never did. Always he compromises, concedes this or that." Jay rested his chin on his fingers, his eyes dark and brooding. "Now he tries begging Caesar for what he wants. But he gets nothing. The issues are already decided. He's just a collaborator."

Allaine thought he had better start being tactful. Riona was looking perturbed. "Our fathers were pushed into decisions by circumstance. Let's not judge them too harshly."

"He's a collaborator," repeated Jay.

Allaine had gradually acquired all the things necessary for their journey. He ordered Octavian to pack the wagons. He discovered turmoil inside, with a frustrated Octavian ineffectually kicking a chest, which obstinately refused to go into the too small space he had allotted it. Allaine removed the rolled up blankets, and stowed the chest in its rightful place, underneath the seat.

"It must take a considerable effort on your part, to be able to do a job as badly as this," he observed.

"I'm sorry, Master. I can't work out where everything goes." But he was sure he could have done so in the past. Octavian was beginning to be worried about himself.

"Why not?"

"There are so many things."

"Why should that make any difference, Octavian?" Allaine looked at the goods heaped on the ground. "You find the ordering of this too much to sort out?"

Octavian felt there was something he was missing. "Yes, Sir."

"You lack discipline, Octavian."

Octavian bent down, picked up a whip that was lying on the ground, and silently handed it to his master.

"That, too. But I mean internal discipline. Don't you know what that is?"

Octavian shook his head. "No, Sir."

"What do you do when you go to bed?"

"Go to sleep."

"But before that. You review the day's events in your mind, don't you?" This had been their very first exercise, when he started school.

"No, Sir."

"I see. Well, take all this out, and start again."

"Yes, Master," said Octavian. He wasn't sure doing it all again wouldn't have the same end result.

Allaine was frowning at him. "I suppose I am going to have to teach you." He didn't sound very pleased about it. "We will start tonight. Oh, and when you've finished, you'd better take the prisoner back. What's his name? Hugo, isn't it? He'd better go back."

Octavian froze, looking at him in horror. "Back where, Sir?"

"Back to the other prisoners, of course." Allaine was getting quite irritable. Octavian seemed very slow to understand anything today.

"No, Sir. No, please," Octavian panicked, dropping swiftly to his knees in front of his master. "Please, couldn't you keep him as well?"

"No, certainly not. I have neither the time nor the inclination to force another of you into slavery. The Gods know you are all hard enough work as it is."

"Master, I beg you, please, please keep him." What a bloody idiot he was, not to have sorted this out before.

"Why, Octavian?" Allaine was by now very annoyed. "How on earth have you managed to become so attached to him, in such a short time? He doesn't seem to have been much help as far as I can see. In fact he seems completely useless."

"I'll make sure he's not a nuisance. He's not been well, has he? He's not very strong yet. He'll learn, Sir. I'll train him myself," Octavian pleaded. "You won't have to do anything. I'll make sure..... I'm sure I can manage ....." He didn't feel he was getting anywhere, Allaine still looked annoyed. "For the Gods' sake, Sir. Please, please!" Octavian broke off, his voice choked. He was feeling quite desperate.

"I presume you have some reason for these histrionics?" Allaine snapped at him, but already he was becoming curious.

Things seemed to be getting more and more disastrous.

"I'm sorry, ...I'm sorry, ...I'm so sorry." Octavian was in despair. "I should have told you before. I don't know what to say now that won't make it worse."

"Try!"

"I've known him for years. We've been friends for years, since we were children."

"Oh, for heaven's sake, Octavian," Allaine said, angrily. He folded his arms, and leant back against the wagon. "How can I make a judgement, if you fail to give me all the relevant information?" He looked at his slave in exasperation. "Come here!"

Octavian stood before him, head bowed. Allaine gripped his arms. "What position did he hold in the legion?"

"He was the Senior Tribune, Sir," Octavian confessed.

Allaine shook him roughly. "Just when were you proposing to tell me?"

"I'm sorry,...... I'm so sorry," Octavian faltered. He was very near to tears now.

"I suppose if an oath taken at the altar doesn't command your loyalty, beating you is unlikely to improve matters," Allaine said savagely, "though it might make me feel better."

"What can I do to make it right?" Octavian begged his master, a picture of misery.

"Pack the wagons properly for a start! And stop looking so bloody soulful!"

"Yes, Sir." Octavian was distraught.

Allaine became a little calmer, seeing how upset Octavian was. "After that, I will give you my decision."

Allaine stalked away, thinking hard. So he could have his revenge, after all. He could hurt Octavian, plunge him into despair, if he ordered him to return Hugo to the other prisoners, to be slowly and humiliatingly destroyed. Octavian would be devastated. But for some unfathomable reason, he no longer wanted to hurt Octavian. He hadn't even physically punished him for his failure to clean the surgical instruments, though it had wasted a precious hour of his time.

If he took on Hugo, he would be travelling with two slaves who had yet to prove their loyalty. Allaine was sure Octavian and Valerius would keep their oaths. He couldn't imagine either of them would think to harm him in any way, let alone try to kill him. He wasn't bothered about Darius. How that young man had ever thought to become a soldier he couldn't imagine. Probably pushed into it by his father, he supposed. But Allaine knew very little about Hugo, who presumably was another highborn Roman, if he was a friend of Octavian's. Hugo might possibly prove dangerous, although as far as he could see, at the moment the man spent all his time in a corner of the tent, looking miserable.

Two hours later Allaine returned to find order instead of chaos. "Amazing," he remarked. "Come on, we'd better go and find your friend, and tell him his fate." He deliberately said nothing more about a beating, thinking it would do no harm for Octavian to feel apprehensive for the rest of the evening.

When they returned to their quarters, it was to discover Hugo crouched in a corner as usual, but white-faced and doubled up in pain. Allaine walked over to him at once, and bent over him in concern. This man was to be his responsibility as well, though he hadn't as yet told Octavian.

"What is it, Hugo?"

The pain was so piercing, Hugo was unable to answer. He rocked himself backwards and forwards, trying to cope with the fierce spasms coursing through his abdomen.

"Give me your hand. Come with me," Allaine ordered. "We need to get this sorted. Octavian, you'd better come as well."

Hugo's other hand was still clutched to his stomach, but Allaine managed to lift him to his feet, and lead him outside to his examination table. It took a lot of probing questions before the full story came out. The Gauls had known that Hugo was an officer from the tattered remnants of his uniform, and had accorded him specially harsh treatment. Hugo had not only been frequently beaten, but sexually assaulted as well. He was miserable with pain; the after effects were getting worse and worse.

"Put your hands down by your side, Hugo," Allaine ordered. "That's right." Patiently he showed Octavian how to palpate the abdomen. He started to explain the clinical findings. "So far we have found considerable gaseous distension and abdominal resonance, but no other abnormality."

"That's good then, Sir?" Octavian asked.

"Yes, that's very good. It's going to be alright, Hugo."

Allaine persuaded his patient to roll onto his side.

"Now Octavian, come here and look at this. He was raped with some force. It has caused a bad anal tear. Do you know what they used, Hugo? Some instrument as well?"

Hugo had difficulty answering. He was now in tears, as well as in agony. He was feeling so humiliated in front of Octavian. Allaine felt the first stirrings of pity for this emaciated shaven creature, whose bruised and battered body was now racked with sobs, but he thrust them out of his mind. This was a senior Roman officer. More culpable than Octavian, probably.

Allaine sent Octavian away, and spent some time getting Hugo calmed down. He was able to conclude the examination, and explain the treatment to his new slave, but then told him the condition he would impose as punishment.

"Hugo, you have only two choices. You may stay with me as my slave, like Octavian, or you can go back to being a prisoner. If you choose to stay with me, I will not permit you to kill yourself." Allaine was adamant. "You must give me your word on this."

Hugo reluctantly agreed to slavery. He felt his courage had worn out. He couldn't bring himself to face any more humiliation. There was nothing heroic about submitting to further abuse. From what he had seen so far of Allaine, he could expect to be treated fairly, at least. When they finally returned to the tent some time later, Allaine advised everyone that Hugo was to remain with them. Octavian walked over to his master, knelt at his feet, kissed his hand, and thanked him from the bottom of his heart. He hoped the beating he was expecting any moment would hurry up, and be over and done with. He was on tenterhooks.

After supper that evening, Allaine snapped his fingers. "Octavian!"

Octavian leapt to his feet. Oh, fuck it, he thought, still inwardly cursing himself for his own stupidity. Now he was for it, a beating, or worse. So humiliating! His guts contracted in fear. He felt sick, even though he'd hardly eaten.

Allaine could feel the tension in the air. He knew everyone was expecting the worst. He looked at his pale, sweating, trying not to look scared slave, and said, "Come with me."

He was pleased to find an unprotesting Octavian following him out, as meek as a lamb to the slaughter. He shepherded him over to the barn, and pushed him down onto the bench at the back. Then he sat next to him, and proceeded to give him a lecture on loyalty, which made Octavian feel contrite and remorseful.

"So, I am not expecting you to be disloyal to your friends, of course not," Allaine finished up. "That wouldn't be right. But if there is a conflict between what they need, and what I need, you must tell me first, and leave me to be the judge of the best course to follow. You trusted me with Val, didn't you, when he wanted to get through to Caesar? Why didn't you trust me with Hugo?"

"I don't know, Sir."

"There must be a reason."

"I suppose I thought you might kill him. By some unpleasant method."

"Have you seen me kill anyone else, Octavian?"

Octavian looked at him, then quickly looked away again. "Those prisoners." His voice shook a little. "The ones burnt to death in the wicker cage."

"Oh, I see. You were not supposed to witness the

ceremony," Allaine said, vexed. He paused, wondering how to explain to Octavian, so he would understand. "Ambiorix wished for ten prisoners to be sacrificed to the Gods in thanksgiving for his victory. It is the custom in North Gaul. It wasn't my decision, but there is no way I could have stopped him, even if I'd wanted to. The chosen victims are not supposed to feel pain, otherwise the Gods would be offended. Having been burnt myself, I thought it would be better if they felt nothing at all. So I picked out the ones I could put into a deep trance, and drugged them as well."

"Do you think they felt anything?"

"No. There was no sound, apart from the roar of the flames. No screams or cries of fear. So no, I don't think they felt anything. Rather strangely though, Darius became fully conscious as he was being transported to the altar, even though he was heavily drugged. So, I asked for him. Tomorrow I will have to ask for Hugo."

"Yes, Sir."

"Then you must trust me with Hugo."

"But I do." Octavian's expression was grave in the dim lamp light. "Of course I do. Why else would I beg you to keep him?"

"So what has changed?"

"Sir, it is infinitely better to be your slave, than to be Ambiorix's prisoner. I know now that you wouldn't harm Hugo without just cause."

"Good." Allaine nodded slowly. "He seems to have no fight left in him, at present, so he should be easy to train. He is to have nothing at all to eat for the next two days."

"Oh!" It was a cry of anguish. The thought of Hugo being starved any more, was too painful. "No, please, Master. Couldn't you punish me, instead of him?"

"No doubt I could," Allaine said, amused. "But it seems a dubious method of effecting a cure for Hugo's parasitic worms."

"Parasitic worms?" Octavian said in surprise. "Is that what's causing the pain?"

"Partly that, and partly the anal tear, I think." Allaine frowned, thinking back. "He was very distressed when I showed them to him, almost hysterical."

"Why? Were they moving?" Octavian asked, equally horrified at the thought.

"Of course they were moving. They were wriggling, Octavian. That's what worms do. I wonder why he was so upset. He surely must have seen much worse on the battlefield."

"Perhaps he hasn't your analytical medical mind, Sir."

"I suppose not. I'm not starving him to punish him, Octavian. He has accepted slavery, which will be punishment enough. I'm trying to cure him. He has endured a great deal, another two days won't make much difference to his well being."

"How will you cure him?"

"With a medicine made from pine resin. We must delay our departure, until he is purged. I've explained it all to him. He seems willing to accept the treatment, and as you have made yourself responsible for him, you can look after him."

"Of course, Master."

Allaine laughed. "It will be your job to make sure the worms are no longer moving."

"Yes, Sir," Octavian agreed, with an inward shudder.

Allaine became serious again. "But be careful. Hugo feels dishonoured, degraded at the moment. So try not to humiliate him further."

"Yes, Sir," Octavian agreed again.

Allaine looked at him with approval. "You're a good friend to have, Octavian. But I need you to be a good slave, as well. You must learn to concentrate. No, don't start apologising," he said, as Octavian attempted to speak, "it's up to me to train you. As you discovered this afternoon, you are more capable than you think. I am forced to admit, though, that sometimes your behaviour seems inexplicable to me."

Allaine touched Octavian's dark curls. "Your hair is growing. In three month's time, no one will know anything bad ever happened to you." He ran his fingers lightly over the ridged scar tissue. "Tell me, Octavian. When you were surrounded by thousands of hostile troops, just why did you remove your helmet?"

"It was hot, Sir."

"Oh, Octavian!" Allaine groaned.

Octavian's face broke into a grin. "I know. Completely idiotic. But I'd had no sleep. I'd spent the night trying to get the men into some semblance of order. Then we marched out of camp, moving at a snail's pace. When the lines halted, I'd been yelling myself hoarse at the same stupid men. They were commanded to form a circle, but instead they were trying to get their precious possessions out of the baggage wagons. The sun was beating down. I was hot. I couldn't think straight any more." Octavian looked at his master, with a tiny self-deprecating smile, and shrugged his shoulders. "So I took my helmet off." He paused, looking back into the past. "And then you arrived. Why was that, Sir?"

"I have this urge to go home, but every time I'm about to set out, something stops me. I felt impelled to go back for you. Then Valerius turned up. Now Hugo." Allaine smiled. "I have some sympathy for Ulysses. I suppose by the time we do set off, Caesar will have arrived to stop me."

They sat in companionable silence, pondering the arrival of Caesar. Allaine would be dead, killed in some disgusting manner - Octavian thought - Servilius would be heartbroken, as would Val, Darius would go back to being a victim, Lady Riona would be forced to marry a man she loathed, Hugo would kill himself, and he would go back to killing Gauls. Whining fucking Gauls.

In that instant Octavian discovered he had no desire for Caesar to capture his master again. Strangely, he couldn't bear the thought of him being hurt again, tortured again. It had all been so bloody unjust in the first place. Amazing, really, that Allaine was so normal. And although he had thought he was going to be beaten this evening, he knew the punishment would have been acceptable, reasonable even. He was prepared to voluntarily hand his body over for chastisement, without protest. He did trust Allaine. He felt emboldened to ask a question that had been puzzling him for many days.

"Sir, why did you want Guéreth to buy you? Because of Lady Riona?" Octavian hazarded. "You don't seem to like him much."

"But I didn't want him to buy me." Allaine sat frowning. "I can't stand him!" Octavian gazed at him. He could hardly contradict his master. "Why do you think that, Octavian?"

"I was talking to that little medical clerk."

"Pius."

"Yes, Pius. He told me how much the dealer was asking for you, and I said 'Where am I going to find someone with that sort of money?' and you said 'Guéreth,'" Octavian explained. "It's the only thing you did say."

Allaine shook his head. "I have no memory of it at all. How odd. I usually have total recall."

"You were very fevered, Sir."

Allaine rubbed his face with his hands. "I'm sure Guéreth has many good qualities. Well, I know he has. But...." He hesitated, searching for the right words. "To me it seems much worse, that he should be fighting against his fellow Gauls, than it does for you Romans to come here, uninvited, and try and conquer us. You are from another country, with different customs, different values. You are ignorant of us, and of our civilization. But he should know better. Does that make sense to you?" Allaine wasn't sure why he was trying to justify his dislike of Guéreth to his Roman slave.

"He has always been so kind to Marcius. Like a big brother, Marcius said, only better."

"What would you do if Guéreth ordered you to kill me?" Allaine asked.

"I'd come and tell you," Octavian said immediately. "But

379

he's not that stupid."

"Then feel free to like him, Octavian, as long as your loyalty is to me first. But don't expect me to."

"Thank you, Sir." Octavian paused, thinking. "There's something more I should tell you." Now he was going to betray his best friend. Please let me be doing the right thing, he begged the Gods. "Do you know Marcus Metius, the slave dealer?"

"Marcius's uncle? Yes, you could say I've come across him." Allaine laughed to himself.

"That's what I was going to tell you. That he is Marcius's uncle."

"Marcius told me before you were all captured. I think he was trying to impress me with his rich relation, as he wasn't succeeding in any other way. But I'm glad you thought to tell me."

Octavian breathed a sigh of relief.

"Now, enough of this frivolity, my pet. We had better get to work." Allaine enjoyed seeing Octavian's smile of amusement at the epithet. His slave was getting used to him. "And afterwards you may go and say goodnight to Marcius," he added, "otherwise I doubt if he will sleep."

"I don't seem to be thinking very well at present," Octavian admitted.

"Then this will help," Allaine told him. "But you have made a series of good decisions, today. There's not much wrong with you."

Allaine gave him the first elementary mental exercises to do. It didn't seem too difficult to start with. He merely had to lie in bed at night, review the day's events, and think how to improve on them. Then he had to tell it all to his master, before sleeping. It had an immediate effect. He found that before doing anything, he had already thought of a way to do it better. He became more efficient with hardly any effort on his part. He was quite pleased with himself.

The following day Allaine returned from Headquarters, to find Octavian bent over a foul-smelling bucket, busily engaged in stirring its contents with a stick.

"Well, anything moving?"

"No, Master. But there seem to be more worms than shit."

"From what he said, I think Hugo has had this condition for some considerable time. Long before he was captured."

"He's very distressed, Sir."

"I'll talk to him. You'll need to keep an eye on him while we are travelling, and we will repeat the treatment once we are home."

"Where is home, exactly, Sir?"

"In Switzerland. About ten miles north of Aventicum. It's a piece of blackened earth. We had to raze our house to the ground, before we left, to set a good example to the general populace. I suppose there may be a pile of burnt wood lying around."

"You must have been sad."

"No. I was angry. The whole plan seemed such a stupid idea to me. And it seemed like running away. But I couldn't convince anyone. No one listens to an eighteen-year-old. Anyway, we leave here in two days. Tell the others."

BOOK 3: CHAPTER 5

Winter 54 BC

As they were going to be spending a great deal of time travelling together, Allaine and Guéreth were keeping an uneasy truce. There were two wagons now prepared and packed ready for their journey, one for Guéreth and Riona, one for Allaine and Jayven. The women were told they could sleep where they could find a space. But Allaine mostly intended to stop at houses and farms, where they could find warmth, food, water, fodder for the horses and mules, and bathing facilities, a pool anyway. It was too difficult to transport enough food for animals and people. Guéreth and Val, being mostly in the wagons for the entire journey, were given comfortable straw mattresses inside. Ambiorix provided them with pack animals, more horses, and an armed escort to the borders of his territory. He came to wish Allaine a safe journey, presenting him with a further large supply of Roman gold, captured from Cotta and Sabinus's camp. Allaine had already commandeered a lot of equipment, most of the medical supplies, and a chest full of books.

Ambiorix was in an ebullient mood, telling Allaine if he would only wait, he could have another six thousand Roman slaves. He had wiped out one legion, now he was about to destroy another. The siege was going well, the siege terrace completed, ready for the final attack, the poor starving Romans staring death in the face.

He embraced Allaine warmly. "May the Gods guard you, protect you, and keep you safe on this journey, and for ever more, Allaine. You deserve no less, my dear boy. I'm sure you will find your brother, maybe even others. You've already found one relative. So go with a good heart, my young friend. Our prayers will go before you."

Allaine thanked him sincerely for all his help. "You have been like a father to me, Sir. I am so grateful." He couldn't say any more, he was overcome. Ambiorix patted his shoulder, and then helped him to mount up. Jay knelt and kissed Ambiorix's hand, then he mounted the beautiful horse that Caesar had given him. The wagons and pack horses were given the order to move off.

As they left Octavian twisted round in the saddle, looking back the way they had come. He thought about his friends, fighting desperately for their lives in the stricken camp. There would be no Allaine to come to their rescue. Rescue, a strange word to come to mind when thinking about Allaine. His master had certainly rescued Darius, and agreed to take on Hugo. But on the other hand, he had appeared to be perfectly happy to connive with Ambiorix, in the terrible sacrifice of those Roman prisoners in the wicker cage. Octavian wasn't sure in his own mind if he was being rescued, or suffering awful punishment. He wasn't sure Allaine knew, either. To be honest, slavery was no longer that awful. At times it was quite entertaining.

After two days Allaine decided to change things round. Guéreth and Valerius were bored, so Allaine put them together during the day, and told Guéreth he was to teach Val and Hugo the language, as he had done so well with Marcius. Guéreth found it difficult to raise Hugo's interest, though. He seemed sunk in apathy.

Allaine thought he could find out more about his Roman slaves on the journey. He continued Octavian's education while they were riding together, and most nights after they had dined. He was surprised to find how ignorant Octavian was, of even basic philosophical concepts. He had to teach him about deductive reasoning, Socratic, Platonic, and Aristotelian philosophy, Epicureans, Cynics and Stoics. Although Octavian knew the names, he had only the vaguest idea of their thinking. Allaine couldn't imagine what he had done with his time in school. He was worried.

"Perhaps your head injury has caused some memory loss."

"No, Sir. I don't think so. We were lazy, we just mucked about," Marcius explained.

"But didn't you want to learn?" Allaine asked, astonished.

"We had David, you see, Sir. He did all the work for us." Octavian frowned, trying to work it out. "David is the reason we're here."

"We rely too much on slaves, I suppose. We have tutors, physicians, sculptors and artists, but many are Greek slaves. Scribes write our letters for us," added Marcius, quickly. He didn't want to think about David. It still upset him terribly. But Allaine was not so easily diverted.

"Tell me about David. Who is David? Why is David the reason you are here?" Allaine heard Marcius draw his breath in sharply.

"He was Marcius's slave. Such a lovely willing kid, and so clever." Octavian tried to explain about David, and the reason for his dreadful death. But he could see his friend becoming ever more upset as he talked. "I was forbidden to see Marcius by his stepfather. He thought I was a bad influence. My parents took me off to Greece, to take my mind off it all, and stay out of trouble."

"What sort of trouble?"

Octavian had to explain his night in prison. "And because we were away, we didn't help Marcius. And because Marcius sold himself to Guéreth, I decided to join my eldest brother here in Gaul, and not my other brothers." Octavian thought he had better change the subject quickly. "But you're right, Marcius, we do rely too much on slaves. I remember Mother was horrified when Chrys...." He stopped abruptly. He had never before mentioned his wife's name to her brother.

"When Chrys what?"

Oh well, he can only beat me to a pulp, thought Octavian. "When Chrys said she would feed the baby herself."

"I have a nephew, then," said Allaine, "or a niece?"

"We have two sons, now."

"Two sons, that's good. And what are their names?"

384

"Octavian and Allaine." There was silence. "We thought you were dead." Still silence. "Sir," he added, and waited for all hell to break loose.

But Allaine sat lost in thought. Eventually he asked, "Did going to Greece take your mind off David's death?"

"No. He haunted me night and day. He was only fifteen."

Marcius muttered something, got up, and walked away.

Octavian looked at his master.

"Go and help him," said Allaine.

Octavian found Marcius outside, deeply upset. "I was so bloody helpless. I could do nothing for him. Oh, David, David!"

Octavian realised with a jolt, he had never spoken of David to his friend. He had been afraid of breaking down himself. He said nothing, just put his arms round Marcius and held him close.

Marcius kept having to rethink his feelings about Allaine. He knew that even Guéreth was amazed at his medical skills, which seemed little short of miraculous. Marcius hated the brutal methods by which Allaine had trained Octavian and Valerius, but had to admit to himself they had learnt in days how to act as a Gallic slave, in a way that had taken him months to work out. And Allaine had taken on Hugo, who was proving to be a disaster as far as usefulness was concerned, just because Octavian had begged him to. So far Allaine hadn't hurt Hugo in any way.

Marcius couldn't help but be pleased to be spending his time with Octavian. He had found it a little bit awkward to be a slave, whilst his best friend was a Military Tribune, not that Octavian had ever shown the slightest concern for their difference in status. He was a truly wonderful friend to have, thought Marcius, and vowed to help him as much as possible.

Octavian was surprised and shocked to find Riona knew more about philosophy than he did. It was now a long time since he had been punished in any way. He began to relax a little, and even enjoy his master's company. Allaine tried to answer any questions he cared to ask, but eventually had to explain that, though touched as he was by Octavian's great faith in his abilities, he was not omnipotent, and did not have the answers to everything.

The weather was kind to them. Apart from a few slight snowfalls the roads remained clear, although muddy and full of potholes, making the journey uncomfortable for Valerius to start with. But Guéreth's fractured femur had begun to unite, and the splints kept his leg fixed, so he was less affected. He was becoming quite adept at using his crutches. They made good progress, managing over thirty miles some days, although crossing and fording the rivers barring their route sometimes took all day to complete. Allaine knew that as the roads got steeper, they would travel much less distance. Each morning the invalids were provided with hot bricks or stones to keep them warm, and Allaine had purchased a quantity of furs, wool rugs and blankets, as well as fur lined cloaks for each of them. Servilius was overwhelmed when he received his cloak. Nothing so splendid had ever come his way before. The puppy and the women spent a lot of time next to Valerius. Gold was welcome everywhere, and they were able to eat well. Allaine asked for news at every town and village. Eventually they heard that Caesar had managed to relieve Cicero's camp. Allaine wondered wearily why the news didn't surprise him. How Ambiorix could lose when in such a commanding position seemed quite baffling. He wondered if Caesar had some divine help. Perhaps Caesar was right. Perhaps he was a God, after all. Allaine found this thought very depressing.

Ambiorix had sent messengers ahead of them to smooth their path home. They travelled through the land of the Treveri and Sequani, taking a considerable detour to avoid Labienus and his legion. Allaine sent outriders from the escort on ahead, to announce their arrival, and arrange for their accommodation. Everywhere Allaine was received with great honour. People were amazed at his re-emergence from the dead almost, with many thinking he must have supernatural powers. They were often housed in the homes of the local magistrates or priests, and usually provided with an armed escort to the next town.

At last the roads started climbing upwards. Their progress became slower. The cold mountains could be seen in the distance, gleaming with fresh snow. The air got chilly, the sun turned silver, the sky a deep piercing blue. Octavian backed the wagon horses into their traces, without any problem for once, and burst into song.

Jay laughed aloud. "He's happy," he told Allaine.

"It would seem so," Allaine replied, smiling. "He has a beautiful voice."

"Yes. You know he sang the lament for my uncle, Dumnorix?"

"No, I didn't know that." Allaine was amazed.

"Dumnorix liked Octavian. He liked him a lot," Jay explained.

At this point Octavian turned round, saw he was the object of attention, blushed and abruptly stopped singing.

"Don't stop!" Allaine called. "Sing whenever you like, Octavian. It is lovely to listen to." But Octavian felt embarrassed, and didn't sing again that day, until the evening, when Jay insisted, accompanying him on his harp.

"Why don't you sing us the song you sang for your wife on your wedding night?" Jay asked maliciously, after Octavian had sung a couple of songs. "'The girl of my dreams,' wasn't it?"

Octavian discovered just how much he disliked Jay.

"He sang it with such feeling," Jay continued. "One would almost have thought he was in love with his barbarian princess." He smiled sweetly at Octavian. Octavian thought about wiping the smile off his face with his fist.

Allaine covered Octavian's clenched hand with his own. "Remember what I said? You must let it wash over you."

Octavian realised his master had given him a shield. He

looked at Jay, and saw a jumped up junior chieftain, and felt better. His hand uncurled.

Allaine thought Octavian was being poorly rewarded for singing so beautifully.

"Do you know a song 'The land that I love?'" he asked. "The guards used to sing it in the prison. It seems strange that anything pleasant came out of that place, but I liked to hear them sing."

By the time Octavian sang the last verse, all the Romans were joining in.

"A whole flock of nightingales," Jay said, laughing.

In return for the hospitality he received, Allaine would see a few cases early in the morning, at first light, before moving on. He always made time to instruct Octavian in the niceties of history taking, examination, prognosis and treatment. He found himself enjoying teaching such a responsive pupil. Octavian remembered what he had been taught, and asked intelligent probing questions. Allaine found himself having to think hard, and to question some medical practises on his own account. Octavian was good for him.

Allaine was glad to hear Caesar had retired to Samarobriva for the rest of the winter, not daring to return to Rome, in case of another insurrection. It seemed a nice long way away. But they also heard that Caesar had first carried out a few mopping up operations, burning every Eburone town and village he could find, and butchering every inhabitant. He hadn't found Ambiorix, though.

Allaine began teaching Octavian about idea and form. He was a remarkably patient teacher. Discussion after dinner became quite lively, Guéreth, Jay, Allaine, and even Riona usually arguing heatedly about the finer points, but everyone allowed to join in.

"Now, Octavian, you have to learn self examination. Why you do what you do. Have you done this before?"

"No, Sir."

Allaine sighed. "We had better start with something simple. You talked about David the other night as the reason for your being here, but why did you join the army? Do you like killing people?"

"No, Sir, not really. Men of my class have to serve three years, unless there is a good reason not to, like a crippling disease, for instance."

"But you've been in the army much longer than three years, Octavian."

"Yes, Sir. It's because I'm a magistrate."

Allaine was puzzled. "How can you be a magistrate, and in the army as well?"

"I'm an Aeduan magistrate, not a Roman one." Octavian shrugged his shoulders. "I get elected every year. I don't know why."

"It's because your judgements are considered fair. You are an excellent magistrate; you are thought to be one of the best. You listen carefully to both sides, your conclusions are just, and the penalties you impose are appropriate," Jay said. "That's why you are elected every year, my friend."

Octavian was highly gratified. Jay had never praised him before. In fact he wasn't aware of Jay ever taking him seriously before.

"That's true," Guéreth added. "He is very good, trusted by both Aeduans and Romans. That makes him quite a rarity. So Caesar persuaded his father to let him continue for another three years."

"Very well then," Allaine carried on with the examination. "Social pressures made you take this course, and continue with it. You didn't have much choice. But did the idea please you, anyway?"

"Well, I thought it would be exciting."

Allaine smiled at that. "And is it?" he asked softly. Octavian failed to answer.

"Why Caesar's army, why the Fourteenth?"

"My brother was already in the Fourteenth. He said Caesar was making allies of the Aeduans. I thought I would be able to find Marcius, and buy him back. I spent three years saving up for him."

"You astonish me, Octavian."

It was Octavian's turn to smile. "No, he astonished me. He didn't want to be bought. He was very happy with Guéreth. Anyway, it turned out he was far too expensive. And all the time I was imagining whips, and chains, and tortures, he was having a great time with the Aeduans, mostly with Prince Jayven, I understand."

Jay and Marcius looked at each other at this point, and then both burst out laughing.

"Now I am astonished, Octavian," said Guéreth, frowning. "I thought you boys were writing to each other."

"I thought he was just putting a brave face on things. He didn't tell me much."

"You wouldn't have understood, anyway. It's all so different," added Marcius.

"And what makes Marcius so expensive? Has he some special attributes that have been hidden from me so far?" Allaine inquired drily.

"It was his scarcity value as a Roman slave, Sir," Octavian said grinning. "I'm afraid you've ruined the market."

Allaine laughed at that. Octavian was pleased to think he could make him laugh; Allaine was usually so serious. But now he was serious again. "But you don't ill treat your slaves, Octavian, as far as I am aware. Why did you think Guéreth would be any different?"

"No, I don't beat them, of course not, not the twins anyway. I probably should beat the other one. He's a fucking idiot." Still, the man was presumably dead now.

Allaine spread his hands. "I thought he was sensible enough. He is very good at lip reading. He didn't wish to remain with you, so I gave him to one of the Eburone noblemen. He appeared to find him satisfactory. Unfortunately I was only able to improve his hearing slightly. He remains very deaf."

"You mean the Dolt?" Octavian asked, incredulous. "Why didn't he want to stay with me?"

"I understood his name to be Borus," Allaine said. "He doesn't like you very much, and as you were in a vulnerable position, I thought it best to let him go."

"Oh." He'd never realised the Dolt was deaf. It explained a great deal. Now he was a slave himself, Octavian was beginning to discover that abusing a servant with whom one was sharing a tent, was not a very intelligent idea. Servilius had told him about the disgusting methods whereby slaves could wreak surreptitious vengeance on their unsuspecting masters. He wondered if someone had served up parasitic worms to Hugo.

"I suppose you think I am an idiot," Octavian concluded.

"I think you sometimes do some stupid things, but you often do some wise ones, so there is hope for you yet. But don't swear in front of Riona. As you may have noticed, she learns quickly. You have brains, Octavian, but for some reason you fail to use them. I must find out why. I will see if I can get any information about your twins."

"Unfortunately, Sir, I left them in Britain, and they disappeared."

"Yes, you told me. I have many friends in Britain who will help me if I ask them." All the Druids in Britain, he thought. Not that Octavian would understand. Still, he was improving.

"They look big, but they're just children really," said Octavian sadly.

Allaine poured the rest of the wine into Marcius's cup. "So, why did you sell yourself to Guéreth? It seems an odd thing to do." He looked quizzically at Marcius, and waited for the explanation. None was forthcoming."You don't have to tell me, of course. And I won't make Octavian tell me either. Don't worry," Allaine said to reassure him. "Octavian, bring some more wine, will you?"

"Well I'm not exactly proud of it," Marcius explained, and launched into the story.

"Drugged, do you think?" Guéreth asked Allaine, at the end of the recital.

"He must have been," Jay said. "If it had been Octavian, now, it would be different. Octavian is typically Roman, volatile, impetuous, scatter-brained, but Marcius is sober even when he's drunk, and I should know," he ended up, laughing at Octavian's angry expression.

"Considering how badly he was wounded, I think Octavian is managing pretty well," Allaine said, "but I agree. There are several drugs that would have that effect. But it sounds so reckless of them. Such a drug could have killed him quite easily."

"I know," Guéreth said. "And he's the stepson of a senator as well, as I found to my cost. But, of course, I didn't expect to see him again, after I gave him the money." He smiled fondly at his slave. "I think you should be proud of yourself, Marcius. You kept your word, and you were so young."

"Astonishing, really," Allaine agreed. "That was very brave of you, Marcius."

"I didn't have many other options, though, Sir," Marcius explained.

"Wouldn't Octavian's brother have taken care of you?"

Guéreth interrupted. "I'm sure Gaius never thought Marcius would go through with it, either. So the deed was done, and couldn't be undone."

There was a pause in the proceedings, everyone thinking their own thoughts.

Allaine shifted his attention to Valerius. "Now, Valerius, it's your turn. Why did you join the army?"

Val had drunk a considerable amount of wine, and forgot to be cautious.

"Well, Sir, we only have a small farm. It won't support two

392

families. My elder brother will inherit, so my Dad said I had to join the army. I wasn't going to go, because Dad said I couldn't take Hector. I thought of running away, but we met Tribune Volusenus at an inn, and he said he'd take Hector."

"Oh yes, of course, Hector. I forgot about Hector," said Allaine. "Did he ever get his dog-tag?"

Valerius shot him a look of pure terror. So his master did remember him.

"Did you leave him behind in Cicero's camp?" Allaine went on.

"They'll have eaten him by now," Jay put in.

Valerius paled at the thought.

"Don't, Sir," said Octavian. "You know Val prefers dogs to people. He's with my brother, Val, in Labienus's camp. He'll be fine."

"Is that right, Val?" asked Allaine with a faint smile. "You prefer dogs to people?"

"They're better than people, Sir." Val was staring resentfully at Jay as he spoke. "They don't lie or cheat, or change sides. They're loyal, and they stay loyal."

"Well, that's rubbish, for a start," said Jay angrily. "If I had a bone and you had none, which of us do you think he would go to?"

"He'd go to you, Sir," said Val. "But I could take it off him again. You couldn't."

Allaine was quick to intervene. "Enough, Val, we won't waste time arguing about a dog." He didn't want to have to punish Valerius for insolence, as the man was only just beginning to regain his strength.

Jay recovered his sense of humour, and grinned. "I think you're probably right about that, Val."

"What about you, Servilius? Why are you here?"

"I'm here because you brought me here, Sir," Servilius replied, wilfully misunderstanding.

"And before that?" Allaine asked.

"Sir, you are the only good thing that's ever happened to me. I don't want to think about what happened before."

"We will leave it there, then, for the time being," Allaine said. He looked across at Hugo, but Hugo was looking so fearful Allaine decided to leave him alone.

He was worried about Hugo. Unlike Marcius and Octavian, the further they travelled the more depressed Hugo became. He spoke very little, his face almost expressionless. He seemed to be preoccupied always with his own thoughts, becoming more and more withdrawn. He was able to obey simple orders, but if Allaine wanted him to do anything more complex, he had to make sure one of the others was around as well, to help. Octavian was finding his friend difficult to cope with. He felt so responsible for him, but had no idea what to do for him. He tried to jolly him along, but it didn't work, just revealed the depths of Hugo's despair.

They were staying at a pretty little town east of Besançon. The chief magistrate had welcomed them, delighted to have such a distinguished guest. At dinner that night Allaine noticed Hugo's hands were grimy, as Hugo was pouring the wine into his cup. He pulled his slave up abruptly.

"Hugo, you will not serve me with dirty hands. Octavian, take him outside, and scrub him clean."

When they came back, they found the talk had turned to liberty, freedom, slavery, prisoners of war, and their ill treatment or otherwise. Octavian thought the conversation was coming far too close to home. But it was Riona that shocked them all. Riona had been listening quietly to the conversation, but she exploded with a suddenness that surprised the men.

"And how is it any different?" she asked. "My brother was taking me to be married, to a man I've never seen. Why is that any better? What is the difference between marriage and rape?"

"But your parents have chosen for you," said their host. "Surely they have chosen the best thing for you?"

"I didn't have a choice," stormed Riona. "Nobody asked

me what I wanted. Why should I have to sleep with a total stranger. I don't suppose you liked it, when Caesar did it to you, Allaine."

He was so surprised, he spoke without thinking. "I couldn't care less what happened, Riona. I just wanted it to stop hurting. Nothing else mattered."

"Oh, Allaine," said Riona, and started to cry. He walked over to her at once, and gathered her into his arms.

"Stupid girl! You shouldn't ask the question, if you don't want to hear the answer," he said. He lifted her chin and kissed her lips. She wept into his shoulder. "Stupid girl," he repeated, stroking her hair and cuddling her.

Allaine could see Valerius looking at him with a puzzled expression, and frowned slightly at him, shaking his head.

"Be quiet, Val," he said, which confused the others, as Val had said not a word.

"Come on, Riona, stop crying, love," Allaine said, kissing her wet cheek. "We have to thank our hosts, and look pleased."

The next morning Allaine took Hugo to task.

"I don't ask a lot of you, Hugo, just for you to keep yourself and your clothes clean. If you fail to do this, I will punish you. Do you understand me, Hugo? This is important."

"Yes, Master, I understand," Hugo agreed.

That evening Hugo again appeared at dinner, dirty and dishevelled. Allaine took him outside. He refused to allow Octavian to accompany them.

"Hugo, do you remember what I told you to do this morning?"

Hugo looked at him, scanning his face, trying hard to get a clue.

"No, Sir. Was it something important? I don't seem to be able to remember things anymore," Hugo confessed. His voice dropped to a whisper. "The worms are eating away at my mind, Master, aren't they?"

"Rubbish!" Allaine was very sharp with him. "There are

no worms in your mind at all."

"But I can hear them, Sir," Hugo protested. "They're gnawing away at my skull. They keep me awake."

Allaine looked into the fearful eyes of his slave. "I will have to rid you of them, then," he said. "Try not to worry, Hugo. Leave it to me."

Allaine returned to the others.

"Go and clean him up, Octavian, and in future, keep him clean."

This was proving to be a difficult case. He had thought, initially, that good food and fair treatment would restore Hugo to some semblance of normality. Astonishing how quickly Hugo had been rendered a human wreck. Allaine could see that his mind was attempting to withdraw from the world, but he didn't think Hugo was in control of his own thoughts. He decided to talk the matter over with Octavian.

BOOK 3: CHAPTER 6

Helvetia (Switzerland) Winter 54 BC

There were a couple more incidents before they reached the Swiss border. One day, when they had stopped to water the wagon horses, the puppy bundled down the wagon steps, and set off. Valerius chased after the puppy through the woods, and arrived back with it in his arms, but with bluish lips, and fighting for breath.

"I don't feel so good, Master," he gasped. Allaine was quite cross with him.

"You were dying, Valerius, only two months ago. Your lungs were almost liquid. How do you expect to go from severely ill to well again in such a short space of time? It will be months before you are completely fit, and in the meantime don't overdo it. Go and rest in the wagon, and take that stupid animal with you. And keep him on his leash in future."

Two days later, as Octavian got up from the table at breakfast, the floor rushed up to meet him. He grabbed onto the edge of the table to try and steady himself. Allaine was by his side in an instant. Octavian felt strong arms encircling him, and his master's voice coming from a long way away.

"It's alright, it's alright, I've got you." Then a pause. He felt a chair being pushed against the back of his legs, but the whole room was now rotating slowly. He tried to explain, gesturing with his arm.

"The floor. It's going round."

"Sit down now, Octavian."

Octavian collapsed heavily onto the chair, and then passed out, his head lolling against his master's chest, his warm body slumped unconscious.

"We need to get him over to a couch. Marcius, can you help me carry him?"

"Yes, of course, Sir." Marcius was pale and anxious, but

able to function quickly.

Octavian was laid gently on the couch.

"What is it, Sir?" asked Marcius, worried out of his mind. His friend had a strange greenish tinge to his complexion, and his breathing was stertorous.

"He's fainted," said Valerius knowledgeably. "Isn't that right, Sir? It's a faint, isn't it, because he hasn't passed urine, and that's the difference between a faint and a fit."

"Well remembered, Val," said his master. "Yes, it looks like a simple faint. Don't look so worried, Marcius. He will come round very soon."

Sure enough, at that moment Octavian opened his eyes and groaned.

"Just keep still now, Octavian," said Allaine.

"Where am I?" asked Octavian. He looked from side to side, bewildered, then held out his hand.

Allaine grasped it firmly. "You're with me."

"Oh," said Octavian. "Good," he added. "That's alright, then." He closed his eyes again, and lay back with a small sigh.

"Obviously still a bit confused," Jay said sweetly.

Allaine laughed, and repeated, "Lie still, Octavian." An unlooked for wave of affection for his slave swept through him. He waited, half smiling, conscious of Marcius hovering anxiously at his shoulder. After a short while Octavian opened his eyes again.

"What did I do?" asked Octavian, still dazed.

"You stood up, and then you fainted."

Octavian tried to understand. His thoughts felt muddled. "Why, Sir?"

"You drove the wagon for the first time, yesterday. Perhaps that was a bit too much for you at present."

"But why should it be too much for me?"

"Octavian, you've had a severe head injury. It would be astonishing if there were no after effects. This is just a minor setback, nothing to worry about." Allaine sincerely hoped he was right about this. "We won't travel today."

"I'm a nuisance," said Octavian.

"You certainly are," Allaine agreed. "You, and Val, and Hugo." That made Octavian try to sit up, but Allaine pushed him back against the cushions. "Just be patient."

Riona came and stood beside Allaine, with her hand on his shoulder. "Shall I cut his hair, today? Then he won't look quite so lopsided."

Allaine agreed, laughing. "There you are, Octavian, a nice exciting day for you. Lady Riona will cut your hair, and then Val can read to you for a bit. I have some poems by Catullus he can read." Although perhaps Octavian would find some of them a bit too exciting. "Otherwise you are to do nothing."

"Actually, Sir, I'm not very good at reading." Valerius was embarrassed to confess his weakness.

"We will ask Guéreth if we can borrow Marcius for the afternoon, then, and you can take his place, Val. Meanwhile we will find the local holy place, so Hugo and Darius can take their oath of loyalty to me." Allaine took Hugo aside. "After your oath, you will undergo purification."

"What do you mean, Sir?"

"I think you still feel soiled, debased, contaminated from your experiences, don't you? It's pulling you down, and making you miserable. It is preying on your mind, making the worms you hear. This ceremony will help you."

"I don't think anything can help me," Hugo sighed.

"It won't do you any harm, Hugo." Allaine went off to make the arrangements.

When they returned after several hours, Hugo couldn't explain at all what had been happening to him. It was clear something drastic had occurred. Hugo was cheerful and smiling. That evening he washed himself scrupulously before dinner, although unfortunately he forgot to put his trousers back on afterwards. Allaine ordered Octavian to ensure Hugo was properly dressed in future, as Hugo appeared to have become a little disinhibited after the purification. However at supper Hugo joined in the conversation for the first time, so there was some improvement.

"What happened?" Octavian asked Darius later.

Darius was unused to being the centre of attention. "Hugo had to lie down on the altar, like, after we was sworn. And then he was washed all over, and that. And the Master was saying words to him. Seemingly it's all to make him feel better about hisself." Darius paused, remembering. "Then we all had a drink. Good stuff, it was, too."

After a good night's sleep Octavian felt fine again, but he was a little worried. He had never fainted before. He watched his master's face, as Allaine checked him over. Finally Allaine made him stand with his eyes closed. He remained almost motionless, with no swaying.

"I can't find anything wrong with you, my pet. So you may get dressed now," Allaine said.

Octavian was pleased to have his health confirmed. But Allaine didn't want to take any chances. He stopped Octavian, as he went to get his horse.

"You will ride in the wagon today, Octavian," he said.

"No, Sir. I feel fine. I'm sure I can manage....."

Allaine slapped him hard across the face. He was dammed if he was going to allow Octavian to get away with that sort of insolence. For an instant he could see the astonishment in his slave's brown eyes.

"You will ride in the wagon," Allaine repeated angrily.

Octavian flushed and stiffened to attention. "Of course, Master. Whatever you say. I just meant that I feel good."

"No, Octavian, you feel well," Allaine corrected him. "You are certainly not being good this morning."

Octavian dropped to his knees and bowed his head. "My apologies, Master." He had been in danger for the moment of forgetting what he was.

Allaine was mollified. He decided to explain. "If you faint and fall off your horse, you will be even more of a nuisance."

The possibility hadn't occurred to Octavian. He leant back on his heels, and gazed up at his master in consternation. "Do you think it will happen again, then, Sir?" he asked. "You said there was nothing wrong with me."

"I said I couldn't find anything wrong with you. I'm not infallible, Octavian. As I have no idea why it happened in the first place, I have no idea if it will happen again. We will just have to wait and see. And while we are on the subject of behaviour, you may now start Hugo's training."

Octavian looked baffled. "Sir?"

"You assured me you would be responsible for his training. Have you forgotten?"

"No, Sir." Octavian remembered just in time.

"Good. You used to be a Military Tribune, so I presume you must have some idea how to train a man. You may now start to do so."

"Yes, Sir." Octavian decided that agreeing was the safest policy, though how the hell he was going to train Hugo he couldn't imagine, Hugo being older and senior in rank to him.

Marcius thought he had better take the heat off Octavian. "Why do you bother with any of us, Sir?" he asked, greatly daring.

"I ask myself the same question every morning," Allaine replied. "If I ever discover the answer you will be the first to know it. I am well aware of what you are doing, Marcius. Don't think just because you are Guéreth's property, you are immune from me." He turned away to the others. "Darius, come here!"

Darius started to quake. His master terrified him.

"You had better ride Octavian's horse."

"I dursn't, Sir." Darius was almost in tears.

Allaine was becoming exasperated with his Romans. He was beginning to feel like getting rid of the lot of them, dedicated or not.

"And why the hell not?"

"I don't know how, Sir." Darius was now weeping openly.

Jay started to laugh. "One bad, one mad, and one sad," he said. "You're not doing very well this morning, Allaine."

Allaine looked at him, and groaned in mock despair. But then he pulled himself together, smiled in turn, and stopped being angry.

"At least you haven't done anything wrong yet, my little one," he told Darius. "It's time you learnt to ride. Come and say 'Hello' to Octavian's horse. Unlike Octavian, he is very well behaved."

Allaine led Darius over to the horse, choosing to ignore Octavian's look of smouldering resentment.

Marcius grabbed Octavian. "Say nothing," he hissed.

"I'm not mad," Octavian replied, crossly. "That's Hugo."

"Stroke him," Allaine ordered Darius. "Look. He likes to be stroked and patted. He won't bite."

Darius tentatively stroked the horse. The horse gave a soft whinny, and shook his head, causing Darius to step backwards in alarm.

"See? He likes you," Allaine insisted. He could see Darius remained unconvinced, but he ordered him to mount up, and put the horse on a leading rein. "Just for a couple of hours, to start you off," he explained. "That will be enough riding for your first day."

With that Allaine walked to his own horse, and indicated that the cavalcade was to move off.

Marcius decided to leave well alone. He climbed up onto the wagon, sat on the seat beside a subdued Octavian, and picked up the reins to drive the horses.

"Fuck!" Octavian was annoyed with himself. He sat rubbing his cheek.

Marcius said nothing.

After a mile Octavian spoke. "The trouble is, you know....." He paused, then started again. "The trouble is, and you

402

will probably think I'm insane, Marcius....."

Marcius thought he knew what was coming.

"I can't help liking him," Octavian finished, and waited for his friend's reaction.

"Well, that's obvious," said Marcius.

"Is it?"

"And, of course, it's equally obvious he likes you."

"How do you make that out?"

"Look," said Marcius. "Just now he gave you an order and you flatly contradicted him, in public, what's more. And all you got was a slap. Now I think I'm fairly easy going, but if one of my servants had done such a thing, he'd have got a thrashing off me. It was bloody cheeky."

"I suppose you're right."

"It's not just today," Marcius said. "He's taken on Hugo, only because you asked him to, and I'd have thought he finds Hugo nothing but a nuisance. And remember when you forgot to clean the instruments? You didn't even get slapped."

"Yes, that's true." But Octavian couldn't remember his master showing any sign of being pleased, let alone actually liking him. Though he had thanked him for his help when Val was so ill, and he'd said Octavian was a good friend to Hugo. "Look Marcius, you are going to have to help me with Hugo. I've no idea how to turn a Senior Tribune into a Gallic slave, especially one that doesn't seem able to think properly. I can't start beating him up, can I?"

"My master has never laid a finger on me, but I worked out most things for myself after a month or two. I think we'll manage it somehow. I'm sure your master isn't expecting you to use his methods. He's not daft. He knows you wouldn't be able to hurt a friend."

"I hope you're right."

"Does he remind you of Chrys, in any way?" Marcius asked.

Octavian thought about it. It was difficult for him to think of Allaine and Chrys as brother and sister, but there were sometimes little flashes of speech from Allaine that reminded him of his wife, more especially when he was speaking Greek. But at present he mostly spoke Latin or Gallic. He only slipped into Greek when he was instructing Octavian in medical matters.

"Not really. He's so masculine, isn't he? And she's so very....." His voice trailed off, as he was seized with such longing for Chrys. How he wished he could hold her in his arms again. It hurt to think of her. Would he ever see her again? It seemed unlikely. Marcius was still looking at him, waiting for an answer. He would have to think what to say. "They've got the same grey eyes, but apart from that there seems to be no similarity. He looks more like his elder sister, Eloise, I think." The wagon wheels jolting over the hardened ruts in the road, jolted his mind. Realisation struck him like a thunderbolt. "He dropped the book!"

"What?"

"Antinous. He dropped the book when I told you Eloise had been killed. You said something about my Chrys and her sister, and I told you Eloise and the boys were dead. So he knew then." But thoughts of Dumnorix's beautiful wife, her two beautiful boys, and their dreadful end made Octavian feel so depressed, he hardly spoke again for the rest of the day.

"Stop sulking, Octavian," Allaine admonished him at supper that evening, irritated that his slave still occasionally exhibited juvenile behaviour.

"I'm .." He got no further. Marcius seized hold of him, with a hand over his mouth. Octavian pushed him off in fury.

"Will you stop doing that," he said angrily.

"You were going to say the wrong thing," Marcius whispered.

Octavian was full of indignation. "I was going to say 'I'm sorry if I seem to be sulking.' What's wrong with that?"

Allaine was looking justifiably annoyed, Jay thought.

"Oh, I don't know," Jay put in quickly. "You are still disagreeing with your master, even though you are doing it politely. What do you say, Allaine?"

"I say 'Don't quarrel with Marcius,' Octavian," said Allaine. "You need him. And especially don't quarrel with him at the supper table, otherwise we will all get indigestion. So don't do it again."

"No, Sir. My apologies."

"There's nothing wrong with your hypothetical reply," Allaine added.

"Oh, good." Octavian became calmer, turning to Marcius, with a small smile of triumph. "You see?"

Marcius apologised to Allaine, and then quietly to Octavian, who forgave him instantly, gripping his hand.

"Idiot," Octavian whispered in his ear.

Most unusually, Octavian couldn't get to sleep that night at first. The straw-stuffed sack that served him as a mattress, seemed to be full of lumps in the wrong places. His thoughts turned repeatedly to his relationship with Allaine. The most surprising thing was that the longer they travelled, the happier he felt. It was partly the journey itself, going through country he had never seen before, every day a new vista, a new village. Partly also the company, Marcius, whom he had always loved, Prince Jayven, with his sparkling good humour, defusing any awkward situation, Guéreth being kind, Allaine continually fascinating, teaching him medicine, philosophy, Gallic culture, and this strange new personal control, the control and order of his own mind and thoughts.

Mainly though, he knew also the great relief to be away from the sickening smell of blood and death; the stench of rotting corpses, the reek of burning flesh, the shouts of men and the screams of women, the cries of little children crushed between opposing armies. To travel upwards, leaving behind Autumn with its fungal scents of decay, towards Winter, with its chill pure air, crackle of frost under foot and hoof, tumbling mountain streams of icy clear water. He hadn't realised it before, but he had had enough of fighting.

In some strange way Allaine himself seemed part of the purity he sought. Octavian felt refreshed, alert, alive, the pages of his mind constantly filled with new experiences, new thoughts, new ideas. All due to Allaine. But to actually enjoy being a slave? Crazy!

Octavian had to stay in the wagon for a few days, and be bored stiff, until Allaine was satisfied with his progress. Octavian eventually begged to be allowed to ride again, and explained that he wanted his education to continue. He swore he'd had no further feelings of faintness or dizziness, so Allaine decided to take the risk.

Darius walked over to the horse, and felt pleased with himself, when he managed to mount it without any help. He was just picking up the reins, when Octavian came up to him.

"Get back in the wagon, Darius, I'm riding him today."

"Says who?"

"Says me," Octavian said with a smile, and put his hand up to pull Darius off the horse. Darius was only just learning to get his balance. He fell heavily to the ground, with a sharp cry of anguish. He sat up, white faced, clutching his arm.

"Oh, shit!" said Octavian.

His master's voice came from behind him. "Do you think you could kerb your tendency to bully those smaller and weaker than yourself, Octavian?" Allaine snapped.

"Me?" squeaked Octavian. He had always regarded himself as exceptionally benevolent.

"Yes, you!"

Octavian was already kneeling by Darius's side, brushing him down, and apologising. He jumped up, full of contrition.

"If he's broken anything...." Allaine continued, menacingly.

Fortunately Darius, although tearful yet again, proved to be bruised, but otherwise undamaged. As Allaine examined his arm, he realised he had been at fault. One horse, two riders. He should have given clearer instructions, and said so.

"Do you think you could ride Guéreth's horse, Octavian?"

"I don't see why not," Octavian said, guardedly.

"I will seek his permission," Allaine said. "Now what?" seeing Octavian's bemused expression.

"But he's your prisoner, Sir. Why seek permission?"

"Because it would be the height of bad manners, if I did not. The horse is his property."

"But what if he refuses, Sir?"

"Then we will have to waste half a day, buying a horse." Really, sometimes Octavian seemed remarkably stupid.

Octavian decided he would never, ever, understand the Gauls.

Guéreth was pleased to know his horse would be exercised by a competent rider. Allaine borrowed a spare horse from the escort, to allow Valerius to start riding as well, watching out carefully, to make sure none of his slaves looked too tired or ill at the end of the day. Octavian was forced to admit that so far, Darius had done no damage to his horse's mouth, in spite of his own dire predictions to the contrary.

Before they reached their new home Octavian felt as if he had been turned inside out. He wasn't sure if it was an improvement, but he still had no way of telling if Allaine was pleased with him or not.

Darius was beginning to enjoy riding a horse. It was wonderful to sit looking down on the world. He also began to feel a little more confident, especially when his master praised him. He agreed with Servilius. Life had never seemed so good.

There was a great deal of fuss made when they reached the Swiss border. Outriders were dispatched to Aventicum, to announce their presence. The chief of the Sequani arrived to make a speech, hoping they had found everything to their liking. Allaine replied suitably. The chief then advised them that a hunt had been arranged the next morning, to do honour to Allaine. Allaine thanked him with great formality.

When they reached their luxurious accommodation, Allaine dismounted, drooping a little, then leant wearily against his horse, one arm round its neck.

"What's the matter, Allaine, aren't you feeling well?" Jay asked in alarm. Allaine was usually so hardy. During their journey, it was mostly Jay who suggested they stop to rest the horses, and themselves.

"No. I want to go home. The last thing I want to do is hunt. I haven't held a spear for five years," Allaine said in despair.

"Just be grateful it's a proper hunt," said Jay, relieved. "When we visited Rome, we had to put up with mock hunts in an arena. It was deadly in all respects."

"I must sound like a spoilt child. But to be so near...." Allaine's voice trailed off.

When Allaine asked his Romans if they wished to hunt, he found them full of enthusiasm.

"Yes, please, Sir. Don't worry, Sir. We can take care of you, if you like," Val assured him, his eyes sparkling in anticipation of the thrills ahead.

"Val, I'm not sure if you are fit enough yet." Val had only been riding for a few days. But he looked so miserable, Allaine relented. Octavian promised to look out for him.

Jay suggested Marcius should join them, to his delight. Guéreth gave his permission. He was even more depressed than Allaine. For once Allaine was sympathetic. "Only another four months, and you will be able to ride again, the Gods willing. You are doing very well." Guéreth merely gave a disgusted snort.

Allaine ordered his slaves to behave well, and not disgrace him. They were to obey Prince Jayven, as Jay agreed to be responsible for them. Allaine allowed Octavian and Marcius to retrieve their own swords from one of the chests in his wagon.

"It's beautiful," said Allaine, as he held Octavian's Aeduan sword.

"Yes, Sir."

"Do you know what the markings mean?"

"Yes, Sir. Prince Dumnorix told me."

"He must have thought highly of you."

"But he hardly knew me when he gave it to me."

"Then you must have made a big impression in a short time."

They spent a happy evening, sharpening their weapons, speculating on their success, or otherwise, and boasting about their exploits in hunts past. Hugo came to life, testing the balance of a spear, and carefully weighing a sword in his hand. Allaine thought he looked more alert than he had ever been since he had taken him on.

They had good hunting, three wild boar, and a stag, though the stag had seen better days. They started at daybreak on horseback. Hugo was the successful deer killer, with a superb accurately thrown javelin, impressing everyone else in the party. He grinned happily up at Allaine, when his master came riding up to congratulate him. Allaine dismounted to collect his own weapon, which had gone wildly astray. He had wrenched his shoulder as well with the throw, but endeavoured to keep his thoughts hidden. They brought back the deer carcass to the village, and broke their fast with bread, meat, and beer.

The rest of the hunt was on foot. Half the village beat through the forest, while the other half spread nets on the outskirts, in an effort to catch the wild boar. The hunters stood back, armed with their spears, ready to hurl them at any animal that escaped the nets. The most dramatic moment came in the middle of the afternoon, when a boar broke from cover, and charged straight towards Allaine, who sidestepped neatly, and thrust his spear deep into the animal's chest. The boar's impetus made it somersault in the air, before it landed on its back. Then it slowly collapsed, falling sideways, legs quivering and jerking in its death throes. Octavian and Marcius came running up, out of breath, and full of anxiety. Marcius slit the boar's throat, to make sure of it. Allaine was feeling pleased with himself. People crowded round, congratulating him on a good spear thrust.

"Very impressive," Jay remarked. "I wonder what would have happened, had you practised."

"I would have missed, I expect, like I did this morning," said Allaine, with a laugh. "It was a fluke. My shoulder's really sore, though."

He had no qualms about allowing his slaves to keep their swords. He dutifully presented the carcasses to the villagers, thanking them for a memorable day. Two boars were removed, to be smoked for the long winter ahead, but the stag and the remaining boar were roasted in the village square. The entire village population appeared in order to feast, dance, and generally drink themselves silly.

Allaine was feeling tired and happy, when a commotion at the village gates revealed Coevorten, with a host of men, come to escort him home. Allaine could hardly speak, he was so overjoyed. He hugged his brother with fervour, rejoicing that at last, after so many years, he was seeing a member of his own close family.

"Little Allaine!" Coevorten smiled up at him. He held him at arm's length, scrutinising his face. "You don't look so bad. I hear you had good hunting today." Then he laughed and hugged him again.

It was so good to feel Coevorten's strong arms embrace him. He was so alive. But Allaine could see that the dreadful experiences had taken their toll. His brother was now grey haired and bearded, his face strewn with lines of anxiety. But his smile was sweet.

The next day normal relations were swiftly resumed. Coevorten wanted to imprison Guéreth as soon as he found out who he was, but Allaine wouldn't allow it. He insisted Guéreth was a virtual prisoner, because of his fracture, and anyway, he would soon be his brother-in-law. That was another cause for disagreement. Coevorten felt his brother was much too important a man to throw himself away on an Aeduan, even if she came from a noble family. He was horrified when he found out about Allaine's Roman slaves.

"Look what happened to the Veneti," he said. "All the council members executed, and the population sold!"

"What would you have me do with them instead, brother?" Allaine answered, laughing. He felt in such high spirits. Now he was home at last, he could overcome any difficulties, even an anxious elder brother. "I could have put each of them on a horse, and sent them off to Caesar. They wouldn't have got ten yards. I could have kept them chained, but travelling with chained men is slow, and anyway, someone would have had to look after them. I could have just come home by myself, of course, but these men are important to me."

"They will have to be killed. No one must know they ever survived."

"They are dedicated. So, touch them, and I will kill you!" Allaine told him cheerfully.

"Allaine, you're mad!"

"Yes, you're right. I think I was a bit mad. But not now, now I'm sane. They are dedicated, and I have sworn to prevent any harm coming to them, from anyone. From anyone, Coevorten."

Coevorten tried to think up arguments to overcome him. But Allaine was no longer an eighteen-year-old, willing to obey his big brother without question. He was a priest, a powerful man, becoming well known throughout the countries he had just travelled.

"How, important to you?"

"Valerius is special. I owe Val a debt so huge I can never repay it," said Allaine.

"Why, what did he give you?" Coevorten asked, puzzled.

"He gave me Humanity. It was in short supply at the time," Allaine responded. "I will explain the others later." He thought it best not to give Coevorten too many shocks all at once.

BOOK 3: CHAPTER 7

Helvetia (Switzerland) 54 BC

The Helvetians were still rebuilding towns and villages, but several good harvests had made a big difference to their well being. The mood was optimistic. The Germans had been fully occupied by Caesar, and had left them strictly alone. As had Caesar.

By now the whole country had heard of Allaine's return. People lined the streets of the towns through which they passed, waving and cheering, blowing the long alpine horns, or pounding drums in excitement. Allaine had to keep stopping, being greeted by Council members he knew, young nobles he had known all his life, friends he had thought dead, men who had escaped the holocausts, men he had fought with. There was so much emotion, so much rejoicing, so much pure happiness, that Allaine felt exhausted by the time they reached Coevorten's house in Aventicum.

They stayed the night with Coevorten, and his wife and young family. Coevorten discovered just how well-trained Allaine's Romans were. They, in turn, were beginning at last to realise the enormous importance of the man they served. Not Antinous any more, but Prince Allaine. They obeyed orders swiftly and cheerfully; their manners were perfect. They also knelt unprompted at their master's feet, and kissed his hand when dismissed. Coevorten had to admit he found them very impressive.

The next morning Allaine said he wanted to get back to his old home, and start the rebuilding process himself. He knew he would spend all his time disagreeing with his brother, if he stayed any longer.

"You're too late, I'm afraid, Allaine," said Coevorten.

"What do you mean?"

"Wait and see," laughed Coevorten.

"Wait and see, wait and see," echoed the children. "It's a surprise, Uncle Allaine, a big surprise," said one. "Shh, we're not to say anything," whispered another.

"I will just have to be patient, I can tell," Allaine smiled. It was good to be with children again, his own kith and kin, what's more. Happy, excited, well fed, rosy-cheeked children, not the thin miserable creatures he had left behind five years ago. To Allaine's surprise Coevorten suggested they all travel the ten miles to the site of his old home, children included.

Coevorten didn't tell Allaine anything. He let him find out for himself. Before they ever got to the gates of the town Allaine could see the new house at the top of the valley, rising above all the others. He urged his horse forwards. The gates swung open, to the sound of cheering. The whole populace were standing outside in the streets, waving and shouting excitedly, some openly weeping tears of joy, to bring him home. His heart was pounding. He could see tiny familiar figures in the far distance, waiting with smiling faces full of delight. When Allaine saw Tzïnne, Grandmother, and even Noemon beaming up at him, he could hardly speak, he was so overwhelmed with emotion. He dropped the reins, and slowly got down from his horse, feeling a little unsteady, drunk with happiness. For so many years he had thought them dead, foully massacred in that terrible night, on the banks of the Saöne. He thought they had perished with the thirty thousand other victims. His eyes blurred with unshed tears. At the edge of his vision he became aware of Riona. As he turned to look at her, she clambered down from the wagon, and raced over to a woman, with two blond boys by her side. In an instant they were locked in each other's arms.

"Oh Eloise, Eloise!" cried Riona.

Allaine was swiftly surrounded by his family, his sisters kneeling at his feet, only to be lifted up laughing, and kissed and hugged and kissed again. He hastily forestalled Grandmother from attempting the same thing. Finally he walked over to where Noemon knelt, unseeing through the tears coursing down his cheeks. Allaine pulled him up, caught him in his arms, and embraced him.

Eloise's boys hesitated, a little shy of this tall imposing uncle of theirs, till Allaine beckoned them forwards. They dutifully knelt in turn before being kissed by the uncle they couldn't remember.

Almost immediately afterwards, one of the boys spotted the little group of accompanying men dismounting, and cried out in joyful astonishment, "Oh, look! Look! It's Octavian!"

Allaine had some idea of what to expect, but Coevorten was taken aback. The boys ran over to Octavian at once, and hurled themselves on him. Octavian hugged them both fiercely. He felt a welling up of happiness. His wards were alive, and clearly thriving, judging by the welcome he was getting. But he was worried they would get into trouble.

"Go and salute your Chief, properly, boys," he said. "You should have done that first." He could see Coevorten looking at him askance.

"Octavian!" Eloise went over to him in turn. To her surprise, he knelt and kissed her hand. "Octavian, what are you doing, and what are you doing here?" Eloise asked him. Then she noticed Jay, with Guéreth and Marcius. "But this is wonderful. We were so worried, we thought you might all have been killed. Allaine, you have kept us in the dark," she laughed at him.

Allaine looked at them all, then at his beaming Grandmother, at his two beautiful happy sisters, at his shy nephews, and at his slaves. He felt some of the ice crystals in his heart melt and dissolve.

The crowd of excited, happy, chattering people moved away into the house. Octavian stood quietly by the wagons, deep in thought. He sent up a prayer to the heavens, to thank the Gods for sparing his wards and their beautiful mother. He felt so grateful their lives had been saved. But concomitantly, how did he now feel about Caesar? He was very troubled. He wished he could talk it over with someone who would understand. He would try and get hold of Marcius tonight, if it were possible.

An officious looking man came up, and ordered Octavian to unpack the wagons. Marcius had already gone inside the house, having been told to help Guéreth. Octavian assumed the order originated with his master, and must be obeyed. To stop him getting above himself, he supposed. He wondered if Allaine thought he was getting too cocky after the hunt, and wanted to remind him of his servile status. He spent the afternoon heaving goods and chests out of the wagons, and into the Great Hall of the house. The women helped him with the smaller things. By the end he was dirty, clammy, and sweating, despite the cold. The officious looking man reappeared, and said Octavian could now groom the horses. Octavian was feeling exhausted. He needed a rest, and some food and drink wouldn't go amiss either, he thought. There was some sort of disturbance at the house entrance. A boy hurled himself through the doorway, leapt down the steps, and came running up to them, panting for breath.

"Please, Sir. Are you Octavian, by any chance?" the boy asked, his chest still heaving from exertion.

When Octavian replied in the affirmative, the boy sighed with relief.

"The whole house is looking for you, Sir. Your master wants you straight away."

The officious man looked a bit surprised at this.

"Are you sure, boy?"

"Yes, Sir. Prince Allaine wants Octavian. He's very angry."

Octavian brushed some of the dirt from his tunic and trousers, and followed the boy to where his master was seated, surrounded by his family, everyone trying to talk at once. Octavian bowed, and stood quietly to attention. Allaine raised his eyebrows when he saw his slave, and spoke to a man standing at his shoulder. The man came over to him.

"Would you come with me, Sir?"

"Where to?" Octavian enquired.

"To the bath house, Sir. Prince Allaine thought you would like a bath, and some fresh clothes before dinner."

"A bath house?" Octavian exclaimed.

"Yes, Sir. There's always been a bath house here, as long as I can remember. It's the only building that didn't get fired, when the rest of the house was burnt to the ground."

So, there were some servants here, who had survived the massacre, as well as the family members.

Octavian thoroughly enjoyed his bath, and the full services of a very pretty masseuse. Also a thoughtfully placed carafe of very good wine, and a wine glass, helped assuage his thirst. Afterwards he was led to a large hall, which appeared to be where the family dined. There were a lot of people, most of whom he didn't recognise. But he knew Coevorten at the head of the table, with his wife and the lively children. He saw Marcius with Guéreth near to his master. Allaine glanced at him over the heads of the people, and gave him a brief approving nod. Octavian's guide showed him to a place, and thereafter attended to him. The dinner was many courses long. His master didn't send for him.

Octavian decided to talk to the man on his left, a man with only one arm. The man introduced himself as Noemon. He was speaking the purest Greek. It turned out he had been on the bank of the Saöne, during the slaughter, although he had lost his arm many years before. He explained he was Allaine's tutor, in days gone by, now the tutor of Eloise's boys. He told Octavian a great deal about the family. But Octavian said nothing about Chrys. He wasn't going to discuss his wife with the tutor.

At the end of the meal Octavian was shown to a small room, where Valerius was already fast asleep on a large mattress of sheepskins stuffed with horsehair, that they were to share. Ajax was snoring peacefully at his side. Thick fur rugs were piled on top. It looked warm and inviting. Octavian was very thankful to say his prayers, get undressed, and extinguish the lamp. But he was feeling a bit bereft. This was the first time in months that he had gone to bed without his master saying 'Goodnight. Sleep well,

Octavian.' Perhaps now they were in Switzerland, his master would push him away. He admonished himself for being ridiculously childish. Just then a servant appeared with a lamp. Ajax woke up, alert at once. Allaine came through the doorway. Ajax pattered round for a caress, his claws sounding loud on the wooden floor. Allaine gave him a pat.

"Grandmother must never know you are here inside the house," he told the dog. Ajax gave a short sharp bark, signalling his agreement.

"Quiet, you wretched animal!" Allaine knelt down by the mattress, one arm round the dog. Octavian sat up.

"Are you alright, Octavian?" Allaine asked. "Have you everything you need?"

"Yes, Master, thank you. I'm fine."

"May the Gods bless you and yours, Octavian. Goodnight then, sleep well."

Octavian kissed the hand held out to him. After Allaine left, he fell happily asleep.

Octavian woke up. The room looked unfamiliar, as always. But no, this time they were staying put. This time they had come home. To their master's home, anyway. Apparently a brand new home, smelling deliciously of lavender and winter sweet, pinewood and resin, with wooden floors, wooden walls, and wooden ceilings. He wrapped himself in a blanket and slipped off the mattress, careful not to disturb Valerius. Ajax was on the floor, as close to Val as he could get. He lifted his head, and whined softly in his throat. Octavian stooped down to stroke him, and got a wet nose nuzzling into his hand.

He pushed open the shutters, breathing in the cold mountain air with pleasure. In the far distance the sun was peeping over an icy ridge, rimmed with golden light. Soon it would be flooding down the valley, coating the houses in a warm glow.

Marcius padded in from the room next door. "Beautiful,

isn't it? Let's get dressed and look round."

"Do you think anyone will mind?"

"No, come on. Darius can stay and look after my master."

Octavian dressed quickly. They wrapped themselves up in their cloaks, and made their way to the massive oak door, which was unbarred for them by the guards. Fresh snow had fallen in the night. The ground was white, sparkling with frost crystals. Their breath hovered in the air. Fingers froze. Snow crunched underfoot as they explored the house and stables. To start with, they made their way to the incongruous building, sitting by the side of the house. From the outside it appeared to be a perfect Greek temple, that had somehow detached itself from the Ionian Coast, and become marooned here in the Swiss mountains.

"Is it a temple, do you think?" Marcius asked.

"No, it's a bath house. I had a bath in it yesterday. I didn't realise how extraordinary it looked. It was dark outside, when I was taken over."

They walked round the back of the building, and found a small mountain of chopped logs, waiting to feed the furnace. The red sun was over the ridge now, burnishing to gold the pretty little wooden houses of the village, warming the stone cottages, and turning the snowy thatch into ruddy shining hay. It looked as if the whole village were on fire.

No, don't think of that - Octavian stopped himself hastily. Don't think of Caesar and his legions, marching up the valley, burning everything, destroying everything, and everyone.

There were many outbuildings and workshops, a smithy with sounds of hammering, a tannery from the smell, a cold store. They found barns, some with sheep and some with cattle, judging by the noises emanating from them. A stockman emerged from one, carrying milk in two heavy wooden pails, and wished them a good morning. Hens clucked around at their feet, hoping for corn. A disordered pile of huge charred beams, patterned with rime, spoke eloquently of the past.

The bakery was separate from the house, exuding a

tantalising smell of fresh baked bread. The baker saw them from the window, and beckoned them in. It was cosy inside with the heat from the ovens. Octavian had difficulty understanding the man, the dialect was so different. The baker gave them hot rolls to eat, and smiled to see their pleasure. Then he presented them each with a large wooden tray, piled high with risen breads and rolls. They made their way round to the back of the house, finding it difficult to hold onto the trays, and not slip in the snow. Eventually they found the kitchens, and much activity. Maids were scrubbing a vast table, which was being laid with cheeses, pâtés, cold meats, apples, pears, and dried fruits. They were told to put the trays of breads down on the table.

A beautifully dressed elderly lady entered, holding an ebony stick in one hand. She was surrounded by anxious attendants. All the servants leapt to their feet, and stood rigidly to attention. There was complete silence. This was Allaine's grandmother, Octavian realised. He had seen her briefly yesterday, before being told off to unpack the wagons.

"Good morning, my children," said Grandmother. The servants all responded. Grandmother held her arms wide, and said the morning blessing. That was the signal for everyone to help themselves to breakfast. People sat down on the wooden benches, and chatted to those around them. It was all very cheerful. Marcius was used to it, and tucked in, so Octavian did the same.

It took Octavian a moment to realise the elderly lady was addressing him in Greek. He hadn't been expecting it. He knew what to do. He walked over to her, knelt at her feet, and kissed the hand she held out to him. She patted the seat next to her, so he sat down. She questioned him closely about his origins, family, upbringing, and schooling, then turned her attention to Marcius. She appeared to be satisfied. Then took him by surprise.

"So, you are married to my granddaughter." She said it as a statement of fact. Octavian agreed.

"How is my darling Chrys?"

He felt he would have to tell the truth to this rather

419

formidable old lady. "Mother says she has been sad since the birth of our second son. She gets homesick. And of course, she hasn't seen much of me, recently."

"And your presence would cheer her, you think?" Grandmother could tell he was worried.

"Yes, of course." But he wasn't sure, really.

Grandmother smiled. He spoke well, excellent Greek with a pleasant Roman accent, she noticed. Apparently a highborn Roman, from good family. He was very handsome. Chrys probably would be cheered by his presence.

"My dear, women often become a little cast down after a birth. Don't worry, it will go as the child gets older. How long is Allaine going to keep you away from your wife?"

"I don't know, Madam, he has never discussed it with me. I've only been with him a short time."

The servants all leapt to attention again when Allaine entered, with Jayven and Guéreth, now much more dexterous with his crutches, Hugo and the others trailing uncertainly in their wake.

"And where are my granddaughters?" Grandmother asked laughing, knowing perfectly well.

"Still in bed, I hope," Allaine smiled back at her. "I believe the girls stayed up half the night, catching up with each other."

Of course, he had talked with Noemon far into the night as well, learning what had been happening here at home, while he was away. Noemon could now add Allaine's name at the top of the carefully preserved lists of all those who had come back to Switzerland with Coevorten. Listening to the story of their escape from the carnage brought memories and emotions back so vividly. He knew he would have to be careful to remain fair in the treatment of his Roman slaves. The past must not hold the future to ransom. They had been pretty good, on the whole, he thought, apart from poor Hugo, who was still a lost soul unless close by his master, or Octavian. But even he was improving after the hunt, although still lacking in self control, apt to swear a lot, sometimes in front of Riona, so occasionally he had to be corrected. Their journey had inevitably thrown them all together. Allaine sometimes found he forgot to dislike them quite so much, even, he forced himself to admit, enjoying their company, especially Octavian's, whose questions were becoming ever more esoteric. But it was extraordinary how they all tried so hard to obey his orders, right from the beginning. Their military training, he supposed. Presumably his Romans regarded him as some strange type of legate.

"And what are your plans, my Grandson?" Grandmother asked her favourite.

"I must go and give thanks to the Gods for my return, Grandmother. I never dreamed it would actually happen."

"I prayed for your return every day, Allaine."

"I know you did. I could feel your prayers," he replied. "But I thought they came from another place." He leant over and kissed her wrinkled cheek. "And then I thought I might have a day to rest, but the steward says that already petitioners are arriving. I'll need a building with good light. So, I'd better draw up some plans. Octavian, come here to me."

Octavian moved quickly to stand before his master. Allaine took hold of his wrist.

"Where did you disappear to, yesterday?"

Octavian cast his mind back. It was already difficult to remember, he had seen so much in such a short space of time.

"I was told to unpack the wagons, Master."

"By whom?"

"I don't know his name, Sir. The man sitting at the far end of the table."

"Fetch him here."

"Yes, Sir."

Octavian returned with the steward.

"Epheus, this is Octavian Volusenus," Allaine said. "He is my brother-in-law, and my dedicated slave. He takes orders only from me."

Octavian encountered a look of startled horror from the steward.

"Master, I am so sorry!"

"It doesn't matter," Allaine reassured his steward. "We all make mistakes."

"And the others, Sir?"

"Take their orders from me alone, to start with. They don't yet know the language."

"I'll inform the household of that, Master."

Allaine nodded. "Do so. Octavian, show me your hands."

A little surprised, Octavian held out his hands for inspection.

Allaine was relieved. "Not too bad," he said. "But no suturing until these abrasions have healed, my pet."

"Why is that, Sir?"

"You would risk an infection in those cuts. I'm not having that, having got you this far." Allaine turned back to the steward. "Epheus, Octavian will need an attendant. He needs some one to look after him, and take care of his clothes. See to it."

Allaine continued holding Octavian's hands in his own, staring into his eyes. "Something's wrong, Octavian?"

"Yes, Sir."

"Go back to Marcius now. We will talk after breakfast."

Octavian bowed and obeyed.

"You nearly caused a riot yesterday, when you disappeared," Marcius told him. "Prince Allaine was furious that no one knew where you had got to. Where had you got to?"

Octavian explained. Marcius thought it very funny. Octavian told him about the bath house, and the masseuse.

"I hope I'm allowed these luxuries," said Marcius enviously. "Almost worth unpacking the wagons."

"I wouldn't go that far," grinned Octavian.

Hugo and the other Romans stood looking bemused, unsure of what to do, faced with a hall full of noisy people, all speaking incomprehensibly. Allaine addressed them in turn.

"Listen, you four. You need to learn to speak the language a bit better. So we will follow Marcius's example. It worked well for him. You will speak only Gallic during the day. You may speak Latin at dinner, and afterwards. And Valerius, I want you to learn to read as well."

Val initially would be allowed only to play with the children for the next few days, until his master was sure of his recovery. Then he was to join them for lessons from Noemon. Allaine explained to Octavian afterwards, that even some healthy people got breathless in the mountains. No one knew why, but it was usually strangers, people unused to the strong mountain air, he thought. He didn't want any setbacks with Val. Octavian was to accompany his master. He was becoming more and more useful. He could already change some dressings, bandage neatly, and do simple suturing. Allaine found him to be surprisingly interested in the order and disorders of the human body. Strange, considering he had seemed so uninterested in learning as a youngster. He decided to start him off reading the treatises of Hippocrates and his fellow physicians.

Allaine addressed his prisoner. "Guéreth, with these icy conditions outside, I'm afraid I must confine you to the house. I cannot risk you falling."

"Oh, for the Gods' sake, Allaine!" Guéreth swore softly, so Grandmother couldn't hear, but he was not happy.

"In a month we will be able to see if you can weight bear. Then maybe it will be safe. In the meantime you may work your way through all the books in the house."

Guéreth looked anything but grateful for this offer. "What about Marcius?"

"What about him?"

"If I am not allowed to go out of the house, Marcius is going to become very bored."

"But won't you need him?"

"Not enough to keep him occupied. Darius can look after me."

"I'll take him off your hands again, if you like," Jay said.

"What will you be doing, Sir?" Guéreth asked his prince, anxiously.

"Coevorten wants me to train the cavalry."

"Sir, Caesar will never forgive you, if you fight against him."

"Let's look on the bright side, Guéreth," Jay said laughing. "Perhaps we will win."

"No," Guéreth said. "You won't. Look at Ambiorix. How could he lose? But lose he did. Win one skirmish, then everyone gets drunk. They think they've won the war. No structure. No discipline. No tenacity. No cohesion. He didn't even bother to fortify his camp." Guéreth looked at his young prince, and his heart sank. "You are beautiful, Jay. Even more so than Allaine. Caesar is utterly ruthless. He will destroy you, and take pleasure in doing so."

"Well, I'll just have to make sure I never get captured. Like Ambiorix." Jay looked at his former comrade in arms. "Do you seriously think, Guéreth, that I could go on sitting in his tent, stroking Hector, and pretending not to understand Greek? After he had Dumnorix killed? But stop worrying about me. Coevorten says he wants his cavalry trained to fight the Germans, not the Romans. He won't want to take on Caesar again. Not after the last time. And don't worry about Marcius. I won't let him do any fighting."

"I hear you are to marry your Aeduan girl after all," Grandmother said to Allaine, wanting to turn the conversation away from war. "Does Coevorten agree?"

"Of course not." Allaine was highly amused. "When did he ever agree with me? But I don't care if he does or not, I'm still going to marry her. Riona's brother isn't exactly pleased, are you, Guéreth?"

"If my father gave consent, who am I to withhold it?" said Guéreth. But Allaine knew that inwardly Guéreth was seething, outraged to think his own sister would ally herself to his disloyal slave, an enemy at that. They'd had a furious shouting match, with Guéreth calling his sister a traitress, which didn't go down very well with Riona.

As they came down the steps, Octavian lost his footing on the black ice, and fell heavily, colliding with Allaine, and knocking him to the ground.

"That was really painful," Allaine complained, sitting up and rubbing his elbow. "You're a dangerous person to have around, Octavian. Always hurling people to the ground. What happened?"

"I slipped," gasped Octavian. "I'm so sorry."

"Perhaps you haven't got enough nails in your boots," said Allaine, getting up. "No, don't move. You don't appear to have any nails in your boots."

"What do you mean, Sir?"

"Stay still," Allaine commanded. He knelt down in the snow, and removed Octavian's boots. Then he disappeared into the house. He returned again quite quickly, holding a pair of boots in his hands.

"Try these for size. Look, do you see? There are nails sticking out of the soles, so you get a good grip on the ice. We keep them by the main entrance. Just change your boots for this sort, if the ground is frozen. But don't ever wear them in the house. It's a capital offence."

"It is?" Octavian said, aghast.

"No, you idiot. That was a joke. Are you alright? Still in one piece?"

Octavian recovered and got up. "Bruised pride only, Sir. Are you alright yourself?"

"I'm fine. How do you manage in Rome?"

"We don't get much snow in Rome, as a rule. I can only remember a few winters when we had any, and it didn't hang around. In fact in the summer, we have to buy ice in."

"Buy ice?" Allaine laughed at the ridiculousness of it. "We

don't have to do that here. But snow can be dangerous. Sometimes we have avalanches, when the snow cascades down the mountains, burying everything in its path. The cold kills many people in the winter, especially the very old and the very young, and despite the nails, the ice causes many fractures. You may not do as much stitching, but you will learn a lot about orthopaedics this winter. Shall we go now?"

"Yes, of course, Sir."

They started walking downhill. Octavian found immediately that his feet felt secure. He no longer slipped and skidded. He was thinking. His master always treated him with a great deal of courtesy. He even treated that imbecile, Darius, with courtesy. Allaine hadn't punished him for knocking him to the ground. If the Dolt had done the same thing to him, Octavian wondered what punishment he would have meted out. Something unpleasantly cruel, he surmised.

"Where are we going, Sir?"

"We will go to the Bailiff's office, first. He has thought of some outbuildings that might suit us temporarily, whilst we are having one constructed to our specific requirements." Allaine continued the lecture. "Of course snow is very convenient for transporting goods and people. Sledges can be pulled over the ground easily by draft animals. But mostly, oh, it's just so beautiful. The mountains. So white, so bright, so clean, so pure." He smiled at himself. "I don't suppose I'm making any sense to you."

"Your bath house is beautiful. At first I thought it was a Greek temple. It looks just like the ones I saw all over Greece."

"Did Chrys tell you the story?" Allaine asked.

Octavian shook his head. "No, Sir."

"My grandmother is Greek, as you have discovered. The story goes that Grandfather fell in love with her at first sight, when he saw her in the market place at Massilia. Her father was quite agreeable to his daughter marrying a Helvetian prince. Apparently Grandfather looked very rich, and had masses of servants with him. But Grandmother wasn't at all keen on the ideadf. Grandfather promised he would build her a temple here, so she could worship her own Gods. But Grandmother said she didn't want a temple, she wanted a bath house. So they compromised," Allaine finished, with his faint smile. "You will find Grandmother is made of steel."

"Is Marcius permitted to use it?"

"I'm sure we can stretch a point. Is he jealous of your new status?"

"No," Octavian said. "I've known Marcius all my life. If there is anything bad about him, I have yet to find it."

"I agree with you. He is a good man, and a loyal servant."

They arrived at the bailiff's office, a wooden shed abutting the stables. The sun was causing the snow on the roof to melt. Octavian got an ice cold drip down the back of his neck, as he passed through the doorway. The bailiff greeted Allaine with great deference, and showed him a map of the near estate, and told him where to find the buildings he thought might prove suitable. He produced a wineskin of wine, and two earthenware beakers, and then left them sitting in front of a cosy fire of coal, the smoke drawn up to a smoke hood in the roof. Octavian hadn't seen coal before, and wanted to know all about it.

Allaine poured out the wine for them both.

"This is unusual, Sir."

"We are not going to suture anyone today, Octavian. Now, tell me what it is that is causing you so much anguish."

Octavian sat and talked. It all came tumbling out, just as if he were talking to his father. It didn't seem to matter that Allaine was the same age. Octavian thought his master was wise way beyond his years. He told him about his dreadful feelings of guilt after the massacres. How he now felt torn into pieces. How he hated the Eburones for destroying his beloved Fourteenth legion, slaughtering his friends, but how he could also see that Ambiorix had some justification. Like Guéreth, he dreaded the thought of the Helvetians fighting Caesar. He kept seeing both sides. He was sickened by the way Caesar had ordered the death of his wards, and their mother. He told Allaine of his vision this morning, of Caesar stampeding up the valley, killing, burning, destroying.

"I'm a Roman, an Aeduan, and your slave. But somehow they don't mix very well. I don't really know what I am any more," he ended in despair. "I still don't seem to be thinking properly."

"There is nothing wrong with the way you think. You grasp complex philosophical concepts without any problem. Drink some more," Allaine commanded.

"Drink some more?"

"Wisdom is found at the bottom of the glass, not at the top," Allaine said, gravely. "Or in our case, the bottom of a wineskin."

He waited patiently, staring into the flames, while Octavian obediently drained another beakerful.

"Now, what about me?"

Octavian swallowed, closed his eyes, opened them again, and stared straight at his master.

"You tortured me. You forced me to take an oath, to serve you for as long as you wish."

"So I did," Allaine agreed.

"I should hate you."

"But you don't."

"No."

"And that worries you?"

"It hardly seems natural."

"Oh, I think it is, Octavian." Should he enlighten him? No, not yet. "I was tortured as well. I remember so clearly how grateful I felt when he eventually stopped. It wasn't as if there was anything I could do or say to stop him, unlike you and Val. It was entirely up to him. And then he gave me wine to drink with opium in it, and the pains began to subside. I was so grateful then, I could have kissed his dick."

He could see he had thoroughly shocked Octavian, who

was looking at him in horror.

"Fortunately, I didn't have to."

C   "What do you mean, unlike Val and me?" Octavian asked, desperate not to visualise his master's words.

"For you two, it depended entirely on how much you were prepared to put up with. If you remember, I stopped as soon as you agreed to do what I wanted. The same with Val."

"No you didn't!" Octavian protested. "You said 'I'm afraid I am not yet fully convinced of your sincerity.'" He could remember all too clearly the dread of hearing those words, the realisation that there was to be more pain, more torture.

Allaine shrugged. "Well, almost as soon as you agreed. I had to be quite sure you meant it. But Caesar wanted nothing from me, nothing at all. I remember I kept apologising, but I don't know what for. Anything really to stop it, but it didn't stop." He became silent, staring into the flames, remembering. After a time he sighed and continued. "However, that's enough about me." He leant forwards, and refilled the beakers. "I'm sorry I had to hurt you so much, my pet, but I still don't know what else I could have done. You hated being chained. And although you were wounded, you hadn't reached Hugo's advanced stage of disintegration. For him, all I had to do was give him the choice, stay with me as a slave, or go back to being a prisoner. No choice really, is it?"

Octavian shook his head.

"Ambiorix was so worried about my safety, he only gave me two options as well, to keep you all alive. Either you were to be chained, or you were to be totally obedient. Do you wish I had left you dead and rotting in the ground at Atuatuca?"

"No, I don't." Octavian looked straight at his master. "I feel more alive now, than I have ever felt before."

Allaine was pleased. "It's because everything is new to you. It makes life very exciting, doesn't it? A bit like when you joined the army? At first, you don't know where you are, but after a while you get used to it, I presume."

"No. It's nothing like joining the army," said Octavian. But he didn't elaborate. He wasn't going to tell his master how he had always felt like a duck amongst the hens in the army, never able to fully join with the other officers. How it had all got so much worse after marrying Chrys.

"No? Well, anyway, there is a solution for you, but it's quite advanced. I'm not sure you could manage it, so we may have to compromise, like my grandparents. It worked for me."

Allaine decided it would do Octavian no harm to hear some of the truth. He drank some more wine himself, while he thought how to explain.

"Apparently Caesar ordered the governor of the prison at Arles to dispose of all the prisoners, me included. I think we were all supposed to be killed, but instead we were all sold to a dealer, acting for Marcus Metius, for ten gold pieces. I was bought by Antistius Petronius. That was a problem. At first I was so ill, I couldn't remember what had happened, or why. But he treated me so well, so kindly. When my memories eventually returned I discovered how much I had suffered. Unjustly, I thought. And I hated you, all of you Romans, because of what you had done to me, to Chrys, to my family, and my country. I had to go on treating Romans. But that wasn't difficult. I could enjoy their screams and struggles, even as I was curing them."

"Oh, for the Gods' sake," groaned Octavian.

Allaine ignored him, and carried on. "But there was my master, Antistius Petronius. A Roman, but a man who had shown me nothing but kindness. He loved me, because I was a mystery to be solved, and I loved him, for what he was, a thoroughly decent human being. He was like Marcius; I never found anything bad in him. He judged no one. He treated everyone who came to him as well as he could, whatever their station in life. He was as kind to the slaves, as he was to the generals. As good to the Aeduans, as he was to the Romans. So in my mind I built a wall, with him on one side, and the rest of you on the other. Do you understand any of this?"

"Quite a lot of it," Octavian said.

"I don't think you could do that. You would have to build two walls, which is not at all easy. So what we will do is this. You will live in the present, and you are to train yourself not to think too much about the past. Your present life is here with me, not as a Roman, not as an Aeduan, but as a Helvetian slave only. You need no nationality to function. You will stop worrying, Octavian. Worrying is a waste of effort. It doesn't alter events in any way. Leave Caesar to me."

"I suppose you hate him most of all?"

"He is convinced that whatever he does is right, by divine will. He thinks he is Alexander, reborn, and it is his duty to conquer the world, and fulfil his destiny. So he told me. I don't need an augur to tell me the future. He will destroy my country, and most of the good men in it, but then he will destroy your country, in the same way, with war. Finally, he will destroy himself. So no, I don't hate him. But I am still terrified at the thought of him. He still gives me nightmares." Allaine sat pensive for a time, then asked, "Do I still give you nightmares, Octavian?"

"No. I feel perfectly safe within the parameters you have set." Octavian stretched his legs out to the fire, inspected the contents of his mug, and then drank to the dregs. "I wouldn't dare disobey you, though."

"See? I was right. Wisdom is found at the bottom of the wine skin," Allaine said smiling. "I would like to be around at Caesar's end, though, so I can gloat. I'm looking forward to it. You must look forward as well, not back. Here you are my slave, but only until I let you go."

"Let me go?"

"I can't keep you forever. Seven years is the usual period for a dedicated slave. You only have six years and nine months to go. How old will you be?"

"Thirty one, Sir." Ye Gods, Octavian Junior will be twelve years old. Chrys will have forgotten him!

"Then you will still have plenty of time left to achieve your ambitions. What is your ambition?"

My ambition is to take Chrys and the children, to settle on her estate in the Loire valley, and produce the best wine in Gaul, Octavian thought. "I'm not very ambitious, Sir."

"That's not good enough, Octavian. It is when men like you shirk their responsibilities that we end up with tyrants and dictators."

"Men like me?"

"Yes. Good men. Just men. Kind men. The world needs you. Don't opt out."

Octavian was amazed by his master's words.

"When is your birthnight?"

"The same as you, Sir. December the twenty third. Saturnalia. When I was little I always thought the celebrations were specially for me."

"You are my twin." Allaine was staring at him.

"That's right, Sir. Just that we have different parents," Octavian smiled. But Allaine continued to stare. "Has it some special significance, Sir? In Gaul, I mean?" Octavian thought Allaine was looking a bit pale.

"Yes." He didn't elaborate, either. "You will be my groomsman when I get married."

"I will?" Octavian found his brain reeling at the sudden change of subject. The wine he supposed.

"Of course." Allaine was surprised. "You are my brother-in-law. You won't object?"

"Of course not, Sir." He managed to sound convincing, but it seemed a course fraught with danger. What if he made a mistake? "It will be a great honour. I hope somebody will tell me what to do. Do I have to make a speech?"

Allaine laughed. "No, my pet. Coevorten will do that, as he is the elder brother. Now, don't start worrying about that as well. I'll make sure you know exactly what to do. And at a wedding, any mistakes are forgiven, and laughed at. Who was your groomsman, when you married Chrys?"

"Prince Dumnorix."

"You don't do things by halves, do you, Octavian?"

This time there was a much longer pause, as they both sat thinking.

"I always assumed that being a slave would be easy, but it's not," said Octavian, eventually.

"Oh I don't know," said Allaine. "I think I'm managing quite well, myself. I'm even beginning to like my master. Especially as he thinks I'm almost as beautiful as Jay."

Octavian laughed. "I was forgetting."

"I expect Guéreth spends most of his waking hours imagining how he will kill me. But you are right. To Marcius he is like a kind elder brother. And for that I must honour him. Come on. We had better stagger out, and look at some of these buildings."

Allaine had twice mentioned Chrys, but Octavian refused to take the bait. Coevorten was about to take his leave, but Allaine stopped him. He summoned Octavian to kneel before them both, inwardly pleased to see his slave was slightly unsteady. Octavian had drunk a great deal more than he had.

"This is Octavian Volusenus," he told Coevorten.

"Oh, yes." Coevorten didn't want to know.

"He's married to Chrys."

"Married to Chrys?" Coevorden stared at Octavian in astonishment. "I thought you said he was a Roman Citizen."

"Yes, he is. He was a Military Tribune, before I got hold of him."

"Then how can he be married to Chrys? I thought they had a law against marrying out of their tribe?"

"Yes, they're surprisingly backwards in some ways. It's interesting," Allaine smiled. "Can you explain, Octavian?"

Oh, you fucking bastard - Octavian thought. He started off slowly, very unsure of himself. "Caesar gave Chrys to me."

"Why you, Octavian?"

"I suppose he wanted to give her to the most stupid junior

officer in the army, and he came up with me." He looked steadily at Allaine. "I am stupid," he said. "I didn't realise you were making me drunk for a purpose."

"You are anything but stupid, Octavian," Allaine said, reaching over and lightly touching the side of his slave's face.

Octavian sat back on his heels, thinking how to put it. "Chrys said to make it right, I had to consult her male relatives. She said I'd killed most of them."

"To make what right?" Coevorten asked.

"That we weren't married." Octavian frowned. He was feeling very drunk indeed. He must be careful.

"I consulted Prince Dumnorix. He turned me into an Aeduan, and I married her by proxy."

"Why?" Allaine asked.

Octavian sighed. "I thought she'd be pleased."

"And was she?"

"No. We had a row about it."

Coevorten laughed. "She hasn't changed much, then." Although he was well aware one didn't usually have rows with slave girls. Or wives, for that matter.

Allaine slipped his hand into Octavian's and gripped him firmly. Octavian felt a cold chill in his heart. Something was happening, but he wasn't sure just what was going on.

Allaine looked into his brother's eyes and asked, "Is there a penalty?"

"You aren't going to kill him, are you?" Coevorten retorted, "whatever I say."

"No."

"You could horsewhip him."

"I could. I don't wish to."

Coevorten looked into the anxious brown eyes of the man who had the temerity to marry his half sister. Octavian looked completely harmless, kneeling obediently on the ground in front of him. But Coevorten knew it was an illusion. All the resources of Republican Rome stood behind him, powerful ghosts.

"Prince Jayven confirms he was dealt with?"

"Yes. By a tribunal, arranged by Dumnorix. In court."

"An Aeduan court?"

"Yes. An Aeduan court."

"Then the case is closed."

"Hah!" Allaine exclaimed in relief, as he released Octavian. The danger was passed.

"Did you tell your parents you had married her as an Aeduan?" Coevorten demanded, his curiosity aroused. "Your parents are living?"

"Yes, Sir. Yes, I told them."

"What did they think of that?"

"They were a bit surprised. They don't really understand. About Aeduans, I mean. They've never met any. They think they're barbarians." He scowled, remembering his parents' ignorance. "Mum wanted me to marry Lucy. That's Marcius's sister." He looked at Coevorten. "You don't know Marcius. He's my best friend. His step father is fucking bonkers." Careful now, he was rambling. "I was engaged to her for a bit, but I think it was just because Mum wanted to get her out of the madhouse."

Coevorten was looking baffled. "I've got four brothers, no sisters," Octavian continued. "None of them are even engaged, let alone married, and they are all older than me. Chrys is the only girl of the house, so of course........" His voice trailed off, "and the children......" He wasn't explaining very well. "Dad calls her his Princess."

"There are no other girls in the house?" Coevorten said in surprise.

"Of course there are other girls in the house, but they're not married to me!" Octavian frowned, how to say it? "Chrys is the only daughter my parents have."

"And you like Chrys?"

"Like her?" Octavian looked at him, as if the man must be mad. He swallowed. "Even thinking about her hurts." He couldn't go on, just stared at the floor.

"And does she like you?" asked Allaine, gently.

"She tolerates me," said Octavian, with a bitter smile. "Apparently I am marginally better than the prison. I nearly killed myself, to become an Aeduan, but Chrys said it didn't make any difference. She said she's still a slave, and so are the children." He sighed again. "She's right, of course. But I just don't see what I can do about it. I've made Junior my heir."

"What children?"

"Octavian and Allaine, apparently," said Allaine. "And this Octavian is my birth twin. I found that out this morning."

"Merciful Gods!" Coevorten exclaimed.

"So you see, brother, he is important to me."

"Yes, I see that. He becomes important to me, as well," Coevorten added. "So who is Junior?"

"Octavian Junior, our eldest."

"And what does it imply, that you have made Junior your heir?"

"Everyone will think I've been killed, won't they? My father will apply to the state for Octavian to be made a citizen, when he is eighteen."

Coevorten grinned. "You need to move your household to Gaul, Octavian. Then Chrys will be a princess, and the children will be princes."

"I'll still be a slave, though," Octavian smiled.

"Well, you can't have everything."

"That's what Prince Jayven says."

Coevorten stood up. "Come here, Octavian."

Octavian went to him. Coevorten pulled him forwards, and kissed him on both cheeks.

"Welcome to the family, Octavian."

"Thank you, Sir." Now he was crying again. Hell!

Coevorten put his arms around him, and gave him a brief hug. "I always said anyone who married Chrys has my deepest sympathy," he said, chuckling. He patted Octavian on the back. "I see I was quite right."

They both accompanied Coevorten to his horse, and the group of armed men waiting patiently to escort him home.

Coevorten mounted his horse, and gathered up the reins. He looked down at Allaine. "Go on, then. Tell me the rest. I know you're holding something back."

"There's Darius."

"I suppose he's the king of Persia."

"No, he's just an ordinary legionary. Like Valerius."

"And?"

"Well, there's Hugo."

"Cotta's right hand man, I suppose."

"That's right. The senior tribune of the legion."

"For the Gods' sake, Allaine!" Coevorten turned angrily to Octavian. "How do you let him away with this stuff?"

"But how can I stop him, Sir? I'm his slave," Octavian protested.

Allaine grinned. "Oh no. You can't blame me for Hugo. Hugo was entirely Octavian's idea."

Coevorten surveyed them both. "The Gods choose our relatives. We must abide by their decision, unfortunately." He was smiling, though. He saluted them with his whip, before riding away.

Octavian was still a little groggy from the wine. "I've never known you to be devious before, Sir." It was an accusation.

"Sometimes it is necessary."

"What *is* the penalty?" Octavian asked with trepidation.

"For rape? Blinding with the irons, followed by castration. Whatever you were charged with in the Aeduan court, Octavian, it certainly wasn't rape. I'm not worried about the castration part, though maybe Chrys would be. But I didn't drag you all the way here to be blinded. You would be no use to me at all."

Octavian was gazing fixedly at Allaine. He was almost as white as the snow.

"And if he'd ordered you to impose it?"

"You surely know the answer to that question by now, don't you, my pet?"

Octavian looked into his master's cold eyes and realised that, on the contrary, he had no idea of the answer, and was much too apprehensive to ask and find out. But surely a blind groomsman wouldn't be much use? He had thought this morning that he and Allaine were beginning to become more like Marcius and Guéreth. Friends, despite being slave and master.

Allaine smiled at his anxious expression. He put his arm around Octavian's shoulder. "Idiot," he said. "I have sworn to protect you, so I would refuse, and then I would be at war with my brother. Bad for us, and worse for the country. So I thought we had better get the matter cleared up. Coevorten wants to go home, he doesn't want to hang around convening a court hearing, so it looked like a good time to get you off the hook. It's called politics." Allaine's eyes crinkled into laughter. He ruffled his slave's hair affectionately.

"It's a good thing you are so sweet, when you're drunk, Octavian."

BOOK 3: CHAPTER 8

Rome, Winter 54 BC : Spring 53 BC

When news reached Rome that six thousand men had perished in the forests of North Gaul, there was deep mourning and a desire for revenge. Caesar wrote from Samarobriva to ask for, and was immediately given, permission to raise three new legions - the Senate making not the slightest protest. So Caesar wrote to Pompey, and received his assurance, that he would raise one of the legions on his behalf in Italy, and dispatch it to Gaul with all speed.

Caesar was angry. Deeply, deeply angry. He was already forty-six years old. Time was passing by. He had wasted time in Britain, a country too far away, and too poor, to be of much use to Rome. The conquest of Gaul should have been a simple affair. Why did these men persist in refusing the hand of friendship he offered. Surely they could see from the way he had treated his allies the Aeduans, what great advantages there were to be had in acquiescing to Rome's justifiable suzerainty. A whole legion wiped out. The Eagles gone forever. How could Sabinus have been so criminally stupid? How was it that the more experienced Cotta let him make that final catastrophic decision? Why didn't the senior centurions make their generals stop and think? As for Ambiorix, let him watch out. Caesar would make sure the whole tribe suffered for the misdeeds of their leader. He would punish the Eburones until they cursed the name of Ambiorix.

As soon as Titus Volusenus saw the army messenger was clothed in black, he knew the news would be terrible. But which son? Please the Gods, not both!

So it was Octavian, his darling youngest son. Titus had such a piercing pain in his chest. It wouldn't go. He kept rubbing at it with his hand, to no avail. He called the family and servants together, and read out the brief message. Chrys just stared at him.

439

She seemed made of ice. She made no sign she had even heard him. Claudia broke down, harshly sobbing with an awful grief. The servants were subdued. Most of them thought that as masters go, Octavian was by no means the worst. They had enough sense to realise an extravagant show of sorrow would not help the mistress, who was loved by most of her household. The children didn't understand. Little Allaine was much too young. Junior was trying hard to make sense of it, and kept asking, "But what does it mean, dead?" And then, "What is a soul?" None of the explanations were satisfactory to him. Then he wanted to know exactly where his soul was, until Chrys called to Greta to take him away. She couldn't cope with him any more. She was numb with grief and shock. Somehow the thought that Octavian could die, had never really crossed her mind. He was always so alive, so active, talkative, laughing, loving.

Volusenus went round to break the awful news to Ursula. The Fourteenth legion had been massacred. There were a handful of survivors only, just a few had made it through the woods to Labienus's camp. All others were dead, including his own boy, Octavian, and his friend Marcius, and Marcius's owner as well, apparently. Ursula was stunned at first, she couldn't seem to take it in. For years she had been depending on having Marcius back again, as soon as Sperinus was dead. She had clung to the thought of her husband's death and her release, her freedom, the freedom to see her beloved son again. But now, now her boy, her wonderful boy..... Titus held her, weeping in his arms. He had just done the same for his wife, and he thought his own heart was breaking as well. He was saddened to note Chrys seemed quite unaffected. He was a little surprised too. He had thought Chrys had some feeling for Octavian. He was just a sentimental old fool, after all.

Titus arranged for Octavian and Marcius to have a joint funeral. He thought such great friends in life shouldn't be parted by death. The memorial cenotaph would depict Octavian in military dress, with Marcius by his side, to be built near the family mausoleum. Titus wondered if Guéreth should be included as well, but Ursula was vehemently against the idea. She wanted no Gauls to sully her son's shrine.

Octavian Junior was fascinated with the priest's preparations, convinced all these grown ups were going to magically conjure up his father. Titus allowed him to be the caller for Octavian. Junior called his father's name, but wouldn't stop, as he thought he had to continue until his father appeared. He became inconsolable when he discovered it was not to be. On the ninth day after they received the terrible news, the two families held the customary banquet at the Volusenus family vaults, Ursula being adamant she wanted nothing whatsoever to do with the Sperinus family's tombs.

Ursula discussed matters with Andreas and Lucy. She needed someone of her own generation quite desperately. They all agreed to continue with their original plan. Ursula knew her brother would care for her. His descriptions of the comfort to be obtained in his house at Bibracte, sounded most alluring. She longed to be pampered again. They would travel in the spring, once the roads became easier to negotiate. Letters from Marcus Metius assured them he was longing to help them. They must not worry in the slightest about travelling to the country of the Aeduans. It was perfectly safe for them to do so. He would provide servants to escort them, to make sure all was well on their journey.

Treveri Territory (Luxembourg), Spring 53 BC

Labienus turned his horse round and surveyed the advancing enemy with grim satisfaction. They had been enticed across the river, thinking he was making a retreat and were now advancing uphill in a totally unfavourable position for battle. He drew his sword.

"Right, you bastards," he said to his troops. "See those

silly buggers that don't know any better than to fight uphill? We're going to make mincemeat out of them. We're going to chop their balls off and use them for marbles."

Everyone was quiet. He knew what they were waiting for - his famous imitation of Caesar's high-pitched voice. He held his sword out towards the enemy.

"Fight under me as bravely as you would under Caesar."

"Hooray!" the men shouted.

"Imagine he is here. Imagine he is here watching every one of you in battle."

The men cheered loudly, hurled their spears and launched themselves into the fray. Labienus winked broadly at the senior tribune.

"I don't know what the enemy feel about it," he remarked, "but they certainly scare the shit out of me."

Gaius kept his horse reined in. He gazed down the steep hill. What fools the enemy were to think Romans would ever retreat. The Gauls were still scrambling up the steep-sided river bank, leaving themselves nowhere to go when attacked. Gaius gripped his spear tightly. Hatred welled up in him, flooding his veins, making his heart beat faster. He could hardly wait for the order to come. At last the harsh trumpets sounded the signal to advance. He charged forward, leading the cavalry. His spear shot claimed the first victim on the opposing side. Gaius unsheathed his sword. He fought like a maniac throughout the day, hacking, cutting, killing, his mind a fog of malice, his sword dripping hot blood.

The river flowed red with the blood of the enemy, Eburones, Atuatuci, Nervii. But it wasn't enough. It was nowhere near enough. He would go on killing Gauls until there were none left to kill.

The next morning the camp servants were sent across the river to scour the enemies' camp for plunder. They came back with Borus.

BOOK 3: CHAPTER 9

Spring 53 BC

Lady Volusena was seriously worried about Chrys. When her husband told Chrys she had been freed in Octavian's will, her eyes lit up with happiness.

"I can go home now, then?" she said, and sank into despondency again, when told she couldn't.

She hadn't been right after the birth of the second baby. For many days afterwards she had been prone to fits of crying, which Lady Volusena thought common enough, but which didn't resolve until Octavian was home again. Fortunately his period of leave started not long after the baby was born. With his arrival Chrys came back to life, especially when he suggested the baby be named after her beloved brother. Sadly, they had seen little of Octavian in the intervening period, and now Baby Allaine was two years old, and a baby no longer.

With the news of Octavian's death, Chrys became a frozen ice maiden. Now she was apathetic, and sat staring out of the window into the garden.

Octavian Junior noticed the difference in his mother. "Why does Mother keep looking into the garden? "

"She's looking for it to snow," explained Claudia. She couldn't imagine why, nasty greyish stuff.

"What is snow?" asked Junior.

Chrys got up and left the room.

It took a long time before Lady Volusena managed to persuade her husband they would have to take Chrys back to Switzerland. He couldn't make her understand how hazardous an undertaking it was.

"But dear Ursula is going north."

"Yes, but to an established community. Where she has a close relative. Where there are many Roman traders. This is a journey into the unknown. We can rely on Roman protection only as far as Geneva."

"I'm sure we could stay with Chrys's relatives, darling."

"That's the point," said her husband. "Chrys doesn't even know if she has any relatives. And if we survive this experience, and there's no guarantee that we will, we may not be allowed to return with our grandchildren, let alone Chrys. Have you thought of that?"

"Of course. I know that. But Octavian would want Chrys to be happy. We must do this for them both, even if....even if....." But she couldn't say the words. Claudia adored her grandchildren.

Titus had had enquiries instituted and discovered there was a half-brother. He hadn't told Chrys, because he thought it would make her frustration worse. He allowed himself to be convinced. Rome, after all, didn't appear to be particularly safe these days, with the riots in the streets. Also, the death of his youngest son had broken something inside him. Titus found it difficult to care about danger any more. He knew he was being irrational, but he had a desperate desire to stand on the spot where Octavian was killed. He wished to say 'Hail and Farewell' to his beloved son, in the beautiful words that the poet Catullus had composed, when standing by his own brother's grave in Africa. There wasn't the slightest possibility of it happening, of course, but Titus felt that at least when they went north, he would be a little nearer to Octavian. The thought gave him some small comfort.

Titus found Chrys trying to teach Junior a board game, with little glass counters, but Junior was having great difficulty getting the hang of it.

"Chrys, my love, Claudia and I have reached a decision. We think it best to take you back to your home country, so....."

He wasn't allowed to continue. Chrys leapt up, put her arms round his neck, and burst into tears.

"There now, Chrys, my darling girl. Don't upset yourself so much. There now, my love." Titus produced his usual handkerchief, tucked it into her hand, and patted her back, until she became calmer.

"I thought Mother *wanted* to go home," Junior said, baffled by his mother's apparent distress.

"I do, darling. I do," Chrys reassured him, smiling through her tears. "I am just so happy."

Junior stared at his mother in surprise. It seemed a very odd way to show it, he thought. He only cried when he was unhappy. He quite often was unhappy. His Daddy was dead. He didn't like that thought at all, but every night, when he was tucked up in bed, the realisation would come to him, and he would quietly cry himself to sleep.

Once the decision had been made, Titus and Claudia flung themselves into action. It helped. It helped a great deal. It took their minds off Octavian's death, for a tiny space of time. Chrys even found it helped her a little, to make plans. By tacit agreement Octavian was hardly spoken of, as Claudia was inclined to stop what she was doing, and break down, whenever his name was mentioned. They saw a lot of Ursula, Andreas, and Lucy. Chrys did not like Ursula at all. Ursula had referred to her as the obstacle to Lucy's happiness, and called the children the little obstacles, while chatting to Lady Volusena in front of her. Chrys found her appallingly rude. Even Claudia was taken aback. She liked Chrys very much, and was almost reconciled to Octavian's choice of wife. He had been remarkably constant, to her surprise.

Chrys began to like the other two members of the family. She liked Andreas especially. He was sensitive and kind. Now there was no chance whatsoever of marrying Octavian, Lucy started to enjoy being with Chrys and the children. She had spent so much time without any social life to speak of. It was good to be able to discuss many things with Chrys, who still knew much more than she did, especially about political and philosophical topics. Neither Lucy nor Andreas were bothered about Chrys being from Gaul. They were well aware the Helvetians had nothing at all to do with their brother's death. Chrys spoke such pure Greek, it was hard to remember most of the time that she *was* from Gaul.

Titus wrote to all the friends he knew who had villas on the route, and was given many other names by other friends. Titus had a lot of friends, some of whom had also lost sons. They formed a tight knit little inner group, and met to get drunk together, to assuage their grief. He would miss them on the journey, particularly Flavius Domitius, Hugo's father. They had always enjoyed each other's company, just like their sons. Flavius understood Titus adored Chrys for her own sake, as well as Octavian's, and it mattered not one whit whether she was from Gaul, or Germany, or Greece. She was a wonderful girl, and a superb mother to her sons. Titus would never hear any criticism of his Princess.

Claudia, Ursula, and Lucy found that discussing what clothes to pack, and which servants to take, made living a little bit more bearable. The nearer the date came for their departure, the happier Chrys became. A long letter arrived from Marcus Metius, with many instructions, and injunctions, and some well-dressed and well-organised servants, to help the exodus. Metius had written to ask Titus if he were able to procure various spices he had been unable to obtain in Gaul. Titus thought that might also be a good present for Chrys's unknown relatives. They had already packed books, and bolts of material. Spices would take up little room, and might be very welcome.

They travelled with Ursula and her family, and were met at Arles by Marcus Metius, delighted to see his sister and her children again. Children no longer, of course. How they'd changed, since he last saw them, Andreas now a man, and Lucy a very pretty woman, he thought. He supposed he would have to find another husband for her. Perhaps not one in the Army, this time. Military husbands didn't seem to last long, these days.

Metius confirmed what they all knew already. The Fourteenth legion was no more. Their sons had perished, killed by

446

Ambiorix and his barbarian hordes. Their mutilated bodies lay unburied, their precious Roman blood seeping into the soil of this alien land, far, far from home. Ursula felt hatred flare up inside her. But she would have to continue being civil to the Gauls they met, though she was barely civil to Chrys.

Chrys could share with no one her devastation at the news of Octavian's death. She was aware Lucy was also distraught. Chrys knew Lucy had cherished hopes of replacing her in Octavian's affections. It didn't used to bother her at all. Only now she had lost him was Chrys aware of just how much she loved him. She hugged her grief to herself, especially as Junior was so unhappy, despite being told by Titus he would now be Octavian's heir. How would that make up in any way for the loss of his father? But every mile further north made Chrys a tiny bit happier.

She had been turning over many things in her mind on the journey.

"Dad," she said, when they arrived at Arles, "this is where my brother and I were imprisoned. He died here. I would dearly love to have a priest send his soul to the other world. He was a priest himself." A very proper priest, she remembered, sadly. "He didn't have a chance to be a priest for very long, poor boy."

Metius knew just the man. "Of course. I will arrange it." He thought it would greatly please the Aeduans, when they got to hear about it.

Two days later, Marcus and Titus in their black togas of mourning, accompanied Chrys and the children to the simple white stone altar. It was placed on the shore of a small lake. Titus was alarmed to find a crowd of men congregated. Several were richly dressed, and greeted Metius by name. Many approached Chrys, kissing her hand, or her cheek. She recognised several of them from Eloise's wedding. Marcus Metius had paid a great deal for the ceremony, a simple sacrifice of a beautiful black bull. The contrasting colours of the bull, the red blood, and the white stone, all repeated in the shimmering images reflected in the almost still water, made an indelible impression on the mourners, an image they didn't forget for a long time.

Junior never forgot it. It gave him nightmares for ages afterwards. He couldn't see how Mummy's brother could benefit from the death of this gorgeous animal. Obviously the bull didn't want to be sacrificed. It bucked, and struggled, and made horrible sounds of protest. As Uncle Allaine was already dead, why did he need a dead bull? It's not as if he could eat it, could he?

Chrys found it deeply moving. She was happier now she had performed this last rite for Allaine. All the correct Roman rituals were performed for her husband, but Allaine, her dearest brother the priest, had nothing till now that she knew of, though she supposed Coevorten would have arranged something. She wondered if Allaine's soul would meet Octavian's. And if so, what would they say to each other? She was smiling at the thought of the two men she loved best in the world, meeting. She supposed they would hate each other on sight.

Titus sent up prayers to the heavens for their own lost young men. Metius arranged an enormous funeral feast afterwards, but Chrys found it difficult to eat. She was gratified that he had tried so hard to please her.

"I'm so grateful to you, Sir," she said. "I've no doubt my brother Coevorten has performed the rites in Aventicum, but I know it should be done as near as possible to his place of death."

"So the priest said, my dear. You did quite right. But come, you must eat a little, to give honour to your brother, and the occasion. His soul is quite safe now, is it not?"

He held her hand, looking deep into her eyes. There was no point in telling her that her brother had survived, only to perish with the Fourteenth legion. He didn't think it was only her brother she grieved for, anyway. Ursula couldn't understand her brother's actions. When would they ever be able to bury their own dead? Never, as far as she could see.

Metius tried to explain the politics of this huge country to his sister, with little success. Lucy was able to understand, that

448

they had friends as well as enemies in this land. That the Aeduans were friends and allies of Rome still. But she knew her brother thought only of avenging Marcius's death. He was shattered by the loss of his big brother, and could see the havoc the news had wreaked on his mother. Her relief at the death of her dreadful husband had been so short lived.

Titus Volusenus had written to Gaius as well, and was delighted to find that he would meet them at Bibracte, and stay for a few days. Gaius hoped by this to be able to persuade his parents to immediately turn round and head back to Rome. He was horrified at his mother's plan, remembering quite clearly how abysmally the Romans had fared, the last time they went into the High Alps.

They found Gaius waiting for them at Marcus Metius's sumptuous house in Bibracte. He hugged his parents. It was so lovely to see them. But he could tell from his father's sad eyes, and his mother's look of anxiety, they were no more over Octavian's death than he was. He kissed Chrys and the children, and said how glad he was to see them all, but Chrys knew better. He was looking at her now as a part of the enemy; he had never regarded her as Octavian's wife, merely his concubine. She was well aware Lady Ursula regarded her in the same light.

"And who's this?" Gaius found himself staring into the beautiful brown eyes of a beautiful brown haired girl, who looked vaguely familiar. His heart gave a quite unfamiliar lurch.

"Darling, it's Lucy of course, Marcius's little sister."

"What happened?" asked Gaius, bewildered, disconcerted by the strange tight feeling in his chest.

"She grew up, of course," said Andreas, with an irritated frown. Was the Tribune making fun of them?

Now Gaius knew who she was. This was his little brother's betrothed, till her stepfather stepped in and forbade the match. But Octavian had always talked of her in the most disparaging terms. Gaius felt odd, weird, off balance even. He'd seen it happen to Octavian of course, dozens of times, until he

449

met Chrys, and then it stopped. But it had never ever happened to him. Frankly he preferred boys, at least he thought he did. At the moment he wasn't really sure about anything.

Lucy stepped forwards with a shy smile, unaware of the havoc she was causing in Gaius's breast. She thought he looked rather nice, a little bit like Octavian, actually, with his big brown eyes and delightful smile. Although he was taller, and older of course. But she thought she would have known they were brothers.

Gaius was not pleased to find Lucy might be snatched away from him, just as soon as he found he wanted her, but no, apparently the new fiancé, Hugo Domitius, had also been killed, having been with Octavian. By the time he had chatted to her at dinner a few times, and found her to be surprisingly well informed for a girl, Gaius decided to make his feelings known to Metius, and met with instant approval. He discovered Lady Ursula was equally desirous of the connection. She would have to have been quite stupid not to realise Gaius was falling in love with her daughter. He made little attempt to hide his feelings from anyone.

Lady Volusena was becoming a little more cheerful at the thought of marriages and more grandchildren. Perhaps a girl? After five boys Claudia had given up hope, but there was always the next generation to fulfil her dreams. Gaius thought he had better find out what Lucy herself might feel.

He was completely unsuccessful at changing his parents' minds. They felt they had come so far, the journey might as well proceed as planned. He promised to expedite Andreas's entry into the army, though, and said he would look out for him when the time came. But he didn't think Andreas would have much left to wreak vengeance on. Caesar was instituting a punishment campaign for all the tribes involved in the destruction of the Fourteenth legion. The entire summer was to be spent burning and butchering.

Metius arranged a trading convoy to accompany them to

Geneva, where they were met by envoys from Coevorten, a group of virile young men, in boots, trousers and tunics, with heavy fur cloaks slung over their shoulders, and armed to the teeth. They looked just like Lady Volusena's idea of barbarians, and she was a little nervous. But they leapt off their horses and approached Chrys, dropping to their knees, kissing her hands, and laughing. Junior was overawed, and hung back, trying to hide behind his mother, but Chrys brought him out, telling him not to be shy. The leader knelt before him, and asked if the little prince wished to ride with him on his horse.

"Would you like that, Sir? He is a nice gentle beast, and he would be greatly honoured if you would ride him with me."

Junior had never been addressed as 'Sir' before by a big man. The servants at home called him Junior. And certainly no one had ever knelt respectfully before him. Mummy had said things would be different in Gaul. So far, Gaul had seemed much the same as home, but perhaps now it would change.

"Can I, Mummy?"

"Of course," said Chrys, "but Allaine is too small."

Coevorten had picked men who could speak Latin. After greeting his princess and the little princes, the leader turned with a charming smile to greet the Volusenus family, and formerly welcomed them to Helvetia. The envoys explained they would accompany the party to Aventicum, where they would meet Coevorten. It was quite a way, so arrangements had been made for them to stay the night at an inn.

It was a tiring journey. Junior was fast asleep on the horse, held safely in the leader's arms. The sun was setting behind the mountain ridges as finally the wagon oxen ambled up the hill towards their destination. There was a figure standing at the door of the inn, waiting to greet them, a man shading his eyes. The nearer they approached, the more familiar he seemed. Now there was no doubt at all.

It was unbelievable! It was a miracle! It was Octavian!

He wished his parents had stayed in Rome.

The leader gently shook Junior awake. "It is time to greet your father, Sir."

Octavian moved towards them, and saw his father's smiling face and brimming eyes. He helped his father dismount, and went over to greet his mother. She nearly fell out of the wagon in her excitement at seeing her youngest again. Chrys felt unaccountably shy of this bearded man. He didn't look like Octavian. He was somehow different. His mother had no such misgivings.

"Octavian!" said Claudia, embracing him warmly. "I knew in my heart it couldn't be true. My dear boy, you look ill. You haven't been eating properly. These army people, they get everything wrong."

Octavian grinned weakly at his father, and then looked past him to where Chrys was standing, patiently waiting, now holding Octavian Junior's hand. She wasn't smiling. He hugged and kissed his father, who patted his cheek and told him it was good to see him. Octavian could see how much he meant it. He went over to Chrys, hoping he wouldn't find her expression the same as her brother's used to be - indifferent. He wasn't sure. He kissed her cheek, then picked up his little son. He hugged him desperately, clutching him close, then gently lowered him to the ground. Junior thought he must still be asleep, and dreaming. Octavian managed to kiss Little Allaine, who was wriggling wildly in Greta's capable arms, struggling to get free. With his heart thumping madly, he turned to face his wife.

"May I take you to your brother, Chrys? He wishes to see you alone."

"Well, dear," said his mother, "I really think perhaps your father should."

"No!" Her son stopped her abruptly. "Chrys first, then Octavian."

He walked along the corridor with Chrys, wavered for a moment, then stopped and broke down, to the astonishment of the inn servants.

"I can't bear to lose you, Chrys, I can't bear it," he said in despair. Tears welled up in his eyes.

"Octavian? Is it something bad?" He thought she sounded concerned.

He took her in his arms. He couldn't think straight, he felt so much emotion at seeing her, holding her. The words came out all anyhow.

"No. It's nothing. Just that you don't care, do you? Not about me. You never did. Why should you, after all?"

"Octavian!" She felt so relieved. It was her husband, thanks be to the Gods. "For heaven's sake, Octavian." She held him tightly. "What a sensible woman your mother is. She always says men are stupid. And so you are. What do you mean, I don't care? Of course I care." Couldn't he see how much she cared?

He pushed her away, holding her face in his hands, looking into her eyes. "Do you mean it?"

"Of course I mean it." She was smiling at him through her tears.

"Do you love me?"

She was grave again. "Yes."

He wiped the tears from his own eyes, and then hugged her to his heart. "You don't have to anymore, you know."

She started to laugh. "Octavian, will you shut up. You're beginning to annoy me."

She touched the gold chain round his neck. What an adorable idiot he was, she thought. I don't suppose he has any idea that people will think he's a slave.

"Come on." He took her hand and kissed it, and then pulled her through into the garden. He hadn't told her which brother.

"Allaine," she said, transfixed. "Oh Allaine!"

Octavian went back to see his parents, and tried to give them some idea of his present circumstances. His father, he could see, was trying to understand. His mother brushed it aside.

"It will just be a question of money, dear. Let your father

453

handle it, he's used to dealing with natives. He was quaestor to the Governor of Cilicia, you remember."

Octavian Junior came through to conduct them to his Uncle Allaine, clearly pleased with his new relative. Any thoughts Lady Volusena had entertained about her son's status being of only a temporary nature were quickly dispelled by the controlled young man, who was behaving with chilling courtesy. He didn't look as if he was a problem that could be disposed of very easily. Claudia became a little frightened, and gave a little shriek when Jay came in, a sword by his side. He towered over her, but went to address Octavian Junior.

"Greetings, Cousin," he said, arm outstretched in salute.

Junior looked at him in awe. "Really?" he asked. "Are you a real relative?" One who acknowledged him? Amazing!

"Really," Jay laughed down at him.

Junior smiled blissfully. When his Daddy's brothers were home on leave, they cheerfully called the children 'Octavian's bastards,' and laughed that Octavian had 'gone native,' prophesying he would come round eventually. Junior had already surmised that a bastard wasn't a good thing to be. He wasn't sure if it was better or worse to be called a 'little obstacle' by Lady Ursula, especially when she pushed him roughly out of her way.

Octavian blushed for his parents' ignorance, and tried to apologise to his master. His father was cautious, and checked himself before speaking, but his mother wasn't quite so astute. Allaine told him it didn't matter, which made it worse.

Allaine unbent a little at dinner that night.

"We usually dine with our slaves," he said to Lady Volusena. "I hope you don't mind."

"Not at all," said Claudia, secretly appalled.

Allaine smiled faintly. "I know it's not a Roman custom, but it will enable Octavian to eat with us."

Claudia looked at him in alarm. She hadn't given too much credence so far to Octavian's words, sure that her husband would be able to negotiate some kind of agreement. But this man didn't appear to be at all malleable.

Octavian sat next to Chrys, hardly able to keep his hands off her. She was so beautiful. He loved her so much. It seemed little short of a miracle, after all he'd been through, to find himself sitting at dinner, next to his beloved wife, as if life had returned to normal.

Allaine asked Titus if he would be willing to break the bread to start the meal. Titus did so, and followed it up with his usual blessing. "We thank the Gods for their bounteous gifts of food and wine. May they bless this house, and all who dwell in it."

Allaine looked at him in approval. "May I translate it for those who don't speak your language?"

"Certainly, Sir."

"No," Allaine said, pleasantly enough. "I call you Sir. You call me Allaine. But if you feel able to address my brother Coevorten as Sir, he will be delighted."

Jay set about charming Octavian's mother. Being extremely good looking, as well as speaking exquisite Greek, he soon succeeded. Claudia began to think that maybe Helvetia wasn't such a bad place after all. So far the inhabitants appeared almost civilised. She still worried about her son, though. She knew he was ill at ease. Apart from admonishing the children, he said nothing. Allaine noticed as well.

"Are you feeling alright, Octavian?"

Octavian smiled. "Mother says I look ill, Sir."

Allaine was startled. He hadn't noticed anything wrong with his slave.

"You think he looks ill?" he asked Lady Volusena. Perhaps she could see something he had missed.

"Mother says I can't have been eating properly," Octavian added, with a grin.

Jay and Allaine burst out laughing at this. As she looked at her smiling son, Claudia was forced to concede that, in fact, he looked a picture of perfect health.

"That's good," said Allaine. "He was very sick for a time."

"I think you look gorgeous, darling, though I'm not sure about the beard," Chrys told Octavian.

"You'll just have to get used to it, Chrys. It's orders."

"Whose orders?"

"Lady Riona's orders." He wanted to fold his wife in his arms, and cover her with kisses. She looked so lovely.

At the end of the meal the children were kissed and sent to bed, with Greta in charge. Octavian was struck by the conversation Allaine was having with his father.

"I told Octavian I was going out with the foraging party," Allaine was explaining. "I wanted to see Ambiorix. He has known me since I was a child. I wanted to borrow a horse from him to get home." Allaine smiled. "I would just have been another runaway slave."

"You were a slave?" Titus said in surprise. This man appeared far too impressive to have been anything so lowly.

"I am still a slave. I am owned by Guéreth, the Aeduan. But he is also my prisoner, having been captured himself by Ambiorix, which complicates matters." Allaine could see Titus was confused.

"I'm sorry. Please continue."

"Then I heard Sabinus had persuaded Cotta that the legion should leave the camp, and march to join Cicero, or Labienus. Absolute madness, of course."

Titus was worried, not sure how much he could say. "We heard Ambiorix had promised safe conduct."

"I don't know, I wasn't there. But he may well have done. You see, once Caesar had seized the German ambassadors, he was declared unfit for honour in Gaul. That is an edict, issued by the Druidic Council, which means no one need keep any sort of bargain with him, or his army."

"Yes. Dreadful man. He's ruined our country's reputation for justice." Claudia was indignant. "Even some in the Senate said he should be handed over to the Germans, isn't that so, darling?" She turned to her husband for confirmation.

Allaine stared at her in surprise.

"He had Octavian imprisoned once, when he was just a boy."

"Yes, he told me about it. That must have been a great shock." Allaine spoke gravely, but Claudia thought he might be teasing her.

"Yes, it was shocking to me," she said, vehemently. "He was put in the Mamertine Prison, and Caesar said, 'The prison for traitors.' I thought he might be killed. I loathe Caesar!"

"Darling!" Titus thought his wife was getting a little too heated. Octavian stared at his mother in concern. "Mum!"

"I'm not the only one," declared Claudia. "One day he'll go too far."

"I agree with you," said Allaine. "Though maybe Octavian won't. Caesar told me he was a God. Very dangerous people, the ones who think they are Gods."

"Thought he was a God?" Claudia's eyes opened wide in surprise. "Well. That just shows you. The man's a megalomaniac!"

"Unfortunately for my country, he is a brilliant general as well, though," Allaine offered, "and inspirational to his soldiers."

"Can you tell me what happened?" Titus wanted to get away from Caesar.

"When the legion arrived to take up winter quarters, Ambiorix tried to explain that his country was on the brink of starvation. The harvest had been exceptionally poor, and feeding six thousand foreign soldiers was going to be quite a problem. But Sabinus was so rude to Ambiorix, so disgustingly rude to his face. He treated him like dirt, in front of everyone. Ambiorix is a proud man, with good reason to be proud. He feels a strong sense of duty towards his people, and has always striven for their welfare, much more so than some other tribal chiefs. I don't blame him in the slightest for his subsequent actions."

"So what did you do?"

"Well, the legion marched out at dawn, in this long slow file," Allaine started.

"That was another stupid mistake on Sabinus's part," Octavian interrupted. "No one had got any sleep. They were faffing around all night, deciding what to take with them."

"Yes," Allaine agreed. He thought he'd better overlook the interruption, as Octavian had hardly spoken all evening. "You do wonder why Caesar ever gave him a command."

"Or why Cotta didn't overrule him," Octavian added.

"Well anyway, I had to find Octavian, which was difficult, because for some reason he was miles back down the column. And no sooner had I found him, than he was badly wounded by a sling shot."

"Badly wounded?" said Claudia, startled. "Where?" She hadn't noticed any sign of wounds.

Chrys looked anxiously at her husband. Octavian smiled back at her, picked up her hand and kissed her fingers.

"I'm fine," he whispered.

"He sustained a fractured skull and......" Allaine stopped. He could see Claudia turning pale. "Well, there is no need to go into details. He's perfectly healthy, now. Don't worry, Lady Volusena. Fortunately he was riding next to Marcius, who can act quite well in an emergency."

"Marcius?" said Claudia, faintly.

"Yes. Marcius Carvilius, Octavian's friend Marcius. Don't you know him?" Allaine asked, surprised.

"Of course. He practically lived in our house when he was little. What happened to him?" Titus asked with trepidation.

"Oh, nothing happened to him. He's fine."

"He's at my master's house, Dad, with Guéreth," Octavian spoke again, "and Hugo Domitius."

"Hugo? Oh, dear," said Claudia.

"For heaven's sake, Mother. Why 'Oh dear.' What's wrong with Hugo?" Hugo was a touchy subject with Octavian.

"Darling, do you remember Lucy? That girl you were

458

betrothed to, before you met Chrys?"

"Marcius's sister. A little brown mouse, rather stupid. Of course I remember her. I might be a slave, but I've not gone gaga," Octavian said crossly.

"She's not stupid, Octavian," Chrys objected. "She's a clever girl, and she's very pretty. She's helped me a lot with the children, because we travelled with her, Lady Ursula, and Andreas, as far as Bibracte."

"Andreas?" Octavian frowned. "Well, I hope he's improved. He was a horrible little squirt."

"He seemed alright to me," Chrys said, surprised. "What's wrong with him?"

"Maybe he's matured, but years ago, when we were little, he was always wanting to play with Marcius and me. The trouble is, he's so much younger. We'd play with him for a bit, then he'd get hurt, and go and complain. He was forever trying to get David into trouble. Jealous, I suppose." Octavian sat scowling, thinking of times past. "I've often wondered whether...."

"Well don't!" Allaine cut in, sharply. He continued, speaking in Gallic. "It won't help Marcius, it won't help Andreas, and it certainly won't help David."

"He wants to join the army, and avenge his brother's death," Chrys dropped into the ensuing silence.

"What an idiot!" Octavian declared, directing a challenging look at his master.

Allaine was annoyed with him. He didn't think it would greatly improve Romano-Gallic relations, if Octavian ended the evening being thrashed for insolence.

"Well, darling," Lady Volusena continued, unabashed by her youngest's bad temper. "Lucy's engaged to Hugo Domitius, but as he was presumed dead, your brother Gaius has fallen in love with her, and has just got betrothed to her himself."

"No, Mum, not Gaius. He doesn't do girls."

"Well he does now," said his mother. "And there's no need to disparage your brother at the dinner table."

Allaine and Jay's eyes met across the table, with mutual recognition. Jay was by this time finding the Volusenus family quite hilarious, and trying not to show it.

"But this is outrageous!" Jay broke in, crashing his fist down on the table, and making them all jump. "I am the love of Gaius's life. Octavian, how many times has he told me so?"

"Every night for the last ten years, Sir," Octavian answered promptly.

"Maybe not quite so much." Jay graciously waved away a few year's worth of declarations. "Who is this Lucy person. Does she look like Helen of Troy? If not, I am insulted." He grinned wickedly at Gaius's mother.

Claudia was the mother of five sons. She was used to being teased. She was unmoved. "No, dear. Maybe not Helen of Troy. But she's a very nice girl, all the same."

"Mum," Octavian said, appalled. "You can't call Prince Jayven 'dear.'"

"But of course Lady Volusena can call me whatever she likes. I am enchanted." To prove it, Jay kissed Claudia's hand. Claudia blushed like a girl.

"But to get back to where we were," Titus asked, wondering why his wife was encouraging the handsome young man to flirt with her. "Why did you need to find Octavian?"

"I wanted some revenge," Allaine explained, with his cold smile, "and he seemed the best person to provide it."

The room went silent again. Octavian stared into the ice grey eyes of his master. Titus plucked up his courage, took a swig of wine, and asked. "Did you get it?"

"No, not really." Allaine made a sweeping motion with his arm. "Octavian, being Octavian, bubbles up like a spring, whatever happens to him. He is quite irrepressible." He paused to smile at Octavian's astonished expression.

"Unfortunately, Octavian keeps spoiling everything, by being happy, and bursting into song," Jay added.

"I don't keep bursting into song!" Octavian protested.

"Yes, you do. You don't even know you're doing it."

Octavian looked to his master.

"Yes, you do, actually. But don't stop. I like it," Allaine said. "In fact, instead of getting revenge, I found myself nursemaiding one of his friends, this Hugo, who is a very poor creature at present, I'm afraid."

"Why, what's the problem? He used to be such a lovely boy," said Claudia.

Allaine and Octavian tried to explain Hugo, and his condition, without going into any horrific detail.

"When I found him he was being treated quite savagely," Octavian said. "He wasn't very well either, was he, Sir?"

"No, he was in a bad way, physically," Allaine told them, "so we managed to sort that out. But then he became miserable, and more and more withdrawn, so I tried to do something about that as well. Now he is cheerful, but confused. I don't know which is worse, really."

"I think he's better being cheerful," Octavian declared. "He is much improved when we are hunting, isn't he, Sir?"

"Yes, that's true. I swore to make him of some use, but so far I have been mostly unsuccessful," Allaine went on. "He can't concentrate for any length of time. Perhaps you can help with him? Do you intend to make a long stay with us? I am getting married at the end of September. I would like Chrys to be there, if that's possible."

"Getting married, Allaine? Who to?" Chrys asked, fascinated.

"To Riona. That's Guéreth's sister."

"Eloise's friend? The one Father wouldn't let you marry? The one you raved about?"

"Rave? I don't rave, Chrys."

"Well, you did about her. 'Hair like spun gold, beautiful eyes, so graceful when she walks, and when you mentioned Plato, she knew all about him.' Don't you remember being so cross with Zinny, because she told you to stop boring on and on about a girl

461

we'd never met?"

"That's her," Allaine laughed. "Guéreth doesn't want me to marry her, and Coevorten doesn't want me to marry her, either. But I am just going to please myself. And Riona," he added.

"Why are you waiting till September?"

"Coevorten wants to make it a big event, for some reason. As I've disagreed with him about everything else, I thought I'd better let him have his own way about one thing. Riona seems to like the idea, as well." He grinned at his sister. "And it will really annoy Guéreth."

"What's she like?" Claudia asked, thinking of the bales of material they had brought as presents for Chrys's relatives.

"She's the most beautiful girl in the world, of course," said Allaine, cheerfully.

"That sounds like an excellent reason to marry her," Titus offered with a smile.

"She's tall, blonde, and yes, she probably is the most beautiful girl in the world, always excepting Chrys," Jay corrected. "She's also charming, intelligent, and she's got quite a temper. They should have great fun together," he added, grinning.

The talk became much more friendly, now that politics had been left behind.

After dinner, Chrys walked over to Allaine and announced, "I will be with my husband tonight."

"Of course. But won't you find the stables a bit chilly at this time of year?" he teased, grinning at her.

"Allaine?" said Chrys, a little unsure of this new powerful brother of hers.

"Go and sort out the sleeping arrangements, then," he said, sensing her uncertainty. "And remember, the best room is for Octavian's parents, not for you, my girl."

Chrys was relieved. "If there is a best room. We may all be sleeping together. What about you, Allaine?"

"I can sleep anywhere. Oh, not near Greta, though. She snores too loudly."

Chrys went to hug Titus to bid him goodnight. "Thanks for bringing me home, Dad," she whispered in his ear.

"It's a pleasure, my darling. Goodnight, Princess," he replied, and gave her his usual kiss.

"Come on, Mother," said Chrys. "You'd better see what suits you. This isn't a very big inn."

"I want a cubicle at least," put in Octavian, "or it will be the stables for us after all, Chrys."

She swung round laughing. He could no longer resist. He caught her in his arms, and kissed her. He no longer gave a fuck what anyone thought. This was his wife. She was his own Chrys, and she loved him. He was never sure before. Now he was certain. It was a wonderful feeling.

Chrys had her arms round his neck, her body pressed tightly against his. "Oh, Octavian, I can't believe you're real. Don't vanish overnight, or anything, will you?" Chrys felt frightened of her own happiness. It was all too amazing. Not only to have Octavian back from the dead, but Allaine as well.

Allaine was a little surprised by his sister. He remembered Octavian's words when he described their relationship. It was obvious Chrys did a lot more than tolerate Octavian. She looked to be very much in love with her husband. Sadly, he remembered how Eloise had looked just the same, madly in love with Dumnorix. How cruel life was. No, how cruel death was. How cruel Caesar was.

Octavian thought he'd better make an effort to get back into his master's favour. He crossed the room, knelt at his master's feet and kissed his hand. "Goodnight, Sir."

"Goodnight, Octavian." He didn't add his usual 'Sleep well.' They had both reverted to Gallic. "I'm sorry I had to shut you up," Allaine added, "but I thought your parents had enough to contend with tonight, without adding speculation as to whether or not Andreas was responsible for David's death."

"Yes, Master. You were quite right, of course."

"I'm glad you agree." Allaine was relieved to find Octavian hadn't forgotten his manners entirely.

He pulled Chrys towards him, and kissed her cheek. "Goodnight, my lovely sister. I'm so glad you came home."

Chrys left the room, hand in hand with Octavian, giggling a little, like a young girl.

"Shall we finish the wine, Sir?" Allaine suggested to Titus. "Are you staying, Jay?"

"No, my dear. I think I'll go to bed. I rather fancy that little brunette, the one that spilt the sauce." He bowed deeply to Titus. "Goodnight, Sir. I hope you enjoy your stay with us."

Allaine dismissed the servants, then waited till the room was clear. "Well, what do you think of him?" he asked Titus.

"He didn't say a lot."

"It is difficult for him. You have certain expectations of him, but my requirements are different. He will need some time to adjust."

"You seem to have taken great care of him."

"No. I forced him into slavery. He could choose slavery, or torture. He chose slavery in the end, as all men do. That isn't exactly looking after him."

"May I ask how long you intend to keep him?"

"I haven't yet decided. Seven years is the usual tariff for a dedicated slave. You know what I mean by a dedicated slave, such as Octavian?"

"Marcius tried to tell us, years ago. A prisoner of war, is that right?"

"That is correct. He has sworn to serve me, and I have sworn to protect him. Octavian is a man who keeps his promises, even those made under duress." Allaine paused, thinking how to frame the next words. "However, I think you have taken great care of my sister."

"We have five sons, and no daughters until Chrys came along. She is a joy to have around. And she's a wonderful mother."

"But weren't you shocked when Octavian married her? Surely from your point of view, your son was marrying a barbarian?"

"Of course. Horrified might be a better word. Especially as Octavian used to fall in and out of love on a regular basis. But that all stopped with Chrys. I'm not sure if you've noticed, but he adores your sister, and has from almost the first moment they met."

Allaine laughed. "I would have to be blind not to see that. I hadn't realised Chrys felt the same way. It is a revelation."

"We stopped thinking of Chrys as anything other than our dear daughter. Octavian and Allaine are our only grandchildren. We have much to thank Chrys for."

They stayed for an hour, talking together, both still very cautious with each other. But Titus retired to bed, not only happy to have found his adored son, but also thinking that Octavian would be safe in the service of Chrys's brother. How strange the way things had turned out. He must give thanks to the Gods in the morning, he decided.

In the pokey little room Greta's snores woke up Junior. The oil must have run out, because the lamp was out. He was in complete darkness, and he badly needed to pee. He got up off the mattress, and felt about with his arms, encountering the door frame almost immediately, and the nasty musty smelling leather curtain, that acted as a door. Junior knew leather came from dead animals. The soft slimy feel of it made him shiver with terror. A dim light from one of the other rooms shone through a rip in the curtain, so he skirted round it cautiously, in case it came alive again, and tried to eat him. He hastened towards the light and pushed open the door. He found his new uncle sitting up in a vast bed raised off the floor, attempting to read by the multiple flames of a large lamp.

Allaine looked at the white-faced little boy. "What's the matter, Octavian?"

Junior explained his predicament, so Allaine pulled out the wooden bucket for him from under the bed.

"I expect you would like me to stay with you, in case you are afraid of the dark," Junior stated hopefully, when he had finished with the bucket.

"An excellent suggestion," Allaine gravely replied. Thankfully Junior climbed into bed, and snuggled down next to this large practical uncle of his. "Is anything else worrying you, Octavian?" Allaine enquired.

Junior knew Uncle Allaine was a very important man, because Daddy had said so. He decided this uncle was bound to be good at answering the difficult questions Greta just laughed at, and then ignored. "Were you ghosts, you and Daddy?" Junior asked. "How did you get back alive again?" He was filled with anxiety. Would they stay alive, or suddenly be transformed into corpses again. Junior had seen a corpse, and didn't much like it.

Allaine spent some time talking to his nephew, soothing his fears away, until Octavian Junior's eyes closed, and he fell back to sleep. The next morning Greta roused her mistress to confess that Junior had been stolen during the night. Chrys and Octavian were in a panic, until Junior was found, curled up fast asleep in Allaine's arms.

"He was frightened," Allaine explained. "He didn't know where you were, so he found me instead." He decided not to alarm them about the extraordinary fears that invaded their little son's peace of mind. The turmoil of the world was inevitably going to seep through the cracks in the nursery walls. Junior and Little Allaine would not be exempt. Fortunately Junior came to regard his large uncle as a rock of safety in the turbulent sea of his imaginings, and often sort refuge there, from the battering waves of anxiety that sometimes threatened to engulf him.

As she travelled to Aventicum, Chrys found everywhere reminders of her nightmare journey. Initially she felt her homecoming tinged with sadness at the sight of blackened buildings, and such sparsely populated valleys. But the people were thrilled by her return as well as Allaine's, and the horns resounded throughout the mountains in jubilation. A mass of people collected to greet her. She couldn't have been given a warmer welcome than if she had been a conquering hero. Anyway, all around were the signs of rebirth. Both buildings and babies.

They were ushered in to meet Coevorten, Allaine's half brother, the Chief Magistrate and most important man in Switzerland, Octavian had assured his parents. Allaine greeted his brother, then Jay did the same. Next Octavian was brought forward to kneel and kiss Coevorten's hand. As he stood up, Coevorten moved to embrace him, and kiss him on both cheeks, then made some remark about his newly shaven chin, which caused all four men to shout with laughter. Octavian's reply caused another bout of hilarity. Titus could see his son was quite at home in this august gathering of princes.

Lady Volusena watched anxiously as Chrys greeted Coevorten. "Will we have to kneel too?" she asked Allaine, who laughed aloud. The idea tickled him that Claudia should try so hard to conform to local custom. To start with, she had been such a determinedly Roman matron, but latterly had made a huge effort to become a little more amenable. Allaine kissed her hand.

"Don't let Octavian bully you into doing anything you don't like," he said. "You are honoured guests."

They stayed a few nights with Coevorten, as Allaine and Titus thought Claudia could do with a rest from travelling. Junior was a little shy of his new cousins to start with, but they had been very sternly ordered to be kind to him. He found he could understand a lot of what they said, because Chrys often talked to him in her own language. He came running up to his father.

"Did you know I'm a prince, Daddy?" Junior asked excitedly.

"No, my son, I think you've got that wrong," Octavian

answered.

"Of course he's a prince," Allaine corrected. "You remember what my brother said? Move your household to Gaul? Your son is Prince Octavian here in Gaul, whatever he is in Rome." Junior had confessed to him his slave status, one of many anxieties he had. "And Little Allaine is Prince Allaine. But, Junior, as I told you last night, being a prince can be hard work when you're grown up. Just have a look at my brother. He has to solve everyone's problems, and it's not easy."

"Uncle Allaine, I'll stay here with you until I'm grown up, and then I'll go home."

"Very logical," Allaine laughed. "You'll be staying all summer, anyway."

"Oh, good," said Junior, and capered off again.

"What's it like, the new house?" Chrys asked Allaine, trying to steel herself to face the changes.

"Much like the old one, only a lot bigger."

"Why a lot bigger?" asked Chrys, astonished.

"Grandmother insisted. Evidently she told Coevorten to have faith I would return. She walked every day to the altar on the hill, to pray for you and me. Quite a walk for an old lady," Allaine smiled ruefully. "It's just as well we've returned. I think it was getting far too much for her. Still, although the house is larger, we may have to build on some more bedrooms. I'm not sure where we are going to put everyone. Although your in-laws might prefer to sleep in the Guest House."

"What about Grandmother's bath house?"

"Still there, looking as incongruous as ever, but working well. No problems. Apparently, when Grandmother returned, she and Zinny slept in it, until Coevorten came back to sort things out." What a nightmare that must have been for his brother, he realised, trying to hold together a country that had immolated itself, with fire and war.

"Do you remember what you said, the last time I saw you. You promised one day we would meet again?" Chrys said.

"Of course I remember," Allaine replied. "I thought it might help to have something to cling to. A bit of hope, even though there wasn't any at the time."

"It did help. And then I had Octavian to cling to. But then when we heard he was dead as well...." Chrys started to cry. "And I couldn't even cry, because Junior was beside himself with grief, and Mum and Dad.....Mum was in such a state....."

Allaine took her in his arms. "So why are you crying now, Chrys?"

"I don't know!" Chrys wailed.

"Here, Octavian, look after this stupid woman of yours," Allaine said. "She makes a lot less sense than Junior."

Octavian obligingly put his arm round his wife's still slender waist, and kissed her cheek. "Don't cry, darling. There's no need to any more, is there?" He settled her comfortably against him, both arms round her now.

"No, Allaine. I want to know what happened to you." Chrys wiped her eyes with her hands.

"You must have heard what happened," Allaine said softly. "I thought all of Gaul could hear me screaming."

Chrys picked up his hand, and kissed it. "After that, Allaine," she said.

"I was sent to the prison in Arles."

"I was there, too," said Chrys. "But only for a few days. Then I got bundled off to Rome."

"I'm not sure how long I was there, because I decided to go."

"How do you mean?"

"I obliterated the prison from my mind. It was like putting myself into a trance," he explained to Octavian. "Unfortunately, not having tried the technique before, I couldn't get my mind back again when I wanted to. I had no idea who or what I was. From what I can make out, Caesar ordered the prison to be emptied, to be ready for the next campaign. He either forgot about me, or didn't care what happened to me. Apparently the prison governor sold all the prisoners to a man called Marcus Metius, a slave dealer, for ten gold pieces." Allaine laughed. "I'm a lot more expensive now."

"I've met him," said Chrys, in surprise. "That's Marcius's uncle. I met him in Rome first, when he brought Marcius around for a visit, and then we went back to his house. He was very attentive to me, wasn't he, Octavian?"

"I suppose so. Probably trying not to offend his Aeduan customers." Octavian didn't like to think of his Chrys associating too closely with slave dealers, even though Metius was Marcius's uncle.

"I thought he was rather nice. He cared a lot for his family. And when we arrived at Arles, I asked Dad if I could arrange for a sacrifice for you, Allaine, to ensure your soul departed safely on its journey. Metius arranged it all, and a funeral banquet afterwards."

"And what about me?" Octavian objected. "Didn't I merit a funeral?"

"You had an enormous funeral in Rome, a joint one with Marcius. Your memorial has you and Marcius together. Dad insisted. He thought Guéreth should be depicted as well. But Lady Ursula refused. She hates us all. All Gauls. She thinks we're all the same." Chrys sat remembering how awful it all was. "Junior was in a terrible state. I was so worried about him, I almost stopped worrying myself. I couldn't even speak about you, because every time I did, Mother went to pieces. I thought one was supposed to go numb with grief, but it didn't work for me. I thought of you every waking moment."

"Oh, Chrys," groaned Octavian. He hugged her tighter.

"Go on, Allaine, what happened after that?"

"But Metius knew perfectly well I didn't die in the prison at Arles," Allaine said in surprise. "I'd met him years ago. He sold Noemon to me. How old was I then? Eight? Do you remember, Chrys? Grandmother said I had to learn Greek, so I had to find a tutor."

"After Mother died?"

"Yes, that's right. And when I started school I rode with him in his chariot from Bibracte to Paris, because he wanted Father to provide an escort for his goods. I think he must have remembered me, because he kept me with him for a few days. He told me he didn't want to get mixed up in politics, and offend Caesar. I'm sure he knew who I was. Anyway, he then sold me to this medical officer, Antistius Petronius, one of the best men I have ever met, the perfect master for me. He was such a lovely man, one of those brilliant teachers, truly brilliant. He was fascinated by his subject. He thought I was a fascinating subject as well. I was with him for three years. Some memories came back, I could remember playing with you in the snow. We were sledging. You fell out, and cut your mouth, and said it was all my fault."

"It was."

"No, it wasn't. Anyway, stop interrupting. I still didn't know who I was. Then Octavian intervened."

"I did?" Octavian was surprised.

"First you brought over the twins, in the middle of the night. I discovered I could speak their language, and I knew it was the language of South Britain. I couldn't see any Greek knowing that. Then you wanted them dedicated. As soon as the priest lit the oil, it all came back to me."

"You said it was an earth tremor," Octavian frowned.

"That's what it felt like to me. I think you told me your name then, but it didn't register at the time. But then when you were seasick, you told me your name again, and I remembered years ago, the centurion saying that Caesar was giving Chrys to Tribune Octavian Volusenus. So your fate was sealed."

"But you couldn't have known how idiotic Sabinus was going to be, could you, Sir?"

"No. My idea was to poison the lot of you at Riona's wedding."

Octavian and Chrys looked at him in horror.

471

Allaine lifted his hand, and then let it fall back. How to make them understand? "I was half mad, I think, after Petronius died."

"Oh, he died," said Chrys.

"Yes, he died. It happened so quickly. I did all I could to save him. To no avail. And yet," he sighed, "and yet the strange thing is, it worked for Valerius. There must still be things we don't know." Allaine sat quietly looking into the distance, remembering those dreadful few days, and his desperate struggle with Death. "After that there seemed no point in living, no point at all. I had lost my country, my family, my freedom, my beloved master, and now I was losing my girl as well. I was sold to a man I despised utterly. Thoughts of revenge seemed the only reason to stay alive. Not a very good reason, as it turned out, subsequently."

"Go on."

"What happened next? Oh, yes. Guéreth. Do you know Guéreth, Chrys?"

"No. I don't believe I've ever met him. Did he come to Eloise's wedding?"

"No. Guéreth went to collect Riona to marry her off to this Tarleton, and Octavian went with him to see Eloise and the boys."

"How are they?"

"They are all well, and as happy as they can be. Eloise will never get over losing Dumnorix, though, and the boys miss their father. They love Octavian. He is a great help."

Octavian looked at his master in surprise. He didn't think anyone had noticed his affection for the boys.

"The Fourteenth legion marched to Atuatuca, and you know the rest."

"So where did your other Roman slaves come from?" Chrys wanted to know.

"From Ambiorix. I discovered he would do almost anything for me. Servilius was one of Cotta's servants. I knew him before he was captured. Valerius tried to carry a message from Cicero's camp to Caesar, and got caught. Darius didn't want

472

to be sacrificed, and Hugo is a friend of Octavian's."

"You didn't bring them here?"

"It wouldn't be fair. Coevorten hates Romans, especially Roman soldiers, or those who have been soldiers. He can just about manage Octavian."

"Why don't you hate them?"

"Why don't I hate them?" Allaine repeated. He thought for a bit, working it out. "It's because of Petronius, I think. He was such a good man. So I started seeing them as individuals, not as a mass of people. Some good. Some bad. Some evil. Most a mixture. I decided they were just like us, after all."

BOOK 3: CHAPTER 10

North Gaul, Summer 53 BC

Caesar spent the spring and summer chasing phantom armies. Reports of rebellions came in from every part of the country, only to disappear as soon as he arrived. The armies melting into the woods. He knew what they were doing, of course. They thought they would keep him busy for a year, while the tribes trained their men for total all-out war. Well, he would be ready for them. They could gather as many armed men as they liked - they would be no match for his legionaries.

He desperately wanted to capture Ambiorix, and punish the Eburones, but Ambiorix refused to fight. Then illness swept through the Roman ranks, causing a rash, vomiting, high fever, and cough. But sometimes it became much worse, with brain fever, or pneumonia. There were many deaths.

Caesar left Quintus Cicero in charge at the still well-fortified Atuatuca camp, with the heavy baggage, and all the sick and wounded. He conducted the search for Ambiorix and his allies by splitting the army into three parts. He sent Labienus and three legions in one direction, Trebonius with three in another, and took the remaining legions himself, promising to return in seven days. Time after time, when he arrived at a village, according to the natives, Ambiorix had only just left. They would look into the distance, as if expecting still to see him. It proved equally impossible to conduct a punishment campaign against the Eburones. Their forests were impenetrable, with no adequate roads through them. There was no great stronghold to be breached, no fortified town to be captured. The population were scattered in small pockets throughout the land. But they could still fight! Any straying legionary in search of plunder, was quickly surrounded and killed. And Ambiorix got clean away. The necessarily small parties of cavalry chasing after him, were apt to disappear into the woods, and not come out again. It was all very frustrating.

To cap it all, German fighters crossed the Rhine in search of plunder, and were told by the Eburones that the whole of Caesar's baggage was at Atuatuca, with no garrison to speak of, just a lot of sick soldiers. It was theirs for the taking. Cicero, having fought so well throughout the winter, made a strategic error. He listened to one of the Military Tribunes. One of the stupid ones.

"Sir," said the tribune, "we've been cooped up here in camp for a week. It's not as if Ambiorix is surrounding us like last year. He's vanished. Now the country has been pacified, why can't we get out? The men say it's worse than being blockaded."

Traders had miraculously appeared again, pitching their tents outside the camp ramparts, shouting out their wares and displaying their slave women for the soldiers. The men were forbidden to exit the camp, but they were getting restless.

"I suppose it can do no harm," Cicero replied. "Very well. Take half the legion to those fields on the other side of the hill. They can cut the corn ripening there. That way we will have a good stock for the winter, and it will deprive the local population of their food. They will starve."

"What about the sick, Sir. Couldn't you allow them to visit the traders, at least? And the animals could do with some good pasture. The cattle need fattening, and it wouldn't do the horses any harm to get fresh grass."

"You may send some of the camp servants out with the cattle and horses then. Make sure to keep a lookout at all times."

"Certainly, Sir." Ye Gods, what an idiot, thought the tribune. Cicero's gone soft after last winter. Must have put the wind up him properly. Who does he think is going to attack us, the Germans? He laughed to himself.

The German cavalry soon discovered the information they had been given was correct. They attacked Cicero's camp with great enthusiasm, but failed initially to penetrate the defences. The traders were annihilated. The Germans circled round the camp perimeter, gathering all the plunder they could lay their hands on, women included. The troops inside were in a state of utter confusion, convinced they would be destroyed like Sabinus and Cotta's men. Afterwards some claimed to have seen the ghosts of their dead comrades from the Fourteenth.

The Germans spied the cohorts returning from the fields, discovered how small their numbers were, and gleefully attacked on all sides. The foolish tribune mustered the newly recruited legionaries and tried to make a stand, first on high ground without success, but then he ordered his terrified men to make a run for the camp. They were all hacked to pieces. Some veterans managed to form a wedge, and drive through to the gates, followed closely by the camp servants. They survived to fight. Now the camp fortifications were properly manned again, so the Germans retreated, very happy with their plunder. They swept back across the Rhine in their many boats. When Ambiorix heard about the debacle he was highly amused. He hadn't reckoned to be grateful to the Germans, but they had done him a great service.

Caesar had no idea of the catastrophe. He sent his cavalry on ahead, to announce his imminent arrival. Gaius arrived that night, and banged on the gates of the camp, demanding to be let in.

"Who are you?" asked the terrified guards, still reeling from the day's narrow escape.

"It's me, Volusenus. Come on, open the gates. You know me!"

"Oh, Gods protect us! It's the ghost of Volusenus. The army must be destroyed. Don't let him in. Run and tell the Commander. Ask what we should do."

"I'm not a fucking ghost," yelled Gaius. "Let me in or I'll get a battering ram to these gates, and have the lot of you decimated!"

A centurion rushed to Cicero. "Sir, the ghost of Octavian Volusenus is at the gates, demanding to be admitted."

Cicero went white. But he could not be accused of

cowardice. He hastened to the gate with the centurion, and peered out into the gloom.

"Who's there?"

"For fuck's sake! Will you let us in? It's bloody cold out here, and I'm hungry," Gaius bellowed.

"It's Gaius, you fools," said Cicero, much relieved. Gaius found the whole camp in a state of alarm, convinced Caesar was dead, and the army vanquished. Why else would the Germans attack the camp?

Cicero lost well over a thousand men that day. He had failed to follow orders. Caesar was furious with him when he arrived. Cicero had a most uncomfortable interview with his commanding officer. Caesar couldn't say so publicly, of course. He had no wish to alienate Cicero's brother, Marcus, the famous orator. He needed all the political allies he could get in Rome.

The guards apologised to Gaius, but so many men assured him they had seen Octavian's ghost, and others from the lost Fourteenth, he began to look for the ghosts himself.

By the end of the summer Caesar was frustrated and furious. He summoned all the tribal leaders to a national assembly. One of them was shielding Ambiorix, he knew. Impossible to tell which of them it was. He decided to give the lot of them something else to think about over the winter months.

Gaius looked at the twins in exasperation. How come Octavian's slaves kept turning up, but never Octavian. He'd got no information out of Borus. He got none from the twins either.

"Where the hell did they come from?" he asked the legionary.

"They arrived off a ship at Samarobriva, looking for their master, Octavian Volusenus, Sir. They've been prisoners in Britain. We thought we had better bring them along to you."

Gaius beckoned to the interpreter.

"You'd better tell them Octavian is dead."

The interpreter translated. The twins conferred with each

other. Gaius could hear the word 'Octavian' several times.

"They say he is not dead, Sir. They say he sent for them."

Gaius exploded. "He's dead, you stupid cunts. Can't you get that into your thick heads. It was your friends, the Eburones, who killed him. Allies of the Veneti, aren't they? If you dare mention his name again to me, I'll knock your heads together till you see sense."

The twins were baffled.

"They want to know what they should do, Sir," the interpreter explained.

"Take them to my tent, and tell them to keep out of my way," snarled Gaius. He never could stand the way the twins always jabbered together, before saying anything to him. They irritated him even when Octavian had been alive. Anyway, he thought his brother had spoiled them. He thought a good dose of discipline wouldn't come amiss.

Labienus called Gaius to his quarters. "Do you remember Commius, that treacherous little bastard we used against the British?"

"Why treacherous?" asked Gaius. "I thought he was on our side. I thought he'd been quite useful."

"Don't give me that crap, Gaius. You know he's a twisted bastard, I know he's a twisted bastard. He'd sell his own mistress for a denarius, and probably does. Want some of this? Tastes good. Snails or something. They eat some queer stuff, don't they?"

"Squid," said Gaius.

"Snails, squid, same difference." Labienus chewed for a bit. "According to my informant,"

"Metius, I suppose."

Labienus ignored him. "Friend Commius thinks he's clever. He's been writing letters to the draughts player."

"Chess. Vercingetorix."

"That's who." Labienus grinned. "You might as well knock

him off."

"Vercingetorix?" asked Gaius, shocked.

"No, stupid, Commius."

They met in a clearing. Commius came over, grinning as usual.

"What's with all this cloak and dagger stuff, Volusenus?"

"Hello, Sir. Caesar told me to tell you........." Gaius extended his hand. As Commius grasped it, the senior centurion struck down sharply with his sword, onto his unprotected head. Commius stood dazed momentarily, blood pouring from the scalp wound, but his bodyguards were already moving. The first horse knocked the centurion to the ground, and got between Gaius and his victim. Gaius drew his sword in alarm, but the man was more interested in getting his chief to safety.

"Sire, your horse."

"Bastards. You treacherous fucking bastards," yelled one of the bodyguards, charging forward, sword outstretched.

"No, come, quick! Let's get the chief to safety. There could be a whole legion here for all we know."

His men heaved Commius onto his horse, and hastily led him away. Gaius looked at the departing horsemen, and then at the spots of blood on the ground. Gaius had some idea of the words his commander would choose to describe the encounter. Something along the lines of "You stupid bugger, Gaius. You fucked up."

Labienus watched the tribune's face, as he gave his report. Gaius had been fighting continuously in Gaul now for five years, with only two short spells of leave. Labienus knew the death of young Octavian had cut Gaius to the heart.

"Tribune, in view of what you have just told me, I propose to write to your commander-in-chief, recommending that you be awarded a citation for bravery."

"Thank you, Sir," said Gaius, his voice choked with

emotion.

"Gaius!" Labienus placed his hands on his tribune's shoulders, and gripped him, looking into his miserable face. "You can't win them all, old son. You can't win them all. Any news of Jay?"

"No, Sir."

"He'll turn up."

"Yes, he'll turn up on the other side," said Gaius wearily.

Labienus was worried by his favourite tribune. It was so unlike Gaius to fail in any project. He was always so reliable. Give him an order, and he obeyed unhesitatingly, without thinking. He didn't sit around arguing about whether or not it was morally justified.

"Come on, Gaius. Metius has sent us two wagon-loads of his best wines. Let's see if we can't finish the lot by morning."

Helvetia (Switzerland), Summer 53 BC

Octavian Junior remembered that summer for the rest of his life, as the most magical he ever experienced. To start with there were his cousins, Aunt Eloise's boys, aged eight and six, not too busy to play with a five and two year old. Their other cousins came often to play as well. Junior loved having proper relations. When his Daddy's brothers were home on leave, he was told to go away, and not be a nuisance to them. He wasn't allowed to call them 'Uncle,' because in Rome he was only a slave. Uncle Allaine, and Uncle Coevorten were quite different. Junior loved it, that he and Little Allaine were princes. He enjoyed being called 'Prince Octavian,' or 'Sir,' by the household servants.

The children sometimes had the services of Valerius to call on, a grown man, with an amazing dog called Ajax, that could do all sorts of tricks already, even though he was only a puppy, Valerius said. Valerius knew lots of games to play, with wooden swords for mock fights, or balls to throw or kick, sticks to be spears, circles of wood to be discuses. He taught Junior to swim in the cold waters of the lake nearest the house. But best of all, Junior thought, were the ponies Uncle Allaine gave them, a tiny one for Little Allaine, and a bigger one for him. In no time they could ride with confidence, even Little Allaine.

It was wonderful to have Daddy for the whole time. Even though he often went away with Uncle Allaine in the morning, he was always home again in the evening. There were the grandparents, but now also a great grandmother, who knew so many stories, and Cousin Jayven, with his beautiful horse, a relation of Pegasus, apparently, but he was too young yet to grow any wings. But Junior loved Uncle Allaine the best of his new family, Uncle Allaine, who would scoop him up into his arms, laugh at him, and answer seriously all his questions, telling him he was as bad as his father.

"Is it bad to ask questions, then?" Junior wanted to know.

"No, it's very good. I was only teasing. It's how we find things out, isn't it? When you are older you will learn to read and write, and then you will be able to find lots of answers for yourself, in books. But sometimes no one knows the answers, and you have to work it out for yourself."

"Daddy kneels and kisses your hand. Should I do that as well?"

"No, my pet. Relationships between us adults are rather complicated at present. Just be polite and courteous to everyone, always do what your father says, and you won't go wrong. And try and be a better big brother to Little Allaine. I know little brothers can be exasperating, always wanting the very thing you are playing with. But the older you get the more use they are."

"Daddy is the littlest brother, he says."

"I was a little brother myself, once. But you see, I have now grown bigger than my big brother Coevorten."

After dinner Junior was allowed to climb onto Uncle Allaine's lap, and listen drowsily to the adults, until Greta decided it was bed time for little boys, and sometimes, if it had been a particularly exciting day, he went to sleep in Uncle Allaine's arms, and just woke up for a moment, while being put into his bed. He liked that best of all.

The Volusenus family hadn't known quite what to bring as gifts to Chrys's relatives, but Titus remembered the account Gaius gave of the Aeduans' visit to Rome, and how they had wanted to see plays, and visit museums. So he had selected a number of books, which Allaine fell on with delight, while Lady Volusena and Chrys had decided that silks and finely dyed woollen cloth might be acceptable to any female members of the household. Riona's wedding dress was now being fashioned in great secrecy. The spices were greatly welcomed by the fierce head chef, who had a smile on his face, for once. He anticipated many splendid savoury dishes for Grandmother. Maybe at last she would appreciate his skill, and stop comparing his efforts with the chefs at her father's house in Massilia.

As head of the family, Coevorten had sent wedding invitations far and wide, but he was astonished at the number of distinguished guests who indicated they were coming, many of whom he didn't remember inviting in the first place. But important tribal chiefs could hardly be told to go away again. It appeared that Allaine's wedding was a good excuse for the real Council of the Gauls to be held in Switzerland, far away from the prying eyes of Caesar. The ceremony was to be held at Aventicum, at the most sacred altar in the country.

The children always hung about the stables in the late afternoon, waiting for Allaine, Octavian, and Valerius to return. But this time Junior hurled himself towards Allaine, before he had even dismounted.

"Uncle Allaine, Uncle Allaine, you must come quickly. A very important man has arrived, and Mummy thinks he will kill Guéreth!"

"Who is it? Do you remember his name, Octavian?"

"It's Vercingix, something like that. And he's very important. He's got lots of men with him. Please come quickly."

"Vercingetorix?" Allaine suggested.

"Yes, Sir." Junior wasn't sure he could say that long name, but it sounded right.

Vercingetorix was indeed one of the first to arrive with his entourage, delighted to see Allaine looking fit and well. He hugged and kissed his friend, so pleased to see him again after so many years.

"Allaine, you are like a miracle. We were so sure you were dead. We heard such appalling stories about you."

He pushed up Allaine's sleeve, and traced the lines of white scar tissue up his forearm towards his elbow. He looked deep into his friend's eyes.

"Caesar?" he said softly.

Allaine nodded.

"Are you over it?"

Allaine slightly shook his head. His eyes blurred with tears. Vercingetorix held him tightly in his arms.

"I have bad news to relate, Allaine," he said, when he let him go.

Abruptly he ordered the children into the house, puzzled that they didn't seem to understand him. Allaine intervened, telling Octavian to take them away, and to tell Chrys to stop worrying. He would deal with it.

Allaine took Vercingetorix into the shady aromatic herb garden behind the courtyard, and summoned a servant to provide refreshments, giving instructions for Octavian to attend them. Octavian reappeared carrying a tray laden with a carafe of wine, the best glasses, napkins, and plates filled with the special savoury tarts of the region. A servant appeared equipped with a basin of water and hand towels. Carefully Octavian poured out the wine, served the food, then stood quietly behind his master. After the niceties of hospitality were given their due, and appetites slightly dulled, Vercingetorix told Allaine the dreadful news.

"Allaine, it was simply appalling. Caesar was in a vicious

mood. The last time I met him, he was quite charming, but that civilised veneer has now gone."

He fortified himself with some of the wine, gulping it down before proceeding.

"Caesar summoned a Gallic National Assembly, before returning to Rome this winter."

"Yes. We heard about it, but our delegates haven't yet returned."

"No, I've come here in all haste," Vercingetorix said. "I must tell you what happened." He paused, marshalling his words. "There we all were, sitting or standing around at this Assembly, wondering what Caesar wanted this time, thinking more hostages, maybe, or more secure supplies of corn for his wretched legions. Caesar opened proceedings with a speech, and then took us all by surprise. He said he was arraigning Prince Acco of the Carnutes. You knew him, Allaine?"

"Knew him?" Allaine frowned, noticing the past tense. "Yes, of course."

"Caesar accused him of conspiracy and treason, although Acco was only fighting in defence of his own country. In the sight of all of us, all the Gallic chiefs, Prince Acco was arrested, and found guilty. The trial was a complete travesty of the truth. Caesar ordered him to be executed in the ancient way. Of course we didn't know what he meant at the time. Now we do." Vercingetorix stopped speaking, to get his thoughts and emotions in order again. He was still very affected by the events he was unfolding to Allaine.

"We had to watch, powerless, as Prince Acco was dragged away. He was yelling and protesting, but we were surrounded by the Roman legionaries. We were no help at all. Allaine, they pinned his neck to the ground with this large wooden fork device. They'd tied his hands in front, so he couldn't even bite on them, to stop the screaming. And then they stationed a man on each side of him, wielding the military whip. You know? Those whips with bits of metal embedded in them, designed to cause as much damage as possible?"

"Yes," Allaine said with bitterness. "I have had some experience of their use."

Vercingetorix was arrested momentarily, gazing at his young friend in consternation.

"Maybe I shouldn't be telling you this." He put a hand on Allaine's shoulder. "After all, it's a wedding we are coming to, not a funeral."

"No, go on. Tell me. I need to know."

"Well, then they flogged him mercilessly. I can still hear his screams ringing in my ears. His body was jerking around like a landed fish. It was horrible. Eventually, when he was just a bloody mangled wreck, they pulled him over to the block, and finished the job with an axe, but I think and pray that by then he was too far gone to know anything, I think he was practically dead."

Coevorten appeared, having heard that Vercingetorix had arrived, and was told the appalling news. They talked it over together, examining all the implications. But the message from Caesar was crystal clear. 'Gaul is now a Province of Rome. I will dispense justice. Rebel against me or my rule, and you will suffer the same fate as Prince Acco.'

Not surprisingly the Carnutes were incensed, but then so was the rest of the country.

A few days later Coevorten came again to invite Vercingetorix to the male-only dinner preceding the wedding. They all rode to Aventicum, Allaine taking Octavian and Servilius to attend him. Commius arrived as well, to Allaine's great surprise. There began to be a certain tension in the air, as Commius was known only for the many ways in which he had assisted Caesar and his army.

Allaine told Octavian that part of his role was to serve the wine at the dinner. Octavian hurried off to consult with Servilius, who always seemed to know how to do things. Servilius told him it didn't matter in which order he served the guests, but his master must be served last of all.

As Octavian finished pouring out the wine for him, Allaine held onto his wrist. He called for silence, and rose to his feet.

"This is Octavian," he announced to the assembled guests. "He is a Roman Citizen, an Aeduan magistrate, my dedicated slave, but also my brother-in-law. He is married to my sister Chrys, so will act as my Groomsman." This caused an excited stir amongst his audience. "I must explain that there are several Roman Citizens present in my household, mostly relations of mine. I wish to emphasise that if any of them are harmed in any way whatsoever, I will personally kill the perpetrator."

Commius got up and walked over to face Allaine. "You trust him?" Commius spat at him. "A Roman?"

"Of course. With my life. He is dedicated. He knows what that means," Allaine answered.

"Then you're a fool!" Commius was still outraged at the perfidy of Caesar. "Listen to me, young Allaine, and learn something. Gaius Volusenus, one of your precious Romans, arranged to meet me secretly a couple of months ago. He's a Military Tribune, a man I've fought alongside, a man I foolishly thought of as a friend, someone I could trust. He held out his hand in greeting, and as I took it, I was struck violently over the head by one of his centurions. They tried to kill me. Kill me! One of their staunchest allies! That's the sort of people they are. They know nothing of honour, nothing of loyalty. Trust him and you'll find out. They are treacherous dogs."

"Romans are much the same as Gauls," countered Allaine. "Some good, some bad. I happen to know mine are the good sort."

"I'm going to get that bastard Volusenus, if it's the last thing I do," Commius ended bitterly.

"He'll have been acting under orders," Allaine said. "Caesar's orders, or perhaps Labienus's."

Commius grunted his agreement. Octavian wasn't sure

why this exchange had the effect of eliminating the tension, but now everyone seemed to relax, drink, and enjoy themselves. Allaine called Octavian to sit next to him. Jayven moved over to sit on his other side.

"Just in case you are the bone, this time," he whispered to Octavian, with a mischievous grin. "And whatever you do, don't mention your family name to Commius."

Octavian felt it very strange to be sitting surrounded by men who hated all things Roman, but felt safe from attack all the same, with Prince Jayven on one side of him, and his master on the other.

Vercingetorix leant across and asked, "You really do trust him, then, despite what friend Commius says?"

"Yes, I trust them all."

"What do you mean, all?"

"I have five Roman slaves. They were captured by Ambiorix, and given to me."

"Why was Ambiorix so generous?"

"I was at school with his sons, if you remember. They should all be arriving soon, for my wedding."

"But you won't take your Romans to the sacred grove, when you are prepared for your wedding night, will you?"

"Octavian is my brother-in-law, and my birth twin. He has agreed to be my Groomsman."

Vercingetorix looked at Octavian with interest. "Allaine, I have a few things to say. I hope you don't mind me muscling in on your wedding?"

"Of course not. But I would have thought the more important question was, would you trust Commius?"

"He could be of immense use. He has fought with Caesar, and knows his methods. He can raise many men, even some from Britain, if necessary."

Allaine looked round in amazement at the assembled guests. There were over a hundred of the most important men in Gaul.

"If Caesar were here with the Tenth legion, he could solve his Gallic problem once and for all," he remarked.

That made Vercingetorix laugh.

By the eve of the wedding, the vast majority of Gallic leaders had arrived, together with Ambiorix, as well as his sons. Coevorten was able to thank him formally for all the assistance he had given his brother, and offer safe haven to any Eburones, should it be required. Aventicum became a very busy town. It was probably impossible for Caesar not to get some inkling of the event. Vercingetorix held a series of conversations with all he met. But that evening, by the altar, after Allaine had been purified, and robed with Octavian's help, Vercingetorix made a speech which had little to do with the forthcoming nuptials.

"My fellow countrymen, we are met here to honour Allaine of the Helvetii, and his lovely bride, but also to avoid Caesar. We are skulking in the sacred groves of our own country, lest we be overheard by his spies. For many years we have lived relatively amicably in this huge, beautiful, fruitful land of ours. We are a collection of small states, united by two common languages, and a common culture. Our Druid priests hold sway over the whole of Gaul, and are respected and revered in Britain as well. Caesar has managed to divide us, and pick each clan off a few at a time. He makes some provocative move, waits for the hostile reaction, and then smashes us to bits, calling our defence an uprising, a rebellion against Rome, selling the prisoners-of-war as slaves, or slaughtering them, men, women, and children alike, until we witnessed the final degradation of our country, the awful death of Prince Acco at our recent assembly. A warning to any of us impertinent enough to fight for ourselves, our wives and children, our land, our laws, our religious beliefs. My friends, if you like, we can be like the Aeduans, and the Remi, accept the Roman yoke, and hope that a few crumbs will come our way. Give our children as hostages, and feed Caesar's legions, so he can make war whenever and wherever he feels like it. If you find this acceptable, I suggest you talk to Prince Jayven. I have another thought for you, though. That if we combine together, become as one country, with one army, we will be able to smash Caesar and his legions, drive them back to the Mediterranean, maybe even restore the Province to our control. But this is not something we are used to do. It will need iron discipline, and strong will. When we all disperse after this wedding, please take this message back to your people. The time has come to say 'No More.' I will be waiting in Gergovia for your answers."

Afterwards Vercingetorix sought out Octavian deliberately, and sat by him.

"Well, there you are, Octavian. Insurrection, sedition, rebellion. What do you think of us? Do you think we are fools, not to accept the Roman yoke?"

Octavian found Vercingetorix one of the easiest of men to talk to. Allaine was occupied with receiving the congratulations of his peers. He thought a robust exchange of views would do neither man any harm, so he left them alone. Octavian found himself pouring out his heart to this extraordinarily sympathetic charismatic man. He even told him about his tendency to cry at the slightest provocation, because of his head injury. Afterwards he wondered if Vercingetorix had hypnotised him in some way, but his master thought not.

"He's not a Druid, Octavian. He is a man politically astute, able to put people at their ease, and then inspect their inmost thoughts. It's quite a skill. Did you find out anything about him? No? I thought not."

Octavian discovered the major part of his role was to be charming to all the guests, and solve any diplomatic spats, caused by past tribal differences. His experience as an Aeduan magistrate helped him considerably, as Allaine had known it would. Octavian made a few more friends during the course of the evening.

Vercingetorix ambled up at the evening's end. Allaine called Octavian over.

"Here, Octavian, this is a present for you. Thank you for all your help. You've far exceeded my expectations, tonight." He held out a beautiful gold cloak brooch on the palm of his hand, intricately worked and patterned in the Celtic manner.

"It's lovely, Sir. Thank you." Octavian's eyes watered yet again. "Oh shit! I wish this would stop. It's driving me mad."

Allaine laughed, and proceeded to fasten Octavian's cloak with the new brooch. "Not that you need a cloak, tonight. It is still so warm, fortunately."

"He looks so sweet," Vercingetorix grinned. "Quite endearing."

"He does, doesn't he? But don't be fooled. He is very hot tempered, aren't you, Octavian?"

"Am I?"

"You are improving. But I think you could control your anger more if you tried. But no more lessons at the moment, my pet. I have other things on my mind."

"You like him, though, don't you, Allaine?"

Allaine slipped his arm round Octavian's neck, and kissed his cheek. "Of course I like him. Why else would he be here? I love him like a brother, don't I, Octavian?"

"No, Sir. Much better than a brother." Octavian laughed aloud.

Vercingetorix looked at them both, as they stood there grinning at him, Roman and Gaul twined together. How many dead Romans and dead Gauls would there be, he wondered, before the two countries were like them, marching arm in arm in friendship? Too many. Unbidden thoughts flashed into his mind. Thoughts of corpses piled high, of scorched earth, ruined buildings, desolation. He had tonight set it all in motion. He fully realised that it would be death and destruction, until one or other army should yield. And as the war was to be fought on home ground, the casualties of war would include many non-combatants, old men, the innocents, women, children, and babies. Villages would be burned, towns plundered. It would happen. It was inevitable. He stopped smiling.

The two men looking back at him caught his mood, and sobered up. Allaine became serious at once.

"I think you'd better send Octavian home, now, Allaine." Vercingetorix was grave. "We need to sort out a few things, and he won't want to have to keep our secrets."

Allaine agreed. Octavian was dismissed, to return to Coevorten's house. "So, you envisage total war, then, for the whole country?"

"What else can we do? I see no alternative. Can you, Allaine?"

Allaine shook his head. "No, none. But that is just what Caesar wants of course. He wishes to finish the conquest of Gaul as soon as possible. He is getting old. There isn't so much time left for him to conquer the entire world, is there? That is his ambition, to be the second Alexander. To a certain extent we are playing into his hands. We will need to be a cohesive force. We have never done such a thing before, but I agree with you absolutely. It is the only way."

Vercingetorix leapt onto the altar. He raised both hands. The crowd of men hushed at once.

"My friends, the Carnutes have decided on the date to instigate the attack on the Romans, to avenge Prince Acco's death. Let us swear to them here and now, that we will fight together, and support each other in this endeavour. We will not run to Caesar when hostilities commence. We are fellow Gauls, free men, and we wish to remain free."

Coevorten led the cheering. Allaine administered the sacred oaths.

By common consent there was no talk of war when the final day of the wedding dawned. Marcius was feeling almost as happy as the groom. Guéreth had freed him the day before, in front of Octavian in his capacity as an Aeduan magistrate.

"You could free me as well," Allaine suggested, with a

grin. "Then your sister won't be marrying a slave."

"No, I'm not going to free you. I'm going to kill you," Guéreth replied.

Allaine knew he meant every word. He just laughed. "You'll have to wait a bit for your opportunity, then."

Guéreth said nothing. But inwardly he became even more angry, and ever more determined. One day, he would have his revenge on this slave of his.

The children were madly excited, each having been given a little role in the celebrations. The bride looked beautiful, the groom handsome, the wine flowed freely, and the guests mingled happily with one another, Helvetians, Aeduans, Arvernians, Eburones, Senones, Carnutes, and many more, all the tribes managing to forget differences for a time, as decreed by the priests. The feasting and speeches went on most of the day, the dancing most of the night. Octavian led the singing, while Jayven and many others played. Claudia was startled to find herself led out to dance by the groom, and Titus by the bride. Fortunately they had been primed by Grandmother, so had some idea of what was expected. To start with Claudia concentrated on not making a complete fool of herself. Allaine was a graceful dancer, so she felt in capable hands. In a very short time she could manage to offer a few scraps of breathless conversation.

"I have five sons," Claudia told Allaine, as she began to negotiate the steps with comparative ease. "Only Octavian is married, and that by proxy. I feel cheated."

"I hope this makes up for it, a little."

"Actually it does. Your bride is a beautiful girl. I hope you will be as happy as we have been."

"Yes. It is good to see you both together. You are a testament to a happy marriage."

Eventually she had to admit defeat. "Allaine, darling, you will have to take me back to a chair, now. I need to sit down."

"You are a wonderful dancer. It was a great pleasure," said Allaine, not just for courtesy's sake. He secretly enjoyed being called 'dear,'and 'darling' by Octavian's mother, even though it horrified Octavian.

Riona was beginning to flag a little by late evening. Her brother seemed to be dancing just as well as ever, she thought, his leg so well healed there was only a tiny amount of shortening, hardly perceptible. Allaine was annoyed to see him frequently partnering Eloise. He also thought Jay was paying a little too much attention to Zinny. At this rate there would be more Aeduans than Helvetians in his family. There were masses of children, all tearing around with boundless energy, all getting on well with each other, as it should be, Romans and Gauls intermingling. Why can't it be like that for adults, Riona wondered.

"Had enough?" asked Allaine of his bride.

"I'll drop dead with exhaustion if I dance any more."

"Good."

He jumped onto one of the tables, called for silence, thanked them all for coming, and making the days so memorable, and wished them all good fortune. He then swept up his bride in his arms, and carried her to the waiting carriage.

Allaine lay naked on the bed in the lamp light.

"I'm somewhat flawed," he said with a smile. "Perhaps not what you had hoped for."

Riona looked at him. She couldn't begin to imagine what it must have been like to endure so much. Amazing, really, that he was still sane, still capable of loving. She ran her fingers lightly along one of the scars on his arm, bent her head, and kissed the ridged tissues. She felt such love for him, overwhelming love. Could she hope to make him whole again?

"You are perfect in every way," she said, smiling down at him. "And I will love you for ever."

"Oh, Riona, Riona, my love. I am so glad you chose me."

Valerius found Allaine's woman, the one he had kept

exclusively for himself, sobbing her heart out in a corner of the stables, when he came to put away the carriage horses. He lifted her up, all wet and sticky. He thought he had better try and give her some comfort, but one thing led to another, as he confessed to his master the next day.

Allaine thrashed them both.

BOOK 3 : CHAPTER 11

Helvetia (Switzerland), Autumn Winter 53 BC : 52 BC

The wedding guests departed. But although it seemed an oasis of tranquility, up here in the high mountains, the rest of Gaul was in ferment, as Allaine was increasingly aware. If his Roman relatives were to survive, he would need to get them away, and soon. And the more he thought about it, the more he wanted them to survive.

He summoned Octavian to his room, and told him of his decision. He made Octavian kneel, but it had never really given him any satisfaction. It was appropriate for the occasion, though. Octavian felt his heart racing. He thought he knew what his master was going to say, and he dreaded the words.

"I find, after all, that I have no real use for you, Octavian." The man looked stunned as if he had hit him. "Or for Valerius." He hadn't yet made up his mind about the others.

Octavian dropped his eyes to the floor. He felt the old despair returning. He had failed again. He had been trying so hard. Trying to be like Marcius, trying to have the same trusting relationship his friend enjoyed with Guéreth. He had got nowhere it seemed.

Allaine began to realise something was wrong. "Octavian, you don't understand. My words are supposed to make you happy. It means I will free you. You will leave with your parents."

"I don't want to leave." There. He'd said it. It was the truth.

Allaine looked into his eyes, startled at what he saw. This was going to be a problem.

"Octavian, I'm afraid you must."

"I have sworn to serve you," said Octavian desperately. "You said seven years. I've only been with you for a year."

"I will rescind the oath on the day you leave. I can free you at any time. That has always been my right."

"You will obliterate me from your mind, won't you Sir?"

"I don't want to, Octavian. I may have to."

"I don't know how to do that."

"Well, you can come and obliterate me with your legions," Allaine said softly.

He saw something then in Octavian's eyes, some deep hurt.

"Don't I even help you with the sick and wounded, Sir?" Octavian asked miserably.

"Yes, of course you do. You help me a great deal. I couldn't have managed without you, not well, anyway." Allaine was beginning to wonder how to put this right. "I assure you, I am not looking forward to your going. I wish with all my heart you could stay. Listen Octavian, you are changing, day by day. You're becoming more and more help to me. If I don't give you back now, I will have lost the chance for ever. I'm worried I've left it too late, already. How can I keep you, when you and your family have done so much for my sister?"

"Will you keep my sons?"

"No, of course not! I won't even keep your wife."

"Valerius worships you, practically."

"Valerius worships anything that's set in authority over him. I'm sure you'll help him find someone."

"No, Sir. You're wrong there. It's you he worships."

Allaine sighed. This wasn't going at all the way he'd expected.

"Octavian, you heard the speech Vercingetorix made on the eve of my wedding. Don't you realise the whole country is now up in arms? I must get you all away as soon as I can. You are no longer safe, even with me. Your family is no longer safe. I couldn't bear it if anything bad happened to any of you." He leant forwards, and touched the gold chain round his slave's neck. "I'm so sorry, Octavian, I can't take you with me. I wish I could. But where I am going, not even this will protect you, and that was the first thing, if you remember, I swore to do."

"Are you going to fight, Sir?"

"No. I can't do that and heal as well."

"Master, I don't think I can, either."

"Octavian, you will be fine. Once you are back with your own people, it will all come back to you."

"No, it won't."

Allaine took Octavian's hands in his own, and lifted him to his feet. He put his arms round his slave's shoulders. He was beginning to have some idea of Octavian's feelings.

"Octavian, I can't keep you. It wouldn't be right, it wouldn't be fair, my pet. You shouldn't want to be my slave. You will be fine, I promise you."

But Octavian knew better. He would never be the same again. He would always yearn for the high mountains, and his master's friendship. Allaine had come to mean so much to him. He had taught him so much. The thought of being without him, and his guidance, made his soul weep in distress. He was better than a brother, better almost than his own wonderful father. Allaine was the epitome of everything he wanted to be, a man who healed. And now Allaine wanted to return him to the killing fields.

"Octavian, you're looking soulful again." Allaine couldn't raise a smile from his slave. "Come on, now, don't be so sad. When you were captured, I had to make a lot of decisions in a hurry. No doubt some of them were bad, though I have never regretted for an instant owning you. But you weren't born and raised to be a Gallic slave. I wasn't raised to be a slave, either. But I had been one for so long, I was worried I had forgotten how to be free. It came back so easily, being a prince. It will be just the same for you."

Allaine guided him over to the couch. "Now I need your help. So come and sit down, and tell me what I am to do with Hugo. I will keep Servilius. He tells me he doesn't want to leave me, either. But unlike you, Octavian, he has nothing to go back to, but a cruel slavery. He was savagely treated before, and he is such a decent young man. It hasn't affected him badly, as far as I can see. It makes some men vicious themselves, if they've suffered vicious treatment. He isn't like that. Darius, I'm still am not sure about. Perhaps you could look out for him. He was made a scapegoat by his centurion. And suffered even more than Servilius, in some ways. Perpetually humiliated. I have been told there is one such victim in each centuria. Is that true? That one legionary usually has to die, to encourage the others?"

"Yes," said Octavian. He tried to think, to sound sensible. "They pick on the weakest. The men are more terrified of the centurions, than of the enemy. That's why we win, I suppose." He sounded anything but happy about it, Allaine noticed. "As for Hugo, It's a problem. He still seems so...." He paused, searching for the words, "so damaged, somehow, doesn't he?"

"There is no way he is fit to command anything at the present, least of all legionaries. Tell me about his family. Can he opt out of the Army and return to Rome, for example?"

They sat together, chewing over the problems for a last time, Octavian thought. They decided Hugo was to return as well. Octavian would try and look after Allaine's freedmen, to the best of his ability. Allaine thought if he had some extra responsibility, it might take his mind off his anguish at leaving him.

Octavian was ordered to supervise the packing of the wagons and mules. The Romans made preparations to leave. Everything was wrapped and beautifully packed, including some exquisitely worked gold jewellery, and some lovely furs, that Claudia thought would be the envy of all her friends. Guéreth was going as well. Allaine couldn't be bothered keeping him any longer, and had managed to secure Coevorten's agreement. He didn't want the Aeduan, either. Guéreth was already desperate to get back into action. Now he could ride again, Allaine thought he would become unbearable once all his friends had left. Jayven made a half-hearted attempt at persuading him to fight with his fellow Gauls, but Guéreth wouldn't hear of it. And he was no more reconciled to his sister's marriage, even though she was so evidently happy.

Allaine came to see how Octavian was getting on. All was neatly stowed away.

"I'm afraid you will have to get them to take everything out again, Octavian."

"Why, Sir? It all fits quite well this time, I thought."

"Yes, it is excellent. You have done so much better than the last time, haven't you?" They looked each other, and laughed at the memory. "But can't you feel the air?"

"Feel the air, Sir?"

"Yes, the air! Snow is coming, heavy snow. The passes will be blocked, long before you arrive."

Octavian gazed up into the vivid deep blue sky. As he looked, a solitary snowflake appeared out of nowhere, and fluttered down onto his hand, melting into nothingness. A gentle cold wind lifted the hair from his forehead. He grinned at his master.

By nightfall it was pouring with huge flakes of snow. The temperature dropped sharply. Snow cascaded down roofs, balanced on trees, dropped softly onto the ground below, blocking windows and doorways. The world became enrobed in a bright white cloak.

This early winter storm and succeeding snowfalls made safe travel impossible. Coevorten suggested they all abandon the attempt, and remain with his brother until the passes were open again in Spring.

Relationships changed after the wedding. Titus and Claudia were careful to stay in the background and slowly began to be treated as members of the family. Now they were used to hearing their son address Allaine as Master, and sounding as if he meant it. It was rather more shocking to hear Allaine giving orders to Octavian in that quiet authoritative voice of his, and realise that no matter what, Octavian would always obey. There was no question ever of going absent without leave. The family became less guarded in their conversation, sometimes revealing a small part of the terrible sufferings. One night Eloise told them how Marcus Metius had planned their escape, putting them up in a remote farmhouse, until he was sure their wagon had been pushed over the cliffs, and the soldiers returned to barracks. Claudia looked at Eloise's two cheerful blond boys sitting at the table, and felt sick.

At breakfast one morning Junior decided it was time to find out the answer to another puzzle.

"Uncle Allaine, what are those white marks on your arm?"

"They are scars, Octavian."

"And what are scars?"

"When skin is badly damaged, it heals up with scar tissue."

"How did you skin get badly damaged, Uncle Allaine?"

"With hot metal."

"Oh," said Junior. He carried on eating for a bit, then frowned, trying to work it out.

"Where did it come from, then, the hot metal?"

"It was heated up in a fire."

"Did it hurt?"

"It did a bit," Allaine smiled at his little nephew.

Junior looked at him, wide eyed. "Why did they want to hurt you, Uncle Allaine?"

"I was told it was to punish the man who had married my sister, my brother-in-law, Prince Dumnorix." Though he couldn't remember where exactly this information had come from. There were still a few small holes in his memory.

"But that's not fair."

"Life isn't always what we would want it to be, Junior. Sometimes it hurts."

One day, when the weather had warmed a little, Allaine told Octavian it was time they gave medicine a miss for a change, and got some fresh air instead. Octavian followed behind his master, riding one of the sure-footed mountain ponies. They rode north for a long way, climbing ever higher. Eventually they came to a vast cleft in the mountains. The air was so cold, full of delicate particles of light, tiny sparkles of shimmering ice crystals, stirred up by the wind. They were shivering despite their fur cloaks, even though they were riding in full sunshine.

"Here we are. This is the place," said Allaine. "Look up there."

He pointed out the massive blocks of palest blue ice, much bigger than any temple, poking out of the snow above them, appearing to tumble down into the valley.

"It's a glacier," Allaine explained. "A river of ice. It moves slightly over the years. I want to see if the ice cave is still there. Chrys and I found it years ago, when we were children."

After half a mile of carefully picking their way up into the ravine, Allaine found what he was looking for.

"Come on."

They ducked into the small triangular entrance. Inside the ice opened out into a great cavern, an enormous amphitheatre. The blue light filtered dimly through the walls. Octavian shivered again.

"Come over here," Allaine called to him. He was standing in front of an irregular wall of ice. Octavian could see the names inscribed in enormous Greek characters, 'Allaine' and 'Chryseis.'

"I hadn't had Noemon long. We weren't sure of how to form the letters. But it's not bad for young children. Now, write your name as well," Allaine ordered.

Octavian removed the dagger from his belt, and obediently carved his name next to the other two.

A deep hollow creaking sound rumbled above them, like distant thunder.

"Perhaps we had better leave, before the mountain king

takes us for his own," Allaine whispered.

Octavian wasn't at all sure as to whether his master was being serious, or having a joke. He found his master's sense of humour difficult to fathom, at times. He felt much happier, though, once they were outside again. They left the cave and headed home, stopping in a warmer sheltered spot for a bite to eat, near to a rushing stream of melt-water. Allaine brushed the snow off a rock, spread his cloak out, and pulled Octavian down to sit beside him. The bread and slices of smoked pork tasted heavenly to Octavian, as he shared the meal with his master. He looked out over the tranquil sea of whiteness, delicately patterned with the tracks of small animals, just a few birds in the sky making any movement. The chattering noise of the stream, and occasional cry of the birds were the only sounds. He felt an inward peace seep into his soul.

"I hate war!" Allaine declared suddenly, with savage intensity, breaking the spell. "Such a waste. Such a terrible terrible waste."

Octavian wondered what in the world had caused his master to speak with such vehemence in the midst of the quiet landscape. It was some time before he found out.

Cenabum, principal town of the Carnutes, Central Gaul

An odd noise invaded Andreas's dream and woke him in the night. He was disorientated to start with. They had travelled to Cenabum three days ago, for his uncle to conclude some trade agreements. Marcus Metius thought Ursula and her family would find much to interest them in the picturesque old town, so they were all happy to accompany him, especially as he travelled so luxuriously. There were usually bargains to be had in the local markets, he told them, and the food was superb. His enthusiasm for all things Gallic was becoming infectious, with even Ursula sometimes expressing a grudging admiration.

The bedroom was unfamiliar to Andreas; there was no lamp lit, but bright moonlight seeped through the shutters, striping his bed and the floor with regular thin bars of light. He could dimly see the outline of furniture. What had woken him? Yes, the sound of horse's hooves in the courtyard, and now heavy footsteps hurrying to his uncle's room. He sat up in bed, straining to hear, listening intently. He thought he could hear further sounds, sounds that shouldn't have been there in the middle of the night. Far off, distant shouting and screaming, the crackle of flames, and the crashing of buildings. Something bad was happening.

His uncle appeared in the doorway. "Andreas, we must go, we must leave immediately."

His servant Samuel was awake now.

"What is it, Sir?" Andreas asked. "What's going on?"

"We are being attacked. Roman traders slaughtered throughout the town."

"Where will we go then, Sir?" Andreas asked fearfully. Slaughtered. What a horrible word. He didn't want to be slaughtered.

"The roads south are blockaded. We will head north and east, and make for the Helvetian country."

"Can I take my servant?"

Metius looked at the frightened boy on the mattress in the corner of the room. "You may take him if he can ride a horse. I have a wagon always prepared for this. Ursula and Lucy will go in it with their maids. Now, no more discussion. Get ready as quickly as you can."

The horses' hooves were muffled with cloths. His mother and Lucy appeared, with a couple of frightened sobbing girls, told to shut up at once, if they didn't want their throats cut by the Gauls. The shouts and screams got louder, came nearer. The women scrambled into the wagon, the men mounted up, Metius gave the order to leave without a moment's delay.

The streets were strangely deserted, as they made for the northern gate. No one challenged them. It seemed most of the town's inhabitants were either out marauding in the southern part of the town, or were hiding behind closed shutters, not daring to move. Andreas breathed a sigh of relief as they left the town behind them. Metius had taken only a few outriders. The other servants would have to shift for themselves.

The roads got steeper, the air much colder, and villages with taverns, willing to accept Roman gold, increasingly hard to find. News of the uprising was beginning to catch up with them. The journey became hellish, the mules and horses having huge difficulty picking their way along the frozen roads and through the snowy passes. Metius now sought isolated farms. He talked to Andreas one evening, when the women had retired shivering for the night.

"We cannot expect to enter the Helvetian country unchallenged. We have no way of securing their approval in advance. But I am hoping that, as they have some obligation to me, we will be treated fairly."

This didn't sound very reassuring to Andreas. "Do we have any other options, Sir?"

"We could kill ourselves," said his uncle.

BOOK 3: CHAPTER 12

Helvetia (Switzerland), Winter 53 : 52 BC

The messenger was explicit. Would Prince Allaine ride at once to Aventicum, where Coevorten was holding the assizes. There were some Roman captives. Coevorten wished his brother's assistance in dealing with them. He was to bring his surgical implements.

Allaine walked into the Great Hall. Octavian and Chrys had just come in after playing with the children, their clothes covered in snow. They were laughing hysterically together, looking blissfully happy. Chrys brushed snow from her cloak onto the floor.

"These horrible boys have been pelting me with snowballs," she protested. "Look at my cloak. I'm soaked."

A servant dashed to relieve his princess of the heavy wet cloak. Octavian handed over his snowy cloak as well, and then threw Little Allaine up in the air. The child shrieked with glee, as his father caught him.

"Darling," said Lady Volusena. "I wish you wouldn't do that. You might drop him."

"Of course I won't drop him, Mother," said Octavian, hugging Little Allaine tightly to his chest. "Anyway, I can remember Dad doing the same to me. You didn't tell him off."

"They seem so much more precious, somehow." Claudia tried to explain the difference between one's children and one's grandchildren.

Grandmother agreed. She found that she often agreed with Lady Volusena. A woman of great good sense, she had told Allaine.

"Octavian, I am sorry to interrupt," started Allaine.

Octavian shrugged his shoulders, spread his hands, and said, with a charming smile, that it was not a problem.

"Darling, don't do that," Claudia reproved her son.

"Do what, Mother?"

"Be so Gallic. You are worrying Allaine."

"No I'm not!"

"Yes, you are a bit, darling," Chrys laughed at him.

Allaine found Claudia to be very astute on occasion. He was seriously worried about his slave. He could now hardly tell the difference between Octavian and Jay. There was no doubt about it, Octavian was turning into a Gaul. The sooner the passes opened the better. Every day that passed would make it harder for him to turn back into a Roman military tribune.

"Well anyway, could you find Val, and get the horses ready," Allaine went on. "Make sure you both wear warm clothes and boots, and good waterproof cloaks, those waxed ones."

"Where are we going, Sir?" Octavian was surprised. They had brought the children in as the weather was deteriorating so much.

"To Aventicum. Apparently there are some Roman prisoners there. It sounds as if some are wounded, so take all my equipment, plus dressings and bandages." He shook off further questions. "I know no more than that, we will have to find out when we get there."

"But Allaine, it's already starting to snow heavily," Chrys was worried. "The road will be blocked soon."

"We may have to stay over, so don't worry if we're not back. I'll take care he comes to no harm." He grinned at her. "If we've not returned after a couple of months, you can send someone to dig us out."

Chrys smiled at that. Allaine, previously so serious when he first came home, was at last becoming the Allaine of old, still serious, but more relaxed, cheerful, and happy, able to make the occasional joke, even. Mostly thanks to Riona, Chrys thought, but also to Octavian. She was pleased that the two men she loved most in the world, liked each other so much as well.

Riona appeared, coming to find out the reason for the group of men in the courtyard. She had overheard Allaine's last remark.

"I think I'd better kiss you goodbye, Allaine, if you are planning to be away for two months."

He pulled her towards him, kissing her and laughing at her. "And what do you know about snow, my heart? Nothing. You think it's there to make everything look nice and clean and beautiful."

"And so it does. Even Lady Volusena agrees. But Allaine, where are you going?"

Allaine explained as much as he could.

"Shouldn't the men be fed before their return journey?"

"No, love. We had best be on our way. We will eat at Aventicum."

Coevorten had sent a party of men-at-arms to escort them. It was snowing heavily, then the wind got up to mischief, whipping up snow from the trees, the rocks, the ground and ridges, hurling ice pellets into their faces. They were glad of their cloaks and hoods. The horses slipped and slid over the frozen surfaces. Landmarks soon became obliterated, and visibility poor. It was getting difficult to see more than a few yards ahead, through a world of whirling whiteness, but Allaine knew the road well, and made sure the others came after him in single file. The road went close to the river in several places. He didn't want any one of the party falling through into the icy waters. It took them over two hours to travel the ten miles to Aventicum.

In typical Helvetian fashion, the road to the Courthouse was being cleared, even as the snow was falling. They arrived in early afternoon, chilled to the bone; the sky already dark with unshed snow. Servants ran out to meet them, hearing the jingling harnesses telling of their arrival. Allaine dismounted, telling the others to follow him. Their cloaks were shaken and taken to be dried off. Slaves came with warm towels for their hair and faces, and welcome mugs of mulled ale.

The Roman prisoners were standing close to the door, under heavy guard, a shivering woman trying not to cry, a group

507

of terrified girls, a youth, a young man, and an anxious looking, beautifully barbered, grey-haired man, whom Allaine recognised at once as Marcus Metius. The three males all appeared to be injured in some way, their arms and faces bruised and cut. Allaine heard Octavian gasp in surprise behind him. He turned swiftly.

"You know these people, then?" he asked quietly.

"Yes, Sir. Marcus Metius, a Roman merchant."

"The slave dealer? Yes, I know him," said Allaine. "And the others?"

"His sister, Lady Ursula, that's Marcius's mother, Sir, and his brother and sister, Andreas and Lucia. I think the other girls must be their maids. What on earth are they doing here?"

"Fighting a battle, by the looks of it. We'll find out. Wait here with them, Octavian, but don't talk to them, as they are in the custody of the Court. It looks as if all the men are injured, and need attention. I'll go and speak to my brother."

The prisoners had no idea who the dark-eyed man was, standing quietly behind them. He didn't say a word. Allaine approached Coevorten, who was seated on a platform above the throng, with well-armed attendants by his side. Allaine waited, until noticed and summoned. He walked forward and knelt at his brother's feet. Octavian couldn't hear what was said, but they seemed to be having a long discussion. Allaine was shaking his head when he came back, he didn't look very pleased. He started to issue orders in his quiet voice. Orderlies sprang to attention and rushed to obey. Octavian was no longer surprised at the effect Allaine had on his subordinates.

The saddle bags were brought in. A servant appeared with a stool. Allaine looked to where Andreas stood, blood slowly dripping down his face, onto his clothes, and ending in a pool on the courtroom floor. His hands were tied in front of him. One glance at his white anxious face, was enough to show Allaine he was in a considerable amount of pain.

To start with Allaine paid no attention to the others. He spoke only to Andreas.

"Come here," he ordered.

Andreas knew instantly this was a man who had to be obeyed. He walked over and stood silently before him, trying not to think of what the immediate future might hold.

"What's your name?"

"Andreas Carvilius, Sir." He managed to speak, without his voice shaking.

"Come and sit down, Andreas. Val, make a compress, and hold it on this head wound, will you? Make sure it stops bleeding."

Metius knew he had seen Allaine somewhere before, but a long time ago, he thought. Recognition caught him by surprise. He was astounded to see Allaine fully recovered, tall, strong, and powerful.

"I know this man. His name is Allaine," he whispered to Ursula.

"Will he help us?" asked Ursula, in despair.

"I don't think claiming acquaintance with him will assist us much. The last time we met, I sold him." But he had treated Allaine kindly, when he'd had him for the few days before selling him to Petronius. He wondered if that would help at all. Probably not.

Allaine moved to stand in front of him, a slight smile on his face, aware the slave dealer recognised him.

"Well, Metius. We appear to have reversed roles. Are any of the women hurt?"

Metius started to apologise.

"No. Save it for my brother. Just answer the question," said Allaine.

"Your brother, Sir?"

"My brother Coevorten, the presiding magistrate. Now, about the women?"

"They are frightened, Sir, but not hurt." Metius thought he'd better obey. So Allaine was Coevorten's brother. Fuck!

Allaine approached the group of girls. Two of them started

to sob, but the well-dressed one, Lucy, he presumed, just stood, pale and shaking. Chrys was right about her. Marcius's sister was indeed a very pretty girl. She was slight, delicate looking, staring at him with terrified big brown eyes. She backed away from him, until stopped by the courtroom wall. He found himself feeling sorry for her.

He held out his hand to her, and said gently, "Come with me, my pet."

She was frozen with fear. He repeated, "Lucy, come with me now. I don't wish to have to carry you."

How did this tall blond man know her name? Obediently, she held his hand. What else could she do? She couldn't fight him.

Together they walked through a doorway, and immediately afterwards the curtain was closed behind them. They were in a large chilly room. The window shutters were wide open, snow drifting in from outside, and melting to a puddle on the ground. A brazier stood at the far end, under a hole in the roof, with Allaine's instruments in a basin of simmering water on the top. Lady Coevorten sat in a chair next to a long table, with her eldest daughter by her side. Lucy felt reassured to see them. It didn't look to her like a rape scenario.

Allaine spoke kindly to her. She wasn't going to like his information. But he thought she was unharmed. He could see no signs of blood on her clothes.

"Lucy, I'm sorry, but the Court insists you be examined for any evidence of assault. And unfortunately, this being a Gallic court, they won't take a woman's word for anything, so I have to be here. This lady will have a look at you. But if you *have* been injured, my pet, it will be me that puts you back together again." He thought he'd better warn her.

Lucy looked stricken. "What do you mean, assault?"

"I mean, have you been injured? Have you been raped? Are you still a virgin? We need to find out."

Why Coevorten considered it necessary, he couldn't imagine. She was so pale, he thought she might faint. "Come and sit down, Lucy. On this table, pet. That's it. That's a good girl."

Gently he pushed her hair back from her face with his fingers. "It will be very quick. It won't hurt you at all, I promise, and I will go to the other end of the room. You won't see me. Can you manage that, Lucy?"

She was moving her head from side to side, like a trapped animal, desperate to escape. There was no help for it. She was going to have to say it. What was this nice kind young man going to think of her? She took a deep breath. "I'm not a virgin," she whispered to him.

Allaine was taken aback. He gazed at her in consternation, absorbing this new information. He wasn't expecting anything like this. He could see the girl was very distressed. "So are you married, Lucy? Who is the lucky man?"

"No, I'm not married." Her eyes filled with tears, which spilled down her face. Allaine thought quickly. Claudia had told him that only Octavian was married. He doubted if Gaius Volusenus would risk intercourse before marriage with a girl of good class. It would be madness. Chrys had given him some information about Lucy, that until Sperinus died, she was hardly allowed out of the house. No servant would touch her after what happened to David. That left one of her brothers, or....

"Was it your stepfather, pet?" So that was it. The madman. What a lot of damage he had wreaked on this family. "Oh, poor Lucy," Allaine said softly.

She sobbed in his arms. She didn't know how this strange man knew all about her. Maybe he was an angel, or a God. He was so comforting, as he held her and soothed her.

"Now, my pet. You need to tell me a bit more. Could you be pregnant? When did Sperinus die, exactly?"

Bit by bit he got the story out of her. Apparently it had gone on for years, starting as soon as Marcius sold himself. She was twelve years old at the time. "He kept saying he would kill me," she wept, "because I had dishonoured the family. And if I said anything, he would kill Mother as well."

"Did you tell Gaius?" Allaine asked her. Lucy was amazed. How did this man know about Gaius? No, she hadn't dared, she said. She didn't know what to do. Allaine was the first person she had ever told. But she was sure she wasn't pregnant. Sperinus had died more than a year ago.

Lady Coevorten tried to help, but couldn't do much, other than make sympathetic noises, as she didn't speak Latin, Allaine assured Lucy. He told his sister-in-law, that as Lucy was so distressed, they would simply take her word for it nothing had happened to her. He succeeded eventually in calming Lucy, and drying her tears, telling her no one else need know anything about it. If she would give him her word she hadn't been assaulted by the guards, that would be the end of it. But he would have to tell Coevorten.

"We won't decide what to do about you just yet, my pet. There are other things to bother us at the moment. We need to get the injured sorted out, don't we? Perhaps you can help me with that?"

Octavian stood with Val by the prisoners, silent, but with his mind racing. This was Lucy, after all. He had been betrothed to her himself, once. Was his master raping her? If so, what should he do about it? Val grabbed his arm, speaking in Gallic.

"Shouldn't we do something, Octavian?" he whispered. "You said she's Marcius's sister."

"No." He remembered his master's words. "We must trust Prince Allaine."

After a short while they could hear the sound of low sobbing. It went on for an eternity, it seemed to Octavian. Still he didn't move or speak. A servant came out of the room and disappeared, to reappear a short time later, with what looked like a goblet of wine on a tray. Then two men arrived, carrying an enormous amphora between them. Octavian could smell the familiar vinegary smell. Now there were some splashing sounds. The sobbing had stopped.

Allaine appeared in the doorway. Lady Coevorten moved past him out of the room, with her daughter. Octavian experienced a wave of relief. There must be another door.

"Octavian," she said, pleased to see him. "How are you? And your charming family?"

He knelt and kissed her hand, and made a suitable reply.

Allaine took her over to Ursula. Chrys had told him how impolite Ursula had been on their journey. He wasn't going to waste any time on her.

"Ursula, this lady will take you and your maids to her house, now. Her daughter has a few Latin words, but the only other person who can speak Latin in their household is my brother Coevorten, and he is the presiding magistrate. How much Gallic have you learnt, since you have been in the country?"

None, apparently. "Then you may spend the afternoon learning how to say please and thank you," he told her brusquely. He wondered if she had known about Lucy, and said and done nothing.

"Octavian, bring the two youngsters in, will you? Val, you come as well."

"What are you going to do with my son?" Ursula asked in panic.

"His injuries need attention," Allaine said, impatiently. "Do as you're told, and go with Lady Coevorten."

Octavian? - thought Andreas to himself. He tried to see the face of the man behind him. He hadn't appeared to be anyone he knew.

He caught at Allaine's sleeve. "If I'm to be killed, Sir, may I first say goodbye to my mother?"

Allaine looked at the young man, who was trying so hard to be brave. "I don't know what sentence the court may have in mind for you, Andreas. But as my brother has ordered me to ride ten miles through a blizzard, and spend the afternoon putting you back together again, I would be most annoyed with him if it resulted in your execution. So come with me, and don't be so melodramatic. We are not acting in a Greek tragedy." Allaine was losing patience. The light would go soon, and it would be infinitely more difficult to suture by lamplight. What a nuisance this little family was proving to be.

Allaine took his arm, and guided him to the side room, where the servants had already set out his instruments. The table was used by the Court, when questioning recalcitrant witnesses, and was equipped with restraining straps. The room's appearance did nothing to reassure Andreas, who stood clenching his uninjured hand, attempting to stay calm, attempting not to show how desperately afraid he was, despite the reassurances of the tall blond man. Octavian came into the room, leading his injured servant. Andreas could see Lucy sitting in a chair, sipping at a beaker of what appeared to be wine. As far as he knew, she had never drunk wine before. She didn't look like a girl who had just been raped.

"Lucy is going to help us," Allaine said, seeing his glance. "Octavian, get them both stripped, will you?"

Andreas recognised his brother's friend with a start. "Octavian," he said in amazement. "It is you! What are you doing here?"

"Hello, Andreas. It's a long story. Let's get you sorted out first." He could see Lucy's eyes widen in astonishment.

"Octavian?" said Lucy, bewildered.

"Hello, Lucy."

"Octavian!" At last she recognised the black-bearded young man, who was helping her brother undress. "But you're dead!"

"Apparently not," said Octavian, smiling at her.

Allaine made Andreas sit on a bench, naked, but wrapped in his cloak.

"Now, Lucy. Yes, it's Octavian. Never mind that at the moment. There will be time for explanations later. I want you to clean your brother up. Can you get rid of all the blood on his face and body? When you have done that, you must cut his hair around this head wound, do you see? Then I will know what I'm dealing with. Can you manage that?"

"Yes, Sir," Lucy said meekly. It was all too puzzling.

"That's a good girl."

Allaine turned his attention to the terrified servant. "What's your name, my little one?"

"Sam, Master. That is, Samuel."

"Sam will do very well. Come over here, now."

Allaine removed the boy's cloak, folding it into a pad. Then he made him lie on the table, with his head resting on the cloak. All the time he was talking to him, quietly reassuring, saying he wouldn't be hurt, asking about his journey, and how he was captured. Sam began to feel calmer, no longer so scared.

"It must be tiring, having to fight after such a long journey," Allaine suggested. He could see the boy's eyelids begin to droop. He started to stroke the boy's face. "It won't take long to sort you out, my little one. But I don't think you would find it very interesting, so I think you had better get some sleep, while we stitch you up. Close your eyes, now, Sam, and go to sleep."

Lucy looked over at them, astonished to see Sam's eyes closed, apparently fast asleep. She was even more sure a God had come to help them.

"Let's get started," Allaine said briskly.

Valerius fastened the straps around the slave's inert body, just in case the pain broke through the trance. Allaine started suturing, with Octavian cutting the stitches, Val supplying them with the required instruments, and threaded needles. Lucy and Andreas looked on amazed. The work was soon completed, with dressings and bandages fixed firmly in place. Val lifted the boy up. Allaine ordered him to be laid on his own cloak, along a side wall. He thought the boy might as well continue to sleep.

Allaine beckoned to Andreas. "Now, let's take a look at you."

There was some bruising on his body, but the main injury was to the right hand. Allaine frowned over the deep cuts to palm

515

and fingers, which were still bleeding slightly. There was also the deep gash in the scalp, more easily seen, now the bleeding had stopped. Lucy had made a good job of cutting her brother's hair.

"Andreas, I'm afraid your hand is in a bad way," Allaine told him. "I am going to have to suture each cut. This will be painful, but as the cuts are clean edged, it should be easy to give you a hand that works again. Afterwards you must do exactly as I tell you."

Andreas felt relieved to think there would be an afterwards. His injured hand was immersed in a bowl of vinegar, Allaine telling him that it might sting a bit. It was agony, as the acid seeped deeply into the cuts. Then he was strapped down. Allaine began the suturing. But inevitably the feel of the needle biting into sensitive flesh proved too much altogether. Andreas started to cry out against the pain. He pulled and tugged at the straps. Octavian was having difficulty holding his hand still. Allaine paused.

"We'll stop for a bit, Andreas, so you can get yourself back together again."

"I'm sorry, Sir."

Allaine was sympathetic. "Unfortunately for you, hands and fingers are some of the most sensitive areas of the body. So don't apologise. Any one of us would react in the same way."

"Could you tell me what will happen next, Sir?" Andreas asked anxiously, appreciating the kindness of Allaine's words.

"You will need to kneel in Court, and express contrition for daring to invade the country without permission." Allaine smiled at the thought of this tiny invading army. "We will endeavour to make you look inoffensive."

"Yes, Sir. And then what?"

"That I don't know, it's up to my brother. He's the chief magistrate."

"But why are they here, Sir?" asked Octavian.

"It appears the Carnutes have attacked the Roman traders in Cenabum, killed a lot of them, and plundered their stock,"

Allaine explained. "They killed Gaius Fufius Cita, the man in charge of Caesar's commissariat, but one of his servants was able to flee, to warn Metius."

"Why would the Carnutes do such a thing?"

"Were you there, when Vercingetorix was telling us about Prince Acco? Oh, yes, of course you were."

"Yes, Sir. This is revenge for Prince Acco's death, is it?"

"Yes." Allaine had known the exact date the Carnutes were going to attack, the day of the ice cave. "Apparently Metius only just managed to get his family away in time, but found all the roads blockaded, except for the high pass route. That's why he's here. I suppose hoping the fact that he saved Eloise and the boys can be set against his expediting the murder of my father."

"He murdered your father?" Octavian was horrified, and Andreas was terrified all over again, just when he was beginning to feel safe.

"He sent a masseur to my father as a gift, and the masseur poisoned him. He confessed while under trance, when as you probably know, it is impossible to lie." Although the masseur had declared Metius knew nothing of the plot to kill Orgetorix, his instructions had come from Caesar.

Octavian and Andreas were silent. Presumably the masseur had met some horrible end. They didn't want to know the details.

A servant walked in. "Sir, your brother asks how long will you be?"

"Another hour, I should think. There is still Metius to be seen to."

Allaine called Lucy over. "Now, Lucy, I want you to watch closely. When I have dealt with your uncle, I will need to go and make some arrangements about where we are staying tonight. Octavian will sew up your brother's scalp wound, and you will cut the stitches."

Lucy came over to where her brother lay strapped down, his left hand gripping the edge of the couch tightly, his right hand

517

stretched out, covered with lines of small neat stitches.

When Allaine had finished the suturing, he once again immersed Andreas's hand in vinegar.

"Yes, I know, I know," he said in sympathy, as Andreas tearfully protested, "but we don't want any infection to set in. You've done really well, Andreas. Not much more now."

He gently dried the wounds with a towel before putting on the oil soaked bandages.

"So they won't stick," he explained. "Val, go and get Metius in, and strip him."

Metius was pale, but saying nothing. He had heard Andreas's cries from where he was standing, at the back of the Courtroom, and wondered when it would be his turn. He was unsure of what was going to happen to them all. He wanted to feel his way carefully. Allaine inspected him closely. Two gashes, both of which needed stitching.

"What a fortunate decision of yours, to sell me to a medical man," Allaine said sweetly to his victim. "I will be able to demonstrate to you, just how well he trained me."

"Indeed, Sir." Metius looked quite ill.

After an hour the servant returned to escort Metius back to the courtroom, as Allaine had finished with him. Coevorten was now ready to question him.

Allaine watched as Metius left. "You'd better go with him, Val. He looks as if he might pass out at any moment. Now, Lucy, you know what to do? I'll leave you to it, then, Octavian."

When the three of them were left alone, Lucy felt bold enough to ask questions.

"Why are you letting that man give you orders? Is he some kind of God?"

"No, it's because I am his slave."

"How can that be," said Lucy, astonished. "He's a barbarian, isn't he?"

"No, Lucy, he's a Helvetian, a prince, a very important man. His name is Allaine. I was captured a year ago, when the

Fourteenth legion was destroyed. I was taken prisoner, and given to Prince Allaine by Ambiorix, otherwise I almost certainly would be dead. No, cut it a bit shorter than that."

"Is he a doctor?"

"He calls himself a healer; it's similar, I suppose. He is also a brilliant physician, truly brilliant."

When Allaine returned some time later, he inspected the scalp wound, and murmured "excellent," which made Octavian feel absurdly pleased.

"Lucy, is this your first surgical procedure?" Allaine asked her.

"Yes, Sir."

"Well done, then. Come on, now, Andreas. We need to get you dressed and get your arm in a sling. And I think you can have something for the pain."

Andreas recoiled at the bitter tasting wine, but Octavian intervened. "Yes, it doesn't taste very nice, but swallow it down quickly, Andreas. It makes a great deal of difference, makes it bearable."

A little later Allaine was able to say, "There now, you look very sweet, I think you'll do."

Andreas was taken into the court, and helped to kneel at Coevorten's feet alongside his uncle, whose arms were outstretched for mercy to be extended. Coevorten had finished examining Metius. He found him guilty only of entering the country without permission, and resisting arrest. He pronounced the sentence; a large fine, and confiscation of his goods. Metius breathed a sigh of relief. He hadn't been at all sure of the mood of these Gauls. Hearing Andreas's screams for relief hadn't helped him endure a very uncomfortable afternoon. He'd understood the jeers of the crowd, and the lurid suggestions for his punishment, slavery or torture seemed to be a popular remedy for past sins. He got to his feet, bowed, and expressed his profound gratitude to the court, and sincere apologies for invading the land of the Helvetians without due process. Coevorten pronounced that the prisoners were to be released into the care of Allaine, to his brother's astonishment. He ordered Allaine to make sure they behaved themselves in the future.

"Why me?" Allaine asked his brother, feeling annoyed. "My house is pretty full at present."

"I cannot stand them, Allaine. I can't bear to be near them. I hate Romans. You seem to like them."

"I most certainly do not. I like a very few of them."

"Yes. All the ones you've met so far."

"Rubbish! What about Octavian? I thought you quite liked him?"

"He's different. He's one of the family. I'll put up with these others until the snow clears, and you can reach your house. Then, for their sakes, get them away from me."

At dinner that evening, with snow still falling silently outside the windows, Allaine explained there was now no way any of them could leave Switzerland.

"I'm afraid all the passes will be blocked. The drifts will be much higher than a horse or wagon. You must resign yourselves to staying here until the passes are open again, and most likely that won't be until the Spring."

This caused consternation. "But where will we stay, Sir?" asked Ursula.

"We will be able to get to my house in a day or two, I expect," replied Allaine. "I'm afraid you have to stay with me, as I am responsible for you. But I think the Volusenus family will be pleased to have some friends to help while away the time until they can leave." He smiled to see their astonished expressions. "Octavian's parents are still here. They are equally trapped, though they don't seem to mind too much, do they, Octavian?"

"I think they are having a good time with the grandchildren, Sir. And Mother loves having all the girls around her." And he knew his father found Allaine as fascinating as he did himself. They talked for hours together.

Allaine dropped the thunderbolt. "And I am sure Marcius will be delighted to see you."

Ursula looked at him in anguish. "Surely my son is dead?" She looked from Allaine to Octavian. "We heard he was killed. All of them were killed. Everyone with the Fourteenth legion. Isn't that so?"

"But I'm not dead, am I?" said Octavian, gently.

"No, Marcius is not dead, I can assure you. He is very much alive," Allaine said. "He's at my house, with his master. Do you know Guéreth? Have you ever met him?"

"Yes." It was Lucy who answered. "He visited us in Rome, just after he bought my brother. And he used to write to us, giving us news of him."

"You will see them both in a few days. There should be enough of a thaw to enable us to travel along the valley."

Ursula was overcome. Lucy had her arms around her weeping mother. It had all become too much. Too much fear, too much worry. Now too much relief. She was still unsure whether to believe Allaine, or not.

Coevorten thought it was time for conversation to become less emotional. "Very good wine this, Metius," he said.

"I would be delighted to obtain some more for you, Sir." Should I ever get out of this mess, Metius thought to himself. The pain of his wounds was getting worse. He felt a bit light headed.

Allaine decided that now he had got hold of Metius, he would not let him off lightly. "But I am curious," he said. "You told me you had to sell me, because you don't dare to get mixed up in politics. You said Caesar might be angry to find you had kept me alive."

"Did I?" Metius was surprised. He wasn't usually so indiscreet.

"Oh yes. You used to talk to me as if you were talking to yourself. How is it, then, that you connived at my father's murder?"

Metius thought the truth might be best. "I was told the

masseur was to be a spy only. I was never told he was a poisoner. In fact I was horrified by your father's death."

"Of course we knew he was a spy. I thought he was too timid to kill. A misjudgement on my part, I suppose," said Coevorten.

"And on Father's," added Allaine. "Don't trust Romans bearing gifts. If you get some more wine for us, Metius, Marcius will have to taste it first."

Metius thought he'd better offer something of value. "I believe young Vercingetorix is making quite a stir. He has been in communication with many of the clans. His secret meetings deep in the woods, aren't always as secret as he believes."

The Gauls smiled at that. It didn't look as if Caesar had any idea of the Gallic Council meeting in Switzerland. Allaine steered the conversation to more general topics, to the relief of the Romans.

After dinner Allaine went with Valerius to see how Andreas was coping. Andreas was nearly asleep. He had managed to eat a little. His hand was beginning to swell, and throb, so Allaine persuaded him to take some more opium, and administered some to Sam as well.

"Now, Andreas," Allaine started sternly. "What have you learnt today?"

Andreas looked blank for a moment. Oh yes. "Vinegar is an antiseptic?" he suggested.

"Good, what else?"

"I don't know, Sir."

"I thought you might have learnt not to grab a sword with your bare hands," said Allaine.

"It all happened so quickly. I didn't have time to think. I'm sorry I've been such a nuisance."

"I hope you manage to get some sleep. This is my servant, Valerius. He is going to stay with you both tonight, so if you need any help, just ask him. Goodnight, Andreas."

"Goodnight, Sir."

Andreas lay in the dark, listening to Valerius's quiet breathing, and Sam's snores, as the opium began to take effect. He went over the terrifying events of the last days, the headlong rush to escape the massacres, the gruelling journey, the horror of being captured, the uncertainty, the fear. Now he felt safe. He savoured the word. He felt safe. He *was* safe. His mother was safe. His sister was safe. His uncle was safe. It was a pleasant feeling. Drowsily he wondered about Allaine. He appeared to be a powerful man. Not one to disobey. Octavian seemed to like him. It was all very puzzling. He would find out more tomorrow, but just now, just now he would sleep.

Allaine was conducted to the guest room. He sat down on the bed, rubbing his face with fatigue. Octavian knelt at his feet, and took off his boots. Then he helped his master undress.

"Where are you sleeping, Octavian?"

"In here, on the floor, Sir, if that's alright?"

"You'd better share this bed, then. It's big enough for three. As long as you don't wake in the night and think I'm Chrys."

Octavian laughed and started to strip. "Won't you be wanting one of the women, Sir?"

"I'm exhausted. What about you?"

"I'm pretty tired myself, though I haven't had to concentrate as much as you."

"Then let's sleep. Goodnight Octavian. Sleep well."

"Goodnight, Master." Octavian extinguished most of the lamps, rolled himself up in a blanket, lay down beside his master under the furs, and was almost instantly asleep.

"Octavian!"

Octavian woke up, confused. "What the hell? Oh, sorry, Sir. What's up?"

"Go and let that bloody dog in."

"Sir?"

"Ajax! I don't know how he got here, but he's howling outside. Go and let him in, before he wakes the entire house."

Octavian got out of the comfy warm bed in disgust. He lit a candle from the single oil lamp, pulled on his trousers, and found his way to the front of the house with some difficulty. It was so dark, with very few lamps lit in the rooms he had to pass through. He shook the porter awake. Together they unbarred the door. A very wet dog burst through, barking vociferously. Octavian went to quieten him. Ajax shook himself at that moment, splattering Octavian with freezing cold water.

"Go and find Val," he ordered the dog, "and you may jump on him with my blessing."

Ajax gave a short sharp bark, and dashed off.

"Was it Ajax?" Allaine asked sleepily, when he returned.

"A very wet cold Ajax. He shook himself all over me. I told him to go and jump on Val."

Allaine chuckled. "I wonder how I am going to placate my sister-in-law. Dogs aren't usually allowed inside. Quite a dog to come through such appalling conditions unscathed, though."

They slept again, with no more disturbances.

Fortunately Lady Coevorten was so amazed at Ajax's feat when she heard about it in the morning, she suffered him to stay with Val. Andreas was happy to have anything at all to take his mind off his hand. Val was immensely proud of his dog's achievement.

Within three days they were all back at the house. Allaine didn't think Andreas could have managed before, as he was in so much pain. He asked if Allaine could cut his hand off, at one stage, he was feeling so desperate. Allaine insisted on bathing the hand in vinegar night and morning. But by the third day the pain became bearable. Even so, Allaine kept him sedated on the journey, and he travelled in a wagon with his mother and sister. Allaine sent some of the escort with Valerius and Ajax on ahead, to announce their arrival.

Marcius was waiting in the Great Hall with Guéreth, consumed with impatience.

"Marcius! Oh, Marcius!" Lucy ran to him, as soon as the party entered the hall, and flung her arms round his neck.

He had to detach her, whispering, "No, Lucy. That's not how we do things here. Quiet now. And when you speak, speak Greek." He conducted her back to Allaine, who was looking irritated. The Helvetians will think our family have no manners at all, Marcius thought.

Allaine presented Marcus Metius to Grandmother, saying he was the man who had rescued Eloise and the boys. Grandmother wasn't impressed. "I believe you killed my son," she said, addressing Metius.

"He was the unwitting instrument of Father's death, Grandmother."

"Tuh!" said Grandmother in disbelief.

"He most likely saved my life, as well," Allaine added. "And he paid a lot of money for my funeral. Chrys said it was a splendid affair." He was smiling at her so nicely, and who could resist her lovely Allaine. She held out her hand for Metius to kiss. Allaine was relieved. They were all going to be stuck together for months. There needed to be peace between them.

Metius presented his sister, and niece, and explained there was also a nephew, who was too ill to be formally greeted at present. Ursula was shocked to find she was supposed to kiss Grandmother's hand, and did so with bad grace. Lucy made up for it by kneeling before Grandmother, and begging her pardon for her lack of manners. Her Greek was perfect. Grandmother became gracious. Riona and Chrys stood politely waiting with the children, who now knew just how to behave. Junior was grinning happily at his father, but said nothing.

At last Guéreth could bring Marcius forward, to kneel at Allaine's feet, and beg permission to greet his family. The meeting became very emotional between Marcius and his relations. Ursula could hardly believe her son was alive and thriving. It seemed to her as if some powerful deity had taken a hand in events. But it turned out the deity in question was Allaine. She didn't think she would ever be able to thank him enough, but he brushed it aside.

"It was purely for my own selfish reasons," he claimed. "I wanted Marcius to look after his master, so I didn't have to, that's all. He had a very unpleasant time with me, so I don't think you'll find him grateful," he added.

Having greeted Ursula politely, Chrys went to Lucy, and kissed her in welcome. Junior bounced up to her as well, and gave her a hug. He liked Lucy.

"Do you know I'm a prince, Lady Lucy?"

"That's splendid, darling," said Lucy. "I expect you like being a prince, don't you?"

"Yes," Junior replied. "It's much better than being a bastard. That's what I am in Rome."

Junior spoke with the clarity of a child. His words hung in the air. There was an embarrassed silence. Marcus Metius was looking at his sister in consternation. He knew she hated all things Gallic. Surely she couldn't have been as stupid as that!

Allaine scooped his nephew up into his arms. "Let's discuss your status after supper, my pet," he said, looking at Octavian's furious face. "I think we are all very hungry."

Titus and Claudia, having politely hung back, were now ushered forwards by Grandmother to greet their friends. Titus thought he'd better have a word with his son himself, about Junior's devastating utterance, and decided to solicit Allaine's assistance.

Allaine was in great demand after supper. Riona asked him where he thought everyone was going to sleep. Allaine said the new arrivals would have to share the Guest House with the Volusenus family. He was sure Claudia could settle everything satisfactorily. And he wanted Metius in bed soon, as well as Andreas and Sam. They were all feverish now, as he had expected. He would see to them in the morning.

Marcius sought an interview as well. He knelt at Allaine's feet, and thanked him tearfully, for his kindness to his mother, brother, and sister. Allaine had also purchased the family's servants, Marcius discovered, as they had been rendered confiscated goods.

"I don't know how I can ever repay you, Sir. Romans don't seem to have done any good to you, or your family."

"You forget, Marcius. My sister was welcomed into the Volusenus family." Allaine patted his shoulder. "And you gave me a great deal of help with Guéreth and Octavian. You managed to reconcile both of them to their fate. It would have been impossible to travel without you."

"Yes, Sir." Marcius wasn't too sure whether he had done something good or bad.

"Marcius, if they had been killed, it would have been a terrible waste of two good men. There aren't enough of them in the world."

Marcius smiled at this. "I think you're right, Sir."

Jay wished to speak to him alone.

"You realise these men could be dangerous, Allaine?"

"Are you worried?"

"Yes. Guéreth has vowed to wreak vengeance on you. Then there's Marcius, and now his brother and Metius, as well as all those servants you have so kindly purchased."

"But if they attack us, they would have to be prepared for them all to be killed as well. There's no way they could escape from the country at present."

"I think the Guest House should be guarded."

"I agree, but not for your reasons. Let's face it, Jay, the whole country is preparing for total war. I don't want some idiot thinking there are a few easy Roman targets to be killed, like they did in Cenabum."

At last Allaine could help Titus. By unspoken consent he had Junior on his lap. Octavian ruffled his son's hair.

"That was a strange word you used this afternoon, Octavian."

"A strange word, Daddy? What word?"

"The word bastard. I wondered where you'd heard it."

"It means something bad, doesn't it?"

"Sometimes. It all depends on the context," Octavian said, frowning. "So, who called you a bastard?"

Junior was a sensitive little boy. "I could whisper it to you, Uncle Allaine."

"That sounds like a very good idea."

"It was my Daddy's brothers, Sir. Gaius, and Claud." Junior's whispers were loud enough for them all to hear.

"Your other uncles?"

"No. They're not uncles, Sir. They are Daddy's brothers."

"Oh, I see."

"Did Lady Ursula ever use that word, Junior?" Titus asked.

"Oh, no, Sir. Lady Ursula just calls me a little obstacle." Junior was confident of this, but becoming frightened by all the attention.

"Now that is another strange word," Allaine put in. "Why are you an obstacle, my pet? Do you know?"

"Yes. I am a little obstacle. So's Little Allaine. And Mummy is an obstacle, as well. Mummy says Lady Ursula is very cross with us, so we must stay out of her way. It's something to do with Lady Lucy. But I like Lady Lucy. She doesn't get cross." At this point Junior dissolved into tears.

"Hush, now," Allaine spoke soothingly, and waited for the tears to cease. "Don't worry about it, my pet." He kissed his little nephew. "But these are grown up words that only grown ups know how to use. So don't go calling any of your cousins an obstacle, or a bastard. That's all. You're not in any trouble. Go and find Greta, now, and tell her it's time for bed."

"I'll fucking kill them," Octavian exploded in fury, as soon as Junior had left. "How dare they!"

Allaine called him to order immediately, and said, "Octavian, if the State doesn't recognise your marriage, there's no reason why your brothers should, either."

Octavian glared at him. "Very well, Master. You're right of course. But can't the swines keep their filthy remarks to themselves, instead of upsetting my children?" He was still angry. "And as for that prize bitch, Ursula,"

"Octavian, that's enough. She is a guest in my grandmother's house, and a great friend of your mother's, I believe. You are sounding as bad as your brothers, now."

"Master, she is always on at Mother, for me to divorce Chrys, and marry her precious daughter. That's why..."

"Yes, I know perfectly well why they are obstacles. But I expect good manners from my slaves. Be good, Octavian, or accept the consequences." He couldn't make it clearer than that.

Octavian came to him immediately, knelt, and apologised.

"And to your father," ordered Allaine. Octavian obeyed.

Titus was amazed at his son's subservience. He spread his hands wide. "You know what they're like, when they're all together. Unfortunately Junior was in the salon at the time. Claud said, 'I hear Octavian's gone native. Is this one of Octavian's bastards?'"

"And you let Claud away with that?"

"No." Titus looked at his son's still stormy expression. "I punched him in the face. Unfortunately he has a head like a rock, and I broke my hand."

"No, did you, Sir?"

"I did. I regretted it for days afterwards," Titus smiled. "And I told him if he ever said anything like it again, he could leave my house for good."

Octavian kissed his father's cheek. "Thanks for that, Dad," he said.

"No wonder Junior thought it was something bad. I expect that's why he said the word so publicly today. He's a child that likes everything to get sorted out properly. A bit like his father," Allaine ended with a smile.

Allaine ordered Octavian to go away, but asked Titus to remain, as he wanted some advice himself. Titus was flattered to think he could advise this extraordinarily self-contained young man, who managed to control Octavian's anger so well, a lot better than he could himself, he decided.

Allaine dismissed the servants. "Titus, I believe that in Roman law a father is fully entitled to kill his children, or his wife, if they displease him sufficiently."

"That is correct, Allaine."

"Are uncles entitled to kill their nieces for the same reason?"

Titus looked at him in consternation. "Can you give me an example of what might cause such displeasure?"

"Suppose his niece had been assaulted by her stepfather for some years, and was no longer a virgin?"

"That bastard Sperinus!" Titus was almost as incensed as his son had just been.

"I have only asked hypothetically." The recollection of Petronius using the words so frequently slid unbidden into Allaine's mind. How complicated life was. Why was he bothering about Lucy, anyway? "Perhaps you could give the matter some consideration, and then let me know your thoughts?"

Titus agreed to do so. Allaine decided to let the matter lie for the time being.

Titus wondered if Gaius would still be willing to marry Lucy. It seemed unlikely. He wasn't sure in his own mind if he would allow such a marriage for one of his sons. But then Octavian had never sought his permission to marry Chrys, and his marriage was an unqualified success. Mostly because Chrys wasn't just beautiful, she was a fascinating girl from a different culture. She possessed a questioning mind that never ceased to learn and ponder. If ever Octavian tired of her looks, he would still find plenty to entertain him. Octavian wasn't likely to do any such thing. He appeared to be even more in love, now Chrys reciprocated so heartily. Titus knew Claudia was anticipating more babies, maybe even girls, she'd dared whisper to him, in their cosily shared bed one night.

BOOK 4
REBELLION

BOOK 4: CHAPTER 1

Gergovia, (Clermont-Ferrand), Winter 53 BC

Gergovia, a heavily fortified Arvernian town a thousand feet up on the edge of the Auvergne mountains, was becoming political. People were everywhere busy on the streets, arguing, sometimes violently, the prospects for and against more war. Unknown young men appeared, bearing arms and equipment for battle. The city fathers were becoming nervous, and decided to call a Council meeting.

Vercingetorix climbed up to the defensive ledge on the inside of the town wall. He propped his elbows on the parapet, and leaned over, looking out across the plains to the far distance. It was a scene of tranquility. Men, oxen, and horses were going about the business of ploughing, ready for the winter sowings. He could hear their voices, carried on the air. Soon, he thought, these fields will be red with the blood of my countrymen. Was he justified in doing any of this? Inflame passions for a last chance to reclaim what they had already lost in part? Freedom, liberty, they were big words. Easy to make speeches. Much more difficult to fight Rome. What difference would it make to the peasants, after all? Would it be merely a change of servitude? Did Caesar ask these questions, before plunging the country into bloody rebellion? Of course not. What did Allaine say? 'He thinks he is Alexander reborn, his destiny is to conquer the world.'

A man climbed up onto the ledge beside him, and tapped his shoulder.

"The Council have had their meeting, and wish to speak with you, now, Sir. I have been sent to fetch you." With many armed men standing behind him, Vercingetorix noted. They were taking no chances with him.

Vercingetorix took hold of the messenger. "Look," he said, pointing with his arm into the distance. "What do you see?"

The man screwed up his eyes, peering at the tiny figures on the horizon. "It looks like people, Sir. Men, marching, I think. And some on horseback. With pack animals?"

Vercingetorix smiled in satisfaction. He was getting his answer, then.

He entered the Council chamber, and bowed to the assembly. The city fathers were seriously alarmed, he knew, feeling they were far too near Caesar's legions for comfort. These terrified old men had no desire to support a rebellion, especially one led by a young man, untried and untested. His uncle moved forwards to speak to him.

"Vercingetorix, we are all agreed, are we not, gentlemen?" He turned to receive the murmured assurances of his colleagues. They knew that pledges of support for this young firebrand were raining in from all over Gaul, together with excitable young men. "You are causing dissent, stirring up trouble. We do not approve of your actions. We seek only peace for our people. Our decision is unanimous. You are forbidden the city, and must leave at once, and take all your followers with you."

"Certainly, Uncle. Whatever the Council decrees, of course," Vercingetorix replied, ostensibly obedient, but with his soul seething internally. What cowards they were, these greybeards. All they could think of, was their comfort and security. They cared nothing for their own people, the peasants whose well-being they should have ensured. The little people, who would be bled by the Romans, till they starved. Forced to work their own pitiful scraps of land for the conquerors, then made to sell their children into slavery, when the taxes proved too big a burden. It was happening in the Province for all to see. Roman rule meant the rape of the country. In the end, it would affect the city fathers as well. But he kept his thoughts. Why waste breath on these sycophants, sucking up to Caesar. He would follow the example of the Carnutes, under their prince, Gutuater. He wouldn't let them down. "Fetch my horse, boy," he said quietly to his servant.

Vercingetorix rode out through the city gates, down the steep slopes, with his servants, his secretary, and his too few adherents. He pulled up his horse two miles from Gergovia, at the first village on the road of the plains. He walked into the nearest house, bowed, then smiled at the occupants.

"As you may know, my name is Vercingetorix," he told the astonished farmer. "You have the honour of becoming my headquarters." He ordered his bearer to plant his standard before the doorway, so all could see. "And in the meantime," he turned, with his charming smile, to his bewildered hostess, "perhaps you would care to offer me some of that excellent rabbit stew I can smell."

Vercingetorix didn't have long to wait for more answers to his plea. In a very few days so many men poured in from every tribe, all seeking to serve under him, and pledging allegiance, that he was able to march straight back to Gergovia, retake the town, and throw out all those who had opposed him, including his uncle. He found it very satisfying. The old men scurried down the hill road, with their hastily packed possessions, their wives, and frightened servants. Within twenty days Vercingetorix had the support of all the tribes of the West, the Parisii, Turoni, Aulerci, Lemovices, Andes, and Pictones. Prince Gutuater joined him with many of his fellow Carnutes. General Drappes, leader of the Senones, turned up with his large infantry forces.

Lucterius the Cadurcan arrived with a contingent of cavalry. He called for a council meeting of all the young chiefs present. He was a good orator, but really, he thought as he looked around, I don't need a good speech to inflame these men. They are already on fire.

"Gentlemen, we have come in answer to a summons, a summons issued by our friend and ally, Vercingetorix the Arvernian. A call to forget differences, a call to unite. Believe me, gentlemen, we must unite if we are to succeed in our purpose. There must be no half measures. But also a call to arms, to repel the Roman invaders, who are raping our country, and breaking our laws. Caesar has dared to have Prince Acco flogged to death." There was a howl of anguish from the Carnutes at this point in his speech. "Caesar thinks to depose our properly elected magistrates, and impose his own petty kings, in their place." He looked all around at the sea of eager faces. He held his arms wide. "From now on I will call you all my brothers, for brothers we must be in this purpose." He drew his sword and raised it in the air. "Together we will fight, each of us to our last breath, if necessary, to defeat Caesar, the stealer of our lands, our laws, our freedom." At this point he paused, so everyone could cheer, and clash their weapons together. "To do this we need a leader, a man of skill and strength." He turned to face Vercingetorix. "I choose Vercingetorix as my king, as my commander-in-chief, as the man who will free Gaul." He hurled his sword to the ground in front of his newly appointed king, where it quivered, glinting in the sun. Then he walked forwards and knelt at the feet of Vercingetorix. The cheers of the crowd were deafening.

One by one the bearers from each tribe brought their standards to the altar, and stacked them together, in a most sacred binding promise of loyalty. After the ceremony of allegiance, Vercingetorix conferred with the chiefs.

"Look at this list. I've asked for each tribe to provide us with specific numbers of infantry and cavalry. Do you agree with these estimates?"

"You are asking a lot from the Helvetii and the Nervii. They lost enormous numbers fighting Caesar, and the Helvetii still have to keep their borders secure from the Germans." Lucterius was worried. No point in demanding impossibilities.

"Very well, I'll cut it to eight thousand only from the Helvetii. Prince Jayven is in charge of their cavalry, and has been training them all summer. So they should be pretty efficient. But the Nervii are fantastic fighters. I am loth to do without a single man."

"Isn't Prince Jayven an Aeduan?" asked one of the other

chiefs.

"Yes, he's an Aeduan, the only son of Diviciacus. Up until now he has obeyed his father, and fought with the Romans. But he is twenty-six years old, and has decided to think for himself. He chooses freedom, and wishes to fight with us. But he has seen the way Caesar uses his cavalry for the last five years. He is proving to be an efficient and able cavalry commander. I've seen his cavalry corps in training. The Helvetians have no problem taking his orders. He is sworn to serve his kinsman, Allaine of the Helvetii, the healer."

"How are you going to keep us all together? There have already been one or two sporadic fights break out between different factions."

"I'm afraid there will just have to be discipline, iron discipline. Severe punishment for any infringement of my orders, or the orders of any of my generals. And I mean severe. Death at the stake for disobeying an order, death for cowardice, death by torture for the last man to appear here to fight. I agree with you. We are a disparate lot. This is a new venture for us. But we must try to be like the Romans. We need to break the army into manageable units, with a proper structure, that can be the same whichever tribe a soldier is in. We cannot keep stopping and worrying about which tribe a man belongs to. This army must be the Gallic army, and that's all."

"What about weapons?"

"I suggest each tribe be given a target of weapons to be produced by a given time, and they should be standardised as far as possible, shields, lances, spears, and swords. But also we need archers, scorpios, catapults, and the ability to make siege engines, with breast works, woven screens to protect the men whilst they are working. We must learn from our foes to dig trenches, and fortify camps, to build siege towers, if necessary. Look how close Ambiorix came to success. We have the means, if only we are resolute in the execution."

"What do you want to do first?"

"We will need money, coinage. We will ask all for a contribution, then melt it down here in Gergovia, and mint our own coins. The first military action will be to march to the Bituriges tribe. I have heard they are thinking of joining us, as are also a number of Aeduans, despite them having been allied to Rome for so long. I suggest you, Lucterius, try out the defences of the Province. It will be a good way to test the mettle of our troops. Drappes, I would like to put you in charge of disrupting any Roman reinforcements that get through from Italy. The rest of us have all winter to prepare arms and armour, to train the men and get them battle ready. Then, when Caesar returns from Italy, we will be fully prepared to repulse him and his army."

By the end of the evening, anyone who had doubted the ability of Vercingetorix was completely won over by his enthusiasm and competence. He knew exactly what needed doing, and made sure it was done at once.

Caesar heard the news of the uprising of the Carnutes under Prince Gutuater, while still in Rome. It was just as he had expected, indeed, just as he had hoped, had manoeuvred into being by his very public and bloody execution of Prince Acco. A rebellion he could put down with his usual ruthlessness. But the rebellion had occurred much earlier than he had expected, in the middle of winter, not a great time for campaigning. And it was rather a pity he'd had to sacrifice Gaius Fufius Cita, and Marcus Metius, two able men. Why didn't they have contingency plans at the ready? Very short-sighted. The rest of the Roman traders were no great loss. But, oh, what a glorious excuse for war. The Senate could hardly argue now.

Caesar decided he had no alternative, but to hurry back to Gaul. He couldn't allow Vercingetorix the luxury of time to train his army. First he had to repel Lucterius and his forces, which he did easily enough, by reinforcing the defences of the Province, but then he was faced with the Cevennes mountains, passes blocked by walls of snow.

Centurion Pullo lashed at the soldiers and slaves indiscriminately.

"Get on with it, you lot, and stop moaning. This pass is going to be cleared, because Caesar has ordered it." But he was worried. There was no knowing from one day to another, how high the snow drifts would be in the next section of road, if it could be called in any way a road. There was no attempt at a decent surface anywhere, as far as he could see. What wasn't covered with snow and ice, was covered with deep frozen ruts of mud, with large craters under a light snow covering, that his men and mules fell into. They were digging deep, six feet deep in some places. Pullo just knew a path had to be cleared through these viciously icy, cold snow mountains, that blackened men's faces, fingers, and feet with frostbite. These barricades would have to be tackled and overcome, whatever the cost in limbs.

"Sir, I think another one has broken something." Yet another legionary, clutching a wrist this time. There were too many casualties, breaking a wrist, or an arm, or a leg. They slipped around on the ice in their stupid boots, unable to get a purchase. Hands and feet froze in the cold, and ceased to work, spades slipped from their grasp, boots from underfoot. Pullo sent for the Helvetian slaves.

"Alright, you lot. How would you cope with this?"

They laughed at him. What idiots the Romans were. "Put nails through the boots, so you get a purchase on the ice. Make mittens and boots from sheepskin, and stuff the boots with straw for more warmth. Don't let anyone work for too long when the temperature drops. Rotate the diggers, and warm them up between sessions. Drive oxen ahead. If they can, they will trample a path through the snow for you."

"Make snow shoes," suggested another.

"What are snow shoes?" asked Pullo.

The slave walked off, and returned with the wide, flat-meshed shoes that gripped the snow.

"These," he said.

Pullo went off to see the supplies officer. It was all very well, but what if it snowed again? They could so easily become completely stuck, up here in the high passes. Had Caesar thought of that?

In the end, after much struggling and cursing, they managed to get through, with the baggage intact. Caesar's luck held, further snowfalls were light, and few and far between. They were over the Alps, and into Gaul. They had come to the lower ground of the Arverni country, of Vercingetorix's country.

The fox was back in the hen house now, with a vengeance. And the hen house was full of plump chickens, ready to be torn to pieces.

First, though, Caesar would need to gather his legions, scattered in their winter quarters, protect his supply routes, and find some cavalry reinforcements. He could tell from the mood of the Aeduans, that his treatment of Prince Acco had affected even these, his staunchest allies up till now. He thought they might even make an attempt on his life. He left young Brutus in charge while he hared off to Vienna, picked up his cavalry, and the German reinforcements, and then hastened back to summon all his legions together. He rode day and night without stopping, through hostile Aeduan territory, until he reached the land of the Lingones, and two of his legions. He sent for the two on the borders of the Treveri, and the six from the Senones territory. Now he was back in Gaul, with his ten legions. He felt the old familiar sense of exaltation. Let battle commence!

The first town to be plucked was Vellaunodunum, encircled in two days, and capitulated in three. The Gauls were made to surrender all their arms, all their horses, and hand over six hundred hostages. The second town was Cenabum.

BOOK 4: CHAPTER 2

Helvetia (Switzerland), Winter 53 BC

The children did everything conceivable with snow. Building snow queens, snow kings, ice palaces, spending the day sledging or fighting with snowballs, skating on the lake, playing strange games with stones skidding across the ice. In mid December there was an enormous festival with bonfires, roasted oxen, cheerful men and laughing women, children gleefully dancing about, skidding, sliding, happy that their mothers and fathers were happy. But when the passes opened intermittently, envoys arrived, and the Romans' charming hosts would disappear. Octavian caught the tail end of a conversation between Allaine and Coevorten, when he came in answer to a summons.

"He wants eight thousand from us."

"But we lost so many at the beginning."

"He wants you, too."

"But he knows I'm not a fighter."

"No, for your surgical skills. Prince Jayven will lead the cavalry."

They broke off when Allaine spotted Octavian.

At first the Volusenus family were delighted to have their good friends share their temporary exile. With them all living together relationships changed again, gradually at first, but then more dramatically. Octavian and Valerius accompanied their master every day to his hospital building. Allaine was correct. Their work mostly involved injuries from accidents, rather than war, although the occasional fights amongst the peasants sometimes ended in blows from weapons. They also dealt with acute and chronic disease. Very occasionally they were called in to births going disastrously wrong, usually far too late for the situation to be in any way retrievable. Allaine made sure Octavian knew how to reach a diagnosis, by a careful history of the illness, and a thorough examination. Octavian became keen on learning as much as he could. He found it all very interesting. He was allowed to do more and more of the suturing, and could reduce simple fractures. His knowledge of anatomy improved every day. Now Allaine valued his opinion. They discussed difficult cases together, before deciding on a course of treatment.

Noemon was told to take Val for lessons as well as the children. Valerius could scarcely read. After his lesson, he would join his master and Octavian at the hospital. He was adept at bandaging by now, good at threading needles and passing the instruments required for surgery, or heating the cautery irons to the correct temperature. He became very useful, but Allaine wished his reading would improve, so he could study like Octavian. Val found it a great struggle, but persevered. Anything to please his master.

Allaine didn't wish his Roman slaves to forget completely their other skills. Having given the problem a lot of thought, he sent for Hugo.

"Hugo, I wish you to teach Darius how to fight. I understand from Octavian that you are excellent at drilling men, and having seen your prowess on the hunting field, I feel sure you could teach him sword play, as well as throwing a javelin. Can you do this for me?"

"Yes, Master," Hugo replied, eager to do anything. He didn't feel very useful compared to Octavian, his master's obvious favourite. Some memories were seeping back slowly into his brain. He badly needed some self respect to counteract them. "Don't you think the others could participate as well, Sir? It would give them some physical exercise. They don't get much at present, working with the sick as they do."

This was the most sensible suggestion Allaine had ever heard Hugo make. Smilingly he thanked him for his advice, and agreed.

"You are quite right, Hugo. After all, I wish them to return to the army, once the passes are clear."

"And me, Sir? Will I be going as well?"

"Why not, Hugo? Do you think you are ready to resume your duties?"

Hugo looked steadily at him. "You don't think so, do you, Sir?"

"Not quite. But I think you will be soon. You will be ready by the Spring."

"Sir, it makes no sense, what you are saying. If you return us to the Roman army, we will be fighting you, and your fellow countrymen, won't we?"

"You're right, of course. I am hamstrung by my own decisions. I had to make so many so quickly. I mistakenly assumed Ambiorix would win, and Caesar would retreat. But it was not to be. I've sworn to protect you all, and there is no way I can do that here, for much longer. Every day grows more dangerous. I have to give you back."

Noemon also taught Tzïnne still, so Lucy asked if she too could carry on studying. She also wanted to learn the language, and become fluent like her big brother. Lucy was maturing. It took little time for her to become aware that Octavian would never, ever, divorce Chrys, and really, she couldn't find it in her heart to blame him. She was half in love with Chrys herself. Would she ever marry, she asked herself. Would any man ever be persuaded? As she had no idea of the answer, she sought out Allaine, and asked him what he thought.

So one night, after the children had gone to bed, and when Allaine had plied his guests with wine, he steered the conversation round to moral sexual behaviour, which provoked a lively discussion. It was easy to see the men held radically different views from the women.

"You are so absolute," Allaine declared, when Metius claimed that for his part, he would only marry a virgin. "I'm sure you are not a virgin. Why insist on a woman being pure, when you are not?"

"And what is wrong with marrying a divorced woman?"

Ursula asked indignantly. "Or a widow, for that matter?"

"Presumably because she has had intercourse with another man. It appears to be of vital importance in all cultures," Allaine suggested. "For instance, what if a man, on his wedding night, found that his supposed virginal bride wasn't as virginal as he had been led to believe. What would he do? What would any of you do?"

"It wouldn't bother me, Sir," Valerius responded, looking wistfully at his master.

Allaine laughed. "I'm sure we'll manage something, Val," he said.

Val looked immensely pleased at this. The others were baffled.

"I've no idea," said Octavian.

"Divorce her straight away," Metius declared.

"I'd kill the bitch," Hugo proclaimed, to gasps from the girls.

"Hugo, dear!" Claudia exclaimed.

"Hugo, perhaps you could confine such descriptions to the stables. I will not have them in my house, at my table," Allaine said. But it was his own fault, after all. He could hardly punish Hugo for confirming his suspicions so swiftly.

"Oh, I'm sorry, Master. I mean, I think it would be only proper to dispose of such a woman. After all, if she was deceiving me about something so radical, how could she be trusted about anything else?"

"It is the lie, then, that distresses you, Hugo. If she had confessed before marriage, would that be enough?"

"Jupiter, no! I'm with Metius, a virgin or nothing. Otherwise how would one know if a subsequent child was yours or this other chap's?"

"I suppose that is a valid point. What happens with divorced women, Ursula, if they remarry, and are then found to be pregnant?" Allaine enquired. "There is no provision for divorce in Gaul, though a widow or widower may remarry without controversy." His main query had already been answered loud and clear. He didn't care where the conversation ended.

Marcus Metius and Titus Volusenus disagreed about the relevant laws, and Allaine allowed the conversation to drift.

"I'm stuck with you, then," Octavian whispered to Chrys.

Chrys giggled. "No, it's the other way round, I'm stuck with you." He looked so adorable. Such a good, kind, big-hearted man. She loved him so much.

"There's no hope for us, then," Octavian said, smiling. He gazed in wonder at his beautiful wife. What had he done to deserve her? How had she ever managed to forgive him for that terrible initial encounter? He couldn't begin to imagine.

"Are you hanging out for a virgin, Zinny?" Jay asked plaintively. The men found the thought hilarious. Even Allaine was grinning. Tzïnne blushed furiously as the laughter eddied around her. She wasn't used to this sort of conversation.

Grandmother put a stop to it. "That is quite enough," she proclaimed, frowning at Jay. "I do not consider this a suitable topic for the young unmarried people present."

At the end of the meal Hugo asked his master if he had to sleep in the stables again, that being his usual punishment for swearing inappropriately.

"No, Hugo. Tonight it is so cold you would be frozen to a block of ice by the morning. Just be a little more careful in future."

Hugo was relieved. He'd avoided the stables for months, now, and had no desire to renew his acquaintance with the hard cold lumpy ground.

Allaine saw Octavian staring at him, apparently suspicious. He wasn't altogether surprised when Octavian tackled him the next day.

"Were you thinking of any particular situation last night, Sir, when you made us all drunk?"

"I didn't make you drunk, did I?"

"You aren't going to tell me, then?"

"Why not? After all, you are concerned to some extent. Weren't you betrothed to Lucy, before you married Chrys? And then Lucy was betrothed to Hugo, before your brother became interested in her. Metius has asked me to marry them. I think he realises Ursula is beginning to annoy me, as well as you and Chrys, and he is worried I might take it into my head to do something barbaric, shall we say?"

"I feel pretty barbaric about Lady Ursula, myself."

"Yes, I sympathise. Unfortunately, once Marcius was out of the house, Lucy was assaulted regularly by her stepfather."

"Oh, for the Gods' sake!" Octavian was shocked.

"Poor little thing," Allaine continued, "she is no Lucretia. But if you look at her wrists you will see some scars where she made tentative cuts, but lacked the courage to carry it through to suicide. I don't blame her for that, at all. She was only twelve at the start. He carried on for some years, sadly. He threatened to kill her each time, telling her she had brought dishonour to the family. He said it was all her fault for ensnaring him, that she was a witch, casting a spell on him. What a disgusting man he must have been."

"Vile!" Octavian agreed.

"I am quite sure Lucy was in no way to blame. And I do not wish my little Lucy to be killed. I like her. Do I tell Metius the reason why I won't marry them?"

"I suppose you would have to, otherwise he will continue in his efforts to marry her off. Poor Lucy, she has been unfortunate in her choice of husbands."

Allaine looked surprised. "It seems to me she has had no choice at all."

Lucy was getting sick of her mother's machinations. In the Guest House Ursula spent much time extolling the virtues of her daughter, and the vices of that red haired barbarian witch. Titus was getting increasingly fed up with the woman. Her attitude was making Chrys quite frosty. Lucy decided it was time to face up to reality. When she discovered Andreas and her mother conferring in whispers, she thought they were hatching some plot involving her and Octavian.

"Mother, I'm glad to have this chance to talk to you both," said Lucy bravely. But she didn't feel very brave inside. "I know you would like me to marry Octavian. But he will never divorce Chrys, and indeed, why should he? She is a wonderful wife, and mother, and she loves him with all her heart."

Ursula started immediately to point out the many advantages to be had in never giving up hope.

"Mother, surely you know now that I have no hope. How can I think of marrying anyone? I would have to tell them about my stepfather, and you saw Hugo's reaction last night."

Her mother stared at her. "Oh, Lucy," she said, and started to cry. Lucy could see there was no need for explanations for her mother. Andreas was looking mystified. Lucy lost her nerve. She turned and fled from the room, lay on her mattress, and sobbed and sobbed. Andreas came to comfort her, and learnt at last the cause of his sister's misery. Andreas found he wasn't that surprised. He must have felt the undercurrents of tension in the house, without being aware there was more than one cause. But all could be traced back to his mad stepfather.

"I wasn't plotting, Lucy. I was trying to tell Mother to behave a bit better," he explained. He had found it increasingly difficult to side with Ursula, aware she was antagonising everyone.

Lucy became very sad over the next few days. She thought wistfully about Gaius. She knew he loved her, he had told her so clearly. Would he still love her once he knew her secret? Judging by Hugo's reaction, it seemed unlikely.

Allaine began to notice Hugo staring at him frequently, lost in thought. He decided to watch Hugo training the others. As soon as Hugo noticed him, he threw a spear over to him. Allaine caught it.

"What's this for, Hugo?" Allaine asked.

"Sir, you need to train, just like us."

"No, Hugo. I don't fight."

"I know that, Sir. But the war may come to you, whether you fight or not. We would like you to be prepared, as you are preparing us. So, throw the javelin."

"You had better remove everyone in the vicinity for at least half a mile," Allaine replied, laughing.

"I saw you hunting. You're not that bad. Go on, Sir. Throw the spear."

Allaine took off his cloak and outer tunic, rolled up his sleeves, and picked up the spear.

"I had no idea you were such a bully, Hugo. Where is the target?"

Hugo laughed, and pointed it out. Allaine hurled the spear, and missed the target, but not by much.

"Your action is excellent," said Hugo. "Darius, now try to copy Prince Allaine. Remember you start out virtually facing the opposite direction, and use your whole body. Uncoil yourself with a whipping movement from the hips, then use shoulder and arm muscles for the thrust."

They watched as Darius obeyed. "Good, Darius. You're getting better all the time. All you need is practise, like you, Sir," Hugo said to Allaine. "I heard you were a good swordsman, as well."

"It was such a long time ago."

"If you think this is good for us, it must also be good for you. It is getting lighter in the mornings. Won't you spend an hour with us, before your hospital work?"

"Oh, very well, Hugo. If I must," Allaine agreed. It did seem a sensible idea. Fortunately his wife, sisters, and grandmother, together with Epheus, his steward, ran his household to his complete satisfaction, only occasionally seeking his advice or decision. And when he made time to inspect his vast estates, he discovered the excellence of his bailiff. Although he had many judicial and priestly duties to attend to, a large amount of his time was spent with the sick and injured. He could probably spare an hour most days.

Allaine thought Hugo was beginning to turn back into an army officer, and wasn't altogether surprised when Hugo begged him for an interview.

"Sir, Octavian said you took my memories away, because they were too painful, and I wasn't coping with them. Is that right?"

"That is correct, Hugo. You were becoming so withdrawn, you were no longer functioning, even on a primitive level."

"Do you think I'm well enough to have them back? I feel well, Sir, and strong. I feel I can manage."

"Suppose I told you what happened to you. Then you could decide."

"I'll go with that, Sir."

"Very well. After supper."

Allaine brought Octavian as well. Together they told Hugo about the appalling condition he was in, when Octavian found him a prisoner, and what had happened subsequently, sparing no details. It didn't appear to bother him, not even the worms. Allaine decided the time had come for Hugo to face up to reality.

"Very well. I will count to three, Hugo, and then all your memories will return."

The instant he finished counting Hugo cried out loudly, "No, no, no!" He went white with shock, then gradually his face flushed. He buried his head in his hands and groaned aloud.

Octavian was alarmed. "What's happening to him, Sir?"

"We will find out in a moment. Just give him some time to sort himself out."

They waited. Hugo gradually became aware of his surroundings. He lowered his hands. His expression was tragic.

"You will feel off balance to start with, Hugo, so stay still now," Allaine advised him.

"You wouldn't let me kill myself," Hugo said, looking at

his master accusingly. He appeared grief stricken, in terrible distress.

"Why should I?" Allaine flared up immediately. "I wasn't given any such choice."

Hugo attempted to explain as guilt overwhelmed him. "Sir, Sir, I was responsible for their deaths. Six thousand of my men. You must allow me to kill myself."

"I will not." Allaine was angry. "Your punishment is to live, Hugo. To atone for the wrongs you have committed against me, my family, and my country. In my judgement you do not deserve a quick death."

Hugo gave in. He got up slowly, walked over to Allaine, and knelt before him. "Please, please let me die, Master," he begged. "I can't bear this disgrace. I tried before, truly I did. But it's no use. The thoughts never leave me, that it was all my fault."

Allaine became calmer. "No, Hugo. You have sworn to serve me. Do you remember?" Allaine grasped his hands. "What use are you to me, if you are dead? No use, Hugo. I will not release you. You will remain alive."

Hugo's face crumpled. He pulled his hands free, covered his face and began to sob, deep tearing sobs, completely distraught.

"Oh, fuck!" said Octavian. He sank to his knees in front of his friend. "Don't, Hugo, don't," he said in anguish. He held the sobbing man in his arms until gradually the emotional storm ceased. Once Hugo was weeping almost silently, Octavian got to his feet, and fetched a bowl and cloth from the intrigued attendant, who couldn't understand a word of what was going on. Gently Octavian bathed Hugo's face and hands, speaking soothingly to him as if he were Junior. Allaine waited patiently until Hugo was quietened.

"Come here, Hugo," Allaine ordered, and pulled him up to sit beside him. He put his arm round the shoulders of the overwrought man. "At least he is beginning to talk about it now," Allaine said to Octavian. "That's good." He could see Octavian was becoming ever more upset. Allaine spoke gently. "Hugo, tell me. Why do you take that responsibility onto yourself?"

"I sided with Sabinus. Octavian said I was mad to."

"Hugo, you were given enough corn for a few days only. You could eat the horses, but that wouldn't last very long amongst so many. It wasn't a mad choice you made. Ambiorix is the man responsible for the deaths, not you. Cicero's camp so nearly succumbed, but they held out partly because they had much more in the way of supplies. It wasn't a stupid decision, whatever Octavian says."

Hugo looked unconvinced.

"I heard the arguments raged all night. Either course was fraught. I will not release you from your promise, Hugo. The only man who should commit suicide is Sabinus, and he is already dead. That is my last word on the subject."

It wasn't, of course. It took many more words from both Octavian and Allaine before Hugo could be persuaded. At the end of the evening Allaine was satisfied that his slave was beginning to blame himself less. It would have to do for now.

Riona suggested to her husband that Val be allowed to marry Allaine's slave girl, as he now had little use for her. She was a sweet shy girl, with a pleasant nature, who adored Allaine, and appeared to be at the same stage of pregnancy as Riona herself. Val was overjoyed when he heard of his good fortune, and the girl seemed quite pleased. Allaine married the pair of them at the altar, and promised to sponsor the infant when it arrived.

Volusenus asked if he might come and see Allaine and Octavian at work in the hospital. Unlike the Roman temple of Healing, no Gods were held to be resident, although he knew prayers were offered up. He was astonished to find how skilled his son had become. To start with, Octavian was suturing a complicated injury sustained by a ploughman, when his horse pulled the plough on top of him. Then he lectured to the students about subsequent wound care.

Allaine was examining a shepherd, brought in by his distraught sons. The shepherd had been marooned on the mountain when a snowstorm broke. He had severe frostbite of hands, feet, and nose. Allaine explained he could amputate all four limbs, but the man preferred to be killed, as otherwise he would die slowly in agony. Titus watched amazed, while Allaine held the man in his arms, recited the prayer for the dead, and as soon as the man made the response, slipped a dagger under his ribs, straight into the heart. Gently Allaine lowered the corpse to the bed, and closed the unseeing eyes. Then he called to the weeping relatives, telling them they could now take the body for cremation.

"What would happen in Rome?" Allaine asked Titus. He could see the process had disturbed him.

Titus shook his head. "We don't get frostbite in Rome."

"But what happens if someone has a painful incurable illness?"

"I believe a surgeon will open their veins, and they will bleed to death."

"Rather slow, and not very pleasant, I would have thought," commented Allaine.

"I expect they drink a lot of wine first."

But then Volusenus watched as Allaine performed an amputation on a man whose arm had been crushed in a rock fall. Allaine kept up a running commentary for Titus, and for the group of young students, priests like himself, Allaine explained, who wished to become healers. Allaine and Octavian worked swiftly, Octavian anticipating every move of his master's, and supplying him wordlessly with the correct instruments. It was an awe inspiring performance. Despite the snow people trekked from miles around to see Allaine. The queue was never ending. He had already trained up several medical orderlies; some were competent nurses, some could do basic wound dressings. Servilius kept the records beautifully. But as Titus walked around the hospital, he soon realised Octavian was the principal help.

Allaine was going to miss him in the Spring. He was such a help, Titus began to worry that Allaine wouldn't let him go after all.

They stood together as Octavian started on the final stitches of a knife wound he was suturing.

"You seem to have trained my son very well."

"Yes," Allaine sighed. "It's going to be hard without him. He is so good."

Octavian glanced up at this. Praise from Allaine was rare indeed.

"Unfortunately it doesn't much help his career in the Army. So I'm glad he has renewed his weapons training with Hugo, and the others. I can't have him killed the first time he goes into battle."

A few days later Allaine noticed his slave couldn't stop coughing at breakfast, and looked decidedly the worse for wear.

"Go back to bed, Octavian," said his master.

"Oh, thank the Gods," said Octavian, still coughing.

"No, thank me!" said Allaine. "Idiot."

Octavian laughed, but that made him go off into another paroxysm of coughing. He bowed, and went back to his bed, still coughing, and rubbing the front of his chest. Allaine rode back at midday to see how he was getting on. He brought some medicine with him.

"Why does your medicine always taste so foul?" Octavian asked.

Allaine was amused. "I would put honey in it if you were a child, but you are not."

"What is it, Sir?"

"An infusion of willow bark. It's a good antipyretic."

"How are you managing without me?"

"Not easily. I have to do all the difficult cases myself, at the moment. But the pupils are coming on. They can do a lot of stitching now. They will have to substitute for you when you leave. Unfortunately, so far no one has your flair."

"Why can't I stay, then?"

"Don't start, Octavian."

Allaine sat on the bed, and gazed at his slave in dismay. "Come on, Octavian. Surely it is better to be a free man, than a slave? Aren't you fed up with me telling you what to do all the time?"

"Don't be stupid." It took Octavian moments to realise he had been appallingly rude. He flushed. "Sorry, Master."

Allaine laughed at him. "I can't punish you any more, can I?" he said. "Chrys would never speak to me again." But then he became serious. "What is it, Octavian? What's bothering you so much?"

"Do you remember, Sir, when you first taught me self examination? You asked if I had joined the army to kill people."

"I was merely trying to shock you into thinking."

"Yes, I know. I don't think I do like killing people, actually. And especially not Gauls."

"Whining fucking Gauls," said Allaine, half to himself.

"Precisely. How do you think I felt when Sabinus said that? My children are half Gallic, my wife is wholly Gallic, and, frankly, I am quite proud of being an Aeduan as well as a Roman." Octavian found his eyes were welling up with tears, as usual. "How can I make you understand?" He banged his fist on the bed in frustration.

Allaine was worried. It had not occurred to him Octavian would be so sensitive. And he thought he knew the man.

"You said you couldn't be a healer and fight as well. I'm not sure I can, any more."

Allaine nodded in sympathy. "I know, I know. But look, if someone attacks me, I will have no hesitation in fighting back. You will be just the same."

Octavian looked into the troubled grey eyes of his master. How could he persuade him?

"Caesar ordered the death of my wards, and your sister Eloise. The death of Dumnorix, our brother-in-law. How can you make me go back to him?"

"Because I have to. Your father wishes you to finish your stint in the army, and then take up a civilian role as quaestor. And I agree, Octavian. I have told you before not to opt out. I wish you to take your proper place in the governance of your country. It is important, vital, that the good men are in charge, not the Caesars of this world."

"But I want to heal, like you. I know I can never be as good."

"Of course you can be as good. You must go on learning. But it can no longer be with me, Octavian. I'm sorry, I'm sorry. But you must go back. I will miss you more than you will ever know, but I cannot and will not keep you."

"But you'll keep Servilius?"

"You cannot compare yourself to Servilius. What does he have to go back to? He wasn't well treated. He doesn't seem to relish the thought of a return to Roman slavery. Octavian, you will know soon enough. The whole of my country is in a ferment, arming, training, ready for total war. They wish to deal with Caesar once and for all. I must try to get you and your family away as soon as possible. Every day it is becoming more dangerous for you. As soon as the wagons can get through I hope to be able to get you safely to Geneva, and then hand you over to Roman protection."

"But I'll be fighting against you."

Octavian went off into another bout of coughing, he was becoming distraught. Allaine patted him vigorously on the back.

"I have sought my commander's permission to release you all, and he has given it."

"You mean Vercingetorix?"

"That's right." Vercingetorix didn't think a couple of officers and a couple of legionaries were going to make any difference to the final outcome of the war.

"You are my master, my teacher, and my brother," said Octavian in despair. "I thought you were my friend as well."

Allaine took his slave's hands in his own.

"We are just gaming pieces, Octavian. Moved around the board by the Gods for their sport. They give us hope, only to dash it, and love, only to destroy it. For a while we were able to be together as captured pieces. But now the Gods are setting out the board again. And you are on the white squares, whilst I am on the black."

He gripped Octavian's hands tighter.

"But this I swear to you. However we are moved, and whatever happens to us, you will always be my brother, and I will always be your friend."

"Then what is the point of self examination, if I can't do anything about it?" Octavian was still angry and resentful.

"It can't be bad to know yourself, Octavian, wherever you are or whatever situation you find yourself in. Stop worrying about it now. Concentrate on getting better." Allaine ended on a lighter note. "And kindly don't get pleurisy. I don't want any more sleepless nights."

BOOK 4: CHAPTER 3

Cenabum (Orleans), Carnute Territory, Winter 53 BC

When the news first reached Gaius of the assault on Cenabum by the Carnutes, and the slaughter of the Roman traders, he thought he would go mad with grief. Lucy, his sweet little Lucy. His girl callously killed, before he had even kissed her. Why was Metius in Cenabum, he raged at his slaves. Why couldn't he have stayed safely in Bibracte? Why did he risk his family's life? Gaius knew the answer. Money. It was always money with these men. Money, profit, gold, all they ever thought about. How to get and stay rich. Lucy was sacrificed to avarice. Gaius now knew what heartbreak meant. His heart was broken. It hurt, it hurt so much! He was shocked by the intensity of his feelings. He wanted to lie on the ground, and howl his grief to the world. But he couldn't. He couldn't tell anyone how deeply damaged he was. Roman officers were expected to behave with decorum, not go about snivelling at misfortune. He hugged his grief to his heart. He could feel it gnawing away at him.

When Caesar announced that Cenabum was to be the next targeted town, on his way back south to confront Vercingetorix, Gaius found a strange thrill seeping into his bones, into the very marrow of his soul. He swore to himself he would make the citizens pay for their temerity in striking such a savage blow against him and his family. This war was now deeply personal. He had so many to avenge.

The town was rapidly encircled by the Roman troops. The legionaries started their usual preparations for a siege. The townspeople were quite unprepared, having thought that the siege of Vellaunodunum would take weeks to resolve. Their only escape lay in the bridge from under the town walls, crossing the Loire. Caesar was like a cat, waiting at a mouse hole. To his soldiers' disgust he kept two legions permanently under arms, day and night, despite the difficulty they had in getting any sleep. As soon as Caesar discovered that the citizens were trying to slip out silently in the middle of the night, his troops seized the bridge, fired the gates, captured the town, and just about every inhabitant. The plunder exceeded all expectations.

Gaius inspected the prisoners. Some of them were families grouped together, clinging to each other in terror. All were to be sold. He found what he was seeking, a good-looking young man with a pretty, very pregnant wife, and two small boys. He ordered the man to be brought over to him. The prisoner looked at the grim face of the Tribune, at the military whip in his hands, and knew it was going to be bad. His little boy realised it too, and clung desperately to his father's legs, yelling "No, no, no," at the top of his voice.

"No, Fáelán, stay with your mother," said the man, trying to detach his son. Gaius understood, picked the boy up, and carried him over to the pretty woman, whose face was white and strained with fear. "Stay there," he ordered. But as he turned to deal with the man, Fáelán ran straight back. The boy hung onto his arm, clinging to his sleeve, as Gaius tried to shake him off. The centurion accompanying Gaius prised the child away, and struck him heavily across the face. The mother screamed. The man ran to his little son, and picked him up once more, trying to wipe away the blood running down the child's face with his hands. He was talking to him rapidly, trying to persuade the boy that it was nothing, no problem, Fáelán was just to stay with his mother. The sobbing boy clung to his frantic mother, his blood soiling her dress. The last sight for her husband, as he was led away to his doom.

"This is for Lucy," said Gaius as he wielded the whip. A livid mark showed up on the prisoner's skin. "And Octavian, and Guéreth," he continued, "and Mum, and Dad...." His voice broke with emotion. He had to stop for a moment, get himself together again. He had heard nothing from his parents, since they

557

disappeared into Switzerland. He could see tiny rivulets of blood hanging in little curtains from the whip marks across the man's back, coalescing, trickling slowly down towards the ground, while the prisoner cried with the pain of it. Blood! Pain! That was better, what he needed. Gaius got a grip on himself. He carried on until the prisoner's screams ceased, and his naked bloodied body slumped unconscious against the whipping post.

"Keep him alive," ordered Gaius. "I haven't finished with him."

"And his family?" asked the centurion.

"Yes, them as well. I'll need them, too."

Avericum (Bourges), principal town of the Bituriges, 60 miles South East of Cenabum, (Orleans)

By the time the important town fort of Noviodunum in the Bituriges region had surrendered in another remarkably short space of time, Vercingetorix knew his plans would have to change.

The people of Avaricum heard the new orders. Vercingetorix explained that the one sure way to defeat the Romans, was to starve them. All towns and villages in the path of Caesar's army were to be destroyed. The peoples' possessions and food supplies were to be hidden from the Roman enemy, deep in the forests, as the Gauls instituted a scorched earth policy.

"I know how terrible this is for you all," Vercingetorix said. "But we must make this sacrifice, so that we prevent our wives and children being carried off as slaves, and ourselves killed. That is what will happen if the Romans conquer us."

Twenty towns were fired in a single day to deprive Caesar and his troops of his precious corn. As it was the middle of winter, there was no grass to be cut, no grain in the fields. His foraging parties needed stores from barns. Vercingetorix sent out his cavalry to make sure they didn't get any.

He ordered a second council of war to discuss whether or not Avaricum was to be fired as well. The inhabitants were desperate to save what they considered their greatest and most important town, the finest in Gaul, they thought. They argued that its defensive position made it impregnable, being virtually surrounded by river and marsh, in which there was only one narrow opening. Despite their tearful pleas Vercingetorix was against the idea, convinced the town should be fired. Then the leading citizens fell to their knees in front of him, and begged that their beloved town be spared. After much discussion Vercingetorix was swayed by the views of his generals to be sympathetic towards them, so he gave in. He made a careful choice of the officers in charge of the town's defences, and set up camp sixteen miles away, with firm liaison measures in place, so he knew every hour exactly what was happening in the town.

When the Roman army arrived, Caesar immediately ordered work to be started on the construction of a massive siege terrace, and the many wooden mantlets, the wheeled sheds needed to protect the soldiers bringing up building materials. Day by day the siege terrace took shape, rising at right angles to the city wall, despite the constant barrage of javelins raining down on the builders from the ramparts above. Then two towers were successfully erected on the terrace, both several stories high. All this heavy physical labour gave the men huge appetites, unassuaged by their meagre rations. Caesar sent out foraging parties at irregular intervals, and in varied directions, but Vercingetorix kept watch, and sent out his cavalry, either to capture them, or to hack them to pieces. Caesar ordered the Aeduans to supply him with food. For once, they ignored him, as did the Boii. He thought seriously about raising the siege. His men had no bread for days, only surviving on meat from thin mangy cattle that had to be brought in from far afield.

Vercingetorix ran out of supplies, so moved his camp nearer to Avaricum, but settled it on a hill, in a most advantageous position, surrounded by marshes. He took personal command of his cavalry, and left the camp, seeking to ambush the Roman foragers. Caesar set out silently at midnight with his infantry, and came in sight of the enemy camp at dawn. But this enemy had broken down the causeways over the marshes, and posted patrols at any spot that could be forded. If the Romans attacked, they would get stuck fast in the mud, and be sitting ducks. Caesar beat an undignified retreat.

Instead of praise, Vercingetorix was upbraided by some of the chiefs for removing the cavalry, and leaving no one in command at the camp. Carefully, he explained his reasons to these idiots. "We were out of forage, so we had to move the camp nearer. But I chose the perfect site, defended by Nature herself. I left no one in command, in case someone impetuous should attempt to fight the Romans, when there was not the slightest necessity to do so." He brought forwards his Roman prisoners. They looked pitiful, having been kept in chains and given nothing to eat. They explained Caesar had promised to lift the siege after three more days, if he had no success by then in obtaining further food supplies.

The prisoner's wife stared at him with enormous terrified eyes. She remained oddly motionless, as still as a statue. Gaius lifted the spear, and thrust it straight at her distended abdomen. The point sliced through the foetus with ease, and then came to a juddering halt, as it hit the woman's backbone.

Gaius woke up at once, drenched in sweat, despite the cold damp air. The images were still fixed in his mind. He could feel the spear scraping past skin and gristle. A dream, a dreadful dream. He had never done such a thing in his life! The rain was thrumming loudly on the roof of the tent, the sturdy construction groaning and creaking in the howling wind. The nightmare left him feeling quite shaken. The hammering of the rain, and the wind flapping round the tent skin, sounded deeply menacing to his already overwrought brain, making him more disturbed. He was fully awake, now. The light from the single oil lamp flickered, throwing grotesque shadows onto the black leather walls. It was some time before he could thrust the vivid pictures out of his head, and get back to sleep.

Gaius was exhausted after the fighting the next day. They seemed to be getting nowhere. They'd had ten days of incessant, freezing cold rain. He waded through the mud, wrapping his cloak tightly round him, fighting against the icy squalls. He made his way across to the wooden holding cell, where his prisoner was being kept. The man was lying outside on the ground, now hardly stirring as Gaius walked over to stand next to him. The rain pelted down, mixing with the tears squeezing out from under the prisoner's eyelids. His eyes were the only thing that moved. He could no longer walk, Gaius knew. The last time he had whipped him, the man had to be dragged to the whipping post, and his body slumped against the ropes tying him up. Now he had no strength left even to try and shift out of the way of his tormentor. His lips were bluish in colour, and when Gaius touched him, his skin was cold as marble. He was still alive, though. Just.

"I said I wanted him alive," Gaius shouted at the guards. "Bring him inside, out of the rain, for heaven's sake. Get him near a fire and get him warmed up. He's dying of cold out there."

The guard proffered the whip, but Gaius shook his head. "He can't take any more at present. I want him brought back to life, first."

Fáelán stared at him with enormous terrified eyes, as he was fastened to the spit. The flames licked round his slender body, but his head weirdly distended, distorted, the eyes still looking straight at Gaius as his head exploded.

Gaius was jerked awake again. This was beyond a fucking joke! He sat up in bed, and let out a cry, as he saw eyes staring at him from the other side of the tent. It took him some moments to realise it was one of the twins. Relief and fear mingled. He found himself shivering, he wasn't sure why. He didn't know which twin it was. He had never bothered to find out how to tell them apart.

"Go back to sleep," he ordered. The twin lay down again. Gaius got up and retrieved the blankets, that yet again he had dislodged. The twin was whimpering. Gaius walked over to the huddled pair, and knelt by the side of the mattress.

"What's up?" he asked, with irritation.

"Cold, cold, so cold." Now the twin started to sob.

Gaius reached out and touched him. His scanty clothes were soaked with ice cold water, and his skin was stone cold to the touch.

"Jupiter," Gaius exclaimed. "You're soaked to the skin. What are you thinking of, you idiot."

His angry voice woke the other twin. An ice cold drop landed on his head. He looked up to see the small tear in the tent fabric, the slow drip, the sagging blackened stretched leather, now pooled with water. He was exasperated to hear Borus snoring away. But there was little point in waking him. He was too stupid to understand anything. Gaius kicked his old servant awake instead.

"Get up! Sort these two out. They're freezing!"

He sat on his bed, wrapped in a blanket, while the man pushed up the tent fabric. They heard the water sloshing down the tent wall. The rent would have to be mended in the morning, there was nothing to be done tonight.

"Find a pail, you cretin!" Gaius ordered. "You," he shouted at the wet twin, "get your clothes off. Come on, hurry up." The twin looked at him fearfully. "Why the hell can't you understand good Latin. You've been here long enough." Gaius walked over to him, and started to untie the youngster's thin tunic. Drustan pushed him away.

"No, I do," said Drustan.

Gaius walked over to his bed, and pulled off a blanket to wrap round the shivering twin. Their clothes appeared to be quite unsuitable for this horrible weather, Gaius thought moodily to himself. He supposed he would have to do something about it. What an infernal nuisance they were. Their straw mattress was sodden, as well. However, they would just have to sleep on the ground. He couldn't do anything about that in the middle of the night. He made them sleep next to Hector. At least the dog would keep them warm.

He lay awake, pondering the meaning of his nightmares. The Gods were telling him something, he thought, something vital. There was a message, but what was it exactly? He began to get some inkling, just before he fell back to sleep again. It was Octavian, of course. Why hadn't he understood before? Octavian was telling him to stop torturing the prisoner. Gaius smiled to himself. How like Otto. He always was a softie. Never disciplined his servants properly. Positively spoilt the twins. Always so good natured. Look at the way he treated Chrys. More like a wife than a slave girl. Ridiculous! And as for his children! Pampered, they were, mollycoddled even. Making Junior his heir, for Gods' sakes. He found his cheeks were wet, remembering his adored little brother. Very well, if that's what Octavian wanted.... Gaius went back to dreamless sleep.

The next evening he took his bread ration over to the prison hut. Food was getting hard to come by for the troops, he knew. Officers were still well fed, but the foraging parties were being cut to pieces by Vercingetorix's cavalry. He worried now that his prisoner would die of starvation, instead of cold. The prisoner looked at him with dread. He was more conscious now, and a healthy pink colour. Gaius sat on the floor next to him. He waved away the interpreter.

"When I joined the army, do you know what my father said to me?" Gaius asked the prisoner. He didn't wait for an answer. "He said 'Don't do anything that would make me ashamed of you.' That's what he said." Gaius paused, thinking to himself. Could he make his prisoner see sense? About Octavian? About everything? After a while he went on speaking. "I wonder what Dad would think of me and you." He stretched out his legs, folded his arms, and leant against the wall of the hut, staring unseeingly into space. At last he sighed.

"It will be hard to make you understand," he told the prisoner. "You see, it all started years ago...." He spent half an hour telling the prisoner about his first meeting with the Aeduans. "So you see, that's how Guéreth and I became good friends," he finished up. He sat quiet again, lost in memories. The camp trumpet signal broke in on his thoughts, and brought him back to the present. "Oh, well, I'd better be getting on with things, I suppose," he sighed.

The prisoner was looking at him in terror.

"I've enjoyed talking with you," Gaius told him. The prisoner said not one word.

Gaius tucked the bread into the man's hand, but the man made no attempt to eat it.

"Go on. It's for you," Gaius said impatiently. "Eat it!" But the man turned his head away, and again Gaius could see the tears gathering, and rolling down his cheeks.

"Well, I'll leave you to it." He turned to address the guard. "Where did you put his family?"

Gaius followed the guard over to the stable, where his own string of horses were kept. He found the woman huddled in a corner with the two boys, trying vainly to get some shelter. The stable was open to the air on the leeward side, and the straw was sodden. They stared at him with frightened eyes. Gaius got angry.

"This is no good," he shouted at the guard. "They'll die of cold. Do something!" The horses shifted nervously in their stalls. "Make sure this shelter is waterproof. Oh, and make sure they're fed, or there'll be trouble for you, big trouble."

"Yes, Sir!" The guard hastened to reassure this very oddly behaving tribune. But it was well known in the camp that Gaius Volusenus was one of Caesar's favourite officers. However mad his orders, it would be as well to carry them out. The family were terrified by the angry shouts, cowering in their corner, the woman trying to shield the little boys with her body. Gaius went to her, and crouched down to her level.

"Look, I've explained it all to your husband," he said. "We'll need to sort something out. Alright?" She looked at him blankly. "We'll sort something out," he repeated.

The rain eased off slightly. After twenty-five days the siege terrace constructed by the exhausted legionaries, was now virtually complete, and almost touching the city wall. Gaius accompanied Caesar on his rounds that night, as he exhorted the men to make the final push. Again two legions had been kept under arms day and night, ever since the siege started. Men were bad tempered, short of sleep, and hungry. They still managed to put on a good face for their commander, though. Caesar stalked along the siege terrace, grinning with pleasure. Victory was in sight again, and not before time. Gaius stopped abruptly, sniffing the air. Something wasn't right. Unbeknownst to the Romans, while they had been building upwards, the ingenious enemy had been tunnelling downwards underneath the town walls, and had undermined the siege terrace. Now they were busily setting it alight.

"Sir, I can smell smoke," Gaius yelled.

Just then there was a great shout from the Gauls, as they poured out of the city gates to attack, hurling lighted torches, pitch and straw, onto the flammable terrace. They fought all night, encouraging each other as the Romans were pressed back, the siege towers burnt, the mantlets destroyed. A Gaul stood on the wall by the gate, hurling lighted pitch and tallow onto the terrace. He was killed by an accurately aimed bolt from a Roman scorpio catapult. Immediately another Gaul took his place. And as he was killed, another. Again and again. They didn't lack for courage, these Gauls. But try as they might, they couldn't break through the Roman lines. They fell back at dawn, back behind the city walls. The men decided to abandon the city, and retreat to join Vercingetorix's camp, only a few miles distant. But they were prevented by their wives, who didn't want to be left to the mercies of the Romans. They knew only too well what their fate would be.

Gaius managed to snatch some sleep during the day. His clothes stank of smoke, but at least he had no more nightmares.

The rain became torrential. Caesar at last saw his chance. The siege works were completed, the fire damage repaired. He moved one of the towers forwards. He hid his mass of soldiers in the remaining mantlets. He told the troops there would be huge rewards for the first men to mount the walls. Then he gave the order to attack.

Legionaries streamed out of the mantlets onto the walls of the town. They fought like fury. They were hungry, cold, wet, and very very angry. The defenders were swept off the walls. The Gauls attempted to form wedge formations in the town, but saw in alarm that the Romans occupied the entire length of the city wall. Escape was cut off.

Gaius came up to his Commander. "The town wishes to surrender, Sir. Shall I order the signal to cease fighting?"

"No." Caesar smiled with grim satisfaction. "No, Gaius. Young Vercingetorix needs to be taught a lesson. I am not always merciful. These ignorant peasants must learn the consequence of thwarting my will. How dare they defy me for such a length of time?"

"They are hard fighters, Sir."

Caesar agreed, grinning. "Victory is so sweet, especially over such a worthy enemy. We need to send out a clear message to any who are foolish enough to dream of joining in this rebellion against me. That when they wake up, they will be annihilated!"

"Very good, Sir."

"So let the men carry on fighting. I'm sure they will enjoy their revenge."

Those trying to get to Vercingetorix were hacked to pieces by Caesar's cavalry. The infantry assaulted all trying to flee from the town gates. Out of a population of about forty thousand, only eight hundred escaped. The rest were butchered, old men, women, and even the children. No one was spared.

Vercingetorix and his generals waited on the road before their camp, to give comfort and succour to the desperate refugees. Even though it hadn't been his decision to defend the town, he felt the heavy responsibility for so many fruitless deaths. How to help the afflicted? The bereaved? How to make it all make sense? He would need to try and lift their spirits in the morning. But for tonight it was commiseration, friendly arms around drooping shoulders, warm embraces for the weeping, hugs for those numb with grief and shock.

Vercingetorix called the tribal chiefs together the day after the defeat. He had to do something to overcome the pessimism of his troops. His men were devastated by the massacre.

"Now listen to me. We must not be disheartened. We were not defeated by superior courage, or in a fair fight, but by siege craft, about which we know all too little. But we will learn from this. It confirms what we already knew in our hearts. Romans are brutal savages, who kill not only fighting men, but women and children as well. But try not to let the loss of this town and its people upset us too much. I know it's hard, but in a great war such as ours, there will always be the occasional reverse. So steel yourselves. We will win. In the end, we will win through and avenge these innocents. Our cause is just. All the time I am working to bring over the tribes that have so far refused to join us in our enterprise. Soon all Gaul will be united. We will have plenty of reinforcements. In the meantime, to get back to the practical, you must do as I ask, learn from this, as I said, act like the Romans and fortify this camp."

Vercingetorix clothed and armed the shattered refugees. He continued to make overtures to the other tribes, and was invariably successful. This dreadful reverse wasn't blamed on him at all, but on the townsfolk, who had insisted on the town's defence. Indeed, his reputation was considerably enhanced, as he had said originally that Avaricum should be fired, like the other towns. And then he advised that it be evacuated. Even with this terrible defeat he had readily confronted the setback, and not tried to minimise it in any way. He ordered reinforcements from the various tribes, stipulating the exact number he required, and sent for all the archers he could muster, to quickly replace the losses he had suffered.

Gaius stood in the market place at Avaricum. Such a quaint little town it had been, with its checkered walls of wood and stone, grey and white layers alternate, one above the other. There were the public spaces, the fountains, the court house, assembly rooms, and sports arena, and all the cheery little wattle houses with their pointed roofs and painted walls. Now the cobbles were slippery with blood, the hundreds of corpses lying everywhere despoiled, slashed to death with huge gaping wounds, their jewellery hacked off, their clothes ripped or removed. He walked past the heaped bodies of the old, the young, the babies, and felt sick with himself. Thank the Gods the weather was too cold for flies, but he kicked away an opportunistic rat, feasting on the cold corpse of an infant. The legionaries were still rampaging around, drunk with looted wine, exultant with bloodlust, hunting for anything that moved. They felt invincible.

He rode back to his quarters, and then went to see his prisoner. The man was lying quietly. He started crying as soon as Gaius approached. Gaius squatted on the ground beside him, and summoned the interpreter.

"Tell him he is the bravest man I have ever met," he told the interpreter. What would Octavian do now? "Tell him I would consider it a great honour, if he would agree to serve me."

The prisoner took no notice, and continued to sob. Gaius patted his shoulder.

"He'll come round," he told the interpreter. The interpreter thought it extremely unlikely, but didn't say so.

As Gaius entered his tent, he found one of the twins crouched over, doubled up in pain, with the other twin holding him close.

"Now what?" Gaius said in exasperation. "What's up with you, Drustan, Ninian, whatever your name is."

Drustan looked at him in disgust. "No food for Gauls," he said.

"What do you mean?"

"No food! Five days! No food for Gauls."

"Do you mean you've not had anything to eat? For five days?" Gaius turned in amazement to his old servant. "What are they saying? Is this true?"

The servant nodded. "That's what they said, when they gave out the rations. No food for Gauls," he finished complacently.

"You fucking idiot," yelled Gaius. "They don't mean the slaves. You're in trouble for this, my lad. Go and get them something now, soup, bread, whatever." He kicked the man out of the tent. He thought with horror, the twins had been serving him his food every evening, without a word of complaint. They must be starving.

He knelt on the ground beside the twins. "Look, twin, whatever your name is, I'm sorry. I'm sorry. He's an idiot. You must tell me these things." He stroked the boy's face. "You must tell me, savvy?"

Drustan looked at him contemptuously, and rolled over his brother's forearm, showing the scar of the wound, beautifully sutured by Antinous Allaine. "Ninian," he said. He extended his own forearm, free of blemish. "Drustan. It's quite simple really, you stupid Roman dog," he finished in Gallic.

But that was one of the few phrases Gaius knew. He had heard it often enough from Jay, when he was laughing at him. He pulled Drustan to his feet, and slapped him hard.

"If you are ever rude to me again, my lad, I will take the skin off your back with a whip," he shouted. Drustan continued to stare at him resentfully. Gaius lifted Ninian onto his own bed.

"What am I going to do with the pair of you?" he asked. It was becoming increasingly difficult to keep his hatred of all things Gallic in check. If only Octavian hadn't been killed, if only Guéreth hadn't been killed, if only Jay hadn't changed sides. If only Lucy........No, he mustn't think about Lucy; he felt such anguish when he did, it frightened him.

His servant returned, clutching a loaf of the coarse bread, and a bowl of some warm stuff, that smelt vaguely like broth. Gaius held Ninian in one arm, and spooned broth into him with the other. "Any good?" he asked, anxiously. Ninian gave a weak smile. "Right, Drustan, for you, too. You, idiot, get another bowl."

"Borus give bread," said Ninian, wiping tears from his eyes.

"Oh, did he? Thank the Gods one of you has some sense, then." He went to where Borus was shrinking back into the corner of the tent, trying to appear inconspicuous to this angry officer, in case he should be kicked again.

"Good work," Gaius shouted at him. Borus nodded his agreement with relief. He had been worried about feeding the twins, when Gaius's other servant was adamant they should have nothing.

Oddly enough, making sure the twins ate, gave Gaius a happier feeling inside. This was the first time one of the twins had let him touch them, without becoming stiff with apprehension. He knew Octavian had treated the twins affectionately, patting their cheeks, tousling their hair, even kissing them on occasion. He thought undoubtedly Octavian missed his own children. But if he tried to show any tenderness, the twins were terrified. Probably thought they were going to be raped, or worse. He wondered what Octavian would have thought of him. He had been dreadfully careless of Octavian's property. He would be more careful in future, he promised himself.

Gaius thought he'd better check up on the prisoner's family. He had ordered them to be fed, but now he wanted to make sure he'd been obeyed. Rations had been so poor, the guards might have kept any food for themselves. He was accompanied to the stables by one of his centurions. They could hear strange sounds as they approached. A child was sobbing loudly, while overlaid were peculiar animal noises of distress. Gaius started to run. When he rushed in, he found the woman writhing around on the ground, her fingers scrabbling in the dirt floor. Fáelán was howling. The other little boy was crouched next to his mother, clinging to her skirt in terror. The woman groaned and moaned aloud.

Gaius slipped to his knees beside her. "What is it?" he asked urgently. "What's going on? What's the matter?"

She grabbed at his hand, and hung on to him, squeezing so hard it hurt. The pain eased off for a tiny space, then came again. Again the woman groaned. Her hair was wet with sweat, her eyes wide with despair. The centurion thought he knew what was happening.

"She's having the baby, Sir," he whispered.

"What?" Gaius looked at him in alarm. Babies were outside his experience. He found them terrifying. Tiny things, that could yell blue murder, even though they couldn't talk. Especially if he tried to pick one up. "We need a woman," he said desperately. "Where do we get a woman? What about what's his name's wife, you know, that officer in the Sixth?"

"Lady Sempronia? She's in Bibracte, Sir."

"Who, then?"

The woman clutched his hand again. He thought she would break his bones, her grip was so fierce. She cried out sharply, and then again. Her legs bent upwards. She screamed in agony, then gave a long drawn-out wail, her breast heaving convulsively. Her cries abruptly ceased. She lay back on the earth, quite still. Gaius thought she had died at first, but no, she was still breathing.

"Look, Sir," whispered the centurion. He indicated the woman's skirt. Something appeared to be moving very slightly inside. Gaius pulled up the skirt.

"Oh, God," he said. "What the hell do we do now?"

The tiny baby lay inside its mother's skirts in a dark pool

of blood. Its arms extended suddenly, as the material was lifted off its body.

"Do they always look like this?" Gaius asked in dismay. "Is it normal?"

The baby was streaked with blood, mixed with a creamy whiteness over parts of its skin. Black clumps of hair were stuck down to its scalp. A twisted bluish glutinous rope went from its abdomen, and disappeared between the mother's legs, into her interior.

The centurion wasn't much wiser than his superior. "I think they get washed, don't they?"

"But it is still attached," said Gaius.

The woman moaned again, and the placenta slithered out to join the infant.

"Oh, that is revolting," Gaius declared.

Something hit him sharply on the head. He got swiftly to his feet, to find Fáelán gripping tightly onto a stick he had found. Gaius wrested it from his hands with ease. "Leave my Mummy alone," yelled the child, and burst into noisy sobs again, terrified of the consequences of his action. Now the baby joined in, with a weak wailing noise.

Gaius had had enough. After all, he was an officer. Much simpler to give out orders. "Right, get this baby cleaned up, and the mother as well," he told the centurion. "I'll take the boys away. Give her a bit of peace." He remembered his mother telling him frequently on his last leave, to give Chrys a bit of peace. He wondered if the prisoner's wife would be equally weepy, and didn't feel quite ready to cope with her, if she was.

He lifted the smaller boy into his arms. The child was too frightened to protest. Gaius took hold of Fáelán with his free hand, and pulled him away. The mother looked at him in fear. She tried to sit up.

"Don't hurt them," she pleaded.

Gaius guessed her meaning. "They'll be fine. I'll get them something to eat. Not to worry." He gave what he hoped was a reassuring smile. "Bring the baby to me, when it looks more the thing," he said to the bewildered centurion.

An hour later the centurion brought the cleaned up baby to his superior. The baby now looked like it was supposed to. It had stopped crying. "It's a girl," whispered the centurion.

"Oh, that's brilliant," Gaius exclaimed. "My mother has always wanted a girl."

He took the baby over to show the prisoner. "Look what we've got," Gaius said proudly. "It's a girl. It's yours. Do you want to hold her?"

The prisoner looked at him in horror. Was this Roman going to murder his child before his eyes?

Gaius tried again. "Isn't she sweet? Look at her little hands. She's even got tiny fingernails. Amazing! You'll have to give her a name, won't you?" He placed the baby on the prisoner's lap. The prisoner looked hesitant, and then pulled back the blanket to see the child's face. The baby opened her naked lashless eyes.

"Looks like you," said Gaius, affably. The man needed a bit of encouragement, he could see. "We'd better drink her health."

Borus appeared with a tray, a jug, and two earthenware beakers. He poured out the wine for his mad master and the prisoner. Gaius held out the beaker to the prisoner. The man took it in his hand.

"Cheers," said Gaius. The prisoner said something in return, the first thing he had ever said. Gaius looked to the interpreter. "He wished you good health, Sir," said the interpreter.

"That's good," said Gaius. "I feel we're getting somewhere. Better get her back to her Mum, now." Tenderly he lifted up the baby. "Ask him what the baby is called," Gaius said to the interpreter.

"She is called Dòchas," said the prisoner, who started to weep again.

"Dòchas, that's a nice name," Gaius said. "What does it

mean?"

"It means 'Hope,' Sir," said the interpreter.

Gaius's good intentions about the twins vanished a few days later, when they approached him, with an interpreter in tow. Unfortunately for the twins, a rather bad interpreter. Gaius was extremely busy, organising the distribution of the supplies the army had seized from the laden stores in Avaricum. Caesar wanted to give his debilitated army the chance to recuperate, after the appalling depredations of the winter campaign. He knew his men were in no fit state to fight at present.

The interpreter spoke first. "Sir, these slaves ask for your permission to leave camp. They have received news that their master is near, and they wish to join him."

"Oh, for fuck's sake," said Gaius. "When will they get it into their silly heads that Octavian is dead. I haven't time for this. I'm busy." He turned to the twins. "Clear off, do you hear me, you stupid cunts. Fuck off out of my sight." He turned back and continued to give orders to his centurions, without another word to the interpreter.

"What did he say?" asked Drustan anxiously.

The interpreter was puzzled. "He said you were to go."

Drustan was delighted. "He said we had his permission to go? Is that right?"

The interpreter was a slave, an Arvernian from South Gaul. He wasn't very sure of some Latin words, but the twins had clearly been told to go away, he had understood that much.

"Yes, you have permission to go."

The twins were a mile from the camp, when they were spotted by a routine patrol sent out to forage in the surrounding countryside. The decurion in charge didn't understand what they were saying, but he knew these were Tribune Volusenus's slaves, and was sure they wouldn't have been sent out alone by him. They were tied up and hauled back to camp, to be arraigned in front of a furious Gaius.

This was shocking. The twins were obviously deserters, spies going to join the enemy's camp, which wasn't that far away. He knew that as such they should be crucified, but he couldn't bring himself to give the order. He thought he would just have to treat them as runaway slaves, not spies. Labienus sent for him. Gaius was not surprised to find him unsympathetic, the Commander's message was unequivocal.

"Gaius, don't start going soft on me. You have to put such feelings aside. I know they're a good looking pair, but you can easily find other bed companions, for the Gods' sakes. Caesar insists. Your slaves must be crucified. Vercingetorix's camp is so near. We cannot encourage spies and deserters. An example must be made of them."

Gaius's face set in an uncompromising frown. "They're Octavian's. I'm not having them crucified. He won't want that to happen. He'll never forgive me."

"Caesar's orders must be obeyed."

"Tell Caesar to get stuffed. I'm not obeying any such order."

"What a stubborn bastard you are, Gaius." Labienus was shocked and angry. "Alright, I'll tell him. Don't be surprised if he insists. And if he does I'll see to the punishment myself. And you'd better pray he doesn't want you flogged into the bargain."

Gaius had never before disobeyed an order. This was something quite out of the ordinary, Labienus explained to his commander, something to do with the death of young Octavian, he thought. But such rank disobedience in a senior officer should be put down ruthlessly.

Caesar roared with laughter, when he heard what Gaius had said. He could see Labienus thought it was no laughing matter, however.

"Sometimes a little insubordination is necessary, my dear Titus. I would be loathe to upset Gaius. I am so very fond of him. We will just ensure that any other such spies are treated with the greatest severity, tortured rather than flogged, then crucified."

That evening Gaius had the twins brought out of confinement. He pronounced the sentence. They were crying and protesting, but he took no notice. In the morning they were to be scourged, and then branded on the forehead as runaways. He thought he was being merciful.

BOOK 4: CHAPTER 4

Spring 52 BC

At last came the news they had all been waiting for so impatiently. The passes were now negotiable to traffic. They could return. Lucy didn't want to return. Nor did Chrys, nor did Junior, nor did Val, nor did Darius. And most definitely, nor did Octavian.

Lucy enlisted Grandmother's help. "If I go back to Rome, Madam, I know my mother will make me marry a disgusting old man, a cousin of Senator Sperinus. Then when he is dead, she thinks I will be able to persuade Octavian or Octavian's brother to marry me. But I've heard the cousin is almost as mad as my stepfather was."

"Do you have any other plans, my dear?" Grandmother asked. She approved of Lucy, who spoke beautifully, and always treated her with the greatest deference.

"If you permit it, I would like to stay here. I am learning the language. I can help Lady Riona when the baby arrives. I'm really good with babies. Ask Chrys."

"For my own part I would be pleased to have you stay. But your mother must consent."

Now Lucy found her mother. "Mother, I think it would be much better if I remained here in Gaul. I will be near Marcius and Andreas, and of course nearer to Octavian and Gaius, while Chrys is miles away, back in Rome."

Ursula thought delightedly, that at last her daughter was seeing sense. "I'm not sure how easy it will be to see the boys," she demurred.

"Uncle Marcus has gained permission from Prince Coevorten to set up trading posts here again, Mother." Lucy didn't add that Coevorten had stipulated this wouldn't be until the war was won by the Gauls. "He will be here frequently. But I can stay with Uncle Marcus in Bibracte, as well." Although Lucy knew that Uncle Marcus was not the slightest bit interested in the welfare of his niece, now he knew she was damaged goods.

"Would Prince Allaine be willing, darling?"

"I think so, Mother. I have already asked his grandmother, and the idea pleases her. Prince Allaine quite likes me, I think."

"Darling, you mustn't under *any circumstances*, consider Prince Allaine as anything other than a friend." Lady Ursula was a little concerned. Could Lucy have an ulterior motive, she wondered. Allaine was an exceptionally good looking young man, with his blond curls, and Grecian features. And he did seem fond of her Lucy.

"Don't be silly, Mother. He's a barbarian," Lucy replied, hoping to have put enough scorn into her voice to allay her mother's suspicions. She's got a mind like a cesspit - Lucy thought to herself. But then poor Mother had had such a rotten time. Perhaps it was no great surprise.

Allaine was pleased to hear that Lucy wished to become a more permanent member of his household. He was impressed with her efforts to put the past behind her, and become useful, though never likely to be married. He encouraged her to speak Gallic, and continue with her studies. He thought Riona and Eloise and Zinny would welcome her company. She was such a slight thing, he thought there would be no risk to her staying, even though she was a Roman girl.

Riona was furious. They had a blazing row. Allaine couldn't imagine at first why Riona should be in the slightest bit jealous of a girl who aroused no sexual feelings in him, whatsoever. He had already foisted his woman onto Valerius, at Riona's instigation, and he was really fond of her. He had hoped to use her if Riona became too tired during her pregnancy, but now his woman was pregnant as well, whether with Val's child, or his child, no one would ever know.

"Lucia is a victim, a patient, if you like. Of course I'm not interested in her, a tiny little thing like that. She's like a doll to me. She needs protecting."

He'd been doing quite well till the last sentence. Riona exploded with anger.

"She's a schemer, like her mother. She wants a man, and any man will do. Well, she's not getting you."

"You're jealous!"

"Of course I'm jealous. Alright, it's not rational, but you weren't exactly rational about Tarleton, were you? And I'd never even met him."

Allaine had to admit there was truth in that.

"And I'm getting uglier by the day," wailed Riona, collapsing into tears.

Allaine could see things were getting serious. He took her in his arms, and kissed her. "You silly gorgeous girl," he said. "Don't you know you get more beautiful every single day? I love you, Riona, so much, I don't know how to tell you. I will never love anyone else. You are the only girl for me. You have always been the only girl for me."

He apologised to his wife, and kissed and cuddled her until she was soothed better.

"I'll watch out for any plots on my virtue, my love. But I will be gone all too soon, to join Vercingetorix and his forces, so I will be safe from any schemes on Lucy's part. So please, darling Riona, can we stop wasting precious time arguing about things that aren't going to happen?"

Allaine told Chrys what she already knew in her heart, that she had to return to Rome, with her husband's parents, and the children. Chrys knew she would never see Allaine again, or Grandmother, or her sisters, despite Lady Volusena's earnest assurances, that they would all be very welcome at her house in Rome. How could she bear to part from Octavian? When he made love to her now, her own intense pleasure made him ecstatic as well. "We are an amalgam," he told her, "stronger, shinier, harder, and more beautiful together." At times in bed it was difficult to stay quiet, and not wake the rest of the household.

Allaine and Jayven travelled with the Romans to Geneva, with a large and heavily armed escort. Coevorten refused to take any chances with his brother's life. The rest of the party waited at the inn, while Octavian, Valerius, Hugo and Darius were taken to the sacred grove for the their manumission, and the Ceremony of Departure. Allaine freed each of them in turn. He knew them all inside out, not just as slaves, but as fighting men, having trained with them most mornings throughout the long winter. They had been his constant companions. Of course, they knew him equally well, his strengths and weaknesses. Valerius was sobbing throughout, not even stopping when Allaine presented him with the dog. If anything it made his sobs even louder. When Allaine fastened the cloak round his shoulders, Octavian broke down as well.

"Listen to the words, Octavian. I am releasing you from your oath. You are free to go." Allaine lifted the gold chain over his freedman's head. "Hold out your hand," he ordered. He put the chain into Octavian's palm, and closed his fingers over it."Keep it as a reminder. Don't forget all I've taught you. And don't worry. We will not meet on the battlefield. And I assure you I will never be taken alive again. Once is quite enough."

Octavian couldn't stop crying. Allaine put his arms round him, and held him in a final embrace. "You'll be fine, Octavian. You mustn't worry. You'll be fine. As soon as you are addressed as Tribune, it will fall into place again." Octavian merely hugged him tightly for a bit, until he had recovered his composure.

Allaine looked round at his little group of Romans, and thought how much he liked them all, loved them all, even. "Don't any of you get killed," he ordered.

"No, Sir," they agreed, smiling through tears.

"And don't any of you get captured."

"No, Sir," they chorused again.

"But if you are, or if any of you ever have need of me, send for me, and I will come."

Octavian was confused. "You haven't rescinded your part of the oath, then, Sir, have you?"

"No. It is not permitted. I am bound in duty to all of you for ever, through life, and after death. That is our custom and belief."

Allaine held his arms wide in the final blessing. "May the Gods go with you, my children, and keep you safe, now, and for always."

They all knew the response. "So be it, Master."

Of course by rights - Hugo thought to himself - he should kill his former master. Allaine was an ally of Ambiorix, and now, no doubt, an ally of Vercingetorix. Enemies. Hugo knew what would happen, if he attempted any such thing. He would be cut to ribbons by the others, if he so much as lifted a finger against Allaine. Anyway, if it hadn't been for his master, he would have suffered a miserable death. He was grateful to Allaine for restoring his health, mental and physical. What an amazing man he was, for a barbarian. No, Hugo corrected himself. Allaine was an amazing man, in any culture, Roman, Greek, Gallic. It was a privilege to know him.

At last the travellers arrived at the final parting. The road dropped to the lake. It was possible to see in the distance, tiny figures, marching behind Roman standards, Caesar's reinforcements arriving from the Province. Coevorten had finally allowed Metius to arrange for his servants from Bibracte to meet them at Geneva, and escort them back to Rome.

They said their final farewells. It was Darius's turn to look miserable. He would have to face his centurion again, and didn't know how he was going to cope. To cheer Darius up, Allaine told him he was to keep the horse he was riding, as he now knew how to look after it, and could ride it properly. Darius was overcome.

"Can I call him Bucephalus?" he asked wistfully. It all seemed too good to be true.

Allaine burst out laughing. "Of course you can. You can

call him anything you like, Darius."

Junior burst into tears. "I don't want to be a slave," he wailed.

Allaine picked him up in his arms, and kissed him. "Junior, you are Prince Octavian, like your father." He encountered a startled look from Octavian. "Don't forget it. I am a prince, and I am also a very bad slave, as Guéreth will tell you."

"You're a slave?" Junior was so surprised, he stopped crying.

"That's right. But remember, Junior, you are also a prince, wherever you are, and whatever country you are in. So don't forget to act like a prince. How do princes act. Do you remember?"

"They have to solve problems."

Allaine smiled. "You can leave that bit till you are older."

"Be courteous to all, and be kind to your little brothers," said Junior.

"Good. You've learnt well. Now in Gaul we never say 'goodbye,' only, we say 'till we meet again.' So, my little Prince Octavian, goodbye till we meet again."

Lady Volusena was feeling most hospitable, sad to be leaving her new friends, but pleased to be going home again, part of the way with her beloved youngest son, who was to rejoin his legion with his comrades. Allaine had given his permission. So, it appeared, had Vercingetorix.

"Darling Allaine," Claudia said to him, "you must come and visit us in Rome. I'm sure you would be pleased with the public buildings and temples. And no doubt you will be wanting to see Chrys again, and the children. If that dreadful man starts bothering you, you must come to us at once, all of you. We have plenty of room."

Allaine kissed her hand, and then her cheek. "You have a very kind heart. All I ask is that you take care of my sister and the children. I am so grateful for all you have done for my family." He shook hands with Titus, both of them sad to think how unlikely it was that they would ever be able to meet again.

The jarring note was provided by Guéreth.

"Goodbye, Allaine," said Guéreth. "When we do meet again, I swear I will have you killed."

Allaine just laughed. "You're consistent, anyway. Just make sure you keep doing those leg exercises. And don't fall off your horse again.

Octavian said an emotional goodbye to his parents, and his wife and children. He was to travel with Guéreth, Marcius and his fellow Romans.

"Do you think you'll join the army, now you are free, Marcius?" Octavian asked his friend.

"No thank you. I've been a slave for eight years, and I don't wish to exchange one form of slavery for another. I wish to be my own master for a bit."

"But you'll stay with Guéreth?" Octavian asked in alarm. He didn't think he could cope without Marcius, always cheerful, always level headed.

"Of course. But I'll know that if I should wish to, I could leave at any time."

"You'd have a problem leaving in the middle of a war," Guéreth remarked, overhearing the conversation.

"But I could pass for a Gaul, any time, couldn't I, Sir?"

"Yes, of course you could. Both of you."

"What I don't want to be, is a slave dealer, but I'm sure Uncle Marcus has that prospect lined up for me."

"Listen, Marcius, when everything has settled down, Chrys and I are going to take the children to her estate, the one Dumnorix assigned to me for her dowry. It's beautiful, bordering the river Loire. Very productive land. I'm going to plant a vineyard, and make the best wine in Gaul. Why don't you come there as well? Chrys wants to be near Switzerland, so she can see her family."

And you want to see Allaine - thought Marcius, but

refrained from saying so.

"What about your parents? I thought your father wanted you to take up a civilian appointment."

Octavian laughed. "As we've produced their only grandchildren to date, I expect we will see quite a lot of them as well. I think Dad will change his mind, once he sees the size of the estate. And I expect I will still be an Aeduan magistrate. That should satisfy him." And Allaine, he hoped.

Marcius wasn't so sure. "Alright. If that's what you end up doing, I'll join you. I love this country." He could see Guéreth's smiling look of pleasure at his words. "And the people."

"Shake hands on it, then," Octavian said. He brought his horse up alongside Marcius's. It was awkward, but they managed it, and broke away from each other, laughing. Octavian felt much happier.

The others were now to be given an escort by Marcus Metius's men as far as Arles, and were then able to have a military escort back to Rome.

"Perhaps it will be a girl this time, darling," said Lady Volusena to Chrys.

Chrys was surprised. She had only just felt movements, and had told no one.

"It would be so nice to have a girl in the family," said Claudia.

By the time they got to Genua, Chrys was bleeding heavily. They would have to stop and await events. Claudia was a great help to Chrys in the dark hours, when she got frightened thinking of the future, and wondering if she would still be in it.

When she wasn't comforting Chrys, Claudia spent a lot of time on her knees in the temple, begging the Goddess Juno to spare her beautiful daughter-in-law.

"Never mind the baby," petitioned Claudia, desperately. "We can manage without a little girl. But we can't manage without Chrys."

BOOK 4 : CHAPTER 5

Spring, 52 BC

Allaine, Jayven, and the rest of the Helvetian contingent, hastened to join Vercingetorix's forces. Allaine went with Jay, and reported to Headquarters. Vercingetorix rose up at once, and embraced them both, so pleased to see them.

"What did you do with your Romans, then, Allaine?" he asked. "Did you get them away safely?"

"Yes. We took them to Geneva, and said our goodbyes."

"That must have made you sad."

"Yes. But I had to let them go. Thank you for allowing it. If I had brought them here, how long do you think they would have survived, chain or no chain?"

"No time at all, I'm afraid. But you will miss your Octavian, I think?"

"I miss him already."

"Come and sit down, Allaine. You too, Jayven. Have something to eat, and then let's talk."

"What's the situation?" Allaine asked, after they had been wined and dined.

"This campaign is going to be a bloody affair. We lost many at Avaricum."

"They should have taken your advice."

"Yes, of course they should. But I had no way to compel them to give up the town that meant so much to them. Now I need every available man. I know you won't fight, Allaine, unless as a last resort. I want to make sure, though, that the wounded are properly cared for. I don't want any man to feel he is expendable. Everyone who fights with me is precious in my eyes. I want them to be secure in the knowledge that we will always do our utmost to use their lives, solely for the good of the country they love so much. Many will die. Their lives must not be wasted for no good purpose. They are giving themselves into our hands, so we must do our best for them, and for their families."

"Quite a responsibility," said Allaine. "We have to be mobile. I'll need pack horses and wagons, then, fully equipped with splints, bandages, and medicines. We have cautery irons, suture material, retractors, but we will need supplies of vinegar, oil, and medical unguents. It would be good to have a secure place where the unrecoverable can die in peace. If they are badly wounded, but survivable, it would help to get them home. They wouldn't be able to continue fighting, and they would just hold us back. Minor wounds can be turned around quite quickly. I have brought some surgeons and medical orderlies with me. I can teach more, as we go along."

Vercingetorix was surprised and gratified. "You seem to have thought it all through already."

"I've been thinking about it all winter. I've brought a great deal of materials with me, as well."

It was still raining. On the other side of the river in the Roman camp, the guards were staring at them nervously through the mist. These men looked solid enough, but were they? Surely they had all been killed. Could they be the ghosts everyone was talking about?

Hugo found it amusing. "Boo!" he shouted at them. The guards shrieked in panic, turned round, and hared back inside the camp gates.

"That lot should be on a charge," Hugo grinned. "Look, I'll go straight to Headquarters, inform them of our arrival, and get Andreas commissioned."

"What will you tell Caesar?" Octavian asked his superior, anxiously.

"The truth. We were captured, rescued by a Helvetian, and taken by him to Switzerland for our safety. We had to work off our price, but he has been extremely reasonable, treated us with great kindness, and let us go as soon as the passes were clear. Will that do, Octavian?"

"Will you tell him the name of our rescuer?"

"He won't ask. He won't be that interested. You go and find your brother. Take the rest with you. Andreas, come with me."

As Octavian approached the row of officers' tents, he had a premonition of disaster. He could hear two voices, one high pitched, screaming, again and again. The other youngster calling out his name, "Octavian, Octavian," with the familiar North Gallic lilt he knew so well, crying, and sobbing, and protesting. Fear engulfed him. He knew instantly it would be his twins. Why did nothing go right, ever? He started to run. Ajax ran with him.

His brother was standing near the whipping post, with Hector squatted beside him. A slim figure was jerking against the ropes in agony, his golden skin criss-crossed with bloody welts, as the centurion lashed at him with the scourge.

"What the hell do you think you're doing?" yelled Octavian, hysterically. "Cut him down. Cut him down at once."

Ajax barked in excitement. The centurion moved swiftly to obey, while Gaius stood rigid with shock at the sight of his brother. Valerius hastily tied Ajax to the whipping post, then moved to deal with Hector's ecstatic welcome.

Drustan slumped to the ground semi conscious, making strange moaning noises between tightly clenched teeth. Blood streamed from the multiple cuts on his back, the rain turning the blood into tiny red rivulets that trickled down his sides. Octavian walked over to his inert body, and fought for control. He knelt down, Allaine's voice ringing in his head, saying 'reassure first, keep calm, slow deliberate movements, quiet voice.' He dredged up the new words he had learned last year, from the depths of his brain.

"Hello, Drustan. It's alright. Everything will be alright. Octavian is here now to look after you. Don't worry. Don't worry." He twisted round to face the centurion. "Get a stretcher and take him to the hospital tent, then wait for me. And don't you dare touch him! Val, go with him. Organise bandages and dressings. You know what I need."

"Sir!" Val slammed to attention, saluted, and knelt by Drustan. Now the boy was more conscious, and having difficulty keeping still. He writhed with the pain, making odd sharp cries, in terrible distress as he tried to breathe.

Octavian walked over to where Ninian was kneeling on the wet ground, his hands tied in front of him. Tears were streaming down his face, as he continually called out his master's name.

"Octavian," he sobbed, "Octavian," he repeated, over and over again.

Gaius tried to intervene. "Look, Otto, I can explain...."

"Come near me, and I'll kill you," Octavian snarled in fury.

At that moment Ajax sank his teeth into Hector's hindquarters. A ferocious dog fight ensued. Octavian was oblivious to it all, oblivious to Val seizing both dogs, and forcing their obedience. He had eyes and ears only for his twins.

Octavian bent over his slave, and raised him up to a standing position, then slashed through the cords with his knife.

"It's alright, now, Ninian. Everything is alright now. I'm here. Octavian is here."

But Ninian continued to repeat his master's name, unable to think or speak coherently, totally overwrought. Octavian held his slave firmly, and recited the formal words of welcome. He could feel Ninian's body trembling under his hands.

"Ninian, you must try and be calm. We need to help Drustan, don't we? Take some deep breaths, my pet. Slowly, slowly, now. There, that's better. That's much better."

Ninian was clinging to him, like a limpet from one of his own rocky shores. His sobs lessened as he began to regain some sort of self control, his master's words finally penetrating his consciousness.

"Octavian," he gasped, in startled recognition. His master

was with him. His prayers were answered.

Octavian looked past him to a wooden shelter, with a legionary standing underneath next to a brazier. The irons were protruding obscenely from the red hot coals. Octavian turned to confront Gaius.

"You unspeakable bastard," he shouted, beside himself with anger. "How dare you hurt my twins."

He picked up Ninian's pathetically thin tunic from the ground. It was soaking. He threw it down again in disgust, stripped off his own cloak, and fastened it round Ninian's still shivering body.

"Darius, get some tunics and trousers out of my pack, and bring them to me. Come on, now, Ninian. We must go and deal with your brother. He will need your help."

Taking Ninian by the wrist, and ignoring Gaius completely, he strode across the parade ground, towards the hospital tent.

When Hugo arrived at the hospital, he found Drustan screaming in pain, as Octavian scrubbed at his back with vinegar. He waited to speak until the cries subsided a little.

"We are to share a tent for the time being. I've co-opted Val and Darius."

"He'll make a bit of noise, tonight, most probably," Octavian said. "You might not get much sleep, Sir."

"That's alright. As long as you're happy with him."

"Happy!" Octavian exclaimed.

"You know what I mean. When Val's finished, he can help Darius stable the horses." He thought the other twin would faint, he looked so white. Valerius pushed Ninian down onto a bench, and told him to put his head between his knees.

Octavian got up in the middle of the night to dose Drustan again. He held the whimpering boy in his arms, until the drug took effect. Allaine was right, he thought. He had turned back into a tribune without a moment's pause. Ditto Val and Darius, legionaries again. And Hugo had slipped effortlessly into his role as Senior Tribune. Octavian discovered he liked Hugo being in charge. It made everything so much easier.

Two days later Hugo found Octavian in the hospital again, changing Drustan's dressings.

"Tribune, you are wanted at Headquarters."

"Not till I've finished this," Octavian replied curtly.

Hugo nodded, there was no great urgency. They walked together over to the Praesidium.

Octavian saluted and spoke. "Hail, Caesar."

"Octavian, my boy." If his commander was amazed to see him, after an eighteen month's absence, he had no intention of showing it. "You are needed. These Aeduans wish to speak to you."

To everyone's surprise the Aeduans came forward, knelt, and each in turn kissed Octavian's hand.

"Why this greeting?" Octavian asked, but he thought he knew.

"Sir, you are the brother of Prince Allaine of Helvetia?"

"Brother-in-law," Octavian corrected, smiling.

"Yes, Sir. So, you are Prince Octavian, here in Gaul."

Caesar was pleased. He had no idea what was going on. But this was the way his officers should be treated by the barbarians, with proper respect. Octavian spoke fluently to the Aeduans in their own language. He then explained the problem to his commander.

"Sir, apparently there is a conflict. There are two important men, both claiming to be the elected principal Aeduan magistrate this year. They wish me to adjudicate on the dispute. It doesn't sound as if I will have any difficulty. The law is perfectly clear on the matter. The only problem being that one of my servants is sick at present."

"You can have Borus," said Gaius.

"Borus?"

"Are you as deaf as he is?" Gaius barked at him. Octavian

had taken leave of his senses. He refused to speak to him, or say where he had been for the last year and a half. Guéreth wouldn't enlighten him either, being too ashamed to admit he was a prisoner of his own slave.

"You can take the Dolt to serve you. You'll make a fine pair."

"Thank you, Sir," Octavian said coldly. "Caesar, do I have your permission to leave for Decetia?"

Caesar thought for only a moment. "Philemon, come here."

The secretary walked swiftly to his master, dropping on his knees before him, stylus and waxed tablet poised ready in his hand.

"Make a note that I leave the fighting front with the greatest reluctance, but this affair needs the hand of Caesar. Octavian, I am sure you would do your best, my boy. But we must tread carefully with our great allies, the Aeduans. This affair must be resolved to the satisfaction of all, unless any of the disaffected join forces with Vercingetorix. I will accompany you, therefore, and take the matter into my own hands. I doubt if they were expecting a mere tribune to decide the issue."

Octavian didn't bother to correct him. He thought the less Caesar knew the better, as far as he was concerned. The Aeduans were surprised to find Caesar would forsake the war with Vercingetorix, as he had just scored a notable victory. Octavian wasn't surprised in the least. To him the army appeared dispirited, undernourished, and weakened by the long siege without adequate food. The euphoria of victory had evaporated. Reflection had found the outcome too close for comfort. The Gauls learnt so quickly. He thought also, that some of the legionaries felt a bit guilty, ashamed at their rampage through Avaricum. It wasn't only Gauls that could feel for the innocents. It was a time to take stock, and replenish supplies, without losing face.

Octavian was right about the dispute. He thought he

detected a spark of fury in the two claimant magistrates, when they were told Caesar would arbitrate, instead of him. The matter was settled within the hour of the Council meeting. Convictolitavis was duly pronounced Chief Magistrate. As Octavian made the announcement, it appeared to be well received, the Aeduans being fully aware that Caesar had bowed to Octavian's superior knowledge of Aeduan custom and law. The Aeduans weren't quite so pleased to discover that now they were to provide Caesar with all their cavalry, and ten thousand infantry, to protect his supply routes.

Octavian returned to camp with his commander.

"Apparently you are an honorary Aeduan, my boy," Caesar said, as they were riding back together.

"Oh, really, Sir?" Octavian replied, trying to sound non-committal. "They must be confusing me with my brother Gaius." He looked into his commander's shrewd eyes. He wasn't fooling him for an instant.

Octavian took the opportunity to try and alleviate Borus's deafness. Each night on the journey he poured warm olive oil into his servant's ears. As Allaine had done the same, Borus wasn't frightened by the procedure. Once back at camp Octavian used a small syringe to remove the softened wax.

"Any improvement?"

Borus was beaming. "I can hear you, Master, a bit."

"Have you always been deaf?"

"No, Master. It was after Master Claud hit me round the head. Your distinguished father was very angry with him."

Octavian held his slave's hands. "I'm sorry, Borus. Now things will be better between us, do you think?" He wondered why his brother Claud was such an unpleasant man.

Borus kissed his master's hands.

Drustan had made a partial recovery, while they were away, competently nursed by Val and Darius. But he was scarred for life.

"They can't cope with you being away, Sir," Val told

Octavian. "They're like children, aren't they?"

"They were only thirteen years old, when they fought against us in the battle of the ships. To all intent and purposes they are children still. They are only sixteen, now. Did you find out how they were treated?"

"Something bad happened in Britain, when they were captured. Your brother didn't harm them at all, until just now, when he thought they were running off to Vercingetorix, but it seems as if he was a bit careless, not knowing much about Gallic culture. They went without food during the siege for a few days, but it was the fault of your brother's idiotic servant."

"Borus?"

"No. Borus gave them some of his own rations. The other one said there was no food for Gauls. But the Tribune sorted that out. Only he made them sleep with Hector. He said it would keep them warm."

"What a fucking idiot."

"Your brother has slave children as well."

Valerius related to Octavian all the information he had gleaned about Gaius and the prisoner. "The men think he's gone mad. He's sent the wife, baby and little boy to Bibracte, to stay with Lady Sempronia, but he's taking the prisoner and his son as servants."

Val thought Gaius must have missed his family so much, he needed to acquire a new one. Of course Gaius would have thought Octavian was dead, and probably his parents as well. Coevorten had forbidden the Romans to communicate with the outside world, until their return to Rome.

Octavian thanked Borus for helping the twins. Borus turned his master's bedding inside out, and removed the lice he had placed inside the blankets. Then he gave Ajax the stew he had been ready to serve. He had liberally laced it with his own saliva. He'd give Octavian another chance to behave.

Caesar divided his army. Labienus took four legions to

fight against the Senones and the Parisii, in an attempt to prevent these tribes from reinforcing Vercingetorix's army. Octavian was delighted to find Gaius was going with him. The tension between the two of them was becoming unbearable, but Octavian refused to budge. He wouldn't speak to Gaius, until Gaius admitted he was wrong.

Gaius decided to have one last attempt to speak to Octavian. He went into his brother's tent to try and mend matters before leaving, and found the tent abnormally tidy. He nearly walked straight out again, thinking he must be in someone else's tent, but he caught sight of Drustan, lying on his face on a palliasse. Nothing was out of place, the reports were neatly stacked, armour and weapons hung in good order and gleaming with polish, bedding, cushions and couches straight and uncluttered. Previously Octavian's tent had resembled a rubbish dump, a bit like his own, he thought. There was no disputing the fact that Octavian was different. His brother had changed. Not entirely for the better, the stubborn bastard.

The other officers noticed a difference as well. Octavian seemed not just confident and competent, but organised. He also didn't suffer fools gladly, and had developed a rather sarcastic manner when speaking to the new draft of Junior Officers. They began to be afraid of displeasing him, not relishing his cutting comments on their incompetence. The centurions became slowly aware they were dealing with an officer who knew just what to do under the most trying circumstances, and reacted accordingly, giving him the greatest respect.

Caesar took his remaining six legions to march towards Arvernian country, to Gergovia, along the course of the river Allier. Vercingetorix camped his army on the opposite bank, and broke down all the bridges. The armies could see each other's camp fires, across the river.

"He's there, somewhere," Octavian said. "I wonder what he's doing?"

Marcius slipped his arm round his friend's shoulders.

"Probably looking across at us, wondering what you're doing." Octavian laughed. "Aren't you going to make it up with your brother, Octavian?"

"Why should I? He won't admit he was wrong."

"Perhaps the twins made a mistake?"

"They are adamant. The interpreter said they had been given permission to go. It is Gaius who made the mistake, not my twins."

"Do you think we're going to spend the summer marching up and down this river bank, while Vercingetorix camps opposite us?"

"No. There's a plan. We are to conceal two legions in the wood, and send on the rest, looking as if it's all of us. Then, in the night, we build the broken bridge up again, on the old piles that are still standing, get across, make a camp, and send for the rest of the army."

The plan worked. Now Caesar was on the same bank as Vercingetorix. But the Gauls had no desire to fight a pitched battle on open plains, sure they would lose. They marched speedily to Gergovia, Vercingetorix's home town.

BOOK 4: CHAPTER 6

Gergovia (La Roche-Blanche), South Central Gaul, Summer, 52 BC

Gergovia was a natural fortress, perched a thousand feet up on a mountain. Vercingetorix knew every inch of it so well. He stationed his forces in three camps around the town, outwith the town ramparts, but within the additional six-foot high stone wall fortification a little lower down the slopes.

Caesar arrived soon after with his six legions. He began the construction of his fortified camp on the plain opposite, each legionary knowing exactly where to go and what to do. He made the camp big enough to hold his six legions comfortably, with a decent space left for prisoners and cattle.

Andreas took one look at the vast ranks of enemy, and felt very scared. "There's masses of them, Octavian. How does Caesar think we can take on all those forces?"

"You must stop calling me Octavian, Andreas," said Octavian in irritation. "You address senior officers as 'Sir.'" This must be the tenth time he'd had to tell Andreas off. "He'll have some plan, I expect. But I agree, it doesn't look too promising."

Andreas didn't want him to agree. He wanted his senior to banish his fears, like Allaine always did.

Hugo had a quiet word with Octavian. "Stop being so hard on Andreas. You were pretty useless yourself when you first arrived in Gaul, don't forget."

Octavian told Andreas to go and befriend one of the new Juniors, a lad called Laurence, who was obviously terrified as well. He thought helping someone else might help Andreas.

Vercingetorix sent out some of his cavalry to harass the legionaries building the camp, and succeeded in killing quite a few, before withdrawing into the safety of the fortress. Andreas became even more alarmed.

"When we fight, you will stick with me," Octavian reassured him. "I'll make sure you come to no harm."

That was a lot better - Andreas thought. Why the hell hadn't Octavian said that in the first place?

It wasn't just Andreas, Octavian found, that looked at him as a substitute for Allaine. Valerius, Darius, and sometimes even Hugo, sought his advice and support. Octavian went to see General Quintus Cicero, and reminded him of his promise to Val, so Val was now a standard bearer, a soldier of some consequence, and earning a lot more money, which he gave to Octavian for safe keeping.

In Gergovia Vercingetorix summoned the tribal chiefs each morning at daybreak. He collected and disseminated information, and gave out his orders, explaining his plan of campaign.

"We have already been successful in our first skirmishes. I want the cavalry sent out every day against the enemy, with archers amongst them. This is to be a war of attrition."

He sent for his M.O. "Here, Allaine. This is a good place for our badly wounded to die in peace. We can hold this town with few forces."

"Good. We'll ask some of the women to help nurse them."

"Go and find a building you think best suits your requirements."

Allaine prowled around the town, until he found what he was looking for, a large airy brick built barn, with wide doors big enough for a wagon to pass through, and huge shuttered windows, giving excellent light, and shelter from the elements, if necessary. He set up the hospital, with the sign of a serpent coiled round a sword, painted boldly onto the door, and another sign hanging from an overhead beam, so everyone knew the building's purpose.

Caesar made a night raid, and seized a small steep hill opposite the town, to prevent the Gauls reaching part of their supplies of water and food. He constructed a small camp on the top, protected and connected to his larger camp by a twelve foot deep trench, so his troops could pass from one to the other, without fear of assault from the enemy cavalry. His men were getting fed up with the constant requirement to dig deeper and deeper trenches, so the camp servants were enjoined to dig in addition. Octavian ordered Ninian and Borus to help. Drustan wasn't yet fit for heavy work, but was well enough to fish in the local streams. He knew how to conceal himself from any of Vercingetorix's cavalry, but the horsemen didn't come down the mountain very far from their base camps, relying mostly on the archers to cause havoc. The twins knew everything about fishing. Octavian ate delicious trout, eels, lamprey, or crayfish every night, or sometimes a plateful of river mussels. It was so good to have his twins back again.

Octavian hadn't appreciated just how furious the Aeduans were, at being palmed off with Caesar, instead of himself. The new Chief Magistrate of the Aeduans, Convictolitavis, was particularly incensed.

"Why did Caesar involve himself in our dispute?" he harangued his fellow countrymen. "It's all very well seeking the help of Prince Octavian. He's an Aeduan, a magistrate, and well connected, known to be impartial, and respected by all. But Caesar! Do the Senate ask us to decide on Roman problems?" He didn't wait for an answer. "If we Aeduans side with Vercingetorix, we can throw these blasted Romans out of the country. We are the most important clan in Gaul. Our support would tilt the balance. Vercingetorix will be victorious, and we will be with him."

"We agree with you," said the eager young men. "What can we do to bring this about?"

"We must bide our time," said the Chief Magistrate. "We must be as cunning as Caesar."

The Aeduans were unaware that Metius had planted well-paid spies as slaves in the households of all the most important families. The spies reported these seditious speeches to Metius, who forwarded the information to Caesar.

The Aeduan Chief Magistrate in turn sent a message to the commander heading the ten thousand strong Aeduan infantry marching south to Gergovia. The commander claimed in a speech to his men, that two young noblemen had been accused of treason by Caesar, and killed without trial. The Aeduans were furious at the news. Their commander suggested they march immediately to join with Vercingetorix. His suggestion was greeted with huge enthusiasm.

As soon as Caesar heard about the disinformation campaign, he marched straight out of camp with four legions and all the cavalry, leaving only two legions behind under the command of General Gaius Fabius. He couldn't afford to loose all the Aeduan infantry to Vercingetorix. His troops were delighted to leave Gergovia behind. They didn't care how far they had to march, as long as it was away from what they thought of as a hopeless situation. They arrived in time to prevent the bulk of the Aeduan infantry from deserting the Roman side, but many of them had already decamped to join Vercingetorix.

The Chief Magistrate continued to promulgate the false rumours of Caesar's execution of the two young noblemen. He encouraged the populace to rise up against any Romans living in Aeduan territory. Most were enslaved or killed, and their property confiscated.

In Bibracte Marcus Metius knew there was no point in running. The entire country was in revolt. He couldn't escape this time. He explained their perilous situation to Lady Sempronia, who had come to his house in the night, seeking refuge. The hostage children staying in his house were terrified. The prisoner's wife intervened, and told them not to worry. She ordered branches of yew and oak to be nailed to the main entrance. She stood or sat at the door of the house every day, with Dòchas cradled in one arm, and a spear in the other, and dared any Gaul to cross the threshold. None did.

"This house is under the protection of the Goddess Andarta, so depart in peace," she said to anyone who thought they might easily obtain a load of expensive Roman possessions. "No one in it is to be harmed."

The marauders slunk away, apologising for the disturbance.

The Gauls in Gergovia were well aware that now the Roman camp held only two legions. The two camps were so vast, the soldiers manning the ramparts were spread so thinly, they couldn't be relieved, fighting continually, day and night. Octavian felt exhausted. He had never fought so hard or for so long without rest. He thanked the Gods and Allaine for Hugo's training. It was good, too, to have Valerius and Darius at either side, knowing how dependable they were.

Andreas was frightened again, as his sensible, kind, reassuring brother Marcius had left with Guéreth and the cavalry. The Gauls advanced a little more each day. He looked down at the enemy hordes in despair. His mouth was dry, his guts churning continually in anxiety. He'd had no sleep for four days, unable to rest even when given a short respite from duty. He couldn't stop his panicking thoughts racing through his mind. He was sure they wouldn't be able to hang on defending much longer. He decided to face up to the consequences.

"Octavian, I mean, Sir," Andreas corrected himself hastily. "We can't keep on without sleep. What will we do? Surrender?"

He got short shrift from his senior. "Don't be such an arsehole, Andreas. And don't mention the word surrender in the hearing of the troops, or I'll have your guts for a necklace. We fight to the last man."

"But Prince Allaine....."

Octavian interrupted. "Prince Allaine isn't going to be hovering around, waiting to rescue us. He'll be up in the town, tending the wounded. If the Gauls break through into this camp, Andreas, we will all be slaughtered where we stand."

Slaughtered. That ghastly word again. Why did he join the army? What the hell was he doing here? Andreas no longer knew.

Octavian turned back to encourage and praise the men. They were manning the catapults, and scorpios, causing the Gauls to fall back from the camp walls. But many of his men were getting badly wounded, with spears, arrows, and sling shot hurled at them by the enemy. Hugo conferred with General Fabius. They desperately needed help, so would have to take a risk. Fabius ordered a small party of horsemen to be sent out from the back of the camp, as silently as possible, to meet with Caesar. They got away safely and managed to find his returning legions after travelling for some thirteen miles. Caesar hurried to the rescue. At last the camp's defenders could get some well earned sleep.

Now Caesar had his six legions again, together with what was left of the Aeduan infantry. He needed to teach Vercingetorix a thing or two about war. After his men were rested, he rashly decided to make an assault on the town. A decoy of cavalry was set up, in a pretence of attacking a high ridge, which most of the Gauls were busily fortifying, thinking it was a weak point, difficult to defend. Then Caesar transferred his troops in small parties to the other end of the town, and made the attack. The soldiers had no trouble climbing over the six foot defensive wall, and fell upon the half empty Gallic camps in search of plunder. One Gallic chief, who was having a siesta, fled from the scene clad in only his shirt. The Roman soldiers pushed forwards to the foot of the ramparts.

Some of the women in the town, observing the advance of the enemy from the top of the ramparts, were terrified out of their wits. They remembered Avaricum, and the fate of its inhabitants. One or two were lowered by friends from the town walls, to give themselves up to the Romans, and hopefully escape death. But the Gallic troops quickly realised what the Romans were up to, and rushed back to man the defences. There were so many of them, and they were in such a commanding position, Caesar saw the day was lost. He ordered the trumpets to sound the retreat. The Tenth legion stopped at once, as they were with him, close by the trumpets, but the others pressed on, not having heard the signal. They hoped to scramble up the town ramparts and seize the town. The soldiers were eager for more booty, and more women to rape, more hapless victims to thrust their short swords into, up to the hilt.

One of the centurions called out to his fellow soldiers, that he would be the first onto the town wall, and thus get a huge reward from Caesar. The centurion climbed up, and stood for an instant at the top. He was killed almost immediately, his body hacked to pieces, and thrown down, together with those of his foolhardy companions. The Romans continued to fight on, regardless of the consequences. More and more were killed. They were in a hopeless position.

Altogether Caesar lost forty-six of his centurions that bloody day, and more than seven hundred soldiers, with over six thousand wounded. More than a sixth of his army out of action or dead. Once the fighting had ceased, with the officers and centurions still yelling hoarsely at the men to get back to the shelter of their camps, Andreas searched for Laurence. There was no trace of him. No one saw what happened to him. No one much cared.

The Gauls moved over the mountain slopes, collecting their wounded and dying. Inevitably they came across wounded, still living enemy. Some were killed instantly, some were forcibly carted up the slopes, taken into houses to be tortured for entertainment, or to become slaves, some were taken to the hospital. Laurence was pinned to the ground by a spear. He fainted away when they pulled it out of his shoulder.

Vercingetorix joined Lucterius and the other tribal leaders. They leaned over the town ramparts, and watched the Romans scuttling down the mountainside, retreating back inside their fortifications.

"They've lost a lot of men, today," said Vercingetorix,

grinning in satisfaction, "with many more wounded."

"At least forty centurions, we reckon, Sir. I wonder why Caesar tried to storm the town. A recipe for disaster."

"I'm glad he did," smiled his commander.

"We've won, Sir, thanks to you," Lucterius said. There were cheers and tears. Then wild celebrations.

Vercingetorix went to inspect the hospital and comfort the wounded. Many injured were being carried or stretchered in. They were assessed straight away. If there were deemed no chance of recovery, they were sent away again, to die. He found Allaine and his surgeons up to their elbows in blood, their overalls drenched, as they stemmed bleeding, and stitched up and bandaged wounds. There was no time to hypnotise anyone. The screams and cries could be heard some way from the building.

Allaine looked up briefly to see his commander.

"They've withdrawn," Vercingetorix told him.

"Tell the dying outside," Allaine said. "Give them a reason to die."

"Very well. Are those Romans?" Vercingetorix asked in surprise, noticing the uniforms under the blood and dirt.

"Yes. I'm doing nothing with them, until I know your mind. I'm not wasting catgut on them if they are to be killed."

"They're wounded, then?"

"Yes, but their wounds are recoverable. The men want to keep them, or sell them."

"How did they end up here?"

Allaine laughed. "I've no idea. One of them's an officer. Look."

"You'd better have that one, then, Allaine, as you seem to know just how to handle them. Tell the men they can have the prisoners if they wish, but they are to make sure they are properly secured. We don't have a lot of chains available, or prison space. I don't want to hear of any Roman slaves killing their masters."

"Good," Allaine declared. "I hate waste." He walked over to the vat of vinegar, and rinsed his arms and hands, then removed his blood-soaked apron.

He approached the absurdly young looking officer, who was white with blood loss and shaking with fear, convinced he was already in Hades.

"What is your name, my little one?" he asked gently.

"Laurence, Sir," whispered the boy. Oh thank the Gods, someone spoke Latin. "That is, Laurentus Cornellius Calusa."

Laurence was gripping tightly onto the wooden bench with the hand that still worked. He had already discovered to his dismay, that his other arm no longer functioned.

Allaine lightly caressed the boy's cheek. "I think Laurence will be sufficient," he said, smiling. He could see he would have no problems at all with this particular prisoner.

By now it was obvious there was no way the Romans could take Gergovia. Caesar paraded his men, telling them although he was impressed with their display of courage during the battle, it was their foolhardiness and impetuosity that had caused such havoc to his army. They were to ensure in future that they minded his own and his officer's orders, listened carefully for the signals, and not take the conduct of the action upon themselves.

Caesar was well aware this disaster was mainly of his own making. Although he blamed his troops, he should have ensured that his advancing army were always within earshot of the signalling trumpets. He should have realised a frontal assault on such an impregnable fortress was sheer folly. Audacity does not always equate with success.

"How do we withdraw, Fabius?" Caesar demanded. "We don't wish to make it look like a retreat."

But it was a retreat. There was no other word for it.

"Why not offer battle, Sir? Draw up the troops in battle formation. Vercingetorix isn't fool enough to take the offer up."

"Splendid. We will do so, Fabius. An excellent suggestion."

Caesar pulled out his army, and marched northeast to Aeduan territory. He was back at the River Allier in three days, repaired a bridge, and marched the army across.

Many of the Aeduans openly joined the rebellion. Deputations were sent to Vercingetorix; the Aeduans wished to join the victorious alliance. They attacked and slaughtered the small Roman garrison left behind at Noviodunum by Caesar. They released all the hostages, and sent them to the Aeduan magistrates at Bibracte. They had a wonderful time seizing Caesar's personal possessions, most of the stored grain, and all the horses. They ordered the town to be fired, to prevent the Romans making use of it, evacuated the people, and hid the excess grain deep in the woods.

Vercingetorix left town to carry out negotiations with his putative allies. Allaine stayed in Gergovia with the wounded.

Labienus and his four legions in the East were having no luck, either. He discovered all the tribes were ranged against him. In particular the Belgians, the most fearsome fighters, had assembled a formidable force. He soon realised there was to be no hope of conquest, and had a job to get back to his heavy baggage at Agedincum. He marched his men as quickly as possible to join up with Caesar.

Octavian was enjoying a delicious supper with his slaves, of fresh trout fried with oil and herbs, a fact noted with envy by Gaius, when he came into his brother's tent. The twins had never exerted themselves in a culinary manner for him, but then why should pigs know how to cook? Gaius was dying to tell Octavian of his adventures in the North, of the brilliant strategic manoeuvres of Labienus that had enabled them to fool the enemy, and return safely. He wanted to hear how his little brother had fared in the South, but the look on Octavian's face stopped him in his tracks. Octavian and his servants all rose to their feet.

"Can I help you, Sir?" Octavian enquired in a voice of ice.

Gaius could see it was still no good. Without a word, he

spun on his heel, and left. Octavian sat down again, and gestured to the others to do the same.

"Fucking pillock," was his only comment on the disturbance.

"What does it mean, Master? Fucking pillock?" Drustan asked.

Ye Gods, he would have to be careful, how he spoke in front of the twins. "Never, ever use those words, my pets. It is very rude. Very insulting."

"He call us 'stupid cunts,'" Drustan said, looking demurely through his long lashes at his master to see the effect.

"Oh, did he?" said Octavian wrathfully. "You must never say that either, my children, for the same reason. You hear me?"

"Yes, Master," the twins chorused, then grinned at each other.

"I apologise for my brother's bad manners," said Octavian, frowning.

The twins carefully stored up the information for future use.

The Aeduans invited Vercingetorix to Bibracte. Just about every tribe was now involved in the uprisings. The Aeduans used their influence, and the hostages they had obtained, to persuade any tribes not already committed, to join the alliance. A Pan-Gallic Council met at Bibracte. Allaine was happy to leave his patients and attend as the senior Helvetian delegate. He visited Marcus Metius, pleased to find that he and his household were safe. He ordered a Helvetian contingent to guard them, to ensure they remained safe. He was given a wonderful dinner, treated as a most honoured guest.

"Oh, I've been given another Roman slave," he told Metius. "A very young one. His name is Laurence Cornellius. If you have an opportunity, perhaps you could let his parents know he is safe. They will be worried about him."

Metius said he would do his best to see the information

reached Rome. He wondered how to frame the news, so as to keep Allaine from future harm. He alone had faith in Caesar, knowing him to be far more ruthless than Vercingetorix. Caesar would have fired Avaricum, and executed any councillors who opposed his orders. Metius didn't think the Gauls would win in the long run, especially not if they fought a pitched battle. They were so guileless, so gallant, and so gullible. Caesar tricked them at every turn. Metius loved some of them dearly. But they weren't the stuff of conquerors. They were altogether too decent, too chivalrous.

Despite their prestige the Aeduans were rejected as commanders of the Gallic army. The rest of Gaul chose Vercingetorix. No great surprise there. The young Aeduan noblemen were a little chagrined, and reluctant to take orders from an Arvernian, but did so in the name of national unity. Vercingetorix was pleased with their cavalry force, and thanked them for their efforts on his behalf. He ordered all the other tribes to supply him with cavalry and hostages. He said he would keep the infantry he already had.

"We must prevent the Romans getting corn or forage," he said. "That way we will drive them back to their own lands."

Vercingetorix ordered a widespread attack on the three tribes in the Province. This succeeded in preventing Caesar from getting any reinforcements in that direction. The Helvii were routed, the Allobroges succeeded in keeping the Gauls out, by posting pickets all along the Rhone, but all roads south were blockaded. Caesar would get no help, nothing from the Province or from Italy.

However Caesar managed to summon some German cavalry from across the Rhine. Their horses were unsuitable, not trained for the sort of close cavalry work required of them. Caesar requisitioned horses from his tribunes, and anyone else unfortunate enough to own a horse. He started to march the army south, to relieve the Province. Octavian was furious at being ordered to give up most of his horses. Darius was inconsolable to lose his one and only. Octavian promised him he would get him another, when the war ended.

Vercingetorix assembled his cavalry and infantry ten miles from the Romans, in the country of the Sequani. He called his cavalry officers to a council of war.

"We are near the moment of victory," he said. "The Romans are trying to flee to the Province. This is good, but if we don't defeat them now, they will be back in increasing numbers next year. But to ensure they never return, we will attack them while they are marching, encumbered by their baggage. You know their cavalry won't dare leave the ranks to fight. We will halt their infantry, and prevent them continuing on their march South. But more likely they will run, to save their own skins, and then we will strip them of their supplies, without which they will not be able to survive."

All the cavalry took an oath, that they would ride twice through the enemy lines, before they would see their wives, children, or parents again.

The next day Vercingetorix drew up all his infantry in front of his camps. He divided the cavalry into three sections. Two sections attacked the Roman column on each side, the third section formed a barrier across the rear. Caesar divided his cavalry in the same way, and launched a counter attack. He ordered up the infantry if he saw any part of the column wavering. The German horsemen managed to overcome the Gallic cavalry on high ground, and charged, scattering the enemy. This put heart into the Romans, and encouraged the rest of the cavalry to repulse the attack. The Gauls were terrified they would be surrounded, and dispersed rapidly, losing many men in the process.

Vercingetorix was horrified at the defeat of his cavalry, the part of his army on which he had placed the most reliance. How could it have happened? Defeated by the Germans, for the Gods' sake! Not even trained men! He hastily evacuated his infantry camps, formed up his troops, and marched them to Alesia, a

608

nearby fortress town, stronghold of the Mandubii, ordering the heavy baggage to be packed up and brought to him immediately.

Caesar secured his own baggage, putting a couple of legions in charge on high ground, and followed after, managing to kill considerable numbers of the enemy at the rear of their column.

Allaine was so thankful to Hugo for his training throughout the winter months. He organised the defence of the baggage and the wounded, managing to hold off the Romans successfully, until he reached the safety of the Alesia town gates.

BOOK 4: CHAPTER 7

Alesia (Mont-Auxois), Summer, Autumn 52 BC

As soon as Caesar arrived at Alesia he realised there was no way he could take the town by direct assault. It perched on a high steeply sloping hill. The Gauls had already fortified their camp below the town ramparts on the east side, with a deep trench and a wall. These Gauls were learning the art of warfare far too quickly.

Caesar summoned his generals and senior officers. "We have to be prepared for another long siege, I'm afraid," he advised them. "The troops will complain more than usual, as we have to carry out very extensive earthworks, I should think more than ten miles in diameter."

He showed them the plan devised by his engineering corps, a deep ditch round every part of the hill that could be accessed, eight main camps, and many redoubts, to prevent any surprise attack.

Vercingetorix sent out his cavalry in an attempt to disrupt the Romans' earthworks, and get food supplies, only to be defeated, again by the German reinforcements. He decided to send the cavalry away, before the encirclement was completed, to summon help. He sent for his generals, and the tribal chiefs.

"I have made a careful calculation," Vercingetorix explained. "We have enough corn for a month, maybe a bit longer, with strict rationing. I will share out the cattle immediately, as there is no fodder available. I want all the cavalry to leave tonight, before we are completely enclosed. Tell the other tribes we desperately need help, if we are not to succumb to the cruel vengeance of the Romans. Remember Avaricum."

The partings were emotional, they hugged and kissed each other, and wished each other good fortune. Many were in tears, at the thought of leaving their comrades to face the Romans.

Vercingetorix was insistent. "Allaine, you will go out with the cavalry."

"No, Sir."

"Allaine, you are very bad at taking orders. You will go out with the cavalry. You are too important to the world. I will not let you be captured. Do you hear?"

Allaine was close to tears himself.

"I feel I'm deserting you, just when I'm needed most."

"Nonsense. Go with Prince Jayven to Bibracte, and tell them to send an army as soon as possible. Go back to your mountains, to your brother Coevorten, and get me some more Helvetians, you are such great fighters. But once there, you are to stay there, do you hear me, Allaine? Run your hospital. Perfect your techniques. We still have a chance of winning. As long as my country fights to relieve us. So go with a good heart, my dear friend. And my thanks for your brilliant work."

They left at midnight, slipping silently out from the town gates, horses' hooves deliberately silenced. Jay took his leave of Allaine. He was going straight to the Aeduans, to recruit as many young nobles as possible, together with their men. He intended to implore any waverers to join the war, and relieve Alesia. Allaine went to Gergovia first, to check up on his patients, and pick up his new Roman slave. Having a captive Roman made him feel much better.

Caesar grinned in delight, very satisfied with his plans, when told the Gallic cavalry had dispersed. "We've got them, now. There's no way they can get any more food, and there are eighty thousand of their infantry to feed, plus the population of the town. We will starve them into surrender."

Every able man was impressed to make the entrenchments. A twenty foot wide trench encircled the town, with deep perpendicular walls. Two other trenches were dug further away, one filled with water diverted from a stream. Behind the trenches a huge rampart was erected, with the branches of trees projecting outwards towards the town, to deter the enemy from climbing over. More trenches were dug, filled with sharpened spikes, to impale anyone or any horse trying to cross. The ground between the trenches was covered with three foot spikes, protruding from the earth. Iron hooks attached to thick blocks of wood, were scattered everywhere.

Now the Romans needed to protect their camp from outside attack. The relieving army would soon be arriving. They must be prepared. So Caesar ordered further entrenchments facing outwards, over fourteen miles in circumference.

Guéreth was finding the brothers' feud increasingly difficult. Octavian spent a lot of his spare time with the Aeduans, not that there was much spare time. There was so much timber required for the defence works, he told the twins and Borus to assist with its cutting. He wouldn't allow any of them to dig, though, this time. The Gauls didn't watch the trap being sprung without attempting to do something about it. They charged out of the town gates, attempting to disrupt the diggers. It was dangerous work. Both sides suffered casualties. Every Roman was required to provide themselves with enough provisions for a month, and with sufficient fodder for the horses. Octavian liked his food, so abjured the twins to provide food for two months, just in case. The twins arrived back one day with a nanny goat, in milk.

"What's it going to eat?" Octavian asked in surprise.

"Goats eat anything," the twins told him. Each day they pegged the goat out on another piece of ground. They milked it every day to make cheese. They trapped birds in nets, by putting out crumbs of bread or dried peas. There was no point in fishing near Alesia as the Gauls had netted the streams running through the small amount of territory they held. The twins brought back a sackful of apples, and fermented them in a barrel, making a surprisingly potent drink. There began to be a certain amount of rivalry between the twins and Gaius's prisoner, as to who could provide the best meal for their masters.

Gaius was worried about Fáelán. The boy found the awful preparations for battle terrifying. Gaius had hoped he would have a chance of getting him to his mother in Bibracte, but there had not been time. Fáelán found it difficult to eat the coarse bread, and strange bits of meat he was given. He felt scared all the time, despite his father's and his master's constant reassurances. If only *they* had a goat, thought the prisoner.

Gaius decided to have one last try. He had to make it sound official to start with, or Octavian wouldn't even let him open his mouth.

"Tribune, I've a non-combatant in my tent, a servant of mine. He is having difficulty eating. His father thinks he could do with some of your goat's milk."

"Bring him here," Octavian replied, brusquely.

Gaius returned with Fáelán and his father.

"What are you thinking of, bringing a child like that here?" Octavian asked. He hadn't known Fáelán existed, as Gaius hardly allowed the child out of his tent, worried he would be molested. He was a pretty little boy, and the men had had no access to women for weeks, now. No traders were stupid enough to come to Alesia.

The twins were intrigued. Ninian held out his hand to the boy. "Come, come see the goat," he coaxed. Fáelán trustingly put his hand into the big boy's hand.

"I'll order the twins to look after him, and give him milk, if you wish, Sir," Octavian told his brother.

So he was still a Sir. No thaw in relations. At least Fáelán might improve, even if nothing else did.

Far away from Alesia the Gauls convened a council to summon men for the relief of their commander and his infantry. But getting everyone's agreement, and mobilising the troops all took precious time. Agreement was much more difficult to come by, when Vercingetorix wasn't there to inspire them. Commius, together with the two young Aeduan nobles, Eporedorix, and

613

Viridomarus, who had taken Noviodunum, and a cousin of Vercingetorix, Vercassivellaunus, were given charge of the army, together with military advisors from each tribe. They set out for Alesia full of confidence. Their numbers were vast, causing logistical problems, that their leaders weren't all that successful in overcoming.

By now after a month, Vercingetorix had hoped to be relieved. There was no more corn. Every dog, cat and mule had been eaten. The few horses remaining were severely undernourished, their coats and eyes dull, their muscles wasting away. Even the rats the people caught were starved, and provided little in the way of nourishment. There were no fish left in the streams, and few birds in the sky. Their situation was now desperate. Vercingetorix called a council meeting of all the chiefs.

One of the chiefs suggested they start eating those unable to fight. He was very eloquent on the subject. At the end of the meeting, despite Vercingetorix's vehement protests, that these were the very people he was fighting for, the council overruled him. It was decided that those unable to bear arms, the old, the women and children, should be evicted from the town. Vercingetorix was in despair. Morcant, Jay's cousin, came to sit by his side, a hand on his shoulder.

"We have no choice, Sire. We have no food to give them. We have no food for ourselves. We might hold out for a couple more weeks, but the children will surely die. Caesar will take them in, Sire. Caesar will feed them."

"Don't be a fool, Morcant. Caesar will do no such thing. He regards us as subhuman, an inferior species. He has no kindness in him. He is pure ambition. And thus pure evil as far as we are concerned. Look at his treatment of Prince Acco. Look at his treatment of the babies at Avaricum. He knows no mercy if he doesn't get exactly what he wants."

Octavian saw the town gates open, and got his men ready to repulse any attack. But there was no attack. Instead, a stream of pitifully thin people filed out of the gates, clutching infants and babies to their breasts, holding starving children by the hand. They tried unsuccessfully to get through the fortifications, and stood helplessly, weeping, pleading, begging the legionaries for food. But Caesar ordered the guards to allow no one through, and no one was permitted to throw any food to the starving. Anyone caught being stupid enough to do so faced a severe penalty. The women pulled down their dresses, exposing breasts, and pulled up their skirts exposing everything else, to no avail. It just wasn't worth the risk, even in the dark.

"He'll take them back in," Caesar assured Octavian, when he came to ask if a passage could be made through the Roman lines, to allow the Mandubians to escape.

"But if he doesn't, Sir?" Octavian was in despair. "They'll be crushed by the fighting. It won't look good back in Rome, Sir."

"Octavian, you are becoming too enamoured of our enemies for my liking. Let us hope the issues will be decided within the next few days. Then we can relieve their distress."

"Surely, Caesar, we can open a passage through our lines, and let the Mandubii out. They are non-combatants, women, children, old men incapable of fighting."

"My dear boy, you must try and curb these excesses of sentimentality. We are trying to win a war. If Vercingetorix won't feed his people, why on earth should I? He will take them back into the town, and thus shorten the siege, and reduce the casualties amongst our own men."

"He won't take them back," said Octavian bitterly. "He knows this is his last chance."

At last the relieving army arrived. The besieged were delirious with excitement. The next day the cavalry on both sides fought on the plain in front of the town. Vercingetorix led his troops out, carrying woven willow platforms and grappling hooks, to try to overcome the Roman defence works. The battle went on all day. It was won eventually when Caesar's German horse charged together, and broke the Gallic lines. They were

615

pursued back to their camps. Vercingetorix led his disheartened troops back inside the town.

There was a day of relative inactivity, just a few skirmishes, as the fighting men tried to rest and rebuild their stamina, but then the Gauls set out at midnight to attack again. It was too dark to see. The fighting went on all through the night. Vercingetorix led out his troops again, but at dawn the Gauls were forced to retreat back to the plain, having been repulsed by stones, missiles, javelins, and the spiked ditches. Those in Alesia had to go back as well, leaving behind many dead, and most of their equipment. They were rapidly running out of weapons as well as food, and also the willows and wood used to make the ramps to try and bridge the trenches.

After another council of war, Vercassevellaunus was told to take sixty thousand of the best fighting men, ascend a hill where the enemy had two legions posted, and attack at their weakest point. This was the deciding battle. Vercingetorix made one more supreme effort to break through the enemy fortifications. The Romans were attacked from the front and the rear, but held their places. Labienus was sent to strengthen the hill with his men. Caesar was always there, in his scarlet cloak, rushing up and down the lines to send reinforcements to the point wherever it seemed the Gauls might break through.

When it looked as if the Roman line would be breached, Caesar sent out the cavalry outside the outer ring of defences, and took the Gauls by surprise. Attacked from both sides themselves, their line broke, and scattered. Now the Roman cavalry were in pursuit, and chased the Gauls all the way back to their camps, capturing many prisoners, and seventy-six of the Gauls' battle standards.

Vercingetorix gave up hope. He called his starving men back into the town. The next day he assembled them all together, and made his last speech to his devastated troops. Many started to cry openly, even before he had finished.

"Men, I am proud to have fought with you. We have done our utmost to win this battle. But I can't sacrifice any more of you. I began this campaign, not for my own personal glory, but for my beloved country's prestige, and for the liberty of all. I have failed you, and must now accept the destiny the Gods have allotted me. You may either kill me, or deliver me alive to Caesar."

Morcant stood up, protesting violently. "No, Sire, no. Please, please don't sacrifice yourself like this. You have done your utmost. It is we who have let you down. We have not fought hard enough. Give us another chance. Lead us out tomorrow. We will die with you." He choked, as tears started to stream down his cheeks.

The men shouted their agreement. But Vercingetorix merely shook his head.

"No, Morcant. There have been deaths enough. It is decided."

A deputation was to be sent to the Romans, asking for terms. The small group of men rode down the hill to the first of the Roman defence works, carrying the battle standard, with the black flag of surrender attached. They reined in, bewildered and confused, on the far side of the deep trench.

"Well, lads, we've been given an order," said their leader, "probably the last one our Commander will ever give to us. So we will just have to carry it out."

No one made any effort to help them. The legionaries stared, grinning at the spectacle. The Gauls had to abandon their weakened horses, and climb down the steep slopes of the trench, then pick their way carefully over the heaped bodies of their comrades, crushed and impaled on the sharpened stakes, grotesque in death. They tried to avoid getting their clothes and feet caught on the slippery protruding limbs, or the iron hooks underneath. They waded across the deep flooded ditch filled with stinking liquids too foul to contemplate, and stood muddy, dishevelled, soiled and shamed before the Roman lines. A centurion conducted the group to the Praesidium, to kneel frozen-faced at Caesar's feet. They were offered no food or water, before being ordered to return to the town the way they had come, to await Caesar's pleasure. A foretaste of what was in store for them all; total humiliation for the defeated, the vanquished, the conquered.

Once the last of the dejected delegates had clambered back out of the last ditch, the Roman engineers, smiling with satisfaction, set to work to bridge the trenches.

Caesar sent back Gaius and Octavian Volusenus.

With a heavy heart Octavian accompanied his brother and their escort, riding slowly up the steep hill to the gates of Alesia, carefully picking his way to avoid the maimed, mangled, vile-smelling corpses, both humans and horses, lying on the ground in varying stages of decomposition. Clouds of buzzing flies rose into the sultry air. Crows flapped away as they passed, only to return. The enemy had no strength left to bury or burn their dead.

The twins had burnished Octavian's armour, and his horse's accoutrements till they glistened and gleamed in the strong October sun. The red-dyed plumes of his helmet were blood coloured, immaculately brushed and trimmed. Even his horse's coat shone. He looked every inch a conquering hero. A lone bugler played a dirge as they approached the Gallic headquarters, passing through rows of silent sullen men, their faces masks of hatred.

The brothers dismounted. Octavian stood quietly while a slave attendant hastened to remove his cloak and unbuckle his helmet. He took a deep breath, and with a feeling in his gut that he was about to be sick, he walked through the entrance of the building.

Vercingetorix rose to greet him.

"Octavian!" he said, serious but smiling a little, pleased to see such a familiar face.

"Octavian!" Gaius echoed aghast, as he watched his brother sink to his knees in front of the Gallic commander.

Octavian kissed the hand held out to him, and rose to his feet, to be pulled forwards and kissed on both cheeks. Several men then came up to him, greeting him with familiarity, and shaking his hand, or kissing him. They looked weary, some wounded, all thin and drawn, but they made an effort also to be courteous to Gaius, and bowed to him politely.

"You are well?" Vercingetorix enquired.

"Yes, Sir. I'm fine. A few scratches, that's all. May I present my brother, Gaius Volusenus?"

Vercingetorix held out his hand, saying, "Welcome, Gaius." Gaius took it in his own, expecting a bone crushing grip, but received a friendly clasp instead. He was feeling things weren't quite going the way he'd expected. "I presume you are here to tell me my fate?" Vercingetorix continued, looking from one to the other.

"Yes, Sir," Octavian answered. "We're here to discuss the terms of your surrender. My brother doesn't speak Gallic, so I thought I would explain them to you, and one of your interpreters can say it back to him? So we all know exactly what we have agreed?"

"Yes, that's a good idea," Vercingetorix responded in perfect Latin, to Gaius's surprise. "Now come and sit down, both of you."

They were led over to a long table, on which were wine goblets full to the brim, plates of tiny savoury rolls, and the familiar spiced sausages.

"No shellfish for you, I'm afraid, Octavian," Vercingetorix said. "Now, eat, drink, and then talk."

"We can't eat their food," Gaius whispered to his brother, in horror.

Octavian turned on him. Hadn't his brother learnt anything at all, while in Gaul? He'd been here long enough.

"It would be the height of bad manners to refuse. Eat, and say 'Thank you' properly when you've finished."

"If you're sure," Gaius said doubtfully, and reached for the sausages.

"Made from dead Romans, Gaius," teased a dark-haired Gaul, with his right arm in a sling. "Very tasty."

"You bastard, Morcant!" Gaius recognised Jay's cousin, as his hand hovered over the dish. He felt slightly sick.

"You can't say that!" Octavian said in alarm.

"I assure you it's not human meat," Vercingetorix said soothingly to Gaius, as he noticed his hesitation. "Although I'm afraid it was suggested at one point."

A loud rumbling noise came from the stomach of one of the Gauls. Vercingetorix turned round and said something, which made everyone laugh, including Octavian.

"Now," Vercingetorix said, when they had finished eating and drinking. "The terms."

Octavian turned a little pale, and tried to brace himself. "Yes, Sir. Caesar desires that the Aeduans and Arvernians are to be separated from the others. They will be handed over to their tribal chiefs. The rest of the captives will be given as booty to the legionaries. I suggest that if you agree to this, it would be best if no one declare themselves an Eburone."

"And what does Caesar suggest for me?" Vercingetorix asked.

"He wishes you to surrender to him publicly, this afternoon if possible." Oh fuck, thought Octavian, as his eyes welled up.

"And then?"

"He says you will be imprisoned. He presumes the Senate will award him a Triumph. You will be made to walk, or be dragged behind his chariot through the streets of Rome, and then you will be killed."

"By what method?"

620

Octavian was finding it increasingly difficult to get the words out. "By strangling, or beheading. A quick death, eventually. He promises." A tear dripped down his face, and dropped onto the table. "Oh, hell!"

Vercingetorix leant forwards, and covered his clasped hands with his own.

"Don't get upset, Octavian. I know my role. I am the sacrificial victim. But you mustn't worry. You know I won't be there. I will have gone long since."

"Yes, Sir. I know," Octavian said. He compressed his lips in a hard line in a vain effort to stop the tears.

Gaius thought it was time to intervene. "Hey, you! Pull yourself together," he hissed to his brother.

"It's not his fault, is it? It's because of his head injury," Vercingetorix assured Gaius.

"What head injury?" Gaius asked, very confused. How was it the Gallic commander knew more about his brother than he did himself?

Octavian wiped his face on a napkin, and sniffed vigorously. "Sir, do you have any news of my master?"

"I sent him away with the cavalry. I think he has already paid too high a price for being captured, don't you? He will be back in his mountains by now."

A man stepped forwards. "May I speak, Sir?" His commander nodded. "You have a niece, Octavian. I was at the naming ceremony. She is called Claudia. Prince Allaine said in his speech, that it would please his Roman relatives."

"It pleases us very much." Octavian waited, while this was being translated back to Gaius, who was even more bewildered.

"Who are we talking about?" Gaius asked.

"Prince Allaine, Chrys's brother. He married Guéreth's sister, Riona, and they've had a baby, and called her after Mother."

"But I thought he was dead."

"Obviously not," Vercingetorix said, with a slight smile.

"Ask about Jay," said Gaius.

Vercingetorix shook his head. "I've heard nothing. We were unable to communicate with the relieving forces. He went out with the cavalry as well, of course." He looked at the Roman delegation. "Congratulations. You have won a great victory. I wish you'd look a bit more pleased about it, Octavian. The terms are a little more generous than we expected, so..." He turned to his companions. "If we are agreed, Gentlemen?"

There was a murmur of assent.

"I accept the terms offered by Caesar. I will personally surrender myself to him this afternoon. However I respectfully request that Octavian be put in charge of the prisoners."

"Me?" Octavian's voice came out at a much higher pitch than normal. He cleared his throat, and tried again. "Do you mean me, Sir?"

"Yes, you. Of course you. You speak the languages, you know the people. You are respected."

"Is that a condition of your surrender, Sir?" Gaius wasn't sure how Caesar would react to this.

"No, Gaius. I'm in no position to impose conditions. It is a request, nothing more."

"Caesar would like you to dine with him this evening, Sir," Gaius added.

"Dine with him?" Vercingetorix asked in astonishment.

"You must have got that wrong, Gaius," Octavian interposed. He couldn't imagine Caesar being polite to a conquered barbarian enemy. Look at the disgusting way he had just treated the delegates.

"Well that's what he said. He told me he writes these commentaries at the end of each year's campaign. I believe he wants to check that he has the facts correct, and he would like to hear about your speeches. They are reckoned to be inspirational. I believe Caesar has the greatest admiration for you, Sir," Gaius ended.

"Unfortunately he said the same to Prince Allaine. So I don't think I'd better set too much store by that."

"I think he will be trying to humiliate you, Sir, at least," said Octavian. He spoke in Latin, not wanting the others to understand. "He'll have you in chains, on the ground. Don't expect any mercy from Caesar."

"I am sure you are correct, Octavian. If he wishes to hear my speeches, my secretary has notes of them all. I would like you to have him, Octavian. He is my most prized possession. If you are assigned to look after the prisoners, he will be invaluable to you." Vercingetorix beckoned to a nicely dressed very slim young man, who stepped forwards. Octavian could see from his expression how distressed he was. Vercingetorix took the man by the wrist. "Here, Octavian, this is Gregor, my secretary. Take his hand."

Octavian did as requested.

"Gregor, this is Octavian, your new master. You will serve him as well as you have served me."

"Yes, Master." Gregor looked horrified at Octavian for an instant, then he knelt on the ground, and dutifully kissed Octavian's hand. Octavian gave him the formal Gallic words of welcome, which made Gregor look a little less frightened.

"What will you do when your army service comes to an end?" Vercingetorix asked Octavian, as Gregor went to pack his equipment and fetch his horse.

"I'm going to bring Chrys and the children to the beautiful estate she brought me as her dowry, land near the Loire. And I will plant a vineyard. It will be my kingdom. No one will ever be unjustly killed there, neither slave or freeman. This I swear to you, Sir."

"Goodbye, Octavian, you give me hope for the future. Goodbye, Gaius. May good fortune go with you both."

The little knot of Roman emissaries waited patiently until Gregor brought up and mounted his horse, a sad-looking hack. Then they returned to their camp. The camp servants had already started the unenviable task of dismantling the fortifications, salvaging the stakes and hooks, to be packed up with the ballistae

and the rest of the heavy baggage.
    Octavian felt utterly miserable.

BOOK 4 : CHAPTER 8

Alesia, Autumn 52 BC

Hector was getting old and stiff. If he had belonged to anyone other than Tribune Gaius Volusenus, he would have been cooked and eaten by now. He knew not to stray far from the Tribune's tent. He couldn't understand Valerius's attachment to a dog as inferior as Ajax.

Jay's horse had been found wandering disconsolately round the battlefield, after the headlong retreat of the Gallic cavalry, but of Jay there was no sign and no news. No one seemed to have noticed what had happened to him. With a heavy heart Gaius called to Hector, put him on his lead, and walked over to the compound where the mass of prisoners were being held. He was frightened of what he might find.

Gaius was surrounded by a sea of hatred. He walked slowly up and down the long lines of defeated, dispirited men. He had almost given up hope, when Hector lifted his nose and scented the air. Then the dog made off, limping stiffly along, tugging continually at the lead. Gaius allowed himself to be pulled along. Hector was making a strange whining noise in his throat. He seemed to be looking ahead to where two decurions were standing in front of a group of prisoners.

Gaius heard one of them say, "I like the look of this one, myself."

Hector gave a deep warning growl. The decurion grabbed hold of Jay's hair, and forced his head back. Hector yanked so hard, he pulled the lead right out of Gaius's hand, and bounded off. He was still a big heavy dog. He leapt straight for the decurion's throat and knocked him to the ground. The decurion screamed in agony, as Hector's teeth closed on his skin. His companion unsheathed his sword.

"Stop that at once," Gaius yelled at him. "Put that sword away."

"Call the dog off, Sir," the other decurion shouted in panic.

Gaius ran up, and grabbed Hector's collar. At first Hector wouldn't release his victim, keeping up a continual fierce growling, while he was standing over him, jaws clamped together. Blood poured from the decurion's throat. Gaius had to shout and punch the dog's head to make him obey and let go. Deep teeth marks punctured the decurion's neck.

"Get him over to the hospital tent," Gaius ordered.

The injured decurion managed to sit up, very shaken. He was led away by his companion, clutching his neck, and swearing vociferously.

Jay was sitting on the ground, holding tightly onto Hector's lead. Hector was standing in front of him, barking madly, and then began licking his face with enthusiasm. Gaius followed slowly. He could see that Jay was not amused. He went to pull the dog away, but Hector gave a little whine of happiness, and lay as close as he could get to his adored friend, trying to shove his head under Jay's arm. Gaius could see no sign of injury, and felt a wave of relief. But the next part was going to be much harder. Jayven wouldn't look at him.

"Jay, Caesar has ordered that every soldier is to have a prisoner of their own, to keep or to sell. You are mine."

Jay said nothing.

"Jay! You're coming with me." Gaius knelt down and pulled Jay's chained hands into his own.

Jay spat in his face.

Gaius slapped him hard. Hector growled, and then barked. He wasn't going to allow his favourite human to be hit.

Jay grabbed his collar, and hung on grimly. "Fucking bastard," he snarled.

Gaius called a centurion over. "Get up," he ordered, and dragged Jay to his feet. "Get the chains off this prisoner and take him over to my quarters. Make sure he behaves," Gaius told the centurion. Damn Jay for making him lose his temper.

Gaius walked to the Praesidium to find out if there were any further orders. There weren't. He didn't mention Jay.

His brother was in charge of the prisoners, as Vercingetorix had suggested. He appeared to be making an excellent job of it, giving his orders clearly and crisply. There was no necessity for Gaius to intervene. Octavian told him sharply he needed no help from someone who, he said sarcastically, couldn't even communicate with most of the captives.

Gaius returned to his tent. There was no mistaking the malignantly of Jayven's gaze. There was naked hatred in his face. Gaius had thought it would be a simple matter. He began to realise his mistake. Jay sat with his arms folded, trying to keep his shoulder still. He assumed that eventually Gaius would get tired of his silence, and have him taken back to his men. He was finding it difficult to control the pain from his wounds, but he could feel the bleeding had started again, seeping from his groin down to his thigh. Fortunately his clothes were dark, and so far Gaius hadn't noticed. When the prisoner served the food, Gaius pushed it away with an angry gesture. Jayven also refused to eat. Gaius sat on the bed, staring at the wall of the tent. Octavian wouldn't speak to him, now Jay wouldn't speak to him. The prisoner looked miserable, Fáelán wouldn't eat. What the hell was it all for? All the fighting, all the killing. He felt so depressed. Most of his Aeduan friends were either dead, or had joined the revolt. Only Guéreth stayed the same, but even he was finding this victory hard. To Gaius's astonishment a standard bearer in full regalia, and with his standard in his hand, marched into the tent, and saluted. Then broke into a beaming smile, and pulled off his headgear.

"Permission to speak to Prince Jayven, Sir?" Valerius asked.

"Help yourself," responded Gaius morosely. The news had got out, then.

Val walked swiftly over to Jay, slammed onto his knees in front of him, took hold of his hand, and kissed it. Hector wandered up to greet him with a friendly lick, smelt Jay's blood, now dripping onto the ground, and started a low soft whining noise in his throat.

"Hello, Sir," said Val happily, not in any way concerned about his reception, and Jay's scowl. "It's so good to see you again. We were so worried, weren't we Sir?" He turned to Gaius for confirmation. "And when we couldn't see your horse anymore, we were worried out of our minds. Anyway, he's outside."

"Whose outside?" Jay found himself asking. Val's smile was difficult to resist.

"Your horse, Sir. I've been looking after him, ever since we got him. I knew you'd be worried and want him back."

Val was looking at him with something like adoration. He considered Jay to be at only one remove from Allaine. "I'm so glad you're here again, Sir. And look!" Val walked over to the standard, and brought it for Jay to see. "That's my standard. See? Its the Eagle! I've been made a standard bearer for the whole legion. Even though I didn't succeed in getting through Ambiorix's lines, General Cicero made me a standard bearer anyway. Octavian asked him to do it. Isn't it marvellous?"

"Marvellous," returned Jay, wearily.

"That's why I brought it to show you. I knew you'd be pleased," Valerius said, with growing confidence. "Would you like to see your horse....?" He paused, staring at the ground, and then at Jay. "Sir! You're bleeding!"

"What?" Gaius jumped to his feet.

"Look," said Valerius in alarm. "He's bleeding all over the floor. Why didn't you say anything, Sir?"

"Maybe I didn't want to," said Jay.

"Quick, Tribune. Send for Octavian." Valerius was now kneeling on the ground, the heel of his hand pressing hard against the bleeding point in Jay's groin.

"Don't be daft, Val, we need a surgeon," Gaius said in panic.

"We need Octavian. He knows more about wounds than

any of those idiots in the hospital tent. He was trained by Prince Allaine himself. What do you say, Sir?" Val asked Jay.

"Get Octavian by all means, and keep it in the family." Jay gave a bitter smile.

Octavian appeared nowhere near soon enough, as far as Valerius was concerned. He immediately took charge.

"Hello, Sir. I think we had better get you over to the hospital tent, where the light is better. Then I can see what needs doing. You come too, Val."

"I'm coming as well," Gaius insisted.

"As you wish, Sir," said Octavian, with indifference.

"Could you organise some more light, Sir?" Octavian asked his brother with great formality. "And I need these instruments doused in boiling water. There's no great urgency, now the bleeding has stopped," he added in irritation, as Gaius started to yell orders.

Gaius looked at him with incredulity, wondering how his brother had acquired such self assurance, and such a beautiful set of surgical implements.

With the help of the orderlies Octavian and Valerius got Jay stripped, and everything prepared.

"I need your permission, Sir," said Octavian to Jayven.

"Balls!" Gaius interrupted. "He's a prisoner. Just get on with it. If you know how, that is." He was worried Jay might refuse treatment. Worried also that Octavian would be out of his depth.

"Do what you like," said Jay, in his tired voice.

"I'm going to castrate you, with a blunt scalpel," Octavian responded immediately.

Valerius laughed. Jay gave the ghost of a smile, and his dark eyes opened. "Octavian," he warned.

"Just checking, Sir," said Octavian, smiling sweetly. "We will suture the hip wound first, and make sure the bleeding has stopped, then the shoulder, and lastly I will lance the abscess." He faced Valerius. "Ready?"

"It's just like old times, isn't it, Octavian," said Valerius gleefully. "All of us together again."

Gaius took up his position next to Jay, and armed himself with a bowl of water, and some damp sponges.

"First we need to disinfect the wounds," Octavian explained, "which will hurt a lot," he added, pouring raw vinegar into the bloody mess of flesh. The barbed spear had struck the pelvic bones, and veered upwards. Gaius caught Jay's hand as he felt for something to grab. Jay groaned aloud, trying vainly to cope with the deep pain.

"You bastard, Octavian," Gaius shouted, as his hand was crushed. Octavian ignored him.

"Now, Sir. I am going to strap you down. I can't have you moving about, while I'm stitching you back together."

They worked quickly, as a perfect team. Val threaded the needles, cut the stitches, and held the retractors. Octavian brought the flesh together with deep sutures, put ragged skin edge to edge, until the gaping wound disappeared, leaving only a neat double track of stitches winding round the hip bone.

Jay found it impossible to keep still, or to keep quiet. He writhed around in huge discomfort, but it often became too much to bear altogether, and he cried out. Gaius held his hand in a tight grip, and mopped the sweat from his forehead and face, wondering all the time where in hell his brother had learnt this astonishing skill.

"How are you feeling, Sir?" Octavian asked, before tackling the shoulder wound.

"Defeated!" Jay glowered at him. "Conquered, vanquished, crushed. How do you expect me to feel?"

"Sorry, Sir. I meant how do you feel physically?"

"Never felt better," said Jay, crossly. "Stop asking me stupid questions, and get on with it."

Octavian and Val looked at each other, and grinned. Their patient was doing alright, so far. They moved to deal with the shoulder.

"I think he's died," said Gaius in a panic, as Jay lost consciousness when the antiseptic was poured in.

"He's fine, Sir," Octavian responded, and carried on working. He felt a hand on the back of his neck.

"Fuck off, Ruteus."

"My dear boy!" Caesar remonstrated. Octavian looked up in alarm to see that Valerius had risen silently to his feet, and was standing at rigid attention. "No, don't get up." Octavian felt the fingers pressing him down. "You should always ascertain to whom you are speaking, before telling them to fuck off."

"My apologies, Caesar," Octavian stammered.

"How is the patient, Gaius?" Caesar moved to take a seat beside Jay.

"Octavian seems to think he's alright, Caesar," Gaius responded. "He doesn't look very well to me."

Octavian began to get irritated again. "He's fainted, that's all. May I continue, Caesar?" It was much easier to suture an unconscious patient. Octavian was angry to think time was being wasted. Caesar waited patiently for his prey to revive.

Jay struggled back to a bad world. He opened his eyes to see his mortal enemy gazing down at him, smiling, gloating at his discomfiture.

"Jay, my dear boy. I'm so glad you've come home to us." Caesar bent forwards, and kissed Jay full on the mouth. Jay's hands curled into balled fists.

Thank the Gods he's strapped down, thought Octavian.

Jay was looking venomously at Caesar.

"I can speak Greek," he said. If he'd hoped to disconcert his captor, he failed miserably.

"Of course you can, my dear boy," Caesar replied with a gentle smile. He so enjoyed the look of hatred the prisoner gave him, as Jay turned his head sharply away. Wonderful to have such power over such a man. He knew they were all wondering what he was going to do to Jay. They were remembering that brave young Helvetian. Unfortunate that the young man had been destroyed with the other prisoners. He had forgotten all about him. An error. Philemon had been severely punished for that error. Caesar smiled at the memory. However, this was different. There was no need to punish the Gauls any more for the time being. The issue had been decided. Gaul was his now. And if anyone disagreed with this in the future, they would find that mercy did not extend to them.

"Listen Jayven, I used you and you used me. But I stand by what I said. I wish I had son like you, courageous, principled. You are young, Jay, and resilient. One day you won't hate me so much. And although it is right and proper to die for one's country, my dear Jay, it is infinitely preferable to live for one's country. Gaul needs men like you."

Jay said nothing, just glared.

"Ah, Jay," Caesar continued to smile. "If looks could only kill, eh?" He looked round at the others. "Now Gaius, Octavian, I insist you two join me for dinner tonight."

They muttered their thanks.

"You as well, Jay, dear boy."

"Caesar, I must protest. He will be far too ill."

"Pity. His general will be there." Caesar laughed at their horrified expressions, and walked out of the tent.

"I'm going to throw up," said Jay.

"I don't blame you," Gaius replied.

Octavian knew better, hurriedly moving to unbuckle the straps. "Val, get a bucket," he ordered, and heaved Jay to a sitting position.

Val thrust the bucket under Jay's nose just in time, as he started to retch.

"Here, Sir," said Val, when Jay had ceased. "Have some water, rinse your mouth out."

Gaius was ineffectually rubbing Jay's back, saying, "It's alright, Jay, it will be alright."

"No, you idiot," snarled Jay. "It couldn't be more fucking

wrong." He started to cry weakly.

Gaius looked at him in despair. He had known Jay for years, had watched him grow from a charming youth into a battle hardened warrior. Jay was the love of his life, he realised in that moment. Yes, he had loved Lucy, but this love was quite different. This love was a man's love for his friend, a love that needed no physical act to cement it. A love so deep, he would never be able to express it in words. He knew he would do anything for Jay. Lay down his life for Jay. Kill for Jay.

"Jay, listen." Gaius grabbed his shoulder. "I'll kill him. Say the word, and I'll kill him for you tonight."

"Don't be so stupid."

"No, I mean it, Jay. I've never meant anything more in my life. What's he done for me? Lucy's dead. Half my friends are gone. My brother won't even talk to me. And you hate me, don't you? I can't stand that. You hating me. I can't stand it," he repeated, his voice rising in hysteria.

Octavian looked at his brother in shock. Val thought it was time to intervene, and spoke rapidly to Jay in Gallic. "He's been a bit loopy, Sir, ever since we were captured, according to the senior centurion. You mustn't mind him. We won't let him kill Caesar. That would be disastrous."

"Why would it be disastrous, Val?" Octavian asked. "It's beginning to seem like a good idea to me, too."

Val returned to Latin. "Well, apparently all the Aeduan and Arvernian prisoners are to be handed over to their tribal leaders. We wouldn't want anything to go wrong with that, I'm sure."

"Where did you hear that?" Jay asked, leaning limply against Gaius.

"From Rufus. He's Labienus's man," Val explained. "He always knows what's going on before anyone else."

"It's true, Sir. Those were the terms we offered to Vercingetorix."

"Oh." Jay became silent.

Octavian and Val finished their work, by neatly bandaging

the wounds. Octavian persuaded his patient to take some pain relief.

"Otherwise you will keep the Tribune awake all night."

"Good," said Jay. They got no thanks from him. He was stretchered back to Gaius's tent.

Octavian realised that the last thing he wanted to do, was to have dinner with his own commander, whilst the heroic leader of the Gauls was kneeling on the ground, chained and hungry. When Gaius and Octavian arrived at Headquarters though, it was to find the Gallic commander had been and gone, having evidently said something to cause Caesar huge embarrassment, and make Labienus grin from ear to ear. Octavian was relieved. Apparently Vercingetorix had indeed been chained, he found out afterwards. It was not a pleasant meal. Caesar was in a foul mood. Octavian was glad to return to the more congenial company of his twins, Borus, and now Gregor. He could already see that his new servant would be an enormous help to him.

BOOK 4: CHAPTER 9

Roman camp near Alesia, Autumn 52 BC

Now Caesar had discovered Octavian's facility with both Gallic languages, and his logistical skills, he put him in charge of all the prisoners, in part to satisfy Vercingetorix's request. He thought it a reasonable one. Octavian was to separate the Aeduans and Arvernians from the others. They were to be handed over to their respective tribes. Caesar intended to keep his promise, but he wanted also to make sure Prince Jayven and his associates acceded to his authority. He sent for Diviciacus. All other prisoners were to be distributed to the legionaries, as plunder.

Octavian set to work. It helped to keep his mind off the miserable thoughts circulating in his brain. There were so many prisoners. He was aware that he didn't have much time to deal with the starving. He found Gregor invaluable, as promised. He asked Marcius for assistance. He requisitioned Val and Darius, both of whom were fluent Gallic speakers, and Andreas, who had managed to pick up quite a bit of the language as well. To his amazement some groups of civilians, and even a few small children, had survived, sheltering from the clash of armies in the rocky ravines around Alesia, living on water and air, he supposed. He fed them first, then found some former civic leaders, older men, and put them in charge of enough food for a few days for the surviving non-combatants, and ordered them to return to their town. He promised to provide more food, as it became available.

Caesar ordered the legionaries to gather all the provisions from the deserted Gallic camps on the plain, and cut corn for bread, and grass and grain for the horses. They were told to round up any cattle in the vicinity, and bring them in. Octavian put in a plea for any lactating cows or goats. He knew Gauls, unlike Romans, were happy to drink cows' milk. Separately he gathered the centurions from each legion. He explained that each soldier would be responsible for the care and feeding of a prisoner. No slave dealers were any where near, and it would be some time before they appeared, and even longer before the soldiers could off-load their captives for money. In the meantime, if the prisoners were not well looked after, they would simply die, and become worthless, especially the starved ones from Alesia.

Octavian ordered a hospital tent to be set up and equipped for the prisoners. There were many sick, unlikely to recover, but also many wounded, and many who could be treated quite easily, he thought. It seemed a pity to waste any. He discovered and co-opted several surgeon prisoners, most of whom turned out to have been trained by Allaine, though unfortunately, only for a short period. Still, they knew the basics, and one of them, Trevorius, he thought was quite promising. He arranged for latrines to be dug by the prisoners, food and water distribution areas to be fixed. He obtained some army clerks to keep the records. He installed the dairy cows and goats in a field next to the Roman camps, and ordered the prisoners to milk them. He sent small gangs of prisoners out into the surrounding countryside, under the watchful eyes of the legionaries, to cut hay for his animals, and arranged for others to coppice osiers to make temporary shelters from woven willow. It was very hot for October. The blond prisoners were getting burnt, and the sick prisoners were desperate for some shade.

As he was walking through the lines of captives, checking their well-being, he came across one man pouring sweat, shivering with rigor, and highly fevered, with a companion out of his mind with grief and helplessness.

"Is he wounded?" asked Octavian, thinking to get him to the hospital tent.

"No, he's sick!" The companion turned on him angrily, speaking in good Latin. "Sick of the lot of you. Why don't you all fuck off back to Rome."

"Is he a relative?"

"He's my brother." It was too much, hearing a sympathetic voice. The young man buried his face in his hands, and cried.

"Right. I think you'd better come with me. I'm requisitioning you both," said Octavian.

There were many more prisoners than legionaries. The excess were to be divided amongst the military tribunes and the centurions. Octavian was sure he would be due a couple, if not more. One that spoke Latin, colloquial Latin at that, would be worth a bit. More likely, he could find him useful. The twins were slowly learning some Latin, Borus was still pretty deaf. It would be good to have another slave who could do some physical work, and speak his language. Maybe the brother could as well. He went back to his tent with the distraught prisoner, the guards, and the sick brother on a stretcher.

"Drustan, Ninian, I want this man cooled down. He has a high fever. Strip him, take a cloth, and bathe him frequently with water. It will help," said Octavian to the brother. He ordered the twins to get some food into his new acquisitions, if possible. Octavian looked at the shattered young man. He was standing in an odd position, his shoulder turned towards the wall of the tent.

"You're injured."

"What?"

Octavian held his arm. "I'd better sort you out as well. Come with me."

"But my brother?" The man was frightened, now. His bravado had vanished.

"After I've attended to your wounds, you may rejoin your brother. Now, do as you are told."

Labienus strolled over to the prisoners' compound, where Octavian was issuing instructions, seeming to know precisely what he was trying to achieve. An unchained prisoner was standing quite still, patiently waiting to be noticed. When Octavian had finished his orders for the day, he turned to greet the prisoner. Labienus watched in fascination as Octavian transformed into a Gaul before his very eyes. Octavian gave the little courteous Gallic half bow, and held out his hands with the upward facing palms.

"What can I do for you, Trevorius?" Octavian enquired, speaking and sounding perfectly Gallic.

"Sir, we are running low on a few things, suture material, swabs and bandages, lint and oil."

"I'll see to it. Do you have a list?"

Trevorius had found out almost as soon as Octavian had been put in charge, that the Tribune with an amazing command of his own language, was very fond of lists. As long as Trevorius supplied a list of requirements and handed it to Octavian, the Tribune would stare at it, frowning, and during the day everything requested would appear. Two days ago Octavian had frowned as usual, then said "Well I'm not sure about the dancing girls, but I think I can manage the rest!" Trevorius looked at him in horror, grabbed the list back and then realised that Octavian was laughing at him. He had laughed in relief himself. He handed over the day's list of medical supplies required.

"Trevorius you will now stop working, and go and get some rest."

"Sir, there are still many wounds to be stitched and bandaged. And sick men to be attended to."

"Come on, Trevorius, you are exhausted. You can't keep going for ever. You will make yourself ill, and then where will we be? Don't argue with me. That is an order."

Octavian switched to Latin, and became a Military Tribune once more.

"He's a great guy," he remarked to Labienus, who had been quietly listening to the exchange and not understanding a word. "He's a pretty good surgeon."

"Where's he from?"

"He's one of the Carnutes." Octavian summoned a soldier. "Take this man and find him somewhere comfortable to rest. And I mean comfortable."

"Take him to my tent," put in Labienus. "Tell Rufus to get him something to eat." He grinned at Octavian. "If he's a great guy, as you say, he needs to be looked after." Labienus had already decided to keep the man for himself.

Octavian was surprised. He had always thought Labienus was totally without pity for the barbarians, as his legate termed the remarkably civilised Gauls.

"Why do we have a herd of cows, Tribune?"

"Since Caesar put me in charge of the prisoners, I have been working on the premise that they are to be kept alive. As the ones from Alesia are suffering from severe starvation, milk is a food that most of these wretches appear to be able to tolerate. Once they manage to keep it down, they progress to something more substantial."

"And why the latrines for the prisoners?"

Octavian looked at him in astonishment. "We don't want illness to spread through the camp. Our men would be affected as well."

"Very well, Tribune, you seem to know what you're doing, and why you're doing it. You can keep the cows."

"What about the rest of it?"

"Yes, all of it."

"Thank you, Sir," said Octavian.

"What are you doing now?"

"I'll be attending to this man's injuries. He needs some stitches."

Octavian moved into the hospital tent with his new slave, and reported to the leading surgeon in charge, explaining who he was and what he wanted. But the surgeon knew already. Octavian had lent his set of surgical instruments to Trevorius. Most of the prisoners knew about Prince Octavian. He pushed his prisoner down onto one of the trestle tables, called for an assistant to keep him still, and started to work. Labienus wandered in to see what his tribune was up to this time, and watched astonished in turn, as Octavian quickly disinfected the gaping hole, trimmed the edges of the wound, sewed the fascia together with catgut, and then closed the skin with neat double sutures, despite his patient's

639

inability to keep still. Octavian glanced up to see his legate standing before him.

"Cut for me," ordered Octavian. "About a fingernail's length from the skin." Labienus obediently picked up the scissors and cut the stitches as Octavian inserted them.

"Why do you do it like that?" asked Labienus.

"The skin heals badly unless the edges are fixed together and raised. Otherwise the edges grow underneath each other, causing more infection and worse scars."

"When did you learn to do this?"

"When I was a prisoner." The look on Octavian's face warned him not to pursue the matter further.

No wonder the legionaries were complaining that the prisoners were being better treated than they were, especially if wounded.

Octavian invited Trevorius to dine with him. He found it difficult to prise him away from his legate's clutches. Labienus ordered him to be returned before nightfall. Octavian wanted the Gallic surgeon to give him some inside information. He thought he had established a fairly good working relationship. He didn't feel the man felt any great antipathy to him, at least he hoped not, but their relationship might be different now Labienus had secured property rights over him. A legate trumped a tribune every time, even a tribune in charge of all the prisoners.

"Do you have any objection to my slaves dining with us?" asked Octavian. "It is my custom, but I can alter it if it makes you uncomfortable."

"No, I have no objection," replied Trevorius. "It is the custom in my country as well."

Octavian broke the bread, blessed it, and passed it first to his guest, then to Gregor and the others. The twins were surprisingly good at cooking, especially fish. They served the meal with their best party manners. Really, thought Trevorius to himself, this officer is almost civilised. After the wine had been served and drunk Octavian broached the subject he most wanted to ask about.

"What am I doing wrong, Trevorius?" he asked. "Every so often I see I am causing offence, but no one is brave enough to tell me the problems. Perhaps you will manage it?"

"It seems a bit churlish to mention it," Trevorius answered. He had no desire to upset the apple cart. Octavian had been so helpful, doing and ordering much more for the prisoners than he had ever expected. Especially doing more for the sick and wounded.

"I wouldn't ask you if I didn't want to know. You won't offend me by telling me."

Trevorius took the plunge. "The carts that go round each morning collecting the dead. As far as we know the bodies are taken away to be burnt?"

"It's very hot, Trevorius. I don't think we can keep them hanging around."

"No, Sir. But some of us Gauls do not consider cremation a good ending. Some think that burning will destroy the soul, and because of this there will be no chance of being reincarnated. Also, unless a priest is present to guide the souls to the afterlife, whether the bodies are buried or burnt, their souls will still be trapped for ever in their bodies."

"I see. This is much more fundamental than I had thought. This will have to be put right. Is there any way it can be done retrospectively?"

"Sir, you would have to ask a priest. I don't know enough of these matters to be sure."

"Are there any such priests among the prisoners?"

"I know of one at least."

"Will you bring him to me tomorrow, please?"

"Of course."

"What else?"

This was going to be much more difficult. "We do not like the centurions who treat our young men like women. It is considered very degrading. Such a man who has been abused in this fashion ....." Trevorius stopped speaking. He could see the twins looking at him in horror. It occurred to him that perhaps this was something the Tribune approved of, even maybe did himself. The twins looked very sweet with their blue eyes, dark lashes, and blond curls. Not that they looked in any way female, but still.

"If you can tell me which particular centurions these are, I will put a stop to it immediately."

Octavian was furious. He had given strict instructions about this very subject, well aware that it was anathema for a young man to be raped in Gaul. The victim usually had to go through a particularly unpleasant purification rite, he had heard from Allaine, although his master had not gone into any details. Presumably Allaine had had to undergo such a rite himself, like Hugo. There were huge numbers of prisoners. There was no way he could keep them all tied up or chained. He needed their cooperation, at least until the dealers arrived, and they became slaves. After that, of course, anyone could do whatever they liked to their own property, but they would no longer be his responsibility.

The next morning Trevorius identified the centurions, whom Octavian arranged to be publicly flogged. He would make sure he was never disobeyed in the future. When Labienus enquired as to their fault, he was told they had flouted his direct orders. The centurions themselves were left in no doubt exactly what orders they had transgressed. None of the four bothered to appeal. They could see from the face of their officer it would be no earthly use, and submitted to punishment accordingly. Such punishment of centurions was a rare occurrence. The legionaries were shocked and stunned. If this was what Octavian did to his centurions, what on earth would he do to ordinary soldiers? Henceforth they all behaved with great circumspection, careful to treat the prisoners at arms length.

The priest was most helpful, a tall grey-haired man with a

tired face. He assured Octavian he could perform the sacred rites, and would need very little in the way of materials to help him. If he could perhaps be allowed to go into the woods and fields, to gather the necessary leaves and herbs? Octavian thought of the last time he had allowed someone to go and gather herbs. Memory came back with startling clarity. The awful feeling of falling into the black pit of unconsciousness. The appalling awakening. He shook his head vigorously. The priest thought he was being refused permission. Just in time Octavian realised.

"I will be pleased to enable you to do this," he said, and sent the priest out with Valerius and Ajax.

When the priest returned later he tentatively approached Octavian, and asked if he would be willing to be at the committal proceedings. Octavian wondered why, until he discovered his part was to sing the lament, to which he agreed. But the wagons transporting the dead became fewer and fewer in number, and emptier and emptier. At last every prisoner was disposed of.

Valerius wandered over to find out which of the prisoners was allotted to him. It appeared to be a very young, very thin one. One from Alesia he supposed. He pulled the prisoner to his feet.

"Greetings. What's your name?"

The boy looked at him blankly. So he was from the North somewhere. Valerius looked around.

"Can anyone speak this boy's language and translate for me?" His knowledge of the Northern language was limited to the small amount he had picked up in Ambiorix's camp.

"I'll translate," said a voice.

With the assistance of the translator Valerius discovered the boy's name was Cadell, he was seventeen, and from the Veneti. That was good, because Valerius knew Octavian's twins were also from the Veneti. He could borrow one of them to help. Val asked the translator to explain his new master was called Valerius, standard bearer of the Sixth legion, that he was sure Cadell had fought bravely. Would he please tell his new

643

acquisition Valerius meant him no harm. All around them prisoners were being pulled, kicked, or coaxed by legionaries, desperate to get their prisoners fed and watered, in case their property died on them before the slave dealers arrived.

"Ask him what he needs most at the moment."

Apparently Cadell needed the latrine as a matter of urgency. Valerius guided him over to the latrines, showed him the sponges, and left him to it for a bit. He showed him where to wash, and then took him to his own place in the tent. He managed to get him to eat a little bread soaked in broth, told him to stay put, indicated his own mattress, and ordered the boy to sleep. When he came back, the boy had disappeared. The other legionaries were sympathetic.

"That's what comes of trying to be kind to them. They don't understand kindness. You should have kept him chained up, if you wanted to keep him. And beat some sense into him."

"Oh well, easy come, easy go," said Valerius, and returned to work. He was found several hours later by one of the camp servants.

"Sir, there's a prisoner looking for you. He says his name is Cadell. He wants Valerius, standard bearer of the Sixth."

Val went with the camp servant. He found Cadell with a little boy in his arms, a very skinny sick boy, pale and floppy.

"Oh for fuck's sake," said Valerius.

"Brother," Cadell managed to say in Latin.

"We can try, but I think he may well be beyond hope," said Valerius. Cadell seemed to understand. He knelt on the ground, placing the child at Valerius's feet, and begged him desperately for help.

"Please, Master, please."

Valerius took the child in his arms and returned with Cadell to his quarters. He attempted to feed the child some bread dipped in wine, but the boy seemed too weak even to swallow.

"Stay," Val commanded. He went off to find Octavian.

"Octavian, I need help. Actually I need milk. Do you think

your twins could get some for me?"

"What is it, Val?" Valerius rarely imposed on their previous relationship, only when he was in deep trouble.

"The prisoner I was allotted has brought me his brother, a wee boy of about six or seven years, I should think. The boy is starving, so weak. I might be able to get some milk into him. He can hardly swallow at the moment. I know he may well die, but I feel it's worth a try. They are Venetians, like the twins."

Octavian nodded. "I'll get them to bring some over. Where is the boy?"

"In the tent of the third cohort. From what I can make out, his brother hid him in Alesia, and shared his rations with him."

"If his commander had found that out, they would both have been tortured to death."

"Yes, I know. He must love his little brother very much to risk such a thing."

Half an hour later Drustan arrived to find Valerius sitting with the child on his lap, wrapped in a cloak. Drustan proffered the milk, then noticed Cadell. The two boys looked at each other in disbelief, and then fell into each other's arms, partly laughing, partly crying with joy. Valerius demanded an explanation. Drustan attempted to give one in halting Latin.

"He cousin, Sir. Far off cousin?"

"A distant cousin?"

"Yes, Sir. I not see him from battle of ships."

"That's good, Drustan. This little one must be your distant cousin, too."

Cadell was explaining the same thing to Drustan, who was very concerned.

"Let's try and see if we can get some of this stuff in him. Pass me a spoon."

Valerius spent the afternoon feeding spoonfuls of milk to the child. It seemed to be working. At least he was still alive.

Octavian summoned the twins. "I want to talk about a painful subject, my children," he said. "I want to know exactly what happened to you when you were prisoners in Britain."

The twins looked upset.

"Now, start from the beginning, and tell me everything."

Hesitantly Drustan started the story.

BOOK 4 : CHAPTER 10

Roman Camp near Alesia, Autumn, 52 BC

Caesar allowed Jayven to stay with Gaius, until Jay's father Diviciacus arrived to fetch him home, which meant that Octavian had to see a lot more of his brother. Gaius always managed to be around, whenever Octavian checked up on his patient's progress. He wondered sometimes if Gaius was having him watched. Gaius's prisoner needed help with the nursing, so Octavian found a reasonably fit and intelligent Aeduan, and sent him over. Fortunately, the Aeduan was enchanted to be serving his prince, as Jay was a horrible patient, cross, querulous and exacting, now he was beginning to recover. It was some time before Jay realised the situation between the brothers. To start with he was too ill to notice anything, feverish and weak from blood loss. Then he concentrated on being as unpleasant to Gaius and Octavian as possible, but Gaius ignored the insults hurled at him. Gradually Jay got bored with being rude, especially when Octavian said he was ashamed to be related to him. He began to sit up and take notice.

"But Gaius, you don't even say 'Oh God, no!'" said Jay, when Octavian had departed.

"He won't speak to me any more," explained Gaius. "Not unless he has to."

"Why is that?"

"It's a long story. I'll tell you over dinner. Come on, Jay. Octavian says you must eat something."

He tried to explain. Jay was thoughtful, and refrained from insults, for a change. When his father arrived, Octavian didn't think Jay was yet fit to travel, so Diviciacus was given accommodation in the camp. He brought his Aeduan nobles with him, ready to take the captured Aeduans back to his own country. Caesar made it clear, that they would be returned only if Prince Jayven agreed to fight alongside him in subsequent campaigns.

Jay decided to enlist his father's help with the brothers. He explained the problem as he saw it. Then he sent for Valerius.

"You must find the interpreter, Val. It can't be any of the official ones, because they would have cost the twins money, and I doubt very much if they had any at the time. So scour the camp for some kind-hearted soul, who volunteered to help the twins for free, and I suspect, someone whose Latin isn't all that good."

Diviciacus summoned the brothers the first evening he arrived, announced his son had raised a complaint against them, in that they were in dispute, and said as he was one of the principal magistrates, and as the complaint concerned Octavian, a fellow Aeduan magistrate, he would convene a court hearing in the morning, listen to the arguments, and pronounce judgement.

The next morning Diviciacus opened proceedings. Guéreth was appointed to act as interpreter for Gaius. Octavian felt quite nervous. The last court hearing he attended as a defendant, ended in him being flogged.

"Gaius Volusenus Quadratus. Tell us why you have quarrelled with your brother Octavian."

"We disagree about something, something quite fundamental."

"You must explain what that is."

"When Octavian's twins turned up, I took them in. Then one day they ran away. They were recaptured about a mile from the camp and brought back. They said I had given them permission to leave. I had done no such thing. So I arranged for their punishment. Octavian came back in the middle of things. He refuses to accept that the twins lied. I know they lied. Octavian prefers the word of slaves to that of his brother. So we quarrelled."

"Now send for your twins, Octavian. We will hear their version of events."

Drustan and Ninian were escorted into the tent, both looking very apprehensive. Drustan stopped dead as soon as he saw Gaius. Octavian moved to reassure them. He could see

Drustan's eyes fixed on him, anxious scared eyes. He had seen that look before, many times, while assisting Allaine. He had an idea. He wasn't sure if it would work, but it seemed worth a try. He told Diviciacus his idea, and got permission to proceed.

"Drustan, come over here," Octavian ordered. The boy obeyed immediately. "Now I want you to lie down on this couch." Drustan was startled. He lay down, still looking at his master, but becoming ever more alarmed.

"Keep looking at me, Drustan. Don't look round. Just look at me. That's right. Now there's nothing to worry about, my pet. Nothing at all. You must trust me."

Was he doing it right? He didn't know. He reached out his hand and began gently stroking the side of his slave's face with the tips of his fingers, pushing the blond hair back from his forehead, talking all the while in a calm soothing voice. Drustan didn't take his eyes off his master's face. He lay still, rigid and afraid. Now to see if it worked.

"You feel sleepy, Drustan. Your eyes are heavy. You want to go to sleep. You are so so sleepy."

Drustan was beginning to calm down and unwind a little.

"Now you are going to sleep. But while you are asleep, you will talk to me, and answer my questions. Close your eyes."

To his relief Drustan obediently closed his eyes. They watched as the tension slowly left the boy's body. The lines of anxiety smoothed from Drustan's brow. He became completely relaxed. His breathing slowed. He appeared to be sound asleep. Octavian picked up his slave's hand. It was quite limp. He let it drop slackly onto the couch, all muscle tone gone. It was uncanny. Ninian gave a little gasp of fright.

"Everything is alright, Ninian," Octavian reassured the anxious twin. "I'm just going to ask your brother some questions, and then I will wake him up again. Don't worry."

He picked up Drustan's hand again, and held it in his own all through the questioning.

"You may open your eyes now, Drustan."

Drustan's eyes had a glazed expression. He stared at the tent roof, taking no notice of those around him.

Diviciacus spoke. "The court agrees the witness is in trance, and will speak truthfully."

Octavian took Drustan through the events of the morning, on the day his slaves walked out of the camp. After each of his questions there was a pause, while Guéreth translated for Gaius.

"You asked to speak to Gaius Volusenus, about an important matter?"

"Yes. We told him we had been given word by one of the priests, that our Master was very near our camp, and would reach it the next day. The Tribune said we were talking rubbish. He said Octavian was dead. He was very angry."

"But the interpreter said you had permission to go?"

"Yes, we had permission to go."

"Can you say exactly what the Tribune said. Can you try and say it in Latin?"

There was a long pause.

"He said 'Clearov, ju hear me, stupid cunts. Fugg off outa my sight.'"

"Clear off, do you hear me, stupid cunts? Fuck off out of my sight? Is that what he said?"

"Yes. Clearov, ju hear me, stupid cunts. Fuck off outa my sight."

Octavian looked over to his brother. Gaius had his hands over his face.

"And what did the interpreter say?"

"He said 'The Tribune says you are permitted to leave.'"

"How did Gaius treat you before that day?"

Drustan sighed. "I think he tries to be kind, but he is stupid, not like Octavian."

"How not?"

"We are just a nuisance to him. We remind him that Octavian is dead. He is very angry that Octavian is dead. And we are not his slaves, we are his pigs. We do not eat with him. We must not say his name. We must sleep with the dog. We are animals, but not slaves."

This admission caused a tear to slide sideways down the face of his slave, onto the couch.

"You mustn't worry about that then, Drustan. It is past. Octavian is back now. Are you happy now?"

"Happy that Octavian is back. But we cause trouble between our Master and his brother. I don't know how to put it right. Ninian says perhaps we should lie and say we didn't have permission, but then how could Octavian ever trust us again? I don't know what to do. I don't know what to do." Drustan was crying openly now. Octavian thought it was about time to put his experiment to an end.

"Listen, Drustan. You have done very well. It is not up to you to put things right between Octavian and Gaius. They should do this themselves. I don't want you to worry about it any more. Do you understand me?"

"Yes, Master."

"Now when I snap my fingers, you will wake up. And you will remember this, because I don't think it will cause you any hurt." To his intense relief Drustan opened his eyes and sat up abruptly. The boy gazed at the faces round him and got frightened again, clutching Octavian's arm. Octavian remembered the next bit.

"Drustan, move slowly or you will become dizzy. Sit up slowly. That's better."

They were all looking at him in amazement.

"Where on earth did you learn to do that?" asked Gaius.

"I didn't know I could do it. I watched Allaine. He often uses it when he has to stitch wounds, or reduce fractures, or cause too much pain to be able to operate. It doesn't always work, even for him."

It seemed strange to have this new power, but he wished Allaine was there to explain it all. He seemed not only to be acting like Allaine, but speaking like Allaine as well.

651

At this point Val burst in, saluted his senior officers, walked over to Diviciacus, knelt, and kissed his hand.

"I've found the interpreter, Sir," he said, beaming with his success. "He's one of the Arvernians." Val carefully refrained from explaining that the man had deserted to the other side, and was found amongst the prisoners.

"That's very strange," Gaius started. "I searched for the interpreter myself."

Val explained rapidly in Gallic, so Gaius wouldn't understand. He went out of the tent, and returned with his prize. Octavian hastily assured the frightened man that he wouldn't be charged with desertion.

Gaius recognised the man as soon as Val presented him. The interpreter confirmed what they all already knew. He had told the twins they had permission to leave the camp. Diviciacus enjoyed summing up the case. Gaius had to stand at attention and listen to a homily on the importance of giving clear instructions, and making sure they were understood by the recipients.

"How long was the boy unable to work?" Diviciacus asked Octavian.

"About a month, Sir."

"Then Gaius, you will make reparation to your brother of one hundred sestercii. Is that satisfactory to you, Octavian?"

"It's not the money, is it?" Octavian said angrily. "Gaius is a blithering idiot. He must have known the twins were miserable. Why didn't he find out the reason? He doesn't even know that dogs are considered unclean, and have to be housed outside. He's as thick as two short planks when it comes to people."

Drustan heard the angry words, and became fearful. "We have made it worse, Octavian," he whispered.

"No, you have made it much better."

"Well, I think Gaius owes the twins an apology," said Jay.

"I have to agree with you. Is there some special way I should apologise?" Gaius asked anxiously, trying to make amends. He knew the Gauls' love of ceremonies for just about anything. Jay was sorely tempted to make one up, involving copious amounts of mud or ashes, or even dung, preferably to be poured over the head. Oh, well, another time, perhaps.

"I wish to make a formal apology to Drustan and Ninian," said Gaius. He walked over to Drustan and held out his hand. "I'm sorry, Drustan. It was entirely my fault. Please forgive me."

Drustan shook his hand reluctantly. But when Gaius tried to apologise to Ninian, the boy put his hands behind his back, and shook his head vigorously.

"No, you a fucking pillock," shouted Ninian.

Octavian stepped over and slapped him, causing a nose bleed. Ninian burst into tears.

"No, don't hit him," Gaius stopped his brother. "He's right. I am a fucking pillock. It was all my fault. I'll have to be more careful in future. I'm sorry, Otto. I'm really sorry. I was ordered to have them crucified as spies and deserters. An example made. I refused. I thought I was doing the best I could for them."

Octavian felt relief pouring through him. He had missed Gaius so much, he realised. It was so good to get him back again. He walked over to his brother and hugged him.

Gaius bowed to Diviciacus. "Thank you, Sir, for giving me my brother back."

"Perhaps you could attempt to learn our language, Gaius. So many problems arise because of misinterpretation. And, Octavian, you should encourage your slaves to learn Latin."

"Yes, Sir."

Jay was moved to his father's tent. He managed to thank the brothers somewhat ungraciously, for their care of him. Diviciacus was worried about his son. He reminded him so much of Dumnorix.

When they had gone, and the twins had been calmed down, Gaius pushed his brother down onto his bed and said, "Now, Octavian. Who the hell is Allaine?"

Gaius made a lot of discoveries that evening, about Chrys's brother and Octavian. But the news that caused him the most excitement was that his Lucy was safe, if it could be called safe, marooned somewhere in Helvetia.

"She's fine, she won't come to any harm there," Octavian assured him. "She's with Guéreth's sister."

"What?"

"My master, Prince Allaine, married Guéreth's sister. Remember? I told you. They've a baby girl called Claudia, after Mother. Lucy is with them."

He thought he'd better inform Gaius of the major drawback to his girl. To his great surprise Gaius dismissed it as of no consequence, excepting that his Lucy must have suffered dreadfully at the hands of the madman. He told Octavian he wanted to rush off immediately, and carry her back to safety. Octavian told him to calm down and behave like a normal human being.

"You wouldn't be normal if it was Chrys in trouble," Gaius shouted at him.

Octavian agreed. It seemed best to go along with his brother. He didn't want any more upsets. But he was becoming anxious about Chrys and his parents. It was strange that no letters had yet reached them from Rome.

BOOK 4: CHAPTER 11

Winter 52 BC, Summer 51 BC

News of Caesar's decision as to the disposal of the surrendered and captured Gauls soon reached Marcus Metius in Bibracte. Caesar had won. Rome had won. Gaul was conquered. Metius organised his staff, and set out for Alesia. No doubt many of the prisoners would be beyond salvaging, but with any luck he might make a big enough profit on those left saleable, to recompense him for the losses he had suffered in Cenabum. As soon as he arrived, he asked to speak with Marcius and Octavian.

Octavian took him over to the prisoners' compound, and explained his arrangements. Valerius wasn't the only one to decide to hang on to his newly acquired property. But many legionaries were only too happy to hand over their prize. Solid money was a much better bet than a man liable to get sick or die, as so many prisoners insisted on doing, despite Octavian's best efforts. Many Gallic fathers came from all over the country, looking for their sons, seeking to buy them back. Some succeeded. Octavian reluctantly handed over his two new slaves to their uncle, after freeing them both. He refused to accept any payment. Metius purchased all available, and arranged for their transport to Bibracte, where he sold many of them on to his colleagues. Unfortunately the price for untrained men who couldn't speak Latin dropped rapidly, as the market was already saturated.

Several of the captured Aeduans and Arvernians now released into the hands of their chiefs, made it their business to seek out Octavian, and thank him for his efforts on behalf of all the prisoners, themselves included. Prince Octavian was becoming a man of considerable consequence in Gaul, a fact of which the Roman authorities remained blissfully unaware.

Caesar arranged for Vercingetorix to be transported to Rome, ordering the greatest care to be taken with him. When he was awarded his triumph, which he assumed was a foregone conclusion, he wanted to exhibit him to the populace, before having him killed. In the meantime, like Marcus Metius, he decided to set up his headquarters at Bibracte, in Aeduan country in the very heart of Gaul.

Marcus Metius was pleased to discover his nephew and all his young friends had escaped serious injury in the fierce fighting. He invited Gaius, Octavian, Guéreth, and Marcius to join him for dinner. Gaius took his prisoner and Fáelán to the house. Lady Sempronia brought out the prisoner's wife, and explained how she had saved them all from annihilation. The woman came into the room, carrying Dòchas in her arms, with her little boy hiding behind her skirts. The baby glanced all around the room until she saw Gaius. Then she fixed her gaze on him, and gave a baby gurgle of pleasure.

"See," said Gaius. "She remembers me, don't you Dòchas? I was there when she was born," Gaius informed them proudly.

"You were there?" Octavian exclaimed. It seemed so unlikely.

"That's right." He turned to the woman, and spoke in halting Gallic. "I there when Dòchas come, yes?"

The woman laughed and nodded. "Yes, Master, you were there."

The baby held out both arms to him. He plucked her up from her mother, hugged her close, and kissed her. The feel of his beard on her skin she thought very funny. She crowed with laughter. Then she reached out two tiny hands to touch his chin.

"Don't you like my beard?" Gaius asked her, smiling fondly. The baby turned her head away. "I'll have to shave it off, then."

He thrust the baby into Octavian's arms, and caught the prisoner by the shoulder, propelling him towards his wife.

"Go on. Kiss her," Gaius commanded.

The prisoner wrenched himself free, and snatched Dòchas back from Octavian. He stood, glaring at Gaius.

"No touch her!" the prisoner shouted.

Octavian bowed to the prisoner, apologised, and explained that Gaius wanted him to greet his wife, that was all. The prisoner was disconcerted, looking from Gaius to Octavian. He made up his mind, gave the baby back to Octavian and walked over to his wife. They looked at each other for a moment, then fell into each other's arms and clung together. Gaius looked on benignly, while Fáelán slipped his hand into his master's, and smiled shyly at the company. Octavian suggested the family be accommodated on Chrys's estate, to which Gaius promptly agreed.

Gaius indicated the prisoner to Octavian. "Could he be dedicated, like you had the twins?"

"It's a very important ceremony, Gaius. Our master said he was bound to us in life and after death. I'll go through the words with you, and then you can decide if you can keep the promises you would have to make."

"Doesn't he have to promise anything? I thought he did."

"Of course. He must dedicate his life to your service. That's what it is all about."

Gaius was beginning to get used at last to the constant references to 'our master' expressed by Octavian and Val. Hugo didn't appear to be quite so badly affected.

The prisoner refused point blank to be dedicated. From the expression on his face Octavian got the feeling he was outraged at the very suggestion. He wasn't sure the prisoner was all that safe, but Gaius dismissed his fears as groundless.

Despite the twenty days thanksgiving he was awarded by the Senate for the conquest of Gaul Caesar was well aware that still some of the Gallic nations refused to bend the knee to the might of Rome. He decided to stay at Bibracte for the winter, hoping his interests in Rome would be adequately looked after by his friends. In this he was doomed to disappointment. Infuriating that Licinius Crassus had been killed last year, while fighting the Parthians, just when Caesar needed him most. And after his daughter Julia's death, he had grown increasingly apart from

657

Pompey. Now he viewed him more as a rival, no longer as a favoured son-in-law. Despite the promises made three years ago, Pompey's actions while Consul this year had been anything but helpful to him. And Pompey held eight full legions in Spain. Was he for Caesar, or against him? Time would tell.

Caesar dispatched the legions to their winter quarters, all over Gaul. But as already reports were coming in of yet another armed rebellion, he started his military campaign again at the end of November, after only a short period of recuperation.

The troops were fed up and exhausted, and not a few of them knew how close they had come to disaster at Gergovia and Alesia. Caesar's stock wasn't quite so high. However, he was now so rich! He gave a liberal distribution of money to each soldier, and ten times as much to each centurion. Nothing binds loyalty so much as monetary reward, he reflected.

Aware of his soldiers continuing grumbling he decided to unleash his legions on the soft underbelly of Gaul. He left his close friend Mark Antony in charge at Bibracte, and set out with two legions north west to the Bituriges region. He ordered that no towns or villages were to be fired, to avoid the smoke warning other inhabitants of their imminent danger. So the soldiers surprised men tilling the field for the winter sowing, women suckling babies, children tending cattle. All were plundered, men, women, children, horses, cattle, gold, silver, the lot. The Romans seized everything they could lay their hands on. There was nothing left, a wasteland. No people, no animals, no corn, nothing but empty land.

Caesar returned to Bibracte, arranging for the storage of his plunder, and the sale of the prisoners. He then marched north to confront the Bellovaci, who had joined forces with Commius, Rome's former ally, now her fiercest foe. Despite the terrible defeat at Alesia, the Bellovaci had amassed a considerable army, and were renowned for their fighting prowess. They had only given Vercingetorix two thousand men, as they wished to fight the

Romans separately on their own account. It took a great deal of effort and some little time to defeat these fierce warriors. Commius escaped to fight another day.

Organised resistance to Roman rule was now all but over in the north. But the terrified inhabitants no longer felt safe in their towns and villages, after hearing how the Romans had ransacked the Bituriges territory. They deserted their towns, and set up small communes instead, to avoid Roman rule. Caesar decided to pillage the land of the Eburones for the third time, determined to leave nothing but barren land there. He rampaged among the Western tribes, obtaining submissions and hostages. Then he returned to the country of the Carnutes, insisting they give up Prince Gutuater. Just to rub it in, he made sure they knew their Prince would be treated in the same way as Prince Acco. Their revolt had been for nothing. Gutuater was handed over, and beaten to near death, before being executed.

In the south of the country the Gallic general Drappes had successfully raided Roman supply columns and baggage trains from the Province, all through Vercingetorix's rebellion, causing terrible logistical problems for the Romans. More worryingly, Drappes now joined forces with Lucterius, both of them expert warriors, and together they carried on ruthlessly with their raids. Caesar sent his legate Caninius south with two legions, to pursue and deal with the menace.

Caninius attacked and defeated Drappes and his forces, but Lucterius escaped. The rest of the Gauls retreated to Uxellodunum, a town easy to hold, as it was perched on a hilltop, with steep rocky sides. Caninius made three camps, and invested the town with siege works. Caesar sent two more legions to help, and then decided to finish the job himself.

Caesar marched to Uxellodunum with all the cavalry, leaving behind two legions of infantry to follow him. The town was now completely surrounded. But the stubborn inhabitants had obtained masses of food supplies. It would be many months before they were starved into submission. The alternative was to cut off their water supply. Caesar stationed archers and slingers to kill townspeople coming down the steep slopes to get water, but they were still able to get a small amount from a spring higher up, much more easily defended. The Romans were forced to build a siege terrace sixty feet high, which proved very difficult as the defenders rained down missiles on the builders from the town walls. But the terrace succeeded in concealing the digging of tunnels at the base of the hill, the Roman engineers hoping this way to divert the spring. The townspeople knew nothing of this work.

A ten storey tower was built on top of the siege terrace, fitted out with the deadly scorpios. So now the Romans could hurl missiles down with great accuracy at anyone trying to get water from the high spring. The citizens began to get thirsty. There was nowhere near enough water for the people, let alone the cattle and pack animals. In their desperation they hurled burning materials down to set the siege terrace on fire, setting off barrels filled with lighted pitch, to fetch up against the wooden base of the tower. This worked brilliantly; the siege terrace was ablaze from end to end. So Caesar ordered some of his infantry to climb the steep rocky walls and yell as if they were about to attack. The people hastily withdrew to man the walls, which enabled the Romans to extinguish the flames. By now many in the town were dying of thirst. At last the Romans' mining works caused the last spring to dry up. The flow turned to a thin trickle, then stopped completely. There was no water. Not a drop. The Gauls thought this to be a sign from their Gods, rather than the work of the enemy. If their own Gods were against them, there was no hope at all. Uxellodunum surrendered.

Caesar sent for Octavian. "Ah, Octavian," he said, apparently delighted to see him. "I presume you are happy to be in charge of the prisoners, as usual?"

"Of course, Caesar, if you feel I am capable of the task."

"And would you say, my boy, that I am renowned throughout Gaul for my clemency? That I have treated the conquered barbarians with great tenderness, considering their shocking rebellion against the Republic of Rome?"

"There's no question, Caesar, but that you are known for your kindness and mercy towards the defeated."

"I'm glad you agree, Octavian. In that case, I think an example must be made of these stubborn criminals. You will arrange for their hands to be cut off." He smiled to see the shock reflected in Octavian's face, blanching almost white, as the blood drained from his cheeks. "Afterwards they are to be dispersed, to tell anyone idiotic enough to still harbour thoughts of rebellion, to think again."

"Who says they are criminals?" Octavian asked desperately.

"I do," said his commander. "Anyone who disobeys my orders is a criminal, a rebel, a brigand. As such, they must be punished with the greatest severity."

"Caesar," said Octavian. He saluted, and left headquarters, still in shock. He went over to his tent and sat on the bed for a time, trying to collect himself. His slaves were disturbed by his silence, but looking at their master's expression, didn't dare say anything. He's like a malevolent scorpion - Octavian thought to himself - always a sting in the tail. But it's nearly over. Nearly over. Not much longer, and I will be shot of him forever. How the hell was he going to tell the prisoners? Well, the sooner the better.

He walked over to the compound, where the prisoners were under heavy guard. He made his way to the place where the senior officers were chained.

"I have some very bad news to convey," Octavian said. "Caesar has ordered that anyone who carried arms in Uxellodunum, is to have their hands cut off. I will have to arrange for this tomorrow. I can only give you my apologies. I simply don't know what to say."

The officers were aghast. "Both hands?" whispered one.

661

"Yes, both hands, I'm afraid so."

"Oh God," said the man.

"At least it will teach the rest of Gaul never to surrender," said the most senior officer. "Have you any news of Commander Lucterius, Sir, or Commander Drappes?"

"Drappes has killed himself. I believe there to be a bounty on Lucterius's head. Caesar expects him to be given up soon."

They were stunned, but being Gauls they still didn't forget their manners. "Thank you, Sir, for coming to tell us yourself," said the most senior officer.

"I have a plan," said Octavian. "If you will cooperate."

They became interested immediately. "What is it, Sir?"

"I suggest we start with the worst affected. Can you identify the men most ill at present, and likely to die anyway? I suggest they are punished first. Caesar wishes the mutilated to go to the country, and show the populace the punishment for rebellion. If every one dies, his plan will fail. I need about a hundred victims. I am aware that they are victims. I can promise they will be cremated in the presence of a priest, to preserve their immortal souls."

He ordered plenty of water to be distributed to the prisoners, apart from the one hundred chosen ones.

Octavian went back to his tent and summoned his little group of flawless Gallic speakers together, Andreas, Val, and Darius. Andreas looked at him in disbelief.

"He can't," he said. "He just can't. Doesn't he realise how hated he will be? How hated we will all be?" He sat looking at his own hand, the thin white lines of scars. He opened and closed his fist. It worked perfectly, as always.

"These are his orders. They must be carried out. Better that it is us. I need groups of eight soldiers. Two to keep the axes sharp, two to do the chopping, two to get them over to the cauldrons of pitch, and two to carry them out of the way. An hour at the most for each group, and they will need to be rotated. Then after four hours change them for fresh troops. I doubt if even our men will find chopping hands off unarmed prisoners a pleasant experience." Octavian told them his plan. It was the best they could come up with.

Octavian started proceedings at first light. The camp rang to the sound of screams. Some men fainted, some wouldn't stop bleeding. Octavian had the first hundred heaped together, then sought an interview with his commander.

"Hail, Caesar." Octavian saluted smartly.

Caesar was irritated. He had things to do. "What is it now, Tribune?"

"Sir, the prisoners refuse to cooperate."

"What do you mean?" snapped Caesar.

"They insist on dying, Sir, despite our efforts to prevent them from doing so."

"I will come and see." He wouldn't put it past Octavian to make it up. He knew his tribune didn't really have his heart in this war, and was quite desperate to leave the army. He must think of another way to thwart the boy.

Octavian was right, he could see. In fact he watched himself as five prisoners were brought forward to the five separate chopping blocks, suffered the bilateral mutilation, had their arms thrust into the boiling pitch, and quietly expired.

"We could try one hand only, the right hand," Octavian suggested. "It will speed things up considerably, and may be more successful."

"Oh, very well, very well. Get it over and done with, and get them dispersed as soon as possible."

"Certainly, Caesar," Octavian replied. Once Caesar had departed Octavian ordered any prisoner without a beard to be excluded, as being too young to bear arms. Then he assigned one unharmed youngster to each of the prisoners that had survived the double dismemberment. There were very few. Now he concentrated on keeping the rest alive. He remained on hand all day, supervising the proceedings. Once he knew how long the initial process took, he worked out how many teams he would need, to have the whole ghastly business finished by the evening. Andreas was enjoined to make sure the axes stayed sharp.

After their punishment the captives were moved to the shade, and allowed to recover for a few hours. Legionaries were stationed to dole out water, and assist when necessary. Val and Darius were on hand to persuade the victims to drink, as soon as they regained their wits. Also to ensure that the bleeding had stopped. After a while the men were offered a little food to eat. They were given a small supply of corn to take away. There were thousands of victims.

The most senior officer asked to speak to Octavian, requesting that he and his fellow officers be dealt with last of all. "When the axes are blunt," he said with a half smile. "There is nothing else I can do for my men."

"No blunt axes, I assure you," Octavian replied. He made sure the officers were also each given a young unharmed helper. These were the men who had to somehow lift up the spirits of their mutilated troops, and persuade them life was still worth living. He thought the most senior officer would succeed. He found him impressive.

The Romans returned to their quarters at the end of the day, with the sounds of the axe and the screams still ringing in their ears, the smell of the blood and the pitch still invading their nostrils.

Octavian walked with the others back to his tent to find Gaius and Marcius waiting for him. Andreas went straight to his brother, to be comforted in his arms. Octavian collapsed heavily onto the bed. He stared unseeing into the distance, remembering the long lines of terrified hapless prisoners waiting for punishment, knowing there was no escape; the looks of total despair on the faces of the first hundred victims. He started to shudder with the horrors of the day, and couldn't stop at first, racked with torment.

"The fucking, fucking bastard," Octavian burst out. He couldn't keep it in any longer. "I hate him, I hate him, I hate him."

He beat with his fists on the bed. "I'd like to kill him."

He looked up briefly as Gaius inserted a large beaker of wine into his nerveless fingers.

"Drink the wine, Octavian, it will help," said his brother.

Octavian obeyed, gulping down the wine in desperation. He sat forward, shoulders hunched, head bent, saying nothing more for a while. Then he looked in anguish at the others. "What's Allaine going to say about this, when he hears? Oh, God!"

It was Darius who helped most.

"No, Sir. He won't blame you. He's always fair, is Prince Allaine, as you know, Sir. He'll know who give the order. He'll know you done your best for the poor sods."

"I suppose you are going to tell me the end justifies the means," Octavian accused Gaius, as Gaius refilled his brother's cup.

"I hope to God this finishes it," said Gaius. "I don't think I can stand much more of this." He was worried about Octavian, hating to see him so distressed. He knew his brother was a lot more sensitive than people realised.

Two days later Lucterius was betrayed by his fellow countrymen, and delivered up to Caesar. Another of the conquered to be tied behind Caesar's triumphal chariot.

Caesar was pleased to discover Titus Labienus had successfully vanquished the Treveri in the north. He took his troops to ravage the country of Aquitania, not that they'd done anything bad, just omitted to send hostages. Rather foolish of them. But he left the Helvetians alone.

Caesar went to Narbonne at end of summer. He went from assizes town to town, settling disputes, and making sure that any who had had the temerity to fight against him, were punished with the utmost rigour. Then he travelled the length of Gaul to join his troops in the country of the Belgae. He dispersed his legions to winter quarters, covering every part of the country.

BOOK 4: CHAPTER 12

Belgium, Winter 51 BC

Caesar, having whisked through Aquitania in the autumn, eventually retired to Nemmetocenna in the northern most part of Gaul for the winter months, spending the time writing complimentary letters to each of the Gallic tribal governments, and bestowing expensive presents on all the principal citizens. There were no reports anywhere of further revolt against Roman rule, mainly because the Gauls were now back to ruling themselves. He ensured that the tax burden was light, and promised many future advantages for the country as a whole.

Commius the Atrebatian was delighted to hear the news that the legate Mark Antony was to winter in Belgium within his territory, with four legions. He was even more delighted to learn that his great enemy, Gaius Volusenus Quadratus, was appointed commander-in-chief of Mark Antony's cavalry.

Commius set about seeking revenge for the Roman perfidy. He gathered together many disaffected young men, and formed a large cavalry contingent under his own leadership. They had a wonderful winter, attacking a number of supply convoys, which were on their way to provision Antony's camps. Commius took great pleasure in distributing the food and goods to his people. But all the while he was seeking a return match with Gaius Volusenus Quadratus. Commius couldn't get over the Romans' treachery. He had extended the hand of friendship to Caesar, rendered him innumerable services, fought for him, supplied him with cavalry in Britain, when his own failed to turn up, and for a reward he was inveigled into a trumped up meeting and nearly killed. Hatred of all things Roman burned in his heart, but especially of Gaius Volusenus Quadratus.

The remnants of another skirmish reached the safety of Mark Antony's camp. Yet another baggage train had been set upon successfully by the Gauls, all the goods lost, and the vast majority of the men. Something would have to be done. Antony summoned the head of his cavalry into headquarters, feeling aggrieved.

"Look here, Gaius. We can't have this rogue Commius cantering about over the countryside, looting our property, and killing our men. What are you going to do about it?"

"I know. He's so elusive. I wish I could find his camp, then we'd have him. We've tried different routes, but I think myself he is watching us all the time. He waits to see what direction we go in before he sets off. Can I have a free hand, Sir? I'll try questioning the locals, but it won't be pretty."

"You can have whatever the hell you like, as long as you get rid of the bastard."

"I'll see what I can do, Sir. I should have got rid of him when I had the chance. He's been nothing but trouble since."

The following days saw Gaius with his cavalry units, repeatedly attempting to engage with the enemy, without much success. The Gauls seemed to melt away into the woods. The local inhabitants pleaded ignorance of the whereabouts of Commius's base camp, though Gaius knew perfectly well that he must have one somewhere. Torture got him nowhere, and just alienated the populace. But as the days grew shorter, the Gauls became increasingly daring. Bloody encounters with small detachments of Commius's cavalry, became ever more frequent.

Gaius decided to set up an ambush himself, the next time a supply convoy was due to arrive. He concealed his forces in the almost impenetrable woods, on either side of the road. They didn't have to wait long before a small group of enemy horsemen appeared, cantering easily along the route. Gaius found himself staring straight into the smiling eyes of his enemy. He charged, only to find Commius fleeing before him. Gaius wasn't going to give up easily.

"Come on, you bastards," he yelled to his men. He urged his horse forwards, and set off in hot pursuit.

After a quarter of a mile Gaius realised he had gone so fast in his desperation to catch his old enemy, he had lost contact with most of his men, apart from Jay and a few others. Then he saw that Commius had pulled his horse up in a small clearing amongst the trees, and was turned to face him. He had been led into a trap himself. Many men and horses appeared out of the woods, surrounding their Commander. Gaius thought this was probably the end.

"Jay, get the hell out of here," he ordered. "It's me he wants."

"No, get stuffed, Gaius. I don't leave you to fight alone," returned Jay.

Commius smiled at his adversary, then raised his spear.

"Gaius, you are very stupid this morning," he said, and charged.

Gaius froze, staring at him in horrified disbelief.

"No, no, no!" yelled Jay.

Gaius screamed in shock, as he felt the spear enter his thigh. The force of the blow caused him to fall off his horse. The pain was so searing, so white hot, so bad he couldn't think, his brain filled with agony. Jay took command at once, ordering the handful of men left to form a protective screen of cavalry round Gaius's body on the ground, but Commius appeared to be satisfied. The Atrebatians retreated, some of them engaging unsuccessfully with the Romans, now desperate to save their Commander, but Commius had no trouble getting clean away.

"Get this bloody thing out of my leg," screamed Gaius. But Commius had made sure his spear was heavily barbed. Jay posted lookouts at the corners of the clearing, in case the enemy returned to finish them off, then set to work.

"Keep him still," Jay ordered. One man lay across Gaius's torso, another man lay across his lower legs.

It wasn't easy to cut out the head and part of the shaft with his knife. There didn't seem to be any alternative. Jay steeled himself against Gaius's protests. The spear head's removal caused terrible pain, and left a huge gaping wound, which bled copiously. Jay was no surgeon.

"We must stop the bleeding. You, help me."

Another of the men knelt with Jay, at Gaius's side. They both pressed down hard, eventually managing to partially arrest the blood flow. Jay fashioned a rough and ready tourniquet around the top part of Gaius's thigh. He mounted his horse, and received Gaius half fainting from loss of blood, in his arms. The men managed to strap the two of them together, before they set off.

It was a long nightmare ride back to the safety of the camp. Gaius cried out frequently at the beginning, with the speed of the riders and the awful state of the roads. The double weight caused Jay's horse to stumble from time to time. It was near dusk, the light was going and it was difficult to see their way. Jay was fearful every moment lost was tipping the scales further into disaster, as his friend's life hung in the balance. When they arrived back at camp, Gaius terrified Jay by losing consciousness completely. His deathly silence became more frightening than his screams.

Jay rode straight over to the hospital tent, thankful to hand over the patient to someone who knew what he was doing. The wound was roughly sutured and bandaged by a medical orderly. Ruteus came to see the patient. He didn't like Volusenus. He didn't like the other Volusenus either, interfering little busy body, always criticising his techniques. He waited patiently till Gaius came round, and gloated to him that he would soon be removing the offending limb.

"Jay, keep that bastard away from me," begged Gaius. "Get Octavian."

"He's not back." Yet another worry. Where the hell was Octavian? If he hadn't tangled with any of the enemy, he should have been back long before dark.

Octavian returned late with his group. They had pursued a breakaway gang of enemy cavalry, which now appeared to have been in the nature of a decoy. They had ridden miles, always just about to attack the enemy, when the enemy would fly off again.

Octavian was cross and weary. When he heard the news about his brother, he rushed to see him.

Gaius was back in his own tent. He had regained full consciousness. He was in a great deal of pain, and a foul mood, in consequence. He hadn't relished Commius winning the war between them. Defeat never featured in Gaius's mind. So when his little brother appeared to worry and commiserate, Gaius was ungracious, snapping and snarling at him.

"Did they disinfect the wound?" Octavian asked anxiously.

"How should I know. I suppose they did. I was out of it. I wished I'd stayed out of it. It's bloody agony!"

"I'll get you some opium."

"No, I'm not having any of that stuff. It can kill you."

"Don't be stupid. It will help with the pain."

Of course, Gaius was right. It could kill you, and sometimes did just that. The dose was difficult to standardise. Octavian thought his brother didn't look too bad. Perhaps Jay was mistaken in the severity of the wound. After all, Allaine had never called upon Jay to assist in surgery. Octavian wondered whether to have a look at the leg, but Gaius had had enough of being mauled about, and told him to fuck off. So Octavian rather angrily fucked off. He was only trying to help, after all.

They had lost a lot of men. Mark Antony sent off a dispatch to Caesar the next day, telling him what had happened, and requesting cavalry reinforcements.

BOOK 4: CHAPTER 13

Belgium, Winter 51 BC

Ten days later Mark Antony received the reply he was hoping for. There had been a few desultory skirmishes with small pockets of the enemy, but fortunately no great Gallic force appeared. The cavalry reinforcements were on their way, the messenger assured him, their arrival imminent.

But extraordinarily, on the same day, to Antony's great surprise, envoys arrived from Commius, asking for terms. They explained Commius was quite happy to desist from further depredations, and now he had his revenge on Gaius Volusenus, he wanted to make peace, as long as he never again had to see another Roman in his life. He intended to retire with his entire force, to his kingdom in Britain. But if Antony wouldn't agree, Commius was happy to stay and make his life hell throughout the winter.

Jay was tending his friend, trying to get him to drink, without much success. Gaius looked dreadful, in obvious pain, pale from blood loss, feverish, toxic, with his features drawn sharply into relief by the tight skin of his face. His brown eyes were dulled, and sunken in their sockets. He wandered in and out of delirium.

Octavian looked at his brother's leg. It was even worse today, if anything, he thought. The flesh was changing colour from scarlet to dusky purple, the tissues tense and swollen, the veins distended. He touched the skin lightly. Gaius gasped in agony, his face distorted, sweat pouring off him.

"We need Antinous, Sir, don't we?" said Pius, the little medical clerk.

"What?" Octavian was startled. The shock of Antinous's name rang in his ears.

"Antinous, Sir. There's many a limb he's saved from the surgeons. He's around here somewhere," added the clerk, slyly.

"What do you mean, he's around here?" said Octavian. He crossed swiftly over to the clerk, gripping the man's shoulder. He shook him hard.

"What are you getting at? Hurry up and tell me." Octavian was rapidly losing patience.

"He's around here somewhere, Sir," persisted the clerk. "With Commius, to my way of thinking."

"Why do you think that?" Octavian was astounded. What he wouldn't give to have Allaine here right now.

"It's the sutures, Sir. I'd recognise his work anywhere. A work of art, I always used to say."

"Show me," demanded Octavian. He wanted to shake the information out of the man.

The little man became dignified, pulling himself upright, and straightening his clothes.

"Certainly, Sir. If you'd care to come with me, I will show you."

Octavian followed the clerk out of the hospital tent. They made their way to where a group of chained prisoners were sitting disconsolately on the ground, waiting to hear their fate. The clerk walked over to one, and pulled up the sleeve of his tunic, exposing a long row of neat double sutures, the edges of the wound elevated and perfectly aligned, despite the irregularity of the underlying lesion.

"Those stitches should have been taken out days ago," said Octavian crossly. "Bring him over to the hospital tent." But he knew who had inserted them, and his heart started beating faster.

When the prisoner arrived, Octavian pushed him down onto a bench, then picked up a pair of forceps and a scalpel.

"It's alright," he said, quick to reassure, noticing the look of extreme apprehension on the prisoner's face. "It's pretty painless having them out." He proceeded to demonstrate the truth of his statement. "It's a beautiful bit of stitching. May I ask who did it?" Though already he knew the answer.

"Allaine of the Helvetii, the Healer," the prisoner replied.

"And where is Allaine now?"

"In camp with Commius, I should think, Sir," said the prisoner. "At least that's where he was when he put my arm back together."

"How long ago was that?"

"Two weeks, Sir."

The prisoner was returned to his companion hostages. Octavian went to see Mark Antony. He requested permission to go with the envoys to Commius. But Antony wanted to know why, so Octavian explained that he had information about Antinous, a brilliant Greek army surgeon, who he had reason to believe, was with Commius, having been captured by Ambiorix.

"I don't want my brother to lose his leg, Sir, if it is at all possible to avoid it. But at the moment Gaius isn't exactly rational. This doctor is renowned for his expertise in conserving limbs others had thought to amputate. He is also good at persuading his patients to agree to his treatment."

"Don't be ridiculous, Octavian. Commius has clearly stated he wishes to sue for peace, and will stop harassing us, as long as he never has to be in the presence of another Roman. If you go to his camp, he will kill you; and furthermore, that will be the end of any peace treaty."

Antony was well aware of Octavian's anxiety about his brother. In fact as far as he was concerned, Octavian had been completely useless as an officer, ever since Gaius returned with the wound. He went from being the most efficient of them all to the most incompetent. He couldn't seem to keep his mind on what he was doing any more; he kept gazing into space instead of listening to his superior. Now for the first time in days Octavian looked fully awake, attentive and alert.

"No, Octavian. You would ruin everything. I forbid it."

Octavian saluted and withdrew. Mark Antony hoped that would be the end of it. He didn't want an uncooperative Octavian. Now Gaius was out of action, they needed all the officers they could lay their hands on, even hopeless ones.

Octavian didn't waste too much time thinking. He had never disobeyed an order so flagrantly before. He wondered what the consequences would be. But before seeking his legate's permission to leave the camp, he had made up his mind on the course of action to pursue, should he be forbidden to go. He sent for Valerius and Ajax.

Octavian held out the thin gold chain. "Do you still have yours, Val?"

"Of course, Sir."

"Wear it then. We are going to find Allaine."

Valerius was unfazed. "Where is he, Octavian?"

"In the camp with Commius. We will need to wear suitable clothes, Val. If they find out we are Romans, they will kill us. Be ready to slip out of the camp. The envoys are leaving soon. We must be further down the road."

Ajax was already sniffing the air and straining at the leash, aware that something exciting was going to happen.

The envoys were surprised to find themselves accosted by two young men and a dog, kneeling in the road next to their horses, half a mile from the Roman camp. They were both wearing the thin gold chain round their necks, proclaiming their slave status. They stood up, bowed deeply and one of them approached the party. He explained they were freedmen of Allaine of the Helvetii, and they needed his help.

"My brother is very sick, Sir," said the man. "My master always promised his help, if we needed him. But we don't know the whereabouts of Prince Commius's camp."

The men spoke well, with the Southern Gallic speech. Their request appeared a reasonable one, so as their mission had been successful, and they were all in a good mood, the envoys agreed to the young men accompanying them. They rode into Commius's camp; they would never have found it unaided. It was well concealed, deep in the woods. The Gauls learnt fast. The camp was fortified, with a fifteen foot wide ditch, the steep sides

674

perpendicular, and a concomitant rampart. Vicious sharpened stakes protruded from the ditch to trap the unwary. A removable wooden bridge, laid over the ditch, led them to the camp gates. The envoys pointed out the medical quarters, then left them to their own devices, and went to report back to Commius.

Ajax started going berserk with excitement, nearly pulling Val over.

"He's here, Sir," said Valerius triumphantly, almost as excited as the dog.

"Well, hang on to the dog," said Octavian. "He'll knock someone down, then we'll have real problems."

Ajax pulled them towards a tent, open to the elements on two sides. Octavian felt tension mounting inside him. He could feel his heart beating faster. There right in front of him was his master. Allaine was working on a very young man with a severe upper arm injury, the wound deep, the flesh torn and ragged. He turned round when Ajax barked a stentorian welcome behind him. He didn't seem that surprised to see them. He spoke quietly to the Romans.

"Val, tie that brute up outside. Then come and help keep this man still."

"Yes, Master," responded Val, obeying immediately.

"I don't mind the dog," said the patient.

"He's young and stupid," Allaine replied. "He'll have everything over. Octavian, wash your hands and then come and hold this retractor."

"Yes, Master," agreed Octavian. He slid into his place beside Allaine as if he had never left his side. Allaine said nothing, but continued to work at restoring muscle and joining skin together. The young patient was in severe distress, moaning between gritted teeth, his good arm lashed to the examination couch. He looked at Octavian.

"Tell me a story," he gasped. "Something to take my mind off this, please."

Octavian racked his memory for the ones Chrys told to the

boys. "Once upon a time there was a king. He had three sons. He told them to go out into the world and search for the Elixir of Life...."

Octavian carried on with the story, but managed to assist as well, working without thinking about it, automatically handing over the right instruments. "So the first son found the elixir of life in the blue ice cave."

Allaine looked at him in surprise.

"But as he was frozen solid, it was no use to him, or anyone else," Octavian continued. "The second son sailed the seas. He sailed far beyond the blue horizon, and found the elixir of life on a tiny island. But as a storm blew up and wrecked his ship, it was no use to him or anyone else, as he could never get back home again. He was marooned on the island for eternity."

Allaine began to close the skin. Octavian lost concentration, he was feeling so nervous. He picked up the scissors, saying nothing for a time.

"And the third son?" Val asked anxiously. "What happened to him?"

"Yes, what happened to him?" asked the patient, his face contorted with the effort to attend to the story, and not the pain.

Allaine paused for a moment, smiling a little.

"He stayed at home, and married a good girl. They had a little baby daughter. When the old king saw her for the first time, he asked what the baby was called. 'She is called the 'elixir of life,' his son replied. And the old king saw that it was true."

Val and the patient gave relieved sighs in unison.

Eventually Allaine was satisfied. Val helped the youngster to sit up, while Allaine and Octavian carefully bandaged the wound, and strapped the injured arm to the patient's chest. At last the patient was given some pain relief. The young man leaned back gratefully against the pillows of the couch, as the pain gradually settled, and became manageable.

Octavian thought his heart would stop as Commius strolled into the tent. But there was no sign of recognition.

Commius glanced curiously at Octavian washing the instruments, and Valerius rolling the bandages.

"Hello, Garmanos. How are you feeling, my boy?"

"Better now, Father, thanks to Allaine."

"Is that your hound outside, Allaine?" Commius enquired. "It's enormous. I don't know why I haven't noticed it before."

"Yes, it's mine," Allaine answered. "I was given it by one of the Eburones, a grateful patient."

"Is my son fit to travel?"

"No, he needs a few hours rest at least, and he would have to go in a wagon. He can't ride yet."

"Why not?"

"Because he is likely to faint with the pain, and fall from his horse. If he breaks a leg as well, he will be in real trouble. He should really be in bed for a few days."

"Ah, I understand. Thank you, Allaine, I am so grateful to you." Commius wandered over to watch Octavian putting the instruments back in their case. "Oddly enough we seem to have successfully negotiated a truce with Mark Antony. I've given orders to break camp."

"Where are you going, Sir?"

"To Britain, to my kingdom there. Will you join me? You will be very welcome."

"I don't think so, Sir."

"Well my dear boy, you will be welcome at any time."

"Thank you, Sir. I'll remember that. I wish you and yours good fortune."

Commius walked over to kiss Allaine's cheek in farewell, then demanded his purse from his servant, but Allaine shook his head and refused payment. So Commius held out some gold coins to Octavian.

"Master?" queried Octavian.

"Yes, take it."

Octavian knelt and kissed Commius's hand, and thanked him. Valerius did the same.

"Nicely trained youngsters," Commius commented as he went out.

"Huh, I don't remember anything nice about being trained," said Val.

Allaine told the young man's attendants how to care for the wound, and how and when to remove the sutures. He then called for the patient to be carried to his father's tent. When he had gone Allaine walked over to Octavian, took the remainder of the instruments out of his shaking hands, and tucked them into his surgical case.

"Are you trying to get yourselves killed, and is this a unique form of self-immolation?" asked Allaine. He sounded angry.

"No, Master." Octavian sank to his knees in front of Allaine. He was feeling quite desperate. "Master, I need help."

"Is it for your brother, Octavian?"

"Yes, Master."

"And how is he?"

"He's ill, toxic, not making a lot of sense." Allaine nodded, understanding.

"His thigh is swollen, tense, and excruciatingly tender," Octavian carried on, his voice thick with strain. "And Ruteus wants to amputate, but it would be such a high amputation, I can't see my brother surviving."

"And what exactly do you want me to do?"

"If you would come and have a look, Sir, and see if there was any chance, any chance at all of saving his leg, I would be very grateful."

"I'm not sure I can regard your brother as one of your dependants. However you must think highly of him to risk yourself like this. So yes, Octavian, I will come with you."

At which point Octavian surprised himself and Allaine by bursting into tears of relief. Pressure had been building in him throughout the afternoon's events. He had contravened a direct command from his legate, and was probably in great danger of being court-martialled. What would he do if Allaine refused to help him after all, had been the thought uppermost in his mind all the time.

Allaine hauled him to his feet. Val fetched a towel from the table, and silently handed it to Octavian.

"Octavian, I do not perform miracles," Allaine said.

"Yes you do, Master," said Octavian from behind the towel.

Allaine pulled his hands away from his face.

"Octavian, you must be clear about this. Just because I see your brother does not mean that his leg will be saved, or even that he will survive."

"I know that. But at least it won't be my responsibility any more, I mean, medically speaking. He expects me to do something. But I can't, I can't. I can stitch people up, but that's about my limit, as you know, Sir."

"Nonsense. You can do far more. But treating relatives can be difficult, I agree. And, Octavian, risking your own life to save your brother's leg is very stupid. Don't do it again."

"No I won't, Master." Octavian wondered fleetingly why being told off by Allaine should give him such a warm feeling of security.

"Now, let's see if we can successfully leave this camp, without trouble."

Servilius and Noemon greeted them with evident pleasure. There was another young servant, who looked vaguely familiar, but Octavian couldn't place him. Val and Octavian helped them pack up their master's possessions into panniers. Everywhere were signs of activity, tents being dismantled and folded, equipment being loaded onto wagons. They rode out of the camp with the laden pack horses and Ajax, unchallenged by anyone.

Guéreth arrived at camp at the head of the cavalry reinforcements. He found Prince Jayven at headquarters, just returned from patrol. Jay explained how Gaius was injured.

"He looks dreadful, Guéreth. He is dying. I don't hold out any real hope. I will be over myself, once I have my men settled."

Mark Antony had Guéreth escorted over to the hospital tent. Now his reinforcements had arrived, it didn't look as if they would be needed. Prince Jayven had found no sign of enemy cavalry. Guéreth was anxious to see his friend, while Gaius still lived. He wanted to say goodbye. They had been through so much together.

He found Gaius looking so ill, it seemed most unlikely he could make any sort of recovery. While he was attempting to talk to him with little success, a disturbance occurred at the tent entrance. Guéreth half turned, frowning in irritation as some people walked in, the light behind them shadowing their faces. There appeared to be three Gauls, one tall and blond, with two dark-haired slaves, both wearing the chain. Some other servants followed them in.

A little medical clerk almost ran over in his eagerness to shake Allaine's hand.

"Antinous," Pius shouted joyfully. "Oh, Sir, it is wonderful to see you again."

"Antinous?" Guéreth was stunned, momentarily. He turned to look more fully at the tall blond Gaul. There was no doubt. It was Antinous Allaine, his renegade slave.

Octavian looked at Guéreth in horror. He swivelled round to face Allaine.

"He wasn't here, Sir. I swear he wasn't here."

Guéreth moved swiftly to confront Allaine. He stood before him, with his hands on his hips, and his face thrust forward belligerently.

"Why are you here?" he demanded.

"Octavian wishes me to see, and possibly treat, his brother," Allaine replied curtly.

"I warned you how I would deal with you, if we ever met again." Guéreth strode to the tent entrance and called to the legionaries standing guard outside. "You! And you! Come here."

680

He pointed to Allaine. "Arrest this man immediately."

"No," screamed Octavian. "I'll kill anyone that harms him!" He drew his sword. Val did likewise. The legionaries halted abruptly, and stood still, not sure how to proceed.

Allaine swung round straight away. "What the hell do you two think you are doing?" he shouted at his freedmen. He was furious with them. They were in enough trouble already, he thought, having disobeyed a direct order from their general, without making the situation even worse. "Give your swords to me," he ordered.

Octavian and Valerius looked at him, dumbfounded.

"Give them to me at once, do you hear?" Allaine snatched the swords from their lifeless hands, and hurled them down in front of Guéreth. Then he took his own dagger out of its sheath, and threw it onto the ground as well.

"Now. Do you have something to say to me?" he asked Guéreth menacingly. "If not, get out of my way. I've a patient to deal with."

"I certainly do," Guéreth snarled back at him. "I have plenty to say. You might be Prince Allaine the Helvetian, but first and foremost you are my slave. I did you no harm. But you were disloyal, disobedient, mutinous. You betrayed me with your behaviour. I will not tolerate it. I swore to kill you, and that's exactly what is going to happen. I keep my promises."

He waited, but there was no reaction from Allaine, just a contemptuous little smile hovering on his lips.

"However, I appreciate your medical skill," Guéreth continued, more calmly. "I am glad to see you here, because before I kill you, first you will attend to my friend, Gaius Volusenus. If you cure him, I will grant you a quick death. If you kill him, I will have you crucified."

Pius ran out of the tent towards the praesidium as fast as he could go, clutching a piece of parchment in his hand. He rushed inside, not even pausing to explain himself to the guards, and confronted a startled Mark Antony.

"Sir, Sir, you must come quickly to the hospital, if you want Tribune Gaius Volusenus to live."

This unorthodox approach intrigued Mark Antony so much, he agreed to accompany the clerk back to the hospital tent straight away. He found two blond giants facing each other, both apparently in the midst of a furious argument. Mark Antony found an interpreter standing near, and beckoned to him. Then he noticed Octavian, and his standard bearer. Dressed in a most extraordinary fashion. Like slaves. What the fuck was going on?

"What are they saying?" asked Antony.

"No," said Allaine.

Guéreth was taken aback. "What do you mean, no?"

"No. I will not treat your friend."

A howl of anguish came from Octavian. Guéreth was incensed again, but so was Allaine.

"Listen to me, Antinous. You've been tortured once in your life. You will do as I tell you, or I will have you tortured again."

Allaine looked at him with contempt. "Do you seriously think you can hurt me? Look!"

Allaine picked up the dagger he had just thrown down. He thrust it straight into his upper arm, right through. Guéreth could see the point sticking out at the other side. Allaine pulled out the blade, and threw the dagger back down on the floor.

"Or perhaps you prefer the irons," he said. He walked over to the brazier, picked up the cautery iron, and drew it across his arm. Then he thrust it back into the red hot coals. The smell of singed flesh filled the tent.

"Allaine," said Guéreth, now seriously alarmed.

"Perhaps you would prefer an eye?"

"No! No! Oh somebody, stop him!" cried Octavian.

Val ran to Allaine. "Please Sir, please don't do it." Allaine brushed him off, not even looking at him.

Octavian had had enough. "Val, get hold of his arm," he shouted.

They stood one each side of him, each holding tightly onto a wrist. Allaine made no attempt to free himself. He stared at Guéreth, breathing hard, a tower of white hot rage.

Mark Antony thought things were going a bit far. He had just finished perusing the parchment. It didn't make a great deal of sense to him. He held up his hand for silence.

"Stop this at once," he ordered.

Allaine turned on him in fury. "Shut up," he said. "This is nothing to do with you."

Antony was shocked.

Guéreth capitulated, knowing in his heart that he could never go through with his threats. Jay wouldn't permit it, let alone Octavian. "Alright Allaine, you win. If you treat Gaius, I promise I will free you."

"There is only one method by which you can get me to treat your precious Gaius," Allaine spat at him. "If you think so highly of him, you will get down on your knees like Octavian. On your knees, Guéreth," Allaine repeated. "Using the leg that I gave you. And you will beg me to treat him."

Guéreth knew he was beaten. He desperately wanted Allaine to see to Gaius. He thought it was his friend's only chance of survival. He obeyed. He had difficulty kneeling down, Allaine noticed. Marcius had to help him.

Guéreth took a deep breath. "Allaine, I have been friends with Gaius Volusenus for ten years. I love him like a brother. I beg you to treat him, if it is at all possible."

Allaine looked at the top of his head. "Well, since you ask me so nicely, I will be delighted to be of service."

"Oh, thank the Gods," said Octavian, almost crying with relief.

"Let go of me, you two," Allaine said. They released his wrists instantly. "Idiots," he said, affectionately. He stood looking thoughtful. Then he dropped to his knees in front of his master. He placed a hand on his shoulder.

"Guéreth, I'm sorry I struck you, that time. It was unforgivable. I still don't know why I reacted so violently, except that I love Riona so much. Please accept my apologies."

"And are you going to apologise for the rest of it?"

"No," Allaine answered. "If I had behaved as you wanted me to, you would all have been killed. It was a pragmatic decision I made. I hope one day you will see there was no other logical course open to me, if you were all to remain alive."

"That will have to do, then," Guéreth said. "You're a stubborn bastard, Allaine, but a useful one."

Guéreth held out both hands. Allaine and Marcius helped him to his feet.

"I'm getting old," Guéreth admitted.

"Nonsense, Guéreth. You've not been doing the exercises I gave you," Allaine said with annoyance. "How do you expect to remain flexible, if you don't do what I say. Marcius, make him do them, in future."

"Yes, Sir," Marcius grinned.

Allaine was appalled to find he had ordered Mark Antony to shut up. He bowed to him and apologised for his bad manners.

"Your famous Greek surgeon would appear to have an amazing command of the Gallic language," Mark Antony remarked drily to Octavian.

Allaine intervened. "Octavian, will you stop crying and introduce me to your legate and your brother? My arm is hurting like hell, and I'd like to get him sorted, before I pass out."

Octavian looked at the blood trickling down Allaine's arm, and the dreadful burn mark.

"You mean it hurts, Sir?"

"Of course it hurts. It hurts like hell, I've just told you. Do have some sense, Octavian. Before I meet your brother, you can put a couple of dressings on for me."

Jayven arrived shortly after this procedure was carried out. He fell on Allaine with delight, hugging him fiercely.

"Thank all the holy Gods you've come, Allaine. We need you desperately." Then he noticed. "Your arm! Are you injured?"

"It's nothing. Octavian will sort me out after I've seen to his brother. It's so good to see you, Jay," said Allaine smiling.

Antony called for a chair. He decided to stay and watch proceedings. This was interesting. Quite outside the usual run of things. The Greek slave doctor Antinous appeared to also be called Allaine. And was greeted on equal terms by Prince Jayven. And spoke fluent Gallic. Intriguing!

Octavian felt very apprehensive as Allaine approached his brother. What would the verdict be?

"Hello, Gaius." Allaine took in immediately the strained look in his patient's eyes. Like Val, Gaius was scared of illness, but wasn't going to admit it. This was something so out of his control.

"Are you Allaine, Sir?" Gaius could see little trace of the poor burnt youngster he had tried to comfort so many years ago. This was a man in total command of himself and the men surrounding him.

"That's right. Has Octavian told you about me?"

"Yes, Sir."

"Do you wish me to treat you?"

"Yes. Please. I do."

"Then I need to examine you first. This will be uncomfortable for you."

"Whatever you need to do, Sir."

Gaius kept his eyes fixed on Allaine's face. Allaine felt the tumultuous pulse, and then proceeded to examine his patient with his usual thoroughness, causing Gaius to gasp and groan aloud.

"What's the verdict, Sir?" Gaius asked shakily, when Allaine had finished with him, and he'd had a chance to recover a little.

"Gaius, although it appears that the spear wound in your thigh has healed over, that is not the case. Deep inside your thigh, along the line of the spear thrust, a large abscess has formed. It is making you very ill, because the infection is beginning to spread throughout your body. Do you understand me so far?"

"Yes, Sir."

"There are three courses of action."

Octavian gave a sigh of relief, which made Allaine frown.

"None of them are pleasant."

"Go on, Sir."

"As the surgeon Ruteus has so rightly suggested, an amputation would get rid of the abscess. However this would have to be a high amputation, with a great risk of severe blood loss."

"And death," said Gaius.

"And death," agreed Allaine.

"And the other courses?"

"I can open up your leg along the line of the spear wound, drain the abscess, and sterilise and cauterise the tissue. It will not be possible to close the wound. Your leg will then take a long time to heal. If it continued to be infected you would have to have the amputation anyway. But you would be in a worse state than you are now, so your chances of survival would be reduced accordingly."

"And the third?" asked Gaius, but he knew what Allaine was going to say.

"We could just make you comfortable with pain relief, while you are dying. If we do nothing you will be dead in a very few days."

"What would you do, Sir?"

"No, Gaius, it's your leg. You have to make the decision. Do you want some time to think it over, discuss it with Octavian?"

"No, Sir. Drain the abscess, please."

"Very well, Gaius. I'm going to send Octavian away. I don't think he will manage this."

Octavian protested immediately. "Sir, couldn't you make him sleep? Then I could stay."

"I'll try, Octavian, but it seems rather unlikely that I will succeed."

But to Allaine's surprise Gaius was a very easy subject to hypnotise. Octavian was allowed to stay and assist after all. Once he was satisfied with the depth of the trance, Allaine set to work. The incision was vast, the quantity of pus enormous, and the smell disgusting. Allaine looked at Octavian from time to time, but he seemed to be holding up well, even when the cautery irons were applied to rotting flesh. Allaine talked to Gaius throughout, explaining exactly what he was doing and why. He told Gaius he would feel no pain during the procedure, but would understand all that was said to him, and remember it when he woke up.

When he was satisfied that what remained was viable tissue, Allaine packed the wound with dressings of lint, soaked in vinegar, then covered the line of his incision with pads of soft cloth. At last he bandaged the whole. He made sure Gaius was given a drink of wine and opium, laid on comfortable bedding, and then securely strapped down. Finally he told him he would wake him up.

When Gaius regained full consciousness he screamed in terrible agony, the screams echoing round the camp as he called on the Gods to stop the unbearable pain. Allaine refused to allow Octavian to loosen the straps, explaining Gaius would damage himself severely if left to his own devices. Gradually the screams lessened, and turned to sobs, then to a constant stream of profanities. Ruteus walked in, took one look at Allaine, spat on the floor, and walked straight out again. Allaine ordered Valerius to stay with Gaius, and encourage him to drink some water, when he had managed to get the pain under some sort of control.

Antony was finding Antinous astonishing. Again he lifted his hand for silence. This time he was obeyed.

"Antinous Allaine, firstly I would like to express my gratitude for your skills, and the use to which you have put them. Secondly, I wish you to come and dine with me, shall we say in a couple of hours, to give you time to clean up. The clerk Pius has some interesting information that he is dying to impart to you, but it can wait until dinner. If you have no objections, I will invite Guéreth, Octavian, and Prince Jayven to join us."

Allaine looked across to Guéreth, who shrugged his shoulders. "I have no objections at all. Perhaps you could include Marcius. It is some time since I have seen him."

"Marcius?"

"Marcius Carvilius. The nephew of Marcus Metius Celar."

"Certainly. Of course Marcius as well. Then I look forward to seeing you later. Octavian, arrange accommodation for your surgeon."

Octavian steeled himself to sew up his former master's arm. He felt unaccountably nervous. When he glanced at Allaine to see if his work proved acceptable, he met with a sympathetic smile.

"Thank you, Octavian. I couldn't do it better myself. Are you alright? This has been a traumatic time for you."

"It was hell, but I'm alright now. Actually, it's been hell ever since....." His voice trailed off. Really, he must stop acting so childishly, crying all the time. Allaine's words made his eyes water. He cleared his throat and tried again. "I'm so glad you're here. I had no idea Guéreth was expected. I'm sorry about your arm, Sir."

"It feels fine, now you've sorted me out," replied Allaine, leaning over to give him an affectionate hug, and then rubbing his back in commiseration. "Come on, Octavian. Cheer up. Gaius is doing alright so far. I think we can relax now for a bit, don't you? A bath and dinner sounds perfect."

Having ensured that Allaine's servants were being catered for, Octavian and Allaine joined Guéreth and Marcius in the bath house. It was good to get cleaned up, and into fresh clothes.

"I'm sure I know that new man of yours, Sir, but I can't place him."

"Oh, yes. I picked him up at Gergovia. He's a nice

youngster. I think he was a very junior officer. He was badly wounded, poor lad."

"A Roman officer?" Octavian asked in alarm.

"Yes, of course a Roman officer. I'm trying to remember his full name. He's called Laurence something. Oh, yes. Laurence Cornellius Calusa. That's it."

"Sir, you've got to stop picking up Roman slaves. It might be a problem."

Allaine touched the thin gold chain still hanging round Octavian's neck. "I'm afraid they're always a problem, Octavian," he said, his grey eyes dancing with laughter.

Allaine refused to go along with Octavian's explanation for his presence in Commius's camp. As Antony greeted his guest with "Welcome, Allaine of the Helvetii," Octavian gave up all pretence. It was a very good dinner. Mark Antony enjoyed having a guest who knew precisely how the present political system worked in Switzerland, who were the men of importance. He must remember to send Coevorten some expensive token from Caesar.

"Of course we lost our protected status, when we joined with Vercingetorix. We have to keep the Germans out on our own. So far we have succeeded," Allaine explained.

When the dinner was over, Antony summoned Pius.

"This slave has some information very relevant to you, Antinous Allaine."

"Sir, Sir, I'm so happy to see you. I've been searching for you for three years," Pius said excitedly.

"It is good to see you, too, Pius." Allaine was touched by the little man's concern. "But surely you must have thought I was dead? That I had been killed?"

"No, Sir. As I was explaining to the Tribune here, every so often I'd see some of your work on the prisoners. There's no one else like you, Sir. You were at Alesia, weren't you, Sir?"

"That's correct. I was at the beginning. But he sent me away."

"I knew you were there," Pius said in triumph.

"And were you looking for me for any particular reason?" enquired Allaine, smiling at the little man's enthusiasm.

"Well, Sir, I was hoping you might sue that bastard Ruteus for assault."

"I cannot imagine how that could come about," Allaine said with some reluctance. It was a wonderful thought. "Though I fully agree with the sentiments."

"You don't understand, Sir. You don't know. Your Master, Antistius Petronius, thought the world of you, didn't he?"

"And I thought the world of him," replied Allaine sadly.

"He freed you in his Will, and made you his heir, Sir." Pius beamed with pleasure. He had been waiting for three whole anxious years to make this announcement.

Allaine stared at him in astonishment.

"But I'm afraid I didn't find out until after you had gone away with the Fourteenth legion," Pius went on. "Someone hid his Will amongst your notes, naming no names, Sir. Thank the Gods it wasn't destroyed. Antistius Petronius never married, Sir. You could say he was married to his profession. He made you his adopted son. And he petitioned the authorities, successfully as it turns out. That makes you a Citizen, Sir, a Roman one that is."

"A Roman Citizen?" Allaine echoed in disbelief.

"That's right, Sir. Congratulations! And personally, I think that bastard Ruteus...."

"Stop that, Pius. You will get into trouble. He is a bad enemy for a slave to have."

"Yessir. I think the surgeon Ruteus had a good idea of the contents of his Will. Can I say that, Sir?"

"No you can't."

"I'm sure Master Petronius would have told someone, Sir. Did he never tell you?"

Allaine thought back to the terrible night when he had lost the battle to save his beloved master. He remembered the man's agitation, as he lay dying.

"I think he was trying to tell me something, but he had a stroke. He couldn't speak at the end. It was all......" He stopped, remembering with terrible clarity his despair and frustration. "It was all dreadful. The whole thing. It happened so quickly. And I could do nothing for him, nothing at all." Allaine shook his head in distress.

"I've all the documentation here, Sir. It's all in order. You are quite a rich man. Antistius Petronius had estates in North Italy. Yours now, of course. And I've got all your notes."

"My notes," Allaine said softly, "I am indeed rich. You seem to have been very busy on my behalf, Pius."

"Oh well, I think the world of you too, Sir. Always so kind, helpful, courteous. You deserve some good fortune in my opinion."

Marcius stared at the man. He could remember Antinous very clearly, nothing kind, helpful, or courteous about him. Quite the reverse. He was very glad to have left him behind in Ambiorix's camp.

"So, I was never your slave after all, Guéreth." Allaine's eyes shone with laughter. "What a good thing you didn't kill me. You might have been in big trouble."

Guéreth looked nonplussed. "I find all this hard to believe."

"I assure you, Pius is speaking the truth," Mark Antony told him. "I've had a good look at all the documents in question. May I add my congratulations, Antinous. This news must make you very happy."

Mark Antony had found the Will most interesting, now he knew more about the beneficiary. Evidently Antinous had worked for three years as an army doctor under Petronius, who spoke of his slave's skill and knowledge in almost reverential terms. As doctors never lie, Antony realised he had hold of someone special.

BOOK 4: CHAPTER 14

Belgium, Winter, 51 BC Spring, 50 BC

After dinner Allaine and Octavian went to check on Gaius. He was holding his own. Allaine wanted Valerius to sleep in the tent with Gaius for a few nights, to give his servants some well deserved rest. They looked worn out, especially little Fáelán. He couldn't sleep for worrying. He didn't know what would happen if his master died. Something dreadful, he thought, like being sold away from his family.

Octavian came later to see if Allaine had everything he needed. He found Jay and Marcius already cosily installed, chatting away, telling all the news, Marcius explaining the rights and duties of a Roman Citizen to Allaine, who was a bit hazy on the subject, one that had never previously concerned him. And Andreas was renewing his acquaintance with Laurence.

"I'll be able to marry Chrys, now she's a Roman," Octavian said. "As you are head of the family." A terrible thought struck him. "If you agree, of course, Sir."

Allaine found that very funny. "Only if you marry in the presence of your parents, Octavian. Otherwise your mother will never forgive me," he grinned. "How is everyone?"

"You know we have a daughter, Dianthe, after your Grandmother?"

"No, have you, Octavian? That is good news. Who's she like?"

"I don't know. I haven't had a chance to see her, yet. I'll show you the letters from Dad. When they left you, they only just got through in time, before all the roads were blockaded. They got as far as Genua, when Chrys started bleeding. She knew she was pregnant. Luckily they were all able to stay until the baby was born. I think Dad was happy to stop travelling, and explore another city for a bit. Mum says Chrys has been fine this time though."

Octavian saw how neat and orderly Allaine had made his tent already. Allaine sent his slaves to bed, apart from Laurence. They had worked hard today, packing his things up, and making sure all was secure, and then a long ride afterwards. Noemon was still no great horseman. And unfortunately his eyesight was beginning to fail.

Laurence poured out the wine. "You're left handed, I see," Octavian remarked.

"No. I told you he was wounded. Laurence, I want Octavian to examine your arm."

Octavian could see the problem at once. The youngster's right arm was useless, the muscles withered.

"The nerve was severed?"

"Yes. Where?"

Octavian figured it out. "The brachial plexus. He can't lift his arm or straighten his elbow, his arm is rotated medially. And he has some sensory loss."

"Correct. A spear wound to the shoulder. Laurence, take off your tunic." Laurence obeyed instantly, using only his left arm to get undressed. "We've worked out a programme of exercises for him. He has regained a little use. Now my pet, try picking up the cup in your right hand."

It was impossible.

"Show Octavian how you can straighten your fingers. Good. Now flex them. That's it. Now hold his hand in yours, as tight as you can. Excellent. You're doing well." Allaine gave his servant a gentle pat, then explained to Octavian. "He had no movement at all before. A little is coming back, slowly."

"Ah, I see."

"He can't return to the army. He will never be able to hold a sword, or a javelin. There hasn't been any opportunity to hand him back, what with all the continual fighting. He is happy to stay with me, at present. Isn't that right, my pet?"

"Yes, Sir," Laurence smiled.

"Off you go to bed, now. We will pour our own wine."

"It's not easy to have only one arm," Allaine remarked, after Laurence left them. He looked straight into Octavian's eyes. "But much better than to have none. I came back after Uxellodunum. I thought I might be needed again. It was difficult to stay away."

"I was put in charge of it," Octavian confessed. "The hands. It was a nightmare." He shuddered at the memory, the heaps of severed hands, the half fainting men, the screams and despair.

"Yes, I know. We heard. He loves torturing people, doesn't he? He was torturing you." Allaine patted his shoulder in sympathy. "I'm sure you did your best for them."

"It affected Andreas badly," put in Marcius. "Didn't it?"

"Hands have a special significance for me, don't they, Sir? And I hate seeing people being tortured," said Andreas, "ever since David."

Marcius hastily intervened. "I've told you before. You've got to stop blaming yourself for David."

"What do you mean?" Octavian asked, suddenly alert.

"Tell Prince Allaine," Marcius suggested. "See if he thinks you're to blame." He put his arm round his brother's shoulders.

Andreas looked at Allaine, conscious he would have to tell the truth, but desperate for his reassurance. It would mean so much more than the partisan support of his brother.

"Mum had lost a ring, one that Father gave her. I mean our real father."

Allaine nodded, understanding.

Andreas continued. "She was very upset. David worked out that it must have come off her hand when she was washing, so he searched the drains, and found the ring. Mum was so pleased when he handed it to her, she hugged him. I mean, he was just like part of the family wasn't he, Marcius?"

"He was, yes. More like a special toy. It was almost as if Octavian and I could take him out and play with him, and then put him back in the chest. He was so good, so obedient. He did whatever we asked." Marcius sighed. The more he saw of life, the more he felt that somehow they hadn't treated David all that well.

"I was telling Lucy that Mum kissed him. I didn't approve. I was jealous of David. I didn't realise Sperinus was standing behind me. He heard every word. He went demented."

"Why were you jealous of David, a slave?" Allaine asked, going straight to the nub of the matter.

"Oh, it was because he got to play with Marcius and Octavian, and I didn't. Octavian would say I was too young to understand, or too small, or something." Andreas frowned. "Looking back on it, when I think about the way the two of them treated David, it's just as well I was too young."

Octavian blushed for his younger self. He felt quite uncomfortable.

"But you didn't know Sperinus was listening?" Allaine enquired.

"No. But I should have been more cautious. I knew the servants eavesdropped on what we said, and reported back to our step father."

"When did you find all this out?" Octavian asked Marcius indignantly. Why hadn't he been told before?

"The morning I was handed over to Guéreth, Andreas came to tell me. He thought everything was his fault." Marcius hugged his brother. "Didn't you?"

"What age were you, Andreas?" Allaine asked.

"Fourteen, Sir."

"Then that answers your question. Of course you were not to blame. Even if you had deliberately gone to your step father and told him you didn't think your mother should embrace a male slave, you could hardly expect him to have reacted in such an appalling manner."

"He would have killed her," said Andreas, "as well as David." When Allaine put it like that, it did sound like a very stupid thing for his mother to have done. He hadn't ever thought that before.

Jay pulled the other two to their feet, and dragged them off, aware Octavian and Allaine wanted to talk to each other alone.

"What a horrible child you must have been, Octavian," Allaine observed.

Octavian laughed.

"How much longer are you staying in the army?"

"I'll be free in six months. I can't wait."

"Then what?"

"Chrys and I and the children will come here, to her estate. Jay thinks it will be safe. I know you think I should take up a position in Rome, Sir. But if I am to do good, I'd rather do it in Gaul. I love this country, and the people in it. I promised Vercingetorix. What do you think?"

"I think the sooner you're out of the army the better. I don't think there will be any more fighting in Gaul, for a long time. I have heard of no tribes preparing for war. We've had enough. I'm glad you wish to stay here, Prince Octavian," Allaine smiled, "as long as you don't just make wine. You have quite a following already, I understand."

"I'm still a magistrate, but I am now asked to hear cases for most of the country, not just for Aeduans," Octavian explained. "So I'm not opting out." He thought he'd better tell the truth. "But mainly Chrys and I want to be nearer to you and Riona, if you don't object, of course."

"Object? I am delighted. Whereabouts is this estate?"

"We are near the lower Loire, about a hundred and sixty miles from Aventicum by the high pass route, a lot nearer than Rome."

"Three or four days travel on a good horse," Allaine agreed.

Octavian dropped to his knees in front of Allaine, and began to unlace his boots for him.

"What are you doing, Octavian?"

"You are wounded. You need to get to bed. As I am responsible for you only having one functioning arm at present and as you've dismissed your servants, I'd better look after you myself. And tomorrow you will wear a sling on that arm."

Allaine looked at him and smiled. "Of course, doctor." He sat thinking for a few moments, gazing at the earth floor.

"Octavian, I have to say this, I hope you won't be offended. It is abhorrent for me to become a Roman Citizen. I feel as if I have unwittingly become a traitor to my own people, forced onto the same side as Guéreth."

"And Prince Jayven," said Octavian, "and me. But you forced us to swear loyalty to you, Sir. So we changed sides as well."

"I would not have let you fight your own countrymen. That would be so wrong."

"But I stopped Val trying to get through the lines to Caesar, remember? Even though it might have saved many Roman lives in Cicero's camp."

"No, it would have saved nobody. He would have been captured immediately, and tortured to death. I wouldn't have been able to prevent it."

"Loyalty," said Octavian after a moment's reflection, "to a master, to the family, to a commander, to the State. It's difficult when they clash. I think it will be better if we are all on the same side here in Gaul."

"Caesar's term of office will finish next year. What happens after that worries me," Allaine said.

"Will you go home now, Sir?"

"No. The passes are blocked at present. I will stay and make sure Gaius is on the road to recovery, before I leave."

Allaine was in for yet another unpleasant surprise, however. The next morning he was summoned to appear before Mark Antony.

"Antistius Petronius Antinous Allanus, I don't think there is any doubt at all about your citizenship. Therefore, with the powers vested in me, I will co-opt you to work as a surgeon in this camp, for the duration of the winter."

Allaine was taken aback. He felt his stomach curl up in fright. More slavery! He spoke instinctively, outwardly calm. "I will not work under Ruteus."

"Of course not. You will be in overall charge. I agree with Pius. You could bring a successful assault charge against Ruteus, and so I have told him. That should keep him quiet. Perhaps you could teach him?"

"That is unlikely to happen. He drinks far too much. He has the wrong attitude, even for a surgeon. He is reckless with his patients. You really are entitled to force me to work for you, are you, Sir?"

"I am fully entitled to co-opt any citizen of your rank, or below. A senator would be another matter. Obviously no one can force you to do anything you don't want to do. You demonstrated that yesterday. But I can ensure you don't leave this camp. I think you may prefer to stay and do something constructive, rather than sitting about twiddling your thumbs. There are four legions hereabouts, twenty-four thousand men. We share the medical facilities, so you will be busy."

Allaine thought quickly. "Then while you are about it, Sir, perhaps you can co-opt Laurence Cornellius Calusa, to assist me."

"Who's he?"

"A nice lad. A Roman. He has been with me since Gergovia, so badly wounded he is unable to fight again. His right arm is useless. However he is beginning to use his left arm to write with. I find him useful."

"You seem to have a very unorthodox approach to prisoners, Allaine. The Cornellius family is one of the most distinguished in Rome. I will endeavour to smooth things over."

"That's good," Allaine said. He wondered how enslaving prisoners-of-war could possibly be considered unorthodox, as the

Romans did it all the time. "You realise Octavian is a skilled surgeon, do you?"

"That was obvious yesterday. I believe Labienus did mention something about it, as well. Would you by any chance be this Helvetian who rescued Hugo Domitius, Octavian Volusenus, and some legionaries from Ambiorix's clutches, and took them to Switzerland for safety?"

"Perhaps you had better ask Hugo," said Allaine, fully aware that Hugo was stationed in the south of the country. Antony decided not to pursue the matter further, as the outcome seemed entirely satisfactory to all.

To his great surprise Allaine spent an enjoyable winter. Being the chief medical officer was nothing like being Petronius's slave assistant. He managed to get a letter to Coevorten, to explain what was going on. He was a frequent guest of Mark Antony, who found his M.O. a most interesting man. Antony hosted many of the Tribal Chiefs on Caesar's behalf, doling out gold and expensive presents, to try and keep them sweet, with the promise of expropriated land, and low or no taxes into the bargain. He found Allaine's presence at dinners invaluable, with him knowing, or having knowledge of, all the important men in Gaul, most of whom appeared to have been at his wedding. Which makes Prince Allaine a pretty important man as well, Antony assumed.

Allaine discovered it was good to be with his Romans again, all of whom continued to treat him with their usual mixture of deference and affection. He found it hard to understand why he liked them so much. They were still the enemy, after all. But they felt more like family. He even missed Hugo and Darius. He slipped back into army routine, as if he had never left it, his high status an odd mixture of senior officer and Gallic prince.

When Octavian was off duty, he invariably turned up at the hospital to help out and assist in training a new batch of medical orderlies, some of whom were promising, he thought.

Like Allaine he enjoyed teaching, and was a little more forthcoming in his praise of the pupils' efforts than his chief. Allaine enjoyed his company. They worked so well together. He had so missed Octavian after he compelled him to leave his service, and return to the army. He felt guilty that he had forced his freedman into a hard place. He was all too aware of Octavian's feelings about the ever increasing sordidness of the last year's campaigns, carried out purely for enslaving, looting, and plunder, and terminating in that horrendous punishment at Uxellodunum.

Antony kept an eye on Allaine to start with, to ensure that he cured rather than killed his Roman patients; he was a barbarian, after all, however civilised his demeanour. Sometimes Antony came to watch surgical procedures and the occasional postmortem, saying it was the only form of entertainment in North Gaul. Allaine agreed with him. The camp women weren't up to much, even those reserved for the officers, and he found gambling abhorrent. He missed Riona and his sisters. After a very short while Antony allowed him out to hunt occasionally with the other officers, knowing he would return.

Antony departed often to consult with Caesar at Nemmetocenna, concerning their return to full blown Roman politics. When he was away he left Octavian in charge as Senior Tribune, Gaius still being too ill to function in any way.

Cold winter nights were relieved by drunken dinners in the officers' mess. Octavian was always in great demand to lead the singing. Allaine usually exited before Octavian started on his more obscene repertoire. He wasn't a great drinker. But if Octavian stuck to the sentimental, Allaine was happy to listen, and even participate. At Saturnalia, Octavian's and Allaine's birthday, there was almost an unfortunate incident.

"What happened to that beautiful red haired bint Caesar gave you for your birthday that time?" asked an officer who had been present at the evening seven years ago.

Octavian leapt to his feet, fists clenched. Allaine pulled him back down again.

"If you mean my sister, Chryseis Petronius," he informed the startled officer, "Octavian married her."

"Oh sorry, Sir," the officer stammered. "Very sorry. I had no idea. I didn't know she was your sister. Sorry, Octavian."

One evening, after they had chewed over the dreadful siege at Alesia, and the privations suffered by both armies, and Octavian had more than usual to drink, he launched into Dumnorix's lament. He sang so beautifully, many of his audience had moist eyes, even though they didn't understand the words. Allaine found it heartbreaking. So did Jay, he could see, sitting with his hands over his face, and tears running down his cheeks. Guéreth had his head bowed, as if praying. When the last notes were left hanging in the air, Octavian got up to go, staggering a little. Allaine and Marcius moved together to help him.

"Time for bed, I think, Octavian," Allaine said. "We'll give you a hand back to your tent."

Halfway across the parade ground, Octavian burst into song.

"Octavian, the men are trying to sleep."

"Oh, yes. Sorry," said Octavian.

He stopped suddenly, turned to Allaine, flung his arms round his neck, and said, "I love you, you know."

"Yes, I know," Allaine replied. He detached himself from the drunken embrace. "Come on, Octavian. You need to get to bed. You're out on patrol in the morning."

Octavian was looking at him with solemn brown eyes. "I love you like a brother. No, better than a brother."

"Yes, I know. You've already told me. Come on."

"It's not because you're like Chrys, because you're not. You're nothing like Chrys. Chrys is so beautiful. She's so beautiful."

Octavian started singing again, each salacious word perfectly modulated.

"Octavian!" Allaine thought he'd better shut him up quickly, as Octavian was quite capable in his present state, of extolling Chrys and her physical attractions in intimate detail to the entire camp.

"Enough, now, Octavian. I've told you to be quiet."

"Oh, sorry, Master," said Octavian.

A few awkward paces on, Octavian stopped again.

"You said you loved me like a brother, at your wedding. It was a joke, wasn't it?"

"No, it wasn't a joke."

"Oh, good. I thought you'd be angry with me, after Alesia and Uxellodunum."

"How could I be angry with you," Allaine said quietly, "when I had forced you into that position, against your will?"

Octavian sighed loudly with relief. "That's good. I *am* glad. I was worried."

"Don't worry about it any more, my pet. There is no need to worry any more."

Between them they managed to hand him over to the twins, to be stripped and put to bed. The twins grinned happily. They found their master hilarious when drunk. They had learned to skip nimbly out of the way, as he became overly affectionate. Once outside the tent, Allaine and Marcius looked at each other and started to laugh.

"He's such an idiot when he's drunk," said Marcius.

"But a nice one," Allaine agreed. "One of the best."

"He loved Dumnorix."

"Yes, so I heard. He's a very good officer, isn't he?"

"Superb. He wasn't, until you got hold of him."

"What do you mean?"

"You changed him. You changed us. All of us. For the better."

Allaine marvelled as Marcius knelt on the ground before him.

"I'm so glad you came back. We missed you. Goodnight, Sir," Marcius said, and kissed Allaine's hand.

"Maybe you've had too much to drink as well, Marcius."

Marcius laughed up at him, his face ruddy from the flames of the pitch torches around them.

"No, I haven't, Sir."

"Then goodnight, Marcius. Sleep well."

Gaius slowly improved. His fever lessened. He began to sit up, and take an interest in his surroundings. At last he got to grips with the language, now there was little else to distract him. Jayven kept him company, if he had nothing else on hand, playing his harp, and singing simple Aeduan songs. As well as Jay, Gaius had Guéreth to supper more often than not, and sometimes Allaine as well. The two Gauls started to look at each other differently. They disliked each other less. It didn't get any better than that.

There were wild cheers the first night Gaius entered the mess, on his crutches. In a short while he progressed to a stick.

At the end of winter Mark Antony left them to canvas for his election to the priesthood. He was returning to Rome, intending to smooth Caesar's path, when the time came for him to relinquish the Province.

Before he left Allaine sought permission to take Gaius to his own home during the summer, to continue with his recuperation. Gaius was desperate to see Lucy. The Aeduan invasion of Helvetia started in earnest, as Jayven and Guéreth asked if they could come as well. There would be many weddings in the summer.

BOOK 4: CHAPTER 15

Spring, 50 BC to Summer, 47 BC

By the Spring, Caesar was occupied with matters other than Gaul. The problem now was his return to Rome. How to achieve civic power, and consolidate the gains he had made. He was desperate for the Senate to award him a triumph. And he needed to be elected Consul.

The news wasn't good. Admittedly Mark Antony had been made Augur, despite moves against him, and thus against Caesar. Two of his enemies would be Consuls next year instead, Lucius Lentulus and Gaius Marcellus. They seemed determined to deny him all rights and privileges. What fools they were.

His stately journey during the summer through the Province, Cisalpine Gaul, and the Northern Italian towns back to Rome, was a triumph of a sort. The towns and cities put on a huge display of celebrations for his victories. However it was easy to see which way the wind was blowing in the Senate. Against him!

In the autumn Caesar hurried back to Gaul, thence back to Nemmetocenna. He brought all the legions together, and reviewed the state of his army. He was becoming more and more certain that war would decide power in Rome. He wanted Labienus to govern Cisalpine Gaul. Unfortunately Labienus didn't appear to be all that appreciative of Caesar's efforts on his behalf. According to Caesar's spies, he was found to be making overtures to Pompey.

Towards the end of the year, in the Senate, Gaius Curio, one of Caesar's stooges, proposed that since both Caesar and Pompey were in command of huge armies, making the Roman people terrified, wouldn't it be better if both disbanded their armies immediately? The proposal was talked out by Pompey's allies.

However the Senate did try to insist that both commanders give a legion to promulgate a war against Parthia. Caesar was asked to give up not only one of his own legions, Pompey said he would give up the one he had lent to Caesar after the disaster at Atuatuca. Caesar complied, handing over the First and the Fifteenth legions. He returned to Italy, but stayed dutifully outside in Cisalpine Gaul at Ravenna with the Thirteenth. There Caesar was appalled to find that the two legions he had forfeited had been given to Pompey, not to any Parthian war. And Pompey, against all regulations, was sitting in his house in Rome, with the two legions garrisoned just outside the city.

To add insult to injury, Caesar's report to the Senate about his Gallic conquests had been read, but not debated and accepted. Instead the Senate ordered him alone to disband his army, and refused to allow him to stand as a candidate for Consul in absentia, which meant he had no protection from the many charges of bribery, corruption, and war crimes levelled against him. Mark Antony and Quintus Cassius, fearing for their lives, fled from Rome to join Caesar at Ravenna.

Caesar knew what they were doing, of course. It was revenge. They were stamping on his face. This affront to his prestige, his *dignitas,* which was more important to him than life itself, as he told his friends, couldn't be born with equanimity. Did they have any idea who they were dealing with? A man who had conquered vast countries by land and sea, who had defeated Vercingetorix, the great Gallic leader, a man who knew every detail of the arts of warfare. A man who had ensured that he was accompanied by a legion of veterans, with another eight in Gaul he could call on. Legions who had proved their worth in battle time and again. No, the Senate were idiots. Self serving idiots, who needed to be taught a lesson. Don't mess with Caesar, or you will be crushed like a worm underfoot! He sent for the legions wintering in Gaul to join him at Ravenna.

On the seventh of January, only five days after the new

Consuls took office, the Senate moved openly against him by summoning all Romans to arms. The majority of the Senate then fled to Pompey.

Shortly afterwards two Roman knights arrived at Ravenna with a message from Pompey, apparently wanting Caesar to agree to some sort of solution to the crisis.

The discussion rocked backwards and forwards.

"Pompey can't seriously expect me to disband my army, while he hangs on to his."

"I think that's just what he and the Senate hope will happen, Sir."

"Where are his legions? Do we know for sure?"

"He claimed to the Senate that he has ten altogether, the two you gave up, the First and the Fifteenth. Then he has six legions loyal to him in Spain. There is also Lucius Domitius, holding two legions in North Italy." Antony was thoughtful. "At present we only have the Thirteenth. Two against one in Italy."

"He has some important client states in his favour in the East as well, Sir," added Cassius, "now Pompey is married to Scipio's daughter. Scipio is the Governor of Syria. He may also have no difficulty in raising troops."

"I want this message taken back to Pompey." Caesar started to dictate. "Pompey, I suggest if you want peace, then return to your provinces, and disband your army. I am not blind. I can see you are raising troops all over Italy. The Senate has caused the whole state to be up in arms. What is the aim of all this preparation, if not my destruction? Only we two can sort out these problems. I suggest we meet face to face and thrash the thing out sensibly."

He looked over his slave's shoulder to ensure Philemon had the words correctly, not that Philemon ever made mistakes, these days. He knew better. Punishment in the past had been severe, painful and humiliating in equal measure. Caesar smiled his satisfaction, and squeezed his secretary's arm, his fingers biting into the flesh.

"Tell Pompey, warn him, that if he doesn't follow my suggestions there will be war. Civil war. On his head be it."

"We will tell him, Caesar."

The knights returned to Rome, but had to come back empty handed, their mission of peace a failure.

"Caesar, Pompey won't give the necessary assurances, or meet for discussion. He has fled to Capua with the two legions. He said 'Rome cannot be defended.'"

Caesar shouted with laughter. "So he turns tail and runs, before we even make the first move. Well, gentlemen, the die is cast. I will speak to the men, and then we will march across the Rubicon and into Italy. By this time next year, it will all be over."

By the Spring Caesar had taken and secured all the garrison towns in Italy without any problems. Then he marched his army to Spain. Pompey and Labienus with most of the Senate, sailed in the other direction, shipping their forces to Illyricum. They started to raise more troops there.

Gaius didn't meet up with Octavian and Allaine until October, when Caesar was on his way back from Spain, after thoroughly routing the six Pompeian legions there.

Allaine had brought Riona and the children with him, as Riona wished to see Allaine's sisters, and show off her growing family, a boy now, to join Little Claudia. Gaius discovered that Octavian and Allaine had decided to meet up every Spring, before the sowing, and every Autumn, after the harvest, to exchange news and information, and have a good time together, with or without their families.

Allaine had turned down flat Mark Antony's invitation to be the chief medical officer of Caesar's army. Of course Antony had been in Syria when the Helvetians came up against Caesar, nine years ago, now. He probably knew little about what had happened to Allaine after capture.

Gaius found his relatives clustered round a series of

complex designs laid out on the floor. Having greeted him outside with unfeigned pleasure, they swiftly returned to the serious business of choosing which motif.

"Don't you like any of them?" Chrys asked her brother, after the discussion had raged on and on.

"I have something against mosaic floors, especially ones depicting geese," Allaine replied. "I prefer wood myself."

"Wood can look very good, if it is smoothed and polished," Marcus Metius observed. "But a mosaic floor will last for ever." He could see his sale disappearing.

"Never mind about floors," said Octavian. "You decide, Chrys. They all look good to me. Let's go into the solarium and hear the news."

Gaius was laden with presents, the most intriguing being a couple of pig's bladders blown up, and joined by a leather strap.

"Three guesses," said Gaius.

"Some new game?" Allaine suggested.

"Close. I'll give you a clue. This one's for kids."

They had no idea, and rapidly ran out of guesses.

"It's a buoyancy aid," said Gaius in triumph. "It's to help you swim. You shove it under your arms, see? Like this. It's for Dòchas."

He looked at Allaine. "Her Dad says it's OK," he said defensively. "Haetheric," he said in execrable Gallic. "I give to Dòchas? So she swim? Good?"

Haetheric shrugged his shoulders.

"See, Allaine? Her Dad's not bothered."

Haetheric grinned at Allaine, and looked at Gaius with an expression of amused tolerance.

"We discovered the Spanish tribes use these to cross rivers. Apparently they each have one of these devices when they are fighting a military campaign. Brilliant, isn't it?"

"And what does it feel like, Gaius, to be attacking your fellow Romans?"

"It feels horrible, Sir, especially when our own men were

captured and executed by the other side. That was dreadful. But casualties have been light so far. After we cut off their corn and fodder supplies, as well as their access to water, the Pompeians surrendered. Then we heard that the remains of the Senate in Rome had announced a Dictator was required, obviously to please Caesar. So he's off to Rome to become Dictator, then he can stand for election as Consul. Basically there's not going to be any opposition to a man in command of six legions in Italy, is there?"

Allaine laughed. "It seems unlikely. So when he is Consul, what then?"

"I am to pick up any more cavalry I can. Then we are all off to Brundisium to find ships, and pursue Pompey and Labienus in Illyricum."

"Well I hope you settle the affair quickly, one way or the other," said Octavian. "What do you think about Mum and Dad, though, Gaius. Shouldn't they come here?"

"If I think there's any danger, when I get back to Rome, I'll send them to you. And Lucy as well, if she is able to travel. We're expecting a little Roman Citizen," he ended with a complacent grin.

"You didn't lose much time," Octavian said.

"Look who's talking," said Gaius, then stopped abruptly, remembering the first occasion Octavian met Chrys wasn't up for general discussion. He'd have to watch his mouth with Allaine around.

"This calls for a celebration," Octavian declared hastily. "You can try the new wine. It's rough, but I think it will be good when it matures."

Gaius called again, on his way back with Jayven and Guéreth, and a host of Gallic cavalry. They rode into the courtyard in a cacophony of neighing horses, jingling harnesses and thudding hooves, and a flourish of plumed helmets, and scarlet cloaks. Breastplates, swords and spears glinted with menace in the sunlight. The children rushed out to greet them all in great excitement. The adults followed more slowly, but were just as delighted to see them.

"You fight with Caesar, Jayven?" said Allaine, embracing him. "Why? Because of Gaius?"

"No. After I was captured, I had to swear to fight with him in any future campaigns, Allaine. Otherwise he would have sold the Aeduan prisoners, instead of releasing them. So I have no choice. He has ordered me to join him."

"Now I understand." More of Caesar's mental torture.

"At least I get to kill Romans," Jay ended, with a rueful smile.

The Gauls wanted Octavian to look out for Zinny, Eloise, and the children. Gaius brought some surprising news.

"Dad's been made a Senator. So he thinks he will stay put for now, but he'll come to you or Allaine, if things get ropey in Rome. Mum is pleased about the Senator part, but she's very upset as our dear brother Claud is with Pompey, and she's convinced we will meet on the battlefield."

"When you do, run him through for me," said Octavian. But it was brought home to him just what civil war entailed. He was so thankful to be out of it. Although so far there hadn't been too much in the way of atrocities, he had no expectation that such a state of affairs would last. He kissed them all goodbye.

"Keep safe, all of you. Finish it quickly. Oh, and come back victorious. Good fortune!"

It wasn't settled quickly. The war raged over the entire world, apart from Gaul, Octavian thought thankfully. Dispatches from Gaius were few and far between.

Dyrrachium (Durrës), Illyricum (Albania), Greece 48 BC

They were stuck at Dyrrachium on the Albanian coast, trying to enclose Pompey's forces, and getting nowhere. Both armies were short of food and fodder. Pompey's horses were reduced to eating leaves from the trees. Caesar's soldiers were digging up roots of a plant they found, mashing it up, mixing it with milk from mangy cattle, and making thoroughly unpalatable bread with the resulting disgusting dough. Sometimes they threw the bread at the opposing forces. It set like cement if not eaten immediately.

Gaius would have given anything to have the resourceful twins with him. Haetheric was now an armed fighter on Gaius's own cavalry unit, very happy to kill Romans. Any Romans would do. Fáelán had been left at home with his mother and siblings, to his disgust. Gaius's old servant had never been any good at cooking even good food. At present he was hopeless.

Now there was trouble with the Gallic cavalry. Two of their senior officers, Prince Roucillus and his brother, Prince Egus, two chieftains of the Allobroges, were accused of withholding pay and plunder.

Gaius summoned the culprits to his tent, and tried to give them a dressing down, wading in with his usual lack of tact. The chieftains were furious. After all, Caesar had made them both Senators. They were no longer answerable to this jumped up cavalry commander. How dare this officer question them. They yelled back at him.

"How and when we pay our men is up to us to decide, not you, Gaius. We have the plunder safe, and will divide it up when we think the time is right, not when you say so."

"I'm consulting Caesar about this, then. It's not right." Gaius stalked off, annoyed.

He wasn't backed up by his commander. Caesar had more important matters to think about, such as how the hell was he going to get out of this God-awful mess? Their situation was so dire, he had tried to negotiate with Pompey, again without success.

"Gaius, these are exceptionally brave men. They've proved themselves time and again. I think it best to ignore a few little irregularities......"

"Little irregularities," Gaius spluttered, indignantly. "The men have not been paid, Sir. They are angry, very angry."

"Oh, very well, Gaius. I'll have a word with these chieftains, but quietly. I don't want to upset their sensibilities just now."

Really, what was the use, Gaius thought to himself. If they think they can get away with that, they'll think they can get away with anything.

Haetheric was grooming the horses. One of his fellow slaves from the Carnutes approached him.

"I don't know what you think of your master?"

"He's alright," Haetheric grudgingly admitted. Haetheric had refused to become a dedicated slave. There was no way he would ever swear allegiance to Gaius. But he was grateful to a limited extent, at least his master was looking after his family. But he was so far away from Gaul. His constant dread was that he might never see his family again.

"Tell him not to accept an invitation to dine tonight from my master, Prince Roucillus."

"Why not?"

"They're angry with him. They're planning to poison him, cut his head off, and desert to Pompey, taking your master's head with them, as proof of their loyalty."

"Very likely."

"Suit yourself. Don't say I didn't warn you."

When Prince Roucillus appeared, wanting to know where Gaius was, because he wished to mend fences and dine with him this evening, Haetheric lied that unfortunately his master was stuck in the latrine, with a violent stomach upset.

"Perhaps some other night, Sir."

Prince Roucillus stormed off. Haetheric wasn't sure what would happen to him if Gaius was killed. He thought he'd better find out, and soon. He failed to mention the invitation to his master. Roucillus and his brother duly departed in the night, with all their retainers, but without Gaius's head, and joined the other side, able to acquaint Pompey with all the weaknesses of Caesar's position. Which were many.

Pompey said he would have preferred Caesar's head to that of Volusenus's. However he paraded the Gallic princes and their men round his camp, to hearten his forces. Armed with the inside information, when Pompey attacked he was able to inflict huge casualties on the enemy forces, routing them from their positions, causing panic in their ranks, and making Caesar retreat hastily, the troops scurrying back to the protection of their camps. Caesar lost a third of his men, with many more wounded. He had to march his soldiers away silently in the night, like beaten dogs.

Gaius had his work cut out, trying to defend the wounded and the baggage, when Pompey's cavalry eventually caught them up. But to his astonishment, the enemy's main forces didn't arrive to inflict the final blow. Why Pompey failed to pursue the defeated army, no one ever knew. It turned out to be a fatal mistake on his part.

Just one month later, with Gaius and Jayven leading the cavalry, Caesar and his army decisively defeated the Pompeian forces at Pharsalus. It was a hard battle, fought all day long, from daybreak to sunset.

That night Gaius returned to the quarters he shared with Jay, feeling exhausted, hungry, hot and thirsty, to find no sign of Haetheric. He was so sure Haetheric had survived the battle. He had caught sight of him when they attacked Pompey's camp at the end of the day. His servant had no idea where the Gaul had got to. Gaius went to bed feeling a little dispirited, despite Jay saying they would order a search in the morning.

Haetheric woke Gaius and Jayven at dawn. He was clutching on to a dishevelled man covered with cuts and bruises.

"Slave of Prince Roucillus. Carnute like me," Haetheric explained, gesturing to the man. "All night I look for him." He turned to his companion. "Tell him," he ordered the man. "Tell the

Tribune what you tell me before."

Jay sat up cross-legged on his bed, and acted as interpreter. As Gaius listened astounded, haltingly the battered man told of the plot by Roucillus to behead him.

"So," Haetheric said at the finish,"he save your life. I save your life. I say to Roucillus you sick. Now you free us." He stared at Gaius. Did the tribune understand? He didn't seem to be making any impression on his master.

"I want go home," said Haetheric despairingly. "Home to my country. I want my wife. I want my children. So? Now you free us? Yes?"

"Soon, I promise you. As soon as Pompey is caught, we will go home," Gaius told him. "I too want my wife."

Pompey fled ignominiously to Egypt, removing his insignia from his clothes and his horse, first. The Senate in Rome, on hearing the news, hastily declared Caesar to be Dictator for another five years. The Republic was visibly coming to an end.

Gaius heard of the assassination of Pompey while they were on their way to Egypt in pursuit. He found a certain irony when Pompey's head was presented to Caesar. He had so nearly lost his own. There were still Labienus and Pompey's two sons to contend with, of course, together with all the Pompeian forces in Africa, but during the long siege of Alexandria, to Haetheric's relief, Gaius decided to call it a day. He hadn't got over Labienus putting the captive legionaries to death at Dyrrachium. He didn't think he ever would get over it.

Gaius travelled back to Gaul with Jayven and the Gallic cavalry, going from island to island across the Mediterranean, until at last they reached Genua. He was to escort his parents back to Rome, with his mother-in-law Ursula, and a devastated Lucy.

Lucy had laboured for days, long and hard. She couldn't imagine why the Goddesses were punishing her like this. All the appropriate sacrifices had been made, the prayers said. The pain

714

was terrible, overwhelming. It was torture, dying down for a tiny space, giving some hope of relief, but then crashing back into her again, till she could think of nothing but the unbearable pain, no longer even able to know which part of her body was trying to wrench her in two. Ursula and Claudia were at a loss to know what to do. The midwife was equally useless. Octavian didn't know how to proceed. He was desperately worried. They could all see Lucy becoming ever weaker day by tortuous day. But only Octavian realised how closely death was approaching.

Fortunately Allaine had been there, arriving in the nick of time, holding her tight, and telling her he would have to destroy the baby inside her, or the baby would destroy her. Even more fortunately, he magicked the pain away. He tried his best to help her cope with her grief afterwards. It was a girl baby. Lucy felt such a failure. She knew how much Gaius had looked forwards to children of his own. How was it the Gallic women sailed through childbirth, with hardly a loss?

"It will be better next time, Lucy," Allaine tried to comfort her, without much success. At the moment she didn't want there to be a next time. She wondered if Gaius would have preferred the baby to her.

"That is absolute nonsense," Allaine scolded. "Stop it, Lucy."

But then he had to deal with an equally devastated Gaius, who had experienced a sharp pang of jealousy when Haetheric knelt to gather his overjoyed children into his arms. Gaius was upset because his Lucy was upset, saddened by the loss of his little girl, but also grieving on his own account. He had lost good friends at Dyrrachium. The war was becoming increasingly sordid, as Octavian had predicted.

"Labienus had them killed, Allaine. His own men. My men! I suppose you will rejoice at that. You said we would tear ourselves to pieces, didn't you? You were so right."

"You wrong me, Gaius. I hate war. All war. But you don't need a lecture, do you? I can see you are wounded yourself, in mourning for your little girl, and for your friends. It will heal in time, but it will take time to heal."

"I hate to see Lucy so upset. I thought when I married her, that I could stop the world causing her any more harm. She's suffered enough already. But that's rubbish, of course. Living causes harm, doesn't it, Allaine? I agree with you. Wars cause harm as well. Terrible harm. Especially civil wars."

"Come and have a drink before dinner, Gaius," Octavian invited. "You too, Jay. The girls won't want to hear about battles, but we do. You can tell us what happened."

They listened eagerly to Gaius's dramatic account, with occasional interruptions from Jay giving additional information.

"So Pompey sailed to Egypt, and arrived at Pelusium, at the mouth of one of the Nile deltas," Gaius finished. "But when he went in a boat to confer with Young Ptolomy, the Egyptians killed him. Caesar wasn't at all pleased about that. I think he really wanted Pompey in his own hands. I wonder what he would have done with him."

"He'd have to kill him, surely. What else could he do? Pompey would soon have raised another army. There are still his allies in Africa to contend with."

"I expect you're right. It's just as well, then, the Egyptians did the job for him. Afterwards Caesar only had to take one look at Cleopatra, and that was it. He fell for her, hook, line and sinker."

"What's she like?"

"Exotic. Different. Very very sexy, but regal, with it. Like Chrys."

"What do you mean, like Chrys?" Octavian demanded angrily.

"What I say, regal, like Chrys. Exotic, like Chrys. Only with blue black hair, instead of that glorious red, and olive skin, instead of creamy, and huge dark eyes, instead of huge grey ones."

Octavian began to think his brother noticed far too much

716

about his wife.

"You know what Chrys is like if she disapproves of anything. Makes you feel you've just crawled out from under a stone," Gaius continued, oblivious. "And are you trying to tell me Chrys isn't the most devastatingly beautiful girl in the world? Everyone is jealous of you. You must know that."

These final fair words caused Octavian to simmer down. So Gaius thought Chrys was on a par with the Queen of Egypt. Privately Octavian thought Helen of Troy herself wouldn't hold a candle to his Chrys. What Gaius saw in Lucy he couldn't begin to imagine.

"I was so close to her," Gaius went on. "She looks amazing, and she smells delicious. She wanders around in those fine dresses, almost transparent. She doesn't leave much to the imagination."

And nor did Chrys, he thought, the first time Octavian saw her. Better not mention it though, just in case. His little brother had a mighty hard fist, and was looking quite cross, still.

"She wears jewels round her neck, and in her crown, worth the entire Roman treasury reserve, and then some." Gaius grinned to himself as he visualised the Egyptian queen.

"At present Caesar is besieged in Alexandria. There isn't a great need for cavalry just now. I got so homesick for Lucy and all of you, and Haetheric was desperate to see his family. We managed to find enough boats for most of the Gallic cavalry, and we hopped across the Med till we got to Genua."

Valerius was the next to arrive. Having sustained a nasty wound at the battle of Zela, in Pontus, Northern Turkey, he made his way home to Allaine, and his own wife and child. Allaine was pleased to see him, and hear that Val wished to remain with him permanently. He had missed his cheerful freedman with his uncritical adoration. He ordered his chef to include Val's favourite pasta dish at dinner, and took him over to the bath house himself.

"Tell me everything, Val. News has been hard to come

by."

"Prince Jayven and Guéreth are going to Africa with Caesar, Sir," Val said. "Darius is going as well. He's been promoted to Decanus, in charge of an eight man squad."

"Good grief!"

"I know," said Val with a grin. "He told me not to worry. He'd look out for Prince Jay."

Allaine burst out laughing.

"Labienus has joined with Scipio, Cato, and King Juba of Numidia. Apparently they have mustered fourteen legions between them. But the M.O. didn't think I'd be fit for any more fighting, so I've been discharged."

"So what was it like?"

"It's so hot in Egypt, Sir. You've no idea."

"Did you see Queen Cleopatra?"

"Only once. She looked as if she was pregnant. Caesar's, I expect. He's been shagging her almost since we arrived. Unless it's her brother's. The Egyptians are a strange lot. They're in mourning, 'cos their massive library burnt down. But, Sir, you should see their temples. Huge. Enormous statues of Pharaohs, and their Gods. Really weird, their Gods are. Kind of animals and humans combined. So much gold everywhere. And obelisks, enormous stones set up in the forum. Everything is on such a massive scale, not just the library."

"How did you get wounded, Val?"

"It was one of those war chariots, with scythes attached to the wheels, and I couldn't get out of the way in time. There's no one like you there, Sir, or Octavian. So the surgeons made a right old mess of my wound as you can see, even though I was trying to tell them what to do. Apparently I'd say something, and pass out."

Allaine had a good look at the damage. "Yes, I see what you mean. We can sort it out, Val. Don't you worry."

"I know, Sir. That's why I came back. Well, that and other things," Val conceded. "After the battle Caesar reviewed the troops and said 'I came, I saw, I conquered.' We all laughed at that."

Allaine didn't think the troops would be doing much laughing after they went to Africa. As he found out subsequently from Darius, he was absolutely right.

BOOK 4: CHAPTER 16

Rome 46 BC

It was so very hot. The prisoners were brought up one at a time, stiff and blinded by the brightness, hardly able to see. Through his blank blurred eyes Vercingetorix saw his companions for the first time since their capture. They were strangers to him. Had he ever seen them before? He didn't know or care. There was a lot of noise, roars from many people. Idly he wondered where they were, and why. It was so very hot. A part of his brain woke up, remembering cool mountain streams. He stopped sweating immediately, and smiled a little. That's better. He looked at the heavy metal chains on his thin wrists. As he looked, they became wheat stems, and blew away in a cooling breeze. He knew something vital was finishing today. He knew he was pleased it was finishing. He didn't know why, but it mattered not at all. He smiled faintly at his companions. He was glad he wasn't alone. He liked to have companions. This would be a long journey....

It was so very hot. Lucterius looked at his commander. He was slightly jealous, wishing he too had Druidical training, able to transmigrate his soul, even before death intervened. He presumed he looked just as bad as the others did, clothed in filthy rags, and stinking. At least it should be finished today. He had been wanting it to finish every day for the last six years. He tried to whisper a word of comfort to one of his companions, a man in obvious pain from the appalling sores visible under his chains, his bare feet swollen, his chest heaving for air. Lucterius was immediately struck on the head.

"No talking there."

A figure approached the group of huddled prisoners and guards, one of the Military Tribunes of the Fourteenth, by the look of his insignia. He spoke in a voice the centurion recognised with pleasure.

"Centurion Pullo, it seems to me you will have quite a job getting these wretches to their feet, let alone making them walk behind Caesar's triumphal chariot."

"Well, well, Tribune Volusenus. How good to see you, Sir. We were sorry when you left. We missed the singing something awful."

The centurion looked round at his prisoners.

"I know what you mean, Sir. Look at Vercingetorix. Remember how terrified we were, when we saw him charging towards us, on that beautiful horse of his? These prison guards are a hopeless lot. Surely they should have realised the captives were to be kept fit enough for a Triumph."

"I suppose it's been a long time. Much too long, really, to be a prisoner in the Mamertine Prison. I should know. I was there, myself, once."

"Were you, Sir?"

"Just for a night. Even that short spell gave me a horror of prisons. But Caesar should have been awarded a Triumph for the conquest of Gaul four years ago. They should never have been incarcerated for this length of time."

"So he should have, Sir. But these campaigns of his have taken a lot of sorting out. We've been all over the world. And it's not finished yet. Have you any suggestions for these wretches, then, Sir?"

"Here, I have something in this flask that will get them to the steps of the Capitol. Give it to them mixed with some wine."

"Good idea, Sir." Pullo saluted his old officer, and walked off to get the wine from a nearby street vendor.

"What is it, Tribune?" Lucterius asked, his voice thin and reedy in the heat.

"It is oblivion, Sir. It is a gift from Prince Allaine."

"My thanks to you, Tribune. Good fortune to you for this kindness," Lucterius stuttered hesitantly over the Latin words. They were his last.

It was so very hot. The mass of prisoners stumbled their way to their deaths, walking slowly through the baking streets of Rome. Each one was lashed to the long ropes of heavy chains trailing in the dust behind Caesar's chariot. Some of the crowd threw stones, but the soldiers guarding the prisoners stopped most of the missiles with their shields. Vercingetorix found it pleasantly cool when they eventually returned to the prison. He smiled as the thick silken cords were placed round his neck and pulled so tight. Now he would be free at last.

The disgusting noises of men being strangled ceased with the final victim.

"Jupiter, don't they stink," the executioner observed, looking at the heap of corpses. "What now, Sir?"

Centurion Pullo felt sentimental, for once. "They might stink now, my lad, but they were great men in their day. They are to be taken outside the city walls, to be burned at the municipal dump."

The executioner was rifling through the rags clothing the bodies. "There's not much here worth salvaging," he grumbled. "Oh, I don't know though. What's this, Sir?"

He shook out the contents of the soft leather bag he had found, hanging from a cord underneath the prisoner's ragged tunic. The tiny jade chessmen glinted in the light. Centurion Pullo confiscated them immediately. He could sell them for a good price, he thought.

Octavian walked away. He wouldn't stay to see the procession. He could imagine it all any way. He went to a celebratory dinner in the officers' mess that night, but already he was growing away from them. Many of his old comrades had participated in the Spanish, Egyptian, Pontian, and African wars as well, and could talk of little else. The conquest of Gaul was the distant past to them, with so many more campaigns under their belts. War was boiling up again in Spain. There were still Labienus and Pompey's sons to be vanquished. Some were already anticipating more spoils, more bloody glory.

722

He would stay with his parents, and see the rest of the triumphs, and attend some of the games, but he didn't want to see the two thousand strong armies of recent war captives, that were to fight each other to death at the Circus Maximus. He thought how angry Allaine would be if he ever got to hear about it. Even some of the plebs thought it was wanton extravagance on Caesar's part. Octavian wanted to get back to his family, and the peace of Gaul as soon as he could decently manage, without upsetting his mother too much.

Darius was the last to return. He arrived at his former master's home on leave for a short spell. He was anxious to see Allaine, who was equally anxious to hear his first hand account. His freedman's speech in Latin was still appallingly ungrammatical, but Allaine knew he was sharp, with a good grasp of military detail. He installed Darius on a couch, with a liberal supply of wine and food for all of them, and settled down to listen, together with Coevorten and Valerius. Darius spoke well, more concerned with the privations suffered by his horse, than with his own difficulties. He graphically related the salient points of the African campaign, finishing up with the bloody end of the war.

"Finally we gets to grips with the enemy at a place called Thapsus. Caesar couldn't hold us back. We charged, they scattered. Our blood was up, Sir, and that's the truth. But we didn't ought to have done it, all the same."

"What shouldn't you have done, Darius?"

"Scipio's men was trying to surrender. They throwed down their weapons, but we cut them down where they stood. It makes me feel bad when I think about it, 'cos we knew it weren't right. They was legionaries, same as us, following orders, same as us. I dunno what to do about it, Sir. I thought you'd know how to make it right."

"You want me to exonerate you?"

"I dunno, Sir." Darius looked apprehensively at his former master. "Does it hurt?"

"It will have been decided by your officers, Darius, not you. You could all have been stopped by the trumpet signals. If no one gave the order, then it is the officers and generals who are to blame for the massacre, not you."

"That's good to hear, Sir, that it's not all us at fault. Anyways, I've bin called up again. We're off to Spain to finish it, once and for all."

"Have you everything you need? Is Bucephalus recovered, or do you need another horse?"

"He's fine, Sir, thanking you. I've got everything. There's just one thing that's bin bothering me, like."

Darius stopped speaking, and looked embarrassedly at the floor.

"What is it, my pet?"

"You said I'd never make a soldier, Sir," Darius blurted out.

"I was so wrong, wasn't I, Darius?"

"You think I am a proper soldier, now?"

"You are a very brave soldier. I am proud of you."

Darius heaved a sigh of relief. "That's alright, then. I just wanted to make sure."

The Senate appointed Caesar to the office of Dictator for ten years. He brought Cleopatra and her son to feature in his Egyptian Triumph. Her younger defeated sister Arsinöe was exhibited, chained behind his triumphal chariot. But this didn't go down well with the populace. They felt sorry for the poor girl. They could see the chains were too heavy for her thin wrists. When the chariot jerked forwards unexpectedly, making her fall over, she started to cry. Caesar was made to realise their displeasure by the jeers and catcalls of the crowd. He wasn't expecting cries of 'Murderer!' Hastily he arranged for her to be confined in the Temple of Artemis at Ephesus, instead of being strangled like the other principal prisoners.

Caesar installed Cleopatra in one of his many country estates, and then, finding that inconvenient for his nocturnal sorties, much nearer, in a house on the Janiculum. The citizens of Rome lapped up the scandal. After all, he was still married to Calpernia, daughter of Piso. Some of the populace had misgivings about the Dictator's unprecedented term of office. Many more took great offence when he installed a golden statue of Cleopatra as the Goddess Isis, in the temple of his ancestress, Venus Genetrix.

"When will you name Caesarion as your heir," the Egyptian queen demanded yet again, on one of his nightly visits.

He looked at her. She was so young, so beautiful, and so politically naive. He was becoming annoyed with her constant foolish attempts to control him, all doomed to failure. Tonight he didn't feel like prevaricating, he was getting tired of it, but not of her. It was time to make her appreciate her place in his schemes.

"Never," he said, faking astonishment and indignation. "Never. He is a bastard. Hardly an appropriate heir for me."

He could see his words made his royal mistress angry. Good. He would stoke her fire, and then quench it with his lust.

"I am making Gaius Octavius my heir. I've had my will drawn up again," he said, as he smiled that infuriating smile. He liked young Octavius. A beautiful youth. Possibly in love with his famous Great Uncle Julius. Most annoying that his mother wouldn't let him come to Africa, so his uncle could find out for sure.

"But you promised!"

"I have no intention of keeping a promise to a barbarian queen, who wanders around her palaces wrapped only in a carpet. Who knows who fathered the child?"

She sprang at him then, his hot-tempered, spiky, dark-skinned, sexy, oh so sexy woman. He was fully erect so swiftly, as he grabbed her wrists, and pulled her down onto the couch. She tried to turn her face away from him, so he shoved his knee between her legs, prising her thighs apart, holding both her wrists above her head. She started to shout for her attendants, so he covered her mouth with his own. She promptly bit his lip. He leant back on his heels, and slapped her hard across her face. "You bitch," he exclaimed delightedly. "You fucking beautiful bitch." He forced himself into her in an ecstasy of pleasure.

When he'd finished with her, he kissed her breasts and stomach, then he leant back again between her thighs, rubbing his hands up and down her smooth oil-scented body. He knew full well how much she hated him. He boasted to his intimates he had to conquer Egypt every night.

Cleopatra stared back at him, still outraged at his broken promise. She didn't care about the rough handling, he'd been like that from the first. But without his backing, and the backing of his legions, she would no longer be queen of Egypt. When was he going to divorce his wife, or poison her for preference?

As he rode back to town, one of the plebs scattered out of his way by his escort, called out, "Filthy adulterer!"

He had the fellow arrested and imprisoned immediately, on a charge of spreading sedition.

They didn't see Darius again for a long time, not for almost as year, and as Octavian pointed out, one of the longest years there had ever been. He returned after the battle of Munda in Spain, the final bitter end of the Civil War.

When Darius arrived at Allaine's house, it was to find Octavian, Chrys and the children there already, having been invited by Coevorten to attend the sacrificial service in tribute to Grandmother, who had died at the end of a hard winter, a short while before. By now Darius had his own slaves, with their own horses. He had been offered land near Narbonne, but preferred to be in Helvetia. Allaine postponed discussion until after the formal dinner to welcome home his much travelled protégé.

Everyone gathered around, eager to listen as Darius made

his report to the man he always thought of in his own mind, as his personal Commander, the man to whom he must justify himself and his actions.

"Well as you know, Sir, while Caesar was looking the other way, having his Triumphs, Pompey's sons, Gnaeus and his young brother Sextus was gathering forces in Spain. General Labienus was with them. I was glad you wasn't around, Sir, 'cos you wouldn't have liked it. It was horrible. It started off foul, and then got wuss."

Darius stopped to replenish his wine glass, while Allaine sent out for the maps.

"We lost a load of cavalry at first, but then our reinforcements comes from Italy, along with Gaius Octavius. He's a handsome bloke. Very young. Caesar had him in his carriage most days. We reckon he fancies him."

Darius traced the line of battle from town to town, city to city, with vivid detail. His audience were able to visualise the scenes from his colourful descriptions, only too thankful that they hadn't been involved themselves in such a sordid campaign.

"In the end we come to Munda. Pompey had thirteen legions, and masses of light infantry and cavalry. But Caesar couldn't keep us in check. We was right fed up, we wanted it decided, once and for all. We pushed hard on the right wing, then Prince Jay brought up his cavalry on the left wing, and the Pompeians had nowhere to go except to run back to the town. They fled the field. Prince Jay killed Labienus with a beautiful javelin shot, as good as one of Hugo's. He were that pleased with hisself afterwards. He says to me, 'One more down, but still one to go, Darius.' I dunno what he meant."

Darius looked innocently at his master. They both knew perfectly well what Jay meant.

"Gnaeus Pompey fled the battlefield, but he was badly cut about. You won't like the next bit, Sir. I didn't much like it, messell. We had to blockade the town, so we piled up the dead bodies as a rampart. We reckoned there was about thirty thousand of them. We stuck severed heads on top, with their faces pointed towards the town. It went round the town completely."

"That is so disgusting," Octavian remarked.

"It was, Sir. And it was getting hot. The smell was something awful. Then we hears that finally Gnaeus Pompey had been run to earth, and killed. His head was brought to Hispalis. Mind you, his brother Sextus has got away."

"I think you should make an effort to write a full account of all this," Allaine suggested. "It will help with your reading and writing, as well as being an excellent record from the ordinary legionary's viewpoint."

"You'll have to help me then, Sir."

"Very well, Darius. We will make it our winter project."

"That would be great, Sir. I'll call it 'The Spanish War,'" Darius said in triumph.

BOOK 4: CHAPTER 17

Winter 45 BC : Spring 44 BC

Allaine stared at Octavian in disbelief.

"I've been appointed a Senator? Octavian, that's impossible."

"Not at all, Sir. According to Dad, there are another eight hundred and ninety nine Senators now. Rather unwieldy, I would have thought." Although also according to Titus, Caesar's habit of stuffing the Senate with Gauls and other provincials, wasn't going down too well with some of the plebs.

"But he can't know who I am."

"It was Mark Antony who recommended you. He said you had given enormous help to him, to achieve peace in Gaul. And you have served as a surgeon, and then as a senior medical officer in the army in the north, with singular success. And let's face it, Sir, you're plenty rich enough."

"Does one have to be rich to be a Senator?"

"Yes, Sir."

"Stop calling me 'Sir,'" said Allaine crossly. "I feel as if we are going backwards." He was genuinely angry that his life was no longer entirely under his own control. Curse these Romans! He glared at Octavian. "There is no way I can become a Senator. I refuse to contemplate such a ridiculous suggestion. *This* is my country, not Rome."

No wonder Jay had been sitting there with a smirk on his face. Octavian decided to take charge.

"Allaine, sit down and shut up for a moment."

"What?"

"Stop being so angry. Do as I say. Sit down and shut up." Octavian thought fleetingly, that he had never given Allaine an order before. How odd to start when Allaine had just become a Senator.

Rather to his surprise, Allaine obeyed, sitting staring at them all in fury. Lucky they had been speaking in Gallic, Octavian thought. The young tribune detailed to deliver news of the appointment was looking bewildered. He had been told to treat the recipient, Antistius Petronius Antinous Allanus, with the utmost deference. He was alarmed to find the new Senator shouting at Octavian Volusenus, who had been so helpful to him. He glanced at Prince Jayven. He was no help. He was looking back at him with an expression of unholy glee. The young tribune wondered if he had unknowingly committed some gross error. It was well known that the Gauls were a temperamental volatile race. Maybe he had done something to offend. Although all he had actually done so far, was to salute, and hand over the engraved copper sheet, with the confirmation of the appointment.

Jay tried to make things worse, as usual. "I'm sorry, Allaine, but you have to be a Senator first, before you can become a Consul." He looked at the expression on Allaine's face, and laughed aloud.

"Jay, you shut up, too. Allaine, listen to me," Octavian started. "The Roman people have given you an unprecedented honour. This is a wonderful gesture on their part. It is for your country, not just for you. To cement peace between us all. To recognise how important it is for Helvetia to become closely connected to Rome. Please realise that this invitation cannot be turned down. Jupiter! You would start another war! It would be considered the grossest of insults."

His words appeared to be having some effect. Octavian sat down next to his beloved brother-in-law, and laid a hand on his arm. "You don't have to attend the Senate meetings to be a Senator. My father says he can vote on your behalf, by proxy, if you trust to his judgement. But Allaine, you have never yet been to Rome. Wouldn't you like to go this coming Spring? You could take Riona and the children. All being well, we are planning to visit my parents then. They would so love to see you. And Gaius would be pleased as well. Lucy may be pregnant again. She seems terrified of the thought, unless you are around at the end. What do you think?"

"Stop speaking, Octavian. You're going too fast. I want to get my breath back, and my thoughts together."

"Well, when you have done that, you are expected to make a gracious speech to the tribune here, accepting this wonderful opportunity to serve your people. I'm afraid that now includes Roman people as well, Allaine."

Allaine supposed he'd better make a start. He looked into the worried eyes of the young tribune, and coldly told him to stand down. To the young tribune's relief, the rest of the conversation was in Latin. Allaine rose to his feet, and thanked him for his good offices in having travelled so far and so fast to give him the news of his appointment. Octavian arranged for him to be conducted to the bath house.

"What's the news from your father, Octavian?" Allaine asked, having simmered down a little.

"Caesar is back in Rome. Spain is now officially pacified. Sextus Pompey has taken charge of his father's fleet, so he will be a problem, but no one is dealing with him at present. Dad says there are some Senators suggesting Caesar should be made Dictator in perpetuity."

"I thought he was already Dictator for the next ten years. And Consul this year with Lepidus."

"He is. Dad says apparently his supporters think that's not long enough. On the other hand he says there are beginning to be mutterings about Caesar wanting to be king."

"It sounds as if he's already king in all but name."

"Not really. As fellow Consul, Lepidus can veto any law he doesn't approve of, like Mark Antony did last year over Dolabella. And ultimate power still resides with the Senate. What honours the Senate bestows, it can also remove. Dad says opposition to Caesar is growing, even among the plebs."

"I would have thought especially among the plebs. After all, Caesar cut the corn dole, didn't he? That means there are a hundred and fifty thousand people who don't like him at all. Why did he do that, do you think?"

"Perhaps he thought people should get up off their backsides and work for a living. Also, I'm not sure the state can afford it, at present. These endless wars have to be paid for somehow."

Allaine knew that only too well.

Octavian didn't find it too difficult to persuade Allaine to fall in with his plans, especially as Chrys was so enthusiastic. She found she missed the excitement of Rome at times.

"Riona will love it. There's so much to see. And it's high time the children saw their grandparents again. And, Allaine, Mum would love to see little Claudia."

"She's not so little." Perhaps he would go. Octavian was quite correct. He would like to see Rome.

They had a lovely few days making travel plans, and getting into contact with Marcius. Jay said he would travel with them. Caesar had already summoned him to Rome for yet another campaign. In Parthia, this time. Guéreth said it wasn't a problem. He would be happy to stay in Gaul, and solve any that arose, while they were all away. Eloise was due in December, and he couldn't imagine she would want to travel with a tiny baby. Tzïnne opted to stay put, as well. The thought of a mass of Romans still had the power to fill her with fear. Allaine thought Valerius would like to go part of the way with them, and visit his father. The intention was to stay all summer in Rome.

"Will your parents be able to accommodate us, though?" Allaine asked in concern.

"That won't be a problem at all. There must be many empty houses to rent, after so many knights and Senators have been killed."

Allaine notified Coevorten of his plans. He discovered Coevorten was pleased with the news of his appointment. He sent for Riona and the children to join him at Bibracte, to spend part of the winter with Octavian. Then the plan was to travel by the coast roads, properly escorted, and arrive in Rome in Spring. Jay and Marcius would go with them as well.

The party arrived at the beginning of March. Titus and Claudia were delighted to see them all. They exclaimed at the way Junior and Little Allaine had grown, not easy anymore to call him Little Allaine, as he looked as if he was going to follow in his uncle's footsteps. Claudia adored Baby Gaius, and his bigger sister, little Dianthe, named after Grandmother, and so far their only granddaughter. Claudia was enchanted to meet her namesake, now eight years old, and Allaine's two young boys. Allaine hugged his host and hostess, and even hugged Gaius. It was lovely to be surrounded by such warmth. He smilingly explained the reasons for their journey.

"Basically, Octavian insisted. You know what he's like. As he wouldn't shut up about it, I thought I had better agree. Also Riona thought it was time the children met up with their big cousins. And I thought we should all see a bit of the city. Anyway, Riona wants to do some shopping."

"Mother will be pleased about the shopping."

"I inherited some valuable estates from Antistius Petronius, the man who adopted me. I wish to ensure they are being run in the way I would like. Octavian says he will come with me. I would enjoy your company as well, Gaius."

Gaius grinned at him. "What about the Senate?"

Allaine shrugged his shoulders. "I don't know yet if I will take a seat in the Senate. Some reconnaissance first might be a good idea. We've heard that Caesar will be off to Parthia soon, so I think I will wait until he's gone. I don't particularly wish to meet him again."

Gaius found that easy to understand. He was delighted to find Jayven so desperate to see him. His beautiful, laughing Jay, more handsome than ever. They hugged and kissed each other enthusiastically, curled up on a couch together, and didn't stop talking and gossiping for hours.

Allaine enjoyed exploring the city under Octavian's and Gaius's guidance, but they kept away from the Forum. He didn't enjoy a gladiatorial contest, even though no one was killed during the event, but he found the chariot races at the Circus quite enthralling. Titus arranged a visit to the theatre to see 'Phaedra,' which was much appreciated, and another to see a rather crude comedy, which wasn't.

One morning Claudia announced that the girls would go with her to the shops, and then they would take the children to the baths. Afterwards they would call on Ursula and Lucia, despite Chrys and Riona looking anything but enthralled by the prospect of spending an afternoon with Ursula. Still, they agreed it would be pleasant to see Lucy, especially as she was in an interesting condition. They could swap horror stories about childbirth.

A servant reported that Caesar wasn't expected at the Senate today, as he wasn't feeling well. So Titus Volusenus decided it would be an ideal time to take Allaine to see the major sights of his beloved city, and Octavian wanted to see the changes. A great deal of building was going on. Titus was forced to explain that the prison where his young friend's hero had been kept, and then strangled, was in the Forum itself. But Allaine said he was happy to go to a place that had decided so much of his own destiny. He very much wanted to see the Senate House. Titus had to explain again, that it wasn't possible, as one of Caesar's first acts as Consul this year, had been to pull it down and arrange for the building of an improved version. The Senate were meeting at the Theatre of Pompey instead.

"Where is everyone?" Allaine asked, surprised by the empty streets, instead of the previously crowded pavements.

"Today is the feast day of the Goddess Anna Perenna, mostly celebrated by the common people. They'll be out having picnics on the banks of the Tiber, and getting drunk, no doubt."

"Apparently there are some games organised in the

Theatre of Pompey, Dad. I expect we'll meet a few spectators on the way to the Forum," Gaius said.

Their progress was slow. The twins were agog with excitement, and wanted explanations for everything they saw, which involved everyone trying to satisfy their curiosity. There was a constant grabbing of their master's sleeve, and cry of "Octavian, what is that building?" or "Who does that enormous statue represent?"

"So many temples," said Drustan, in awe. He was surprised. Although of course they had always attended the ceremonies at the camp altar before battles, neither his master nor Gaius Volusenus had seemed much concerned with religion, unlike the twins. But clearly this couldn't apply to the majority of the population. He wondered what Prince Allaine thought of it, and decided to find out at a more appropriate time. Prince Allaine never minded answering questions, as long as he wasn't otherwise occupied. He had told Drustan it was part of the master's role to educate, and acted accordingly.

Titus had got used by now, to his sons treating the twins almost like members of the family. Octavian had always been an indulgent master, but Gaius's equally indulgent attitude to the twins surprised him rather. Gaius was usually a strict disciplinarian. Still, it saved Allaine from showing ignorance. He was getting plenty of information. He was astonished by the Aqueduct Marcia, and asked Titus many questions about its construction. Titus thought he'd better invite an architect to dinner. He didn't know the answers.

They wandered into the Forum. There was quite a crush of people. Titus was surprised and alarmed to hear that Caesar was expected after all, but there was no time to retreat. A trumpet sounded.

Caesar staggered, and grabbed at the slave holding the basin. Water slopped over the floor. Philemon looked up in consternation. The dictation wasn't making any sense. A servant

735

hurried towards his master with a chair. Caesar straightened up, and waved him away, only to beckon him forwards again, when he thought he was going to fall. He must be getting old! But he was only fifty six, after all. No great age. His mind flipped back over the years to the beautiful, very young man, wrapped in Caesar's own scarlet cloak, saying to him with a smile of contempt,

"You have the Falling Sickness."

What was the man's name now? His mind refused to remember. It would come to him. Damn, one of the servants must have told his wife. His lovely wife, so much younger than himself. What a stupid woman she was, trying to persuade him to stay at home, sending to the Senate to say he was ill and not able to attend, just because of a couple of dizzy spells. He had to keep the reins of power firmly in his grasp, or the horses would bolt in different directions, the chariot he was driving would topple over, and everything he had worked for would crash to the ground. At the end of the month he was off to Parthia, to put down yet another insolent king, and Rome must be secure before he left. Perhaps he should stop conquering Egypt every night. Maybe every other night, but Jupiter, it was difficult to keep away from her. Even the thought of her made his member stiffen in glorious anticipation. He smiled to himself. No, he wasn't old, anything but. He was a man of vigour! In his prime! Of course he was going to the Senate today. And here was Decimus Brutus, unaccountably nervous, saying the same thing. There was far too much business to be done. No way could Caesar miss a single day. Poor Brutus, he must be overawed by his proximity to a God. His hands were shaking as he held out Caesar's cloak.

Caesar strode purposefully into the Forum towards the Theatre of Pompey. A man delayed his progress, trying to hand him a petition. That idiot Cimber, begging for his brother. Caesar brushed him aside, glanced up and looked over the heads of the crowd around him. He paused, sure he knew that tall blond figure.

Then he smiled a cruel satisfied smile, and lifted his hand in recognition. Allaine, that was it. He knew he'd remember, given time.

Allaine felt a wave of ice cold fear course through his body. He felt weak and dizzy. He wanted to sit down and put his head between his knees. He thought he was going to faint. Titus looked at him in alarm.

"Allaine, you're as white as a sheet. Here, take my arm." Titus grabbed hold of him. Allaine didn't move. Couldn't move.

Caesar passed the ruin of the old Senate House, then mounted the steps in front of Pompey's statue. He stopped transfixed, as full memory came rushing back. Memory he had tried to suppress. He turned round to look again, to see Allaine's ice grey eyes staring back at him. Hypnotic ice grey eyes.

His mind swept away the years. He was lying on his back in the praesidium tent in Gaul. He was so cold, icy cold. Allaine was looking at him with those same ice cold eyes, and that contemptuous smile on his face. Later, Allaine relating the story to Vercingetorix. Both of them laughing at him. All of Gaul laughing at him. Him, Caesar! Gaius Julius Caesar! The greatest man the world had ever known. A God of a man. He was outraged. One of the impious Gauls had been punished for their temerity. Hauled in chains through the streets of Rome, and strangled like a common thief. He felt his anger rising like lava within him, ready to erupt! Ready to explode! Now for the other one.

Caesar raised his hand to summon the guards.

Someone tugged at his cloak. He turned to remonstrate. A shout went up. He saw the knives flash out. A blade slashed his neck. He swivelled round to grab an arm. They came at him in a pack, like wolves.

It was an act, a play. So unreal. It couldn't be happening. Allaine saw Caesar stagger, blood spurting from neck and chest, deep crimson stains spreading over the whiteness of his robes. The men had him down on the ground now, but carried on

737

stabbing in a frenzy of violence. There were so many of them. Their togas scraped in the dirt on the ground, like the bedraggled feathers of massive white birds, pecking at their prey. Then, almost as one, they rose to their feet.

"People of Rome, we are once again free!" Marcus Brutus yelled to the petrified onlookers.

But the shocked Senators not in the plot hurried away, to lock themselves in their homes.

"Let us retreat to the Capitol," said a voice. "Just in case we are misunderstood."

The Forum emptied rapidly. Mark Antony appeared, shouldering his way heedlessly past the twins, who were now standing alert, with drawn swords, ready to defend their master from any attack. He ran to the sprawled figure lying on the steps, almost tripping on his robes in his haste. He knelt on the ground by the body, pulling up folds of Caesar's toga, in a vain attempt to staunch the bleeding. But the bleeding had already stopped. He looked up to see Allaine staring down at him.

"Allaine, come on," Antony urged desperately. "Do something. For the Gods' sake, do something. Bring him back!"

Allaine knelt on the ground by his side. Now he had a patient to deal with, he could act. Antony was a man in shock.

"There is nothing to be done, Mark." He put his arm round the man's shoulders. "He's not coming back. There is nothing I or anyone else can do."

"I suppose he is dead?" Gaius queried. It was so unbelievable. Caesar dead!

"Oh yes. He's quite dead." Allaine closed the staring eyes, and pulled at the toga, releasing some folds of the wet reddened material, to cover the face of the corpse.

"I tried to get to him, to warn him." Antony gazed on the dead body, the bloodstained clothes. His own heart was racing. He began to think more coherently.

"Allaine, what are you doing here? Oh, of course. I forgot.

Gaius, Octavian, get these people away to safety." He stood up. "I will arrange for the body to be taken to his wife."

"Perhaps you should leave the city, Sir. They may be after you as well."

"I won't get far dressed like this, then." Antony gestured impatiently to his consular robes.

"Ninian, come here. You're going to be a Consul for the rest of the afternoon," Gaius ordered briskly, ever practical. "No one will think he is you, Sir, being so young and with his blond hair."

Ninian stripped off his tunic with some reluctance. It was rather a nice tunic, very good quality. He hoped his master would replace it. He handed over his sword as well, then put on Antony's robes, covered with drying blood and dirt. Octavian and Gaius had to help him. Togas were difficult garments. Ninian could feel himself getting hotter in the fullness of the material. He walked over to the corpse on the ground, and spat on it, before anyone could think to stop him.

"Ninian! No!" Allaine shouted at him.

"He kill my father!" Ninian shouted back.

"He killed mine too, Ninian. But we will not abuse his body. We do not wish to be like him, do we?"

"Will you say the prayer for the dead, Sir?" A pale Octavian was bending over him.

"No, Octavian. I will not." Allaine got up, turned on his heel in the pool of blood, grabbed hold of Ninian, and walked back to join a stricken Titus.

"Put your weapon away, Drustan," Gaius ordered the other twin, "and come with me."

Gaius turfed an astonished matron passing by the Forum, out of her litter, and commandeered her slaves. "Madam, Caesar himself has need of your litter," he told her. Then he organised the slaves. "Lift Caesar onto this, and take him to his house. You know where it is? Good. One of you run ahead, and warn his wife."

Gaius came back to his father and Allaine. At last Titus found he could act.

"Allaine, Allaine, he's right. We must go. We mustn't be seen here. This is going to cause an earthquake, and there will be so much damage. Let it not be us, my dear boy."

"I was damaged years ago, Sir. What do you think will happen now?"

"Fighting. More wars. More destruction. When will it end?"

"Come on, Dad. Antony's right. We must go."

"I think we'd better go the back way, Masters."

Titus agreed. The sooner he got his guest and his sons to safety the better.

They held a family conference. Fortunately the womenfolk and children were already home, with Lucy and Ursula as well. Jay was the only one completely unconcerned. He appeared to be surprisingly cheerful. His appetite was in no way diminished, unlike Octavian's. Claudia knew her son was badly affected, when he pushed away the fish from his plate, untouched. Everyone had something to say, except Allaine. He was quiet, saying nothing, still very shaken by the events of the morning. It was Gaius who noticed, who looked after him, seeming to know how he was feeling. Gaius took him out into the garden, while the others were attempting to eat the meal.

"Come on, Allaine, tell me what happened to you. You look as if you're in shock yourself." Gaius was the first to recover. The first to return to normality.

"He knew who I was. He smiled right at me and raised his hand. It brought it all back. As if it had just happened. And I thought, I stupidly thought I had managed to deal with it."

Allaine looked full into his companion's eyes. "He terrified me, all over again. Oh God, Gaius, I can remember every single vile incident, every part of me that was burnt. Every bit that was broken. It all came back. I felt as if I was on fire again." He rubbed at his face with his hands, wiping away a tear. "It's no good thinking to be brave, when you're tortured. It doesn't work, doesn't last an instant. I was reduced to a whimpering sobbing wreck. I would have done anything, anything at all to make it stop. And that knowledge stays with me. I turned into something so pathetic, I despised myself utterly, even while it was happening."

Gaius put a sympathetic arm round his shoulder. "I'm so sorry about that, Allaine," he said. "I'm so very sorry. Don't blame yourself. You were very young, and you fought so hard against it."

Gaius could see a young Allaine clearly in his mind's eye, terrified and in dreadful pain, on the floor of the cell, all those years ago. He'd forgotten the young man's name over time, until reminded of it by his brother, but the image had stayed with him. He had never been able to rid himself of it.

"I don't think being older would have helped in any way," Allaine sighed. "I'd already finished my training."

"No, maybe not."

Eventually Allaine attempted a recovery. He tried to smile.

"Why are you looking after me, Gaius?"

"Because you looked after me, gave me back my leg. You looked after Octavian, you looked after Val. Don't you think it's time someone returned the compliment? I'm your big brother. Everyone needs a big brother, and Coevorten is too far away to be of any use."

"I had other big brothers once. My brother Metilaius and my brother-in-law Dumnorix," Allaine said. "I loved them so much. Caesar had both killed."

"I know, I know. But as my father always says, you can't live life backwards. Stay there, Allaine." Gaius limped into the house. He decided there was no point at all in reminding Allaine it was his big brother Dumnorix's reckless behaviour, that had got him tortured in the first place. Fortunate, really, that Allaine didn't remember. He usually had an astonishing memory. Gaius reappeared, holding two brimming glasses of wine. "Let's drink to the death of Caesar."

Allaine looked at him in shock. "But you fought for him, Gaius."

"That's right, I fought for him. And he's probably the greatest general we've ever had. But Allaine, he was also a vicious twisted bastard. Look at the trouble he's caused. Look at all the people that have died due to him, died horribly, a lot of them. I think the world may be a better place without him. Although knowing us Romans, there's probably someone out there even more vicious and more twisted."

They sat together in the garden in friendly harmony, sipping the wine, engulfed in memories.

"I offered to kill him myself, once," Gaius said.

"You did?" Allaine was startled.

"After Alesia. Jay wouldn't speak to me. He hated me then. I said I would kill Caesar for him. I meant every word of it, and I would have done it, too. But Caesar intended to hand over the Aeduan and Arvernian prisoners, so Jay thought that might well jeopardise things, if Labienus was left in sole charge. Jay says killing Labienus was the best, most satisfying thing he's ever done."

It appeared to be a time for confessions.

"Gaius, I wasn't very kind to Octavian when I first had him, or Val for that matter."

"So did you despise him, when you'd turned him into a whimpering sobbing wreck, Allaine?"

"No, of course not. He was so badly wounded. He had no fight left in him. All I had to do was to suture his scalp wounds and cauterise a cut he had allowed to fester. It was torture for him. I had to deliberately hurt my poor Val, though."

"Yes, I know. Octavian has told me all about it. You managed to put him back together. Val, too. You have an amazing power to heal, don't you, Allaine?"

"It would be comforting to think so. But Octavian and

Valerius have always been fine men. I had known them both to be kind and just, long before they were captured and enslaved. If it were otherwise, I would have left them to rot at Atuatuca."

More silence.

"What do you think your family will do now, Gaius?"

"I think Dad will want to get Mum to as safe a place as possible. I don't think this will be quite like the Civil War. This may come much nearer home."

"I have lands in the Province, as well as in Switzerland. And Octavian has that beautiful estate on the Loire. It might be better if we all retreated to Gaul for a bit."

"I think that's a very good idea. I am sick to death of fighting. They tried to kill me two years ago, and give my head to Pompey, as if I was some sort of trophy. Disgusting."

Later that evening a servant arrived with news and Ninian's tunic, miraculously cleaned and neatly folded. Mark Antony had returned. The servant asked if Mark Antony could call round, and if he would be welcomed. Titus was intrigued, and wanted to hear what Antony had to say. Antony walked in, greeting Gaius with a hug and kiss, and then Octavian and Allaine in similar fashion. Titus invited him to sit down, and eat with them. Antony declined any food. He politely inquired about the family, and the children, whose names he appeared to remember, or had been primed with them by his secretary, as if this were a normal social occasion.

Antony looked at Titus. "Senator Volusenus, Sir, you said today there would be more wars, more fighting. I agree with you entirely that we have had enough of fighting amongst ourselves. We want no more civil wars. What do you think of an amnesty for the "Liberatores," as these assassins call themselves. Will you help me to persuade the Senate? I feel it will be a necessary evil for the stability of the country."

Titus looked dubious. "I suspect the Senate could be easily persuaded. There must have been at least forty Senators clustered around Caesar this morning, all men of great influence and power. It's the plebs, Antony. They will be angry. Their hero has been done away with by members of the elite. But yes, I will help you."

Allaine thought Antony was still looking very shocked. To his astonishment Antony explained that the other purpose of his visit was to speak to him.

"Allaine, or Antistius Petronius Antinous Allanus, I suppose I must call you now. You have worked for the army, worked for me, worked for Caesar. I know he greatly admired you. He often spoke of your courage."

"He did?" This was astonishing. Allaine wondered if it were true, or a convenient fiction.

Not after Alesia, though, thought Antony. Not after Vercingetorix, kneeling in chains on the floor of Caesar's tent while they dined in front of him, had told them all the truth about the night Allaine had spent with Caesar. Caesar had tried to make a joke of it, without success. Unfortunately Labienus had picked up the vase, saying, "Still smells of piss!" The look of hate Caesar directed at his second in command was terrifying.

Antony decided to come straight to the point. "But I have known at first hand, how skilled you are in medical matters. In fact your master, Antistius Petronius, thought no one could hold a candle to you when it came to diagnosis, himself included. As sole Consul, I wish a Postmortem examination be performed on Caesar's corpse. I am here to ask you if you will undertake such a procedure. It seems as if the Gods brought you here for that very purpose."

Allaine sat stunned and silent.

"I know," Antony continued, while his audience remained dumbstruck, "no doubt you are as shocked as the rest of us, Allaine. But it will need to be done quickly, of course. Already the weather is warming up. What do you think? Is it possible? There is little point in me approaching other surgeons. None will consider the task. They would all be too terrified of the consequences to their own practises. But I presume you will be returning to your own country?"

"Very well, since it is you that ask it, I will undertake this task," Allaine replied. "But not till tomorrow morning. I will need good light. Where is the body?"

"It was taken to his home, to his wife, Calpurnia."

"Then I think you should make sure she is agreeable to this procedure, and agreeable to it being done by me."

"That has already been done, Allaine."

"You move quickly, Sir."

"I will come to fetch you tomorrow, with an armed guard in case of trouble. You are right, Sir. The people are furious that their champion has been murdered. There is so much unrest in the streets. However I have read Caesar's Will, and will endeavour to calm them down at the funeral."

"Do you know when that will be, Sir?" asked Titus.

"In five days, on the twentieth of March, in the Forum." Antony, having achieved his objective, got up and left. There was much to do. Calpurnia had meekly handed over all Caesar's papers to him. He had to think of how to deal with young Octavius, still in Illyria of course, but ostensibly Caesar's heir, according to his Will. Best now to seize the treasury. He would send for Lepidus and his legions to keep order in the city itself. What to do with Cleopatra? He laughed to himself. No problem there! But there was also Caesar's own son with Cleopatra, the even younger Caesarion. Not a citizen, of course. But still. Think of all Egypt's fabulous wealth. What could he not do with that? So, keep in with Cleopatra, whatever else.

Allaine lay in bed with Riona, his thoughts churning around in his head. He could order them all out of the room, and do what he liked with Caesar's dead body. But he knew he wouldn't betray Petronius by treating the corpse with disrespect. Riona was attuned to his mood, stroking his hair and face with the tips of her fingers, telling him of her love. She was so soothing, so soft and pliant. He felt as if he were drinking from a deep well of comfort as he entered her, dissolving into him, calming his soul. Even his climax was subdued, but blissfully lasting, as if to compensate.

There was a crowd of men around him, the Consul Mark Antony, of course, and other Senators he didn't know, but including Titus Volusenus, thankfully. It was good to have someone totally on your side. Allaine stood looking down at the wax-like body of Gaius Julius Caesar. For the first time he began to feel a little pity. But not for Caesar. Just for all the dead. How very dead they always looked, as if they could never ever have been alive in the first place.

How much havoc had this one man caused? How many deaths of how many brave people? And cowardly people. And people too young to die, and too old to deserve violent extinction. Hundreds of thousands slaughtered, hundreds of thousands enslaved, and what had it all amounted to in the end, but the death of a man at the hands of his greatest friends. He remembered his own, the thirty thousand Helvetians killed at night on the banks of the river Saöne, the six thousand brave Helvetian men, the Mandubii, the Avaricum citizens, all those from the Gallic tribes, the Belgae, Carnutes, Eburones, Aeduans, Arvernians, Veneti, and so many more. The Roman soldiers at Dyrrachium, at Pharsalus, at Thapsus, at Munda, and so many others. The Roman citizens of Gomphi, Corduba, and Vaga, and all the other cities caught up in the conflagration. So many many dead. Now joined in death by the conqueror.

Allaine asked for a servant to take notes. He hadn't brought Noemon with him. The journey would have been too much for him. Nor had Octavian brought Gregor, unfortunately. Philemon appeared, wax tablet in hand. Allaine spoke to him.

"I wish to have my findings recorded, as I proceed with the examination. Can you manage dictation?"

"Certainly, Master. I was Caesar's own secretary."

"That's good. Let us start then. There are twenty three separate stab wounds. I am going to dissect each of them out, to find out how many of them could have caused death."

General Lepidus walked into the room at this point, and grabbed Antony's arm. They had a whispered consultation about the best places to station the troops. Then Lepidus apologised to Allaine with a charming smile, and left.

Allaine worked with Philemon all morning, as he painstakingly dissected the body, and then resutured the resulting trauma. He was pleased to find Philemon's writing as clear as his own. He told the servant to write out the findings on parchment, and make sufficient copies for everyone present.

"The only deep wound liable to cause immediate death, is this one in the chest, here," Allaine demonstrated to his audience, some of whom started to look a little pale. "But the amount of blood lost from so many wounds would have led to death in any case. Nothing would have prevented it, however quickly treatment was given."

"I suppose that is reassuring to know," Antony said. "That nothing could have been done."

Antony had a sculptor with him, to take a death mask. He ordered a wax figure to be made of Caesar, to stand in the Forum, with the twenty three stab wounds clearly marked. The funeral was to be held in four days time, again in the Forum, Caesar's body to be wrapped in his blood-drenched toga, and cremated with all due ceremonies.

"I'll see you at the funeral," Antony told Allaine. "I will send an escort for you and the Volusenus family."

Allaine looked up and nodded. "Very well, Sir, if you wish me to be present."

Satisfied, Antony left with the rest of the audience, leaving some legionaries to guard the body.

"What happens now to you, Philemon. Are you free, or will you be freed by Caesar's Will?" Allaine enquired.

"No, Sir. I'm a slave, and I am to stay a slave. I expect

Lady Calpurnia will sell me." He remembered with awful clarity, the day he wrote out the Will at Caesar's dictation. His master knew perfectly well he was waiting for those magic words, words promising freedom after a life of hell. But they didn't come. Caesar was a master torturer.

"Would you object to me buying you?" asked Allaine.

Philemon looked at him in wonder. Had any slave ever been asked that question before? His heart leapt within his chest in excitement. "No, Sir. I would be honoured to serve you."

"Very well, I'll see what I can do."

Philemon walked round to his new master's lodgings, his heart still racing. His master had sent an armed escort to make sure his new property arrived unmolested. There were already riots before Caesar's funeral, despite the presence of legionaries on the streets. He had cost Allaine a lot of money. Allaine was delighted with his new purchase, though, when he saw the neat clear letters on the parchments.

"No more work tonight, Philemon. Work only in good daylight, please. Eyesight is important, and not to be abused."

Allaine decided to retire Noemon when he returned home. His secretary's vision was failing rapidly, despite the magnifier he wore round his neck. He would give him some land, a girl or two to keep him warm at night, a few labourers to work the aforesaid land, and an educated slave, to read his many books to him. Oh, and his freedom, of course.

The body was carried into the Forum on an elaborately carved bier, and placed inside a gilded shrine on top of an enormous pyre of wood. There was a vast throng of plebeians in attendance, as well as the public officials. They had come to honour their hero, and stood in silence, listening intently, as Antony stepped onto the Rostra to give the funeral oration. Allaine was placed between Octavian and Gaius, dressed for the first time in a toga, one borrowed from Titus Volusenus, a dark toga of mourning.

The eulogy went on and on. Antony was pausing theatrically after each paean of praise for Caesar's multiple military achievements. His distress was obvious to all. He read out part of Caesar's Will, telling the people that Caesar had such love for them, he had left a sum of money to every single citizen. Many in the crowd started weeping and crying out.

"That's not going to calm anybody down," said Titus, becoming anxious at the volatile mood of the mob.

Two armed men rushed forwards and lit the pyre, once Antony had finally finished speaking. The small twigs and straw in the centre caught immediately. Flames appeared, flickering around, leaping up from the wood, scorching the gilt of the shrine. The crowd groaned in despair and looked around for anything flammable to add to the fire. They found some dry branches, the benches of the judges, even their own clothing.

The roaring flames sucked the dried leaves from the branches into little flecks of red light that spun and floated in the air. The corpse's rust-coloured coverings shrivelled into incandescent wisps. Thin tongues of fire licked round the body, then started to devour it, greedily eating into the waxen flesh, sending a plume of oily acrid smoke and sparks high into the evening sky. Fine black ash drifted down, spattering the onlookers.

"What are you thinking?" Octavian asked Allaine in a low voice.

"How I wish he could feel what it's like to be burnt. Too late, now."

Titus could hear mutterings in the crowd that boded no good for the Liberatores. The amnesty wouldn't hold after all. He decided to usher his sons and friend home. The twins pushed a passage through the crowds of people blocking the surrounding streets, as they made their way back to the relative safety of the house.

BOOK 4: CHAPTER 18

Summer 41 BC

Senator Antistius Petronius Antinous Allanus was a little surprised to be invited to the dedication of the temple to Gaius Julius Caesar at Bibracte. Of course, it was from Octavian, elected chief magistrate this year again, despite his laughing protests at the Aeduan Assembly, that he'd only had a year's respite from affairs of State.

They were all there. Octavian had invited all the old gang. Amazing, really, that so many of his friends had survived the holocausts. Of course he and Riona and the children usually visited the Aeduans twice a year, in spring as soon as the passes were open, and autumn, after the harvest and before the snows came, so he could swap news and discoveries with Octavian, and work together again for a time. They often returned with relatives' offspring for the summer, especially Octavian Junior, who found it difficult to stay away. Jayven and Zinny, Guéreth and Eloise, Octavian and Chrys, Marcius and his wife, and all the numerous children, now growing up rapidly. So far most of them had been lucky. Valerius was the only one to lose his wife, but lost no time in marrying again. As soon as he was invalided out of the army during the civil war, he made his way back to Allaine, and took up his position as if he had never left. Val's farm was becoming productive and profitable.

Tragically, they had all lost a child, or children, in the case of Eloise and Guéreth, but otherwise their wives managed childbirth without problem, though apparently in a great deal of pain. Allaine thought he should find out more about obstetrics, sometime. He had muddled through, using first principles, but he would like to know a lot more. He found the process fascinating.

There was Hugo. He hadn't seen him for years. They embraced warmly. And Darius, now unbelievably a centurion!

Strange how time changed some men, but not others. There was Jayven, exuberant as ever, and Guéreth giving him an affectionate hug. Gaius came limping forwards, so pleased to see him again, flinging his arms round him, and laughing with pleasure. He was intending to stay for a while with Haetheric and his ever growing family in Cenabum, before returning to Rome, Lucy, sons, and patriarchal duties. He had so many letters for Allaine, from so many friends, including one from Laurence Cornellius Calusa, Quaestor in Further Spain, written proudly with his right hand. And here was Marcius in the finest robes, looking very pleased with himself. His uncle had paid for the temple, and was providing the banquet in the forum after the dedication.

"Marcius, you look affluent," Allaine laughed at him.

Marcius grinned back. "You look pretty good yourself, Allaine." It was true, a toga suited Allaine's tall, still slim frame. "I'll have to order my sculptor to immortalise you in marble."

Octavian welcomed him with great formality at first, but after the ceremonies were completed, they were both able to relax.

"I'm so glad you could come, Allaine," Octavian said. "I wasn't sure if you'd feel insulted. But I thought you would like to see all the others. And they wanted to see you."

"Oh, Octavian, of course I've come," said Allaine, giving his brother-in-law an affectionate hug. "Of course I want to see everyone. It's a good excuse for a party."

After the service of dedication, they congregated in front of the marble colossus of Caesar in the town forum, where couches had been laid out for the distinguished guests. The banquet was male only, apart from the dancers and prostitutes, so the talk and the wine flowed freely. Valerius had far too much to drink. So had Gaius. He was gazing in consternation at the statue. It was erect in every sense of the word. It brought things to mind.

"It must be a great consolation to you, Allaine. At least you were fucked by a God," Gaius remarked loudly, to horrified gasps from some of the others. No one had ever dared to venture near the subject before, not when Allaine was around.

Valerius launched himself at Gaius, grabbing his clothes, and pulling him up off the couch.

"Take it back. Take it back at once, you dirty minded swine," he yelled, fist clenched ready to strike.

Junior drew his sword in alarm. Allaine and Octavian moved at the same time.

"Stop this at once, Val," Allaine shouted, grabbing Valerius by one arm. "And put that away, Junior. It won't be necessary."

Allaine and Octavian were now on each side of Valerius, trying to keep hold of him, as he struggled to free himself. He was still fighting mad.

"Val, did you hear what I said?" Allaine rapped out. "Leave Gaius alone."

"No," yelled Val, defiantly. "It's a lie. He'll take it back. He'll take it back, or I'll kill him."

Allaine slapped him as hard as he could, with his open palm across the face.

"I told you to stop it," he shouted. "Oh hell." He rubbed his hand vigorously. "I forgot how hard your head was."

Val's eyes filled with tears. "You can't let him get away with it, Sir. Make him take it back. Please make him take it back."

"For heaven's sake, Val, calm down. You've had far too much to drink."

"He's a bloody maniac," Gaius muttered.

"Gaius, stop making things worse. Val, listen to me. No, listen to me." Allaine had him by the shoulders, now, and gave him a shake. "Would you think so much less of me, if it were true?"

Valerius stopped for a moment to think. "Of course not, Master," he admitted sulkily.

"Then will you please stop attacking everybody on my behalf. The subject doesn't interest me."

"Isn't it true, then?" Gaius asked in astonishment, attempting to straighten out his toga, still pot valiant. He looked from one to the other. "Well, answer me! Is it, or isn't it?"

Allaine looked amused. "Unfortunately, I was denied that pleasure, Gaius," he responded.

Valerius was becoming increasingly agitated. He could hold his frustration in no longer.

"Can't I tell them what happened, now, Sir? Please?"

Allaine shrugged his shoulders. "Oh very well. Why not. What does it matter, after all?"

They were all curious, gathering round to hear better. Val launched into his account. His audience were transported back in time, back more than sixteen years...........

Valerius walked towards the guards, with his finger on his lips.

"Shh," he whispered. "No noise."

They grinned at him. They knew Valerius and Centurion Pullo had already been with the Commander that evening, with the torture implements, and the beautiful blond prisoner, the poor kid. They'd heard the terrible screams. Now all was silent, imagination running riot. They allowed him into Caesar's tent without challenge, thank the Gods. Valerius needed to hunt for Hector's dog-tag. Gaius Volusenus had ordered it, and paid for it. Val had collected it from the silversmith. It cost a lot of money, he knew. There would be ructions for him tomorrow, if he hadn't found it. He must have mislaid it when he vomited all over the floor, and a little bit over Caesar, as only he and the prisoner were aware. They had both looked at the bit of sick adhering to Caesar's tunic, and then the prisoner had shot him a tiny conspiratorial smile of understanding, as Centurion Pullo hastened to get Val out of the tent, and slaves rushed to clear up the mess.

It was dark inside. Only a few lamps lit. He froze, completely still, not daring to move, as he heard the fateful words from Caesar.

"Any mortal loved by a God has to suffer, Allaine. And I'm afraid you will be no exception."

Val heard the soft sound of footsteps on the floor, and then a sigh, and a loud thud. Then there was silence. And then strange animal noises. Seriously strange noises, frightening noises. Something was badly wrong. Alarmed, he walked into the bedroom area, and stood in shock, gazing down at the unconscious figure of his Commander, naked, jerking rhythmically, bubbles of saliva drooling from his mouth, his heels rasping on the floor like a drum beat. It seemed to go on for ever. At last the convulsions stopped. Caesar lay twitching slightly, lying in a small pool of urine.

Valerius looked questioningly at the prisoner.

"No, leave him be," said the prisoner. "He has just had a major fit, and knocked himself out. It is best not to disturb him, in case he has another convulsion."

"What should I do then, Sir?" asked Valerius. "Should I cover him up with something?"

"No," said the prisoner firmly. "But you can cover me up. Go and fetch me a cloak."

When Valerius returned with the cloak, he was surprised to find Caesar now in a much larger pool, with urine on his face, his hair, and all down his body as well. Val looked askance at the prisoner.

"Childish, I know," said the prisoner. "But immensely satisfactory all the same."

Valerius grinned in sympathy. He was amazed the prisoner could be so calm after the horrors of the evening. He was still feeling decidedly nauseated.

"Yes, Sir, I'm sure."

He went away again, and returned with a piss pot. Rather a fancy one. Caesar's own, he presumed. It had carved figures on the sides.

"Is there anything else I can get you, Sir?"

"You may fetch me some of that wine over there on the side table. But don't drink it yourself. It contains a powerful drug."

Valerius returned with a goblet full to the brim. He knelt by the prisoner's poor battered and burnt body, and helped him to drink it all, wrapping his hands over the prisoner's, and gently lifting the cup to his bloodied lips.

"Here," said the prisoner, when he had drunk the wine to the dregs, "Your payment." He fumbled under the cloak, then held out the silver medallion in the palm of his hand.

"Thank you, Sir. Thank you very much. I'd be in big trouble if I lost it."

"What is it?"

"It's Hector's, Sir. It's to go on his collar. See, this is a picture of Hector giving Ajax his sword." Valerius rubbed the medallion against his tunic, and showed it to the prisoner. "And on the other side is Mars, God of War."

"I wish there was a God of Peace," murmured the prisoner.

"There's a Goddess, Sir, although she's not that important. Pax, her name is."

"Who is Hector?"

"He's my dog, Sir. Well, he's more Tribune Volusenus's dog now."

"Tell me about Hector," said the prisoner.

Valerius liked nothing better. He told him all about his wonderful dog, citing examples of his amazing tracking ability, ferociousness if attacked, and devotion to his master. After a little while Allaine drifted off to sleep. Valerius hadn't been dismissed, so he sat on the ground next to the prisoner, and dozed, with the prisoner's head companionably resting on his shoulder. The trumpets sounding the call to parade woke him up. He thought he'd better wake the prisoner, too.

"Shall I bring you something to eat, Sir?" asked Val.

"That would be very nice," the prisoner agreed.

Val went out again, returning with some cold meat and

bread, warm from the oven. They shared the breakfast.

"What happened, Sir?" Valerius plucked up the courage to ask the prisoner.

Allaine smiled, still filled with opium. "He told me he was a God. He looked like one, too. Priapus, I think. He was so excited, I mean so sexually excited. He walked over to me, gave a sigh, and collapsed on the floor. He hit his head with quite a thud."

"That's right, Sir. I heard it."

Val helped the prisoner to drink some water.

The pain at the back of his head woke Caesar up. He felt confused, with a foul bitter taste in his mouth. Where was he, and why was he so cold? Despite the pain, he managed to push himself up a little. He looked down at himself on the cold marble of the mosaic floor. He was stark naked, and soaking wet, even his hair! There was a strange smell, a strong smell, the smell of urinals. Now he sat up and looked about. There was a young man swathed in his own scarlet cloak sitting on the ground opposite him. The man was chained, he realised, and then he remembered who it was. The prisoner was gazing at him with a faint smile on his face. A legionary walked into the tent and moved over to confront the prisoner.

"He's awake, now, Sir," said the legionary to the prisoner. "What should I do now?"

The prisoner tugged the scarlet cloak aside, revealing Caesar's priceless Greek vase, nestling between his thighs. "You can empty this," said the prisoner, handing over the vase, "then find one of his servants, and go over to the hospital tent and fetch a doctor here."

"Sir," said the legionary, and saluted. Allaine smiled at Caesar. Caesar sat upright with one swift movement, and then let out a groan of pain. The legionary hesitated, waiting to see what would happen next.

"If I were you I would move slowly to start with, Caesar,"

said the prisoner. "You have the Falling Sickness. You passed out and hit the back of your head on the floor." He was still half smiling. "You convulsed, and voided urine, thus distinguishing the attack from a simple faint. It would be wise not to be left alone in future, especially not alone with prisoners without scruples, who wouldn't hesitate to kill an unconscious God. It may well happen again, and without warning."

Valerius finished his recital. There was silence as they absorbed the information. It explained a few things, thought Octavian.

"So," said Gaius, "Val was sick all over him, then Allaine pee'd all over him, then used his precious vase as a piss pot!" He let out a peal of laughter. That set them all off.

"Val was the only Roman I came across, who treated me with any humanity, until I was sold to Petronius," said Allaine, when they had all sobered up again. "I knew who he was, as soon as he was captured himself. So, I decided to keep him. And I have never regretted it."

He put his arm round Valerius, and kissed him affectionately. Valerius thought he'd better not explain it wasn't really humanity that had prompted his actions, but Allaine's grey eyes. He had looked like a sad lost dog, not understanding why he was being beaten. Val had seen that look in many animals' eyes.

"What about me?" asked Gaius.

Allaine looked a little disconcerted. "What about you, Gaius?"

"Oh, nothing," smiled Gaius. "Nothing important." He looked up at the statue. "What an evil bastard he was," he said. "What a fucking wanker."

Allaine stood up to glance at the statue. Octavian heard him gasp in dismay as he lurched towards him, grabbing onto his arm.

"Steady, Allaine," Octavian murmured. Unlike Allaine to drink too much. Allaine remained motionless, rigid, looking up still. He could see Caesar's terrified eyes staring back out at him. Octavian followed his gaze, looking up at the statue in turn.

"Do you see something, Allaine?" he asked, puzzled. Allaine was almost as white as the statue.

Allaine forced himself to look again. Nothing. Nothing at all. Only the eyes painted in.

"I thought I could see his eyes staring out at me."

"Just a trick of the light," said Octavian.

Gaius overheard. He became speculative. "What a terrible fate. To be imprisoned inside a statue for eternity. Perhaps mortals aren't meant to be Gods."

"No more than he deserves," said Allaine.

"Why so?" Gaius asked.

"A million of my countrymen slain, a million enslaved, then a bloodbath throughout the Republic, all for Caesar's *dignitas*, his prestige. It is too high a price. And what was the result in the end? Rome ripped apart."

"Hey, no discussing politics, Allaine. Not tonight," Gaius said.

Allaine turned his back on the statue. He'd had quite a lot to drink, but not enough to have hallucinations.

The forum emptied. The laughing groups of men left to go home to friends and family. Allaine slipped his arm through Octavian's.

"I think it might be better if the statue wore a blindfold," he said.

Octavian laughed. "What excuse can we give?"

"Oh, that the gaze of such a powerful God on us mere mortals, might be too terrifying for us."

"Oh very well, Allaine." Octavian smiled to himself. So unlike Allaine to be fanciful. "I'll see that it's done."

Allaine slipped his other arm through Marcius's.

"Don't bother with your sculptor, Marcius. I think I would much prefer not to be immortalised in marble."

As they walked away Allaine felt a tiny thread of memory

tug at his brain. Something to do with Gaius. He must find out tomorrow.

The slaves moved the furniture, and cleared away the debris. There were good pickings tonight. Lots of leftover food, even some dregs of wine. One of them found a heap of small coins on the ground. Life was good, they thought, as they returned to their hovels.

The white marble colossus clad in leather boots and a golden helmet, cast a long shadow over the earth. Stone folds of cloak draped over his huge shoulders, fastened by a golden brooch. He held no weapons, but his left hand grasped the five laurel wreaths, in commemoration of his five Triumphs.

The statue looked out over the lands he had conquered.

Eternity.

A long time, eternity.

Brief Bibliography

1.Commentarii de Bello Gallico
Julius Caesar
2.The Conquest of Gaul
Julius Caesar, translated by S. A. Hanford
3.The Civil War (including the Alexandrian War, the African War, and the Spanish War written by unknown authors)
Julius Caesar, translated by Jane F. Gardner
4. The Golden Bough
J.G. Frazier
5. A Traveller in Rome
H. V. Morton
6. Everyday Life in Roman times
Marjorie and C. H. B. Quennell
7. Doctors and Diseases in the Roman Empire
Ralph Jackson
8. The Georgics
Virgil, translated by L.P. Wilkinson
9. Daily Life in Ancient Rome
Jérôme Carcopino
10. Selected Letters
Marcus Cicero, translated by D. R. Shackleton Bailey
11. The Digest of Roman Law
Justinian, translated by Colin Kolbert
12. Ancient Jewellery
Jack Ogden
13. The Early History of Rome
Livy, translated by Aubrey De Sélincourt
14. De Medicina
Aulus Cornelius Celsus, translated by W. G. Spencer

Especial thanks to Wikipedia and many other Internet sites too numerous to mention.

Printed in Great Britain
by Amazon.co.uk, Ltd.,
Marston Gate.